MISTS OF HEAVEN

Yvonne Kalman

MISTS OF HEAVEN

BANTAM PRESS

LONDON · NEW YORK · TORONTO · SYDNEY · AUCKLAND

TRANSWORLD PUBLISHERS LTD
61–63 Uxbridge Road, London W5 5SA

TRANSWORLD PUBLISHERS (AUSTRALIA) PTY LTD
15–23 Helles Avenue, Moorebank NSW 2170

TRANSWORLD PUBLISHERS (NZ) LTD
Cnr Moselle and Waipareira Aves,
Henderson, Auckland

Published 1987 by Bantam Press,
a division of Transworld Publishers Ltd
Copyright © Yvonne Kalman 1987

British Library Cataloguing in Publication Data

Kalman, Yvonne
Mists of heaven.
I. Title
823[F]   PR9639.3.K33

ISBN 0–593–01301–8

Printed in Great Britain by
Mackays of Chatham, Chatham, Kent

For my father, Colin Wadman Flavell, and for my great grandfather, Joseph Day, who appears on pages of this book.

Part One

ONE

*Near Waitamanui, a coastal village on the North Island of Her
Majesty Queen Victoria's colony of New Zealand
8 December 1854*

'Bejesus, I swear this journey gets rougher every time,' grumbled
Charles Stafford as he flicked the reins and shifted his buttocks on
the uncomfortable wooden seat. 'All this jolting and rocking and
underlating fair reminds me of me wedding night. What d'you
say, hey, Lawrence? Were your conjovial bed like this?'

Absorbed in their own conversation, the two women ignored
his remarks, while Lawrence Rennie simply hardened his distaste-
ful expression. He was lolling at the rear of the juddering cart as
far from Charles as he could get; if not for the fact that the
Staffords offered a convenient transport to town, he would not
have been there at all. He was not of the same class as these
people, and everything about him underlined his opinion – from
his haughty demeanour and his aristocratic features, partly
obscured by a full beard that clung to his chin like a black bee-
swarm, to his clothes, elegant and cared-for if a trifle shabby by
now, though Lawrence had been the epitome of fashion when he
arrived in the colony nine years ago.

Spitting out a clot of chewing tobacco, Charles ruminated, 'I
wager his wedding night were nothing remotely like this. Lazy
fellow couldn't muster up the energy to poke a fire, let alone owt
else!' and he cackled, pleased with his bawdy joke.

Charles was a plain, grey man, thickened through the middle
by his wife Gwynne's abundant cooking, soft-shouldered and

thick-necked with a face crumpled in a perpetually belligerent scowl. They had lived here less than three years, this pioneering venture following other, also disappointing, stints in Nova Scotia and South Australia. Failure clung to him like his body odour. He believed in bad luck and was unlucky.

Gwynne as always didn't seem to hear his carping. A doughy, placid woman of forty-five, she was as accepting and resilient as rising bread. Plain-faced with wispy hair, sharp features set in a broad face, and a distinct peach bloom of sandy hair on her upper lip, she had a remarkably pretty voice, light and chiming like the chords of birdsong that filtered from the dense forest foliage on either side of the rutted track.

By contrast Mary Rennie lingered in her twenties with a hand-some tanned face silk-creased around the mouth and above the bridge of her long nose with extraordinarily beautiful eyes set just a little too close together. She was aware of Charles's every grumbling remark and endured his coarseness with strained irrita-tion, worried that young Lisabeth might hear, but the child was oblivious, intent on playing with a carved wooden duck which she manipulated to open and close its jointed beak. She sat on the hamper between the women.

'Quack? Quack?' she cried, and 'Quack, quack!' she replied. Prettier than her mother, she was a slender milk-coloured child of nine with dark hair that curled in damp tendrils below the rim of her *broderie anglaise* sun-bonnet, and shy blue-black eyes widely set in a tender oval face. 'Look!'she urged, opening a sweating mittened palm to show Gwynne. 'Mr Rennie gave me a whole farthing!'

'Wasn't that generous?' added Mary sourly, and the women both grimaced, for Mr Rennie's meanness was a source of friction between him and his new wife.

Today the group was travelling to meet the *Sydney Belle*, a steam-packet from New South Wales. She would bring not only fresh provisions for the district but also news and mail from Home, together with items of particular interest to the folk in the wagon. Lawrence Rennie expected to receive his usual note of credit which was dispatched quarterly from relatives in Kent, payment to ensure that Lawrence and his dissolute habits remained far from the aristocratic hearth. Charles, however, was spoiling for a quarrel. He hoped to confront the Land Company Agent who was rumoured to be on board this voyage. As he masticated a fresh plug of tobacco he muttered a rehearsal of his blunt accusing

10

speech. *I'll pin the slippery bastard down and I'll make him listen. Bejesus, I will!* he vowed.

To Lisabeth, who regarded everything in the simplest of terms, the outing was a sum of adventure, fun and the hank of bootstrap liquorice her farthing would buy, while to Gwynne today meant the culmination of weeks of waiting. She was serenely happy, her chest thick with a syrupy-sweet anticipation. On the jetty she would meet at last the brother she had not laid eyes on for over nineteen years.

Only Mary made the journey with reluctance. Even the prospect of tonight's social dance in the Waitamanui hall failed to cheer her. She dreaded seeing the ship, dreaded the visit to the tiny overgrown graveyard with the still-raw scar where her first husband, Andrew Maitland, lay buried. It was just a year ago on their voyage out from London that she and Lisabeth had been put ashore here with his body. For Mary grief would be refreshed today and disappointment with this, her salvaged wreckage of a life, would grow even more bitter. *If only I could escape!* she thought dismally. *I thought that marrying Lawrence would be a salvation, but how wrong I was! If only there was some way out of this tedious living death!*

The wagon's progress was laborious. A scrape of primitive track led them down rutted hillsides, along mossy-stoned gullies and across river table-lands that bristled with a haze of glossy flax swords. Occasionally from a ridge's saddle they emerged from the bush for a few yards and saw a view of breathtaking beauty spread before them. Below lay the undulating plumage of the forest, layer upon layer of rain-polished leaves shining like *tui* feathers, while in the distance shimmered the navy-blue sateen lap of lace-edged ocean. To their right jutted a perfectly symmetrical mountain, breast-like, delicately veined with mauve.

'Mount Taranaki,' Lawrence observed loftily, sucking on the stem of an empty meerschaum pipe. Before the plummy tones of his voice had faded the track twisted, the wagon lurched and again they plunged into shade as the dripping bush canopy closed over their heads.

It was perishingly hot and grew hotter as the day ripened. Sargent plodded slowly. In the sunshine steam rose from his back. In the shade they could smell his sweat and the oppressive humid odour of decomposing vegetation.

Mary wrinkled her nose against it. She sat with her back to her husband and flapped a lazy paper fan, arching her neck in the

11

faint current of air. When her daughter bumped against her knee she snapped, 'Do stop fidgeting, Lisabeth! And stop that frightful quacking noise! My head can't stand it . . .' Then to Gwynne she complained, 'I hate this smell – the rotten leaves, the sickening ripe decay. This stench is so exaggerated in summer. Our lives are permeated . . . we draw it in with every breath . . . Oh, I hate it! The woods in England never smelled like this.'

Gwynne nodded, smiling. *I wonder if I'll recognize him,* she thought.

Lawrence cleared his throat. 'English forests are deciduous. These species are evergreens. The flora here present on the fortieth longitudinal —'

'I dream about the English woodlands,' confided Mary in a rush, leaning forward and ignoring him. 'The open leafy spaces, the *civilized* trees – oak and elm and chestnut! And the squirrels . . . The bluebells! I dream about the bluebells most of all. We would gather heaping armfuls of them, Andrew and I would. They would begin wilting almost at once. It was a frightful extravagance but, oh, the luxury of their beautiful blue flowers!'

Lisabeth glanced up at the mention of her father's name, but Lawrence's brown eyes narrowed with annoyance, giving his weak face a transient attractive hardness. No one wished more than he that Andrew Maitland was still alive. Had he not caught measles and perished on the voyage out, then Mary would have not been a distraught new widow and he would not have taken pity on her in a vulnerable moment and married her. Or had cause to regret the impulse.

He pursed his lips and forced his mind towards pleasanter topics. His money. How he would spend it. He began to whistle cheerfully. When Mary stabbed him with an irritated glance he whistled all the louder.

Mary's prattling stirred Gwynne's memories, too. She stared at the work-reddened hands that rested in her lap. 'There were no bluebells in the Isle of Man,' she remarked in her lilting voice, the only really pretty thing about her. 'We picked primroses. And elderberry blossom. I put some on Rhys's cradle, the spring before we left. He was such a fretful restless baby. I would sing to him, talk to him by the hour, but he wouldn't be soothed. Ah, I recall the morning when—'

Mary stopped listening, her irritation deepening. All Gwynne had talked about these past months was her precious brother. Rhys this and Rhys that. Rhys, Rhys, Rhys! If family likeness was

12

anything to go by, he was bound to be as dull and grey and boring as his middle-aged sister. Raising her fingertips to her lips, Mary stifled a yawn.

Gwynne stopped at once. 'I'm sorry. I do go on about him, I know. Only . . . he's the only family I have now, apart from Charles of course.'

'And I be nothing to write home about,' said Charles, his wheezing gravelly voice tinged with resentment. 'I've not scored a century in a Home Counties cricket game, nor graduated from Oxford University—'

'The sixth-youngest man ever to do so with honours,' added Gwynne, her plain features suffused with pride.

Charles flicked the reins harder than necessary, grumbling: 'Marvellous, ain't it? He were a snotty-nose wee brat when we left for Nova Scotia, and now he's probably too grand for us by a half. Coming to stay on our estate, he says. *Estate*, bejesus!' He squirted a stream of tobacco juice in the direction of Sargent's rear hoofs. 'Saints' sorrows, he's in for a surprise! All I can say is I hope that he's within earshot when I meet with that rascal of an agent. Four hundred verdant acres he sold us, at fifteen shillings the measure! The more land I burn off, the more swamp I find, and now Tamati and his Maori tribe of scallywags are telling me they've not seen a penny of that three hundred pounds. *And* they've the blasted impotence to say they want the land back again, of all things! The bloody sauce of it, after all the work I've put in! I'll tell that damned agent once and for all that —'

'Of course, dear,' soothed Gwynne hastily. She was dismayed that Charles had to keep ploughing over the same worries, especially on a beautiful day like today, but she was even more nervous that his language might scandalize Mary.

It did. 'You may tell him and welcome, *and* be as salty as you wish in the telling, but I'll thank you kindly to remember that there are ladies here, and to keep a courteous tongue in your head!' she snapped.

Charles swung around at that, astounded. His was a lumpy moist face like a platter-sized piece of rough-carved pumice, with a scrubby-lichen beard that was always damp with tobacco stains around the mouth. Lisabeth secretly thought him scary-looking, but now, seeing him agape with watery eyes goggling, she couldn't help but giggle, he looked so funny.

Mary cuffed her into silence with a small sharp slap which was executed while she held Charles's gaze coldly. The look was an

13

exchange of mutual dislike which Charles dropped first by turning away and hunching his shoulders as he flapped the reins. The back of his neck below his billycock hat was red with rage. *Uppity bitch!* he thought savagely.

You coward, thought Lawrence in disgust. He'd watched the brief exchange with amusement and would have applauded if Charles had pitched Mary out to walk. He could have done; it was his wagon after all. His gaze flicked on to Mary for a moment. How common she was. Fancy striking her daughter like some ignorant peasant woman. And as for her objections to the language – Lawrence could have told them that any real lady would have maintained her dignity and permitted a silence to indicate her disapproval instead.

Alas, Mary was definitely no lady.

Lisabeth cupped her free hand over her ear to lessen the sting. She was hurt beyond the reprimand. Her mother's moods bewildered her. Sometimes Mary wept like a demented soul, but whenever Lisabeth crept close and tried to comfort her she always shoved her away, while at other times she lashed out at anything within reach with an inexplicable anger. Lisabeth was always shut out. Told she couldn't understand. To the lonely child it was frightening.

The thick bush drew back behind them as they entered a bleak landscape where rough wood-slab cottages hunched in isolation, each in its own sea of blackened stumps. Now the smells of raw earth, manure and damp sheep mingled with a sooty aroma of dead fires. Lisabeth gazed at everything eagerly, knowing from her two previous trips into town that they were very close, that from the top of the next ridge, beyond that cluster of charred *kauri* trees, they would be able to look down on a huddle of unpainted buildings and a long lick of pale sand edged by the frilled sea. Waitamanui.

'That's her, the *Sydney Lass!*' cried Charles when they reached the place.

'Sydney Belle,' corrected Mary, squinting at the bouquet of smoke-puffs and the knife-slice of rippled wake.

'She's so *near!*' breathed Gwynne as she began to draw on her black cotton gloves. 'I'm so excited . . .'

'So near,' repeated Mary dully. Letters from England and goods from England, English people who had been there so recently and might even be going back again soon. It seemed unbearable.

14

Lawrence was pontificating on in his monotonous way. 'Contemplate the barbarity of this scene,' he said, jabbing his pipe-stem at the buildings below. 'This harbour is an exquisite creation of nature, yet ponder the philistinic mind that chooses to erect such hideous monstrosities on its very shores.'

Lisabeth was the only one who listened to him. She understood very little of what he said, and it was always so serious, as if he was a king making judgements on everybody and everything, judgements that were always bad. But his language was magic to her.

To Lisabeth, Waitamanui was a pretty place, quaint and windswept. There was a two-storey hotel with a crinoline of gingerbread-trimmed veranda that, had it been painted white, would have looked like a bride but, being dun-brown, simply seemed to melt into its vast puddle of wheel-churned earth. The three shops were amusingly pretentious with their tall broad facades hiding miserable lean-tos huddled behind them. There were cottages hedged about with *toe-toe* bushes and a lovely wee church, Lisabeth's favourite building with its white spire thrusting from a froth of flower-starred greenery.

'Phallic,' scoffed Lawrence when she timidly pointed it out to him. 'Blatantly phallic. I wonder if these Christians realize how utterly pagan their paraphernalia really is?'

Today the town was crowded. As they jolted past towards the jetty Lisabeth noticed that the stables were busy; white noses blazed from the gloom and there was the hiss of a red-hot shoe as the smith cooled it in his barrel of seething water. People chattered in shop doorways, and dogs lay panting under battered spring-carts. Maoris were everywhere, women puffing on clay pipes as they dandled their babies, children shrieking and old men sitting on flax mats in the sunshine. Lisabeth was fascinated by the *moko*, the tattoo that dribbled from the women's lips like a stain of juice over the chin.

None of the children wore *moko*, but with their confident loud voices and defiant gestures they still seemed alien and bumptious to Lisabeth. Most wore adult clothes cut down for a makeshift fit. Shirt-tails flapped below jackets with rolled-up sleeves, and waistcoats hung over pin-striped serge trousers and skirts that bloomed with smears of dried mud. *They must be sweltering*, thought Lisabeth, whose sprigged cotton gown was already uncomfortably hot.

'Don't stare,' warned Mary, but Lisabeth couldn't help it. A

15

group of Maori youngsters jostled each other, screaming like gulls, as they whipped at a wooden top with plaited flax cords, making it leap right over puddles on the hard road-edge. They seemed to be having such fun that Lisabeth wondered longingly what it would be like to play a real game with other children. She was in awe of them.

The jetty swarmed with excitement. 'More folks here than flies on a carcass!' exclaimed Charles.

'Hardly the simile I'd have chosen to express it,' murmured Lawrence. 'Though perhaps fitting to the occasion . . .'

Mary heard him as she climbed down, skirts modestly hitched to one side. She sliced him a cold look but said nothing.

Already, with the ship just berthed and water still boiling around the stern, cargo was being unloaded. Gwynne pushed through the throng, sobbing with an emotion she could not contain. Charles forged a path beside her. The others hung back.

'Look, Mamma!' cried Lisabeth suddenly, tweaking at the flowing cuff on one of Mary's sleeves. 'There's cages and cages of little brown birds over there.'

'Sparrows,' whispered Mary. 'Sparrows and thrushes!' She took a few steps towards them. 'Poor wretches. They'll be set free in this wilderness in the hopes of making the land more like England. Poor things! They didn't want to come here any more than we did!'

Lawrence had disappeared, gone to find his credit note and then to the hotel to cash it. Mary knew that he would be intoxicated when she saw him again, much later.

Mary looked around for the Staffords. Lumpers pushed by with hand-carts loaded with boxes of nails, kegs of sugar, sacks of seed-grain. Lisabeth felt that they were being swamped in a crush of unfriendly energy, that if her wooden-soled shoes should trip on the uneven planking she would disappear under a stamping of boots and wheels. She clutched her mother's sleeve anxiously. When Mary said, 'We'll wait in the wagon,' she was relieved.

Charles and Gwynne made their way to the gangway, searching the faces of everybody they bumped near to in the throng. They were almost to the foot of the gangway when Charles exclaimed, 'There he is!' and even as Gwynne's heart swelled with sudden joy he added: 'There's the canny bastard. Just you wait, you slimy, evil, conniving—'

'Charles, please!' She puffed up the ridged plank after him, dismay cooling her excitement. She'd hoped Charles's threats to

16

cause a scene were all bluster, she'd prayed he wouldn't spoil her reunion with Rhys . . . Oh, why did he always have to rant and roar like a penned-up bull? It wasn't the agent's fault. They'd been warned the land was isolated, they'd been told it would need a lot of felling and burning to break it into pasture.

She shrank with shame as Charles elbowed his way to the agent's side and clamped a hand on his arm.

'I've a bone to pick with you, you unscrofulous scoundrel!' he bellowed. 'Four hundred verdant acres I purchased, and what have I got instead? Swamp that can't be drained and boulders that can't be bloody well shifted! Let me tell you now that—'

'Sir! Excuse me!' In the rim-shade of his black top-hat the agent's sweat-slicked face was annoyed but not puzzled. He was seasoned in the art of parrying complaints from embittered settlers. Mopping his plump jowls with a silk handkerchief, he affected a friendly smile and suggested that they meet in a room of the hotel in half an hour to discuss the problem in a 'civilized' manner.

Charles greeted this suggestion with a snort. 'Bejesus, but you've got gall! You tried that dodge on me last time, remember? I were cooling my heels – ay, and stoking my temper – for nigh on two hours!'

'Then, I must have been unaccountably delayed. I do apologize, and assure you—'

'Apologize! It'll take more than apologies to—' He stopped as Gwynne clutched his arm with a strangled cry of delight. 'What is it, woman?' he asked irritably.

'Rhys,' she whispered.

While the clash between Charles and the agent took place the young man who had been in conversation with him first looked acutely embarrassed then turned his back and stood at the railing while he pretended to watch the activity on the jetty. He was tall and fair, strong-faced with clear blue eyes and long sideburns that bracketed his high cheekbones. Gwynne glanced at him and noticed that his face turned pink with embarrassment when the shouting began. It made him look so much younger that she stared and kept staring as realization grew in her. Rhys! It *was* Rhys!

He turned at the sound of his name. Gwynne flew to fling her arms around his neck. 'Rhys, oh, Rhys, it is you!' she sobbed. She held him at arm's length and stared at him again, as if unable to believe the evidence of her own eyes. 'I was looking for a lad – a slip of a boy – but you're a grown man!'

'I didn't recognize you, either,' he said, a bashful tone masking

17

shock that numbed him. This old woman his sister? Was this the 'bonny lass' their father had gasped out for on his deathbed? She was so worn, so dowdy, older than he ever remembered their mother as seeming. As for her husband . . . He glanced at Charles, embarrassment deepening to dismay. So this coarse ill-mannered yokel was the brother-in-law he'd travelled halfway around the world to meet. A choking wave of disappointment rose in him. He couldn't speak.

The agent had vanished of course, slipping away as soon as the diversion offered itself as a chance to escape. Charles was so cross when he realized what had happened that he stood scowling blankly at Rhys, and it was not until Gwynne joggled his elbow to remind him that there were other things today apart from quarrels that he pulled himself together enough to rasp a welcome and shake Rhys by the hand.

'Isn't this wonderful?' sighed Gwynne, her dull eyes bulging with unshed tears. 'It's a dream come true! My baby brother here at last!'

Rhys tried to smile back. She has a good kind heart, he thought.

Mary fidgeted impatiently. *If only I could wrest that money away from Lawrence, she thought. I could hide until the ship was ready to cast away from the jetty, then creep aboard and go. . . . Go as far as the twenty-five pounds would carry me. Go anywhere, anywhere as long as it's far enough for me to forget that this horrible place ever existed!*

She sighed. It was a hopeless longing. Lawrence and his money stuck together like a limpet and a rock. He hid it, she knew he did, but so far all her spying and cunning had been unable to find out where. *I'm trapped here*, she thought with the familiar ache of despair. *Unless a miracle happens I'll die here. Oh, Andrew, why did you insist on emigrating when I begged you not to leave England?*

'They look sick, poor things,' mused Lisabeth's voice, intruding on her misery. 'I feel so sorry for them.'

'Who?' Mary looked up, her face vague.

'The little birds.'

They did indeed look ill. Lisabeth was leaning over the side of the wagon watching as the lumpers stacked crate after crate of frail wooden cages nearby. Within the cramped enclosures the birds hunched together like shadows, feathers fluffed up, heads sunk low.

'Excuse me!' Mary called to a lumper, a hulking Maori man with florid facial tattoos that looked odd with his twill suit and battered felt hat. When he grinned at her she said: 'These birds . . . are they to be released here?'

He grinned and shrugged good-naturedly to show he didn't understand, but another of the lumpers heard the question and detoured with his sack of maize seed to say, 'They're being off-loaded to uncover the hatches, ma'am. Then they'll be put back again. It's Auckland they're bound for. Be there in another two or three weeks.'

'Poor things,' whispered Lisabeth. 'They can't even fly about in there.'

'Don't look at them if it upsets you.'

'I can't help it.' Lisabeth looked as if she was going to cry. Her lip trembled.

Mary understood too well. Suddenly she could bear it no longer. Swinging down from the wagon, she picked up one of the cages and jerked at the bars, wrenching them loose along one side, twisting them until they snapped. Then, holding the cage in both hands, she shook it, tumbling the sparrows to the ground. Of the dozen in the cage three fluttered at once into the air, but the others lurched and scuttled under the wagon, flexing their long-unused wings.

'Go!' hissed Mary, seizing another cage and tearing it open, shaking the captives free. A splinter tore one of her gloves, and there was an instant blossoming of blood on the faded velvet fabric, but careless of the pain or the damage Mary ripped open another cage and another.

The Maori lumper saw her and stopped, bemused, shaking his head, reluctant to interfere. Ruins of eight cages lay scattered around her, and she was tugging with bloodied hands at a ninth when one of the ship's officers caught sight of what she was doing and flailed his way shouting through the crowd to interrupt her.

'Leave me be!' she cried when he grabbed her wrists and shook her hard. Behind them on the wagon Lisabeth, thrilled and terrified by what her mother was doing, began to cry.

'Are you insane, woman?' demanded the officer.

'Shoo, shoo!' cried Mary to the birds. To the officer she snapped: 'Let go of me at once! You're frightening my daughter. You've no right to touch me!'

'You've no right to touch this property, either!' He shook her again, harder. She was a damned attractive woman and grabbing

19

her like this – roughing her up a bit – stirred him in a pleasantly diverting way. He tightened his grip on her wrists and pulled her closer to him, leering into her face. Dark greasy hair flopped from below the peak of his cap. His breath smelt of oil of cloves.

Mary hissed at him with a contempt that made him wonder if she could read his thoughts. 'And you have no right to pen up those poor creatures. *Nobody* has that right! They are God's wild creatures and they should be allowed to live their lives in freedom!'

Charles, Gwynne and Rhys, on their way back to the wagon, arrived in time to hear this impassioned speech.

'She's mad,' declared Charles, deliberately loud so that all around could hear him. 'I said she was mad all along, didn't I, Mrs Stafford?'

'Oh dear,' murmured Gwynne, decidedly unhappy. She moved to comfort Lisabeth, who was wailing on the hampers in the wagon.

'I think she's marvellous, whoever she is!' announced Rhys. Before Charles could stop him he thumped a confident hand on the officer's shoulder. 'Let go of her at once. I'll pay for any damage she's caused.'

'Ee, lad, no! Don't be reckless!' hastened Charles, but Rhys shook off his restraining hand.

'Come now, Officer Perkins. You know me. I mean what I say. What are these wretched birds worth to you? Ten guineas the lot?'

The officer's leathery face was thoughtful; his eyes darted around to see if any other of the ship's command were within earshot. 'Ah, well, Mr Morgan . . . They're not ours, sirs, you see. They're bound for a customer in Auckland. I couldn't just sell them to you.'

'You've "sold" half of them already. Say they were infected by some disease and died. Here.' He reached into his fob and drew out two gold coins which he surreptitiously pressed into the officer's palm.

Without another word the officer turned away and began ordering the lumpers to carry on with their duties.

'Stop him!' urged Charles. 'Tell him you've changed your mind. You can't do this lad. Just throw away good money on a packet of wild birds. There's no *reason* to it!' He was wheezing, panicked by the sight of those precious gold coins changing hands.

But Rhys wasn't listening. He turned to Mary with a smile.

20

She was dazed. The young man who had rescued her was tall, so tall she had to tip her face right back to look up at him. His was a square face, strong-jawed with a cleft that had the effect of softening the hard lines of his chin. His nose was straight and proud, his eyes heavy-lidded and his mouth firm-lipped. It was a determined face, Mary decided, the face of someone who was already used to getting what he wanted;but when he smiled the sky-blue eyes sparkled, white, slightly uneven teeth flashed and a dimple appeared at one side of his mouth.

'I don't know how to thank you,' said Mary. He smiled slowly. *He's wicked*, thought Mary in clear intuition. She looked at that curving mouth, the soft brush of moustache, and to her astonishment found herself wondering how that mouth would taste against hers.

'You've hurt your hands,' he said, picking them up.

'Keep them,' she murmured foolishly, but under her breath.

'I'll free the other birds for you. Gwynne, can you please attend to this lady? Charles, you might like to help me.' As he spoke Rhys picked up one of the broken cage-bars and used it as a lever, prising the other cages open in rapid succession as easily as shucking oysters.

Charles protested, but his words were as useless as the barkings of a toothless old dog. 'All that money!' he kept saying. 'All that money just thrown away! You must have money to burn, lad!'

Rhys brushed at some reluctant thrushes, shaking them free of their prison. By now the ground around the wagon was alive with flapping hopping birds and the air was fractured by their chirping. A crowd was packing closer as they watched. Children darted, yelping, as they tried to capture the less strong birds.

'Leave them alone or I'll skin you!' warned Rhys in such a tone that the children desisted.

'I said, "you must have money to burn, lad!"' chafed Charles.

Rhys straightened, dropping the wreckage of the last cage. 'It was all I had in the world,' he said, then flashed another teasing smile. 'No, Brother-in-Law. I've a few sovereigns more. That money was hard-earned but well spent. Very well spent indeed, don't you think?'

Charles scowled. There was no way he could agree with that.

One of the thrushes leaped into the air, then faltered, coming to a wobbly rest on the wagon-rail close to Lisabeth. She sat very still, hardly daring to breathe for fear of frightening it. It had drab feathers, worn into holes where it was moulting, revealing the

21

crêpey pink skin beneath. Through the thin speckled chest-feathers Lisabeth could see the pulsing of its heart. It looked at her while its heart beat fast and its wings stretched tentatively.

'Will it survive?' she whispered.

'Ask your stepfather, dear. He knows the answer to everything.' Gwynne replied. She flung up her hands in her vague little gesture of helplessness, and when she did so the bird took fright and leaped again.

This time its wings remembered what to do. Up and up it soared, then wheeled around far above their heads as its wings pounded joyfully. Soon it had gone, joining into the loose trail of other birds as they flew towards the town.

'What do you think of him?' asked Gwynne, anxious for approval from any source, for it was plain she would get none from her husband. 'Isn't my little brother just the handsomest creature you ever saw?'

Lisabeth studied him solemnly. To her young eyes he looked nothing like a 'little brother' but a proper man, and an elegant one, too, in his burgundy tailored jacket, embroidered waistcoat and ruffled cream shirt. Snug black trousers tucked into tall burnished boots.

Suddenly Mary spoke. She had been standing beside the wagon examining the cuts on her hands and picking stray splinters from her fingers, noting that she was not badly hurt, just uncomfortably sore. She said: 'Your brother is the most gallant man I've ever met.'

Her tone surprised Lisabeth. It was low, thrilling, as if something momentous had happened to her.

Lisabeth looked again at the newcomer. He was facing them, smiling – at Mary, Lisabeth noticed. As he moved towards them, dusting his hands, the sun blazed hotly on the pale gold of his hair, and for a moment he seemed wonderful. Lisabeth thought of pictures of Sir Launcelot in the mouldy-spined volumes of classical literature that Mr Rennie sometimes permitted her to look at. *A knight from a fairy-tale, that's what he's like!* she thought.

Lisabeth had no idea that many thousands of people before her had fitted that same description to personable young men. To her every experience was new-minted, tinged with excitement, and this stranger who had rescued her mother from the nasty bully was indeed a chivalrous legendary figure come true. She knew that he was only Mrs Stafford's brother, but then and there she decided that she adored him.

22

TWO

LAWRENCE RENNIE'S REACTION to the newcomer was less enthusiastic than his wife's. 'You're a fool, young man!' he declared boozily when Gwynne told him how Rhys had saved Mary from the consequences of her act of kindness. 'You're an utter and c-consummate fool! But for your ill-timed intervention, my wife would be inc-carcerated by now and I'd be a liberated man!'

'He's only teasing you,' whispered Gwynne.

'Sure and he doesn't approve of money being squandered, either,' said Charles, still shocked by Rhys's gesture. 'In a place like this, we learn to value a guinea.'

'I've noticed you all have your priorities in the proper order,' said Rhys.

Mary ducked her head over her untouched plate, inwardly consumed by humiliation. *This young man rescued me from an unpleasant situation, so why can't Lawrence at least be civil to him?* she despaired.

It occurred to Rhys that Mary's husband might be afraid of being asked to recompense Rhys for the ten guineas, but he couldn't think of a way to dismiss that worry without insulting Mary still further, so overlooking Lawrence's boorishness he said nothing, merely smiled a tight smile and averted his eyes, glancing instead around the room.

They were jammed into the public saloon at the hotel, sitting elbow-to-elbow at a trestle table with a dozen others. Rhys estimated that there must be upwards of a hundred people in here along with their bundles and baskets. A heap of saddles lay along the hearth. Babies squalled and were shushed. But this was really living, Rhys guessed as he looked at their faces. There were gold scrolls on the windows and a real chandelier – fly-specked but genuine – hanging from the ceiling, and these folk were sitting down to a meal that someone else had cooked. Luxury.

Gwynne beamed back at faces she knew. She felt some of their excitement. They were people like her, people who smelt of sweat and home-made mutton-fat soap, whose faces shone with ruddiness of sunburn and ale and whose loud voices were more accustomed to bellowing at the recalcitrant dogs than to conversing in a room that had a chandelier hanging from the ceiling. Simple, *good* folk.

Mary loathed it all. All week the promise of a 'meal out' had been dangled before her as if it was a privilege she somehow had to earn. (Not that she would try to earn it. She wouldn't.) But here it was set plonk in front of her and it was nothing more than undercooked mutton and pulpy cabbage. Even she could do better than this, and she was no cook. She was astounded to see Charles and Gwynne digging in as if it was a treat when she knew that if he'd been served it at home Charles would have refused to eat such slop. Rightly, too. Gwynne was a marvellous cook; all afternoon she'd been poking around in the trading store replenishing her supplies of not only sugar, tea and flour but also peppercorns, dried figs and apples, bay leaves and cinnamon, while aloud she planned delicious meals to dazzle Rhys.

Rhys. Mary allowed herself a sly sideways glance at him. To her astonishment he was looking at her. With approval.

What beautiful eyes she has, he thought, as she looked quickly away. They were a deep, cool green, large and thick-lashed, but what made them extraordinary was the clear luminous quality of their whites. Most people's eyes were a duller colour, like Gwynne's, or cloudy and cataracted like Lawrence's, or watery pulpy pink like Charles's, but Mary – her daughter, too, he noticed – had limpid eyes of such perfection that they seemed to reflect an inner purity.

In this disagreeable squalor and unpleasant company Rhys was pleased to find something he could wholeheartedly admire, even if it was a married woman's eyes.

Lawrence drank steadily through the meal. His gait was erratic when later they strolled through the moonlight to the vicarage. He waved his arms, proclaiming nonsense. Mary began to talk more vivaciously as if to cover over what he said, to bury his flat ridiculous statements under wreaths of bright chatter. Her laughter trailed like ribbons.

It was a tranquil evening lulled by the strokes and sighs of waves petting the beach below. A membrane of cloud diffused the moonlight, but the mountain stood clear in a setting of stars, its dark base dissolving into the black plain around it.

Mary walked with scrupulous care to disguise the lameness she had suffered ever since Lawrence's horse, August, trod on her right foot when she first attempted to saddle him. Her hands still hurt and had begun to stiffen, but joy rose up inside her, queer, sweet and restless. She affected a skipping step as she cried out: 'Look at the mountain, Rhys! Isn't it the most beautiful thing you ever saw?'

It was a perfectly ordinary thing to say, predictable even, but Rhys was moved by her vulnerability. He sensed that, like those birds she had freed this afternoon, she was yearning to break loose from constraints that chafed at her spirit.

An orchard had been planted on the perimeter of the church land. As they approached a sharp scent of apple blossom drifted on the wind.

Suddenly, Lawrence raised his voice, sharp with aggression. 'You claim to be an Oxford man, I believe, Mr Morgan?'

Dismayed, Rhys replied: 'I could be described as such, but I've never made any special claims to—'

'Kindly hear me out. Contemplate this c-conundrum if you will, then, Morgan. Here in the Antipodean c-colony we encounter each other, two immaculately educ-cated beings in a society teeming with the riff-raff of unenlightened—'

'*Please*, Mr Rennie,' cut in Gwynne, exasperated. All they wanted out of the evening was a little unaccustomed pleasure, but he was ruining everything with his insistence on quarrelling. She'd had enough of squabbles! What must Rhys be thinking of them?

In a softer tone she cajoled: 'Please, Mr Rennie. Promise me that you won't once mention how ignorant you think we all are. Not tonight, please?'

Bravo! thought Rhys. Mary laughed.

Her laugh tumbled into a cold silence and died there.

Capering along behind the grown-ups and enjoying herself by breathing in great gulps of the flowery air, Lisabeth sensed her stepfather's anger and hung back, fearing another of his violent outbursts.

Nothing happened. They all walked a few more paces in absolute quiet until Rhys said: 'I hope it won't give offence, but I've put all that élitist nonsense behind me now that I've left England and—'

'Nonsense?'

'Well . . . yes. The privileges of education mean nothing here in the colonies, do they? I spent two weeks near Sydney and I couldn't help noticing that—'

'Nonsense?' exploded Lawrence. 'You have an Oxford education and you dismiss it as *nonsense*?'

Rhys attempted to laugh.

'And you derive *amusement* from your views?'

Rhys noticed that nobody stood near to Lawrence. Mary's face was indistinct in this clouded light, but he had the feeling that she was nervous, if not actually frightened. He said: 'Permit me to explain my views, please.'

'Oh, please, do! We'll be fascinated,' sneered Lawrence.

'Very well,' said Rhys, uneasy but controlled. 'I'm very young, and my experience is limited, but from what I've seen in New South Wales it's clear that in the colonies men are being measured by different standards from those back home.'

'More is the pity,' Lawrence interrupted.

'Oh, no! It's good! Here men are not measured by the rarefied language they use or the letters they sprinkle after their name, but by their actions, their solid achievements won by the labour of their bodies. It doesn't matter one whit who their parents were or what colleges they were fortunate enough to attend. Here it's character that counts for everything, not privilege. Don't you think that's exciting?' he asked, his voice rushing out in eagerness. 'Why, here in the reaches of the Empire people have shaken off all the petty restrictions of Home and are closer to becoming equals than they have been at any time since the dawn of civilization! It's—'

'It's unadulterated nonsense, the weakest drivel I've ever heard!' said Lawrence furiously.

Everybody was shocked by the violence implicit in his tone. Mary expected him to lash out at Rhys and was trembling with anticipation at the idea, for she guessed that Rhys could knock him down easily – and she hoped he would – but instead of putting up his fists Lawrence turned on his heel and strode back towards the hotel's lighted windows.

Mary said: 'He wouldn't have stayed long at the dance anyway. *He* thinks enjoyment should be a solitary pursuit.' And she laughed.

Charles was too disgusted with both the Rennies to add any

26

comment, but Gwynne explained gently: 'I'm afraid you touched Mr Rennie on a raw nerve, dear. He prides himself on his education. His family . . . well, he's temporarily separated from his family, and his learning is all he has to cling to.'

'I didn't realize . . .' said Rhys, youth and uncertainty showing in his voice. Mr Rennie was middle-aged and schoolmasterly and he should have been accorded more respect. 'Please, Mrs Rennie, allow me to apologize.'

Her hands fluttered like moths in the moonlight. 'Don't apologize! Ask me to dance later, instead.'

She was flirting with him, and the hell of it was that he found it quite delicious. 'I certainly will,' he said.

The vicarage bedroom was crowded as in the yellow glow of lamplight a dozen ladies fussed and primped in preparation for the festivities. Lisabeth sat perfectly still amongst the confusion of petticoats and hair-brushes as Mary dressed her hair in a simpler version of her own style, centre-parted and plaited into ropes that wound around her head in a glossy coronet. Wispy tendrils tickled the back of her neck and escaped in front of her ears. It was not well done but was the neatest Mary's sore fingers would allow. Lisabeth wore a simple gown of blue silk 'filled out' with frilled petticoats made from old starched flour-bags because she was still too young for a real crinoline like her mother's.

Mary's gown was her one good one, and she unpacked it from the willow hamper with care because there was no prospect of her ever getting another one. Lisabeth watched as she eased it over her head then spread the yellow and white taffeta skirts over the wide cage of metal hoops so that it draped evenly to the floor all around.

'You look as pretty as one of Mrs Stafford's blancmange puddings!' she exclaimed. 'They woffle like that when she turns them out of the mould.'

Mary was rubbing crossly at a stain. 'I *will* eat and drink, I suppose . . .' she muttered, twisting to view her back in the pier glass. 'Oh, gracious! My neck is as brown as a Maori's. What will Mr Morgan think of us all?'

Gwynne was heating a curling-iron over a spirit-lamp so that she could frizzle her bangs. 'I think he likes you, and I'm so pleased,' she said. 'I'm afraid he's started off on the wrong foot with Lawrence and, as for Charles, I had hoped . . . But,' she added brightly, 'he seems to have taken an instant liking to you.'

27

Mary bit her lips hard, top then bottom, and ran her tongue around them for gloss. Her eyes looked sly. 'Do you think so?' she said.

'Indeed,' said Gwynne. There was the odour of scorching hair, and when she could relax her concentration Gwynne continued, 'But perhaps it's Lisabeth whose impressions will matter most. Rhys has always said in his letters that he will never think of marrying until he turns thirty. He's twenty-one now, so that makes him the perfect age for Lisabeth. What do you think, pet?'

The idea took Lisabeth's breath away; it was unexpected and utterly thrilling. 'I think he's absolutely—' she began.

'Hush!' Mary snapped, turning so suddenly that she dropped the stopper of Gwynne's perfume-bottle. All the other women in the room hushed, staring at her as she stooped to pick it up.

'Oh dear, it's broken!' she said. 'Gwynne, I'm sorry, but you did upset me properly putting silly ideas into Lisabeth's head. She's only a child! Mr Morgan and her . . . it's ridiculous!'

Lisabeth sat near the fern-draped stage and watched the musicians: the fiddler whose foot jerked up and down in time with his sawing arm, and the fat, toothless man with the purple squeeze-box who winked at her and made her blush every time he caught her eye. The piano was played by the vicar's wife, a soft blonde woman who thumped at the keys with the same grimness she used to pound out the Sunday hymns.

She watched her mother and Mr Morgan. After having the first dance with Mrs Stafford he had every dance with Mary, holding her close so that her crinoline swirled and dipped. Her limp was hardly noticeable at all. She was like a flower swaying in the wind, thought Lisabeth proudly, more beautiful than any of the other ladies in the hall. Everyone was watching them, Lisabeth could tell that they were envious by the way they whispered and pointed.

'I wish that I was old enough to dance,' she said when Mr and Mrs Stafford retreated from the dance-floor to sit beside her on the backless bench. 'It looks such fun!'

'Ay,' said Charles heavily. 'There's fun and there's fun. Some's innocent like, and *some* is sinister. That means it leads to sin.'

Gwynne didn't hear him above the music's din. She was panting as she flipped open her fretted ivory fan and flapped it with vigour. 'Look!' she cried, as Rhys and Mary spun past, laughing. '*Aren't* they enjoying themselves?'

'Ay. That's just what I mean,' said Charles.

As was the custom each of the women attending the dance had brought a 'plate' for supper, one of their best china platters that had survived the journey from England, on which they had arranged a heap of thin-cut sandwiches (ham or tongue), a bouquet of jam tarts or a fat sponge cake dusted with finely grated sugar.

At eleven o'clock these were set out on trestle tables in the centre of the dance-floor under the smoky oil-lamps. Insects looped like dancers in the light, and children hovered, big-eyed, around the feast, hands behind their backs because nothing could be touched until the vicar had pronounced Grace. Lisabeth did not join them. Her head ached.

Mary and Rhys came over to join the Staffords. She skipped, breathless.

'There's no sign of Lawrence yet,' commented Gwynne, for it was unlike him to miss supper.

Mary hitched the shoulder of her gown back into place. 'That really is too bad!' she laughed. Her eyes were very bright, and there was a damp row of little curls across her brow.

'Mrs Zender wants to have a word with you,' Gwynne told her. 'With both of you if possible. She tells me that the district is to receive a schoolmaster. An elderly widower, she said, and he's planning to visit all the outlying homes in turn to set lessons for the children to follow. I know you've been worried about Lisabeth's education, so you'll be pleased to hear all about this.'

'Lawrence won't. A teacher will want paying, and I can't for the life of me imagine him agreeing.' She saw Lisabeth staring up at her and stopped, frowning. The child longed to go to school.

Rhys overheard, too. He drew Charles aside and said: 'What's the situation between the Rennies? They're so ill-matched . . . she's so delightful and he's so . . .'

'You can spit it out, lad,' snorted Charles. 'He's a right bastard and that's faint praise! They've not been married a year. She were a widow woman.'

'Why did they marry, then?'

Charles pulled a twist of tobacco from the wad in his pouch and tucked it into his cheek. 'Simple. He wanted someone to do for him, cook and keep house, and *she* thought he'd take her home to his family in Kent. Trouble is, she's no housewife and he has no intention of ever going home to England.'

'Why not?'

'Believe it or not, he likes the bush. His family send money. It's not enough for him to live well in a city, but ample for a Spartan existence. Spends it all on pipe tobacco and whisky – the wagon will be loaded down with it tomorrow, you'll see.' Charles laughed. 'All right for some,' he added obscurely.

'You don't like either of them. Why don't you like her?'

Charles's lumpy face flushed, and his watery eyes glanced at Mary then away. 'She's . . . she's no business being here. She doesn't fit in,' he said at last.

Rhys laughed tactlessly. 'You fancy her, too,' he accused. 'Well, I certainly do. There's something exquisite about her.'

Bridling at the insinuation, Charles felt his dislike of his brother-in-law increase. 'You're young and reckless, lad. Throwing your money away and now talking like this. You'll throw your life away if you don't take care!'

But in his heart he was envious. He'd never had money to fling about, nor charm. He'd been young once and brimming with hope, but what did he have to show for all his work and dreams? A series of disappointments and a worn-out wife who said her feet hurt after only two circuits of the dance-floor. There was no justice in it.

'What's the matter, dear?' Gwynne bent over Lisabeth. 'Don't you want anything? A sweet pastry or a piece of cake?'

Lisabeth shook her head. She was white and drawn. Gwynne touched her forehead.

'The child's burning up!' she said, but Mary was laughing at something Rhys had said and didn't acknowledge her.

'It's only a sick headache,' protested Lisabeth. 'Do you think I could go out to the wagon now? If I lie down, it always feels better.'

Gwynne went with her; they were skirting the churchyard when Lisabeth uttered a strangling sound and staggered behind a tombstone where she retched up her mutton and cabbage and the lemon barley water she had drunk with it.

'Oh dear,' fretted Gwynne. 'Shall I fetch your mother?'

Wiping her mouth with a shaky hand, Lisabeth said: 'No, thank you, Mrs Stafford. I'll be fine now, truly.'

But Gwynne stayed, helping her off with the blue dress then giving her a leg-up into the wagon. Once the child was ensconced in the nest of bedding she pulled the tarpaulin over her like a tent. 'Goodnight, dear.'

'Thank you for your kindness, and goodnight,' replied Lisabeth.

Gwynne's heart blossomed. As she picked her way back to the hall she suffered a few minutes' sad reflection on her own childlessness. If only God had blessed her with family, then Charles would have been different, she knew. He'd have been happier, more content, not always building up these impossible dreams of being a wealthy country squire and then having the bitterness of seeing those dreams crumble to reality. With children to look after he'd have understood what reality was.

It was all her fault for being barren.

On the dance evenings the vicarage privy was reserved for ladies' use, and lanterns in the shrubbery lit the way. Mary was hurrying back from a visit after supper when Rhys emerged from the hall doorway. He obviously did not see her, for he turned and strode away towards the meadow where the wagons were parked.

Mary paused, calculating. After a moment, she moved, but instead of returning to the hall she circled the church the other way until she, too, reached the paddock. Loitering near the Staffords' wagon, she pretended to admire the moonlit view of the mountain.

When Rhys approached and spoke to her she jumped, startled. It was not feigned; her heart had been cramping tighter and tighter until her whole body was strung to an unbearable pitch. When she moved she could feel herself vibrating like the strings of a guitar. If Rhys stood close to her, she knew that he would hear the blood strumming in her veins, and if he touched her – oh, if he touched her! – she was in danger of flying to pieces.

'It's so hot in there!' Her voice was giddy.

'But out here it's delightful.'

How she loved his voice! It was low and burred around the vowels with traces of an accent he had half-grown at Oxford. She wanted to tell him that it was beautiful, that *he* was beautiful, but she said, 'I do hope you're—' and turned abruptly to find herself leaning against his cologne-scented, ruffled shirt-front.

'You almost tripped.' When he put his hands out to steady her she clutched at him with a swiftness that he somehow expected. 'I didn't tread on your foot earlier, did I? I noticed that as you left the hall you seemed to limp and I wondered—'

'No! Of course not! My shoe is rubbing. It's nothing!' But she moved away a pace, her attractiveness diminished. After a silence

31

she said: 'Is this place as you expected it to be?'

'Nothing like my imaginings, but they were confused in any case.' He reached into a pocket and withdrew a thin cigar. 'Gwynne describes food and Charles's state of health in her letters, and *his* letters hint at terrible happenings, cannibals and hostile tribes. I noticed that the hall is fortified with rifle-slits and so on. Are things as dangerous as that?'

'I don't honestly know,' said Mary. 'Nor do I care! There have been incidents . . . settlers killed, but we've had earthquakes, too, and one can't live in fear, can one? It's this place itself that's the real danger. It's voracious. It swallows people up. When those trees close over my head I begin to panic. Sometimes . . . sometimes I feel that I'm disappearing from the face of the earth.'

She sounded as if she was crying out to be saved. He began to feel an edge of nervousness. To change the subject he said: 'A woman with your spirit need never be afraid of anything. The way you tore into those cages to free the birds was magnificent. How are your hands now?'

In reply she held them up for inspection. They were bare, sensuous in the silver moonlight. 'You wear no wedding ring,' he said.

'Lawrence said I already had one.' Her excitement was intense; her face blazed up at him, and she placed her hands one on either side of his face. Then, with a daring that took her breath away, she slid them around his neck. There! It was done! She had made her move and, having done so, felt an easing of that perilous tension.

Why not? he thought. *Why not?* She was warm and sweet and willing, and desire rose hot and strong in him. As his arms spasmed around her waist her body seemed to flow into his.

Lisabeth, lying close by under the canopy of canvas, heard the whispers, the clatter of crinoline hoops and Mary's greedy laughter. Something magical was happening; she could sense it. Lying perfectly still, she gazed at the slice of star-flecked sky that was visible and listened to Mary and Rhys making love.

Presently Rhys returned to the hall, leaving Mary alone. She stood on the cliff-edge and flung her arms wide to embrace her view of the foaming surf.

'I could die!' she said aloud. 'Oh, if only I could die now!' She turned back towards the wagon, and through the gap Lisabeth could see her face, dreamy with ecstasy. While she watched, Mary

32

drew a long dry breath then suddenly pressed both hands over her face and crumpled forward, sobbing.

At once Lisabeth scrambled to thrust her head out from the tarpaulin flap. 'Mamma! What's the matter?'

Mary gasped in real fright, then relaxed. Her face looked odd, twisted as if in grief, but with a distinct light of triumph in her eyes. The gloating light faded. 'How long have you been there?'

'I had a headache, Mamma.'

'*How long have you been there?*'

'Since supper-time,' whispered Lisabeth.

'You've been spying on me! How dare you spy on me!' And Mary's hand slapped out, cuffing her smartly.

'I didn't mean—' began Lisabeth.

'You didn't hear anything, do you understand me? Do you *understand* ?'

'No, Mamma.'

But already Mary was limping away in the direction of the vicarage, leaving Lisabeth alone and shivering, utterly bewildered.

THREE

NEXT MORNING on the way home the group was subdued. Everybody seemed tired, introverted – all but Mary, who in contrast percolated cheeriness which she splashed around her. She sang, hummed and tried out all the jokes and riddles she could dredge from memory. Warm in the glow of her affection, Lisabeth was delighted to share her joy.

It was a shimmering hot day. The mountain faded, a pale etching on the acid-blue sky. Mary leaned towards Rhys, her face animated. 'The Maoris call it Taranaki, after a fellow named Rua Taranaki who was the first man to climb it. Their legends say that this was originally part of that group of mountains way in the centre of the island, but that one day they quarrelled and—'

'Dash it all, do be quiet for five minutes!' snapped Lawrence, who was heartily sick of the way she was gushing on. The wretched woman had no respect for a hangover.

'Excuse *me*!' retorted Mary. 'I'm trying to entertain our guest and it's hardly my fault if you will make yourself ill by over-indulging—'

'Hush!' warned Charles. 'There's trouble ahead. Maoris!'

They were descending into a steep-sided gully where a brown engorged stream was spanned by a bridge made of logs. It was flat and sideless, and swarming all around were twenty or so Maori people of different ages, men and women, wrapped in cloaks and carrying bundles of luggage tied with flax string. A wagon had broken down on the bridge, and one wheel hung over the side.

'I hope it's not an ambush,' muttered Charles.

'They've had an accident,' said Lawrence. Wearily he climbed down to walk ahead of the wagon. '*Kia ora,*' he called in greeting. '*Aha he?* What's wrong?'

It had been quite an upset. Packages bobbed in the stream, and naked children waded up to their armpits to retrieve them. *Like seals*, thought Lisabeth who recognized some of the people and the horse that stood shuddering on the far bank, a sad black mare with a low-hanging head. Something terrible was the matter with it now. Its neck was slewing to one side and, though the young Maori men around it coaxed it with shouts of '*Haere mai!*' and urged it with sticks, it wouldn't move.

'Its leg is broken!' whispered Mary, aghast.

'They're beating it!' cried Lisabeth, tears starting in her eyes. 'Can't we stop them? It's *hurt*!'

'We'll mind our own business,' muttered Charles, who had a fear and loathing of the natives. Lawrence waved him on to cross the bridge, and he flapped the reins; but Sargent, scenting blood, balked, leaning back on his haunches.

'The poor horse! Can't we do something?' cried Mary.

Rhys and Lawrence grabbed Sargent's reins and tugged, persuading him on to the bridge. He had to be dragged every step of the way.

As they rattled over, Lisabeth stared in horror at the horse, the froth of foam around the mouth and the rolling whites of its eyes.

At the other side of the bridge Sargent jerked his head free, trying to look around at the injured mare. Rhys was moved by the obvious sympathy that flowed between them. 'Was she an old girl-friend of yours, then, lad?' he asked, trying to make light of a situation that sickened him. The youths were still trying to torment the creature into moving. Abruptly, Rhys reached a decision.

'Drive on as quickly as you can,' he called to Charles. 'Don't wait for me.'

With that he turned and dashed back towards the bridge, reaching into his jacket as he ran. From her perch on his luggage Lisabeth saw him withdraw a small brass pistol. Pushing a couple of the Maori youths aside, Rhys wasted no time but shoved the muzzle up against the animal's forehead and pulled the trigger.

There was a single slap of noise. The mare subsided, deflating as if its bones had melted. It uttered no cry.

'He killed it!' shrieked Lisabeth. 'He *killed* that poor horse!'

An eruption of shouting broke out from the river-banks as Rhys loped back to catch up to the wagon. 'Hurry!' he cried as he pelted beside them.

35

'Are you daft or barmy?' shouted Charles, cracking the whip to urge Sargent to plod faster. He felt like plastering the blows around Rhys's shoulders instead. Jaws working with fury, he said: 'Bejesus, it's bad enough that you're hell-bent on tossing money away but now it's all our lives you're flinging into danger.'

'Charles!' pleaded Gwynne, her sharp features bunched with anxiety.

'Stop screaming!' said Mary to Lisabeth.

Rhys twisted his neck to look back. 'We're not being followed,' he reported as he swung up into the wagon. He felt foolish, too, but not in the least repentant. *It had to be done*, he told himself. *Someone had to do it.*

Lawrence was smiling sourly. 'Your precipitous action will be entirely unappreciated. I can guarantee that when this intelligence reaches Tamati's ears all of Hades, as they say, will loose itself upon you.'

Let it, thought Rhys, but he noticed that Charles looked pale, 'Who is Tamati?' he asked.

'The paramount chief of the area. According to the precepts of Maori custom, Tamati owns this entire district and everything within it. Including that wretched beast of burden.'

'Ay, lad,' concurred Charles. 'And he thinks he owns us, too.'

'Then, I'll go to see him,' declared Rhys. 'He's probably a reasonable man.'

'He departed yesterday bound for Patea,' said Lawrence. 'A *tangi*, a wake, will occupy his attentions for a considerable period of time. You would be sagacious, young man, to contrive an early departure to avoid what could be an unpleasant confrontation.'

He wants to be rid of me, Rhys realized with inward amusement. *He's just trying to frighten me away*. He glanced up at Mary and was surprised to see a tight anguish in her face.

Lisabeth sobbed on. The landscape swum around her, her illusions drowned. *How could he be so cruel?* she kept asking herself. *How could he have done such a callous awful thing?*

'Why did he do it?' she asked Mary much later. 'Why did he kill that poor hurt horse?'

They were outside the primitive one-roomed cottage that was their home. Shortly after he first arrived the Maoris had built it for Lawrence, fashioning it in the native style from woven panels of reeds with a thatch of flax matting to deflect the drenching winter rains. It was so cramped and dark inside, so stuffy and dank

36

summer or winter, that unless it was raining most of their time was spent in the open where a black-stained fireplace boiled the laundry copper while another, sheltered by a rusty iron canopy, served for cooking. Like the interior of the cottage the area was bare and ugly. Amongst a litter of bottles and ragged cans scrubby ferns grew wild, and in a neglected garden half a dozen splitting cabbages were almost hidden by knee-high weeds.

It was dusk, and the bush crackled with insect song. Lawrence was away with August somewhere, stashing his crates of whisky. Mary perched on a tree-stump, knees tucked up under her blue poplin skirts, humming as she brushed her hair with slow caressing strokes. When unbraided it was thick and rippling, hanging over her face like a curtain.

'Why, Mamma?' repeated Lisabeth.

Mary raised her head. From where she sat she could see a trace of smoke from beyond the next ridge where Gwynne was cooking dinner for Rhys. Hotpot and apple dumplings, Gwynne had said. Mary had done nothing about their evening meal yet; she was too happy to feel hungry. Later she would scratch up a few cold scraps.

'He did it because he thought it was right, that's why,' Mary said.

'But we could have rescued it and brought it home! We could have nursed it until it was better, couldn't we?'

'What a funny little thing you are,' said Mary. As she drew the brush lazily through her hair she began to sing.

I hate him, vowed Lisabeth wretchedly. *I'll never forget that poor horse. I'll never forget how cruel he was today.* She felt bereft, as if the tall fair stranger she adored had died.

'You smell so good!' murmured Mary, thrusting her face against his neck, laughing in a low gurgle. 'Mmmm, but I'm hungry to be with you. When you didn't come yesterday I was *frantic*. I resolved that if you weren't here today I'd have to make an excuse to visit Gwynne again, just to be near you. I know she's your sister, but we can't have her monopolizing you! You belong to me, too, don't you? Oh, but I *miss* you! I miss you so!' She glanced up at his face, noticed that he looked perturbed so added hastily: 'Not that I'm griping, mind you! You're here now and that's all that matters, isn't it?'

She had met him on the ridge-path as she had done almost every day for the past three weeks. After she had wobbled her way across the stepping-stones above the waterfall and had climbed

37

around the bole of the huge fallen *kauri* tree she would see him waiting for her further on, near a cluster of *nikau* palms. He was always standing still, staring out across the valley towards the mountain with a sober unfathomable expression on his face. Her heart would stop, clogged by the rush of joy that flooded through her.

He's my miracle! she exulted as she hugged herself against him. *I wanted a miracle, and here he is!*

Today, as she tugged at his arm to hurry him along, he slowed his pace deliberately, 'Mary, we must talk.'

'Something's wrong? Gwynne doesn't suspect, does she?'

'Gwynne hasn't one suspicious bone in her body. No, it's not her, but I'm sure that Charles—'

'Then, it doesn't matter!' Mary broke in gaily. Nothing was going to spoil this. 'We'll talk later.' She smiled up at his frowning face as they pushed through the undergrowth, ferns and damp bushes brushing at their clothing. 'Oh, Rhys, I'm so happy I feel ill with it.'

She's like a child, he thought. A passionate, sweet and demanding child.

She skipped on ahead, laughing, teasing, tempting him to run in pursuit, but he followed on leaden feet. He must find a way to put a stop to this swiftly, without hurting her. He was inexperienced enough to believe that such a thing was possible.

Their glade was on a high narrow promontory tonsured around with a thicket of *miro* trees where *tuis* and wood-pigeons set up a taffeta rustling as they visited constantly from one branch to another. By the time Rhys stepped out into the open Mary had unbuttoned her blouse and was slipping it off her shoulders as she gazed down-river in a preoccupied way.

'There's been no sign of the Maoris yet,' she said.

'Never mind them,' said Rhys. He'd resolved that there would be no more love-making, but Mary was already stripping off her camisole. It was old and torn, the sight of it evoked the same guilty feelings in him that her painstakingly disguised limp did. 'Mary, don't . . . Please, let's talk.'

'Later,' she promised, winding her bare arms around his neck and pulling his face down to hers as she chuckled: 'You're *beautiful*. Men aren't supposed to be beautiful, are they? But you are.'

Sunlight bathed her shoulders warm as milk, and her breasts were silk against his chest. There was something so exquisite about her . . . but he mustn't, not today . . .

She reached up to kiss him, and his other self rose up, too, swamping his resolutions as easily as the surf engulfs a paper boat. They sank together to the harsh dry ground, and her thighs moved to enclose him. She was sweet and warm and unbearably good, and he was lost, drawn into the whirlpool's throat, drowning in her while the sound of his own rough breathing roared like the ocean in his head.

'Now you can talk to me!' She was leaning over him, tickling one corner of his mouth with a feathery grass-stalk.

He groaned. The sun was hot orange against his eyelids, but the rest of his body was cold. It shouldn't have happened.

Mary laughed. 'Come, now. Not too exhausted to talk, are you? I know, tell me more about cricket. I love to hear you talk about that, even if I don't understand the half of it. Your face lights up and you make it sound positively splendid. Oh, but you'll be able to show them a thing or two when they hold their annual cricket match on the beach at Waitamanui on New Year's Day. It's all slamming and banging and no finesse, I can tell you! We'll be so proud of you, Gwynne and I!'

I'll have to leave, Rhys realized.

'Better yet, tell me about Oxford. I like the way you describe things. Lawrence can't be bothered, himself. He cracks on that he's a cut or two above the heel of the loaf and someone the likes of me has no right even to share—'

'Tell me about Lawrence.'

She breathed into his ear. 'There's nothing to tell. He's fastened tight into his solitude; marrying me made no difference to his life. I blame the isolation. It makes people very selfish. Lawrence spends all his money on himself. Charles, too, he thinks only of his creature comforts. Even I'm growing selfish and I hate it! I've got to get away from here before this place suffocates me.'

And she wants me to take her, he thought.

'Mary, you must understand something. When I came here it was only for a holiday. I never intended staying long—'

'That's nonsense! Gwynne is expecting you to stay for at least six months.' There was alarm in her voice.

He shuddered. 'Mary, please. I'm trying to tell you the only way I can. This can't go on . . . this secretive relationship between you and me. I'm going to have to leave soon, and—'

'No!' She shoved at him with both hands, pushing him back against the prickly grass, leaning over him so that her dark

39

frightened eyes glared into his. 'No! I won't listen! Don't you understand what's happened? I've been waiting all my life for you and I didn't even know it. You're young and maybe because of that you don't want to acknowledge the truth, but the fact is we *love* each other. It can't be denied, can it?' Her voice shook with a kind of frightened determination, like someone who is balancing high above a void and who daren't look down.

How could he say he didn't love her? 'Mary, you're glorious,' he began. 'You're the sweetest woman I've ever known, but—'

'Then, please don't talk about ending it. Face up to your feelings, Rhys!' She paused to allow him to reply, but he said nothing, just stared unhappily out towards the river. In a panic she said: 'Rhys, don't talk about leaving! It's like dwelling on death when life is at its happiest. You don't know what it was like for me before! Oh, please . . .'

She was crying. Because there was nothing else for it, he comforted her, and she clung to him knowing she was letting herself down but unable to stop.

Rhys stroked her shoulders. He told himself that her unhappiness had nothing to do with him, that he was just one of many different ingredients that went to make up her life. The thought did not reassure him.

I must leave, and soon, he resolved.

FOUR

ON CHRISTMAS MORNING Mary woke feeling ill with worry.
Four days had now elapsed since she broke down and wept in Rhys's
arms, and she had not seen him since. She waited for hours one
afternoon, right through two showers, but he did not take pity on
her. When in desperation she walked all the way to the Staffords'
there was no sign of him there, either. Nor encouragement.

'He's finally taken an interest in the place and gone out to help
Mr Stafford,' reported Gwynne, pleased. 'I can't tell you how
worried I've been that Rhys wasn't happy here. He's been so
moody, so unhappy . . . I can't talk to him, and he takes these
long walks. It's marvellous that they're finally making friends.'

'Marvellous,' agreed Mary sourly. *Well, he's not avoiding me
on Christmas Day!* And grimly she set about angling for an invitation to afternoon tea.

After breakfast Lawrence gave Lisabeth a green glass jar of black
and white sweets – blackboys – and one of his own books, a thick
volume with a stained cover and fraying spine, entitled *Homer's
Reflections*.

The sweets were nice and she allowed herself three before
recapping the jar, but the book was more fun. Though she could
read only an occasional word, she sat in the midday sunshine with
the volume spread heavily in her lap, turning the mould-mottled
pages as she gazed enraptured at the illustrations; scraped landscapes that seemed strangely bare when compared to the suffocating vegetation around here, geometrically perfect buildings that
seemed to have no practical purpose (where were their privies?
Lisabeth wondered) and people draped in bedsheets who stood

41

about with one arm raised. They wore leaves in their hair, a notion she approved.

Pleased to have made her happy, Lawrence sprawled on the ground beside her and drank whisky from the only crystal glass that had survived his exile.

'Christmas deserves to be celebrated with distinction,' he told her as he squinted through the patterned base of the tumbler. He was sottedly drunk by early afternoon.

There were no gifts for Mary, nor did she give any. She spent the morning washing her hair then drying it in the sun before brushing and plaiting it with extra care. Then she put on her only good dress, the yellow and white taffeta she had worn at the dance. It was madness to wear it through the bush, she knew. She would ruin it but she didn't care. Blood was pulsing through her so fiercely that every part of her body was over-sensitive to the touch; the bones of her corset dug in where they had always fitted comfortably before, and the lace edges of her pantalettes scratched the tender skin on the inside of her knees. Even breathing hurt.

Unseen, she slipped away from the house and hurried along the ridge-track, holding the sides of her crinoline close against her body so that they would not spring out to snag her skirts on the bushes that flapped at her ankles as she limped past. Tucked under one arm was a cloth-wrapped package containing her yellow leather slippers. Within sight of the Staffords' neat timber cottage she paused to shuck off her mud-encrusted boots, then proceeded slowly, praying that the blue-painted door would fly open and Rhys would come running to meet her.

Instead she had to knock, and stood staring at the froth of blooms cascading over the path from Gwynne's luxuriant garden. It was she who answered the door.

'Mary! How pretty you look! But where is Lisabeth? I've made her a doll and I can't wait to see her face when unwraps it.'

Mary gaped for a second, then recovered. 'She has another sick headache,' she lied. She'd forgotten completely that Lisabeth was supposed to come today.

It was a miserable afternoon. Mary had no appetite and couldn't taste what she forced down from the spread arrayed on the home-made wooden table. Gwynne had baked fruit cakes, carrot cake, tiny griddle cakes and sweet raisin bread which she offered continuously in turn. Shaking her head, Mary chattered and laughed and, when she paused for breath, glanced hungrily at Rhys who sat by the window gazing out past the opened

42

shutters as if in his mind he was already hundreds of miles away.

Mary was in anguish. A faint breeze stirred straying wisps of hair above his brow, and she longed to reached out to smooth them down. She loved his hair. The texture of it under her fingertips was as sensuous as any other part of him. Through his thin white shirt she could see the outline of his shoulders, the packed wads of muscle that slid under the skin as he moved. It was all she could do to restrain herself from going over to him and kissing him right there, in front of Gwynne's shocked eyes.

In the end she had to ask him – outright, so he couldn't refuse – to walk a way up the track with her. He stopped within view of the house.

Her heart withered. She tried to flirt. 'Don't tell me you haven't missed me!'

'Of course I have.' She was begging. He couldn't bear that.

'Then, you do care for me.'

'Of course I do.' He was about to say more, but changed his mind. There was nothing he could do for her. He'd put aside six pounds to leave with Charles to recompense the Maoris for their horse, and that left him with only a few shillings to spend on the voyage back to Sydney. The irony of it was that if she hadn't freed the birds he could have given her that ten guineas – not much, true, but enough to purchase a passage to the nearest large town for herself and Lisabeth.

Lisabeth. He felt guilty about her, too. The obvious adulation in her eyes that first evening had been so flattering that he'd gone out of his way to chat to her, even offered to whirl her around the dance-floor, but the only looks he'd received from her since he'd dispatched the horse had been glances of loathing. It was his fault; he should have explained, but guilt held him back. This was her mother he was dallying with. How much had she guessed? He'd the most vivid uncomfortable feeling that the child knew everything; those huge blue-black eyes were so expressive – and perceptive, too, he suspected.

'You have so much in your life,' Rhys said lamely. 'Your beautiful daughter, your—'

'Don't do this to me, Rhys,' she hissed fiercely. Then, renewing her light flirtation, she said: 'Come, walk a way further. It's Christmas after all!'

If only he had something to give her. At least he could leave her her pride. She'd gone to such trouble to be attractive to him and

43

what would it matter if they made love one more time? It would be a goodbye gift to them both.

Mary skipped all the way home, humming to herself.

Gwynne was still crying when the wagon reached the edge of Rennie's farm and began to cross the 'corduroy', the long road of logs fitted side by side across a stretch of marshland. Gwynne hugged herself, her moans hiccuping with the sharp wheel-jolts.

'Fine road this,' said Charles expansively. 'Made it myself. Had to. The idle bogger couldn't stir himself to drain the swamp and there were no way around it. Made a fine job even if I do say so myself.'

'Yes,' said Rhys. He patted Gwynne's shoulder. Guilt strangled him.

She clutched at his hand. She'd known he wasn't happy. All those long solitary walks day after day, then in the past week he'd been so remote, so worried. Nothing she said or did seemed to make any difference; she'd tried every delicious recipe to tempt him, but he had no appetite, either.

'I'm so disappointed,' she told him. 'Can't you change your mind? You've hardly been here but five—'

'I'm afraid not.'

'Leave the boy alone,' rasped Charles. He'd be pleased to see the back of him. All he could talk about was how much better things were elsewhere. Looked down his nose at them, he did, and unsettled Gwynne no end. Just hark at her sobbing!

It was early morning. Shreds of mist still hooked on to tree-branches and lay, unrolled, over the swamp in holey rags. The air smelt of mildew.

When the track led them past the clearing the cottage door banged open and Mary emerged. Obviously she had glanced out of the gap between the shutters and when she saw them came hurtling right out without finishing her dressing. Her bodice was only half-buttoned, and her black hair flapped in a loose frowzy plait. Agitated, she made no effort to disguise her limp but lurched and dipped over the rough ground, her skirts snapping around her bare heels and her face twisted in panic. She was gasping as she reached them and hung on to the side of the wagon, gazing up at Rhys.

Charles pulled on the reins to bring Sargent to a halt and stared at Mary from the corners of his eyes. Gwynne was shocked by her friend's dishevelled appearance, but Mary saw only Rhys, Rhys in

44

his best suit with the magnolia silk ruffled shirt and the elegant embroidered waistcoat. His appearance confirmed her fears.

'You're not going!' she pleaded. The heap of luggage was answer enough, but she repeated: 'Tell me you're not leaving!'

'I'm truly sorry. I did try to explain.'

'But you can't. I've something I must tell you. I must!' She tugged at Charles's sleeve. 'Wait for me, will you? I'll only be a moment, I promise. Please wait.'

Charles shrugged. His inclination was to drive on, but curiosity got the better of him. Something was going on here; he'd long suspected it but now he was sure.

The room stank of the chamberpot. Waking to it, Lisabeth wrinkled her nose and thrust her face back under the grimy bedding.

The sound of Mr Rennie shouting at her mother made her peek again.

Mary was dashing about like a whirlwind. Snatching her cape from the peg behind the door, she flung it around her shoulders and stabbed the top button through its slit, then jammed her muddy feet into her yellow leather slippers before whisking her bonnet from its place on the high shelf under the rafters. Craning her neck to peer into the dim mirror, she thrust it on, muttering at her reflection as she frantically poked hanks of uncombed hair up underneath the crown.

Lawrence had closed the door and was leaning against it. When Mary swung the broom to dislodge her ancient carpet-bag from its perch in the rafters he shouted at her again: 'What in the blazes do you imagine your intentions are?'

'I'm going,' snapped Mary, catching the bag and slapping it to knock off the worst of the dust. Tipping out the rags that had been stored in it, she began scooping up her few possessions, a tortoise-shell comb, a silver pin-box, curling-tongs, an ivory button-hook.

Lawrence drew a deep breath. 'Nothing would give me greater satisfaction than to bid you farewell, but not like this. I'll not tolerate the spectacle of you flinging your unworthy self at that pretentious and braggardly young man. His departure brings relief, I must admit, but—'

'You knew?' whispered Mary, a half-folded gown in her hands. 'You knew he was going?'

He's used her and dumped her, thought Lawrence in disgust. *Now he's probably laughing up his sleeve at me*. His face purpled and swelled. Lisabeth gaped at him in fright. It looked as if his great bee-swarm of a beard was stinging him.

'So you've been whoring around?' bellowed Lawrence. 'I'll not have you making a fool out of me!'

'You don't need anybody's help to make you look stupid, Lawrence.' Mary tossed a cloth book of needles in on top of her shawl and clicked the bag shut. 'I'm leaving, and that's an end to it.'

What about me? thought Lisabeth, but in the next instant she was sitting bolt upright in her narrow bunk, shrieking in terror as Mr Rennie grabbed her mother by the throat and bent her over backwards, thumping her head on the table as he repeatedly punched her in the face.

Mary uttered no cry as she thrashed about trying to free herself, but Lisabeth's wailing scratched at Lawrence's nerves.

'Shut up!' he roared as he slammed one last punch against Mary's cheek. She stopped struggling and glared at him from under puffed bleeding eyelids. He stood back a pace, panting, his temper expended.

'See what he thinks of you now, your fine dandified lover,' he sneered. Turning to Lisabeth, he softened his tone. Poor kid. He was sorry for her. 'One thing you should understand, Lisabeth, before you squander your pity on her. She would have abandoned you without a second thought. She forgot your existence.'

He shoved at the shutters and peered out to where the wagon was still stationary beyond the overgrown garden. Rhys was saying something to try to cheer Gwynne. He was laughing.

'Cocky young bastard,' said Lawrence viciously. 'I'll soon wipe that smug smile off his pretty face.'

The cottage door slammed open, ejecting Lawrence. He scooped up the axe from the chopping-block and weighed it lightly in one hand as he strode towards the wagon.

Rhys felt the hair on the back of his neck prickle. The squealing had startled him, but Charles had dismissed that by saying there was a pig-pen beyond the privy. Now Rhys wondered if that anguished voice had been Mary's.

There was menace here, a threat in Lawrence's sauntering gait. Rhys could feel his body tense. He slipped one hand into his jacket so that his fingers lay over the embossed metal of his pistol-butt.

There was a shout of warning as Mary appeared in the doorway.

46

She staggered a pace then paused, pressing a red cloth to her face. 'Go!' she cried. 'Don't wait, Mr Stafford. Just go!'

Lawrence twisted in his tracks and to their horror flung the axe at his wife. It sheared along the muddy ground, fanning up brown wings of spray as it skidded through puddles.

'Good Lord, what's happening?' exclaimed Rhys, standing up. He thumped Charles on the shoulder. 'No! Stay a moment. I'm afraid he's going to hurt her.'

'And you're getting to that ship in one piece,' declared Charles as he applied the whip to Sargent's haunches, stinging him into a shambling trot. He squinted back over his shoulder, saying: 'Don't fret, lad, he'll not cause her any real harm. Sure and he has a vile temper on him but it never comes to much.'

'Interfering only stirs up muck,' agreed Gwynne, though she was sorry that Mary couldn't come with them after all. She could do with a sympathetic ear, and Charles, bless his heart, didn't know the meaning of the word 'sympathy'.

Rhys felt terrible. *I made a fine mess of everything*, he thought, but despite his shame he felt relieved when the cabin and its miserable occupants had been left far behind.

The Maoris were exquisitely polite but, then, they always were. Three of them came to see Lawrence, two with partly tattooed faces and an older man in a shabby grey linen suit and panama hat. Lawrence recognized them all; they had been at the bridge that day when Rhys had shot their horse.

The horse, their *hoiho*, was what they had come about.

He gazed at them, boiling with such anger that he could barely hear them. In the past hour since reaching the river-flats he had attacked this tree with a fury, slashing at the bole so that the chips flew away almost in anticipation of the axe's bite, but as he hacked his frustration only deepened.

He shouldn't have let Rhys get away. He should have lunged at the wagon, should have dragged the cocky young whelp out and hammered his face into the mud. Mary was his wife, dammit, and even if he had no need for her that was no excuse for her to make a fool of him. It was all her fault anyway, if the marriage was a failure. She was so wooden, so reluctant, and he always sensed that she was comparing him unfavourably with her first husband. Damn it all, that was enough to cool any man's blood. After a couple of unsatisfactory attempts he'd given up completely. Wouldn't anyone?

47

Over and over his anger bubbled, and he swung his axe until he was heavy with fatigue and the tree, almost felled now, stood trembling on its whittled axis.

When the Maoris arrived he gaped at them through a red haze of incomprehension. They had to repeat their errand several times.

'Ah, your *moho hoiho*, your stupid horse!' he said, trading insolence for their scrupulous politeness. 'Nothing to do with me. *Haere ra*. Be off with you.'

The older man's eyes glinted hard as pebbles in the bright sunshine. His tattoos had faded to a faint carbon smudge. '*Utu*,' he insisted. 'It is the *ritenga*, the custom. Tamati, he said he must have *utu*.'

'It's threats now, is it?' In his state of agitation Lawrence misunderstood. The word *utu* that they kept repeating had several meanings in the Maori tongue. It meant 'reward', 'cost' and 'payment', but it was also used to describe the Maori eye-for-an-eye system of vengeance where atrocity was matched by atrocity until full-scale wars developed.

'*Utu*,' insisted the man. 'Tamati he say—'

'You may inform Tamati that this is no concern of mine!' declared Lawrence. He tightened his grip on the axe-handle and noticed as he did so that he was shuddering with exhaustion. 'One Mr Rhys Morgan shot your horse, so I suggest you take up the matter with him. Rhys Morgan,' he repeated. 'The tall man – *toa, urukehu*.'

Tall and fair-haired! The young men nudged each other, sniggering. '*Ah, te koe-koea!*' they giggled and flashed sly looks at him.

A *koe-koea* is a cuckoo, one who lays its eggs in another bird's nest. Lawrence knew that they were laughing openly at him, and why. *The bastards!* his brain sobbed as the sides of his skull seemed to press inwards, blinding him. The dirty mocking bastards!

For a moment time was suspended. Nearby the river chattered as it flowed over polished stones, and two fantails flirted as they darted about near the branches of a fallen *rata* tree. One of the young Maoris whispered slyly, and the other one laughed. Lawrence could feel the sun's heat through the crown of his hat; he knew he was about to be sick.

'Get off my property this instant! *Haere atu!*'

He flailed about with his axe, swinging it threateningly first at

48

one then at another of the Maoris, his strength engorged by rage. He could see he had startled them, and this knowledge gave him a small cold core of satisfaction in the centre of his being.

It was to be the last good feeling he would ever experience.

As Lawrence lunged towards the older man one of the others stepped deftly behind him and with both hands grabbed the axe just below the iron head. Lawrence bellowed as he dragged on the handle, struggling with all his strength to gain control of it again.

Though the Maori was fit and agile, it was an unfair contest. Realizing he would not succeed, the young man calculated his chances and let go abruptly when he could see that Lawrence was straining off balance.

Lawrence lurched backwards, stepped, then sprawled heavily over a stump-root, landing on his back. The axe hit him in the throat.

The Maoris watched in disbelief. His head was wrenched sideways between the mossy roots, and the axe-blade seemed to be embedded in his beard. There was a syrupy gurgling in his chest.

The young Maori looked to the older for guidance; receiving a nod, he carefully tugged the axe-head free. Immediately, Lawrence's body slumped and blood flowed over his shoulder.

'Aue,' cried the elder. '*He patunga takekore he tino kohuru.*'*

The younger men ignored him. They muttered together, sweat beading their striped faces, then set about making the scene and the death look like an accident.

A few minutes later the three were on their way home to their *pah* up-river, satisfied that they were safe.

Mary stared at herself in the mirror with eyes that were so pink and pulpy that they resembled bruised over-ripe figs. Ugly little puncture marks from Lawrence's rings dotted her cheeks, and her lips were split, blackened and grotesquely swollen.

Lisabeth watched in silence. Huddled on her bunk, she hugged the rag doll Mrs Stafford had made against her thin chest. It gave her some comfort.

Mary collapsed on a chair, weeping with terrifying intensity. Lisabeth wanted to go to her but was afraid. 'All I wanted was something beautiful in my life!' Mary cried. 'I love him . . . and he loves me, too! I know he does! He would if he knew . . . I know he would! Oh, dear God, I wish I was dead.'

---

*'It is treachery to kill without proper excuse.'

At this Lisabeth shrank in dismay. It seemed unholy and dreadful to wish you were dead. Through the pain of her own rejection she still felt frightened for her demented mother.

It's all his fault! she told herself. Something Rhys Morgan had done had set Mr Rennie into a fury and made him turn on her mother like this. She couldn't imagine what it was, but it must have been enormously bad.

Yes, it was all his fault.

Being an incurable busybody, Charles invented a reason to visit Lawrence next day so that he could nose out further developments. It was a pale Lisabeth who opened the door a crack and said that Mr Rennie had gone away yesterday and not returned.

'Are you sure Mrs Rennie is all right?' Charles persisted, hoping to catch a glimpse of her. She'd be beaten up for sure.

Lisabeth nodded and shut the door.

After musing for a few minutes he decided to go looking, and so it was he who found Lawrence's body lying on his back with the axe at his throat just as he had died. Over the body, not touching it but almost completely concealing it, was the bole of a great *rimu* tree.

'Another day and the wild pigs would have found him for sure,' said Charles aloud as he tucked a plug of tobacco into his cheek.

Something about the scene disturbed him; the accident did not look quite right. If Lawrence was running away from the falling tree, wouldn't he be sprawled the other way, on his face? And why had the tree dropped against the scarf cuts, and in quite a different direction from the other few in this clearing?

'You're going daft in the head,' he decided. Lawrence's rings were still on his fingers and a tentative feel revealed that there were coins in his pockets. If anybody had murdered Lawrence, they'd have picked his pockets for certain.

He was glad Rhys was safely out of the country when this happened. The stupid young pup might have felt sorry for Mary. Lawrence felt sorry for her once – and look what had become of him!

It was good riddance all round.

They moved to Waitamanui, where Mary wrote Rhys a long letter telling him about the baby then waited for him to come to her.

Lisabeth hated the town. She had always envied the town

50

children and longed to go to the vicarage school, but to her dismay lessons proved grindingly boring, just rote-learning strings of facts. She trudged home every afternoon with her face flushed and her head pounding, and pleaded to be allowed to stay away. Mary, who was tormented by morning sickness, was deaf to her complaints. 'You're not there to ask questions. You're there to *learn*,' she said.

She rented a tiny airless room at the hotel. One fixed window overlooked the street, the wharf and the ocean beyond. Mary spent most of every day sitting here keeping vigil.

Summer faded, and the days grew shorter and more blustery. Mary grudged a few shillings from Lawrence's remittance to buy Lisabeth a warm jacket. She was saving everything she could in case Rhys couldn't afford to come and get them and they had to make their own way to him.

Lisabeth developed chilblains on her hands and feet, but no pleadings would persuade Mary to agree to having her stay home. The lessons were free and, besides, Lisabeth had developed a clingy, possessive manner that irritated her mother. She seemed almost terrified to let Mary out of her sight.

Mary swelled. She grew vague. Sometimes she left the window and wandered bareheaded down to the jetty to stare out to sea. People pointed at her and whispered. Children called her names. They tormented Lisabeth, who retaliated by throwing stones and was whipped by the vicar's wife as a punishment.

One day the steam-packet called in from Sydney. Mary was there to meet it, standing dumbly on the wharf as the lumpers jostled around her. When the mail-bags were unloaded she followed the spring-cart up the hill to the store where she asked if there was a letter for her. No? Then, for the Staffords, perhaps? Was there something from Sydney for them?

When Charles and Gwynne came into town Mary was pressed to the glass waiting. A frayed thread of dust inflated as the wagon rolled down the hill into town. As soon as she could be sure it was them she fled from the room, clattering along the bare corridors and down the echoey stairs, skimming across the veranda to limp, gasping, across the road.

Charles stood in a thick wedge of shade, billycock hat perched on the back of his head, ruminating over a letter.

'Is that it?' demanded Mary without preamble.

Charles studied her with distaste. She was ungroomed, unwashed and hatless, clad only in a thin house-dress that

51

positively accentuated her huge abdomen. It was disgusting. Didn't she know a woman should stay decently inside when in that condition?

'Is that the letter from Rhys? Is it? I know that one arrived, Mr Stafford. They told me, and I've been waiting for you for days!'

'Keep your voice down.' People were staring. He held the letter up out of reach and wondered how to get rid of her. Thank goodness Mrs Stafford was still in the store selecting her provisions. She'd only *encourage* the wretched creature.

'May I please read it?'

'Mrs Rennie, really!'

She was shivering in the chill gusts that blew off the harbour. Charles noticed how gaunt her face was and wondered if she was eating properly – she looked starved. Still, that was none of his concern and he'd be damned if he'd get involved.

'You see, I'm sure he'd have replied to that letter I wrote, the one you posted off for me . . . He must have answered! I mean, there was so much . . . Unless he's coming back to surprise me! Only, I must know. There's so much . . . So please let me see what he's written about me.'

Charles smothered a prickle of guilt with a heavy poultice of righteousness. She must indeed be crazy if she believed he'd posted that letter. Rhys wouldn't have wanted to read those rambling torrid outpourings and, as for the 'wonderful news' about the baby, there was no way Charles would pass on information like that. He couldn't allow a lad barely out of his teens to saddle himself with a pregnant, crippled, twice-widowed whore – yes, whore.

'I know he cares for me,' she gabbled, mercifully out of earshot of the interested audience under the shop veranda. 'I know he does! And now that I'm . . . free to marry again I'm sure that—'

'Here,' said Charles in disgust. 'Read it for yourself.'

Snatching it eagerly, she held the pages tight against the buffeting wind. The sentences slid away under her flying gaze until she gaped into Charles's face, stunned.

'I don't understand,' she pleaded. 'He thanks you for settling the compensation for the horse then says he hopes that the Rennies have that unfortunate business well behind them now. He asks you to convey his good wishes! Good wishes!' Her eyes narrowed as they fixed on Charles's face. 'Unless he's never received my letter. Unless you never told him that Lawrence is dead.'

'Don't you accuse me!' retorted Charles, loathing her all the more for guessing the truth and hitting him with it. 'Sure and you're the one in the wrong, *Mrs* Rennie. That young lad, he never cared a jot for you. Why should he, hey?'

His voice seemed to come from a long way off, across a vast cold plateau. Mary hugged herself, shivering. The wind whipped the pages from her numb fingers and sent them wheeling and soaring above the street like sea-birds.

Mary didn't notice. Turning blindly back towards the hotel, she limped quickly, assuming that people were laughing at her and not realizing that it was Charles who caused the mirth as he capered and jumped, chasing his lost pages across the wheel-rutted mud.

When Lisabeth returned from her lessons she found Mary lying on the bed they shared, staring dry-eyed at the ceiling. She was white and still, her eyes filled with a dead acceptance.

'What's the matter, Mamma?' whispered Lisabeth.

'I wish I could die,' Mary said. She began to cry. 'Oh, I wish that I was dead right now!'

'Please, Mamma,' begged Lisabeth in alarm. 'Please don't wish that. You make me so frightened when you say that.'

That night, triggered by anguish, Mary's birth-pains started. She was helped to the vicarage where twenty-nine hours later a two-month-premature baby boy was born. Malnutrition and exhaustion had taken their toll on Mary; she was already dying when the child was dragged from her body.

With a curt warning that her mother was extremely ill, the vicar's wife brought Lisabeth in to see her and left them alone together.

Lisabeth would never forget that yellow-lit room; the scent of sweat and blood and pain would haunt her life. She was confused and terrified. There was no baby – the midwife was in another room working to save his life – only Mary, her eyes black-ringed and hollow, lying in a tall iron bed.

'Come here, pet,' she coaxed as Lisabeth stood reluctantly near the door. 'I want to give you something.'

Lisabeth hung back. Her mother was going to die. She could sense it, *smell* it in the air of this hideous room.

Mary picked at the fastening on the collar of her night-dress. Her fingers were so weak that even such a slight task seemed beyond their capabilities. Finally, she accomplished it and lay resting for a moment before tugging out a small damp cloth bag which hung around her neck from a string.

'Here . . .' she whispered. 'Keep this safe . . . for the baby.'

Lisabeth unpinned the cloth and saw that it contained a curl of fair hair trussed with a twist of grubby thread. She recognized it with an unpleasant stab of shock, and jerked her hands away quickly. Mr Morgan . . . This had to be Rhys Morgan's hair! Nobody else they knew had thick blond hair like his.

Resentment rose so fast in her that she felt giddy. Why did *he* have to intrude now? Why couldn't he be forgotten? He'd gone away months ago.!

'You must give this to the baby . . . promise me . . . The baby is Mr Morgan's, you see. Do you understand, pet?'

'No! No, Mamma, please!'

Mary melted into the pillows. Her breath came harshly. It took an effort for her to continue. 'I love Rhys. I wish . . . I wish I could hate him, but I can't. The baby belongs to him; it's not Mr Rennie's. I know you don't understand, dear, but one day you will. And . . . and one day you'll see Mr Morgan again. You must tell him about the baby.'

'No, Mamma!' This was a nightmare. Her mother was dying, and she didn't even seem to mind! All she wanted to do was talk about horrible Mr Morgan.

'He . . . has a right to know.' The words were laboured, the breathing shallow. 'Promise . . . promise me you'll tell . . .' Her fingers pressed the curl into Lisabeth's hand.

Lisabeth gasped. Mary's fingers felt cold, already dead. 'Please, no, Mamma. Don't die! I'll promise anything! Please don't leave me . . . Oh, please! I promise!'

Mary smiled. 'That's my good little . . .' she said.

It was over.

FIVE

'THEY'RE LATE,' said Gwynne with a frown as she lifted the ladle and tasted the vinegary liquid. 'It's not like Mr Stafford to be tardy. I do hope there's no trouble in Waitamanui. All this talk of war against the Maoris . . .' She stared into the curdling dusk, straining to hear her husband's voice above the chirrup of insects. He should have been back hours ago.

'It won't reach this far, Aunt. Tamati prides himself on good relationships with the settlers,' soothed Lisabeth, who stood beside her at the scrubbed *kauri*-wood bench, shelling hard-boiled eggs for pickling. She smiled at Gwynne's anxious face. 'Don't worry! It'll be something little. Sargent might have cast a shoe and they've had to wait to have another one fitted.' But despite her reassuring tone sixteen-year-old Lisabeth felt a pang of anxiety. They'd heard such gruesome stories of atrocities committed against the settlers, and it was still an isolated track into Waitamanui. She'd never forgive herself if anything happened to Andrew.

'You're a comfort to me, dear,' sighed Gwynne in her sing-song voice as she wiped her hands on the top layer of the three aprons she wore. Bustling to wipe out the wide-mouthed jar she would fill with eggs, spices and garlic-flavoured pickling liquid, she reflected how blessed she had been since she and Charles had inherited poor Mary Rennie's children. It had been literally a godsend because it was the vicar himself who had bullied aside Charles's blustering objections, insisting that they perform their Christian duty by adopting the youngsters. Gwynne was mortified when Charles accused the vicar outright of shovelling responsibility

55

on to his unwilling shoulders, but he quietened when the vicar hinted of more immediate rewards than those in heaven, namely Lawrence's farm and chattels.

Dear Charles! Oh, he still grumbled about having food snatched from his plate to fill theirs, and he pretended he didn't like either of the children, but he was only teasing. At heart Charles was as fatherly as the next man.

'These will do us proud when the hens start sitting,' she remarked as she packed the smooth white globes into the jar. 'And Mr Stafford does have a fancy for pickled eggs . . . Lisabeth! I heard something.'

'Do relax, Aunt.' Lisabeth had heard a rustling, too. 'It's only those new Coloured Dorkings. They roost on the wool-press no matter what I do to encourage them into the hen-roosts with the—' She broke off, her breath catching in her chest.

There was a blur of movement by the corn-rick. Then another, so it couldn't be their shorthorn calf wandering up in hopes of having a few carrot trimmings tossed its way. Lisabeth stayed very still, a half-peeled egg in one hand. Then she saw the face – glimpsed it only for a moment but long enough to see the swirls of tattooing and the gleam of eyes in the fading light.

Gwynne packed in the last of the peeled eggs, saw that Lisabeth hadn't finished and began to help her. 'Perhaps we'd better light the lamps,' she fretted, for that was Andrew's job. 'It's getting too dark to—'

'No,' said Lisabeth in an odd tone.

'Whatever is the matter?' Her voice rose in alarm. 'There *is* something out there, isn't—'

'Hush!'

'Hush?' It was a squeak of fright. 'Lisabeth, whatever—'

'Maoris!' hissed Lisabeth to shut her up. 'But don't worry! I'm sure it's all right.'

The words sounded hollow. All right? Something was very, very wrong if the Maoris were skulking about outside in the dusk instead of marching boldly up to the door as they always did when they wanted something – work, or medicine of some kind – or if they had fish or pork to sell.

'Oh dear!' wavered Gwynne. In the fading light the two women stared at each other, Gwynne trembling, Lisabeth thinking fast.

There was a drill, a series of steps to be followed in the event of possible trouble like this. Months before, when a rash of atrocities occurred in the next-door province of Taranaki, the Staffords had attended a public meeting in Waitamanui on the subject of harassment by the natives and how to minimize the possible damage of a confrontation. Though Charles had scoffed all the way home, Gwynne took the advice to heart. She had wrapped her valuable china and silver fruit-knives in flour bagging and buried them under the wallflowers beside the front door. The task of tending the lamps was given over to seven-year-old Andrew so that Charles needn't notice that suddenly the oil and matches were being stored under a flattened metal can in the implement shed, in a compact cavity that Lisabeth had dug in the furthest corner of the floor. On hot days during extended spells of fine weather Gwynne and Lisabeth carried bucket after bucket of water from the well to douse the thatching and walls of the house. Surreptitiously, piece by piece, the womenfolk had removed everything valuable or inflammable from the inside of the cottage, taking down curtains to be 'mended' and not rehanging them, removing spare table-cloths and spare clothing to the safety of barrels in the shed.

'Mr Stafford is right, you know,' Gwynne had confided to Lisabeth. 'This is just a packet of alarmist hullabaloo, but I've a nervous disposition, dear, and I'd sleep better at night if I knew that my little treasures weren't lying about for the taking. Not that there's any real need to worry . . .'

There was need for worry now, thought Lisabeth, her mind frantically trying to assemble the bones of that long-ago lecture. If only she'd paid more attention!

'Aunt, is there anything we need to rescue? I'll bring the clock, and—'

'My brooch! My grandmother's pearl brooch, and . . . and Mr Stafford's silver shaving-mug.'

'And, if there's any money hidden, we'd better take that, too.' said Lisabeth. Holding her breath, she flattened against the wall and reached to scoop the shaving-mug from the shelf below the window, holding it low so that the embossed surface with its Manx 'three-legged' symbol wouldn't catch the light and be seen by anyone outside. Charles never shaved but he was proud of the mug, a long-ago gift from Gwynne when he first visited her on the Isle of Man.

Clutching it in one hand, she scooped the ormolu clock from the bookshelf and whispered to Gwynne, who was groping under her billowy feather mattress.

'Let's climb out the back window, into the lean-to, shall we? Do you think you can manage?'

'I'll try.' In the gloom she sounded frightened and doubtful for her legs had been giving her so much pain this past year that she had difficulty even bending her knees to sit down. 'Oh, Lisabeth, I wonder where Mr Stafford is? I do hope he doesn't come home right now if there's danger. . . .'

I hope he does, and quickly, too, prayed Lisabeth, thinking how typical it was that in her moment of peril Gwynne had fears only for her husband, but then she remembered that Andrew was with Charles and her mind squeezed tight with a pang of terror. *Keep them away, please God*, she revised her prayer. *We'll get out of this somehow, only keep Andrew safe!*

The lean-to was a semi-enclosed area at the back of the cottage where milk-pans were left to settle before the cream was skimmed off and where butter was churned and moulded into pats with ridged wooden paddles. Against the cottage wall was a long bench and above this a high window that opened beside the two-tiered bunks where Lisabeth and Andrew slept.

With care it was possible to climb soundlessly out of that window and alight on the ground. Andrew had done it many dozens of times until in one moment of carelessness he had stumbled and upset three days' production of milk in a crash that Charles heard where he was breaking clods in the back acre. Andrew had been sent supperless to bed, the window placed out of bounds – and the cottage had reeked of rotten milk for weeks.

'We can do it,' urged Lisabeth, carefully placing a chair beside the bunk and helping Gwynne on to it. If only she knew how many Maoris there were outside and what they were planning to do. It was likely that they were debating whether or not anybody was home – but they must know that someone was here. Even though the lamps had not been lit there was the smoke from the kitchen chimney and the smell of vinegar. That carried for miles.

The thought that they were being watched made Lisabeth feel ill, but she was determined to make a respectable attempt to escape, at least. What had that government man told them at the meeting? She could see him, sallow-faced and pompous, his thumbs tucked under the narrow lapels of his frock-coat. Ah, yes . . .

More unfortunates have been slaughtered as a regrettable consequence of their own fear than from unbridled aggression. Many who have died could have escaped unharmed if they had thought clearly and logically instead of acting in blind panic.

At the time Lisabeth considered this to be a patronizing piece of theory – a slur on the victims of outrages. Now, however, the words gave her encouragement.

As Gwynne leaned on her, trembling, she pushed her towards the upper bunk by guiding her hands and arms, not liking to touch any part of her body. 'Please, Aunt, try to pull yourself up!' she pleaded.

'Help me . . . Push my legs,' panted Gwynne as her body tightened with the strain of effort.

But Lisabeth was reluctant to do that. Instead she stooped and made a stepping-place of her shoulders, grabbing the ridge of the top bunk for support and bending her head forward. 'Climb on to me. Quickly!'

When Gwynne's weight pressed down on her she almost crumpled, but gritting her teeth she forced her legs to straighten and then it was over. Gwynne's felt-soled slippers lifted their burden from her shoulders as she eased herself on to the top bunk.

'The door!' remembered Lisabeth. 'I forgot to lock the door!'

Now it was all coming back to her. The official from the Government had said that the thing to do was to bolt the door, place a lamp nearby if possible and, keeping the rear of the house in darkness, prepare for an escape that way as soon as the Maoris began battering down the door.

The very thought of *that* happening made her sway giddily, and for a second all she could think was *I'm going to die!* but then resolve stiffened her and, leaving Gwynne to tug at the window-catches, she tiptoed back through the gloom to the door and reached to lift the heavy key from its nail beside the lintel.

As she touched the handle, the door swung open. It was silent, effortless, as if the wind had nudged it. Lisabeth stepped back, startled, the key thudding on the stamped-earth floor.

There, filling the doorway, was the tallest Maori she had ever seen.

Because her eyes had grown used to the dimness within the cottage, Lisabeth saw him clearly in the comparatively lighter dusk. She did not recognize him. He was magnificently tattooed – even in her state of terror she noticed that – with intricate indigo patterns of curling lines, whorls and stripes that cunningly heightened the contours of his face, making the nose more hawklike, the chin more arrogant and the forehead and cheek-bones nobler. His eyes, though, were cunning and mean and his hair unkempt. In one ear he wore a loop of string from which dangled a sliver of polished *paua* shell the length and width of

Gwynne's small shoe-horn. This single ear-ring glittered like an iridescent fish, contrasting strangely with the rough brown jerkin and breeches that he wore.

Lisabeth gaped at him, too stricken to scream.

'*Kia ora*,' he said, then laughed. His voice was thick and slurred, the laugh silly. Clearly he was drunk.

'*Ah! Wahine ataahua!*' he giggled, grinning. Purplish tattooed lips drew back over broken teeth.

Lisabeth had understood the greeting *kia ora* and the compliment – 'beautiful woman' – but the leer in his tone made her shrink inwardly, and when he raised a massive hand to poke at her cheek she drew back in disgust.

He laughed again and dropped his hand, allowing it to fall negligently so that the fingers flopped heavily, brushing against her shoulder, her breast and down to her waist before she could move away.

'*Maiaka*,'* he commented dismissively.

She did not know what he said, only that he had decided to leave her alone for the moment, but the liberty shocked her. The implications were terrifying – it was as if he was free to do what he wanted and she would be helpless to stop him.

Stop thinking like that! she scolded herself. In a voice that astounded her by its firmness she said: 'What do you want?' Her insides might be a jelly of congealing fright and fear, *but* she hoped, if she treated this man no differently from all the other Maoris who came to the door on one errand or another, perhaps no harm would come to her.

He gabbled something unintelligible. When she made no response he reached for something that was leaning beside the door, swinging it up so that it was pointing at her. A musket.

Lisabeth swallowed. She could feel the blood draining from her head. *She was going to die!*

The Maori repeated his demands more angrily. '*Waipiro! Tupeka! Wahine moho!*†

Shaking her head to plead that she didn't understand, Lisabeth lifted her hands in a futile gesture to protect herself. Dimly, she saw a second man behind this brute – a younger, untattooed man – and she wondered how many there were. There was no

---

*'Thin', 'Scrawny'.
†'Whisky! Tobacco! (You) Stupid woman!'

hope now. She and Gwynne would be slaughtered, the house burned and their stock destroyed, and if Charles and Andrew arrived home now they would suffer the same fate. Charles carried no weapons, and physically he and the boy would be no match for these two thugs.

Seizing her roughly by one arm, the Maori thrust the barrel of the musket under her chin, forcing her head back. It occurred to her – and she was in such a state of near-hysteria that it seemed funny – that his tattooed nose would be the last thing she would ever see.

'*Waipiro!* he roared, blasting the scent of it in her face as the gunbarrel scraped the flesh of her throat. '*Waipiro!*'

'I don't understand,' she quavered, trembling on the point of complete disintegration. 'Please . . . I don't know what —'

A crash swamped her last words. Not just a little thump but a strident cacophony of jangling metal dishes and splintering timbers, so loud that the clashing din seemed to be inside the cottage with them.

The sudden explosion of noise and the realization that Gwynne must have fallen through the bench made Lisabeth scream, but her cry snipped off short when the Maori twisted her arm, jerking her painfully to her tip-toes. The musket-barrel tore so hard against her neck that she could feel the click of bone and cartilage in her windpipe.

Frantically she reached up to claw at his face. Her fingers grasped the dangling ear-ring, and in a reflex of desperation she yanked at it with a vicious pull that concentrated every scrap of strength she could muster.

The Maori bellowed as his ear ripped. Flinging Lisabeth aside, he clapped both hands against the wound, shouting in Maori. From inside the rear of the cottage the other man shouted back at him.

Lisabeth didn't wait. Sobbing for breath she stumbled outside and dashed around to the lean-to, her tottering legs threatening to give way underneath her. Her throat blazed with hot agony, but she was thinking rapidly. Now they had a chance to escape she must use it sensibly and not be panicked into doing something stupid.

Gwynne was lying in the ruins. Around her Lisabeth could see the great silver discs of pans and the wash of pale milk running into puddles, but it was too dark in here to read Gwynne's expression.

Keeping her voice as low as she could, she rasped, 'Are you hurt?' while at the same time she grasped Gwynne's outstretched hands and helped her to her feet. Gwynne promptly sagged, uttering a tiny gasp of pain.

'Please . . . Please try to run,' begged Lisabeth, scooping an arm around the older woman's waist and hitching her up so that the leverage of her shoulder would give support. Gwynne dragged at her like a dead weight as she staggered out into the open.

Any ideas she might have had about fleeing back along the track in the hope of bumping into Charles had to be abandoned. The Maoris would overtake them before they had covered a hundred yards. They would have to hide somewhere – and close, too.

The well! she thought.

A perfect hiding-place. Only a short distance away beyond the orchard the well had a ledge about four feet below ground level and a cover that could be lowered to conceal them.

But Gwynne was so heavy that their progress was frighteningly slow, one tedious step at a time. 'Oh, please, Aunt!' pleaded Lisabeth, tears jamming in her strictured throat. 'We have to try . . .'

Just then the shouting and crashing within the cottage ceased and there was an ominous silence that meant only one thing. The Maoris had begun to look for them. With only the veil of a single blossoming plum-tree between them and the house Lisabeth knew their cause was hopeless.

Unless she could create a distraction. They were stumbling past the chopping-block where on the base of a felled *totara* tree Andrew split the kindling for the house-fires. Lisabeth could see the axe-handle jutting up where Andrew had left it and an untidy heap of wood beside it. Charles was always scolding about the state of the woodpile.

'Here . . . Hold on to a branch,' hissed Lisabeth, leaving Gwynne and dashing over to the stump where she picked up a solid chunk of wood. If she could throw it far enough in the other direction, the Maoris might be fooled into thinking they had run that way.

Up soared the wood, spinning against the sky. It crashed disappointingly with a muffled whisper into the clump of trees that surrounded the corrugated-iron privy. Snatching up another, she sent that whirling, too, but it took a third attempt before the hunk of firewood landed with an audible thud on the privy roof.

Satisfied that they'd gained another couple of minutes of

freedom, Lisabeth hurried back to discover that Gwynne had recovered a little from her shaking-up and that the circulation was returning to her legs. She was in pain, though. Grimacing, breath sipping through tight lips, she crabbed along, clinging to Lisabeth.

The well-cover was battened timber, hinged with brittle leather strips. Lisabeth raised it far enough for Gwynne to clamber in, then braced it with her arms as she manoeuvred herself over the rim, trying not to glance down at the oily saucer of water far below. The cover dropped silently into place and the two women crouched in the musty darkness holding the cross-bar for support, their thoughts unspeakable, their hearts gushing fear.

Gwynne was shaking; Lisabeth could hear it in the ragged scraps of her breath.

'Shush . . .' she soothed. 'We're safe . . .'

'Oh, Lisabeth! I feel so – so wound up! I want to scream out loud! I can't—'

'Shush! Let's pray, just in a whisper. Maybe that will —'

She broke off with a gasp as the well-cover was abruptly slung aside, opening their concealment to the sky. Gwynne screamed. Rearing and huge with the menace of a mythical giant, the tattooed Maori grinned down at them.

He threw back his head and laughed. A sick hopelessness swelled in Lisabeth's chest as the drunken exultation echoed in a plummeting spiral to the depths of the well.

'*Ah, rua kiore!*'* he declared, enjoying himself hugely. With swaggering arrogance he picked up his musket and prodded Gwynne in the chest with the snout of it. '*E kau! Kiore e kau!*'†

Now Lisabeth shrieked, too, as Gwynne cried out in pain, but they both clung even tighter to the cross-bar. The Maori shoved and poked Gwynne again and again, his mocking jibes mingling with their screams.

Gwynne's doggedness defeated him, and very soon he grew sick of trying to loosen her that way. He made a few ineffectual whacks at her knuckles with the musket-barrel, then muttering to himself dropped it and picked up something else.

The axe! Lisabeth saw the gleam of the iron head as he lifted it in both hands and cursed herself for leaving it on the stump

---

*'Ah, two rats!'
†'Swim! Swim, rats!'

63

instead of tossing it into the gooseberry canes nearby.

Instinctively, she let go of the bar and flattened herself against the damp wall but saw to her horror that Gwynne was still hanging on, frozen, gaping up into that murderous face.

'Let go, Aunt! He'll chop your hands!' shrieked Lisabeth and she tugged at Gwynne's wrists. Above them the Maori was laughing.

Lisabeth closed her eyes. It was a pitiful thing to do but the only way she could block out the nightmare.

Then the shot came.

It was a clean punch of sound. When she heard it Lisabeth assumed for one giddy moment that the Maori had changed his mind about the axe and had shot Gwynne instead, but she opened her eyes in time to see him kneel on the well-rim and lean forward as if someone had clapped him rather too enthusiastically on the back. His head dropped, the tattooed chin resting on his chest before he moved on, soundlessly, to flop into the chasm with such casualness, as if he didn't mind at all. It was not until he broke the water with an enormous slap that Lisabeth realized what must have happened.

Before the surging and flapping of water had stilled there was a second shot and then the first reassuring sound that either of the women had heard in what seemed like hours.

'They're in the well,' said Charles's voice as his head and shoulders appeared above them. 'Sure and they're both in one piece. One piece apiece, that is!'

'Thank the Lord you're safe,' quavered Gwynne as Charles helped her to safety. 'Praise the Lord for both of you!'

Lisabeth stood in the semi-darkness, trembling with an enormous relief that robbed her of all strength. The past minutes seemed unreal now; all that mattered was the wiry warmth of young Andrew's arms around her and his head pressed against her waist. It was several moments before her brain could function sufficiently for her to wonder the hows and whys of their rescue.

Only dimly was she aware of the third person, of the yelps of ecstasy with which Gwynne greeted him, of Charles's rumbling voice explaining.

'A lucky coincidence. Doubly lucky. Rhys were on his way back to Sydney and he stepped ashore here hoping to see us. The cutter he were on hove to here, you see, on account of bad weather ahead and she won't be sailing before tomorrow evening, so he decided to come on home and surprise you. We heard the rumpus when we was still a ways up the track, so we hitched Sargent and crept on up. I was going to whack the feller with a batten, like, only Rhys here got in first and shot him.'

Lisabeth heard no more than the first few words. Rhys! That could only mean one person, the last person in the world she ever wanted to see. It couldn't be true – it *couldn't* – that she would owe her life to this man.

She sneaked a look at him. He was leaning over the well, his hands braced on the rim while he stared down at the figure floating spreadeagled far below. She could see only a fair head and in one hand a small bronze pistol. Yes, she recognized *that*, she thought bitterly. Then he raised his head and grinned up at her, and she noticed with a jolt how handsome he was with such a white careless smile.

His voice was pleasant, too, she noticed unwillingly. Soft and warm with traces of smooth-down accents. 'It's hard to be sure, but I think I got him in the back of the head. Not bad for that distance.'

So he was boastful, too. Lisabeth turned her back on him, still holding tight to Andrew, though her brother, having been hugged quite enough, thank you, was struggling to break free.

'I want to look!' he demanded.

'No!' Lisabeth was adamant. 'Absolutely not!'

But he broke away anyway and left her twisting her hands in anguish. Still shaken by the ordeal, a fresh and stronger fear was bubbling up in her; she was seized by a compulsion to grab her brother and whisk him away, to hide him until Mr Morgan had gone.

'*He belongs to Mr Morgan*,' Mary had insisted as she lay dying. '*He must know. Promise me you'll tell him about his son.*'

Never! vowed Lisabeth now as she turned away, choked by tears of despair. That promise had been forced out of her, and she discarded it when she flung the sweaty rag and loathsome relic it contained into the *toe-toe* bushes below the graveyard on the afternoon of Mary's burial. They were gone, but the revulsion lingered for a long time afterwards.

What never died was the fear that Rhys Morgan might find out about Andrew and take him away from her.

Now he was here, and her blood ran hot with panic.

SIX

FROM THE MOMENT that she first cautiously took the baby into her arms Andrew became the focus of Lisabeth's existence.

She never strayed from his side. If she was weeding the garden, the padded crate that was his cradle would be in the shade close by. When she scraped carrots or peeled potatoes he lay in a blanket on the table so she could talk to him. He slept beside her at night. In her spare time she learned to knit delicate clothes from old unravelled under-bodices Gwynne donated. All her games were played with him.

'She's a little mother,' remarked Gwynne.

If Gwynne felt jealous that she, the stepmother, was pushed away, she was able to smother her envy. She understood something of the grief and loneliness Lisabeth had been through. She did notice that Andrew was being spoiled by having his every whim instantly satisfied, nor ever being corrected, but this she approved. Boys were brought into this world to be spoiled.

As he grew Andrew developed a distinct likeness to Rhys, the same thick buttery hair, the same full delineated lips, strong features and high cheekbones. Lisabeth panicked, terrified that Gwynne and Charles would notice and suspect the connection. 'He's the image of my gran-da,' she explained in a desperate lie. 'He was tall and fair – just like a Viking, Mama used to say. But look, he's got olive skin like Mama's and her green eyes. His eyes are the same shape as Mama's, too, don't you think?'

'Yes, dear,'Gwynne would always say, without really paying attention. She loved both the children with a warm blanket of affection, undemanding and unquestioning.

66

Charles was not sure what he thought. He had read Mary's torrid outpourings of devotion and her confession (though to Charles it read like a boast) that she was carrying their child, but Charles was an unsophisticated fellow who had been taught that babies invariably took nine months from conception to birth. By his calculation, then, the child couldn't belong to Rhys, for it must have been conceived one month before *Sydney Belle* brought him to Waitamanui. Mary must have lied, a pathetic attempt to snare a man who didn't want her.

But whether Andrew was the product of an immoral liaison was beside the point. Charles had detested Mary and wanted not a bar of adopting children, hers or anybody else's. In his view both youngsters should have been shipped right off to a workhouse.

He made the mistake of expounding this opinion to the vicar in front of Gwynne. The very suggestion threw sentimental Gwynne into a fit of weeping that alarmed Charles. He tried everything he could think of to stem her tears, but her sobs subsided only when at length he relented and grudgingly agreed to take the children.

'I'm too kind-hearted for my own good,' he complained.

There were compensations. Lawrence's farm, stock and personal effects. The money Mary had put by. The caches of whisky, tobacco and small sums of money Charles discovered on his excursions around Lawrence's haunts in the bush. Unfortunately, the farm didn't sell, but Lawrence's books and furniture fetched good prices in the hungry market at Waitamanui.

Though he couldn't warm to the children, they were less trouble than anticipated. Gwynne's health was deteriorating to the point where on some bad days Charles would have had to sit down to a bleak scratch dinner if Lisabeth hadn't been there to cook him a proper meal. Andrew was ruined by the womenfolk, cheeky, indolent and downright disobedient at times, but he was already a strong lad who could plough a straight furrow behind Sargent.

Best of all, the children kept Gwynne happy. It had worked out well; by neglecting to tell Rhys that the Rennies were dead he kept his unwelcome brother-in-law at a distance, yet the children kept Gwynne so occupied that she had no time to fret over her brother's prolonged absence. Because he posted her letters he was able to delete any references to the children before he sent them off.

But now his chickens might be roosting around him, thought Charles sourly as he watched Gwynne weeping with happiness in her brother's arms. Already Charles could feel himself being relegated to second place in his wife's affections.

He'd been disgusted to note that young Andrew – an impressionable lad – idolized Rhys on sight, tagging close to him, chipping in with silly questions whenever there was a gap in the conversation. Fortunately, the attraction wasn't mutual; Rhys seemed to have the same distaste for tangible reminders of Mary as he himself did.

Ungrateful child! thought Charles and, grumbling about Andrew's negligence, he picked up the axe and stamped away to replace it on its brace of wooden pegs inside the implement-shed.

Clinging to Rhys like a sailor to a life-preserver, Gwynne allowed him to shepherd her inside. He was calming her shattered nerves with jokes, quiet words, requests for one of her marvellous cups of tea.

Lisabeth leaned against the bole of a peach tree and wished she could run away. Why had he reappeared after so long? In the past seven years there had been odd scraps of letters from all over the world but never a visit. Gwynne had once in a weak moment confessed that Rhys had not seemed happy when he stayed here, and that Charles couldn't warm to him. It was her great disappointment.

Postponing going inside for as long as possible, Lisabeth lingered to help Andrew light the lamps. He was tense with excitement, too, and waved the Maori's musket under her nose in a way that made her heart stutter as he crowed, 'Look at this! I'm going to keep it!'

He was too young to play with guns. 'Uncle Charles hasn't got one of those, dear.'

Andrew scoffed. 'He'd be scared to shoot it! You should see him jump when he fires his scatter-gun at birds! And you should have seen how scared he was when Mr Morgan sneaked up to shoot that warrior! Uncle Charles wanted us to hide.'

'Andrew Rennie! You mustn't tell such wicked fibs.'

'It's true! He said they wouldn't hurt women but if they saw us they'd get ferocious, and Mr Morgan, he didn't say anything. He just went on ahead and *blam! Ahhh!*'

He adjusted the wick; in the orange light his face gleamed with mischievous delight. 'Uncle Charles is a coward, but Mr Morgan is really brave! I say, do you think we might be allowed to call him "Uncle Rhys"? He is practically a relative of ours.'

Forcing herself to be calm, Lisabeth ruffled Andrew's lamp-gilded hair. 'It wouldn't be proper. Besides, he's going away tomorrow and we may never see him again.'

She prayed that would be true. *I have to thank him for saving our lives*, she thought bitterly. *And I hate him! Why should this make any difference? He as good as killed Mama, used her and abandoned her so that she died alone and friendless. If it wasn't for him, she'd still be alive. I hate him!*

Sullenly, with great reluctance, Lisabeth followed Andrew into the house.

'What do you mean, lad?' said Charles, fork raised over a heaped plate of mutton stew and potato dumplings.

As she dished a portion for Rhys, Gwynne fluttered: 'I'm sorry this is all we have for supper. If I'd known you were coming, I'd have roasted one of the ducks.'

'This looks grand.' Rhys smiled at her then turned back to Charles. 'I mean, what are you going to do now? You can't stay here, can you?'

Charles's lumpy features bunched in perplexion. 'Sure and why not? I'll not have one bullying Maori and a young tag-along running me off my land.'

Gwynne looked frightened. 'Mr Stafford, please—'

'It's not as though it were a war party. Oh, sure and there is wild talk aplenty, but that's all it is – talk. What did we have here? A bit of drunkenness, and a few threats to scare the womenfolk. Well, let me tell you, son, I don't scare that easy!'

Andrew began to titter, and Lisabeth pressed a warning foot over his toes.

Gwynne said: 'I thought it was the "Buggane", Rhys, truly I did. I thought my days had come to the tally of their number.'

'The "Buggane"?' interjected Andrew. 'Is that the Manx giant who can flatten trees with one breath and crumble up cottages as if they were breadcrumbs?'

Charles looked annoyed.

'I'll bet Mr Morgan isn't afraid of the "Buggane", are you, Mr Morgan?' piped Andrew.

Hastily swallowing a mouthful of airy, delicious dumpling, Lisabeth kicked her brother's shins and frowned at him. Uncle Charles looked as if he was about to explode.

Then Rhys said: 'The fact is, Charles, you have a dead Maori in your well, and a *live* Maori who witnessed it is somewhere out there. With all the trouble that's going on, do you think it wise to stay here now? You'd be safer to go into town at least until this

incident has been investigated. There are proper facilities at Wai
. . . Waita—'

'Waitamanui,' supplied Gwynne, hovering with the stew-
tureen at his elbow. She glanced anxiously at her husband. Rhys
was talking sense. Settlers were camping in Waitamanui to wait
out the hostilities and so that if war did erupt nearby they could be
easily taken away by ship; but, as it was, on their isolated farm the
Staffords had no way of contacting anyone for help if more of the
Maoris came back for revenge. And they would! Gwynne's aching
knees almost wavered under her at the thought, and her hand
shook as she tipped more meat and gravy on to Rhys's plate. If
only Mr Stafford would listen! Surely he'd see what a valid point
Rhys was making. Surely he'd appreciate that he was concerned
only for their safety.

Charles bristled. 'And tell me this, then! Whose fault is it if
we've a dead Maori in our well, hey? Who put him there?'

Aghast at the vehemence in his tone, Rhys said: 'I didn't mean
to suggest—'

'What you're suggesting', bellowed Charles, warming up, 'is
that we take to our heels and leave everything we've worked for to
be stolen by those dirty murderous Maoris. They'd have our stock
slaughtered, our home looted and burned before we were off the
property! Sure and they're nothing more than a bunch of slovenly
lazy savages, but I'll not run away from them. Especially not if
some trouble-making young upstart tells me to! Furthermore, it's
only—'

Whew! thought Rhys as Charles spluttered on. There was no
point in interrupting him, so Rhys let him rip. The fact was, Rhys
didn't agree with one single thing his brother-in-law said. In his
several visits to New Zealand he had observed a great deal and
enjoyed long interesting discussions with many knowledgeable
men on the subject of the native tribes. Overwhelmingly, one
opinion won through; the Maoris were a fine people with many
noble traditions. They were savage, undeniably. Cannibalism was
a shadow of the present, not a relic of the past. They revered the
ethics of war, and their gods were those of nature, but in cunning,
selfishness, indolence or dishonesty they were neither better nor
worse than the settlers who were steadily encroaching on their
land. Rhys had a sympathy for them.

Charles ranted on, recounting incidents that were supposed to
illustrate what 'yellow-bellied ruffiants' these natives were. Rhys
only half-listened. He wondered what the others were thinking.

Gwynne gave Charles her full nervous attention, nodding as he spoke, but the shocking incident had affected Lisabeth differently. Hunched in the corner with her face averted, she seemed to have withdrawn right into herself. The only time she'd spoken all evening was when she thanked him in a dull monotone, almost curtly.

He looked at her without real interest. She was a diminutive young woman with a narrow, softly shaped face and dark hair pulled back by combs and allowed to fall loosely around her shoulders. She was wearing what looked like a cut-down dress of Gwynne's, an ancient bottle-green that paradoxically made her look younger and more vulnerable. Because her face was averted, he couldn't see her eyes, just her lightly inscribed straight brows. There was a small round mole like the dot of an exclamation mark at the outside end of one eyebrow, on her temple.

Sensing that he was watching her, she glanced up, and for a fraction of a second her dark cobalt eyes looked right into his. In that particle of time he retained the strongest impression of her, the purity of her eyes and the delicate half-moon lids, shaded like petals.

It was eerie. Though her eyes were different from Mary's in shape and colour, for that moment he had the distinct unpleasant sensation of looking through the veil of her features directly into her mother's eyes, but there was something there he had never seen on Mary's face. Hostility.

She hates me, but why? he thought as Lisabeth dropped her chin and looked away again.

But perhaps he had imagined it. He glanced back at her, then to Andrew's eager face. Now, there were Mary's eyes. More slanted than hers but the same blazing deep green, the same clarity. He had to look away this time. Every time he thought of Mary his stomach gave a sickening lurch. To think that every time they'd made love she had been pregnant with another man's child. The very notion made his mind crawl with queasiness. *What a mess*, he thought.

No, he decided. He was sorry about Mary, but he didn't want to think about her. Not ever again.

The longer Charles spoke, the more Gwynne fidgeted, passing a platter of griddle scones and a glass dish of butter, and all the while becoming more and more agitated. Finally, to everyone's astonishment, she burst into tears, subsiding on to her chair in a flap of aprons.

'Oh, Mr Stafford, those men were going to k-k-kill us,' she wept. 'It was more than j-just a scaring they were after.'

'Nonsense,' said Charles, clearly taken aback by this contradiction. 'It were just a couple of lazy rascals out for some excitement. Young Rhys here over-responded when he shot that big—'

'But he j-j-jabbed me in the chest with his musket and he tr-tried to push me into the well. When I wouldn't let g-g-go of the rail he. . . . Oooh, but it's too horrible. Lisabeth, you tell him.'

'They was just scallywagging.' Charles sounded less convinced, but his tone warned Lisabeth not to argue with him.

Instead of speaking out, which would have hurt her throat, Lisabeth tipped her chin up and leaned back, at the same time pulling down the lace-frilled edge of the high buttoned collar, so that the raw scrape along her neck was visible.

'Look!' sobbed Gwynne. 'See what he did to her?' She began to fumble with the buttons on the front of her bodice. 'And I'll sh-show you the bruises where he whacked me with that n-nasty gun!'

'Bejesus, don't do that!' said Charles hastily. He lapsed into a moody silence.

Rhys said nothing, either, but studied Charles, thinking carefully.From his history he knew that Charles had abandoned other farming ventures when things had gone sour on him, and seven years ago Gwynne had whispered that 'Poor Mr Stafford had his worries with this place'. If he was so adamantly against leaving this wretched property, then his fortunes must have taken a turn for the better – or else a turn so much for the worse that he had no capital left to begin again somewhere else.

Not for the better, thought Rhys. This room was shockingly bare. What had happened to Gwynne's treasures? The set of Manx dinnerware that had graced the sideboard – he remembered the primrose pattern well. There was not a piece of it remaining. What about the meat-platter with gold handles and the salmon-dish shaped like a huge green fish?

He glanced around, noticing the absence of other things. A Dresden shepherdess with pink tulle skirts. Scrimshaw from Nova Scotia. Charles's shaving-mug. Things must have come to a desperate state if he'd parted with that.

For heaven's sake, there weren't even any curtains on the windows! Surely they hadn't been forced to sell those, too.

Anger simmered in Rhys's brain. What did the oafish fool

think he was doing, dragging Gwynne from one failure to another and dumping her finally in this godforsaken place in poverty and danger? He wanted hanging.

I mustn't feel sorry for them, thought Rhys. *His own misman-agement got him into this.* He tried to harden his mind against an impulse that was beginning to nudge strongly at him. *She married him of her own free choice*, he reminded himself.

Gwynne was dabbing her swollen eyes with a corner of her top layer of aprons. It twisted Rhys heart to notice how old and palsied she seemed. With a gulping sigh she let the apron drop and leaned back, then met his eyes.

'I'm so glad you're here,'she murmured. 'It's so . . . so good. . . .' Unable to continue, she tried to smile instead.

Rhys couldn't cope with the compassion he felt. It was a roughly sketched smile but filled with such love that Rhys felt all resistance dissolve.

He knew he couldn't abandon her here.

SEVEN

THE DARKNESS WAS SWEATY with the threat of drizzle. In the ferny undergrowth insects scratched and a single owl hooted a question as the two men strolled towards the ridge-track.

Charles was ill at ease. He glanced back to the cottage where under the lamp-glow Lisabeth was brushing Gwynne's hair while Andrew was polishing the musket-barrel with a rag. He wanted to be inside, too, with the door barred and the world shut out.

Anxious to get the conversation over with, he said: 'I suppose you've asked me out here because you're wondering why we never said one word about adopting the children after Mary Rennie—'

'Not at all,' said Rhys. 'I'm not interested.'

'You're not interested in why we never—?'

'No,' repeated Rhys.

'Oh.' Charles glanced into the darkness under the trees. That noise . . .

Get a grip on yourself, he cursed inwardly. *You're not afraid of the Maoris, remember?*

Charles was imprisoned by a dilemma that appeared to have no solution. He couldn't leave the farm, because it couldn't be sold, and even if he abandoned it the items he could salvage – equipment, farm animals and so on – would fetch almost nothing. People everywhere were walking off their farms and trying to sell identical things on a dead market. The last two seasons had been so bad, with rain at harvest time, that all his potatoes and wheat had been ruined. Stated baldly, he had no money to begin again elsewhere. Charles didn't know which was the worse prospect – a quick death at the hands of Maori marauders or an ignominious life of poverty.

But Charles had traces remaining of the optimism that had led him from one fresh start to another. If he abandoned the farm, poverty was certain. If they remained, they *might* be safe. The Maoris might not come back. That young fellow who ran away might not return to his tribe to rally a war party who would descend shrieking one of their hideous *hakas**, demanding *utu*, vengeance.

He glanced back at the comforting lighted windows.

'Are you expecting them back already?' asked Rhys, striking a Lucifer and lighting a pencil-thin cigar for Charles then one for himself.

'Who? Oh . . . the Maoris!' Charles's laugh was unconvincing. 'They'll not bother us – not now there's menfolk here! You know, Lawrence Rennie used to say – not that I were in agreement with much that he said, mind – but he did used to say that if England had waited but twenty years more before colonizing these islands, then there'd have been no natives to worry about. They had muskets, you see, and all they ever did was wage war, tribe against other tribe. Lawrence said that one rascal before our time – Hong Kong his name were—'

'Hongi Hika.'

'That he were responsible single-handed for exterrimenting a quarter of the entire Maori race!' He snorted. 'I just wish he had spent more of his time down this way!'

'There are almost no Maoris in the South Island,' remarked Rhys.

Charles coughed on the cigar smoke.

'No Maoris?'

They were at the edge of a bluff now. Far below a pale river of silver ribbons laced between lozenge-shaped islands of shingle. The owl asked again.

'A few, I grant you, but not many. Odd ones along the coast. Little fishing settlements, that sort of thing.' His cigar glowed as he drew on it. 'Last time I was here Gwynne brought me out here one evening. We had a magnificent view of the mountain from this very spot. I'd hoped the cloud had cleared by now.'

'Sure and it's cloudy most of the time. It's a bonny enough sight, but I forget to look at it often as not.'

'I'm very fond of mountains. They've hundreds in the South Island, you know.'

---

*war chants.

'I've heard.' Charles glanced back at the cottage.

'There are vast prairies of rich soil – no trees to be felled, just tussock to burn off – and at the back of it a breathtaking panorama of these incredibly beautiful mountains. They range across the horizon from the north to the south, and no matter where you are you can see them. They're like a mirage – you advance, they recede—' He broke off, sensing that Charles wasn't listening. Changing the subject, he said: 'I asked you to come out walking now because I wanted to ask your advice, man to man.'

'Oh?'

'Fact is, I've done rather well for myself. There was more than a little good fortune in the goldfields at Bathurst and – but never mind that, I didn't come here to boast. Fact is, I've decided to settle down in New Zealand, and I was hoping it could be somewhere near you people. Gwynne's the only family I have, and I'd find it most pleasant to be able to visit her; but, far more than that, I'd value being able to call on the benefit of your experience and advice. You've a wealth of knowledge about this country and you're a generous man, I know.'

'Sure and I'd be willing to advise you.'

Rhys covered a smile by choosing that moment to puff on his cigar. 'But I'm in rather a predicament, you see. Land sales are frozen in this area, and—'

'The meddling petty Government did that! Sure and the wars aren't going to spread down this far.'

'It makes it difficult for me,' agreed Rhys. 'I'm now obliged to choose the South Island.'

'Ah. You'd be a long ways away then.'

'Exactly. I know it would be a great deal to ask of you but, if you ever did think of moving, it would be absolutely splendid —'

'Never!' wheezed Charles. 'Me, leave this place?'

'I thought it was too much to ask, even as a favour to a brother! Never mind. The fact is,' he sighed, 'land sales out of Christchurch are measured in enormous acreages – thousands of acres in each lot. If I bought a spread, it would be simplicity itself to mark off a good-sized piece for you.' He paused before approaching the crunch point with utmost delicacy. 'Of course there'd be no cost involved to you. I'd regard it as a favour—'

'Bejesus, I'm flabbergasted!' rasped Charles. 'You come here and throw your weight about, murder a Maori and leave the body in my well, upset my wife, then have the gall to braggart about, rubbing my nose in your good fortune at the goldfields. Sure and

76

if that wasn't enough you have the temosity to offer me your charity! Well, I wouldn't accept your charity if I – if I – if I—' He was throttled by rage, shaking like a rat in the jaws of anger.

'It's not charity, Charles! For heaven's sake, man—'

'Not bloody charity? Sure and it's—' Anger made him incoherent. Breath shuddered from his quaking body in asthmatic gasps. How dare he? How dare this dandified upstart with his fine tailored suit and his gold watch-chain strung with nuggets and his flashy smile – how dare he offer him scraps trimmed off his land! It'd be scraps off his plate next, and Charles expected to sit up and beg like a dog.

His temper burst, flooding hot through his head. Before he knew what he was doing he flung down the cigar butt, put up his fists and popped Rhys a smart punch in the nose.

There was a fleeting satisfaction. A crumple of cartilage under his knuckles, blood, the look of utter astonishment on Rhys's streaming face. Then Rhys punched him back.

It was reflexive and very, very hard. Rhys's fist impacted into Charles's flabby midriff like a hammer into a feather bolster, rocking him back on his heels then doubling him over. He half-rolled, half-fell, and lay on his side on the ground with the breath scraping out of him in agony.

'I'm sorry,' said Rhys, standing over him. Blood dripped off his chin. He groped for a silk handkerchief to staunch the flow. 'I am sorry, Charles. I didn't mean to sound patronizing, nor as if I was extending charity, but since you couldn't sell your land here at the moment anyway, and I won't need an entire piece for myself . . .' He dabbed at his nose. 'Oh, forget it. It was an idiotic idea.'

'Mr Stafford, what is it? What's wrong?' Gwynne's voice called from the doorway.

'Nothing's wrong!' replied Rhys, bending to grab Charles's elbow and helping him groan to his feet.

'But we heard shouting.'

'It's nothing.' Hastily staunching the last of the flow from his bleeding nose, Rhys laughed aloud in wry amusement. Yes, he must have been crazy to suggest such an idiotic idea. Of course he loved Gwynne and would like to see more of her, but did he want this dolt as a neighbour? Of course not! And they'd bring along the children, reminders of Mary. That was the last thing he needed. He was sorry about Mary, and genuinely regretted any disappointment he might have inadvertently caused her, but her misery wasn't his fault and he didn't need that girl with her eerie blue-black eyes and her hostile looks making him suffer pangs of guilt. It *wasn't* his fault.

Yes, it was as well that Charles rejected the offer with such a positive *no*.

Gwynne came a few steps down the path and held the lamp high so that great hoops of light rocked and swung over the orchard and the close-tufted blackness of the forest beyond. A huge bush moth swirled like a bird in the beam and was gone. In the doorway behind Gwynne, Andrew stood, legs braced, holding the musket up for shooting.

'Blam!' he shouted. 'Blam! Aaaaaaaaaahhh!'

'Put that thing away!' rasped Charles, lumbering up the path. 'And get inside, both of you. Sure and there's no need to gawp at me like that. Mrs Stafford, you can start packing.'

'Packing? Why?'

'Because we're going to move, that's why. Your brother, he's been doing a little bit of fancy persuading. Seems that he's decided to hie himself down to the South Island to live, and he wants us to go down with him. What do you say to that, hey?' He reached her just in time to snatch the lamp as it wavered perilously in her suddenly limp grasp.

'Say? What do I say, Mr Stafford?' she gasped. Her face was a study in delight. Flinging her arms wide, she rushed to embrace Rhys, crying: 'Oh, but I've prayed to see you again, but it must be the angels in heaven that sent you here today!'

Rhys was still stunned by the abrupt about-face. That punch may have literally knocked some sense into his brother-in-law, but Rhys was already regretting what had happened.

'All the angels in heaven,' cried Gwynne against his shoulder.

Or all the devils in hell, thought Rhys ruefully. What in creation had he let himself in for now?

Now that Charles had warmed to the idea, it was as good as his. They sat around the table while he elaborated on his plans, the cottage they'd build, the crops they'd grow in the fine, rich soil, how they'd prosper with the large market-town of Christchurch to buy all they had to sell.

Gwynne smiled and nodded, but occasionally glanced at Rhys as if wondering whether the finance was to come from him. There was something tentative in her approval; she'd heard all this several times before.

In the corner Lisabeth sat with head bent over mending work

78

that was too intricate for Gwynne's eyesight. She tried not to listen, then tried to fasten on the relief that came with knowing they'd be safe in a district where there was no trouble whatsoever with hostile natives, but that was small compensation in the face of the dismaying news that they would be living near Rhys Morgan.

It was unbearable even to contemplate such a thing, she thought dismally as she jabbed and snipped at the mending. Despair filled her like a dark swamp, but she mustn't cry – that would only draw attention to herself. Her throat ached ferociously under the constriction of repressed tears. If only she could pretend this wasn't happening.

There was no pretending him away. He sat opposite her saying very little, listening to Uncle Charles in such a bemused way that Lisabeth was tempted to hope he was making the whole thing up, that it was all a joke to cheer them up after the horror of the Maori attack and that tomorrow Rhys would walk back to Waitamanui and they'd never see him again. If only!

Snipping the thread, she rolled Gwynne's stocking up with its partner and reached for a working-smock of Charles's that was being patched for the dozenth time. As she sorted for a scrap of a similar butternut colour with which to mend it she glanced up and saw Andrew's face. He was gazing at Rhys with rapt fascination.

'*Andrew*,' she hissed at him. 'It's rude to stare.'

Dismay deepened to genuine terror. *What if Rhys guesses the truth?* she thought in panic. *Perhaps there's some way a father and son instinctively recognize each other. What can I do to stop that happening? If he knows, he'll take Andrew away.*

Her hand shook so that she couldn't thread the needle. *Think! Think calmly!* she urged herself. *There must be some way to put a halt to this mindless adoration of Andrew's. If I can keep him out of Rhys Morgan's way, then the danger will disappear. But how can I —*'

Andrew nudged her, and she realized that Rhys was speaking to her. Reluctantly she looked at his mother-of-pearl waistcoat-buttons.

Deciding that he might as well be pleasant to them all, Rhys was saying: 'Christchurch is a big town, a splendid place, and it should be fun for a young lady growing up.' When she made no response he added: 'There are all manner of entertainments – the opera, plays, pleasure gardens. You'll be able to put your hair up and come out in society.'

He has a brass nerve, she thought furiously. He killed Mamma and now he had the gall to tell me to put my hair up!

But despite her scorn Christchurch did sound interesting and she was secretly crushed when Charles announced: 'She'll be cooking and sewing and dusting just as she does here, and I'll thank you not to put frivolite notions in her head. Sure and I've no money to spare for frippering.'

Gwynne, who also liked the sound of Christchurch, took no notice of her husband's grumbling. 'I'll have tea-parties and be At Home on Tuesday mornings. I've always wanted to be At Home, but we've never really lived anywhere that it was possible.'

Smiling at her, Rhys said, 'You'll need some new china, then.'

'New china? Bless you, no. I've plenty of lovely china, eight of everything from soup-cups to knife- and fork-rests, all with primroses and entwining leaves painted on it. We buried it in the flower garden to be safe from the Maoris. As soon as it's light in the morning I'll start digging it up again.'

Rhys gaped. For a moment he was clutched by the nasty sensation of having been duped, then he realized that any deception was self-induced. He'd jumped to conclusions about their poverty and then, out of misplaced and needless pity, had invited them to share his future. And, like it or not, he was saddled with them now.

He laughed. There was nothing else for it but to laugh. He threw back his head and slapped his knees, and when Gwynne protested that there was nothing amusing about burying plates and cups and saucers in a garden patch Rhys shook his head, laughing all the louder.

The sound of it was infectious. After a moment Andrew joined in, then Gwynne found herself chuckling, too, even Lisabeth at her darning felt a tickle of mirth which she quickly suppressed.

She had to admit it was a pleasant laugh, not skittery like Gwynne's or braying like Charles's. Sneaking another look at him, she had to admit that he was a fine-looking man, too, all gold hair, tanned skin and white strong teeth, with an added quality, an animalistic quality that would have been unsettling if she hadn't already decided that he was completely loathsome. And he had dimples, she noticed before she bent her head over the farming-smock again. Deep dimples that came and went as he laughed.

'Daft, completely daft,' muttered Charles in disgust. Observing that Lisabeth was not laughing, he addressed his disapproval to her. 'The fellow's completely barmy. Sure and I always thought there was something odd about him.'

He doesn't like him, either, Lisabeth realized. *Then, why is Uncle Charles agreeing to go and live near him?*

That question was still bothering her long after the household had retired for bed. She lay on her bunk below Andrew's and listened to Charles's stertorous breathing. He was still awake; not until snores quivered in the rafters was Charles properly asleep.

Occasionally from the other room came a scrap of wakeful sound, footfalls, the dry scrapes of a Lucifer as Rhys lit another of his liquorice-thin cigars.

Pressing a cool damp cloth against her hurt neck, Lisabeth wondered if there was anything that could be done to persuade Charles to change his mind. Probably not; Charles never took any notice of what other people wanted, not even Gwynne as a rule, which made this decision of his even stranger.

In the faint light she could see Andrew's hand where it dangled over the side of the bunk. She reached up to stroke his fingers, and he stirred in his sleep, brushing her away. Her heart swelled with love and dread.

He belongs to Mr Morgan, her mother had insisted. *Promise me you'll tell him! Promise me!*

'You don't belong to him,' Lisabeth whispered in the dark. 'You belong to me, and I'm never going to let him take you away. Never!'

EIGHT

THE *Emmeline* had been rocking at anchor outside Lyttelton harbour, Christchurch's port, all afternoon while the government surgeons wrangled with the captain over the vessel's bill of health.

'There's rumours of a cholera case on board. One of the steerage passengers fell ill this morning,' fretted Gwynne. 'It seems that we'll all be quarantined.'

'Sure and I'll wager that the captain hasn't paid a large enough bribe to the surgeon,' snorted Charles, who stood beside her at the rail. 'If he's like most of the officials I've had dealings with, he'd make a fainting fit out as cholera just to line his pockets.'

Gwynne looked uncomfortable. She wished he'd lower his voice. People nearby were staring.

'He's probably in cohorts with the owner of the quarantine barracks,' claimed Charles. 'Sure and you don't need to tell me a thing about these so-called government fellows!'

Further along the deck Lisabeth was leaning on the railing as she gazed at the coastline before them. It was like a completely different country, more like the parts of Australia she dimly remembered seeing on that long-ago voyage from England.

The *Emmeline* was riding beyond the breakers of a wide bay bracketed by two rugged peninsulas, one of which concealed the harbour within the folds of its hills. Lisabeth could just see the lines of a long wooden jetty and a cluster of houses clinging to the steep bowl sides of the hills above it.

Ahead of the ship spread a ropey line of sand dunes furred with marram grass, while beyond lay a vast treeless plain spiked with plumes of smoke from house chimneys and even further away

swelled golden foothills, smooth as the rest of this strange landscape. At the back were the mountains.

Lisabeth had never seen such mountains, fold upon fold, white
as starched napery, pale as mist, mysterious and distant.

'They're incredible, I can't wait to begin painting them,' said a
voice above her head.

She knew without turning around that the thin, dry voice
belonged to Athol Nye, a spinsterish schoolmaster who, with his
elderly parents, occupied the next table in the cuddy at meal-
times. Once Charles had lent them his luncheon menu when old
Mr Nye had spilled soup on theirs.

Lisabeth was nervous at the thought of conversing with such an
important-looking man, but some comment was called for, so she
said: 'Are you a painting master, then, Mr Nye?' and glanced up
at his face with difficulty, for he was extremely tall and stiff-
necked. It was like looking up at someone on horseback.

'Gracious, no.' His papery white skin flushed as he spoke. He
had a handsome face, rather girlish, with full lips and arched
brows above a long thin nose. Light grey eyes lingered on the
mountains for so long that Lisabeth decided he had forgotten her
when he finally said, 'I instruct in the Classics to sustain my body,
but the arts nourish my soul.'

'I see.' But Lisabeth didn't see at all. It was the kind of thing Mr
Rennie might have said, fine-sounding but incomprehensible.

'You don't paint, do you?' he said, neither glancing at her nor
smiling. 'If you did, Miss Stafford, you would understand.' He
nodded towards the mountains. 'The Southern Alps. That is how
they are named on survey maps, but the common Maori' – he
pronounced the word 'May-oori' – term for them is Aotearoa, or
"The Long White Cloud". Then, again, in legend they are
referred to as "Mists of Heaven". What would you call them, Miss
Stafford, if someone asked you their name?'

She was confused. 'Why, the Southern Alps, of course.'

'Ah, you see!' He flushed, triumphant. 'If you had a true
poetic nature, you would never call them by such a pedestrian
title.'

The slight rankled. 'But you asked me for their name, not for
their description!' she protested, and noted with surprise that the
argument made some impression. Emboldened, she tipped her
chin up and said: 'If you knew me, you might be astonished at
how poetic I am!' And without pausing to judge the effect of
those words she marched back to find Gwynne.

Athol coloured deeply as he resumed his contemplation of the mountains. He'd been put in his place properly, and by a chit of a backwoods girl he was hoping, for some obscure reason, to impress.

Lisabeth was smarting, too. *He thinks I'm uneducated, stupid and dull*, she thought, though these were things she feared about herself, not reflections of Athol Nye's words. Since coming aboard the ship at Waitamanui and finding herself suddenly thrust into the company of brightly spoken and fashionably dressed people, many of whom, like the Nyes, had come directly from England, Lisabeth had felt over-awed and inadequate. She had no hope of hiding her drab hand-me-down wardrobe, so wore Gwynne's old gowns, the navy-blue and the bottle-green on alternate days with her head held high, pretending not to mind that the skirts drooped like folded moths' wings and that her hair hung loose like a child's when all the other young ladies on board (some younger than she) wore their hair up in clusters of curls and glossy ringlets that bobbed as they darted about like butterflies, their wide crinoline skirts dipping and swaying. Lisabeth turned her back on them and tried without success to smother her envy.

Occasionally she heard scraps of their conversation, rich as cake and stuffed with unfamiliar words like 'Dickens', 'Rossetti', 'The Crystal Palace', 'Sloane Square', 'tête à tête' and '*passementerie*' – magic words, romantic, exciting and completely beyond the reach of her comprehension.

'You'll be able to put your hair up and come out in society,' Rhys Morgan had said. No doubt he was mocking her, Lisabeth now decided bitterly. She could never hope to associate with bright clever young women like them.

So during the days at sea while the *Emmeline* sailed south along the coastline, crossed the straits and then traced the rim of Canterbury, Lisabeth kept Gwynne company or played shuffle-board on deck with Andrew.

Now she hurried back to Gwynne.

'Where have you been, dear?' She seemed relieved to see her.

'I've been talking to Mr Nye. Rather, he's been talking to me,' Lisabeth told her.

'Young Mr Nye?' Gwynne looked pleased.

'Bejesus, you can stay away from him,' blustered Charles.

'Oh, *please*, Mr Stafford. There's no harm in a little light con-versation,' said Gwynne who saw the parents approaching. She clasped Lisabeth's hands in both of hers. 'There's the most terrible rumours, dear. They say we're all to be transferred to the quarantine station! Imagine that! Ten weeks at Camp Bay!'

Even at Waitamanui they had heard of Camp Bay where sick and healthy alike were crammed together under filthy and degrading conditions, where fresh meat, vegetables and milk were unavailable, where weevily hard-tack, reject sailors' fare, was the staple diet *and* at inflated prices. The place had been compared, unfavourably, to prison.

'Stop your flapping, woman,' rasped Charles. 'Sure and they'll not send us there. Not while we've silver in our pockets to cross the surgeon's palm.'

The elderly Mr Nye overheard his reassurances and paused, raising an ear-trumpet as a sign that he was about to speak. He was as tall as his son but very stooped, with a shrunken, warped appearance. His thin prim wife hung on his arm as erect as a walking-cane. Neither of them ever smiled.

'Did you mention a bribe, Mr Stafford?'

'We would never pay a bribe,' Mrs Nye put in, nodding her head like a bird placing objects with its beak. She added, as if it was a noble thing to be: '*We* are cabin passengers.'

They look as dowdy as us, thought Lisabeth, noticing the shiny edges on Mr Nye's suit jacket and the cobwebbing of darns at the wrists of Mrs Nye's old-fashioned gown.

'Sure, and that gives us the choice,' said Charles. 'Those poor wretches in steerage won't have any option if the surgeon has his way in the matter. Mark my words, you'd be wiser to pay the bribe than commit yourselves to a term in the quarantine. Neither of you looks healthy enough to stand it, if you don't mind my saying so.'

Clearly they did mind, and shuffled off in haughty indignation. Charles was disappointed when, a few minutes later, word went around that the *Emmeline* was proceeding and there would be no restrictions on any of the passengers, but free transport for all who were transferring to the Immigration Barracks. He had been proved wrong. Charles did not like to be wrong, and he brooded about that as the ship glided into the harbour and the steam-tug chuffed out to begin ferrying the passengers ashore.

Christchurch was the last of the four great colonies to be founded in New Zealand, organized settlements having already been made at Wellington, Nelson and Otago.

Christchurch was unique. The visionaries who planned the

district envisaged a complete slice of England to be built here with an earl and a bishop at the top and at the base a solid foundation of wholesome English labourers. Snobbery was an essential ingredient, allowed for in every stage of the planning.

The raw material for this scheme, the labourers, were not inclined to come here of their own free will, nor could they afford to, however they might want to escape the restrictions of English life for the hope of making something of themselves in a new country. They had to be induced. The Canterbury District subsidized thousands, paying back their fare money on arrival, while others, young female servants, often were granted free passage. In the *Emmeline* three hundred of these emigrants were shoehorned into between-decks accommodation that might comfortably have transported sixty. Only five had died on the voyage, all of them children, so the *Emmeline*'s had been a 'good' voyage.

Because the cabins were situated on the top deck, Lisabeth had seen none of the steerage passengers, though the stench of their filthy quarters drifted up when the wind was in the wrong direction and there was a constant keening of sick and fretful babies – a noise that evoked many complaints from the paying passengers, or 'colonists' as they termed themselves.

Now in the late afternoon, while Charles went to find a hire-cart for their transport, Lisabeth stood on the jetty and watched the steerage passengers unloading, crammed into the steam-tug like cattle, all clutching identical grimy bundles wrapped in stained cloth, all with identical expressions of bewilderment on their faces.

From her perch on the heaped luggage Gwynne watched, too. 'I know how they feel, leaving all that's familiar for an unknown fate,' she said sadly.

'Do you regret coming to New Zealand, then?' asked Lisabeth, who was curious about Gwynne's early history.

'I wonder about the Old Country sometimes,' confessed Gwynne. 'Not that I'd mention it to Mr Stafford, mind, because he'd think I was complaining. But the Isle of Man calls to me sometimes in my sleep . . . Ah, I'd dearly love to see it again.'

'Perhaps you will.'

'Perhaps,' she replied in such a wistful voice now that Lisabeth regretted introducing the subject.

Meanwhile Andrew was fidgeting, for he was an energetic lad who found waiting irksome at the best of times and today had been one long tiring wait that stretched the hours interminably.

He walked along the outer edge of the jetty, balancing on a narrow timber buffer, then found a heap of shingle and filled the pockets of his knickerbockers and, taking off his cap, filled that, too, before running back to where the women were minding the cases and bags.

'I'm going to play skipping stones!' he announced as he squatted beside them and squinted over the sun-gilded harbour as he took aim. But he was too high above the water, the tide was slipping out, and all the stones Andrew tried merely plopped dismally into the water. He took them out of his pockets and arranged them in rows on the buffer-rail, then began to whizz them skittering along the planks of the jetty itself.

Some distance away two people were watching the immigrants with even closer interest. The woman was a florid-faced, amply bosomed woman with improbably bright chestnut hair and a tiny bonnet trimmed with snow fur to match her cape. The man was shorter than his companion with a tall black topper which compensated for the difference in height. When he glanced around in their direction, which he did several times, Lisabeth noticed that he had a round, wrinkled face with the small nose, long upper lip and hard pebbly eyes of a monkey. With one beringed hand he slapped his grey kid gloves against his thigh.

They were watching for young women travelling alone, decided Lisabeth after she had observed them for several minutes. He would whisper to the woman, who then left his side and approached one of the young servant-girls, drawing her aside from the throng. Most of them listened then shook their heads, some violently, but an occasional one pursed her lips, shrugged as if to say 'Why not?' and instead of rejoining the stream of settlers went instead to a large closed coach that was parked in the street near the wharf.

'I wonder what they want those girls for,' remarked Lisabeth as she tried to guess. 'Can you imagine, aunt?'

Gwynne could, and changed the subject before it had begun. 'I wonder what's keeping Mr Stafford?' she worried. 'I do wish that Rhys had been able to come with us instead of having to go back to Sydney to settle his affairs. It's so frustrating having to wait for his return.'

Lisabeth pulled a face, taking care that her aunt couldn't see her. This could have been an adventure if it wasn't for the indigestible fact that the obnoxious Rhys Morgan's presence now hung like a shadow over everything they did. If only Aunt

Gwynne didn't keep dragging a mention of him into everything. Surely they didn't need him and his patronage! she thought in despair. *Surely*. But she thrust him out of her mind. Even nasty thoughts about him (and what other kind were there?) soured her day.

'Aunt,' she repeated with determination, 'just what do you suppose those people—?'

'Look, here he comes!' yelped Gwynne gratefully. 'Mr Stafford, here we are!'

Andrew was still flicking stones along the jetty. Several of them had skidded near to the ugly man, which was why he had glanced around at them. Now, when Gwynne cried out, Andrew pitched his last stone, hard, without taking much care about aim or direction, and instead of spinning harmlessly away it bounced and flipped along on the timber surface, striking the man on the ankle.

He swivelled around, annoyed. Andrew was already running to meet Charles, whooping as he ran. It sounded like laughter.

'Right,' said the man, whacking his thigh one more time with his bunched gloves. He strode after Andrew and reached him when he and Charles were on their way back towards the womenfolk.

To Andrew's astonishment he found himself being seized by the collar scruff and cuffed about the ears.

'Hoi!' bellowed Charles, making even more noise than Andrew but not physically interfering. 'What do you think you're doing?'

'I'm giving your lad the benefit of a practical demonstration,' said the man between clenched, yellowish teeth. 'This, lad, is what happens when you throw stones at people. And this, and this!' And he flailed his gloves with stinging accuracy.

Lisabeth was already there, tugging at the man's arms. 'Leave him alone!' she cried in a fury. 'You just leave him alone! He didn't mean no harm!'

'Guttersnipe!' the man retorted, brushing her hands off his sleeves as easily as if they had been fallen leaves. Andrew flew to her and wrapped his arms around her waist. She stood there glowering at the man.

'What's going on here?' came a cultured, plummy voice, and a rotund man sauntered up. He was dressed in full tropical whites and wore a full spread of beard that resembled a crumpled table-napkin tucked around his shiny apple cheeks. Behind him walked two Indian servants clad in long beige tunics and baggy trousers with scarlet sashes and tall scarlet turbans pinned with gold clasps.

'Fox, isn't it?' asked the rotund man, doffing his pith helmet. 'Mr Thomas Fox?'

'*Councillor* Thomas Fox, as you very well know,' corrected the ugly man, his flat eyes narrowing.

'A temporary title. Very temporary.'

'The voters will decide.' Fox stepped back, adding smugly, 'These folk friends of yours, are they? Then, take care. The smallest reptile throws stones.' And without another word he walked briskly back to his companion.

Sir Kenneth Launcenolt replaced his pith helmet so that the puggaree flowed down his back. It gave him time to survey the Staffords and decide what to do.

'I'd regard it as a personal favour if you looked out for them for me,' Rhys's message had said. 'With hundreds of newcomers arriving in Christchurch every month, my relatives might experience considerable difficulty finding a place to stay.'

Sir Kenneth smiled wryly to himself. He had met Rhys in India, later in London and again in Sydney, and had himself been instrumental in influencing Rhys to choose Canterbury as a district in which to settle. In all their enjoyable association Rhys had never once mentioned family. Now Sir Kenneth appreciated why.

Mr Stafford was obviously a simple yokel; the boy, though a handsome lad, was a brat; and the womenfolk were no more than drabs. As he shook hands with them in turn Sir Kenneth smiled, sincere as the politician he aspired to be, and asked solicitously about their comfort.

Gwynne was not used to such concern. 'My poor feet are killing me,' she confided. 'I'm longing to give them a good hot mustard bath.' Not noticing his wince, she said, 'Are these your darkies? Not Maoris, are they?'

'They're my sepoys,' he responded as the Indians began picking up the luggage. When they were out of earshot he added, 'Damned glad we brought them from Bombay with us, too. Servants are the biggest problem here, you'll find. Can't use a broom or saddle a horse most of them, and the Irish ones only know how to cook potatoes. My sepoys can stuff a pheasant or roast a joint of beef to perfection. They're more *English*, somehow.'

'Bless you,' said Gwynne. 'But we don't have servants. Lisabeth looks after me and very well she does, too.'

She had a pleasant voice, decided Sir Kenneth, warming to her, and noticing the younger woman's sweet smile he liked her better, too. What magnificent eyes she had. There was real intelligence there. Perhaps he shouldn't judge too hastily . . . it was just that they looked dirt poor, and that came as a shock because Rhys was wealthy enough to mingle with the best of society. He never for one moment imagined. . . .

Sir Kenneth suddenly remembered that his wife was at home putting finishing touches to a table set with damask and crystal, silver and flowers in anticipation of welcoming the Staffords with a special dinner. He shuddered.

'Well, let's not keep the maharaja waiting, as we used to say in Bombay,' he said heartily.

They followed the sepoys to a glossy landau. Andrew crowed in excitement as they settled themselves aboard: he bounced on the seats, rubbed his fingers over the oxblood woodwork and grabbed at the polished brass fittings, leaving smears on everything he touched.

The sepoys averted their eyes. Closing the door with a deferential bow to Sir Kenneth, they mounted the carriage, one at the rear and the other taking the reins of the two black horses. The high wheels chewed the gravel-surfaced road.

'Isn't this *exciting*!' whispered Gwynne.

Lisabeth nodded, over-awed. She was nervous of the ridiculous-looking yet dignified man, of his inscrutable, grandly dressed servants, and thought this landau was the most magnificent vehicle she had ever seen. Cautiously she relaxed against the deeply buttoned maroon leather seats and allowed herself to pretend that she was a fine lady in a frothy crinoline-skirted gown riding in her own carriage to a glittering society ball.

Gwynne shattered the dream before it had begun to take shape.

'I wonder what kind of a wagon Rhys will buy,' she murmured in Lisabeth's ear. 'The way he was talking . . . Oh, wouldn't it be lovely to drive to the shops in one of these?'

Lisabeth's mood clouded. *He ruins everything, even my harmless daydreams*, she thought resentfully.

NINE

To AVOID HAVING TO ENGAGE in direct conversation Sir
Kenneth adopted the role of a guide and as they trotted slowly up
the steep road in the mellow afternoon light he told them about the
history of the colony and about the Four Ships that brought the first
wave of organized settlement here some ten years earlier.

Lisabeth listened idly. It was a beautiful evening. On the far side
of the circular harbour sunshine blazed on the yellow hills, but here
velvet brown shadows melted into the pearlescent water below.

'This harbour and all these cone-shaped hills around are the
craters of extinct volcanoes. An interesting phenomenon, don't
you think? You may have noticed a similar outcropping just a mile
or two up the coast.' He paused to point out the three barges which
were now out in the harbour, loaded with the steerage passengers.
'They're off to the Immigration Barracks at Settlers' Bay. From
there they'll be offered employment, homes and so on.'

'Sounds well organized,' commented Charles.

'It should be, but I'm afraid there's rank exploitation going on.
Corruption. The Barracks is owned by a fellow named Fox – yes,
you met him – and he's hand in glove with some of the government officials.'

'I'm not surprised. Sure and he looked like a shady piece of
work,' said Charles.

Encouraged, Sir Kenneth confided, 'I'm standing against Fox at
the next Provincial Council elections. You could say there was a
touch of ill-natured rivalry between us. My platform is that of
stamping out corruption.'

'And good luck to you. That's very combustible of you.'

91

Sir Kenneth covered a smile by patting his beard. 'You people were wise to choose this province to settle in. I took a peek at Otago first, but they're a dour, sour, rum-and-churchy lot, those Free Kirk Scots down there, and of course anything up north is just a raggle-taggle lot, quite disorganized and—'

'We're from up north,' rasped Charles, taking umbrage at once. '*And* we're church-abiding. Sure and what's wrong with that?'

'I'm sorry. I assumed, since you'd come off the *Emmeline* that you were directly — no matter – and no offence, I hope. Only, Canterbury folk like to be told they're the best, you'll find, and now you're Canterbury folk, too.' He noticed that Charles was pulling a plug of tobacco from a twist he had unwrapped in a square of dirty rag, tucking it into his cheek and chewing. Sir Kenneth's heart shrank as he imagined Lady Launcenolt's expression if she could see that. He'd be squirting jets of juice, next.

There was a small hotel at Sumner. Sir Kenneth hoped he could find lodgings for Rhys Morgan's relatives there.

After a long slow climb they reached a plateau where scoured, misshapen rocks loomed like prehistoric sculptures out of a damp grey mist. Lisabeth shivered and pulled her old, darned shawl tightly around her thin shoulders. 'We must be up very high, Sir Kenneth,' she ventured.

'The clouds are down low,' he replied with a smile that tightened his rosy apple cheeks. 'It's a pity, too. On a clear day one can see from Christchurch out there right back to the mountains. A splendid sight. But the clouds do blow in suddenly and then everything is lost to view.'

Lisabeth gazed at the towering mysterious rocks. 'Mists of Heaven,' she murmured.

'Oh?' queried Sir Kenneth. 'You study native legends, do you, young lady?'

Lisabeth shook her head, wishing that she could answer yes. There had been respect in Sir Kenneth's tone when he asked if she studied, just as Athol Nye's tone had been patronizing when he declared there was no poetry in her soul. Looking into herself, Lisabeth realized the limitations of her upbringing in the backblocks where the only skills needed were a deft hand with Blossom's milk-teats and the ability to judge by thumping the base of a loaf whether it was baked through. There was a whole world of which she knew absolutely nothing. Having received only the

92

barest basics of schooling, she was unprepared for life.

And Andrew had received none! Lisabeth began to panic. If she felt ignorant and disadvantaged, it would be much worse for him to be growing up without the benefit of a proper education. A man needed an education for the foundations of a career; he needed to be able to command respect. It didn't matter for her – her 'career' would be to stay at home and look after Gwynne – but Andrew, that was a vastly different—.

'Look, child!' exclaimed Gwynne.

Abruptly the road dipped to follow a scoop of valley that lay slung below the quilt of cloud. Just ahead of them and not far below was a wide shallow inlet veined by channels of dark blue and edged all around by reed-stippled marshland. In the distance lay the plains. 'There's Christchurch itself,' said Sir Kenneth, directing their attention to a thinly spread clutter of buildings which were threaded on a silver sinuous river. 'And here, ladies and gentlemen, is where we get out and walk.'

They had reached the lip of what was now revealed as a hanging valley. Ahead and below the road plunged in a series of twists and dips down the face of a steep cliff until at the foot it levelled out beside a modest two-storey structure which Sir Kenneth told them was the Sumner Hotel.

'Nice convenient place, Sumner. I'll try to get you rooms there,' he said, and when the sepoys glanced at him in surprise scolded them by saying, 'Take this down carefully, Leopold, and you be ready with the chocks, Albert. Not too fast, now.'

They walked behind the landau, which inched down the steep incline with much shouting and whoaing from Leopold who pulled hard on the reins while Albert used a long batten frequently to chock the wheels to a halt. The strain on the horses seemed tremendous.

Gwynne leaned on Lisabeth and glanced doubtfully at Sumner as they descended. The town comprised only half a dozen houses set on a narrow strip of sand between the harbour mouth and these cliffs. On the shore was a boat-shed and a skeletal jetty which probed one of the deeper-blue channel veins. There were a few tired-looking trees and a fenced garden tucked behind the hotel away from the winds. A depressing-looking place, thought Lisabeth.

Waving his walking-cane, Sir Kenneth pointed out places of interest: ancient Maori fortifications long abandoned; Ferrymead, where a barge carried traffic across the river between Sumner and

Christchurch; and this road, nicknamed the Zig-Zag, carved with difficulty at the only practical place on this ridge that separated the port of Lyttelton from the vast rich plains.

'A real bottleneck it is, too,' Sir Kenneth told them. 'See those horses down there? And that cart? They have to wait until we're off the road before they can attempt the climb. There's absolutely nowhere to pass, no room to turn around.'

Andrew was intrigued. 'So, if one cart meets another halfway, what happens? Crash! Aaaaaahh!' And he launched a rock into space.

Sir Kenneth smiled thinly. He was a boy once, though a darn sight better behaved than this one. 'The one coming up would have to back all the way down. So it never, ever happens.'

At sea-level they were met by mock cheers from the folks waiting. Here a brisk wind raced along the ground, wrapping them in a mist of fine sand as they walked the last few yards to the hotel. Along the veranda scarlet geraniums were buffeted by the breeze. Close by, the water patted a long white beach, while nearer still, at the high-water mark, satiny pale driftwood lay in tangled heaps like bare limbs. A group of Maori children were busy there sorting out like-sized pieces, which they loaded on to a small sled.

'Maoris!' exclaimed Charles.

'I think they're from Ferrymead,' Sir Kenneth told him. 'There's a small *pah** nearby. The children collect firewood for sales in town. Make quite a decent—'

'Maoris!' grumbled Charles, staring. 'That brother of yours put us properly crook. He promised that there were no Maoris here!'

Gwynne smiled at Sir Kenneth. 'We've had a slightly disagreeable experience recently,' she explained apologetically.

Lisabeth was astounded. *She makes it sound like a spilled cup of tea at a garden-party!* she thought. *We were almost murdered*!

Mrs Day welcomed them. She was a fair-haired woman of Gwynne's age, sensibly dressed in a brown smock that reached from the point of her chin to the tops of her buttoned ankle-boots. Her face was soft-skinned and kind, a quality she recognized in Gwynne, so the two women warmed to each other at once.

Because Sir Kenneth fled as soon as the luggage was out of the landau, Mrs Day was left with the same mistaken assumption that

*Settlement

94

the Staffords had only today completed an exhausting voyage from England.

'I know how one feels after months at sea,' she told them sympathetically. 'One craves the most ordinary things. A hot bath, a really good cup of tea, fresh fruit, the scent of roses. We can't grow roses here so close to the beach, but I've cut ones in a vase in the parlour, and for newcomers there's fresh apples and peaches put aside. Mabs will heat up some water for—'

'Bless you for an angel, Mrs Day, but we've been only a short time at sea,' confessed Gwynne before Charles could stop her. *He'd* have relished the fruit. 'But if you've another couple of those white starched aprons you might like to lend them to Lisabeth and myself so that we can give you a hand with the chores. It's been too long since I set foot in a kitchen and, to tell you the truth, I feel quite peculiar without my apron on.'

The dining-room was just large enough to accommodate a long table set for twenty, with thick white cups and plates and heavy bone-handled cutlery. On the walls hung several delicate water-colour views of the harbour, while in one corner on a lace-draped stand stood an enormous aspidistra plant with dark oily leaves. Candles in glass-shielded sconces illuminated the room, though a lace-filtered evening sky still lightened the large window.

Lisabeth and Andrew sat at the foot of the table opposite Joe and Alf, the youngest Day boys, lads of nineteen and twenty-one. The two were alike in looks with dark, thickly curled hair, merry green eyes and wide intelligent foreheads.

'Isn't anyone going to sit in the big chair?' asked Andrew wistfully, gazing at the massive carved captain's chair that graced the empty place at the head of the table.

'That's my pa's place. He's up the coast with our brothers George and Robert and with the *Flirt*,' said Joe, the older boy.

'*Flirt?*' questioned Lisabeth.

'A twelve-ton ketch. Our trading boat. She's called *Flirt* because we set her sails to catch the slightest attentions of every breeze,'

'That's a clever name!'

'Our pa's a clever man,' responded Joe. 'He built the *Flirt* himself when we lived near Wellington, then moved us and all our things down here in her.' He smiled at Lisabeth and winked at her, enchanted by her solemn, haunting, navy-blue eyes.

But she looked away at once, shy, and fiddled with the napkin in her lap.

95

'Joseph,' warned Mrs Day, who was ladling portions of cod in curry sauce from a huge tureen. 'He's a scamp, Miss Stafford, take no notice.'

'You lived in Wellington?' asked Gwynne, embarrassed by the way Charles was helping himself to yet another dollop of the delicious mutton stew that had been the first course.

'We came from Kent twenty years ago,' Mrs Day told them with the pride early settlers often displayed. 'Captain Day found us a darling little bay across from the main town of Wellington, but the earthquakes terrified me so – our chimney fell down once, taking an entire wall with it – and then, when the troubles with the Maoris started, that was too much.'

'Bless you!' exclaimed Gwynne. 'I declare that you're a kindred spirit! I've a mortal distaste for earthquakes, too, and as for trouble with the Maoris, when I tell you—'

She broke off, starting with pain as Charles pinched her viciously just above the knee. Glancing at him in astonishment, she met an angry warning glare from his eyes and subsided, deflated, realizing that it wasn't quite proper to tell people that back on their last farm a collapsed well held the grim secret of a dead Maori warrior.

Charles harrumphed. 'And how long have you been here, Mrs Day?'

'We've been here twelve years now,' she said, whisking away his stew-plate and replacing it with another, bearing a steaming portion of cod. 'We saw the Four Ships arrive from the top of those hills, and Joe and the others heaped driftwood on the beach and made bonfires to welcome them. We've seen some changes on these plains, I can tell you. There's talk of a cathedral for Christchurch now! Won't that be a magnificent thing?'

'Aw, Ma! The tunnel under the hills will be more impressive!' argued Joe from the other end of the table.

'Hush, Joe!' His mother was exasperated, but she glanced at him with fondness. 'Are you of the Church of England persuasion, Mrs Stafford?'

Gwynne looked embarrassed. 'We worship the Virgin on the Isle of Man.'

'The Isle of Man?'

'That's where I'm from. Mr Stafford, he's—'

'The Isle of Man!' Mrs Day plonked herself down in her husband's huge chair and patted her damp-beaded brow with the hem of her apron. 'So you're Manx! Your maiden name's not Braddock, is it?'

'No but that's a fine traditional name. Mine was Maughold long ago, but the family changed it to Morgan several generations back. There was a pogrom at the time, and Maughold sounded – well, Jewish.'

'Oh.' She fanned her face with Mr Day's rolled napkin. 'Then, Mr Braddock isn't the relative you're coming here to meet?'

Charles bristled slightly; like all over-inquisitive people he was swift to resent any trace of inquisitiveness in others.

'And who is this Mr Braddock?' he asked as he plucked a chalky cod bone from one corner of his mouth and placed it on the rim of his plate.

'Oh, one of the settlers,' said Mrs Day vaguely. She smiled at Gwynne; it was at her that all her remarks were directed. 'He's a quaint old fellow who comes in here a lot. It's he who did these paintings. Well, fancy your both coming from the same place! Perhaps you'll find you know each other. Just fancy!'

Gwynne beamed back at her. Charles loaded his fork with juicy flakes of cod and slurped curry sauce over the mound with his knife before transporting it to his mouth. As he chewed he looked on uneasily. He didn't like it when Gwynne talked on about the Old Country.

It made her mawkish.

Gwynne made friends with Mrs Day and spent her time chatting to her as together with the sturdy young servant girl they stirred vast saucepans of preserves in the kitchen and pegged snowy sheets on the sagging propped clothes-line below the cliffs. Charles spent his evenings supping ale with Mr Braddock, who rowed across from his property on the headland opposite, but in the days Charles shooed the ginger cat from the only comfortable chair on the front porch and propped his boots on the railing while he dozed, an old copy of the *Lyttelton Times* spread over his face to foil the flies.

Andrew wanted to be out exploring, so Lisabeth, ever careful of his safety, tagged along, too, if her morning tasks were done.

'Mind how you go!' Mrs Day called after them. 'The rocks can be dangerous places, and in the valleys there are wild pigs.'

'Domestic pigs gone wild, just like the "purrs" at home. Mr Braddock told me about them,' said Gwynne with a sigh. Home-sickness was working through her like a fever.

'Don't go into the water, will you? added Mrs Day, her voice rising still higher. 'There can be a nasty rip on the out tide. And, if

97

you see Alf and Joe, tell them their father will be home this afternoon. They'll know what that means.'

Lisabeth turned to wave acknowledgement. Fine breeze-borne grit stung her cheeks and eyes as she squinted back at the hotel. The glassed windows winked back at her. Scarlet geraniums waved. Glare sheeted off the water, and the sun beat hot out of an enamelled blue sky.

After the close confines of the bush all this openness gave her an exhilarating sense of freedom. Spreading her arms wide, she laughed giddily as she raced Andrew along the road and down to the corrugated-iron boat-shed.

'Last one there's a silly-billy!' she called as she slowed her pace just enough to let him win.

When Lisabeth met Joe and his painfully shy brother, Alf, she hoped they'd all be friends, but so far she'd seen little of them because they were gone from the hotel before breakfast and away all day until they dashed panting in, invariably late, and plonked themselves down to mutter a hasty Grace after everyone else had started dinner.

This astounded Lisabeth. Used to Charles's leisurely approach to chores, his 'If it's not done today, tomorrow will do as well' attitude, she couldn't understand why anybody would want to work as hard as these two.

And they relished every bit of it. 'There's plenty of work here, but we still look for more!' Joe said enthusiastically when in a rare spare moment he told her how he spent his days.

The Sumner Hotel overlooked the entrance to a broad, shallow harbour into which flowed the Sumner river. Because land access was so difficult over the hills from the deep-water harbour at Lyttelton, all incoming goods were transferred to whaleboats, barges and cutters to be ferried to Christchurch that way.

'A million pounds' worth of cargo comes into this harbour every year,' Joe told them. 'And every one of those boats has to cross the Sumner Bar. Because we've lived here so long, we know the bar well. It's treacherous at certain tides, and at others boats need guidance to cross. See that red blanket that's hanging over the balcony of the hotel? That's a signal to say the bar's danger-ous, to tell the boats to wait. If there's no danger-flag up, and the boats want our help, they let us know and we row out and guide them over.'

'What say it's dangerous but they don't understand your sig-nal?' asked Andrew.

Joe laughed and ruffled his hair. 'Then, they get wrecked. During a bad storm last winter four boats came to grief within thirty-six hours.One was carrying a load of tea. We fished an undamaged tea-chest out of the surf – Ma's only halfway through it now – but most of the tea-chests were dashed to smithereens. The sand was black for weeks, wasn't it, Alf?'

Alf, who was plaiting a rope, nodded without looking up.

'How much do the captains pay you for towing their boats over?'

'Andrew! You don't ask questions like that!'

'He can, but I needn't answer,' grinned Joe. 'Let's say it's well worth our while.'

'But it must be so dangerous!' said Lisabeth.

'Only sometimes,' and he winked at her. 'But you can worry about me if you like.'

She turned away. *He's a rascal*, his mother had said. Lisabeth tried to follow Mrs Day's advice and take no notice of his flirting – he was playing, she could tell – but what disturbed her was that every time Joe smiled at her in that cheeky way, or winked at her, she thought of Rhys. Why, she couldn't fathom. Joe was delightful, Rhys was loathsome. She liked Joe, she hated Rhys. Then, why did she keep being reminded of him like this? It was infuriating.

In their less busy moments Alf and Joe worked in the boat-shed where they were carving and fitting ribs to the keel of a cutter they had just started building. Most evenings they worked here, too.

Today the door stood open and there was a smell of warm wood shavings but no sign of the boys, nor was their dinghy tied up at the short jetty.

'There they are!' Andrew was staring across the hurtfully bright harbour.

'That's not them.' The rowboat creaked closer, and they saw that it was old Mr Braddock from the headland. Lisabeth wanted to walk away because she was nervous of this peculiar old man. Mabs the servant girl had whispered darkly that he was 'daft in the 'ead'. 'When it rains 'e flings orf all 'is clothes an' capers about like soom demented pixie!' she had said.

But Andrew was racing along the jetty to help tie up the rowboat and to pat Bollan, old Braddock's liver-spotted dog.

'Good day to you,' he cackled to Lisabeth, sweeping off his battered black hat that, like all his clothes, seemed several sizes

99

too large. 'Well, yurr a pretty gel! Yurr get prettier every day!' She retreated, but not before he had pinched her cheek. He was like an ancient tortoise, she thought, with his scrawny neck jutting out of that stiff over-sized coat and those cracked leathery fingers. Every time she admired the watercolours in the dining-room she marvelled that such clumsy-looking hands had executed such delicate work.

'Where's yurr uncle?' he asked. 'I've a proposition furr him.' And covering his freckled bald head with his cavernous hat he stumped off towards the hotel. Bollan ran on ahead, tail switching.

'Look!' cried Andrew when he had gone. 'That *is* Alf and Joe.'

He was right. Out beyond the surf-line was a ketch with brown and white sails and on this side of it, bobbing behind the breakers sometimes visible on the crest, sometimes lost in the trough, was Joe's dinghy, tugging on a line that stretched back to the ketch. Even from this distance they could see the sparkle of water dashing from Alf and Joe's flailing oars and hear the shouts as sailors in the ketch encouraged them along.

'Look at them *go!*' yelled Andrew. He shucked off his wooden-soled boots and his hand-knitted blue stockings and tossed them down on the damp sand, then rolled his knickerbockers up over his knees and splashed out to Cave Rock, which he climbed up on to for a better look.

Lisabeth's throat squeezed shut with fright. The bad rip dragged right past the north face of Cave Rock. She croaked at him to come back, but he ignored her, or didn't hear above his own excited shouting. Scooping up his discarded things, she paced the water's edge fretting.

Joe and Alf swung on the oars. In quick swoops the ketch rolled over the bar and glided into the channel on a funnelling surge. The wind filled their sails. Now there was no need for Joe and Alf to lead them but they rowed the harder, making a game of keeping the rope tight. Lisabeth couldn't see them clearly because of the buckling haze over the harbour, but their laughter bounced off the cliffs behind her.

'Look at them go!' applauded Andrew, scrambling back around the rock so that he could race up the beach keeping pace with them. He splashed ashore, beaming, and at the moment he reached the firm foam-encrusted sand a gust of wind snatched the straw boater from his head and sent it whirling like a wheel across the top of the choppy wavelets. He gaped foolishly as it spun away.

She was so tight with anxiety that her first impulse was to slap him for frightening her so. Instead she grabbed him and hugged him. 'You silly thing!' she cried.

He shook her off and ran impatiently along the water's torn edges. 'Hats are cissy!'he screamed back, his voice as raw as a gull's.

They followed the dinghy and the ketch halfway along the beach to Ferrymead, where Lisabeth was able to shout Mrs Day's message to the pair, then she and Andrew turned and walked back along the beach, she looking for shells, he (encouraged by the find of a toothless grinning boot) looking for valuable flotsam from wrecks.

When they arrived back at the jetty the old rowboat had gone. Stamping on the decking with a force that raised a cloud of gulls from the far end, Andrew shrieked: 'Oh, *blast*! I was going to take it for a ride!'

Lisabeth thought it best to ignore the language and what he said. He was only swaggering for effect. He had so much energy these days, such an enquiring mind, it exhausted her. She resolved to broach the subject of his schooling with Gwynne just as soon as they were settled.

'I wonder if your hat will be washed ashore?' she asked, shading her eyes.

'There's probably a whale wearing it now!'

'Or a shark!' She 'nipped' him with a rigid-fingered hand.

'Or a sea-horse! I'd like a sea-horse to have it.'

They laughed together. Another ketch waited beyond the bar, sails half-furled. Joe and Alf were hurrying to meet it, borne along at a breakneck pace by the mill-race current. Beyond them Braddock's rowboat was bobbing into the safe inlet, far away and merging with the bristling of horizon weeds, but even from here Lisabeth could recognize the figure of Charles sitting erect in the stern, hands braced on his knees.

'What in the world is he up to?' she wondered.

To prepare for their father's arrival the lads had rowed down to Ferrymead and purchased sixpence worth of roses and a crisp fresh lettuce. 'The captain likes the table to look pretty, and he's ever so fond of a salad,' confided Mrs Day. 'So I ask Mr Hopkins at the ferry landing to grow them for me. Lovely rich silt soil, he has, and he grows them under glass, you see, so they're fresh all year round.'

'Spoils' im, she do,' Mabs whispered proudly to Lisabeth. 'And

101

George, too. Always trying ter cheer'im up, she is. Course, '*is* wife kilt 'erself years back. Drowned in the river over town, she were. Ain't never got over the shock.'

'Really?' gasped Lisabeth. Her curiosity was aroused. As she helped Mabs set the table with the heavy china she, too, kept peeking through the curtains to see if there was any sign of the senior menfolk, who would be docking the *Flirt* at Ferrymead before walking home.

'A carriage!' exclaimed Mabs, whirling from the window with a salt-dish in each red hand. 'An' a grand one, too. An' there's the Captain an' George ridin' up in it loike Jacky!'

Lisabeth hurried after her, anxious to see this Dickensian figure of tragedy, and to meet the Captain, whose presence was almost palpable even in his absence.

Her eagerness faltered before she had taken two steps across the worn verandah floor. The carriage was Sir Kenneth's polished mahogany landau, but there was no sign of him. Two men were climbing out, bulky men in rough clothes, both thickly bearded – the older with white streaks through his beard and hair that brushed around the sides of his peaked cap. She knew who they must be – their high, intelligent foreheads and clear sparkling eyes labelled them as Days. But her attention was taken by the other man, the one who was chatting to Leopold and Albert as they unloaded his luggage.

Mrs Day ran, house-cap streamers flying, to meet her husband.

'Ann,' he boomed. 'You remember Mr Morgan, don't you? He overtook us along the way and gave us a ride home.'

Lisabeth turned back into the gloom of the dark-polished corridor. Her brief season of delight was over.

Andrew was in the room they shared. It was a tiny attic room with a sloping ceiling papered with pages of the *Lyttelton Times* and with a casement window that looked on to the sandstone cliff-faces only a few yards away. Lisabeth flung the windows open and took a deep shuddering breath.

'Look at this,' said Andrew. 'It's shaped just like that Maori's gun!' He had found a long branch of driftwood and was using one of Mrs Day's sharp steel knives to whittle it trim.

Lisabeth was too agitated to comment on the forbidden knife or the fact that Andrew had been expressly instructed never, but never, to mention the Maoris for fear that some stray remark might slip out at the worst possible time. She didn't even notice the mess of sand and splinters he had made all over Mrs Day's plaited bright rag rug. All she could think of was that soon Andrew would be gawping at Rhys Morgan again with that undisguised admiration, that she would know that he was slipping away from her and there would be that terrible, impotent feeling of being unable to do one single thing to prevent it.

'Let's go for a walk,' she suggested. *Let's get out of here!*

'It's almost dinner-time,' he protested.

'There's plenty of time. We could hurry up to the top of the Zig-Zag and see how many ships we can count. All right? And let's make an adventure of it, shall we? See if we can creep out without anybody seeing us.'

'Can I bring my musket?'

'Of course, darling. Of course!' She was afraid she was going to cry. *I couldn't bear to lose you*, she thought.

TEN

'WHAT DID YOU WANT TO DISCUSS WITH ME, Charles? Is there a problem?' asked Rhys.

The two men stood on the jetty in a spill of light from a quarter moon. The water around them was chopped into black and silver patches that slurped and sucked at the support-piers. That afternoon had been overcast, but the curdling of cloud had thinned to milk then dissolved, leaving a black sky punctured with pin-pricks of light. Low on the western horizon the Southern Alps were as white and cold as a frozen wave, while to the east three ships poured single splashes of yellow light over the dark flat sea.

Rhys was impatient. He didn't want to talk right now, and especially not to Charles. The journey had wearied him. It had been the stormiest Rhys had ever known, with massive waves that dashed the full length of the decks, and sheeting rain. Promenades on the deck were impossible beyond Sydney Heads and forced to remain cooped up in the cuddy, Rhys would have found the crossing unendurable if not for the delectable presence of a delicious fur-swathed young lady called Leonie Gammerwoth, who was on her honeymoon, a fact made piquant by an invisible husband who was prostrate with sea sickness the entire voyage. Rhys had the pleasure – regrettably chaste – of consoling and entertaining her. Last night they had stayed up late toasting everything from Queen Victoria to cricket, sipping Canary wine from tilting glasses refilled from a teetering, skidding bottle. It was excellent Canary, full-bodied and golden with a smooth Muscat taste, but Rhys was suffering the effects of over-indulgence now.

'I have a surprise,' said Charles.

'A surprise?'

'Something to show you.'

Rhys scraped a Lucifer, lit Charles a cigar and one for himself. 'I hate surprises. Tell me about it now.'

'All right.' Charles was relieved; *he* hated trying to keep surprises secret. 'I've found your land!' he said.

'I beg your pardon?'

'Your land. The land you want to buy. Sure and it's perfect! Ten thousand acres, the choicest spread you could possibly hope to—'

'Wait a minute, here. Don't you think I should be choosing my own land? It is customary, after all, for the purchaser to have the privilege of—'

'Sure but you don't understand, lad!' Charles cleared his throat with a gravelly cough. 'This is special! Sure and it's a lifetime opportunity, a rare bargain even if I say so my—'

'Wait. Start at the beginning.' Rhys's initial annoyance was easing to faint interest. Charles had obviously fallen under the influence of an unscrupulous con-man, but no harm could have been done – Charles had almost no money to lose even if some had changed hands – and the story was bound to be an entertaining one.

He leaned against the wooden jetty-railing, his face illuminated by the glow from the distant dining-room window where the Days were still enjoying their family reunion amid laughter and loud voices.

'Tell me all about it,' said Rhys.

So Charles told him about Braddock.

When he was not much more than a boy Heywood Braddock had been a cabin boy in ships plying back and forth between Europe and the cotton-rich Southern States of America. His family were friends with a certain Captain Bligh and, when a crew was being assembled for the *Bounty*'s experimental expedition to gather breadfruit trees in the South Pacific, Heywood was invited along. Lured by the seductions of Tahiti, he and another friend jumped ship there and had eventually been brought by an American whaling vessel to New Zealand, where Heywood worked part of the time from whaleboats themselves, and part of the time on a land station.

'The boiling-down station was not far from here, across the bay at the foot of those cliffs. Old Braddock's got one of the huge try-pots behind his house with a lemon-tree growing in it, and he said another was to boil up his washing – though by the looks of it, and him, sure and it's been a few years since it was used!' Charles chuckled, then coughed as the down-draught of smoke tangled in his throat.

'But the *Bounty* was taken over seventy years ago! He must be ancient.'

'About ninety or so, but spry with it. Sure and he rows back and forth across here as if it had no more current than a rain-puddle.'

Thirty years ago Heywood Braddock, now well into middle age, had decided that he would never return Home, that the rest of his life could be spent comfortably here. He had taken a Maori wife and had a peaceable, though childless, marriage.

'Twenty years passed. Then the Four Ships came, and with it all the folderol and rules laid down by the Canterbury Land Company. Old Braddock became alarmed as he seen the land all around him being gobbled up by settlers, so he went to court and took out a lease, legal-like, on ten thousand acres. But things turned sour on him,' continued Charles. 'His wife died, and then cockatoo farmers started instigating on his land.'

'Cockies? Like in Australia?' Rhys had heard about them, how like the cockatoo birds that prey on young lambs these squatters move in and pick the eyes out of a run-holding by claiming all the choicest pieces of land.

'Dunno about Australia, but here if they've the money they can buy a few acres of land even if that land be already let to someone else. Happened to the Days, you know. They leased five thousand acres up the coast for grazing back in 1854, but the cockatoo farmers moved in on them and now there be only a few hundred acres of sandhills and swamp left. Old Braddock didn't want that to happen to him, so he took out a mortgage to buy the lot, then found he couldn't afford it. Then back in spring he takes a fall from his horse, so now the poor bogger can't work, can't afford no wages, neither. He's been selling off his stock, and now the mortgage is due. Unless someone rescues him there'll be a foreclosure in a couple of weeks, and—'

'And why should I rescue him?'

'Because you're a fool if you don't,' Charles told him bluntly. 'Because it's the best damned piece of land this side of the mountains, that's why. As I say, Braddock doesn't want to sell it, but—'

Rhys had listened to enough. 'Then, why's he offering it to you?'

106

Accurately reading his tone, Charles bristled. 'You think he's out to skin us because we're new-chums, don't you?'

Us? *Us?* He didn't like being told he was a fool, either; and, yes, he did think Charles was being conned. But, again, Charles was the sort of clumsy-tongued oaf one simply had to make allowances for. What the hell. Silkily he asked: 'If this is such a marvellous spread of land, I imagine there are buyers queuing to snap up the mortgage.'

'Sure and there would be.'

'Then, why offer it to you, Charles?'

'To us.'

'Oh, of course, *us*,' he agreed sarcastically.

To his utter astonishment Charles gave him a reply he never could have predicted. 'Because he's Manx, too. Comes from just out of Douglas. Sure and it's true. He's got those "fylfuts" – those three-legged emblem things – tattooed on his wrists, identical to the one on my shaving-mug. Taken a real shine to Mrs Stafford, he has. Didn't like him at first meself, but he's a sound enough fellow. He were hoping what with you being Manx, too, and in the market for a property, that you might buy his and let him stay there. He's an old man, Rhys, sure and he don't want to move. Not at his time of life.'

Despite his scepticism, Rhys found himself believing every word, and despite his resentment that Charles could have had the utter gall to discuss his business with a stranger Rhys was intrigued. He'd never buy the land, of course – for without doubt it would prove to be inarable and useless – but he'd look at it.

He was intrigued and amused, too.

He was chuckling to himself as he strode along the beach, not sleepy at all now nor yet wanting to return to the hotel where bright light spilling over the veranda and eruptions of laughter indicated that the family were still enjoying their own company.

Lisabeth heard his boots crunching on the damp sand. She heard the chuckling, too, mistook it for sobbing and wondered with wide-eyed apprehension whether George might be walking beside the water. He'd *seemed* cheerful enough at dinner, but who could guess how having a drowned wife might affect somebody?

She was standing on a rock shelf just above wave-level, having walked as far as she could to this point where the path disappeared

107

under the incoming tide. As Rhys approached she huddled back into the shadows, anxious not to be noticed.

The shiny bottle-green fabric of her gown reflected the faint moonlight, and Rhys saw her at once. He stopped. Nothing was said until, realizing she had been discovered, Lisabeth stepped forward.

'Oh, it's you, Lisabeth. What are you doing here?'

'You sound as if you think I have no right to be here!'

'And you sound angry!'

She was. Angry with him for stealing her solitude just as he seemed to swagger through her life casually helping himself to everything else she valued. All she'd wanted this evening was half an hour of tranquillity to listen to the murmurings of the tide. Even that was too much to hope for with him around.

But she wasn't going to dignify this encounter by saying anything further to him. Raising her chin with cool hauteur, she stared beyond him out to the black headland across the harbour and waited for him to move out of the way so that she could retrace her steps.

But she's beautiful! he noticed with an unpleasant jolt – unpleasant because there was a haunting remembrance of Mary in those enormous, thickly lashed eyes. For a second his impulse was to turn on his heel and run, but instead he heard himself say gently, 'And why are you angry with me, Lisabeth?' while at the same time he extended a hand to help her step down from her rock pedestal.

That was the last thing she wanted. Avoiding his proffered help, she backed away, only to feel the jab of the craggy rocks against her back. There was no way out but past him, so without pausing to think she hitched her skirts at the knee with both hands and stepped down boldly into the sea.

The water was only inches deep, but her leather slippers immediately felt so soggy, so squelchy around her toes, that with plummeting dread she feared she had ruined them. Gritting her teeth, she waded out a pace or two and then turned so that she was making a wide arc around Rhys. Chin up, she pretended that this was the kind of thing she did every day, strolling in the ocean in her only pair of slippers, her skirts hoisted to mid-calf.

Then she trod in the hole.

It was where the sea had nibbled and scooped the sand away from around the base of a rock. Incoming surges had covered the rock, and in this light nothing was visible below the water's black

108

foam-marbled surface. Lisabeth's foot plunged right into the deepest part of the trough between rock and sand. Thrown off balance, she stumbled forward and fell, twisting her ankle painfully.

'My heavens, Lisabeth!' Shocked, Rhys started forward, but before he'd rallied himself to move Lisabeth had scrambled to her feet and was dashing away down the beach. She had lost one slipper, her dress was stuck to her body and the water-sodden skirt streamed around her, and she was furious, furious with herself and hating Rhys so hard that the pain of that eclipsed the stabbings in her ankle. He was probably laughing himself silly back there at the spectacle she'd made of herself.

But Rhys was perturbed. She'd treated him with utter loathing. Rhys was not used to dislike, especially from attractive women: and, damn it all, Lisabeth had no call to be cold towards him! He'd saved her life, hadn't he? If not for him, that Maori with the axe would surely have – well, that didn't bear thinking about.

An incoming tongue of water lifted her slipper from where it eddied around the submerged rock and nudged it up on to the sand. Stooping, he picked it up and shook the water out of it. What impossibly tiny feet she had. She was a fragile, delicate creature altogether.

As he strolled back to the hotel another possibility presented itself to him. Perhaps he'd disturbed something just now – a tryst between Lisabeth and one of the local lads . . . Young Joe Day perhaps. He'd seen the way the boy flirted with her over dinner. It could be that she'd crept out to meet him and Rhys had frightened him away.

Rhys realized with another jolt that he didn't like *that* idea at all.

Rhys couldn't resist teasing her. When with the others she stepped into the whaleboat next morning for the trip across the harbour to inspect Braddock's land, Rhys dashed forward to offer his hand to steady her, smiling when she coolly ignored his mischievous gesture. She didn't see the smile because she was scrupulously not looking at him. but she *felt* the mockery of it and as she settled her navy-blue skirts over the toes of her heavy outdoor boots she distinctly heard him murmur 'Sensible footwear today, I see. At least those won't fall off so easily.'

She jerked her head around so that the rim of her bonnet

obscured her face from his view. Tears misted her vision, blurring the mountains into the limpid blue sky. How typically callous of him to jeer about her lost slipper. He probably knew that she waited shivering in the darkness until he had gone inside last night then dashed back to search for it, how she had been up again at daylight frantically scanning the beach. Those were the only slippers she had, and after Gwynne's distress over the loss of Andrew's straw boater Lisabeth despaired of finding the courage to confess this fresh disaster to her.

Joe and Alf rowed. Lisabeth gazed at the clean peaks in the distance while she dabbed her fingers in the water making little waves and ripples until Andrew, who was trailing a hopeful line behind the boat, informed her that she was scaring the fish.

With Charles's prompting, Joe was enthusing about the riches of the land and the sea in this district. Finding Braddock's land had restored Charles's pride in himself; he no longer felt that he was tagging along with Rhys, riding on the coat-tails of his charity. Rhys would buy the land, but it would be all Charles's doing; he would be indebted to Charles because of it, and the uneven balance between them remedied.

'It's all here for the taking,' Joe said. 'Crayfish that climb into your pots, oysters crusted thick on those rocks over there and plumper ones still on the ocean bed. Why, you can't thrust your hand into the sand here without bringing up a fistful of cockles and you can't walk but a few steps at low tide before you step fair on a flounder. There's wild ducks here, pigs—'

'Whitebait,' said Alf, heaving on his cracking oar.

'And the shrimp that Ma boils up for lunch nearly every day. The Baxters at Ferrymead send them forty gallons a time to Wellington. Don't have anything like our fish up that way,' he added with pride.

'Then, how come I'm not catching anything?' complained Andrew.

Lisabeth was mortified at the cheekiness in his voice, but Joe said kindly: 'It might be the bait. What do you say I look at it for you when we reach the other side? You might have better luck on the way home.'

A few minutes later the whaleboat scraped its chin on the sandy bottom. 'Sorry, but this is the closest we can get to dry land,' Joe told them. 'We'll have to carry the ladies ashore.' He winked at Lisabeth.

Rhys saw that. 'I'll carry them,' he said more firmly than was necessary.

Lisabeth had her own ideas. Already she was easing the boot buttons free from their worn leather loops. 'I'm going to wade ashore,' she announced.

'So long as you don't try to swim it,' teased Rhys.

She ignored him.

ELEVEN

Heywood braddock's cottage was tucked into a shelf high on the cliffs, its doorway overlooking the ocean through a twelve-foot-high arch of bleached bone that had been set into the ground some twenty feet away, near the brink of the slope.

'It's a whale's lower jaw,' Charles explained to Gwynne as he waited for her to recover her breath. She was panting after trudging the long haul up the almost perpendicular track that wove around clumps of rustling flax and over the grey twisted roots of the scarlet-blossomed *pohutukawa* trees that leaned out from the cliff-faces. They had lagged well behind Rhys and Andrew, while Lisabeth, torn between wanting to keep close to Andrew while avoiding Rhys, hung back a few yards behind the two.

'Pooh!' said Gwynne. The rank odour of Braddock's cottage offending her powerfully after the freshness of the sea breezes.

Lisabeth would have liked to peek inside, but Ballon the liver-spotted dog snarled a menace from the doorway. The cottage was a brown cob dwelling with two-foot-thick walls that had been made of puddled mud and chopped tussock. Good-sized rocks anchored the uneven slabs of shiny blue slate that tiled the roof. Glimpsed beyond the dog was utter chaos – filthy rags heaped on a sagging bed, hens picking over dirty plates on a cluttered table – but Lisabeth could see an artist's easel, too, and in the gloom the faint lines of pictures fixed to the back wall.

She remembered Athol Nye's words: 'I instruct in the Classics to sustain my body, but the arts nourish my soul.' Obviously old Heywood Braddock considered his soul to be of far greater

112

importance than his bodily comforts. Though she was repelled by the appalling mess and the stench that made her want to gag, an interest in Braddock was aroused in her.

There was no sign of the old man, so they moved on. As soon as the smell was behind them Gwynne sat down on a grassy knoll, declaring that her feet wouldn't carry her another step. She would stay here and admire the view.

'Sure and it's a breathless view, isn't it?' emphasized Charles, adopting the role of a salesman. The sweep of his arm encompassed the glittering ocean, the brooding rocky headland with the cliffs that plummeted to grumbling surf and right around across the plains to the serene mountains. There was Christchurch, a clutter of buildings scattered like blocks on a dark green rug. There was Sumner squeezed between cliff and scallops of beach, with the sign 'Sumner Hotel' just readable at the foot of the Zig-Zag, and there were the mountains, satin-shouldered with frail shawls of mist draped around their peaks.

Rhys was less interested in the view than with the other things he could see, though admittedly the setting was a stunning one.

'What a place to build a house, hey?' remarked Charles.

But Rhys was studying the stands of timber in the valleys that cut the headland into folds. Those trees were fine and tall, good milling timber, and in this virtually tree-less province must be immensely valuable. Where he scuffed it with his toe the soil looked rich, too, dark and wholesome, while where the land sloped down and levelled out the contours were smooth. It would make for easy working. He was impressed.

Lisabeth sat beside Gwynne. The wind pressed like a hand in her face as she gazed down at the visible scrap of harbour immediately below where Joe and Alf minded the boat. Her feet hurt, too, because she had outgrown these boots. She should have stayed behind to look for her lost slipper. It was all Rhys's fault, she thought miserably. If he hadn't pestered her last night, she'd not have had to go out of her way to avoid him.

I hope he hates this place, she thought. *I hope he hates it and he and Uncle Charles fight about it, and he storms off and leaves us. Then we'd be rid of him for ever.*

'Look at those rocks, Aunt,' cried Andrew, who was tossing something up in the air and catching it again. 'See, out on the furthest cliffs! They look like the circle of rocks in your story-book about the Buggane.'

'The Ballakelly Circle,' murmured Gwynne, and Lisabeth

shivered. Andrew was right, they did look like gigantic tomb-stones, and it was easy to imagine the Buggane, the frightful one, lurking there. *Loathsome place*, she thought.

'What are you playing with, child?' asked Gwynne. When Andrew dropped it in her lap she squeaked with disbelief. 'A lemon! Where did you find this?'

'From Mr Braddock's tree,' he told her reluctantly.

Instead of scolding him for stealing it Gwynne rolled it between her palms, sighing in delight. 'In all the years we were at Waitamanui I only ever saw one lemon, and that was a poor shrivelled thing, not plump and firm like this; but, oh, how we exclaimed over it and passed it from hand to hand after church so that we could all sniff the skin. A lemon! What heaven!'

'Prime land,' said Charles to Rhys. 'Sure and it's the best prime land. Goes right to the river this way and half out across the plains.' He was annoyed; Rhys was making no response whatso-ever. After all the trouble Charles had been to, the least he could do was pass a few favourable comments, the odd word of praise.

Despite himself Rhys was beginning to feel the crawlings of an excitement he hadn't experienced since that moment at Bathurst when he'd seen those first nuggets wink up at him from amongst the crumbs of gravel in the crease of his tin sluice-pan. Everything Charles had told him was true, and more. It *was* the best prime land and at the price it *was* too good to pass up. Because it all sloped down away from the cliff-tops to the plain, it would be sheltered from the harshness of the sea breezes. Fencing would be minimal with the ocean and the river forming two natural borders; it was close to the port for shipping produce, close to the town, and water seemed plentiful – he'd already seen three springs while dark green patches on the plain indicated plenty of moisture there.

There had to be a gigantic snag, a hook hidden in this tasty bait. If Braddock was willing to let him have it for the price of the mortgage and for fifty acres surrounding his cottage, then some-thing had to be very, very wrong. From what Rhys had learned during his exploratory investigations in Canterbury he knew that this land had to be worth at least twice that.

'Are those the cockatoo farms?' Rhys nodded in the direction of a cluster of drab cottages and an untidy patchwork of crop-fields on the flat at the foot of this hill.

'Yup,' said Charles around a mouthful of tobacco. 'Picked out a spread near there for myself, too. Sure and it's grand soil there, fine and black as port wine. Silt from the river. Every time the river flooded another layer—'

'I think I am sufficiently acquainted with the process by which alluvial plains are evolved,' Rhys cut in curtly. 'Where is this Braddock fellow? Didn't you arrange to meet him here this morning?'

Charles laughed uneasily. 'He's Manx. "Traa-dy-liooar!" he says. You know, there's time enough, as the saying goes. Only for him, poor fellow, time is running out. Which is why—'

'Listen,' said Rhys.

Below the knoll on which they stood, between them and the plains, was a thicket of native pine-trees, and from close beyond this thicket now came the sound of dogs barking, a high whinnying and something else – a shot or the crisp snap of a stock-whip, followed immediately by the sound of voices raised in angry argument.

'That'll be him,' said Charles, even more uneasily.

Rhys glanced at him. *Yes, there's a catch, all right*.

He scrambled down the bank with Charles puffing behind him. Treading cautiously, brushing the ferns aside, they proceeded until they could see what was happening.

On the sunlit slope half a dozen men on horseback surrounded a horse-drawn sledge on which Braddock was seated in a tattered armchair. Dogs quarrelled around the sledge, while the horse, forced by them to stop, stamped its hoofs and flicked its tail nervously.

Braddock was shouting. In one fist he clutched the reins and in the other brandished a whip-handle, while in the shade of his wide-brimmed hat his gaunt, wrinkled face contorted with rage.

'I say again yurr'll get off my property and take yurr goons with you and yurr'll stay off, do yurr understand?' he shrilled, tugging at his whip-handle.

The business end of the whip was curled around the gloved fist of an immaculately dressed man on a glossy black horse. Fox. Thomas Fox! realized Charles as he recognized the snub-nosed monkeyish face and the pebbly eyes.

Fox laughed as he yanked on the whip, causing Braddock to rise up out of his armchair. 'But I've come on legitimate business, Mr Braddock. First, I need to pick out a site for my house. I rather fancy that plateau up there, though this is a pleasant sheltered place right here. Second, I want to make perfectly certain that nothing is happening behind my back. We have an agreement, don't forget.'

'Agreement!' choked Braddock, tugging futilely at his whip. His arms jutted like twigs from his too-loose jacket-sleeves. 'We got no agreement! Thirty years I been here! I'll die first rather than see yurr on my land.'

'Then, die,' said Fox. 'It's all the same to me. But come the first of next month that filthy hovel of yours will be levelled to the ground. So, old man, you've fifteen days to pack your pigs and your dog and anything else of value and remove yourself from *my* property.'

'Yurr'll never make me!'

'Yes, we will – won't we, gentlemen?' said Fox to the other five men, who were all rough-looking fellows dressed in workers' twill smocks and moleskin breeches, all astride broken-down farm hacks.

'Them!' snorted Braddock and spat to show contempt. 'Those pathetic cockatoos couldn't pull the skin off a bowl of rice custard.'

But it was an empty defiance, and from their hiding-place behind the ferns Rhys knew that the old man was facing a formidable enemy. Here was the hook, the gigantic snag. Anybody who tried to purchase this property was going to find a ton of vicious muscle descending on him. Ugly muscle, too. Those cockatoo farmers were a brutal-looking bunch, and the dogs were the sort that could rip a man's throat open with one bite – big raw-boned mastiffs with scarred snouts and ragged ears.

'So the property's not such a bargain after all,' Rhys whispered to Charles.

'Hush,' warned Charles, too late. At that moment Fox's horse wheeled around, and when Rhys glanced back it was to find himself looking straight into a hard-eyed face framed with side-whiskers as grey as monkey's fur.

'You have wild game in your bush, I see,' said Fox, then he whistled twice, two short sharp blasts. Immediately, two of the dogs ceased their skirmishing and leaped forward to obey.

'Dear God and all his saints,' moaned Charles.

'Don't try to run,' hissed Rhys as the dogs pelted howling towards them. Stiffening his shoulders to show a confidence he did not feel, he stepped out into the open, demanding that the beasts be called off. As he spoke he levelled his pistol at the snarling maw of the faster dog.

Fox dared not hesitate; those dogs were expensive to raise and time-consuming to train to controlled savagery. He snapped an order, and they subsided at once, cringing as they circled back to the sledge.

Fox's glance slid over Rhys and on to Charles. He smiled sourly. 'I see. One of Sir Kenneth's paltry handful of craven voters. But what are you doing on my property?'

'He's visiting me, on my land!' shouted Braddock, reeling in his whip. 'Now yurr'll go, that's what yurr'll do, or I'll be calling out a constable and don't think yurr've got them all in yurr pockets, neither. It's a dim view the law takes of dogs bein' set on innocent folks!'

'Wild pigs in the underbrush,' snorted Fox.

Braddock screamed back at him, and the argument flared again. *The old man's enjoying the spat*, Rhys realized. He noticed, though, that the cockatoo farmers appeared ill at ease while the quarrel swung back and forth, and he wondered what hold this bully had over them. Something monetary, no doubt. He looked like one of the sleek rich. That magnificent stallion alone was worth a fortune, and Rhys was able to appreciate the value of the clothes this man wore.

The shouting match came to an abrupt silence when Gwynne, Lisabeth and Andrew appeared, though Lisabeth immediately pulled her brother back into the bushes when she saw the pistol in Rhys's hand.

Gwynne bustled forward, blinking in bewilderment. 'Mr Stafford, we heard such a noise! What in the world is happening?'

Braddock crowed in delight. 'Why, me darlin', how good to see yurr!' he exclaimed, sweeping his huge dark hat from his freckled pate. 'Do let me introduce yurr to these gentlemen. These are some of the parasites that sucked the very blood from my land – I'll not bother with their names, there's other epithets much more appropriate, but none suitable for yurr ears, darlin'. But this here is Mr Fox, who holds the mortgage on the property until the first of the month, after which' – and he raised his voice significantly – *after which* yurr good husband will own it. Isn't that so, Mr Stafford?'

Charles glanced up at Thomas Fox, and under his scruffy beard his face paled. 'Bejesus, not me! I'm not the purgator!'

Thomas Fox smiled complacently, a man with nothing to fear, no obstacles between himself and the object of his desire. Reading his expression with intense dislike, Rhys wondered how often this despicable man resorted to veiled force in his roughshod drive to get his own way.

117

A haze of anger danced before his eyes. '*I'm* the purchaser,' he said.

Fox laughed. His stony little eyes didn't laugh. They were summing up this tall golden-haired young man who was dressed simply in brown jodhpurs and an open-necked linen shirt under a dark riding-jacket. No. He might have had a certain air of authority when he pointed that pistol, thought Fox, but he didn't look like a potential run-holder. It'd take a man of substance to buy up Braddock's mortgage, and there wasn't a man of substance in Canterbury willing to antagonize Fox. 'Sure, sonny boy,' he sneered. 'You're the purchaser.'

The 'sonny boy' clinched the matter as far as Rhys was concerned. If he had any doubts about buying the land, they were swept away like leaves before a hurricane. 'The mortgage will be repaid in full by the thirtieth,' Rhys informed him. 'And after that this land will be mine.'

Mrs Ann Day was the rarest of landladies. Instead of measuring out niggardly portions she set brimming tureens and heaped platters of the most delectable fare before her guests. Tonight, with George and the Captain still at home, she surpassed herself, serving first a tangy mulligatawny soup and then a feather-light shrimp puff topped with a crust of melted cheese.

When, after that, Mabs staggered in with a saddle of roast lamb which she set before the Captain to be carved, Charles said: 'Mrs Day, you do us right proud.'

Gwynne, who appreciated another cook's skill, said: 'I don't wonder that your meals are famous!'

'Ma's never so great!' argued Joe, a twinkle in his eye. 'It's just that most of our guests have come directly here from a long sea-voyage, so to them anything would taste wonderful.'

'Get away, you cheeky scamp!' said Ann Day affectionately.

Joe ducked as she reached to cuff him. 'Go on, Rhys! Tell Pa how you got the better of Thomas Fox today.'

'It was nothing. Charles probably exaggerated.' *Trust him to gossip*, Rhys thought.

'If it was Thomas Fox, then I'll have to hear about it,' boomed the Captain, pausing in his noisy belabouring of knife-blade against sharpening-steel. 'I've had dealings with him myself, when we was building the lower end of the Zig-Zag road. That man would squeeze blood from a stone if he thought there was profit in it. He's had his palms greased so many times it's a miracle he's able to keep such a tight grip on his money. Tell me what happened, then.'

Briefly Rhys outlined some details of the encounter, while the Captain carved slices from the roast and laid them on plates which Mrs Day passed to him. Finally, when Rhys had finished he said: 'Well done, Mr Morgan. But . . . I'd take care to keep out of his way, lad, if I were you. He's wanted that land for a long time, and – well, it could be right nasty.'

'Thanks for the warning, but it's quite superlative,' put in Charles. 'Sure and we're not afraid of anything, are we, Rhys?'

'If you say so,' said Rhys.

Lisabeth helped Mabs wash the mountain of dirty dishes, while Mrs Day and Gwynne relaxed together over a basket of darning in the parlour and the menfolk clustered on the veranda in the cool darkness, their pipes and cigar tips glowing like fireflies. Usually as they worked Mabs kept up a babbling flow of harmless chatter, but tonight she was strangely silent and kept slipping sly glances at Lisabeth and smirking. Finally, when Lisabeth was hanging her damp apron on a peg behind the kitchen door she said: 'Oi've a secret message for you.'

'For me?' Foolishly, for there was no one in the room but the two of them.

'For you.' Mabs nodded her frizzy blonde head. She had pale lashless eyes like a white mouse's, and she blinked rapidly as she said: 'It's a secret. Soomone wants ter meet yer at the boat-shed.'

'Who?'

''E said oi weren't ter say. It's a secret. Go on. 'E'll be waitin' fer you now.'

'I'm not going to any boat-shed!'

'Shush!' Mabs blinked nervously. 'Don't go, then! But oi would if 'e asked me. Oi certainly would.'

'I'm not you,' retorted Lisabeth, too indignant to thank her for the message. The nerve of it! Young Joe was always flirting with her, tossing her winks and smiles, but he needn't think she would meet him at the boat-shed in the dark. Gwynne had warned her most emphatically against young men who made those suggestions. She was disappointed in Joe *and* in Mabs for encouraging such nonsense.

Outside the kitchen door she almost collided with Andrew, who was thumping down the stairs, his driftwood 'musket' clattering behind him. 'I'm going to show this to Alf and Joe!' he exclaimed. 'Look, it's all finished now.'

She had to hurry after him and grab his arm. 'Joe? You said Joe. Is he out there?'

Andrew nodded. 'He's telling Uncle Charles all the best places round here to shoot wild pigeons and ducks.'

'Are you sure?'

He shook his arm. ' 'Course I'm sure. Let me go!'

Lisabeth swallowed. 'Is . . . is Mr Morgan out there, too?'

Andrew frowned and shook his head. 'I ain't seen him for ages.' Shaking his arm free, he ran away. The door slammed as he dashed out on to the veranda.

Lisabeth slipped into the dining-room. Two of the candles were still burning, left there so that Mabs could see to put the dishes away in the gigantic *kauri*-wood dresser. Deep in thought, Lisabeth moved to the Captain's high-backed chair and sat down.

So it was Rhys who wanted to meet her. She couldn't believe it. *Rhys Morgan!* A thrill of distaste shivered through her, and she pressed her hands together in her lap to keep them from shaking. Huddled in the chair, she stared at the vase of pink and yellow roses and thought: *Why? What did he want?*

When after a time the door beside her swung open she said without looking up: Why did Mr Morgan want me to meet him, Mabs? What *did* he want?'

There was no reply. Someone entered the room, and the door clicked shut. When she looked up it was to see Rhys smiling at her. In the candlelight his face was as golden as his hair.

'Why don't you ask him yourself?' his voice lilted with amusement.

She glanced away, fiercely, and would have jumped up and run but he was leaning against the door, dimpling at her, no doubt. Mocking. Making fun of her again.

'All right. I apologize for demeaning you, but I did want to speak to you alone, and it's almost impossible with all these people milling about.'

Her chin rose. He could apologize all he wanted, but she needn't accept.

'Lisabeth,' he said gently, and to her horror she realized that she was trembling, as if his voice touched some nerve-centre deep within her mind. He said: 'Your hostility towards me is making me feel uncomfortable. I don't like that, and I think you should explain. I've a right to know if I've inadvertently harmed you in some way, don't you think?'

Lisabeth bit her lip and shoved her treacherously quivering

120

hands in her lap. Through the thin wall they could both hear the voices of the men on the veranda but within the room there was only the click of the clock on the mantel to disturb the silence between them.

'Tell me, Lisabeth,' he said quietly, but she only shrank within herself. How could she begin to describe how he had harmed her?

Finally he drew a deep breath and said: 'I can't force the words out of you, but don't think I'm not tempted! Here. Take this. It's a gift for you.'

One of his jokes, I suppose! she thought bitterly as he placed a package before her, for it was wrapped in a page of the *Lyttelton Times* and tied with butcher's string. She shook her head. Even if it was a gold coronet set with pearls, she'd not accept it from him.

'No, thank you. I can't—'

'Yes, you can.' He sounded disgusted with her now, and for some reason that distressed her even more. She should be pleased . . .

'Open it,' he said. 'I promise you it's something you really want.' Before she could refuse it again he left the room, snapping the door shut behind him.

How could it possibly be something I really want? thought Lisabeth. Still seething with conflicting emotions, she picked at the bow in the string. The package unfolded like a flower, and there inside the layers was her missing slipper, dry, stuffed with newspaper and almost as good as new again.

Lisabeth placed her hands carefully on the table, lowered her forehead to them and began to cry. She couldn't understand it. She hated Rhys so intensely. Tonight she had been rude and ungracious to him. It should have been a victory of sorts for her, so why did she feel so terrible?

TWELVE

AT BREAKFAST when Rhys mentioned that he was catching the twice-weekly Cobb & Co. coach service into Christchurch to meet Heywood Braddock he suggested that Charles come, too.

'Perhaps we should all go, Mr Stafford,' pleaded Gwynne. 'Andrew is in urgent need of more clothes, and Lisabeth needs new boots.'

Rhys grinned wickedly. 'What? Lost your boots as well?' he murmured from behind his slice of toast and marmalade.

Lisabeth flushed, but kept her eyes downcast. Lace-filtered sunlight slanted in on her, illuminating her shabby navy-blue gown. Rhys noticed the mends, the painstakingly darned lace trimming, frayed button-loops and mismatched buttons, and he was ashamed he had teased her. Andrew was not the only one in urgent need of new clothes.

He glanced at the boy, smartly attired in a natty sailor suit ('Just the image of one of our dear queen's children!' Gwynne had said), and he thought: *Gwynne means well, but she's spoiling him and turning Lisabeth into a drudge. Can't she see that the girl needs pretty things, too?*

Not that it was any of his affair.

Four sturdy horses stood in harness to a coach that was painted gaudily so that it could be seen from great distances across the plains. Gwynne and Lisabeth stepped up into the cabin and settled themselves beside two women with baskets of brown eggs and an elderly Maori woman with a black head-shawl, drooping black dress and bare feet. Noticing that she did not wear a *moko*, or chin tattoo, Lisabeth felt confident enough to smile timidly at her.

122

On the outside of the cabin was a ladder bolted to the rear so that the men could climb up to the rows of seats on the roof.

'Come in with us, dear,' said Gwynne as Andrew clambered on to the lower rungs. 'You'll fall and deal yourself a mischief.'

Andrew ignored her; only women and little children rode inside.

'Get down!' barked Charles in irritation. The prospect of spending money on the children always put him into a thoroughly disagreeable mood. Without waiting for the boy to obey, he grabbed his coat and trousers and tugged him free of the ladder. Andrew was like a crab held by the shell as with arms and legs lashing he was thrust bodily into the coach. His sailor hat rolled on to the straw-littered floor.

Andrew shrieked with temper. His flailing boots struck Lisabeth on the shoulder as she stooped to retrieve his hat. Mortified that he was throwing one of his 'paddies' in front of Rhys, she hastened to soothe him with promises of sweets. The old Maori woman clucked sympathetically, but the other two breathed through their nostrils and held the baskets of eggs close against their bodies.

'It's something else he wants promising, not sweets,' muttered Charles darkly as he brushed his sleeves. 'Sure and I've never raised a hand to the lad, but I sometimes wonder . . .'

As the coach jerked and swayed along the coast road, Andrew still cried. 'Please don't, dear,' shushed Lisabeth. 'We're going to have a lovely day. Oh, look, there's that team of oxen we saw on our walk yesterday. Ten of them, and aren't they huge strong fellows? And we're coming to Ferrymead in a minute. Joe says that the whole shebang – horses, coach and us in it – will ride across the river on a great big barge. Won't that be exciting?'

But Andrew sulked. All he wanted was to be up on the roof with the other men. To be treated like a *baby* – it wasn't fair!

Through the tantrum Gwynne smiled benevolently. She was brimming with warm anticipation. Christchurch was famed for being laid out for development as a 'typically English' market-town. Gwynne had seen several of those; they were similar to Manx towns. After so many years of seeing nothing but desolate, primitive settlements it would do her heart glad to feast on the view of fine stone and brick buildings, prim terraced houses and neat cobbled streets. *I wonder if they've a proper ale house*, she mused, thinking how that would delight Charles.

She gazed about with eager interest.

123

After juddering off the barge the coach rolled past the Provincial Customs House, a plain wooden building flying the British maritime flag, then entered a dismal plain thick with *toe-toe* bushes, flax clumps and dusty *manuka* scrub. Weed-choke drains followed the raw dirt road intermittently, appearing then disappearing. From time to time a roof was glimpsed back beyond the fringe of scrubby bushes, or a cluster of trees appeared also well back from the road. Every half-mile or so the coach stopped to pick up more people who waited on the road and soon it was jammed so full that Andrew was perching on Lisabeth's knees.

They passed a church spire, also back from the road. Then a wooden fence ran beside them for a few yards.

Gwynne plucked the sleeve of the woman beside her. 'Excuse me, please, but when will we reach Christchurch?'

The woman laughed, showing stumps of broken teeth. 'Oh, dearie me! This *is* Christchurch! We've been driving through it this past two mile. Look, here's the city centre now.'

And Gwynne looked out of the glassless window to see half a dozen wooden shop buildings, larger but not very different from the general store at Waitamanui with the same sloping verandas jutting over the footpath. Her heart plummeted.

As Rhys handed her down to the gravelled footpath she said; 'Everybody kept telling me how *English* this place is! Honestly, Rhys, it's more like a raw country town in America!'

'Then, you shall have to bite your tongue, as I do, when folk say how extremely civilized it is here,' Rhys said.

When Charles and Rhys went to meet Heywood Braddock at the offices of Valentyne & Wood, Barristers and Solicitors, in Cashel Street, Gwynne and Lisabeth set off on their own errands, Lisabeth dragging Andrew, who loudly expressed a preference for going with the other men. 'You're coming shopping with us, because we need to have you try things on,' Lisabeth explained.

First, they set off in search of the Catholic church to see what time devotions and masses were held. 'I'd like to confess, too, if there's a priest to receive me' Gwynne said. 'It's been so long that my soul absolutely thirsts for a blessing. What about you, dear? Have you given more thought to your own conversion to our faith?'

Lisabeth demurred, knowing that she could never become a Catholic. She loved the solemn unintelligible rituals, but the notion of baring her soul to a priest repelled her. It would be unthinkable for her to tell her terrors and hatreds and her intimate secrets to a stranger.

124

'Mamma always said that the Catholic Faith was too rigid in its disciplines.' Lisabeth said timidly. 'I don't think she'd like me to take instruction. I'm sorry, but—'

Gwynne frowned, and sucked on her lip, but she made no comment.

Guilty about disappointing Gwynne, Lisabeth stayed outside with Andrew as her aunt climbed the wooden steps and entered the tiny weather-board church.

It was a grey day swept with a bleak wind that rattled the notice-board that hung from a frame beside the gravel path, and tugged at the spiny broom plants that formed a screen between the churchyard and the road. Lisabeth refastened her bonnet strings while she watched Andrew gallop around the gravestones and iron-fenced grave-plots that were ranged in rows beside the church.

'There's a big hole here!' he yelled over to her.

'Come away, dear,' she called back.

'I'm going to jump into it!' he cried.

'No!' shouted Lisabeth in alarm, clutching up her skirts and hurrying over to where he was tossing handfuls of fresh black earth into the grave. Seizing his arm, she led him away, explaining what the hole was for, that someone had died and there would be a burial today, that the coffin would be placed in there during a service and then the soil put back over the top.

'Good! We can watch, then I can help,' said Andrew. 'I love shovelling dirt.'

'It's private; other people don't go near.' Lisabeth thought of Mary's poor burial, where only the vicar and his wife stood beside her as her mother was interred. It was the loneliest moment of her life.

'Why are you sad?' Andrew wanted to know.

Biting her lip, Lisabeth shook her head. A plain black cart driven by two black horses turned in at the churchyard. On the cart lay a coffin of raw yellow wood, the cheapest, ugliest kind, exactly like Mary's. Overwhelmed by painful memories, Lisabeth turned away, unable to look at the cart or at the black-garbed couple following on foot behind it.

'It's the people from the ship,' Andrew told her as the church door opened and a plump, bespectacled priest came out. His cassock flapped around his prim black boots; he looked harried.

Andrew tugged at Lisabeth's hand. 'It's that man with the funny voice, from the next table in the cuddy. Look!'

Athol Nye loomed awkwardly beside his mother, who was sobbing into a handkerchief. There was no sign of old Mr Nye. *Oh, no!* thought Lisabeth.

'Wait here,' she said. Impulsively she walked directly over to the Nyes and said; 'I'm so very sorry, Mrs Nye.' To Athol she said: 'If it's of any consolation, I share your grief. I clearly remember the deaths of both my father and my mother. Believe me, Mr Nye, I do feel for you.'

For a second she looked up into his face. His light grey eyes stared at her with a bemused, slightly startled expression. Neither of the Nyes said a word in reply, so Lisabeth wondered if she had made some serious error of etiquette. Backing away, she nodded at them then turned and fled past the priest, who was discussing arrangements with the undertaker and the leather-aproned sexton.

'Poor Mrs Nye,' whispered Gwynne, who was pulling her gloves on beside the broom hedge. She shivered; her worst nightmare was that something might happen to Charles and leave her stranded here halfway round the world from Home. All beatific effects of her confession evaporated.

Her feet were troubling her by the time they had walked back to Heath's Drapery and Millinery Store, so she requested a seat and was brought a bentwood chair on which she sat to inspect bolts of tweed and suiting which the assistant brought to the counter and partly unrolled so that Gwynne could feel the quality of the cloth by chafing it between her finger and thumb.

It was an elegant shop. The assistants wore ruffled caps and white ruffled pin-on jabots and cuffs – 'like maidservants in the grandest houses, Gwynne whispered. And they sold the most exquisite goods: silk shawls dripping with beaded fringes, bonnets smothered with delicate artificial flowers and, displayed on padded coat-hangers, their skirts stiffened with wired underskirts, were five elegant gowns in fabric so light and glossy that Lisabeth was reminded of butterflies' wings.

She gazed at them hungrily. It had not escaped her notice how the shop assistant had stared at their clothes as they entered her domain, and faint condescension as she called Gwynne 'ma'am', the off-hand attention that contrasted markedly with the deference being paid to a customer at the next counter, a striking auburn-haired young woman who wore a black sateen riding-dress and a tiny black bonnet. Two assistants scurried to fetch evening gloves for her appraisal, while the lass serving Gwynne yawned, examined her fingernails and dawdled as she fetched the next bolt of fabric.

Lisabeth's spirits flagged. Looking at the perfectly groomed young woman in her fashionable riding-habit, she felt no envy but simply a surge of wistfulness. It would be lovely to have just one pretty gown that swayed and wobbled as she walked; it would be lovely to wear the merest wisp of a bonnet, a delightful confection instead of this heavy old-fashioned thing. It would be lovelier still to put on slim ankled tiny-heeled boots with wafer-thin soles instead of the chunky clunky things she knew Gwynne would buy. There was no point in dreaming, though, she thought with a sigh.

'What's your opinion, dear?' Gwynne was asking her. 'Which would suit Andrew best, the blue tweed or the grey and white suiting?'

'Sorry, Aunt,' said Lisabeth. 'What did you say?'

In the offices of Valentyne & Wood, Rhys was not enjoying himself, either. Braddock kept them waiting an hour, and his chirpy admonishment of 'Traa-dy-liooar!' did not smooth Rhys's impatience as an apology might have done. Braddock arrived on his disreputable-looking sledge just as an elderly widow was being shown into Valentyne's office, so they had another half-hour's delay before it was their turn.

Worse was to come. When the papers were handed around to be signed and Braddock realized that Rhys did not intend to revise his original offer at all, he hastily reconsidered the matter and said that instead of four hundred guineas and fifty acres above the mortgage he now wanted two thousand guineas and a hundred acres.

'I calculated wrong,' he said craftily. 'Yurr know us Manxmen, "Jes the shy", we're careful, like. Never ask too high, yurr understand.'

'You certainly did calculate wrongly,' said Rhys, pushing back his chair. 'I'm "Jes the shy", too. Even more cautious. You told my brother-in-law that all you wanted was to be able to live on that land for the remainder of your days. The four hundred guineas was my offer, a gift for you. I'm sorry, Mr Braddock. I miscalculated, too.'

He nodded a curt 'good day' to Mr Valentyne and was out in the street putting on his top-hat when Charles slapped a hand on his arm.

'What are you doing, lad? The land's still a bargain. Mr Braddock was sure you wouldn't mind coughing up the extra—'

'So you've discussed it with him. I might have guessed that you'd—'

'Hey!' interrupted Charles. his colour and temper rising. 'Just what is *that* meant to inseminate?'

'Insinuate,' snapped Rhys, breaking his own rule never to correct Charles's malapropisms no matter how blatant. 'I'm insinuating that you and Braddock probably calculated my worth and decided how much I might be prepared to bear.' While Charles gasped and stuttered as he scraped a denial together, Rhys added; 'Tell Mr Braddock I hope that he and Mr Fox have a lively and interesting time on the first of the month.'

'Just a minute,' came Braddock's cracked voice from the office interior. 'Please won't yurr come back, Mr Maughold?'

The use of his old family name touched Rhys. He was still angry but he still wanted the land.

'We'll talk,' he agreed.

Charles closed his eyes and offered a silent prayer of relief as he followed him into the office.

Lisabeth and the others emerged from the bootmaker's and turned right to find their way back to Cashel Street. Only a few yards in front of them Rhys was in deep conversation with the beautiful young woman who had been buying gloves at Heath's.

'Ooh!' whispered Gwynne. 'I wonder if Rhys has a young lady? That might be what attracted him to come back here to settle. My, but she's a beauty, isn't she? What glorious brown eyes!'

They're too close together, Lisabeth thought.

'And what a fine figure! Look at that tiny waist,' sighed Gwynne.

Her neck is too short, noticed Lisabeth. *She's years and years older than me and she's got far too much bosom - she's positively vulgar!*

'Let's cross the street here while there's no traffic coming,' suggested Lisabeth, but Rhys saw them and beckoned them over.

'He wants to introduce us,' thrilled Gwynne, but her romantic notions were dashed when Rhys presented the young woman as 'Mrs Leonie Gammerwoth'.

'Charmed to meet you.' She had a soft purring voice, but her eyes were direct and shrewd, dismissing Gwynne with one glance, Lisabeth with two and then alighting on Andrew. 'This must be your nephew. My word, but he's the image of you! The eyes are not yours but look at that hair, those cheekbones. What a powerful family resem—'

For a moment the street dissolved around Lisabeth, but then she rallied swiftly, snatching Andrew's hand and squeezing it to stop him gaping with astonishment at what was being said. She daren't look at Rhys.

She interruped; it was rude, but this was no time to worry about manners. 'Show Mr Morgan your new shoes, Andrew!' she said gaily. 'Look, Mr Morgan, aren't they splendid?'

'Splendid,' he agreed coolly. He hadn't liked what Leonie said, either. It was a preposterous notion; they were both fair, but there all resemblance most emphatically ended.

'*Mr Morgan?*' repeated Leonie, puzzled. What a strange cluster of relatives these were.

'I'll explain,' Rhys told her, inclining his head to excuse himself from Gwynne as he walked away with Leonie on his arm. 'Those two aren't blood relatives. My sister and her husband adopted a pair of orphans when their parents died. I don't know them very well yet, so they still call me ''Mr Morgan''.'

'I see.' Lacing her fingers possessively over his arm, she said, 'That's very admirable of your sister. Interesting, too, don't you think? The girl . . . I mean, to have someone so close who is not a relative. She has quite a passion for you, too, have you noticed?'

Rhys laughed, and Leonie smiled up at him because she adored to watch him laugh. He said: 'My dear Leonie, you are sweet but some of your ideas are completely outlandish. Lisabeth actively dislikes me.'

'Now *you're* being ridiculous,' she purred. 'Dislike you? Impossible! But let's not talk about her. I was going to write you a letter this evening. My husband wants me to persuade you to join his cricket team. Once your fame spreads everybody will be battering on your door, so we thought—'

'I'm sorry, but Sir Kenneth Launcenolt has already asked me, and I've accepted. I say, I don't suppose there's any chance of them both being in the same team, is there?'

Her reaction was unexpected. Inhaling sharply, she almost glared at him as she said: 'We're not on the same side ever, Rhys, not in anything!'

'I saw you in the town earlier,' remarked Sir Kenneth as he accepted a frosted glass from the tray the sepoy lowered before him. 'Thank you, Leopold. Would you please tell Albert that Mr Morgan is staying to dinner? You will stay, won't you, Rhys?'

They were seated on lyre-backed cane chairs on the deep verandah at Benares, Sir Kenneth's home, which was sited on a slope above a loose-slung curve of the Avon river within the borders of town. Rhys loved the house; it reminded him of an elegant hat-box, trimmed as it was with a fretwork of wooden 'gingerbread' lace and festooned with drapings of honeysuckle and wisteria. The gardens were cool and languid, with lawns dipping their edges into the milky river under the willow's trailing fronds. In the shadows peacocks barked strange cries as they dragged their vivid, cumbersome trains across raked pebble paths. Azaleas and rhododendrons held globes of colour aloft, bright as lanterns. It was a fantastic place.

Lady Launcenolt was kneeling on a cushion before a rose bush, tending it like a nurse with secateurs and a syringe spray of tobacco-water mixed with soapsuds. A turbaned sepoy stood beside her holding the syringe and a basket in which she placed the precisely severed twigs she had pruned.

'You were with Juno Gammerwoth's wife,' said Sir Kenneth in an aside that his wife could not hear. 'Dashed attractive lass, that. Don't go much on him, though.'

'I've not had the pleasure of his acquaintance. I met her on the last voyage, but he was confined below the whole time. Seasickness.'

'Seasickness! This more like.' He shook his glass.

'It *was* a rough crossing. What's he like, this . . . Juno?'

'That's a nickname. No idea how he got it. How can I sum him up? H'm. He drinks to excess, he's old – sixty-five if he's a day – and he's – how shall I say it? – unattractive. Yes, unattractive.'

'That's not quite how I pictured Leonie's husband.'

'And he's rich, very rich. That may help you reconcile the Beauty-and-the-Beast paradox. Yes, thought it would. So it's "Leonie", is it? You were having a very jolly chat together, I thought.'

'Mr Gammerwoth wants me to join his cricket team.'

Sir Kenneth laughed. His beard quivered. 'That's one in the eye for them. You'll do us proud, Rhys. Fancy the Canterbury Colonels having the great Rhys Morgan in our team!'

'What I like is that you invited me before you knew I could play.' He set his glass down on the inlaid ebony table that stood between the two chairs. 'I came to ask for a little confidential advice. Very shortly I'll be having dealings with a chap called Thomas Fox. I've had one encounter with him – an unpleasant one, I'm afraid – and, frankly, I don't look forward to our next meeting; but it's – alas – unavoidable. Charles said that you seemed to know the fellow reasonably well, so I was rather hoping that you'd give me a few confidential words of. . . . I say, what's the matter? Why are you looking at me like that?'

'Don't you know about Leonie?'

'What about her?'

Sir Kenneth roared, bellows of laughter that set the fibres of his beard fluttering and shivering and brought Lady Launcenolt up from her knees. She towered above the sepoy.

'Are you all right, Kiki?' she asked.

Sir Kenneth shook his head. 'Tell him about Thomas Fox . . . and Leonie,' he gasped, tugging out a vast white handkerchief and mopping his face with it. 'Oh dear me, oh dear!'

Lady Launcenolt ambled over. She was a big-boned woman with a generous puff of hair as white as carded sheep's wool and a repertoire of dainty little feminine gestures that went uneasily with her size, as ear-rings would look silly on an elephant.

'Leonie?' she repeated, flinging up her hands. 'Why, she's Mr Fox's daughter. His only child. He absolutely *doted* on her, you know. She accompanied him everywhere she went right from when she was practically a baby. Or so they say.'

'Nobody ever thought she'd get married,' added Sir Kenneth, now fully recovered. 'Every man who came near, Fox chased away. I think the only reason old Juno stood a chance of marrying her was that he was the only man who was ever able to get close to her. See, he's so big and old and hideous that I don't think Fox ever imagined that his daughter would give him a second glance. Well, she did. She gave him a lot more than that!'

'Kiki!' reproved Lady Launcenolt, patting his shoulder before leaving them and returning to her rose bush.

The story disgusted Rhys. So Fox was a tyrant with his own, too. Such a tyrant that his daughter was forced to marry someone repellent in order to escape. 'Poor girl. What a way to buy your freedom,' he said.

Sir Kenneth looked at him curiously. 'Don't forget that Juno is extremely wealthy,' he cautioned. 'I'd not feel too sorry for her if I were you.'

'Oi told you 'e'd get soomone else. Oi told you!' scolded Mabs as she scoured the stew-pan.

Lisabeth didn't bother to reply. She polished the ladle with the white dish-cloth and hung it on its hook, then reached for the meat-fork. She was ready to scream at Mabs; for the past hour her nasal voice had been berating Lisabeth for last night's lost opportunity. When Rhys hadn't appeared at dinner Mabs took it as a sign that Lisabeth had driven him away.

'A feller wants encouragement,' counselled Mabs, blinking her pale eyes. 'Mr Morgan, 'e's a feller in a million, 'e is. Oi seen 'undreds of fellers come through 'ere and oi know—'

'I think you're sweet on him yourself!' Lisabeth lashed back in desperation. 'He hasn't noticed you, so you're pushing me at him in the hopes that I'll tell you all about it if anything does happen. Was it *your* idea for him to meet me at the boat-house? Well, I'm sorry, Mabs, but I'll never go along with your plans! I hate Mr Morgan, and nothing he says or you say will ever change that, so won't you get that into your silly head and simply leave me alone and stop mentioning his loathsome name to me, because I wish I'd never heard that name and I wish I'd never set eyes on him and as far as I'm concerned he's the most horrible, nasty, un-un-p-pleasant . . .'

'You're cryin',' mumbled Mabs stupidly.

'No, I'm not'! Lisabeth turned away, scrubbing her face fiercely with the damp dish-cloth.

'Yes, you is.'

'I'm not.'

'Oi don't understand,' mused Mabs. 'If oi 'ated a feller oi'd never cry over 'im. Only if oi—'

Lisabeth fled, slamming the door behind her so hard that the ladle, the meat-fork and the egg-slice jumped off their hooks. As she picked them up, Mabs chuckled to herself.

THIRTEEN

RHYS STAYED IN TOWN.

In his absence they discussed him, gossiping pleasantly over dinner. Mrs Day was of the opinion that Rhys needed a wife.

'I don't think there's a special young lady yet,' confided Gwynne. 'I asked him, and he said there was no one but me.' She smiled. 'Ah, but he's a good lad.'

'Give him time,' said Joe, applying himself to his mutton chop. 'Half the girls in Canterbury will be setting their caps at him.'

'Ay,' said Alf gloomily. 'It must be grand to be tall and fair and have a charming smile like he has.'

'And his education, and his sporting skills . . . and his money!'

'Now, Joe, that's enough,' warned his mother. To Gwynne she said: 'I suppose there's no hurry for him to be married. He has you to look after him. I suppose he'll be staying with you folk when you move over to the farm?'

Andrew's glance snapped up. He had been piling the food on his plate up into mounds and squashing them. 'He'll live with us? Oh, that's wonderful! Now I can call him Uncle Rhys.'

'*No!*' said Lisabeth. Aware that the panic in her tone had attracted attention, she added: 'Not until he asks you to, dear.' She said faintly: 'Is that true, Aunt? Will Mr Morgan be staying in the same house as us?'

Charles answered for her. 'Of course not! Rhys is much too grand to live with us. We're just peasant farmers, simple folk. Sure and he's one of the landed gentry now.'

133

'Oh, Mr Stafford!' Gwynne was stricken.

'You'll see soon enough that I'm right,' Charles told her.

Rhys had not the slightest intention of living with the Staffords. His first impression of Charles had never been revised, but now he perceived that Charles wore his roughness like a badge of honour, taking perverse pride in his inability to get on in the world. He was a bitter man, soured by defeat. Rhys had noticed how he always ranted against those in authority, how he sneered at anybody who had done well in life and automatically assumed that everyone holding an official position was bound to be corrupt.

Sooner or later he'll be thinking that about me, thought Rhys wryly. *I'll be the 'toff', the crooked landowner.*

He was secretly pleased when Braddock tried to raise the agreed price and Charles had been in on it. Trifling though the incident was, Rhys seized on it. Here was the excuse he needed to keep Charles at a very long arm's length. He was almost grateful.

Rhys had never minded helping the Staffords. The money had come easily to him, and he was fond of Gwynne; family feeling stirred in him. He'd carve off a generous slice of the fattest, richest flank of the estate and he'd even lend Charles what he needed to establish his market garden, but he wouldn't have anything else to do with the fellow if he could help it. Charles was an incorrigible meddler; Rhys could do without him, thank you!

Sir Kenneth insisted that Rhys spend the next few days at Benares, an invitation that Rhys was pleased to accept. Most of his luggage was here, so he was able simply to stay on.

It was convenient to be close to town with so much to be done. Stock had to be purchased, and Sir Kenneth knew of a reliable agent, one who wouldn't try to unload flocks of diseased or ancient ewes on him. Fencing material and lumber were to be purchased; again, Sir Kenneth was able to advise. His help was especially valuable when Rhys had to go out to the Immigration Barracks to select workers from the flood of newcomers seeking employment.

'Don't thank me, lad,' Sir Kenneth said as they rolled back to Christchurch in the landau. 'I'm starting my election campaign soon and I'll harvest your gratitude then. Oh, not to knock on doors or write letters or even to stun prospective voters and haul them into polling-booths – though I'll need some of that doing, no doubt! You're standing up to Fox, and that's going to excite a great deal of interest around here. I'd like to have you attend a few campaign socials, balls, dinners, club evenings and so on.'

'I'd be glad to. No, more than that, I'd be honoured,' said Rhys as the high slender wheels rattled over one of the many bridges that spanned the Avon. 'I'm a new-chum and there are many people I'd like to meet. The only folk I know so far are you two, Fox . . . and Leonie.'

'You'll not see either of them at one of my evenings,' laughed Sir Kenneth, slapping his knees.

'She said that you're on opposite sides in everything. Perhaps we'll meet at a cricket game,' mused Rhys. 'Do you ever play their team?'

'On, yes.' He eyed Rhys speculatively. 'Why the interest in the Fox lass?'

'She fascinates me.' Rhys glanced into a closed carriage that they were overtaking. Laughter bubbled out. He raised his hat.

'She fascinates everyone,' Sir Kenneth told him.

Mr Valentyne informed Rhys that before he could subdivide his land to give some to Charles, approval had to be sought from the Provincial Council, though in Braddock's case it would be straightforward because he had long established a residence on the property.

'I see. *Approval.*'

'Yes, Mr Morgan. At the next Provincial Council meeting on, ah . . . let me consult my calendar.'

'Is Mr Fox likely to be at the meeting?'

'Certainly, sir. He's one of the Councillors.'

'Then, never mind,' said Rhys.

He decided instead to buy out one of the cockatoo farmers, Aaron Jenks, who owned a choice thirty acres of river-flat as far away from Rhys's tentative home-site as possible. This was a better idea anyway. It would suit Gwynne to be closer to town and on the coach route, and Charles would have no breaking-in to do because there was already a house of sorts (a tiny cube of central dwelling with lean-tos buttressing the sides), ample water-tanks, a small packing-shed; but, best of all, the land was handily divided into one-acre paddocks each fenced and gated, hedged and drained. Sir Kenneth protested that this was an expensive way to settle his brother's family – Aaron Jenks had held him to ransom over the price – but Rhys argued that Charles had saved him time and money by finding Braddock and his land in the first place so deserved a thank-you.

'Your brother-in-law is a fortunate man,' said Lady Launcenolt at dinner.

'Tell me, Rhys, what do they think of their new home?' She nodded to the sepoy, who glided from a shadowy corner of the high-ceilinged room.

'I don't know what they'll think. It certainly isn't like this.' Rhys's glance took in the pale green walls, the shelves that covered half of one wall, all laden with ornamental elephants in various sizes, the graceful walnut furniture and the elegant candelabra that were banked with flowers. Polished wood, crystal, damask and dull-gleaming silver – the essences of true comfort.

Leopold hovered at his elbow, uncertain. Rhys nodded, and he deftly removed the bowl of soup.

Lady Launcenolt did notice. 'You don't like lentil soup?' Her large hands fluttered in distress. 'I shall instruct Albert. Would you prefer—?'

'No, please. I do apologize, but I ate nothing but pulses, rice and dried beans for over two years in the goldfields. Whenever I taste the texture of them I break out in a sweat of lurid memories – heat and dust and flies. I promised myself that I would never touch them again.'

'Spoken with feeling,' approved Sir Kenneth. 'The Indian Raj cuisine was heavy on pulses, too, so we do understand.'

'Yes.' Lady Launcenolt fingered her five-strand choker of pearls. 'Azura made an indentical vow when she left India for a boarding school in England. Except that in her case she was forced to break her vow or starve! The winters were so bitter, you see, and thick pea soup was often the only item on the menu.'

'Ah, you'll like this better, I guarantee it,' said Sir Kenneth in satisfaction as a dish of fried trout was presented for him to select from.

'Careful, Kiki,' urged Lady Launcenolt as flakes of almond toppled from the fish's golden back to the floor. Averting her attention, she said: 'You'd like Azura, Rhys. She's nineteen and very sweet. Our god-daughter. Her parents have promised to bring her out to stay for a long holiday very soon.' She tentatively patted her puff of bouffant white hair, found and pushed a loose pearl-headed hairpin back into place.

'It's a shame she's not here now, with all the excitement,' continued Lady Launcenolt as she watched Rhys expertly remove a trout to his plate, cargo intact. As she helped herself she said, 'You'd be able to show her about, escort her and so on.'

'Beware the gleam in her eye, lad,' said Sir Kenneth. 'She'll be matchmaking if she gets half a chance! Eat your trout, go on. It's excellent.'

On the thirtieth of the month Rhys rode into town on his new chestnut hack, thinking how little appetite he had for the confrontation with Thomas Fox. It was a cold day, sharp with the needle-edges of drizzle borne in intermittent gusts, and under his oilskin topcoat Rhys sweltered with the delirious ache of a juicy fever. He would have preferred to be in bed at Benares, sipping Sir Kenneth's cure of beaten eggs, whisky and honey, but this interview could be postponed no longer.

He knew where the office was. Many times during the past week he'd detoured to pass it, hoping for what, he wasn't sure. A glimpse of Leonie, perhaps, or of her and her husband, for his curiosity was aroused.

Today, feeling and looking wretched, he hoped he'd see nobody. In his pocket was the bank draft duly signed and stamped, made over to Thomas Fox, esquire, and in his mind rested the hope that the business between them would be as brief and as formal as possible.

The building was white-painted, one-storeyed, with a shop-window fronting on to the street. The wind was stripping yellow leaves from the chestnut tree in the vacant section next door and was using some to paper the footpath and flinging the rest carelessly into the muddy road.

A carriage stood outside, an impressive glossy black carriage with glazed windows and silver fittings. Rhys thought, *an undertaker*, and smiled to himself, for it was just like the carriages used in Europe to carry mourners to a funeral. Someone was inside it, but Rhys couldn't see more than a vague shadow because the rain had started to beat down grimly now.

It swept him inside. Removing his coat, he approached a counter where a hulking dark man was copying figures from one ledger to another. When Rhys tried to speak his throat burned. The pain caught him unawares like an accusation, starting tears to his eyes.

'Morgan,' he managed to say. 'Rhys Morgan to see Mr Fox.'

'*Councillor* Fox. Do you have an appointment?' Though he must have known Rhys did not. The man had a single eybrow that scored a heavy line right across his face.

'Money. I have some money for him,' croaked Rhys. He stood

137

at the shop window to wait. Rain brushed like a stiff yard-broom across the street, obliterating the row of buildings on the far side, churning up the mud. Rain nailed the leaves to the footpath.

A cart rumbled past; the driver's head was pulled so far down into the neck of his coat he appeared headless. Rain bounced off the tarpaulin covering his load.

When it was gone there was no sound but the thrum of rain on the roof. Rhys listened to it, swallowing to ease the burning in his throat. Suddenly the rain drifted away and the sound of voices could be heard, angry voices gusting and shrilling like a quarrelling wind.

' – so *humiliating*! How dare you stop the auction like that! You had no right to—'

'Nor had you! You can't auction off your mother's—'

'Yes, I can! They were left to me! If I want—'

'But not to sell! It's always clearly understood that one day—'

'They're mine, so it's for me to say. You don't run my life any more, Father! You can't—'

'*Not to sell*! And not like that. If you'd taken a discreet notice in the newspaper, it might not have been so disgraceful, but to flaunt our personal possessions in public as if—'

'That's it, isn't it? You've got your image to think of, so—'

At that stage, the receptionist, who had been casting increasingly embarrassed glances from Rhys to the closed door behind which the squabble was raging, finally cleared his throat and tapped on the door. There was immediate silence. He tapped again.

'What is it, Featherston?' came Fox's voice, now flat enough to be plainly recognizable. Featherston opened the door an inch and murmured something.

'Oh, what fun!' cried Leonie. Her burst of giggles was like the gleeful laughter that follows a whispered joke, slightly guilty, very much for effect. 'Do show him in.'

'I'd – I'd rather not intrude,' Rhys managed to say, feeling piqued because he would never know now what the objects at the centre of the quarrel were. Valuable vases? Paintings? Family heirlooms? Jewellery?

'Oh, come in, Rhys! Don't be stuffy! Darling Father and I were just having a friendly chat, weren't we, darling?'

Fox's inner office was a cold white room with a dark polished floor and windows with a view of the rain-sodden racetrack and the grandstand opposite which looked white and wet as a freshly

138

iced cake. On his leather-topped desk rested a brass-bound case which Rhys knew would contain duelling pistols and Fox's booted feet which he did not remove when Featherston ushered Rhys in and shut the door behind him.

'Don't bother to get up,' said Rhys.

Leonie was seated, too. All their energy must be poured into their voices when they quarrel, thought Rhys. She was wearing a wide-skirted dress of a wild honey colour and a tiny bonnet of brown velvet trimmed with damp honey-coloured ribbons. Her magnificent auburn hair was drawn back into a seal-tight chignon, and her eyes still sparkled with the residue of anger. She welcomed Rhys like a saviour.

'I didn't know that you and Father were old friends! See, Father, I'm not the only one to keep secrets; you've been hiding Rhys from me.' Her brown eyes danced over his face. They weren't soft velvety eyes like most brown eyes are but hard as toffee with the same opaque glaze. 'You look sick, Rhys.'

'I have a slight fever. Just a cold, I think.'

'Then, you had better not kiss me; it might be contagious!' she declared, though he had never once kissed her.

'Very well, I shall refrain,' he agreed soberly, realizing that all this pretended intimacy – the frequent use of 'Rhys' – was a goad to irritate her father.

Having abraded him, she applied salt with a will. 'Oh, your poor scratchy voice. Just listen to it, Father! What's that excellent cure of yours for colds? Something with blackcurrant wine, isn't it?'

Fox stood up. Hatless and standing, he was not as tall as Rhys might have imagined – not even Leonie's height – and physically was unimpressive with thinning hair and a hunch to his shoulders that his excellent tailoring couldn't completely camouflage, but there was a menace about him and the same ruthless aggression that makes a certain type of dog frightening. As they looked into each other's eyes Rhys knew that this man would kill him without hesitation if he thought he could get away with it. Despite himself Rhys was afraid.

He looked away, at the cold whitewashed fireplace where a mass of maidenhair ferns quivered like flames in the downdraught from the chimney. Immediately, he could have kicked himself – to have lowered his eyes first was tantamount to yielding under pressure like a schoolboy under a headmaster's gaze.

It had occurred to Fox, too. 'Well, sonny boy,' he said, a

smugness overlaying the tension in his tone. 'State your business and leave; but, if you've come to plead for that filthy, bag-of-bones friend of yours, you'll be aggravating your throat to no good purpose.'

'You know why I'm here,' croaked Rhys. His ridiculous voice didn't help any, he thought in frustration. What a day to be bunged up and feverish when he wanted above everything to exude strength, determination and a manly confidence. Instead he felt foolishly like an unready half-grown bull elephant challenging the lord of the herd.

Fox examined him with patent dislike. Perhaps he *doesn't* know why I'm here, wondered Rhys, though at first the idea seemed incredible. All week he'd been making purchases that only the owner of a large sheep-and-cattle-run would have any use for. Surely news of the vast flocks and herds he'd bought would have reached Fox's ears; the prime breeding stock alone was of interest.

But perhaps not. All deals, every purchase, had been made through agents Sir Kenneth recommended, and in Leonie's words they were on opposing sides 'in everything'.

Rhys said: 'I've come for a signature, that's all.' Stepping forward a single pace he unfolded the bank draft and placed it not on the desk but on the pistol-case. 'A receipt,' he said, laying that on the leather-bound desk blotter. 'Kindly sign that, if you would, and I'll take up no more of your time.'

'Don't run away,' pouted Leonie.

'I'll not sign anything!'

'You'll sign this,' Rhys told him, meeting his eyes without flinching this time.

'Don't be awkward, Father. Sign for the lovely man.'

He glared at her. 'Your husband is waiting outside for you, Leonie.'

'He can wait.' She patted the brown velvet cloak that lay across her lap. This was a treat. It was rare indeed to see someone standing up to her father; the only trouble was, she wasn't quite sure whom she should be inwardly cheering for.

'This,' said Rhys, for Thomas Fox had not so much as glanced at it, 'this is final payment in full for Heywood Braddock's mortgage. Check it if you like. Every last penny has been paid, all the interest, even a penalty rate for the two payments he missed. You'll find it's scrupulously fair.'

Fox was thunderstruck. He could have put on his spectacles and read the document, but there was no need to. It would all be in order – there was no reason to doubt this young whelp's word on that. Anger made him rigid. This was real anger; not the irritation that made him shout at Leonie, but overwhelming rage that solidified within him, immobilizing him and dulling his senses.

'It's that damned Sir Kenneth, isn't it?' he gritted. 'He doesn't really want that land but he'd stop at nothing, no matter how devious, to stop me from getting it.'

If Leonie hadn't been there, Rhys would have let him believe anything, but she was watching and listening – he could see her stunned face out of the corner of his vision. 'It's all my money,' he told Fox, with satisfaction. This was a touché for the 'sonny boy'. 'I've been thinking of buying a good-sized sheep station for some time, and when Braddock offered his land to me it was too tempting an offer to pass up. So if you'll oblige by—'

'You're lying!' He seemed to shrink inside himself, a concentration of venom and rage. 'You're with those Staffords – that much I do know. They haven't got two sixpences to rub between them, sonny boy. So how can you claim to have this kind of wealth? Don't tell me you earned it digging ditches!'

'Something like that,' replied Rhys, thinking of the eighteen-hour days toiling with his pick, spade and gold-pan.

'I thought so.' He nodded at the documents. 'Tell Sir bloody Kenneth to come and see me personally if he's got the gumption. Tell him I'll not sign receipts for any snivelling errand-boy.' He glared with contempt at Rhys, who was at that moment blowing his nose. 'Now get out of my office before I ask Featherston to escort you.'

Rhys sighed. He was dizzy with fever, his throat raged in flames and his head was pounding so hard that it hurt to keep his eyes open. 'The money is mine. I could tell you how I came by it but I won't except to assure you it's legally earned. If you refuse to sign the receipt, I shall take it with the draft to my solicitor, who will take it to *your* solicitor. There is no possible way you can refuse to accept it. If you tear it up,' he added as Fox picked up the parchment-coloured paper, 'then the bank will issue me with another.' He looked at Fox wearily. 'You can't win.'

Leonie stood up. There were tears in her eyes. 'Father's had his heart set on that land for ages,' she pleaded. 'Ever since we first arrived in Canterbury and went on our first horseback rides out into the countryside he's wanted that land.'

'Then, he should have bought it from Braddock properly,

instead of lending him money and hoping to foreclose. He tried to get it for a song instead of paying a fair price.'

'Isn't that what you're doing, too?'

His head felt as if it was being crushed. She was right; Rhys knew that he had been too harsh with Braddock. 'There's an important difference,' he told her. 'Braddock *wanted* to sell to me. He knows that he can stay there for ever, and that I'll look after him well in his last years.' *My God, I will, too*, he vowed. 'Your father, on the other hand, declared his intention to—'

'I'll sign,' said Fox, cutting in to stop him. 'I'll sign your damned receipt, but that's not the end of the matter, I promise you. As for looking after Braddock, he's going to need it . . . And yourself, sonny boy. Don't forget to take good care of yourself.'

'Father didn't mean to sound so . . . pompous,' whispered Leonie in the outer office. 'He's a sweet man, really. Please take no notice of what he just said.'

'I admire your loyalty . . . among other things,' said Rhys, trying to lighten the mood. *Pompous*! The man had just made threats against both his and Braddock's lives.

'You sound as if you don't believe me,' she said tremulously, looking up at him so that he could see the single perfect tear still brimming in each eye. 'You must understand how angry he was, Rhys . . . not himself at all. That land was so important to him. He has a model in the parlour at home of the house he planned to build there on the cliffs overlooking the ocean.'

Rhys said nothing. Taking the balled-up handkerchief out of her mittened hand, he carefully wiped the tears from her eyes then flicked her under the chin. She wouldn't smile.

'Won't you change your mind, Rhys?' she whispered. 'You've just arrived here and you can take your pick of the Canterbury sheep-runs. All father has ever wanted is that one piece of property. It will break his heart—'

He couldn't feel the slightest bit sorry for Fox, but Leonie's genuine concern for her father moved him to say: 'I can't change my mind, but if I ever do decide to sell I'll offer the property to your father. There, does that cheer you up?'

'Is that a promise?'

'Of course it is. I'm a man of few words, but I mean every one of them.'

'My favourite kind.' She slanted a flirtatious glance at him.

He stood on the step and watched her get into the funereal black coach. The coachman materialized from where he had been sheltering from the rain in a doorway up the street. He opened the door for her, pulled the step down and handed her in. Rhys was hoping to see her husband, but the door closed and the coach drove off in a flurry of mud and still all Rhys glimpsed was a shadow.

FOURTEEN

BEFORE RETURNING TO SUMMER next day Rhys rode out to his
new property along the main north road which followed the
western rim of the harbour before striking inland. Here, beyond
the swamp and the mudflats, the road forked, a rutted scrape of a
pathway following the coast while the main road plunged into the
heart of the plains. Rhys paused before taking the rougher road,
for here Braddock's land – *his* land – began, stretching as far
north across the plains as he could see and out to the east where a
rugged swell of hills marked the wild headland. There under the
high blue arch of sky he gazed around him, feeling that quick
panicky feeling of excitement. Here was the raw clay he would
mould with his hands. On this place would he found his future
and the future of his sons. Heart beating in time to the clatter of
hoofs, he jogged on, his mind teeming with plans.

A distance before the headland the road dipped before
petering out in a large cleared area at the foot of a high ridge. Set
around the bare land like sentry-boxes were five almost identical
timber and iron houses, small as railway wagons, drab as old
packing-crates, each crouching in a dismal clutter composed of
identical ingredients arranged in different ways – frames for
drying sheepskins, tin wash-tubs, wood-piles, vegetable gardens
and fireplaces. *A nest of rats, or a den of thieves*, thought Rhys,
eyeing with distaste the muddy yards and the grimy ragged children that stood inside the paling fences, fingers in mouths as they
gaped at him. These were cockatoo farmlets, the Gullicks, the
Thompsens, Leaches, Blakes and Nevins – the names strung
together in his head. A distance apart from these stood a trimmer,

144

larger cottage back from the road surrounded by a flourishing orchard and set in a patchwork of tended fields. Jenks's place. Rhys gazed at it speculatively, and as he rode up the ridge behind the cockatoos' hovels he looked back at it again.

Then, when he reached the ridge-top the spread of his own land was before him again, and he clucked the horse along, his heart singing as he explored every dip on the vast plains. Soon every swell and sag would be as familiar to him as the contours of his own face, but now it was a richness of delight in fresh discovery. It was excellent land, fertile, fed by many springs and streams, pocketed with clumps of trees in sheltered gullies where sheep could shelter against winter snowstorms but for the most part smoothly undulating and covered with a thick carpet of waist-high tussock which would burn off easily leaving sweet green herbage on which his flocks could graze.

I'm going to be the most successful damned run-holder on the entire Canterbury Plains, he thought, anticipation and eagerness to begin emerging through the rottenness of cold fever from which he was still suffering.

By noon his head was aching ferociously again; he left the north-east boundary where a small Maori settlement lay in a wide curve of sandy bay beyond the rocky headlands. That could be explored another day when he was feeling better. Flapping his tired horse into a gallop, he headed for the cliff-top where he had first stood to view the property.

Braddock was there, hunched against the wind as he worked with a tray of watercolour cakes and a pot of water, capturing the image of the sunlit mountains on a paper pegged to his easel. Rhys reined the horse in and dismounted to watch him. He was moving swiftly with direct sure strokes, and the painting took shape in a matter of minutes.

Rhys made no comment; he admired absolute realism and intricate detail in his art. Instead he said, 'It's all settled, signed and sealed.'

Braddock touched-in an area of tussock with a few deft flips of the brush, then removed a tiny insect that was fluttering in the sky blue. 'Yurr done a good day's work, then. Come on down to the house. I'll pour yurr a mug of whisky to celebrate.'

Rhys declined. Taking a leather purse from his jacket, he withdrew two banknotes, saying: 'Tomorrow you're to go into town and buy yourself a couple of large strong dogs. Tie them up by your cottage and take them everywhere with you.'

'Fox making threats again? Yurr mustn't pay no mind to him. I don't need no dog – Bollan's company for me.' At the sound of his name the old liver-spotted dog came snuffling out of the bushes nearby. 'Put yurr money away. That Fox is a pig's bladder full of air. Are yurr staying here now yurrself?'

'Not until tomorrow. The tents and the workers and the fencing gear arrive then. I'm back to Sumner tonight.'

'Then, take my rowboat. Yurr horse looks weary. I'll take care of it for yurr.'

Rhys looked across the harbour at the hotel. Fifteen minutes of rowing would get him there as opposed to an hour and a half's ride around through Christchurch. More probably, his horse was already exhausted, its head drooping. Rhys felt scarcely better himself.

'Thanks. I'll return the boat in the morning.' He glanced again at the picture; he should say something. 'Very nice.'

'Nice!' Braddock cackled. 'Train those eyes of yurrs, Mr Maughold. Those mountains are magic. Poetry. ''Rangi Pokekohu'', my wife Hine used to call them. ''Mists of Heaven.'' There's a Maori legend—'

'Yes, yes,' interrupted Rhys. His headache was intensifying. Braddock tilted his head on his leathery neck. 'Yurr sick.'

'I'll be all right.'

'Take yurrself some lemons from my tree. Mrs Day will make yurr a special potion, cure yurr in no time.'

Rhys had to smile. If he spoke to fifty people in this colony, he'd probably get fifty different cures. 'Take care of yourself, old man.'

'Arr.' He began to pack up his paints. 'Put Fox out of yurr mind. He'll cause yurr no trouble now.'

Rhys wished he could feel as confident.

In the sheltered harbour the water surface was only ruffled, but beyond the sand bar a swell was surging and spray tossed on the wind from the pounding breakers. Rhys could feel it like rain on his face as he sawed at the oars, punching the little craft steadily towards the Sumner jetty. When he was almost there he checked the current; the tide was on the outflow, the rip strong, so he rowed a couple of hundred yards upstream before attempting to cross the channel itself.

Alf and Joe came hurrying to meet him from the boat-house.

Nearby Andrew was amusing himself by throwing chunks of

146

driftwood into the water and shrieking as they bobbed by at a brisk pace under the pilings. He stopped and clattered along the jetty to meet Rhys, but the older lads pushed past him in a tumult of shouting.

'Have you been in Christchurch today? Have you heard the great news? There's been a gold strike – a massive gold strike, too, further down country. Some folks in off a coastal boat told us about it, and already Christchurch is emptying. Everybody's going. *Everybody*!'

'They're welcome to.' He finished tethering the boat and scooped the lemons from the pool of salt water in which they bobbed.

'But you've *been* to the goldfields, so you can give us some—'

'Who told you that?' He knew the answer before he had spoken. Charles of course. Bragging that Rhys had not only been a prospector but had made his fortune that way. Trust slow-thinking fast-mouthed Charles. He'd have a word with Charles, but later, when his head had stopped this hammering.

'You found lots of gold!' crowed Andrew, tugging at Rhys's coat.

Rhys didn't notice him. He'd seen him on the jetty as he approached and, remembering the tantrum at the stagecoach, felt a brief spasm of distaste. What was it about the boy that made him feel so uncomfortable? But now, while Andrew plucked at him for attention, Rhys neither felt nor heard him. Muffled by his cold, he heard only the barked questions that the Days pelted at him as the three walked up towards the hotel.

Disconsolate, Andrew scuffed his new boots on the deck planking and resolved to show them – *really* show them – that he was a grown-up, too. Jutting his lip, he began tugging at the ropes which moored Braddock's rowboat to the jetty.

The group had waded across the powdery drifts of sand above the high-water mark and had reached the road when some innate sense caused Joe to turn and look back. 'Oh Lord, no!' he said. The others stopped, too.

There a dozen yards from the shore the rowboat revolved idly on the current as it rode inexorably towards the open sea, towards the breaker-line that thundered over the bar. In the boat, his face grim with concentration as he struggled to fit a rowlock into the gunwale, stood Andrew. The frail craft, off balance, was dipping under his weight.

The swiftness of response astounded Rhys. Without a single

word Joe was away, dashing down the beach, flinging his jacket down, whirling his peaked cap away, hopping from one foot to the other while he stripped off boots and stockings. Alf was already dragging their own dinghy from the boat-shed along its polished wooden rails down to the water.

Rhys pelted to join him. *The stupid little bastard!* he thought, the frustrations of the last few days, of his cold, of his interview with Fox all peaking into a hard blockage in his chest.

Lisabeth heard the shouts from where she sat on the back steps shelling peas. She paused to listen; it had been a turbulent afternoon vivid with shouts and whoops of enthusiasm as prospective gold-seekers thickened the ranks of wagons, carts and packhorses waiting to ascend the Zig-Zag. But these weren't the yahoos of newborn adventurers. They were screams of pain.

Andrew!

Lisabeth leaped from the step, upsetting the yellow enamel basin and spilling peas and pods over the sandy ground, starting the ginger cat away in fright. Almost tripping over him in her headlong rush, she wheeled around the side of the hotel's verandah. Breeze slapped her face, and the glare off sea and sand momentarily blinded her into a panic. Andrew! Where was he?

When she had crossed the road and was running along the track down to the beach she saw what was happening. The sight almost felled her. Alf was fastening the dinghy to the jetty; Joe, soaking wet and half-dressed, was manoeuvering Braddock's rowboat to tie up behind it; while on the jetty itself Rhys had Andrew by the collar, forcing his head down while he applied hefty wallops with his free hand to the boy's backside.

'Stop that!' screamed Lisabeth, skimming over the sand, her bottle-green skirts flapping around her ankles. Indignation choked her. How dare he? *How dare he?* She could hardly believe that anybody would be so monstrous as to whip a child, and especially a child like Andrew who had not an ounce of malice in him.

She tugged him free; he came away from Rhys's grip at a touch, twisted against Lisabeth, shrieked his anguish against her waist. She pressed his head hard to her with both hands. His skin was on fire, his screams terrible.

She glared at Rhys, unable to speak. It was too enormously horrible. Rhys straightened, chest heaving, face flushed like someone who had just run a long race. Not realizing he was ill, Lisabeth read his expression as evil, his high colour as a lust for violence. A flame of righteousness flared in her; up until this moment she had nurtured an uneasy suspicion that her blind judgement of Rhys had been too harsh, too sweeping, but now she knew triumphantly that she had been right to hate him, justified in her distrust.

Her fingers smoothed Andrew's thick gold hair. His tears soaked through her dress. 'How dare you!' she railed. 'How dare you beat a helpless child!'

Joe and Alf had finished tying the boats up and now stood at Rhys's shoulder, distinctly embarrassed. Joe said: 'Lisabeth, please don't be so upset.'

'I've every reason!'

'He deserved it, Lisabeth,' Rhys told her. 'Joe risked his life—'

She was deaf to reason; the argument inflamed her fury. 'Who are you to judge him? How can you dare to take it upon—'

'Miss Stafford, please,' interrupted Joe. 'Look at it this way. Your little brother is lucky to be alive. Another few yards and the dinghy would've capsized for sure. The waves would've rolled him over and over – I'd never have found him. He'd have drowned in no time.'

'There, you see?' said Rhys. 'What he did was foolish and dangerous. He needed to be taught a lesson.'

She refused to be placated. 'Andrew meant no harm! He's just a little boy. Don't you dare to touch him! Don't you dare to go near him again!'

She really hates me, thought Rhys, and was astounded at how this realization affected him. She looked beautiful in her anger, her enormous cobalt eyes radiating energy, her face white, lips trembling and her hair escaping in tendrils from the combs that scraped it back from her face. Clad in her worn old dress with a ridiculously large starched apron wound about her middle, she looked fragile and vulnerable, clinging to her brat of a brother as if she was a mother protecting her child. *She certainly didn't learn motherly love from Mary*, he thought, suddenly remembering the blithe neglect Lisabeth had received. *Poor kid.*

But despite his compassion his overriding impulse was to grab Lisabeth by those slender shoulders and shake her until the Andrew-worshipping notions of hers were freed from her head. Andrew had deserved the spanking. He mustn't apologize for chastising him.

149

Coldly he said: 'Joe risked his life just now. Don't you think you should be thanking him instead of berating me?'

Lisabeth took Andrew for a walk along the beach. If they went inside, Gwynne and Charles would ask questions.

The wind was whipping across the harbour now. White-capped waves raced each other to fling themselves face down on the sand.

'You had a fight with them because of me,' Andrew said unexpectedly.

'Not because of you, dear.' She squeezed his hand. 'I was taking your side. I'll always take your side.'

He grinned at her. She waited for him to say something else. Finally she probed: 'Don't you think it was wrong of Mr Morgan to hit you?'

Andrew shrugged. Breaking free from her grip, he hurtled along the beach, shouting, kicking pieces of driftwood aside as he ran. After a second's hesitation Lisabeth ran after him, snatched at his arm to force him to stop, stooped so that she could look into his face.

'Mr Morgan was wrong to hit you,' she insisted. 'Don't you hate him?'

'Not really,' he responded sulkily, scuffing his feet in the damp sand.

'Andrew, listen to me! It was terrible of that man to beat you! He had no right to do it. You must keep away from him from now on, do you hear me?'

He wasn't even looking at her. Amongst the traffic on the road came a tiny wagon with a cream canvas cover, drawn by a brisk grey pony. Under the hooped cover swung muslin-swathed bundles, and a large scarred chopping-block sat solidly on the backboard.

'It's Mr Berry the butcher! He promised he'd bring me a candy-stick if I held on to Strawberry and kept him quiet while he worked today.'

Defeated, Lisabeth trudged back to the hotel behind him. *He's poisoned Andrew's mind*, she thought, hatred surging in her. *Now Andrew thinks of Rhys Morgan as a godlike figure, someone who can do no wrong, and even that vicious unprovoked attack didn't open his eyes.*

I must get away, she thought. *Somehow I must get away and take Andrew with me.*

Mabs looked up from the stew-pot when Lisabeth entered the

kitchen. She handed the ladle to Lisabeth to stir while she fed the fire underneath the pot. Flames licked up the sides.

'Mind your dress don't catch,' she said.

Lisabeth stirred so hard that the pot swayed on its long black chain. 'Mabs, how long have you been in service?' she asked.

'Ten year or more, oi s'pose.' She stacked wood in a pyramid shape under the potato-pot and transferred a panful of hot coals to get that fire going. 'It's a fair life, oi s'pose.'

'Do you think I could get a job in service, too?'

'You?' scoffed Mabs. 'After you just run off an' left the peas all scattered to Kingdom Come an' oi 'ad to pick them all up an' it took me near on a 'ole 'alf-hour to finish what you done started an'—'

'I was called away urgently.'

' "Oi were called away," ' mocked Mabs, still cross. 'You ain't suited, Miss Stafford.' Then, relenting, she said: 'What's put such a notion inter your 'ead? Service! You don't want to be doin' for others from 'afore daylight to past dark.'

'I thought you liked it here.'

'Oi do.' Mabs blinked rapidly as she glanced towards the door. Lowering her voice significantly, she said, 'It's a funfair 'ere, long side of some places oi been in. Anyway, you got a good 'ome. You don't need none of this 'ere employment.'

'I want to get away. I have to get away, that's all.'

'Ah,' sighed Mabs, wiping her sweaty brow with the back of a chafed red hand. '*Oi* want to get away an' all. Thing is, where would oi go?'

At dinner the dining-room was jammed full. Even the Captain's chair (which usually presided over an empty place in his absence) had been removed to make way for a bench on which sat three young men, elbow to pressed-in elbow. They, like the other 'extras', were treating themselves to a substantial meal to sustain them on the first part of their journey to the goldfields.

The atmosphere crackled with excitement. In the candlelight eager faces reflected the glow of gold-fever. There was no conversation, just an outpouring of facts reported, rumours acquired, stories heard about the already fabulous gold-find in the south. Ten ounces in as many minutes! Fortunes to be made overnight! Gold lying for the taking, winking out of the black soil like stars glittering in the sky! A goldfield that promised to be richer than the Australian diggings.

Rhys listened to it all through a veil of the laudanum he had sipped to relieve his headache. Unlike Joe and Alf, who were soaking up every detail with an avid hunger, Rhys was detached, weary. How many times had he heard such stories? Why did men do this to each other? he wondered. Up went the cry, and men turned into lemmings rushing to abandon everything they had patiently scrimped to build, hurtling themselves into the jaws of greed.

'You tell us about it, Rhys!' cried Joe, breaking into his thoughts. 'You were at the Australian fields. You know all about it.'

'I don't know much about anything,' demurred Rhys.

But the voices had stilled; all the faces – except the passive downcast one opposite – were turned expectantly towards him. 'Yes, I was at the Australian fields, for thirty-one months. It was like thirty-one years. I can tell you about enervating heat, bone-numbing cold and about hunger so fierce it feels like a sharp-toothed sharp-clawed animal. I can tell you about being robbed, both by thieves who steal up in the darkness and by the daylight robbers who charge five guineas a pound for salt and a guinea a pound for flour, or six guineas for a gin-case, not with the contents intact, just for the empty case! I can tell you about being sick or hurt or, worse, of suffering toothache with no means of relief. But you don't want to hear about any of that, do you?'

Joe was gaping at him. 'But – but you did well there, didn't you? You struck it rich! Tell us about that, Rhys. Tell us how you found your gold.'

'I found gold at the end of that time, when I was almost past caring. By then the searing days and the bitter nights and the hunger had taken so much of a toll of me that at times I forgot what I was there for. It's true, I *was* one of the lucky ones; but if one word I said encouraged any of you to rush down there on that same vague hope of riches that lured me, then I would be seriously at fault. If you do want advice, then here it is: Don't go.'

Joe was flabbergasted. 'How can you talk like that? It wasn't a vague hope for you, was it? No, you can't dissuade us, Rhys. We're going. Alf and me.' And Alf nodded agreement.

Mrs Day heard that. She was at the head of the table dishing great slabs of steaming apple pie into dishes and passing them out. 'You two lads aren't going anywhere,' she said.

'Aw, Ma! *Everybody's* going to the goldfields, and the first ones there will get the richest pickings, so we need—'

'You're not going anywhere,' she repeated. Intercepting Mabs, who entered with two tall white jugs of pouring custard, she took one from her and carried it down to the end of the table to set it with a thump on the cloth between Joe and Lisabeth. 'I'll talk to you later, Joseph,' she said in an undertone.

He plucked at her sleeve. 'You'll let me go this time, won't you, Ma? You stopped me from going to England, but this time surely—'

'I stopped you from going to England because that's the very place we came away from in order to give you a better life! And you'll not go gold-prospecting, either, Joseph Day, not while I've strength in my body to stop you, so eat your pudding and put those foolish notions out of your head.' She spoke quickly, in a low voice, and having said her piece hurried back to finish doling out the dessert.

As Lisabeth stole a glance at Joe she remembered what Mabs had said. *We all want to get away from something*, she thought.

FIFTEEN

WHEN CHARLES WAS TOLD about the Aaron Jenks land he flew into a lather of indignation, snapping recrimination at Rhys, his beard damp with spittle.

'Sure and you promised me a *choice* of your land, you did, and now you're palming me off with the rubbish you don't want!'

Mortified, Gwynne drew Rhys aside and explained that Charles had been in a 'wee mood' ever since news of the gold strike came.

'He's desperate to go, too, you see. He knows he could make his fortune just like you did, only he's embarrassed for funds to finance the journey, unless . . .'

'I thought it was just his way of expressing gratitude,' said Rhys drily. He ignored the hint, tempting though the thought was of being rid of Charles. If he was in need of funds, then he would need assistance with buying seed and implements; and Rhys, after all his purchases, had only two hundred and thirty guineas left of his own money. He would have to begin turning a profit, and soon.

When they arrived at their new home Charles took Andrew off to tour the weed-choked fields and sagging outbuildings, while Lisabeth and Gwynne inspected their new home. The two women looked around the three tiny rooms in silence then went quickly outside where Gwynne subsided on to a stump, flung her aprons over her head and wept.

Lisabeth was equally dismayed. It was obvious that the Jenks family had simply up and run, leaving the place in a filthy state. Rat droppings encrusted the dirt floor, the primitive bunks were

154

strewn with musty bracken and soiled rags, while below them rusty receptacles slopped full of stinking night-soil. From the smell wafting near them now Lisabeth guessed that those same receptacles were habitually emptied into an overgrown drain that ran behind the dilapidated fowl-house.

Here around the woodpile the ground was slippery, rancid and littered with mouldy bones, leavings from the Jenks's table which stood under the overhanging eaves and still bore food-caked chipped plates and a cast-iron pot half-full of something mildewed and stomach-churningly revolting.

Looking around her, Lisabeth noticed there was no privy at all, no house-garden, no kitchen, only the charred remnants of an open fire and no well. Water was caught from the lichen-draped roof in a long wooden trough and funnelled into an enormous barrel. Peeking into it, Lisabeth was immediately repelled by the stench of decay.

Returning to Gwynne's side, she said helplessly: 'I suppose we can tidy it, Aunt. With both of us working at it we can make it nice. At least it's four walls and a roof over our heads.'

Gwynne blotted her face with her top apron. 'Ah, but you're a bonny lass to look on the bright side. I've been sitting here thinking ill of Rhys, but I suppose he didn't know the state of the place. How would he? He's only ever galloped past and glanced at it, and it does seem sound enough from the outside. But how could those people live like this? It's worse than pigs. Pigs never foul their sleeping-quarters. Ah, the lazy creatures! I'd like to meet that Mrs Jenks eye to eye and give her the sharp side of my tongue.'

'You haven't got a sharp side to your tongue,' teased Lisabeth, glad that she was cheered up. 'And if you did meet Mrs Jenks you'd wish her a ''good day'' and ask after the children. She must have a tribe of them! When we go in there again I'm going to count the bunks. There must be at least a dozen.'

'She has fifteen children living, Mrs Day said.' Gwynne stood up and drew in an enormous, deep sigh, gathering strength. 'I think Mrs Day must have known something of what faced us. No wonder, then, that she insisted we borrow her brooms and buckets and scrubbing-brushes.'

While Lisabeth was ladling a pailful of water out of the stagnant tank Andrew came running back ahead of Charles. 'Ha! Ha! Ha!' he cried.

'What do you mean, ''Ha! Ha! Ha!''?' asked Lisabeth, keeping her face averted from the smell.

'You know how you were asking for Uncle Charles to send me off to school?' he chirped, dancing around her gleefully. 'Well, he says there's so much work to be done here that I don't need to go *at all*! So there! Ha, ha! Pooh!' he exclaimed, peering into the tank. 'Ooh, look, there's dead things in there, rats and birds and all rotten!'

'Andrew, do stop fussing! Look out, you'll knock the pail over.'

'I want to pee. Where's the "little house"?'

'There isn't one.'

'Whaat?' His green eyes stretched open.

'There isn't a privy. Mr Jenks was too lazy to dig one.'

'No privy?'

'You heard me!' she snapped. 'You'll have to go behind some bushes. Don't look so astounded. You've done that lots of times before when we've been travelling.'

'No privy? Yippee!' crowed Andrew. 'I like this place! It's like being on a picnic.'

'It's no picnic for us, I assure you,' Lisabeth retorted grimly. 'When you've finished come back here and light me a fire there in the ashes, will you? We've lots and lots of things want burning.' She gazed at the cottage, thinking how much simpler it would be to torch the whole place. 'And don't get too excited at the thought of no school, either. I'm going to have a long talk to Uncle Charles about that.'

Charles ambled back from his own inspection tour, ruminating on his plans as he chewed at the wad of tobacco tucked into his cheek. He stuck his head inside the house and hastily withdrew it again. 'Mrs Stafford, I'm off to town now,' he called. When she hobbled out clutching a broom he informed her that he was going to make a few purchases while the stores were still open. 'That second paddock's just right for cabbages; sure and I'll put this one into broad beans,' he said. 'I'll buy the seed today, make a start. No sense in waiting.'

Gwynne's brow furrowed below the frill of her faded cotton house-cap. Rhys had been adamant that Charles obtain proper advice from the vegetable merchants before deciding what crops to put in. Hesitantly she said: 'Couldn't we perhaps consult. . .?'

'Never mind what Rhys said. What does he know? Sure and aren't I the one who's been in this colony these past ten years? How long has he been here? Five minutes!'

'I don't think he meant it quite like that, Mr Stafford. Rhys was only trying to be helpful.'

'Helpful! Giving me orders, more like. You mark my words, Mrs Stafford, that brother of yours will lose no opportunity to rub our noses in the fact that we're beholden to him.'

Lisabeth couldn't help but agree with those sentiments. With her hair swathed in a dish-rag against the fog of dust she was dislodging she swung her broom along the cobweb-draped ceiling, sending spiders scurrying and horrid sensations of disgust crawling over her body. He might have checked the place out first, she thought bitterly. Gwynne was taking the charitable view, but that was in Gwynne's nature. What kind of person would expect his sister to have to scrape and scrub up muck like this? Or perhaps he thought she, Lisabeth, would be doing it all by herself. That was it. He was living in soft luxury at Sir Kenneth's place with the sepoys at his beck and call, sipping tea and admiring the peacocks and laughing as he pictured her begrimed and exhausted, toiling to clean this filthy hovel.

Hatred of him gave her fresh energy. Every swat of the broom was a blow against him, and when Charles returned at dusk, just in time to accompany them down to the shore to wait for Joe to ferry them back across to Sumner, Lisabeth was still working with a ferocious determination.

Far from living in luxury, Rhys was already settled on the far north-western border of his estate where at the edge of the foot-hills he was beginning to erect the fences that would eventually ring the whole property. Helping him were his two new workers, Paul and Jock McFallish, Highland crofters who had been evicted from their homes in Scotland. Rhys had selected them because they would be accustomed to a Spartan life and both declared a preference for solitude.

'I can promise you plenty of that,' Rhys told them. 'But I can promise you good wages too, and a bonus at shearing time, too, if we get a good clip.'

Before they began setting the fence-posts and stringing wires they spent two hours constructing the rudiments of a shepherd's hut, one of the half-dozen Rhys planned to space over the station so that no matter where the sheep were grazing one of the shep-herds would be able handily to keep an eye on them at all times. The hut was built into the top of a hillock; sods were cut to mound the walls, the floor was tamped down with a fence-post for a battering-ram and canvas was strung up for the roof. Later, before winter set in, a tin roof and chimney would be added, but in the

157

meantime the rough shelter would serve the three men adequately, allowing just enough room for them to stetch out at night on a pallet of chopped tussock.

For a month they worked every hour of every day but Sunday, no matter what the weather, pegging their fence along the hill boundary. On Sundays the stoutly Presbyterian McFallish lads traipsed off at dawn for services in Christchurch, while Rhys slept past noon then rode out to gaze over his golden beautiful land, the sight of which never failed to excite him.

One day he rode down to the Maori coastal settlement where he introduced himself to the folk there – a *hapu*, or fragment, of the Ngai-tahu tribe. There were less than twenty people living in only three dwellings nestled amongst the sand dunes, though the settlement must have been considerably larger in recent history judging by the grey tatters of dilapidated *whares*, or flax and thatch houses, further back from the beach. These Maoris seemed peaceful enough, nervous of him in fact, the toddlers peeking shyly from behind their mother's black skirts while older children stared through ragged gaps in the woven wall-panels.

Rhys inspected the grotesque red-painted carvings that formed a gable arch on the airy echoing meeting-house and glanced over the brush fence at the tiny graveyard with its whitewashed stones and crosses. On the way back along the shore one of the older children came dashing across the sand to intercept him with cries of '*Haere mai!*' as he thrust a wet wriggling flour-sack up at Rhys, then went dashing away again before Rhys could open the string-bound mouth to see what kind of a fish was flapping within. To his delight he found a couple of large crayfish, grey-green, and spiny, fresh from the rocky ocean-floor.

'Canterbury rabbits! I found a burrow and dug them up,' he explained to Jock and Paul when with a flourish of triumph he produced them scarlet-shelled and succulent for dinner that evening.

'Och, that's a guid joke, but ye'll nae fool us,' Jock told him. It was one of the few things he said that Rhys completely understood. Laconic by nature, when the two did speak their accents were so broad that most of what they uttered remained a mystery to Rhys.

After a month Rhys paid them and gave them a day off so that they could take their wages in to deposit them safely in the savings bank. Heartily weary of the food they had been existing on, Rhys decided to pay a visit to Gwynne and Charles to see how they had been getting along.

'And to see if your cooking is still as marvellous as ever,' he added, tossing his broad-brimmed wideawake hat on to a peg beside the door. 'We've had nothing but boiled mutton and damper for weeks, except for some occasional fish we've bought from the Maoris. Our damper is terrible stuff that's hard as clay and tastes of ashes, and the mutton is invariably red-raw in the centre or boiled to rags. We're none of us cooks, I'm afraid.'

'You look healthy enough despite it all,' smiled Gwynne, thinking with a pang that he seemed gaunt and undernourished. His wrists and hands were as bony as old Mr Braddock's, and his eye-sockets had deepened; with his straggly unkempt hair and scruffy beard he looked as disreputable as one of their cockatoo neighbours. In fact she thought, peering closer, he didn't look well at all.

To smooth over her alarm she said: 'We bought fish from the Maoris once – fine plump flounder that a young scamp came to the door selling. When Mr Stafford discovered how we'd obtained it, he was very angry, but, oh, it tasted lovely. But come in, come in! I'll boil the billy for our tea.'

Prising his boots off on the jack, Rhys stepped across the threshold and looked around the prim little room. Flax mats covered the floor. The walls were whitewashed and decorated with pictures of Queen Victoria cut from periodicals, and there in pride of place on a dresser were Gwynne's precious platters and her primrose dinner-set. Everything was spotlessly clean.

'The furniture cost the earth,' said Gwynne, apologizing for its sparseness. 'It's locally made and not well finished, but it's comfortable, so that's the main thing. Poor Charles is so exhausted at nights. I do wish he could afford a hired man to help with the heavy work. If only we had a little more money to start us off —'

'If only we all did,' Rhys interrupted, determined not to get on to the subject. Hearing voices outside, he glanced through the thin muslin curtains and saw Lisabeth and Andrew laughing together as they came up from the fields with a bulging Maori flax bag of *puha*, a bitter sow-thistle that grew like a weed in any once-cultivated areas of the countryside. Lisabeth had one of Andrew's straw boaters tied on with a scarf to shade her face, while Andrew was hatless, the sun burnishing his fair hair.

'They've been a blessing to me,' said Gwynne at his elbow. 'Young Lisabeth is such a treasure, so helpful and cheerful. They've been gathering greens for the hens. We've a dozen pullets – they should start laying soon.'

'How old is she?' asked Rhys as Lisabeth turned to bestow such

159

a loving look on her brother that it twisted his heart. 'Seventeen? Then she should be coming out in society soon, going to parties and balls.'

Gwynne laughed. 'Bless you, dear, but we'll never have the time or money for things like that. Mr Stafford says she'll have to make the best of life here, so don't you go putting any ideas into her head. She's been upsetting the poor man a lot lately with all these notions that young Andrew should go to school. As if he could spare the money for the fees, even if he could spare the lad! He's a capable pair of hands, you know, and a fine strong boy for nine. Lisabeth! Come on in, dear. We've a surprise visitor.'

'Is it Mrs Day?' came Lisabeth's voice, high and eager. She drifted into the room as if borne on a current of cool air, smiling and graceful in her patched, much mended bottle-green gown. 'Oh, how—' The smiles, the joy and her voice faded when she saw him.

'Hello, Lisabeth.' His own disappointment rocked him. Why should he mind that she was so plainly dismayed to find him here? Was it because deep down he felt a nagging guilt about what had happened so long ago, that every time he saw her he was harking back with longing to the demure little girl with the starched bow in her hair who had gazed at him so adoringly that first day at Waitamanui?

But he needn't feel guilty. If he'd injured her through Mary, that debt was repaid a thousandfold when he shot the Maori hooligan and saved her life. He could dismiss her now as an ungrateful churlish nobody – he need never take any notice of her again, so why, then, did he force a smile and say: 'You've got the place looking charming.'

Indigo eyes snapped at him. Her voice was haughty, remote. 'So you saw what it was like before?'

'I heard it was a bit rough,' he admitted. 'But it certainly—'

'A bit *rough*? Is that what you call it? *A bit rough*!' She would have said more but stopped when she saw that Gwynne was staring at her.

Andrew came in from feeding the hens. 'Uncle Rhys!' he cried, dashing to shake hands. 'You haven't been here for ages! We had lots of fun before.' He slid a sly glance at Gwynne. 'We had *no privy*!'

'Andrew!' from Gwynne and Lisabeth simultaneously.

'I helped to dig the new one. Uncle Charles had a bad back and had to lie down, and the cockatoos wouldn't help us, so Alf and

160

Joe came over for the day.' His green eyes sparkled, and he ignored the shushing from the women. 'You should have seen the mess in here! You should have seen the dead seagulls we got out of the water-tank. Joe cleaned it right out for us and we didn't have any water until it rained again. We've got a cat now to chase the rats away. It's a ginger one like the hotel cat, only it's got fleas so—'

'Andrew!' cried Gwynne, but Lisabeth grabbed his arm and yanked him outside.

'I had no idea,' Rhys said.

'Bless you, of course you didn't. Sit yourself down, and I'll wake Mr Stafford to join us for a cup of tea. He's having a wee nap. Then I'll read your tea-cup. Mrs Day showed me how to find your fortune in the tea-leaves. Won't that be fun?'

'Yes,' said Rhys absently, still shocked by what he had heard, but more by what he had seen. Both Lisabeth and Andrew were thin and sunburned, their hands blistered and chafed. By the looks of them, they'd been labouring as hard as he had been.

Charles, when he emerged, looked damply well fed as he always did, his frame well covered by a sagging upholstering of flesh. Rhys studied his hands; because they looked neither work-worn nor soft, it was impossible to arrive at a conclusion. Nevertheless, a suspicion had taken root and was flourishing; Charles was very likely exploiting the youngsters, using them as unpaid navvies and making them do all his hardest work.

After an hour of awkward conversation Rhys made his excuses and remembered an urgent errand that had to be attended to in Christchurch. Gwynne looked stricken, so he said: 'If I come again on Sunday night, will you cook one of your hotpots for me?' Which brushed her disappointment away.

Charles ambled out to the roadway to see Rhys off. There was still no sign of Lisabeth or Andrew, so Rhys took the opportunity to say: 'They're just youngsters still, Charles. You are making provision for their schooling, aren't you?'

He looked immediately defensive, rheumy eyes narrowed. 'Mrs Stafford hears Andrew his lessons every night. That's all that's needed. Sure and look at you, you're a farmer now just like me. What use was all your fancy education to you?'

Rhys decided he would be wasting his breath if he tried to explain the multitudinous benefits of a complete education, his understanding of the world, his training to plan and anticipate unexpected contingencies, his appreciation of literature and the soul's-ease delight of being able to refresh himself with Chopin on the harpsichord or piano. Charles would never understand the vast unseen difference between a mind wealthy in learning and a mind rich in ignorance.

Instead he said: 'What about Lisabeth? I hope you're not making her work all the hours God sends. She needs some time to herself, you know.'

'Sure and she'll get time to herself once the bulk of the work's done. She's struck up a friendship with old Braddock, and he's going to show her how to paint. Bought her a set of paints and brushes and an easel thing out of that money he got from you. Waste of time and money if you ask me,' he added, averting his head to squirt a stream of juice. 'I could do with money like that to fling about. I'd spend it on something sensible – hire a man for the hard work. My back's giving me gyp some days, sure and I —'

'I hope it's better soon,' said Rhys firmly as he swung into the saddle and made that movement one of momentum, flicking the reins subtly to signal to Polka, and immediately they were away.

Charles spat again. 'Sure and it's just as I thought,' he wheezed. 'The uppity bogger doesn't want to know.'

Andrew and Lisabeth appeared much later. 'We met Mr Braddock on the cliffs and he showed me how to hold the brush properly,' Lisabeth reported. 'I painted a little picture of a wave crashing over a rock.'

'Yerrrk, what a mess!' gagged Andrew. He ran out again.

'You're not nervous of Mr Braddock any more?'

'Not since he comes here to visit. He's a funny old man, but I like him. He calls me "darrrrlin' gel". His voice sounds tickly.'

'Sit down, Lisabeth.' Gwynne looked solemn. When she was seated at the table her aunt said: 'I want you to promise me you'll be nicer to Mr Morgan.'

Lisabeth coloured. Ducking her head to avoid Gwynne's eyes, she fiddled with a tea-cup.

'You could have been much more pleasant to him today. It wasn't his fault that we had all this mess to clear up and, even if it was, we should be grateful. Rhys is letting us live here rent-free, and we should at least be courteous to him. Besides which, he's my brother and I insist that he's made to feel welcome in our home.'

Tears were stinging Lisabeth's eyes, and her conscience was burning, too. This was the harshest dear Aunt Gwynne had ever spoken to her. But she couldn't compromise her position. She *couldn't* pretend to like Rhys Morgan. In an attempt to veer away from that subject she said: 'I thought this land belonged to Uncle Charles. He said—'

'Mr Stafford has his pride, dear,' Gwynne reminded her.

How beastly, thought Lisabeth as she chased the ginger cat off the potato-bin and rattled a heap of potatoes into a bowl to prepare for dinner. *He's saved my life, he owns our home, he probably paid for these potatoes, too! If only I could get away from him!*

It seemed an impossible hope.

SIXTEEN

WHEN Rhys rode away he had formulated an intention to investigate the availability of proper schooling in the district, but that same week before he had a chance to make enquiries he took delivery of most of his stock and then his troubles began – such troubles that the youngsters' predicament was driven right out of his head.

Stocking the land was of the utmost priority. When Braddock had claimed the land in the beginning he had had to abide by the laws of the Canterbury Association, which decreed that the land must be used, one sheep to every twenty acres or one head of cattle to each 120 acres. Having absolutely no money to purchase stock, and being in danger of losing his land without it, Braddock was forced to turn to Fox for the mortgage to purchase his animals. The terms of the mortgage were steep, but Braddock might have made a fair fist of building up a run if it had not been for a string of bad luck that set in almost at once and eventually forced him to sell his sheep just to pay the interest on the mortgage.

Privately Rhys suspected that Heywood Braddock's 'bad luck' might have been mismanagement until similar incidents began to happen to him. Fences were uprooted, bodily as if by some huge animal. Stock mysteriously stampeded over cliffs and were killed. His new barn burned down, the load of roofing tin he had ordered for the shepherd's huts vanished shortly after being unloaded, and a mob of prize merinos he had inspected before purchase were, when delivered, a scrawny scabby-mouthed flock, not the same ones at all.

164

Each of these incidents was a blow to Rhys, but their nuisance value was incalculable. Each of them gobbled up precious time he could not afford to remedy the situation. The roofing tin was found halfway down one of the headland craters, the prize merinos were located and swapped for the diseased flock, the barn and fences replaced, but because Rhys already had work to last him and his men some eighteen hours a day the mischief caused serious setbacks.

'The worst of it is that I don't know who's behind it,' said Rhys to Gwynne and Charles over the promised hotpot. 'The damage itself has to be caused by either the cockatoos or the Maoris – there's nobody else within coo-ee of here. I've been down to the Maori settlement and caught them red-handed skinning one of my sheep, but they all swore blind they know nothing about the fences or the fires. I believe them, too, so —'

'So more fool you! Maoris are thieving, lazy and murderous, as well we know. And, while we're on the subject, you told me—'

'That there were no warlike tribes down here and hardly any Maoris, and it's the truth. I've come to a tidy arrangement with them now; they'll provide me with fish and crayfish and they're to receive a sheep once a month for payment – a cull sheep, too, not one of our best in-lamb ewes as that one was. No, it's the cockatoos I'm worried about. You live handy to them. Could you please keep an eye out and report anything at all that looks suspicious? I've been to have words with them of course, but they just glare sullenly at me and won't say anything. Sour, I think, because I bought Aaron Jenks out and not them.'

Lisabeth said nothing. Obedient to Gwynne, she was being scrupulously polite to Rhys, but she would not look at him, nor smile. Now her blood bubbled with the knowledge of a secret. She had seen something. A week ago, when she was milking the house-cow in the wooden pail down in the paddock by the road, Fox had ridden up on horseback. Lisabeth kept very still, anxious not to be noticed, and she was screened so well by the *toe-toe* bushes that fringed the road, and veiled by the dusk, that he had not seen her as she hunched by Bella's warm udder.

Fox seemed to be waiting rather impatiently; several times he started to ride further up the road towards the cottage, then changed his mind and wheeled his magnificent black horse about. Lisabeth finished milking and eased the pail out and covered it with the bead-fringed net to keep the insects out. Immobile in the curdling evening, she waited until, finally, three of the cockatoo farmers came strolling along together.

'You're extremely late,' snapped Fox. 'Did you do what I asked?'

'Oim tullying yer we done it all,' said one. Sam Nevin, thought Lisabeth. 'Twen'ee-foive hud. A shame ter cull them. Gud eatin' they be. A roight shame.'

'I didn't ask for your comments, just the job doing. Here's your money.'

'What hoppens next, thun?'

Lisabeth strained her hearing to catch what was said next, but Fox's horse began dancing about and in the sound of scuffling hoofs the substance was lost.

Now Lisabeth glanced up at Rhys. He looked gaunt and old. *Fox is out to get you, Rhys Morgan. And I hope he does!* she thought.

Several evenings later, while Lisabeth was again tending to Bella, Fox came by as before. This was at the end of a fortnight's Indian summer, an unbroken swath of scorching days and crisp dewless nights, and in their thousands all around, on the umbrella'ing tree-ferns, in the forests of grass and the branches of the orchard trees, cicadas were singing frantic serenades to the summer's demise.

Lisabeth was listening idly, her cheek against Bella's warm soft-smelling flank. She didn't hear Fox's horse, and when she glanced up it was to see his top-hatted grey-whiskered head gliding along above the *toe-toe* plumes. Curious to find out what she could, she ducked out of sight, moved the bucket out of range of Bella's legs and crept along to the edge of the field. A watercress-choked drain prevented her from getting any closer to the road, but clumps of scarlet-blossomed flax concealed her while she watched Fox pull his watch from the fob pocket of his velvet waistcoat. Tonight he had less time to wait.

It was darker than it had been on the previous occasion, no later but the nights were fast closing in. There was, however, enough light for her to see some distance up the road as the three cocka-toos strolled through the gloaming towards Fox. All doffed their shapeless cloth caps as they approached, and she recognized Sam Nevin's bright red hair.

This time, because of the cicadas, she heard almost nothing. There seemed to be an argument of some kind, Fox insisting, the three men putting up resistance. Fox's voice sharpened as the tussle progressed until Lisabeth heard him say: 'It must be now. If the rains come, it will be too late. So do it, and you'll be paid well.' Then he unstrapped his saddle-bag and withdrew several large square bottles which he thrust at them. He seemed angry, and so did they. When the horse galloped off one of the men spat after him.

The incident lay heavy and undigested in Lisabeth's mind. There had been something ugly about the exchange; it frightened her, but she was not sure why.

That evening Gwynne had prepared a 'foine Oirish stew' of lamb and potatoes. To amuse themselves at dinner they all tried to imitate the Nevins' fruity brogue.

'Listen to the thonder! It's about to roine dine!' tried Charles.

'Look at the graws in its notral styat,' said Andrew, who was not very good at accents.

Lisabeth laughed. 'Twen'ee-foive hud!' she cried, then stopped, aghast, remembering belatedly where she had heard those words.

'Twenty-five head?' repeated Gwynne. 'That's the number of sheep Rhys lost, drowned in the swamp the other week. When did you hear Mr Nevin say that, dear?'

'Oh, ages and ages ago,' lied Lisabeth, turning scarlet. She stopped playing the game; it was a stupid game, and she was furious with herself for letting that phrase slip out. How could she be so careless?

When Lisabeth was scrubbing the porridge-pot at the outside bench next morning the two McFallish men swung past along the road with a clattering of hoofs, waving their billycock hats and bellowing a cheery 'Guid morranin'!'

Gwynne returned from checking the nest-boxes. 'Nice enough lads, those, but they've only two words to say for themselves when they're galloping by. They'll not step inside for a sup of tea no matter how I coax them.'

'Perhaps they think you're trying to marry Lisabeth off!' called Andrew from where he swung an axe at the chopping-block.

'Gracious! I hope not!' She clutched her top apron in both hands. 'Now, don't run off, Andrew. It's church today!' She came to stand beside Lisabeth, who was gazing over at the mountains.

'Look how far down the snow is now, Aunt. Winter's almost upon us.'

167

'But it will be lovely today.' Gwynne turned her face up to the dazzling sky. 'Feel the warmth in that sunshine!'

'I saw the cockatoos all trooping off towards town earlier,' Lisabeth told her. 'All of them together, carrying bundles wrapped in dish-cloths and billies, too. One of the young Nevin kiddies said they were having a picnic.'

'Nice day for it.'

'Yes,' said Lisabeth absently. There had been something odd in the demeanour of the families as they hurried by. Not one of the adults had looked in her direction as she stirred the porridge over the open fire, and when the child had called out excitedly to her his mother jerked crossly at his arm, pulling him along abruptly. It was almost like a mass exodus, she thought. Odd.

She was checking outside to make sure that Andrew hadn't left anything lying about – for, should the cockatoos return from their outing first, nothing was safe – when suddenly she smelt a sharp clear aroma of burning. Shading her eyes she gazed out across the cockatoo properties to the ridge where she saw hanging and billowing in the sky a turbulent pall of amber smoke. Along the blackened backbone of the ridge itself writhed a faint erratic flicker of flame.

'There's a fire!' she shouted, running indoors with the clean porridge-pot in her hands.

Charles didn't seem excited. He inspected the distant scene, dourly calculated the wind direction and said that Rhys was a damned fool for setting a fire on a Sunday but it was no surprise to him. 'Sure and I'll wager he's not set foot in a church for years,' he added, slapping on his bowler hat and stumping out to harness Bosun to the pony-trap.

'Uncle Rhys says that masses are the opiate of the ig— Ouch!' And Lisabeth pinched Andrew's arm, abbreviating his irreverent remark.

'He's been talking about firing off some of his land,' said Gwynne. 'He did say it would have to be done soon, before the rains come, so that there would be fresh autumn grass for the sheep.'

Before the rains come! Now, before the rains come!

'What's the matter, dear? You look as sour as a curd-pot. Don't worry; the flames won't turn this way.' She peered through thick lenses. 'You look *ill*.'

'I have a terrible headache,' said Lisabeth. 'It's been at me since last night, and I hardly slept. Could I please stay home today? I'll go for a walk on the cliffs and see if the breeze clears my head.'

'That might be best,' agreed Gwynne, for Lisabeth's face was fiery, stoked with the enormity of her lies. 'Off you go, then, but take care.' Headaches? she mused. Perhaps Lisabeth needed spectacles, too.

She was panting when she reached the hilltop but her breath stilled in dismay as she viewed the plain, where a wide crescent of fire was scything across the tussock with a bright, vibrating cutting edge and a black smoking wake. On the nearside it moved in almost a straight line parallel to the coast and perhaps half a mile inland, kept back by the south-easterly wind, but on the other edge the flames leaped like tops strummed by the breeze, fanning out in all directions.

The wind beat on her back, cold, and she hugged herself, shivering with anxiety. From here the sound of the fire was crackling and alive, a million chirping crickets, and above the dirty turmoil of smoke the mountain-tops marbled in a blur of heat haze. *Fox did this! Fox hired those cockatoos to set this inferno. I knew. I could have stopped them. Just by walking on to the road, saying I'd heard, I could have prevented this. They'd never have dared do anything then.*

Something bumped against the backs of her legs, and she started in fright as Heywood Braddock said, 'Pretty sight, fires, don't yurr think?' and she glanced down to see Bollan pushing his damp freckly nose against her navy-blue skirts.

'Stupid durrned fool if yurr ask me,' added Braddock. 'Should have had more sense than to set a fire with the wind strong as it be today. 'T won't stop while the river now and that's five mile off. Half his sheep are like to burn. Yurr'd think a feller like him would have more sense.'

He has, thought Lisabeth. Half his sheep! She didn't know much about farming, but surely a loss like that would ruin anybody.

'What can he do to save them?' she asked faintly.

'Round them up, chase them over the river. Don't yurr fret, gel. He's got them Scots fellers helping.'

'No, he hasn't,' said Lisabeth suddenly. 'He's got nobody, Mr Braddock. The cockatoos have all vanished, and Uncle Charles . . .' Her gaze swung around to see a feathery plume of dust dispersing on the town road. 'We'd never catch Uncle Charles

169

and Andrew now.' She looked into the crinkled-leather face despairingly. 'We'll have to go and help him. We can't let all his sheep die.'

'Us?' cackled Braddock, bemused. He scratched his freckled pate. 'Don't yurr mind my talk, darrlin' gel. He don't need us.'

'Yes, he does.' Lisabeth was crying now, with guilt, remorse and sheer panic. 'Don't you see, Mr Braddock, Mr Fox and the cockatoos set this fire! They're trying to drive Rhys – Mr Morgan off his land. I know they are! I heard them talking about it.'

'Yurr *heard* them?'

His eyes regarded her shrewdly. They were old faded eyes with a light crusting of cataract that encroached on the round irises, making them patchy and irregular. Set as they were in cracked skin that resembled parched brown mud, they weren't pretty, although once Lisabeth had overcome her aversion to the old man she grew to think of them as kindly and perceptive.

Now she looked apprehensively into those eyes; he was judging her, and he didn't like much what he saw. She shrank, ashamed.

'I didn't realize the significance,' she appealed. 'One evening I heard Mr Fox talking to the cockatoo farmers and I only now understand what it was they meant.'

His gaze didn't waver. 'Yurr owe yurr home to Mr Maughold, gel,' he said slowly. 'Ay, and if yurr darrlin' Auntie Gwynne tells me right yurr owe yurr life to him and all.'

'And you sound just like Auntie Gwynne, too!' Lisabeth burst out in exasperation. 'Always rub, rub, rubbing about being grateful! I suppose we do owe him a debt, but that can't alter the fact that I utterly detest the man—' She broke off, horrified by what she had said. How could she explain the reasons for her loathing to Mr Braddock?

To her astonishment, Braddock was cackling with mirth. 'Detest him, do yurr now? Then, yurr should be dancing with glee, gel, not breaking yurr neck to help him.'

'Oh!' she cried in angry frustration. 'I don't want to help him but – don't you see? – we *have* to! The McFallishes *aren't* there with him. They've gone to church for the day; they always do on a Sunday, and don't come back until amost dark. No matter how much I hate Mr Morgan – and I do! – I can't stand by while his poor sheep burn to death!'

Braddock had stopped laughing. This was serious, then. Very serious indeed. 'Yurr right, gel. He does need us. Come now, help me harness up the sledge. We'll overtake the fire in a jiffy and see what we can do.' He reared back in surprise as Lisabeth flung impulsive arms around his neck. 'There, there, gel! Don't take on so. He's not in any danger, this man yurr so detest, so don't yurr go breaking yurr heart afore there's the need.'

She pulled away at once, haughty with indignation that he was determined to misunderstand. Couldn't he see that she was simply doing what any decent person would under the circumstances? 'Let's hurry,' she said, crisp and cold.

Braddock cackled, laughing at her. She ignored him.

His horse was a solid little roan with a nervous disposition. It jog-trotted briskly down the slope and along the undulating rim of the plain but constantly tossed its head and twisted its neck as far as the reins would allow, tossing them fearful, white-walled, one-eyed glances.

Braddock sat up on the sledge in his mouldering armchair while Lisabeth stood behind, gripping the chair's threadbare back while she braced her feet against the bumps and jolts of the precarious platform. When they set out the fire's front was over two miles away and travelling away north at hot speed, so for a long time they never seemed to get any closer. They galloped along through a sweep of dry land clumped with tussocks and an occasional tea-tree bush or, where the soil was damper, flax or a cluster of cabbage trees, tall spindly trees with long branches culminating in clusters of swordlike leaves held erect towards the sky. To their right lay the sea, bright azure and waving at them from between scallops of sand dunes, while to the left some fifty yards away lay the edge of the fire's leavings, a vast burned hide of blackened earth on which smouldered lumpy blood-red remains of what once were tussock plants.

As they sped through the usually empty landscape their approach startled dozens of creatures that had fled the fire and were seeking new refuge in the skimpy ground-cover. Rabbits and mice started up and fled again running in directionless confusion. Flightless brown *wekas* darted, heads down, across their path, while the orange-legged *pukekos* flashed their white tails as they loped down towards the sea.

Overhead circled other birds: the hawklike harriers, or *kahu* which had been also rudely evicted from their territory; speckled pipits dipping as they flew; and tiny blue *kotare*, or kingfishers. These were outnumbered in hundreds by flocks of flapping, squawking gulls that were already beginning to congregate around the sand dunes. As soon as the ground had cooled sufficiently for them to land they would be foraging in the ashes for succulent roasted morsels: insects, grubs and lizards. For them the fire was a banquet.

After a time they began to close the distance between them and the fire-line. Now the sky darkened as a thin pall of smoke flurried around them, and suddenly the air smelt sooty as millions of specks of burned matter, some still alight, whirled and eddied through the air. Occasionally, where a larger fragment alighted in the dry tussock, a candle-flame flared briefly, as if set there by a conjuror.

A spark whipped against Lisabeth's neck, stinging like a gnat and causing her to swat at it with a suddenness that almost lost her her footing. At that moment the roan whinnied and bucked in the traces.

'The wind's changing, gel!' shouted Braddock. 'It's dangerous. We'd better—'

'No, please! We must go on,' pleaded Lisabeth, coughing as she inhaled a gasp of smoke.

But the roan was frightened. It shied, pawing the air above a tussock plant that was bursting alight directly in its path. The sledge slewed sideways. Struggling to hold the reins taut, Braddock unrolled the stock-whip that was hooked to a peg fixed to the side of his chair.

'Please don't – the poor thing's terrified already,' cried Lisabeth. Oddly, she felt no fear at all, as if the act of dashing to the rescue had coated her in an armour of immunity. Her mind reassured her that so far they were safe; there was no real heat in all this billowing spark-laced smoke, and the crackle and sigh of the flames still seemed distant. What they were experiencing here was just a blow-back, a freak twisting of wind.

Braddock thought otherwise. 'We'll turn back,' he decided, dragging on the reins and forcing the roan to a standstill. 'No sense us risking our lives, darrlin' gel.'

Lisabeth was furious with him. 'We've come so far! We're almost there! We can't—' Seeing it was useless to argue, she scrambled down and ran ahead to seize the bridle, jerking impatiently until Braddock relaxed his grip and the sledge began to move uncertainly forward again. The roan whinnied with a blast of tickling breath in her face and tossed its head with energy that all but broke her determined hold on the leather bridle-strips.

172

Braddock was shouting at her, but she ignored him, concentrating all her attention on the seemingly impossible task of coaxing the stupid stubborn horse forward. How was it done? She thought hard, her mind jumping from the recollection of one of Charles's stories to another. How had he coped when that out-of-control bushfire swept across the road out of Waitamanui, blocking them off from home? Of course, a blindfold!

'All I did were wrap Mrs Stafford's shawl about the creature's face, and from that very second he ambled along sweet as honey,' he'd said.

Lisabeth had no shawl, and her apron had been hung on its peg before she left the house, but she did have her bonnet, her large-brimmed, out-of-fashion bonnet. One hand ripped the string-bow undone, while with the other she tried to control the pitching roan, which took advantage of her loosened grip to misbehave badly, rearing up and plunging down in the traces while Lisabeth was jerked and flapped by one arm like a broken marionette, and it was all she could do to keep her feet, stumbling and stretching as she was flung from crouch to tip-toes, her arm spasming in pain. Bonnet off, she immediately clapped it over the roan's forehead so that the stiff rim covered both rolling white-ringed eyes.

The effect was magical. At once the horse stood bolt-still, trembling, its hide twitching and quivering as if the peppering of hot sparks was no worse than a torment of flies. 'There, now!' she soothed, her smoke-roughened voice alive with triumph as with both hands now she swiftly wound the bonnet-strings around the harness to fix the makeshift blindfold firmly into place. This time when she tugged at the reins the roan stumbled along beside her in blind obedience.

The smoke thickened; abruptly a dense grey quilt wrapped around them, suffocatingly snug, while bright sparks of burning cinder cascaded from the sky, stinging where they landed on her face and hands and causing the poor horse to shrill in fresh fear. For a moment, when she was struggling to breathe, Lisabeth understood what danger they might be in, but just as suddenly as it had clamped down the smoke dissipated again and the giddy panic dispelled.

'On we go!' she cried, her voice raw with smoke. Yanking hard on the reins, she began to run, dragging the roan into a shambling trot.

'Gel, yurr crazy!' yelled Braddock, but when she looked back through the thinning veil of smoke he was grinning his yellowed gap-toothed smile at her.

The encouragement lent her strength and speed. Now she was pulling the horse, now it was dragging her as they lurched over the rough ground. Every step her wooden-soled boots took jarred right up through her body and her head sang with noise: the thump of her pounding legs, the rasping of her breath, and closer now the fire noises – the sharp prickle of snapping tussock blades, the deep sigh of the wind and hissing of the flames. Smoke scorched her throat, but she felt good – strong and purposeful. *No harm can come to us now,* she assured herself as she forced herself on, pushing, dragging, striding forward in the thin grey fog.

Then without warning the wind was pushing at their backs and they were completely in the clear with the sky open and clean above them. Lisabeth blinked sore gritty eyes as she scanned the dazzling sunlit plain for some sight of Rhys. On this dry terrain the sheep would be difficult to see, for their coats blended in almost perfectly with the yellow-grey coloration of the tussock.

They were ahead of the fire now; it had been more frighteningly close than she had realized, but it was moving away now steered by the swing of the wind, a great dark monster of pulsating smoke that reared high above the hills as it danced away across the tussock on a multitude of bright orange claws. For a moment she rested, watching it as she untied the blindfold, her flesh creeping with the relief of danger averted.

'There he is, gel! Look there, along the river-line!' Braddock's face was smeared with soot that caked into all the cross-hatched lines of his face and neck. *What a scarecrow he looks!* she thought tiredly, never thinking that she must look equally grimy. She clung to the horse's drooping neck for support as she obediently gazed in the direction of Braddock's pointing finger. Her legs trembled with fatigue and her fingers seemed oddly stiff as she plucked at the tightly wound bonnet-strings.

She had the greatest difficulty distinguishing what Braddock interpreted as being a figure on horseback. At first she couldn't even see the river through the red haze that was dancing in her vision, and it was not until her brain cleared that she picked out the darker line of flax bushes and cabbage trees that wound across the plain in the middle distance. This side of the river, far towards the foothills, a dark small shape, as insubstantial as a snippet of thread, was moving slowly back and forth.

174

'Listen!' commanded Braddock.

She tried to still the clamour of her lungs and heart to strain for the noise his ear was cocked towards – how could he see and hear such faint small things at his age? – and then there it was, a noise so subtle she had to absorb it rather than hear it, the unmistakable low bleating of thousands of sheep.

Braddock squinted at the tiny figure, then swivelled his head to look at the fast-moving fire.

'Ay, yurr was right, gel. He's going to need our help, I'm picking. And fast, too. There's never a traa-dy-liooar here!'

SEVENTEEN

RHYS WAS EXHAUSTED. His lungs ached and his eyes burned. Though he had wrapped a kerchief around his face to filter the smoke, he was breathing and eating soot. Soot had clogged the creases at the corners of his eyes, matted his hair, brows and lashes, and was gritty on his clothes and on Polka's hide. Soot thickened the perspiration that trickled into his eyes, it leaked into his mouth, and when he patted Polka's neck he saw that his hand was veined with rivulets of sweat and soot.

'It will be over soon,' he promised.

They stood above the river-bank watching a slow grey stream of sheep struggle across the shingly bed. It had been easy rounding the sheep up to this point but, just as leading a horse to water and making it drink were two different things, leading the sheep and making them swim had been acts of completely contrasting difficulty. They would not get into the water at first, and it took himself, his whip and the efforts of both dogs to chase that first group splashing across the shallows before the others, seeing the way was safe and panicked by the heat and smoke at their backs, had funnelled down into the river-bed. Quite a number had been lost, swept away when they missed their footing and their wool became waterlogged, but now approximately half the flock were on each bank with more going through the crossing all the time like sands through an hour-glass. He'd beaten it. Rhys congratulated himself. That wind-change of a few minutes before had removed the immediate danger; with a bit of luck and a steady breeze the fire might bypass this slight hollow completely.

But as he watched the herd, occasionally whistling a direction

176

to the dogs that were chafing reluctant ones along, he felt a shiver go over him, then another, and realized that it was the wind swinging around again and bathing him in a cool draught. After the earlier incessant blasts of scalding air the freshness was welcome, but for only a split second. Then Rhys realized the significance of it, and a far deeper chill raked through him.

Twisting his neck, he saw the dancing fire advancing this way again. *Damn!* he cursed, and dug his heels into Polka's flanks, prodding the chestnut hack into a trot as again he began to ride the outer rim of his herd, chivvying and scolding them with hoarse shouts and crisp snaps of the whip, forcing them to compact forward, to hurry the spill across the river. He didn't hear Braddock calling to him from the opposite bank, nor did he see the confusion it caused as Braddock and Lisabeth forged their horse and sledge through the flock.

A sudden blast of heat swatted Rhys with such force that Polka jumped sideways, neighing in terror. *This is it!* he thought, with bewilderment because it had come upon him much faster than he imagined possible. All along the river-bank the flax bushes rustled then flared into flame. He had time only to swing Polka's head around on a tight rein before a vomiting thickness of smoke rolled over them, obscuring everything from view.

Polka went frantic, plunging down the bank into the thick mass of sheep, wallowing around and over their bodies as if she was floundering through mud, plunging and stumbling as she lurched towards the river.

Somehow Rhys held on. He had lost the reins and clung to the pommel, his knees gripping into the saddle-flaps so tightly that they cramped. Around him was pandemonium, terrified sheep bleating and a hell's-mouth blast of smoke and sparks and unbelievable heat. Suddenly a great tongue of flame licked across the hollow, triggering an uproar of shrieking bleats that completely unnerved Polka. Rearing up on her hind legs, she plunged forward, tucking her head down, kicking up her heels and flinging Rhys from the saddle. He landed across the back of a sheep with a blow so hard that nausea was jolted through his body. Heat raged red before his eyes, there was a strong sheepy smell in his face and his brain buzzed with screaming noise. Then Rhys felt himself being lifted swiftly and gently as if by a giant cushion of cloud that bore him upward. Everything receded behind him. The din, the fetid blast of conflagration, the pain

that racked his body and the panic that paralysed his mind – all of
it melted away into a cool grey mist.

'Dear Lord, we're too late, gel,' muttered Braddock as the flame
reared up like a wave and came whooshing down, sending boiling
smoke racing across the river with a wall of heat that beat them
back from where they stood panting and thigh-deep in milling
sheep at the water's edge. Out of the turmoil had bolted Polka,
overtaking the dogs in her mad flight from the fire. 'He's like as
done for, our Mr Maughold,' he added. 'That's a bad one, that
is.'

'We don't know he's done for,' argued Lisabeth. She noticed
that after that single high lashing of flame there was no more,
though the fire was fiercely spluttering through the flax bushes on
either side of the large depression where the sheep were herded.
Smoke made it difficult to see, but out of the turmoil sheep were
still dashing on stuttering hoofs. Many had smouldering patches
in their wool and all steamed as they plunged into the river below
the smoke-level and floundered bleating through the sooty water.

Lisabeth looked at Braddock. 'I'm going to find him,' she
croaked. 'Stay here with the sledge.' And before he could argue
she had scrambled down the bank and was wading in a cascade of
splashes across the water. Her ankle turned on a rock, causing her
to stagger, then as she reached the opposite bank a fear-
maddened sheep hurtled into her and sent her floundering full-
length into the water, but she pulled herself dripping and sore up
the bank where through flapping curtains of smoke she surveyed
the scene with an ominous clawing feeling of disquiet.

All around the rim of the hollow lay a solid wall of still sheep,
piled up where they had trampled and suffocated each other to
death. She glimpsed the heaped carcasses in swirling snatches as
the smoke billowed and lifted, and the sight sent her optimism
plummeting. All that was alive here was the disorientated remnants of this flock who trotted in blind little circles following each
other, sometimes having the good luck to follow sheep who were
tagging behind the string that were dashing to safety but most
milling uselessly, tongues swollen and lolling, eyes staring in
terror.

Pushing through them as they butted and knocked against her
sodden skirts, Lisabeth called, 'Rhys, Rhys!' in a voice choked
with helpless tears, raw with smoke. Heat smothered her, there
was a terrible odour of scorched wool that clung in her nostrils,

making her heave, but worst was the hopelessness that pressed on her like a heavy hand. This was her fault. Just by walking into the roadway last night and speaking to Mr Fox she could have prevented all this from happening.

'I'm sorry, Rhys, I'm so sorry,' she whispered, sobs lacerating her throat. It was appalling to think that she, who would never knowingly harm a living creature, was responsible for all this carnage, this extravagance of stinking smouldering death.

And probably for his death, too.

He'd saved her life once, and this was how she'd repaid him.

The enormity of her guilt crushed her. She stood dumbly in the middle of the ghastly scene, blinded by smoke and tears. A sheep bumped behind her knees, and she stumbled forward, shoulders slumped, past caring. Then another thumped her, shoving her sideways, and this time when she tried to regain her balance her wet skirts weighted her legs and she fell. Her hands flung out to protect herself, but she landed with a thud that completely dispirited her, and lay there for a long moment, lacking the will to continue the search for what would almost certainly be Rhys's body.

What's the use? she thought. *I'll let Uncle Charles and the McFallishes find him when they come looking this evening. He's dead, and I've killed him. Oh, Rhys I didn't mean to. Truly I didn't!*

She lay crying, face pressed into the sheep-smelling dirt, then wearily decided to go back to where Braddock would be waiting – frantic, too, no doubt. Her fingers grasped what she at first perceived to be a tuft of grass, and she tugged on it to pull herself up, but then realized that what she held between her fingers was cloth.

She sat up and crawled forward to discover that the cloth was part of Rhys's shirt-tail, and that he was sprawled on his side, legs splayed, his body almost obscured by the carcasses of two dead sheep, one at his back and the other pressing over an outflung arm, pinning him down. His free hand was raised, fingers knotted in the wool as if he was trying to push the animal away when death overtook him. Lisabeth gazed into his blackened face then turned her head away and vomited feebly into the dust.

When she had recovered a little she stood shakily and seized the sheep's front legs, dragging it clear. Rhys stretched his arm out, but when his fingers were tugged free of the wool his hand flopped down lifelessly.

179

'Oh, Rhys!' cried Lisabeth in an agony of remorse. Flopping to her knees, she cradled his poor head between her hands, then with the hem of her dress sponged some of the soot away from his face. The cool water partially revived him, and he moaned. It was a tiny sound, almost imperceptible in the tumult of other noises, but Lisabeth knew with a heart-leap of joy that he was still alive.

Gabbling a prayer of relief, she dabbed at his face, her heart swelling with tenderness. One arm stole around his neck and she eased his head into her lap, cradling him just as she used to cradle Andrew before he grew big enough to struggle and push away. Her whole body was thrilling with joy. He was alive! He was all right! She sponged the strong lines and planes of his face and slipped a daring hand into the opening of his shirt to check his heartbeat, and all the while her mind sang with a blithe glorious freedom. It had been hell to know that she had killed him; now she was surely in heaven.

He stirred. She withdrew her hand quickly from where it caressed his warm, lightly matted chest. Gently she resumed stroking his face with her cool damp hem. She had never really looked at him before, and now she examined his features with a devouring interest, as if for this suspended moment he belonged utterly to her. How thick and surprisingly curving his eyelashes were, and how delicate the translucent skin of his eyelids, contrasting with the bronzed tan of the rest of his face. One bold finger traced the full curve of his lower lip and below the sooty tickle of his moustache the finely shaped upper lip, then with her palm she stroked his stubbly jaw, smiling to think that he'd taken Gwynne's horror of his beard so seriously that he'd shaved it off to please her. How dear he was!

She was smoothing the faint squint-lines between his eyebrows with a fingertip when his head stirred restlessly and his eyelids flickered.

She lifted her hand at once. There was a pause, then slowly his eyes opened. They were bloodshot and dazed. He looked up into her face like someone still in a dream. Her heart stopped when she saw recognition in his eyes.

'Mary?' he whispered in a puzzled voice. 'Mary . . . why . . .?' Then his eyes rolled shut and his head lolled heavy in her lap again.

Lisabeth pushed him away with distaste, scrambling from under him and stumbling away through the swirling smoke. Every step she took tore another sob from her body. *Mary!* She was sick, she was disgusted, she wished that he really was dead. He was hateful. She loathed him, she detested him. Why *wasn't* he dead?

Braddock couldn't understand it at all. The lass risked her life to go haring into the maw of the inferno to rescue Rhys but the moment she discovered him alive, it seemed, she lost all interest in him. She wouldn't touch him. Braddock had to manhandle him up on to the sledge by himself and, because Lisabeth refused to sit on the floor and hold his head, Rhys had to be propped in the armchair. Braddock then had to lead the horse while Lisabeth strode out beside them in sullen silence. It was all completely mystifying, and a most unsatisfactory way to travel, especially with an unconscious man being jolted about on the sledge.

'No!' she said emphatically when Braddock suggested they take Rhys down to the Stafford household. 'Nobody's there but me, and I don't want anything to do with him. Keep him at your cottage, Mr Braddock, at least until this evening when Aunty Gwynne returns.'

'What's wrong with yurr, gel?' asked Braddock, sweeping off his cavernous hat and scratching his freckled pate in bewilderment. 'Yurr saved his life. Don't yurr want—?'

'No I didn't!' said Lisabeth with stubborn ferocity. '*You* saved his life, Mr Braddock, and you take the credit.'

'But that weren't right.'

'It's right by me. I want you to promise me that you'll never say a word about this, about my part in it, not to anybody.'

'But, darrlin' gel—'

'Promise me!' she said. 'Promise!'

'If yurr insist . . .'

'I do,' she said and, leaving him to lead the horse, she loped on ahead, her boots striding out across the charred earth. By the time Braddock reached the coast she was lost from sight.

Rhys was suffering from smoke inhalation and severe concussion. He swam back into consciousness shortly after they arrived back at the cottage. Braddock returned from the spring with a dipperful of water to find Rhys blinking up at the branches of the *pohutukawa* tree under which he had been placed.

'Yes,' he said in response to Braddock's question. 'I don't think anything's broken, but I've a headache you wouldn't believe.'

181

'I believe yurr, all right,' cackled Braddock. 'Took a tumble down these very cliffs myself, once. Mind yurr, my head near to burstin' asunder, I did.'

'Is . . . is that what happened?'

'Bless yurr, no. Yurr took a fall from yurr horse. In the fire.'

'Oh.' Rhys propped himself up on his elbows and slowly turned his head from side to side, taking his bearings. The pain in his head was phenomenal. 'My horse? The fire? Oh, no . . .' Sinking back again, he closed his eyes, remembering. A stench of smoke clogging his chest, the horse plunging in panic, cool mist and someone bending over him, touching his face with delicious tenderness. Mary . . .? Why did he think of Mary? She was dead . . . Had he died, too, out there on the plain? Had Mary reached out from beyond the grave to touch him? He shivered.

Braddock tugged the coat he'd covered him with up higher under Rhys's chin. 'Soon as yurr feeling better, Mr Maughold, we'll go on down, see if yurr sister's home.'

'*Lisabeth*,' said Rhys suddenly. 'Lisabeth was there, wasn't she?'

'Here,' said Braddock, slopping the water as he raised Rhys's head to drink. 'Sip this. Yurr'll feel better.'

Rhys pushed it away. 'Tell me what happened today,' he said. 'Tell me everything . . . Lisabeth. What was she doing there?'

'So I knew half yurr sheep was in that place from yesterday when I were out there shooting rabbits,' finished Braddock. 'I got the sledge and rode out, found yurr and brought yurr back.'

There's more to it than that, thought Rhys. *Lisabeth was there, I saw her.* 'What about Lisa—?'

'Yurr horse is safe, and yurr dogs,' added Braddock hastily. 'But five, six hundred of yurr herd are gone.'

'Could be worse.' The pressure in his head was intolerable. A sharp sweet nausea was rising in his throat. 'I could've lost them all. Damned plains fire. I wonder how it started?'

Braddock drew a deep shuddering breath. 'On purpose. I can't prove it, Mr Maughold, but it seems to me that yurr friend Thomas Fox had a pretty paw in this. He's paying the cockatoos to harass yurr, just like they did to me. After the fire was set every man-jack of them went out for the day. 'Course, yurr can't prove it, but—'

'I'll prove it,' said Rhys. He tried to sit up; dizziness swamped

182

him, and he fell back again, but he *was* feeling better. Already the pain in his skull had blunted. Fox! He might have known.

'I'll prove it. And I'll make him pay.'

Braddock cackled. 'Due respect, but yurr'll never manage that.'

'Just watch me,' Rhys told him.

EIGHTEEN

NEXT DAY WAS COLD AND BLUSTERY. Rhys was glad of it; he was flushed with fever and blinded by the same tenacious headache, so the sharp wind kept him alert on the short ride into Christchurch. What he had to do must be accomplished without delay. Later he could collapse.

'You seem ill, Mr Morgan,' said Fox, not bothering to rise when the single-eyebrowed Featherston showed him in.

'Please don't get up,' Rhys said, glancing at where the maiden-hair ferns flickered in the cold white grate. 'I was in a fire.'

'Really?' Fox continued to read his newspaper. As before, his boots rested negligently on his leather-topped desk.

Rhys waited. He nursed his patience carefully. Traffic rumbled by in the street outside. When five carts had gone past Rhys said: 'I'll bid you good day and go to find another buyer. My time is obviously more valuable than yours.'

Boots swung to the floor. 'Buyer?' he said. 'Do you mean that? You've come here today offering to sell your property?'

'Why else would I come?' Rhys asked coldly. 'But since you've got more pressing matters to attend to I'll go elsewhere.'

'No!' said Fox, standing. He wet his lips. 'I mean . . . why are you selling?'

He's no actor, noted Rhys, contemptuously thinking that Fox looked like a guilty ape. 'I'm astonished you ask, Mr Fox.'

'What are you implying?'

'Implying?' Any change of expression hurt, but Rhys forced his eyes wide for an ingenuous expression. 'Implying, Mr Fox? I'm merely astonished that you haven't heard about my run of bad luck.'

'I've heard nothing but, then, I'm a busy man. I've no time for gossip.'

'I'll just bet you haven't,' Rhys said as amiably as he could. Settling himself in the tooled-leather chair opposite Fox's desk, he stared at him blandly.

'What bad luck have you suffered?' asked Fox after a pause. 'Brandy, Mr Morgan?'

'Thank you. Oh, just the usual run of things. Little incidents. I blame the Maoris for most of them, and perhaps an odd poacher or two.'

'Quite right. I believe your predecessor had similar troubles,' he said, handing Rhys a balloon goblet. Rhys noticed that he wore even more rings – on both hands – than Lawrence Rennie had done. As soon as he received the goblet, while Fox was still pouring his own, Rhys began to drink. It was an excellent Cognac. 'To your good health,' said Fox, raising his glass in salutation.

Not acknowledging the courtesy, Rhys said: 'Yes, I do believe that Mr Braddock had his share of worries. You indulge in gossip sufficiently to learn of those?'

The skin over Fox's cheekbones warmed with dull colour. 'The man had the impudence to accuse *me*!'

'Fancy!'

Fox glared at him. 'All run-holders have problems from time to time.'

'But some more than others, eh, Mr Fox?'

'What do you mean? If you've come here to insult me—'

'I see. I *am* taking up your time,' said Rhys, half-rising.

Fox was immediately before him with the chased silver decanter. 'This brandy is over fifty years old,' he remarked. 'It was distilled when Napoleon was still the Emperor of France. Tell me, Mr Morgan, what do you hope to realize as a price for the property?' He settled behind his desk as if in a lair, his face watchful.

He's all but rubbing his hands together, thought Rhys, amused. Feigning innocence, he said: 'Don't you want to hear about the fire? You *do* recall the fire? I mentioned it when I first walked in.'

Fox stood up quickly. It was clear that he was wrestling to control his temper, for Rhys glimpsed his tight angry expression as he walked to the window where he stood staring out at the racecourse, his back rigid.

'I had a little fire yesterday. It destroyed almost half of my stock. Because of the loss I'm going to have to sell. I've no choice.'

'That's a pity.'

185

'No it's not. You want to buy. I want to sell. I was bored with farming anyway.'

'What's your price?'

Rhys looked at his fingernails. 'Thirty thousand guineas.'

'Thirty—' Fox wheeled around. 'But the mortgage was only fourteen.'

'True.'

Fox tugged at his grey side-whiskers. 'That's robbery!'

'It's quite realistic.' He flicked a speck of dust from the knee of his elegant jodhpurs. 'I know you are determined to have the land, you see. If I sold it to anyone else, I'd get twenty-seven; you'd have to offer thirty to secure it then – assuming the first buyer was willing to sell – so this way we'll save a lot of time and trouble.'

'You're a thief!'

'I'm a businessman, just as you are a businessman. *Just* as you are,' he added with deliberate emphasis. 'If you're not interested, I'll go elsewhere.' He shrugged elaborately. 'It's all the same to me.'

Fox glared at him with such naked loathing that for a full minute Rhys was sure he had misjudged. What had Leonie said? *Papa wants that land more than anything in the world . . .?* Rhys was counting on it.

'Very well.' And Fox exhaled slowly.

'Just one thing,' Rhys said, as if there had never been any doubt. 'I need a down payment. A deposit. In cash, now.' When Fox stared he shrugged again. 'There's a private debt I am required to meet. A small thing. I need nineteen hundred guineas.'

'Impossible.'

Rhys smiled. 'Very well. I was going to sell some of my merinos to meet the debt, but Sir Kenneth will understand. In fact he'll be jubilant. He's hinted several times that he would jump at the chance to add my property to his already impressive collection of assets. Thank you for the brandy, and good—'

Before Rhys had uttered three words past 'Sir Kenneth', Fox pulled the bell-rope that hung behind his desk. Featherston loomed morosely in the doorway. 'Fetch me nineteen hundred guineas, now. And a receipt,' ordered Fox. 'Make it out to Mr Rhys Morgan.'

'Rhys Morgan Esquire,' interrupted Rhys.

Fox glared at him.

Rhys leaned back and steepled his fingers together over his

186

mouth, hiding a smile. Despite his ferocious headache he was enjoying himself mightily.

Some time later an elegant black coach rolled up the dirt road and squeaked to a halt on the square of waste ground between the Staffords' and the row of cockatoo cottages. A couple of beaten-looking curs slunk out from under the Nevins' tank-stand and circled warily, taking care to keep their distance from the glossy black horses. Eyeing them – and the surroundings – with disdain, the liveried coachman climbed down to open the door.

'It's that nice Sir Kenneth!' cried Gwynne, removing her top apron and hobbling out to greet him. 'Mr Stafford, we have a visitor!' Charles came out from the implement-shed where he had been relaxing as he perused seed catalogues.

When the coach came by Andrew recognized Polka, saddled but riderless, trailing behind on a long trace-harness. Dropping his push-hoe, he hopped across the rows of young cabbages and raced along the drain-line, catching up just as Leonie Gammerwoth was emerging from the carriage. 'Wow!' he said to her. 'What a beautiful carriage! Is it yours?'

Hearing the enthusiasm, Lisabeth peeked from behind the muslin curtains and her heart beat fast in dismay when she saw Leonie alighting stunningly attired in a pink-sprigged wide-skirted taffeta gown. *How vulgar!* she thought, noting how her breasts swelled up over the deep scalloped neckline. Uncle Charles obviously thought her fetching; he was bowing and scraping as if she was royalty, while Andrew gaped at her in such open admiration that Lisabeth wondered despairingly why the boy unerringly bestowed his hero-worship on all the very worst people.

Because she didn't notice Polka, Lisabeth wrongly assumed that Leonie had come calling on Rhys and was spitefully pleased that he wasn't there, and she'd made the journey for nothing. . . . Unless Auntie Gwynne asked her in! That was very likely, Gwynne being of such a hospitable nature, but the prospect was too horrible, thought Lisabeth, suddenly recalling how bedraggled she looked with hands scorched, face poxed with tiny blisters and her hair in frizzled tatters across her forehead. No doubt the glamorous Mrs Gammerwoth would burst into peals of laughter at the very sight of her, and Lisabeth relished even less the prospect of having to recite over again the lies about how the hem of her dress had caught alight while she was boiling the billy to make a cup of tea, and how she had burned herself as she beat out the flames.

Fortunately, Leonie was no keener to come inside than Lisabeth was to receive her. Though she thought these strangely lower-class relatives were quaint folk, curiosity was not strong in her character, and Leonie only ever bothered with things that interested her – a trait which made her appear stronger and more single-minded than she was.

'I've just come to deliver something special,' she told them, smiling flirtatiously at Charles, amused by his flustering. 'I would have preferred to take him home with me, but my husband is singularly lacking in understanding when I try to adopt stray creatures.'

'It's all right, Mrs Stafford. The lady's merely being divesting, aren't you, Mrs Gammerwoth? She's brought Rhys home,' he added in a hiss.

'Is he ill? Oh dear. I tried to stop him from going into town. He should have stayed in bed . . . He was very sick last night . . . Effects from the fire, you understand, and I pleaded with him this morning not to do anything rash—'

'It's all *right*, Mr Stafford,' insisted Charles as he and the coach-driver carried Rhys between them from the carriage, each with an arm about his shoulders, his feet dragging, his head lolled on the driver's chest. His face was white as mist.

Flicking her pink silk gloves, Leonie said: 'Poor boy. He was in Papa's outer office, stretched out on the couch.' Lowering her voice, she added: 'Papa and he had been drinking brandy to celebrate!'

Gwynne was so perplexed by the notion of Rhys and Mr Fox drinking together that she did not know how to reply. When the coach-driver returned and handed out an unfamiliar black carpet-bag she was even more mystified.

'Yes, it is his,' Leonie told her, her dark-brown eyes sparkling with delight. Events of the morning had put her in a splendid mood. 'In there, Mrs Stafford, are nineteen hundred guineas. Didn't you know?' she added in response to Gwynne's baffled expression. 'Your brother came into Papa's office today and offered to sell him this entire property. This is money on account.'

'He's daft, he's barmy, sure and he's completely deranged!' ranted Charles. 'Unless there's a juicy profit in this for him. Unless—'

'Please, Mr Stafford!' Gwynne shut the bedroom door behind her. She was crying. 'He's not well. Please don't be angry.'

'I'm more than angry, I'm fulminated! After all my hard work he's just up and selling without so much as a by-your- leave . . . And to Fox! I knew all along that he wasn't to be trusted. Sure and I knew—'

'Please, Mr Stafford!' And Gwynne flung herself sobbing from the room.

Lisabeth said nothing. With a large white apron covering her bottle-green dress she was standing at the table kneading bread dough, a mechanical tedious task that allowed plenty of time to think. Right now Lisabeth did not want to think. She could see Gwynne out at the rain-barrel, drawing water into the laundry-bucket as she picked up a pair of Andrew's breeches and began to lather them with hard soap and scrub with the old worn brush. She seemed so upset that Lisabeth couldn't bear to look at her, and instead concentrated her attention on dividing the dough into loaves and setting them to rise. Rhys would never have sold to his enemy if he knew. Lisabeth tried to tell herself that she was pleased, that this could be Mary's revenge for the hurt that Rhys had dealt her. Exhausted, ill and beaten, he was as weak now as Mary had been just before she died. As alone, too, for he had antagonized Charles and turned the family against him. Look at the distress Gwynne was suffering because of his selfishness. A parting of the ways was inevitable now, and with this legacy of bitterness Lisabeth could be confident that they never would see Rhys again after that. *Good.* Wasn't that just what she wanted?

When she had washed her hands and tidied everything away she sneaked another look at Gwynne. She was still scrubbing, still crying. Tormented by guilt, Lisabeth went out to her.

'Don't mind me, dear,' she said, lifting a ravaged face as Lisabeth removed the scrubbing-brush from her grasp and took over the task. 'It's just . . . it's just that it's one of my dreams that Rhys and Mr Stafford would become good friends. Rhys was such a bonny baby, and I'm so fond of him . . . it would mean every-thing to me to have harmony . . .'

'What about leaving here?' asked Lisabeth, for this was the detail that evoked most guilt in her mind. 'Don't you mind the thought of starting all over again?'

Gwynne sighed. She had such a desolate expression that Lisabeth knew the thought was like an insurmountable obstacle, but typically all Gwynne said was: 'It will be so hard for Mr Stafford. Each time we move it comes as a blow to him, one that takes longer and longer to recover from. He's not a young man, you know, Lisabeth. He's not—' And lifting her to apron to cup her face she subsided again into sobs.

Lisabeth was stricken.

Wrapped in a cool grey mist Rhys slept, and as he slept he dreamed. Lisabeth's face came swimming up through the veils of consciousness, surfacing, sinking and resurfacing. She sponged his scorching face. Her every touch was redolent with sweet tenderness. Her unfathomable eyes were alight with soft joy. She saved his life. In his dream the fire almost consumed him; he was suffocating, dying, and she saved him.

It was definitely her.

He woke. Gwynne's face was leaning over him. Gwynne's plump sharp-featured face with the dull eyes and downy upper lip. The lip quivered. Her eyes filled with tears. 'Oh, Rhys,' she said in her lilting Manx voice. 'You've been so ill . . .'

Lisabeth avoided him, speeding through her household chores then fleeing to the fields so that she wouldn't be asked to look in on him. She listened dumbly to Charles's angry ranting, but in her mind all his words turned against her. This twist of events so horrified her that she stopped mentioning Andrew's schooling. And when, on the fourth day, Rhys got up and sat in the sunshine Lisabeth didn't even object to Andrew's rushing over to chat to him.

After dinner that night Rhys walked up to visit Braddock, taking some of the money he had obtained from Fox and a lantern to light his way home. As soon as he had gone Charles burst out in anger again, and Lisabeth wondered if it was cowardice or consideration for Gwynne that kept him from railing at Rhys to his face. 'Thirty pieces of silver!' he rasped at Gwynne, though the significance of this comparison evaded all his listeners. 'He's perfidified us all for thirty pieces of silver.'

Gwynne cried. Lisabeth put a weary arm about her quivering shoulders, and guilt pressed outwards from within her with the uncomfortable urgency of an unlanced boil. She could take no more.

I'll tell him tomorrow. The resolution came to her as she plaited her hair into pigtail ropes and bound the ends with rag. It was a sudden, emphatic decision that she knew was irreversible. Kneeling to pray, she clenched her eyes tight and mechanically repeated her private litany. She felt cold and calm, but when she lay in bed, gazing at the silver hillside beyond the window, a deep chill took hold of her and she wondered whether she could scrape up enough courage to confess.

Long after everyone except her had fallen asleep a lantern-light appeared on the ridge-top and began a slow descent, illuminating a tiny thread of darkness as it came. Rhys.

Impulsively Lisabeth scrambled out of bed and hastily dressed, flinging her bottle-green gown on over her nightgown, thrusting her arms into the tight sleeves (and hearing a familiar faint tearing of perished fibres) and buttoning the neck-to-waist opening with swift practised flicks of her fingers.

Circling around the cockatoos' houses, stumbling in the dark, she intercepted Rhys near the foot of the slope, startling him.

'Lisabeth!' He held the lantern aloft. 'I was thinking about you.'

His voice was harsh. *Mr Braddock's told him*, she thought.

He hadn't. 'What in the world are you doing wandering about out here?'

All resolution receded, leaving her stranded in foolishness. 'I was out walking.'

Stepping closer, he held the light almost into her face, seizing her shoulder and holding her still when she tried to turn away. 'Do you always wear your nightgown under your dress when you go out walking?' he asked, noting the bunched neck-ribbons and twisted collar protruding from the neck of her gown where she couldn't get the buttons fastened. That detail he noticed quickly and in passing; it was her face he was studying, the tiny blisters, the scorch-mark at the side of her chin. She *smelt* charred, or was that him, the stench of the fire inescapably in his nostrils, the images of it superimposed on his vision?

She was saying something. 'I'm worried about Uncle Charles and Aunty Gwynne. I couldn't sleep, so I came for a walk.'

'Ah,' he smiled. Foolish, then, that first flickering notion that she had come in search of him. 'You like walking in the dark, don't you? But you mustn't fret about the Staffords. Gwynne worries quite sufficiently about her husband. Any of your concern would be superfluous, not to mention a monumental waste of energy.'

'You're angry with him, aren't you?'

'Extremely angry. But don't let that concern you, either.' How tragic she looked. The lamplight thinned her, pushed shadows under her cheekbones, hollowed her eye-sockets. She was a waif. 'Hey, don't be upset. You should be happy, a beautiful young

191

woman at your age.' As he spoke the trivial sentences he realized that he meant them. It was important to him that she be happy. '*Are* you happy, Lisabeth?'

She wasn't listening. Her mind was occupied with the far greater problems that seemed to be jumbled together and stuffed into her head. He had to repeat the question, and then she plucked out the uppermost thought and gave that to him. 'I'd be happy if Andrew was going to a proper school.'

He had to laugh. How old was she – seventeen? eighteen? – and worrying above all about her little brother's education. 'Shall I talk to Charles about it? Though I doubt I'll be able to exert much influence there once Charles and I have, shall we say, "unburdened our minds" to each other. There's going to be some real unpleasantness, I'm afraid. Some nasty things have been happening, and I'm pretty sure that Charles has known about them all along.'

'What . . . what makes you think that?'

'There's nothing going on within ten miles that Charles doesn't know about almost before it happens. He's an incorrigible gossip, always eager to pass on tasty scraps of information, so why, then, didn't he bother to pass this on to me? Not that I could expect gratitude. Did you know that gratitude is completely alien to our natures? It's a conditioning, Lisabeth, something we only *think* we feel, because we've been taught to express it. I don't know what Charles was taught . . .' He laughed. 'I'm rambling. Forgive me, Lisabeth. I'm sure you don't need lecturing on the niceties of civilized behaviour.' He stopped. Those great unreadable eyes! He suddenly knew that he wanted to kiss her, to smooth those eyelids closed and to feel her warm breath against his neck. Was this an after-effect of his fever, too, or had the dream of her twined its seductive notions through his mind until all his reasoning was flavoured with her image?

She was breathing hard. He could see her delicate lips tremble, and he wondered. 'Lisabeth,' he ventured. 'This walk . . . did you think you might . . .?' Damn it all. If only he could think straight. 'Did you come to see me?'

A nod. Her face was gilded in the lamplight, all but those huge dark eyes, and they bore twin miniatures of the lamp itself.

It was incredible, through all his surprise, how right it seemed. Placing the lamp on the ground, he stepped towards her and put his hands on her shoulders, in his heart kissing her already. He was stunned when she pulled away, emphatically shaking her head.

'No! Mr Morgan, you mustn't blame Uncle Charles for not telling you about the trouble you've—'

'Mr *Morgan?*' He smiled, bewildered but appealing. 'Lisabeth, we're friends, aren't we? We're more than friends. You *were* at the fire, weren't you? You saved my life, I know you did, though why you invented this other—'

'No!' It was all she could do to keep the tears back. Mary was the one he saw at the fire. Mary's was the face he saw, Mary was the name he spoke. Mary, Mary *Mary!* It was loathsome.

'Lisabeth, what's the matter?'

'Uncle Charles didn't know about the trouble,' she insisted, though privately she had sometimes wondered just how much Charles's keen eyes had seen. 'But I knew . . . I saw Mr Fox talking to Sam Nevin and the other cockatoos – just two of them, a short bald man and the tall thin one with slopy shoulders. It was the same ones each time. I don't know what they said because they spoke softly, but I do know that Mr Fox paid them money to drown some of your sheep and then he gave them bottles of something before they started the fire. Big square bottles. I don't think the cockatoos wanted to make the fire, because they argued a lot about it, but Mr Fox said that it had to be done then, before it rained, or it would be too late.'

Unable to meet his eyes she looked at his waistcoat buttons while she spoke, then at his hands when he raised them and began fiddling with the tiny gold nuggets that were strung along his watch-chain. When she had finished he said coolly: 'And when did you hear him say that?'

'The night before the fire.'

'But you didn't tell anybody? You didn't think I should be warned?'

Guilt crushed her. In planning to confess she believed that the telling would lance her own poisoning, but instead of easing her suffering this inflamed it. Worse, she'd spat it all out at him in a rush, in anger, and without a scrap of remorse, and now she knew with a cold horrid certainty that he would despise her forever. It was one thing for her to think she detested him, but quite another to know that she was the object of loathing. Especially well-earned loathing.

'I didn't know what to do,' she pleaded, belatedly hoping for some small refuge in partial truths. 'I thought those men were old friends of Mr Fox's and I wasn't sure what they were arguing about until next day when the fire started. And Uncle Charles seemed to think you'd started it yourself, which made it all more confusing. So please don't blame him, and please don't sell your property to Mr Fox because he doesn't deserve it.'

'I see.' His smoke-roughened voice was glacially cold. 'The only reason you're telling me this at all is that *you* hope to keep a roof over your head.'

'No!' She was horrified. 'No! I wish I'd told you before, but once I realized the significance of what I'd seen it was too late. All I could do was go and warn Mr Braddock so that we could come and try—' She broke off, even more horrified by what she was saying. Turning away, she fled as if for her life, stumbling miserably through the darkness towards the low huddled shape of the cottage.

'Lisabeth!' he called after her. His shout roused the Nevin dogs and set them barking in a shrill duet, but Lisabeth kept on running.

NINETEEN

'GOOD LUCK TO YOU, LAD!' boomed Sir Kenneth when Rhys
told him what he planned to do. 'Mind you, I'd like to see him in
court – then in jail. That's what he deserves.'

'I considered that, but I doubt I've sufficient strong evidence
against him. The cockatoos would be too frightened to testify,
and he'd have the best legal brains in the colony to fight his case.
I'll have to be content with this, unfortunately.'

'Be careful, hey? There's nothing he wouldn't stoop to in order
to get your land, as well you know. He might get violent.'

'Not in his own office,' said Rhys. But he felt a thrill of
apprehension.

They were sitting on a wooden bench in the vast opaque-roofed
conservatory beside the south side of the house. Though it was
cold outside, in here the atmosphere was warm and misty, heated
by a small cast-iron stove at the far end of the room. One of the
sepoys was stoking it with wood-chips now. Rhys could see his
scarlet turban through the thicket of ferns. Nearby Lady
Launcenolt was watering hanging baskets that cascaded a profusion of seaweedy plants that trailed languidly as though under
water. As she worked Lady Launcenolt pinched her brows together
in a frown. She had a *thing* about Mr Fox. A nasty man.

'Is it legal, though? Fox can't take me to court and demand I
hand over the property to him?'

'No. He'll threaten to, mind you.'

'I've heard his threats.'

'Just as well old Braddock came by to see if you were all right,
hey? You could have been burned to a crisp.'

'Yes,' said Rhys, thinking about Lisabeth. He pushed her away.

'It's a *very* good thing,' agreed Lady Launcenolt, standing before them and leaning forward confidentially. As usual she wore a fussy, frilly gown that did not suit her large frame. 'We would be *devastated* if we lost you. Kiki, have you told the dear boy about Azura?'

'There's no need to, when you manage to weave her name into every conversation,' remarked Sir Kenneth, righteously smoothing his beard.

'Oh, you men are impossible!' Dismissing him, she said to Rhys: 'She's coming later in the year, perhaps for Christmas! It's definitely arranged. Ah, but she's a delightful girl! Tell me, Rhys, is there a young lady in *your* life?'

'Beatrice!'

Rhys laughed. 'I don't mind. No, I have no special young lady, but I'm not thinking of settling down for a very long time.' As he spoke, again he thought about Lisabeth, pushing her away as soon as she slipped into his mind. It seemed that he spent most of his time trying not to think of her yet as soon as he relaxed his guard there she was again. The damnedest part of it was he simply didn't know what to make of her. Perhaps that was her fascination.

'You're trying to bully me, sonny boy,' said Fox in his cold white office.

A thrill of fear slipped down the centre of Rhys's back, but he was determined not to show nervousness. Placing the cheque and the carefully composed 'account' on the desk, he said: 'There's absolutely no bullying involved. I received some money from you on account of certain losses I've suffered. You'll find them all noted there. Damage to my boundary fences, sheep deliberately drowned and run over cliffs, plus the five hundred and thirty lost in the fire. Trifling amounts, but they do add up.'

'You said you'd lost half your herd! Five hundred and thirty is nothing!'

'I was mistaken,' Rhys told him blandly. 'Besides, I wanted to make my intention to sell sound more urgent, therefore more genuine.'

'You never had any intention of selling,' accused Fox from his desk lair.

'Never the slightest.'

'I'll get you for this.' His jaw was clenched so tightly that his sidewhiskers quivered.

'Ah. This is interesting. Here, you see, is where our opinions diverge quite dramatically. I believe that I, Mr Fox, have you. Again, for just a few trifles that all add up. Wilful damage, theft, attempted murder . . .' He shook his head. 'Don't call Featherston yet. I do have proof.' He paused, expecting an outburst, but Fox just glared at him, eyes solid with dislike. 'Incidentally, you were shocked when I walked in the other day and you saw I'd been in the fire, weren't you? Did you assume that I'd be away at church for the day? Is that why you gave Nevin and Thompsen and Blake the bottles of kerosene on the Saturday evening at dusk on the Christchurch road? The irony is that I'm positive that your intent was never to harm me, but in a court of law this would look black for you, Fox, very black indeed. However, I'm a reasonable fellow. Least said soonest mended and all that. I've totted up the damage and given you a cheque for twenty-two guineas, a refund from the nineteen hundred you advanced me. To cover the above-mentioned losses, as arranged.'

'Twenty-two guineas! These claims of yours are outrageous!'

'Perhaps some of the estimates are a tiny bit steep, but I've been advised by Mr Rule the veterinarian that a few of the sheep which survived the fire may still die, so let's just say that this is a once-only payment, shall we? I'll make no further claims on you.'

Walking away from an ugly situation is fraught with more danger than approaching the hazard. From the moment he stepped into the office Rhys worried how he would be able to exit gracefully. Now he took a step backwards, still facing the desk. A shaft of autumn sunlight wavered on the polished floor between them, while from outside intruded the noise of children shouting and the rumble of a coach shuddering along the street.

He could kill me now, thought Rhys, eyeing the duelling-pistol case. He could flip that box open, whip out a pistol and shoot me; he's angry enough to do it.

But all Fox did was pick the cheque up and begin folding it.

Time to go, decided Rhys but, as he turned, Fox pulled the bell-rope and when the door swung open Featherston was hulking large and dark in the doorway.

'Just a minute, sonny boy,' said Fox lightly.

He was as swift as a mongoose striking a snake. At a signal Featherston seized Rhys around the upper arms in a bear-hug that oofed all the breath out of him. Reaching up, Fox prised Rhys's jaws open with unexpectedly powerful fingers and shoved the folded cheque into his cheek cavity, wedging it tightly so that Rhys could not spit it out. 'I never accept cheques,' Fox called

197

after him as Featherston bundled him to the street-door.

It was all so fast, and Rhys was overpowered so brutally, that he felt humiliated by the violation against his person. In the street he plucked the wadded paper out of his mouth – it left a dry uncomfortable patch – and he leaned against a chestnut tree to spit out all traces of peppermint taste that had come from Fox's fingers. He was furious.

At the bank he smoothed out the cheque and presented it to the elderly teller. 'Could you change this into farthings for me, please? Farthings and ha'pennies, if you can.'

The teller looked over his half-scoop spectacles. 'That's twenty thousand farthings and one thousand and eighty-eight ha'pennies, sir,' he calculated doubtfully. 'That's a few more than you'd want to have jingling in your pockets.'

Rhys laughed, but his voice was grim as he spoke through the steel-barred barrier. 'If I can carry them, I'll take them,' he replied.

While he waited in a hansom cab for Featherston to leave the office Rhys read a newspaper and watched people come and go along the street, farmers with wagonloads of produce, 'new-chums' just off a ship, gawping wide-eyed and often in dismay at the scruffy road-verges and wooden buildings, and an occasional carriage with uniformed coachman. Whenever he saw one of these Rhys wondered if a wealthy run-holder rode within.

At three o'clock the black brougham pulled up outside the office and Leonie alighted. Shortly afterwards Featherston emerged, donned a rather battered bell-topper and, pulling his overcoat snugly about his portly middle, set off towards the market-square, leaning head-down into the wind as he went.

The coins were in five weighty canvas bags. Hefting three to the steps Rhys propped them beside the door and went back for the other two, then he untied the leather thongs from the necks of the bags, opening them all wide before he flung the contents of the first over the floor of Fox's outer office. The coins sluiced out like brown paint, slithering and skittering in droplets until they all came to rest, lying in shiny puddles like wet winter leaves.

He worked as swiftly as Fox had worked on him and with as much of an element of surprise; the last of the coins were splashing from their container when the door of the inner office opened and Fox and Leonie, standing shoulder to shoulder, looked out in utter astonishment.

198

Leonie laughed. She had heard the story of Rhys's mortification from her father and was enchanted to see the imaginative quality of his revenge. 'Oh, Papa, he's paid you back in coin!' she exclaimed. 'In *coin*! Isn't he droll?'

'I'll make him swallow every last—' began Fox, rushing forward. He never finished the sentence in word nor had a chance to begin it in deed because his feet slipped on the coins and jutted suddenly out from under him, dumping him abruptly on his back. He swore loudly with vicious anger.

Glancing mischievously at Rhys, Leonie raised her fox-fur muff to smother her laughter. Rhys bowed, smiling like an entertainer receiving applause. 'Please, don't bother to get up,' he said.

Rhys had money for the three cockatoos, too. After ascertaining from the Provincial Council records the exact value of each property, he instructed the bank to make up the amounts in cash, which he stowed in cloth packages in his saddlebags.

In the evening he rode back home. The mountains were rimmed with pink light, and the foothills cast cold grey shadows across the plains. The air carried a strong tang of burning; though the charred acreage was beyond his vision, he could see the sky above still dark with gulls that were now leaving their gorging and flying back to their resting-places, while in the flax thickets of the swamp rustled a profusion of refugee creatures rendered homeless by the inferno.

Submerged in long shadows, the cottages were sepia'd with dusk. Grimy-looking children played outside, flicking marbles and squabbling in the dust. Rhys had to repeat his command twice before the game broke up and the children scuttled inside to fetch their parents.

Rhys remained on horseback, deliberately grim, not even acknowledging Charles, who peered over the hedge of gooseberry bushes wondering what was happening. It was not until all of the cockatoos had gathered into a sullen semi-circle that Rhys spoke.

'This only concerns three of you, but I'll say it to you all. Three families have been involved in criminal damage to my property.' He scanned their faces. Some were craftily watchful, others blank-faced and curious. Sam Nevin, he noted, looked completely innocent, his freckled face composed, his eyes fearless. Rhys continued: 'Those three families are leaving before midnight tonight. Tomorrow at dawn their houses will be burned down.'

'Whud is thus?' said Sam Nevin.

Rhys ignored him. 'Thompsen, how much did Mr Fox pay you to cause the damage? Blake, what did you receive from him?'

Neither replied, but they both slid uneasy glances at Nevin.

Rhys said: 'Very well, I'll guess. I'm deducting the sum he paid you from the value of your properties. Oh, don't worry, I'm *buying* you out, not throwing you out, though that's a concession to your wives and families. If you were single men, I'd see you in jail.'

Sam Nevin found his tongue. 'Thus is ruduc'luss! We've dine nuttin' ter you!'

Ignoring him, Rhys pulled out one of the packages. 'This is yours, Blake. Twenty-five acres at two pounds five shillings the acre. Shall we say less fifteen pounds from Mr Fox?' he suggested, drawing out three notes. 'That leaves—'

' 'E only paid us six pounds,' blurted Blake before Nevin could stop him. ' 'E's not paid us yet for the fire.'

Rhys felt ill. His gaze raked them all with contempt. Tugging the money from all three packages, he flung it in the dirt. 'Get out, all three of you. Now,' he said. 'Yes, Nevin, I know about you, too. And one last thing. You almost killed me the other day. If I ever set eyes on any of you again, I'll repay the compliment. But *I* won't fail. You can bet on it.'

'Oi!' shouted Nevin, his face suffused. 'Jaist a munnut! You coon't—'

'I can and I will,' said Rhys coldly. 'Get out or you're dead, all of you.'

'He threatened to kill them!' repeated Charles gleefully long after Rhys had left for his camp at the far end of the property. 'Sure and he's an implacable man, that brother of yours. Never thought he'd get the better of Mr Fox, though. *He's* a cunning one – Fox by name, fox by nature, hey, Mrs Stafford?'

Lisabeth looked up from the bench where she was grating sugar to mix with stewed apple for tomorrow's breakfast. 'Did you know about Mr Fox's involvement, then?'

Charles flustered, 'Know? What do any of us know?' but in the light of the fire his face was so uneasy that Lisabeth guessed Rhys's suspicions about his brother-in-law were correct.

We all let him down, she thought.

It was almost dark; time to light the lamps and go inside. From the cockatoos' cottages came the sounds of squabbling and a woman's voice raised in a high keening wail.

200

'Poor Birdie Nevin,' remarked Gwynne. 'She's the one I feel sorry for. Sam's been harking on about wanting to go off to the goldfields, and she doesn't want him to go, not with winter coming on and conditions down there being so frightful – he'd freeze to death in the first cold snap, she says. There'll be nothing to stop any of them going now.'

'Uncle Rhys had to turn them out!' said Andrew, stoutly defending his hero. 'He can't ever trust them again.'

Or us, thought Lisabeth. Rhys hadn't been near them since last evening when Lisabeth intercepted him on the hill-path. He'd saddled Polka and left directly for town, and Lisabeth had a nasty intuition that he would make a point of avoiding them all in future.

'Birdie's the one I'm sorry for,' signed Gwynne. She lifted the pot of apple-mush from the fire and prodded the camp oven into place with a stick.

Andrew picked up the shovel to heap embers over it. In the morning the pans of dough within would be baked into fragrant loaves. As he worked he said: 'What about Uncle Rhys, then? Those men were trying to ruin him.'

'Don't waste your pity on him, lad,' cut in Charles before Gwynne could reply. 'That jammy booger – sure and his luck won't never turn sour on him.' Stretching his fingers towards the dying warmth, he said what he invariably did when the gold rush was mentioned. 'Like to have a stab at prospecting, meself. Can't be much to it, really. If that jammy brother of yours can trip over thousands of guineas' worth, I'm damned sure I can!'

Gwynne looked perturbed, noted Lisabeth, though surely by now she must have realized that his plans were only pipe-dreams. Charles liked his home comforts too much to want to abandon them for the rigours of goldfields existence. He'd probably turn back after a week without proper home-cooked food – *if* he survived the journey. No, all his bluster was empty waffle, belittling Rhys's achievements, putting him down.

That *was* it! mused Lisabeth as she replaced the worn sugar-cone in its glass gar and screwed the lid down tight. Charles was consumed with jealousy for Rhys. Secretly he'd like to see him fail.

He probably wanted Fox to ruin him, she thought. *But, then, so did I. I can't blame him if he never comes near us again.*

201

TWENTY

WINTER ARRIVED FOR A LONG BLEAK VISIT. Frost glazed the puddles and sculpted the mud into crystal patterns. Spider-webs, invisible in summer, now draped embroidered veils over the naked gooseberry bushes and hung lace curtains along the fences, lending them a temporary illusion of prettiness.

Then it snowed, and Lisabeth woke one morning to see the dreary little hollow below the ridge transformed. Gone were the black scars where the Nevins', the Blakes' and the Thompsens' hovels had been, gone the weed-choked drains and the scruffy hillside acres – all smothered in a glittering soft whiteness that spread right back to the sharp-edged mountains.

Andrew whooped, rolled, fell in it, his boots kicking it up in mounds like sugar. His breath plumed in the sharp air, and he laughed with delight. 'Look! Look at the rabbit tracks! And the funny marks the gulls' feet make. Oh, Lisabeth, isn't it all a treat?'

Lisabeth decided she had never seen anything so beautiful. Warned by Gwynne that the snow wouldn't last, Lisabeth set out the paints and easel that Heywood Braddock had given her and spent a whole morning capturing the scenes around their cottage in a series of deft watercolours. When the snow melted and all the ugliness pushed through again she was able to look at the pictures and remind herself of those magic few days when their world was pure and dazzling.

The snow dissolved, but the cold remained, bitter and stubborn as a feud. All the family suffered – Andrew tormented by chilblains on raw-scratched fingers and toes, Lisabeth shivering with chills as she tended Gwynne whose rheumatism flared up so painfully that for days on end she was unable to walk and stayed immobile in her musty, uncomfortable bed. Charles suffered least but complained constantly of his bad chest, bad throat, bad head and bad 'influence'. As soon as the weather began to cool he neglected outside tasks to devote all his energy to building a chimney on the side of the house to warm what Gwynne now referred to as the 'parlour' and to make it possible to cook inside. He worked meticulously, but so slowly that the snows had come and gone and still the house was a funnel for freezing draughts and still the rain beat in when the wind blew from the north-west.

'Listen to the poor man coughing,' whispered Gwynne, huddled in the next room. 'He works so hard, Lisabeth.'

'Yes,' said Lisabeth, whose days were spent boiling the billy to brew him endless cups of tea, plucking and stewing him chickens, roasting joints of meat in the camp-oven, preparing vegetables for his prodigious appetite, coping with Gwynne's tasks and her own and then, when she was exhausted and catching her breath, rushing about to do Andrew's work – chopping the wood, feeding the hens and working in the fields.

She didn't mind. She worked with all the will in the world, for it was worth it. Andrew was Receiving an Education!

Lisabeth had found the school – not a proper institution but a class of a dozen boys held at a house on the near outskirts of Christchurch. The master, a Mr Smale, showed Lisabeth his certificates of qualification and agreed that Andrew could join the class on a probationary basis for sixpence per day plus a penny for a hot drink at midday. Lisabeth walked the three miles home with her mind made up and then begged, badgered and nagged until Charles grudgingly relented.

'Don't know why the fuss,' he said to Gwynne. 'Sure and all that fancy book-learning didn't do his father no good. I can learn the boy all he needs to know to get on in the world.'

Lisabeth, who was determined that Andrew was going to better himself, wisely didn't comment. But she was jubilant.

Unfortunately, Andrew didn't share her joy. It was a long trudge to school on winter mornings, and when it rained, as it often did, he had to sit all day in damp clothes. Being naturally quick and intelligent, he learned at a much swifter pace that the other boys, but all Mr Smale's unimaginative lessons were pitched to the lowest common denominator, which meant they were tedious, grindingly dull and repetitive. Used to the freedom of an outdoor life, Andrew grew first bored, then frustrated and inevitably rebellious. Mr Smale caned him.

'I hate him and I hate his lessons!' declared Andrew to Lisabeth. 'I'm never going back, so don't try to make me.'

The pail she was filling slipped from her numb fingers. Freezing water sloshed all over her hem and her boots. 'You can't give up, Andrew! This is your chance in life! You have to stay there. You're doing well, you're learning such a lot. Please, Andrew, don't even talk like that!'

The matter was taken out of her hands. By now the rains had set in with a vengeance – day after day of sheeting rain and nights haunted by the constant mourning sound. The fields flooded; cabbages rotted off their stumpy stalks before they could be harvested. Even in the cold, they stank. Work multiplied until Lisabeth's chafed hands could no longer cope. Back bowed under the lash of rain, she toiled mechanically, clearing drains, gathering cabbages, trimming and packing them for market, ploughing fields ready for the spring crops, but her weary hours were futile. Muttering poverty, Charles yanked Andrew out of school.

Lisabeth was furious. Unable to make Charles listen, unwilling to vent her distress on Gwynne, she poured her heart out to Braddock. He had come calling to sample Gwynne's genuine Manx-recipe soda scones but stopped by the implement-shed to see why Lisabeth hadn't been for any more painting lessons.

'I don't mind how hard he makes *me* work,' she said as she deftly pricked cauliflower seedlings out into trays of sieved soil, 'but it's not fair to snatch away Andrew's chance of an education. He says he can't afford the school fees, but every time he goes into town he comes back with luxuries to pamper himself. Imported biscuits, jams and jellies – the most expensive brand of tobacco. Even English newspapers – though I don't begrudge those, for I get to read them afterwards. Oh, forgive me, I sound ungrateful, but I'm not, really. Uncle Charles has always been kind to us. He's never raised a hand in anger, and we're always well fed.' She sighed. 'It's just that Andrew's a clever lad, Mr Braddock, he really is, and I want him to be able to aim high and be fearless in life, not go along with his eyes fixed on the ground because he's unable to better himself.'

'Ah.' Braddock nodded sagely. 'Yurr want him to be like yurr Mr Maughold, then.'

Lisabeth flushed with hot embarrassment. 'He's not *my* Mr Morgan and he's the last person I'd ever . . .' Her voice faltered as she realized that was exactly what she did want – to mould Andrew into a successful, well-educated and cultured man like Rhys. To outshine him, even, and why not? Andrew *was* his son.

'Perhaps I'm wrong,' she mumbled weakly.

'No, darrlin' gel, yurr right. He's a sharp young sprat and he wants encouraging. Yurr right to fret about it,' He winked and pinched her cheek with his leathery fingers, as if to say: Leave it to me. Lisabeth watched him go, then turned back to her task in despair. What good could he possibly do?

Rhys prospered. It was as Charles said: no matter what blows were struck against him he could twist them to his own advantage. In his first season nature helped him, too.

At shearing time the weather held good and he was able to command premium prices at the wool sales for his clean dry clip of the long-stapled crinkly cream merino wool. His bales were stamped with his own logo – three mountain peaks surrounded in a loose shape that could be either a cloud or a fleece. Buyers from the textile mills in the North of England jostled to bid for them.

Again, in the lambing season the weather helped; the rain eased to a warm, gentle drizzle until the youngsters had enough milk in their stomachs and were steady on their tiny polished hoofs. The lambing strike was so encouraging that Rhys took his first wool-clip cheque and used it to buy another piece of land; five thousand fertile acres in the adjacent foothills.

News of his early success reached the Staffords in a roundabout way, through gossip Charles picked up at the vegetable-markets. Envy seeped through him like a stain.

'What a life,' he commented sourly. 'Here we are toiling in the mud and the sleet, Mrs Stafford, while that brother of yours lies abed and lets the wool grow for him. Do you know what they're saying he's clearing this season? Forty per cent on his investment! Sure and that's a scandal. Money for jam, and it's all right for some!'

But Rhys worked harder by far than Charles ever did, and all the profit he turned was ploughed straight back into his property, into more fencing, irrigation drains, barns, a second team of working horses and even some machinery – a reaping machine and a grain thresher for the wheat he was sowing on the richest part of the plains.

When Charles had a few pounds and shillings in his fob he

spent it quickly on immediate comforts, never planning ahead, so when the time came for fresh seed or potato-sacks for harvest he had to borrow funds from Chase & Hounds, a private finance company who charged twenty-five per cent interest.

Charles slept under a feather quilt and drank Canary wine before his soup and porter with his cheese and crackers, but Rhys bunked down at night in a primitive dug-out shepherd's hut and made one enormous 'cannibal' potful of stewed mutton and potatoes stretch to last him out the week. He returned to civilization only once a fortnight with a sluice in the river and a change into the good clothes he kept hanging from the ridge-pole (swathed against insects in a calico bags). Shaved and feeling exhilarated, he rode into Christchurch to visit the Launcenolts.

Occasionally, if he could be sure that Charles was away in town, Rhys dropped in to call on Gwynne. They joked and laughed, and she chided him about not looking after himself, while he stood at the window of the draughty room and looked out to where Lisabeth was toiling in the fields. He tried not to watch her, but was always drawn to it against his will. Sometimes he wondered if these furtive observations of her fuelled his dreams. Asleep and in the pale hours of dawn she was always on his mind.

'She's a lovely lass, so bonny and good-natured, and she works as hard as a lad would,' said Gwynne, noticing where his attention dwelt. 'We're lucky indeed to have her.'

'Who? . . . Oh, Lisabeth!' And he laughed to show that his thoughts had in fact been miles away. 'Yes . . . yes, I suppose she is a good thing for you, especially while you're so poorly.'

'Good thing? Bless you, Rhys. She's a marvel.'

He chewed his lip. In the field Lisabeth straightened and pressed both canvas-gloved hands into the small of her back. She looked exhausted. 'Does she ever have any fun?'

'She has her paint-box,' frowned Gwynne, to whom 'fun' was an alien concept. 'Not that she has time, mind you. The last time she set up the ease—'

'Shouldn't she be going out? Meeting young people? Courting?' he added bluntly.

He was relieved by her laughter. 'Bless you, no! She's not bothered about being *social*. We're too far from town, anyway,' she said wistfully. All her own dreams of presiding over 'At Home' afternoons had been blighted by the isolation. Who would drive all the way out here to leave visiting-cards in a tray in

206

the hall? 'Sometimes she rows me over to visit Ann Day, though mostly it's Mr Braddock that—'

'She's happy, would you say?' demanded Rhys.

'Happy?'

'Lisabeth. Is she happy, do you think?'

'Oh, Lisabeth,' Gwynne had been massaging her sore knuckle-joints, lost in useless vague longings for a life she would probably never know. 'She's content enough. She has her moments.'

And her worries, he inferred accurately. 'The lad's education, of course,' he remembered aloud. 'How are his studies coming along?'

'They're not,' she told him.

Where Heywood Braddock failed to persuade Charles, Rhys succeeded in one curt conversation. It took place after a chance meeting on the Christchurch road one morning when Rhys was returning home with a wagonload of fencing supplies, while Charles, not long out of bed, was trundling a few crates of early lettuces into the market. Sharp words were exchanged, and Rhys flung a handful of coins into the vegetable-crates. 'Take that, and let's have an end of this exploitation of children,' he said in disgust. 'That boy should be in school, and you know it. There, that will pay his fees for a few weeks and will pay wages if you need extra help in your garden. Though, if you stirred yourself a bit more, you'd have no call to cry "short-handed".'

'What do you mean by that?' Charles tugged at his greasy-looking beard, his face belligerent.

'Sir Kenneth asked me if you've moved into town, you're seen in there so often!' retorted Rhys, and was immediately sorry he spoke. What business was it of his? And why, for that matter, was he interfering in the question of Andrew's education? He didn't even like the child – in fact there was something about the boy that he actively disliked, though he could never quite decide what. Possibly, the thought that Mary had been carrying him all those times when . . . When a mess that was, he thought. Mary. A few hours of giddy pleasure that managed to taint the rest of his life with a flavour of regret. Not guilt, for he could never feel responsible for anything that happened to her afterwards, but it was always there, a faint, disquieting unease, a pervading grubby sadness.

The odd thing was that Lisabeth never affected him like this – his perception of her was always pure loveliness enhanced by a tantalizing sense of unattainability. She was cold to him, and he hated that; yet Andrew idolized him, and equally he disliked that. It was so illogical, ridiculous.

She dotes on her brother, Rhys mused. The lad was all that mattered to her. Perhaps there, if he could overcome his distaste for the boy, there lay the answer to his problem.

Prodding Polka into a canter, Rhys rode off, leaving Charles scowling after him.

Later that spring the colony was swept by drenching and unseasonably icy rains. South at the goldfields rivers swelled and roared through the gorges, plucking prospectors from their burrows and sweeping them away in a freezing brown tide. Further north rain stripped the blossoms from all the fruit trees in the Staffords' orchard and battered the young pea and bean crops into the mud, while Charles hulked in the doorway, cursing.

In Christchurch the docile Avon rose, splitting its cocoon and unleashing a yellow, sinuous monster that lashed at bridges, gnawed away pilings of boat-sheds, then swallowed them whole, and along the way licked up all the flower-gardens within reach of its destructive tongue.

'My azaleas are ruined, and I doubt that these poor soggy roses will ever recover,' wailed Lady Launcenolt when Rhys splashed into town to visit. 'I'd just finished dividing the pansy clumps when down came this vile—'

'Never mind your flowers, Bea,' Sir Kenneth interrupted. 'How have you fared, hey, Rhys? Lost much stock?'

'Fifty acres of wheat will need resowing, but we've been lucky with the sheep. There are a couple of sheltered valleys in that new block, and the McFallishes and I managed to muster all the sheep and lambs up into them. The new shepherds are camping up there keeping an eye on things. I've come into town for supplies and I'll be up there myself tonight. . . . but that's not my main purpose in coming in. I wondered if you'd heard anything specific about the goldfields disaster. I haven't seen a newspaper for days.'

'Yes, of course. It was in yesterday's . . . or was it Monday's?' fluttered Lady Launcenolt, her large mauve hands sifting through the magazines in the rack below the bookshelves. 'I didn't read it properly because we had bad news about Azura . . . She's not coming now until some time next year.'

'Really?' said Rhys, willing her to hurry.

'She's been ill, poor dear. Her father took her in a swan boat at

208

Windsor for a birthday treat – one of those contraptions one pedals with one's feet.' She leafed through some back issues of the *Lyttelton Times*, flapping them noisily. 'A *real* swan took exception to the hat Azura was wearing – at least, we think that's what caused the uproar – and it flew at her, hissing madly. She tried to get away, and fell into the water. The poor girl amost drowned.'

'Oh, how terrible,' said Rhys. 'Can you find it?'

'She ingested such a volume of water, the doctors said it was a miracle she survived. No, it's not. . . . Perhaps Leopold tidied it away.' Ringing the silver elephant-shaped bell on the knick-knack table, she said, 'Of course Azura is in no condition to travel. She's always been susceptible to colds. . . .'

'A weakness of that sort does make things difficult,' sympathized Rhys, then, knowing he should explain his distracted air, he said: 'I've been told that the three farmers I evicted were all killed in that goldfields tragedy, and I'm anxious . . . I hope the rumours aren't true.'

'Oh, Rhys! What a horrid coincidence . . . Azura almost drowning and now this . . .'

Rhys thought there was a great deal of difference between a spoiled rich girl getting damp in a river picnic and this, but he said nothing.

'I'm afraid the rumours are true, lad,' Sir Kenneth told him. 'Our cricket team has been approached with the proposition that we stage a charity match for the benefit of the twenty-one families affected, and your cockies' names are all on the list I saw. Tragic.' He paused for a moment looking theatrical and somehow pompous. 'What about it, hey, Rhys? Soon as the weather brightens up a bit we'll put on a show, get in quickly and show the Province our hearts are in the right place. Of course the publicity won't go amiss, either. With the elections coming up next March I have to consider the problem of getting myself well known. No point in being anonymous, hey?'

Rhys said nothing, but Lady Launcenolt said fondly: 'All of Canterbury knows you, Kiki.'

'These things have to be taken into consideration, Bea.'

While Sir Kenneth ruminated about political gain and Lady Launcenolt fretted that Azura would be missing all the glory, Rhys wondered about the three homeless fatherless families. The chain of events that led them to their nadir had been started with nothing more than a bit of petty bullying between Thomas Fox and Braddock, had almost cost him his life and now had ruined three families. All because, out of misguided generosity and family feeling, Rhys had offered to share his future with the Staffords. How many ways will I have to regret that? he wondered.

'We'll be in quickly with the grand gesture,' decided Sir Kenneth. 'Not that I imagine Fox is doing anything to help. It wouldn't be in his nature,'

The Provincial Charity Fête (might as well give it an important title, argued Sir Kenneth) was held on the first Saturday in November when the plains were steaming, still sodden, in the warmth of early summer.

Feeling much better with the improvement in the weather, Gwynne was anxious for a day out, but Charles declared he'd not a single spare farthing to chip out for any causes but his own, and especially not for those layabout cockatoos.

'But I've heard that Birdie Nevin is living in straitened circumstances in Ferrymead, and my heart goes out to her, Mr Stafford. She always had time for a civil word, and now there she is with seven nippers to bring up.' She reached for another parsnip and scrubbed it with vigour. 'We've a warm and comfortable home and food on the table—'

'There, now!' cried Heywood Braddock, who was at the cottage more and more these days, rambling on aimlessly about his days at sea. 'Yurr cheer up, me darrrlin'. I'll take yurr.'

Charles heard the offer, saw the wink that accompanied it and, come the day, he drove them all to the Fête himself, trussed up in his Sunday best and sulking while the others perched on picnic-hampers in the wagon, bubbling with excitement.

It was a lowering day, oppressive and damp, smothered by the burgeoning profusion of cumulus cloud that had rolled in from the ocean and now filled the sky, erasing all of the early morning's fresh blue. On the inner reaches of the harbour Maoris were pulling in a net. Children stood ankle-deep at the edges, and a small white dog rushed timidly at the ripples, barking in a strained voice.

'They're early to pull that in,' remarked Braddock. 'Looks like a thunderstorm later, I reckon.'

'Rubbish,' muttered Charles.

By the time they reached the park Lisabeth was perspiring under her recently made-over, grey serge dress (another cast-off of Gwynne's), and her face was pink below the rim of her old-fashioned bonnet. At first when she saw the crinolines and pastel ruffled silk gowns, the airy parasols light as cream puffs and the dainty lace mittens she felt that unpleasant souring wistfulness, but Christchurch was thick with the poor, too, and before they had alighted from the wagon Lisabeth had seen a number of young women more shabbily dressed than herself.

It doesn't matter, anyway, she told herself with a proud lifting of her chin. *I'm here to enjoy myself, not to worry about the fact I've nothing pretty to wear. It's not going to spoil my day.*

But secretly she hoped that they wouldn't see Rhys. By comparison with the gaudy plumage flitting around here he'd think she was a drab and dreary sparrow.

Soon she forgot herself, and him. There was so much to look at, so much to laugh at.

Andrew wanted to to on the greasy pole. It cost a penny and if you dislodged three opponents in a row you got your penny back, he pleaded.

'Absolutely not,' said Gwynne, wincing as a loser fell with a shriek from the pole and landed with a drenching splash in a vat of none-too-clean-looking water. She nudged him towards the archery instead.

Charles melted quickly into the crowd – so that he couldn't be tapped for halfpennies, Lisabeth guessed – but Braddock had a handful of coppers and said he wanted help in getting rid of them. There were no toffee apples or sugared peaches – it being so early in the season – but plenty of tempting delicacies were for sale: crisp pork crackling sprinkled with salt, little cakes sprinkled with grated sugar, discs of opaque toffee the size of pennies and slices of pickled meats rolled in a wrapping of dark bread. For those with money there were ices served in little glass dishes in a pavilion near the river-bank, but Braddock's budget didn't run to exotic treats; Lisabeth and Gwynne licked at lollypops while Andrew chewed a bootstrap of liquorice.

They laughed at the oiled pig and the funny see-saw rides, at the donkey rigged up with a double saddle so that two little children could ride, one on each side, at the juggler who kept five wooden blocks and six little cane hoops aloft at once (a trick Andrew avidly watched, intending to practise later at home) and at the man with two little spotted dogs with ruffled collars that stood on their hind legs and bowed. 'As performed before Her Majesty,' the man cried, and when people put coins into his tambourine the dogs bowed faster.

A high keening of bagpipes brought the crowd over to the cricket ground. When Gwynne saw who was playing she was delighted.

'It's our neighbours, the McFallishes! I thought I heard bagpipes the other evening, but Mr Stafford told me I were getting soft in the head!'

'Ay, that you are,' said Charles, catching up to them in time to hear the last remark. He grinned, seeing the dewy lights in her dull eyes. 'Sure and it takes you back, don't it?'

'I close my eyes and I'm Home again,' she said.

TWENTY-ONE

CRICKET IN THE COLONY was played with all the serious respect accorded to it in England. It was a slow-moving and ritualistic game enlivened with as few ornamental flourishes as a composition by Wagner, and in the opinion of many people was equally boring. Rhys loved the game and resented the patronizing attitude that pronounced it tedious.

Today, he resolved, the Christchurch Cricket Club would seize the opportunity offered and display to this crowd of uninterested spectators such dazzling skills that by close of play scores of new enthusiasts would be converted to the game.

'Ignoramuses into *affictionadoes*, eh?' he chuckled to Sir Kenneth as they filed out on to the bright green field. He looked around for Lisabeth but instead his glance fell on Leonie, who was surrounded by so many melon-pink flounces that she seemed framed by her own extravagant outfit. From the cool shade of the white stands she waved; Rhys waved back, then wondered if the salute was intended for Juno Gammerwoth, who had forged out at the head of the Provinces Eleven, their opposing team. He waved again, anyway, then shook hands with Juno, an immensely tall, immensely fat man who wheezed as he moved, but whose movements were surprisingly swift and deft. Juno had a purplish face, a many-creased neck and iron-grey hair that was plastered over his scalp and extended in a hard-looking beard around the line where his jaw would have been had he been much, much thinner. When he shook hands his grip was tight and cushiony, like buttoned upholstery; Rhys imagined bones snapping and pulled his fingers away quickly.

Smartarse, said Juno's pie-slice grine. Rhys detested him on sight. Rhys won the toss and elected to bat.

Cricket is a cautious game, as carefully plotted as chess, with each move deliberately played, each stroke placed with calculation. Coming in to bat third, after swift dismissals by Juno's bowling, Rhys was more intent on racking up a quick, spectacular score than playing a restrained hand.

Juno wobbled and bounced as he ran up to bowl; his arms jerked about stiffly like windsocks in a tornado. The sight of him was a distraction, enough to throw a less seasoned batsman off his concentration, but Rhys watched only the ball as he hunched over his bat, nerves hard and muscles primed. It spun and smacked towards him at dizzying speed, but at exactly the right moment Rhys placed his bat, lifted it with authority so that willow and hide connected loudly and crisply. The ball arched in a magnificent loop up and over the scattered fielders and landed amidst shouts where a group were picnicking on the river boundary.

'A six! Capital, lad!' applauded Sir Kenneth, leaning on his bat at the opposite crease.

Juno glared. He spat viciously on his hands before delivering the next ball. Again it bounced and slapped, and again Rhys moved with precise timing to send it looping gracefully to the same place where now the picnickers were spectators, interested, cheering. A little girl, tripping over her frilled hems, skipped to roll the ball back to the nearest fielder.

The third ball was delivered grimly, flung down like a gauntlet. Rhys picked it up with a deft scoop of his bat and hurled it into oblivion. For the fourth, a high-bouncing, loosely tossed ball, Rhys had a sharp stinging reply. The fifth landed among swans in the river, causing squawks and flurries of white wings.

'Magnificent!' boomed Sir Kenneth, and in the silence following the crowd's ecstatic applause a feminine voice called: 'Well done, Rhys!' Leonie's voice, he guessed, from the expression of hostility on Juno's suffused face.

For the last ball of the over Juno laid down another of his medium-speed spinners. With almost an independent spirit the ball bounced, hesitated, skipped and then bounced in a different direction. Too confident now, Rhys miscalculated and made contact too early – by only a fraction of a second, but enough to flaw his stroke. The ball whirled loose and high. Within seconds it was obvious that it would fall short of the boundary. Fielders ran to catch it on the full.

'You're done for!' crowed Juno, tugging his watch from his fob and checking the time. 'Dismissed in eight minutes! That must be something of a—' He broked off as he watched the three fielders jostling for position. One shoved the second aside in the scramble, and the third, oblivious to everything but the ball, dived into the gap pushing both the others away. He snatched the prize but tripped as he leaned forward to secure it and was scrabbling in dismay as the ball jerked from his cupped hands.

'You fools!' screamed Juno. 'You absolute fools!'

'I'm the fool,' muttered Rhys, determined not to let his concentration slip again.

Watching from their vantage-point on the slope beside the stands, Lisabeth was having a miserable time. Seated in front of her, Andrew was a ferment of unrepressed and gleeful excitement, cheering with every thump of the bat and babbling non-stop praise of his hero. 'Isn't he wonderful, Lisabeth? Isn't he simply grand?' he kept saying as he twisted his glowing face around to glance at her, his green eyes brimming with awe.

Struggling with her consternation, Lisabeth forced a smile. She couldn't condemn his open admiration: unwillingly she shared it, too. That was the worst of it. Nobody watching this display of dazzling cricket could fail to be moved by it. He was brilliant. Out there under the darkening sky his tense figure and laughing face were a magnet for all eyes. He was a perfect hero.

Recognizing that, she felt confused and unhappy. Without understanding why, she felt like crying. When from nearby Leonie called out to Rhys in front of all these people, implying intimacy in a way that shocked Gwynne, Lisabeth couldn't scoff.

Suddenly her drab clothes mattered. She knew that Rhys and Leonie and all the beautiful people in the stands inhabited a world she would never know; the most she could hope for was an occasional peek at them from a distance. Her misery intensified. Though she jutted her chin and told herself she didn't care, the fine brave words dropped into the pit of depression, useless.

At the end of each over the bowlers changed ends. Now Sir Kenneth faced the ball. On his first stroke he smacked a tidy single run which left Rhys again at the batting end. This service he performed each time; one ball, one neat stroke, and the batters exchanged places. After half an hour Sir Kenneth had scored five runs and Rhys a hundred; fifteen minutes later Rhys retired on a total of a hundred and fifty runs, thus denying Juno the satisfaction of dismissing him.

The crowd were on their feet, stamping, whistling, clapping their approval. Andrew flung his straw panama into the air then threaded his way down the slope and dashed on to the field, racing to intercept Rhys as he strolled towards the stands.

A void opened under Lisabeth's heart as she saw them together, both smiling, Andrew's bright face tilted up and Rhys looking down at him. The likeness between them seemed so strong, so obvious that she sneaked furtive glances at Gwynne and Charles, wondering if they saw it, too. For a moment fear made her giddy, but then she realized that the likeness was blatant only to her, and the world steadied around her again.

'Uncle Rhys said I can have a bowl!' cried Andrew brandishing the information like a trophy. He didn't even notice her distress.

'They're opening the earth ovens over there!' reported Andrew, just returned from a visit to the gents'. 'They're shovelling the dirt off the flax mats, and all the steam is frittering up through them. It smells gorgeous! One of the Maori men said there's pork and lamb and chickens and —'

'*Hangi kai? Ah, kapai!*'* chuckled Braddock.

'I don't care if they've diamond-studded beef,' retorted Charles. 'You're not eating that dirty native food if I can help it. Mrs Stafford has packed pies and cheese and a jar of water with lemon and barley in it. Sure and you'll find that perfectly antiquate.'

It's only twopence, and it is delicious, thought Gwynne who would dearly have loved a taste herself. Despite what her husband said she knew that *hangi kai*, or food prepared in the Maori way, was always clean and hygienic. But, as usual, she said nothing.

Lisabeth loved *hangi kai*, too, but she also was silent. Deaf to the discuussion, she was watching Rhys as he detached himself from Leonie's company and continued his progress towards them. It was lunch-time. Leonie had beckoned Rhys over, calling to him and waving her taselled fan; and, while Lisabeth watched, Rhys stooped to kiss her hand, holding her bare fingers for what seemed like minutes – far longer than necessary for a mere greeting. Even from this distance she could hear Leonie's grating throaty giggle, and though Lisabeth willed them to appear there was no sign of Mr Gammerwoth or Mr Fox.

---

*'Earth-oven food? Ah, good!'

216

But now Rhys was on his way towards them. Gwynne was spreading a cloth on the ground. Lisabeth should have been helping unpack the hamper, but she murmured, 'Excuse me . . . I'll be back soon,' and fled with no intention of returning until after he had gone.

Rhys was disappointed. Originally, he had intended to invite Lisabeth to have tea and cakes in the members' room (asking Andrew first as a pretext), but though he waited for fifteen minutes she failed to appear.

Lisabeth walked briskly until she reached safe territory behind the stands, then slowed her pace. Unhappiness blocked her chest; she wished she could go home and walk along the cliff-paths in a bracing wind, alone, instead of jostling through this throng of happy merry-makers.

What's wrong with me? she wondered. I should be enjoying myself.

Breathing in the delectable fragrances of the *hangi*, she felt acutely hungry but she wandered past the trestle tables and tried to ignore the sight of dozens of people clutching little baskets of food which they ate with delight. She walked faster again.

Under the chestnut trees at the far end of the pavilion a selection of paintings were arranged for appraisal and sale. The trees were coming into tender green leaf, and the shadows of the branches criss-crossed the pictures like gently moving fingers. Lisabeth headed for the display. Art could take her mind off her hunger.

Perhaps it was her mood. She didn't like the paintings; they were heavily coloured and so crammed with intricate detail that there was not a tranquil space in them, not even in the skies, busy with clouds. She was frowning over a view of the Ferrymead landing when someone said, 'Miss Stafford?' in a thin dry voice, and before she craned her neck to look into his face she knew that the artist was Athol Nye.

Because she seldom went into town she had not seen him since the day of his father's funeral. Anxious to avoid commenting on his pictures she asked after his mother.

'She's at home. We've settled on a few acres near Sumner and I teach at the boys' school that's opened near there. Hence all these views,' he said, his papery skin flushing. 'She doesn't go out now, and neither do I, much. Times are hard, Miss Stafford.'

'For us, too,' admitted Lisabeth. Then she smiled. 'But we're here, aren't we? Things can't be so bad if we're here at the Fête.'

'I'm only here on business,' he said gravely – a reprimand – but then 'I've just sold two paintings, and I'm starving. What about you, Miss Stafford? Would you risk trying some of that food they're selling? The aroma has been tantalizing me, I don't mind admitting. Do you mind? It's not elegant, I'm afraid.'

'Not the thing to nourish the soul,' teased Lisabeth.

'I beg your pardon?'

He's so deathly serious, she thought. 'Never mind. I'd love some,' she said.

Fifteen minutes was far too long in Charles Stafford's company, decided Rhys, thoroughly fed up with the inappropriate questions he was firing at him. Even if he wanted to discuss his financial affairs with Charles, and he most adamantly did not, he'd have chosen somewhere private. The others were a trial, too. Andrew was over-animated, wanting to replay the innings over and over, while Gwynne was full of gushing praise. But there was no sign of Lisabeth.

By now Juno Gammerwoth and Thomas Fox had emerged from the visiting team's quarters and were ensconced beside Leonie, eating sandwiches and drinking glasses of what looked like cold tea. Rhys decided not to go past them on his return to the club rooms and instead took the circuitous route around the stands.

Near the *hangi* tables he stopped in mid-stride, so suddenly that people coming from behind brushed against him. He noticed neither them nor the angry 'Hoi, why'n'tcha look where'y'r going?' but stood momentarily breathless, gaping at Lisabeth who stood not ten feet away with a square flax basket in her hands, picking morsels from it and eating.

She was *sharing* her food.

As soon as Rhys noticed that, his attention switched from Lisabeth to her companion, a very tall, pale and bookish-looking fellow whom Rhys had seen several times before. They were talking quietly together, Lisabeth doing most of the talking, him doing most of the eating.

So that was the type she liked, thought Rhys, telling himself that it was the unexpectedness of it that shook him. He didn't realize that she even knew any young men. Remembering how he was going to offer her lunch – out of pity, he reminded himself, only out of pity – Rhys somehow felt that she had made a fool of him. Turning, he lurched away quickly, before she had a chance to glance up and see him. Not until he was out on the field again did the dazed feeling lift from him.

Lisabeth waited until the second innings was well under way before going to rejoin the others.

'I hope you're not wanting any pie,' said Charles, swatting crumbs from his beard.

'There's some bread and cheese, dear,' said Gwynne. 'You're just in time to see Andrew have a bowl. Wasn't it nice of Rhys to ask him to be their eleventh man? Rhys has already bowled two of the enemy out.'

'They're not the enemy, Mrs Stafford,' said Charles.

'It seems so to me . . . and Rhys knocked two out right off!'

'Joy in victory! That's the Maughold blood coming out,' crowed Braddock.

Charles glared at him. 'It's *dismissed*, Mrs Stafford, not "bowled", nor "knocked". For cricket you must use the correct termination.'

Nobody listened.

Juno Gammerwoth waddled across the field to pitch, bat jutting and waggling under one arm as he fumbled to button his gloves. 'He doesn't look well,' said Lisabeth, noting his florid complexion. She could see him breathing from where she sat.

'Sure and he's not been swilling tea with his luncheon,' said Charles, who had heard all the town gossip. 'Watch him stagger – he's intoxicating!'

Andrew waited in the slips while Rhys bowled the next ball, Juno's first but the last of that over. Juno tottered on his small feet then regained equilibrium as he swiped. He looked like a large white top, thought Andrew, bracing himself for a catch. Juno missed; the swing was silent. Andrew relaxed.

When after the next over Rhys held the ball out to Andrew, Juno flung down his bat in protest. 'You can't do that! This child shouldn't even be on the field!'

'He's in the team,' said Rhys.

'He didn't bat,' argued Juno.

'He's our eleventh man,' Rhys pointed out. 'We declared after eight, remember?'

The crowd was quiet, listening. Lisabeth could hear a fretful baby way over by the river. She could imagine Andrew's mortification at being the centre of the controversy and wondered why Rhys was doing this. Had he chosen this moment deliberately to

219

pour scorn on Juno Gammerwoth, to humiliate the man in front of his wife? If so, it was a cheap trick, she decided angrily.

'I'll not be bowled to by a child!' declared Juno, but the referee was consulted and after a scuffle of murmured argument Juno took up a batting stance again.

Copying what he had seen Rhys do, Andrew ran up, flung his arms around and sent the ball flying along the pitch. Juno hit it with contemptuous ease and took two runs. As Juno smacked the first crease with his bat and swivelled for the return plunge Rhys saw that his face was purpling and the breath tore out of him in short ragged gasps that sounded like someone ripping a rotten length of cloth into squares. It was a sick sound. Rhys murmured to the umpire who stood near the wickets. 'He's drunk,' the man replied, implying in those two words that he, the umpire, had never taken a glassful in his life.

Andrew weighed the ball in his hands. It was heavy and hard and seemed to be the only real thing in this strange landscape of bright smooth green and the untidy colours of hundreds of people, all pressed into place by the billowing push of the leaden clouds. When there was a flickering of clean light in the dirty sky above the stands Andrew wondered if he imagined it and glanced at Rhys for confirmation. Like all the other hundreds of people Rhys was staring at him. 'Play on,' he nodded as thunder rolled across the field.

Again he ran up with the skipping arm-flailing gait and loosed the ball, but this time it bounced wide of the pitch. The umpire signalled a point. Andrew flushed, and Juno hooted, clapping his hands mockingly. Fox, the other batsman, laughed, too.

When he ran up the third time Andrew could feel his ears burning. He was grim with determination. As he released the ball he heard Rhys say, 'Good, good!' and he stood, panting, arms akimbo, watching the ball.

Juno had taken one of his desperate swipes at it and begun to run, but the ball had flung to the slips where Rhys, handily placed, had leaped and plucked it from the air as it spun over his head. 'Hit the wickets!' he cried, tossing it straight to Andrew.

This was so unexpected that Andrew was momentarily confused. *Right, the wickets!* he thought, getting his bearings as he caught the ball, swung with it and flung it as hard as he could just as Juno was stumbling across the crease. The ball struck him on the side of the head.

Andrew watched stupidly; this old fat man was suddenly tilting forward and stretching his arms wide as he knelt, then flopped forward to embrace the earth. His body skidded right past the wickets. Andrew started to laugh – it looked so ridiculous – but when the man didn't move or speak he was gripped by a panicky intuition that something was wrong.

Pandemonium erupted. The crowd seeped on to the field, rushing over it from all sides like a flood claiming the last knoll. Fox was there first, then a doctor, and Rhys helped them loosen Juno's clothing around his bluish throat.

Lisabeth pelted on to the field, too, pushing her way through, shoving people aside. She felt as if she was clawing her way out of a vast dark dread. 'Andrew! Andrew!' she screamed.

At the moment she reached his side Thomas Fox was straightening. His long upper lip quivered, and his round hard eyes were stony. 'You're a murderer,' he said in a flat voice that caused the crowd to flinch and shrink away. It sounded so much like a judge's pronouncement. 'You, too, Morgan. You put him up to it.'

Before anyone could reply a burst of light exploded overhead and thunder came crashing down on them. 'An omen!' some fool in the crowd bleated, and the others took it up like a chorus. It started to rain.

Rhys put his hand on Lisabeth's arm as she was leading Andrew away. She shook him off and glared into his face, too upset to read his expression, which was of genuine regret and concern. 'It is your fault!' she hissed. 'Why don't you just leave us alone?'

Andrew pulled loose. 'Don't blame him, Sis! It was an accident.'

She was stricken. She gaped at him. Splatters of rain tapped on her bonnet. He gazed at her pleadingly with Rhys's face, Rhys's features set in an expression of determination and their mother's beautiful eyes looking out of that face.

Look at him! she wanted to scream at Rhys. *Look at him! See what you've done?* But at the same time she was terrified that he would look and more terrified that he would see. All she wanted was to get away, but when she grabbed his arm he shook his head, reasoning with her.

'Don't take any notice of what Mr Fox said. He didn't mean it. He was just angry. Uncle Rhys was being kind to me, letting me play.'

Lisabeth was incapable of speech. Dumbly she tugged at Andrew's arm. It was all she could do not to cry. Rain was whipping down hard.

Sir Kenneth appeared before them. He was dressed in his

cricket whites but with his tropical helmet on his head, water rolling from the brim. 'Everything all right?' he said. 'Nasty business, hey. Heart-attack, the doctor thinks. Not your fault, lad. Can I run you people home? The carriage is just near—'

Lisabeth saw Andrew's eyes light up at that and cut in swiftly. Raising her chin, she said: 'Thank you, Sir Kenneth, for your generous offer but we do have our own wagon. Come on, Andrew. Aunty Gwynne will be worried to distraction.'

Fox's shouted accusation had fallen into the aghast silence like a rock into a pond; ripples of it reached out through town and across the province. When, on the day of Juno Gammerwoth's funeral, a pamphlet appeared in Christchurch accusing Rhys and Andrew of complicity in his murder it was not news but confirmation of what everybody already suspected.

The pamphlet was like many that circulated from time to time – anonymous, hurriedly printed on the cheapest paper and scurrilous in the poisonous indictment contained in its few colourful sentences. Rhys found one tucked under the saddle-flap when he tethered Polka outside the doctor's one morning when he went to have a painful abscess lanced. He noticed at once that the pamphlet made no mention of Leonie, and took this as proof that Thomas Fox was the author. Anybody else would have sensationalized his friendship with Leonie and flaunted it as the 'motive', but Fox, of course, wanted to protect his daughter. This pamphlet may have been a preventative, to forestall other, juicier gossip.

'We did it for political gain, apparently,' Rhys told Sir Kenneth, after seeking him out in the solemn gloom of the Canterbury Club. 'The pamphlet claims that Juno was Fox's right-hand man in the coming campaign, just as I am yours.'

'Rubbish!' retorted Sir Kenneth from the depths of his tall leather wing-chair. 'Juno wouldn't have known a ballot-box if one bit him on the nose. Doubt if he's ever attended a political meeting.'

Rhys studied the tip of his cigar. 'Just the same, I think I'd better drop out, stand aside, let someone else take over as your campaign manager.'

Sir Kenneth laughed. His vast mass of spotless whiskers fluttered against his tropical suit. Rhys noticed what a pink clean mouth he had, like a baby's.

'I'm serious,' said Rhys, and Sir Kenneth stopped laughing.

'Don't you see, dear boy, that this will add life to our campaign? All to the good if the public scents the whiff of scandal. Even better that we're running a feud with the opposing candidate. If only we could arrange more drama – a duel perhaps, between you and Fox? Over Leonie, perhaps?'

'Sir Kenneth!' But he saw the twinkle in the old man's eyes and knew it was in fun.

As for Leonie, Rhys had written her a letter expressing deep regret over the incident and offering condolences. He expected no reply and received none, though later he wondered if the letter ever reached her. In the newspaper, describing the funeral, the cause of death was noted as heart failure. Few believed it. Nobody believed what they read in the papers anyway.

Rhys took a copy of the pamphlet to the Staffords' while Andrew was at school. Charles read it in a fury and wanted to wage war with Fox at once, but Gwynne twisted her top apron between gnarled hands and fretted about the effect it might have on the boy.

'You'll pull out of the campaign?' she asked.

'No,' Rhys told them. He was standing in the doorway with his back to them, gazing across the windswept fields to where Lisabeth was patiently plodding behind their horse, Major, the plough steady in her hands. 'What's she doing that for?' he asked Charles. 'That's no work for a girl,'

'Andrew's in school,' he replied, defensive.

'My God!' He turned in disgust.

'Mr Stafford hurt his back, Rhys. He hasn't been able to—'

But Rhys was gone, striding out across the fields.

'Hoi! Mind how you go!' called Charles. 'Do you see that, Mrs Stafford! He's trampling all my young bean shoots. He's not even looking at where he puts his boots!'

Lisabeth looked up wearily when she sensed someone was approaching. *Andrew*, she thought, surprised that the afternoon had passed so quickly. She was smiling a welcome before she recognized the tall figure, the gold hair burnished by the sun.

He smiled, too, thinking the welcome was for him, but her mouth was souring already. With an ache she noticed how handsome he was, and not really like Andrew when he smiled. Andrew didn't have that deep dimple at one side of his mouth, and his chin was rounder. *But when he's older*, she thought with hopeless

223

exhaustion. *When he's older and his features are mature, square and hard, how will we hide it then?*

'What's the matter?' Rhys asked.

I'll never tell you that. Never! Aloud she said, 'What do you want?'

'Stop a moment so that we can talk,'

'I can't,' she said over her shoulder, moving along because if she so much as hesitated Major would stop and the hardest part of ploughing was to get him moving again.

'Lisabeth, please.' Moving in front of her, he grabbed the reins and pulled, halting the horse in spite of her protests.

Her shoulders slumped. She would have sagged to the ground except that it would have meant sitting in slushy churned soil. Instead she let her head droop, stared at her mud-caked hem, as she said: 'What do you want to talk about?'

He told her about the pamphlet. She made no reaction until he added: 'But don't worry about it, Lisabeth. It's a six-day wonder; these things always are. The official verdict is a heart-attack. In the long run it won't matter.'

'It will always matter,' she said, raising her face but looking past him towards the hills. 'When he's an old man people will say: "Andrew Stafford? Isn't he the fellow who killed someone during a cricket match?" They'll never forget.'

There was an undeniable truth in what she said, and the pain in her face moved him to console: 'People aren't really like that. Perhaps the odd one, the gossip-monger, but by and large people's memories are short and selfish, Lisabeth,'

She denied it emphatically. *Not mine!* she thought, for wasn't her memory as long and tenacious as a jungle creeper stretching to keep pace with time, always ready to blossom out with a reminder whenever she weakened? This was the way it should be, that poor tragic Mary should be remembered, always.

'Lisabeth,' he was saying urgently. 'You mustn't blame me.'

The words startled her; she looked into his face and saw the unguarded tenderness in his eyes. The wind was whipping at his hair, and the sun was glinting on it. His skin looked polished. She shivered, hugging her shoulders, wanting him to go away. It was much easier to hate him when he wasn't there. His presence mellowed her, melted her antagonism, and afterwards she was angry at herself for her frail resolve. Lowering her head, she picked at the rag wrappings on her right hand.

'I'd hate it if you blamed me,' he told her.

No, she thought bitterly. *Mamma wouldn't ever have blamed you. She was a fool, she believed in you, believed you cared for her, she'd have let you wipe your muddy boots on her if you wanted.*

Her spine stiffened. Taking a deep breath, she raised her chin to tell him please to go away, but before she could speak Major moved off. He had been standing still, head drooping in the wind, but apparently decided that he'd rested long enough now. Lisabeth started as the reins tugged against her waist, then hurried after him, scrambling and slipping as she frantically tried to control the plough.

It was more than she could manage. While she talked to Rhys she had leaned on the handles and skewed it slightly sideways. The blade had bitten in deep in a soft place and now wouldn't twist back despite her furious efforts to straighten it.

'Whoa!' she cried, butting backwards at the reins, tossing a glare at Rhys, who was not laughing, digging in her heels as Major plodded inexorably on.

'Do you want some help?' he finally asked, then grabbed the reins again, yanking Major to a standstill.

'It's easy when you're not tired!' retorted Lisabeth, feeling foolish and angry as he began to smile broadly. 'I fail to see any—'

'You've got mud on your nose,' he said.

'Where?' She rubbed it and inspected the apron. It was clean.

'Here,' he told her, touching the tip of her nose with a damp forefinger. She looked so sweet and pathetic with her sunburned face and the wisps of hair straying from below her tatty old bonnet – was that the only one she owned? – and with the reins looped and knotted around the waist of that ancient patched dress. He couldn't resist teasing her, though later he wondered if depositing the smudge on the nose was just a pretext to touch her.

He was unprepared for her reaction. Swatting at her face with her bare left hand, she flicked the mud off, but a particle of it flew into her eye, borne by the stinging wind. 'Oh!' she cried as the treacherous lurking tears welled up and spilled over.

'Lisabeth!' he cried, horrified. She shook her head blindly, but he cupped her face in his hands, his fingers clasping her jawline while his thumbs gently smoothed the tears away. He had made her cry . . . His oafish clumsiness had brought her to this. . . .

Too weary to struggle, she allowed him to stroke her face, reluctant and quivering under his touch – like Major, she

225

thought, when he's having a stone removed from his hoof. His fingers were strong and work-roughened; feeling their rough texture against her skin gave her a feeling of illogical kinship with him. His obvious distress moved her.

'I'm sorry,' he was stammering, wounded by what he had done. 'I only meant it in fun . . . I wouldn't hurt you, Lisabeth.'

Her heart quailed at that; with a flush of guilt she recalled all the mean and petty resentments she held against him. To her horror fresh tears came welling up, unrestrained. She was simply too crushed by exhaustion to stop them. Silently she willed him to leave. *I can't cope with him*, she thought.

She wouldn't look at him; those haunting eyes, their beauty only veiled by the tears, were fixed on the mountains. He could sense a dead heaviness in her and knew she was only allowing him to touch her under sufferance. It maddened him. She was so aloof, so infuriatingly unattainable. Was it because of this that he found her so disturbing? If she looked at him the way most women of his acquaintance did – with covetous and flirtatious glances – would he find her unattractive then?

'Lisabeth,' It was an open plea, but stubbornly she ignored it. Stooping, he tried to force her to look at him, but she lowered her screen of lashes until her eyes were almost closed, maddening him still further. Then, in a lull in the wind, he realized he was breathing in her soft sweet breath, and with a groan he bound his arms around her and fastened his mouth over hers.

Her astonishment was total. His body was tight against her – he was so big that he seemed completely to surround her and so strong that when he straightened she was plucked up from where her boots had been rooted in the mud. Boneless, she hung cradled in his arms.

Though his action bewildered her, her own meek acquiescence stunned and shocked her. This was *Rhys Morgan*; he was *kissing* her, and she, stupid as a lamb, was allowing him to do it. Never mind that it was astoundingly lovely. Never mind that his mouth was soft and firm with the tickle of a moustache and that he moved in a lazy, leisurely way against her lips so that her heart and mind floated free and were drawn, flowing towards him . . . Lifted and borne forward in a surge of treacherous emotion . . .

'Stop!' Gasping, Lisabeth twisted her mouth free as she struggled against him, lashing out at his shins with her mud-caked boots, pushing at his shoulders with the heels of her hands.

He dropped her. Suddenly, without ceremony, without apology.

His eyes were cool, his voice colder. 'Don't tell me you didn't enjoy that.'

Hot shame seeped through her as she thought: *He knows! He's kissed so many women that he knew I was responding to his lips.* She scrabbled in her brain for something to refute his accusation; perhaps she could say she was so tired that she didn't realize what was happening until too late. Perhaps she could say—

It no longer mattered. Rhys had turned away and was walking in long squelching strides back across the fields. He was whistling a jaunty, cheery scrap of popular song he'd heard several times at the music-hall in the town square.

Lisabeth felt crushed. Her first kiss, her very first real kiss, and it had to be a bruising, humiliating experience with the man she loathed more than anything in the world. She didn't know which was worse – her perilous almost submission to an alien – *utterly alien* – emotion that compelled her to respond to his unwanted embraces, or the casual way he dismissed her and walked away. If he'd apologized, she might have salvaged some of her pride by scornfully rejecting his apology but, as it was, he'd left her with the feeling that hers had been a cheap kiss easily won and not worthy of the smallest consideration.

For a moment there flickered in her mind the question of what might have happened had she not kicked out at him. It was a tantalizing idea, but she snuffed it out angrily.

'I wish . . .' she said aloud. 'If only . . .' But she was too tired to finish. Scorching with shame and suddenly overwhelmed by a regret she could not understand, she sat down on the wet furrowed ground and wept.

Part Two

TWENTY-TWO

Ｂｙ DECEMBER THE LAND WAS WARM AGAIN. All scars of the plains fire had healed. When Rhys was boundary-riding he saw wild flowers winking amongst the regenerating tussocks while birds rustled up out of the marshes as he rode by – ducks, snipe and quail, and once a flock of parakeets hiccuping as they skimmed over his head. In the hollows where the fire had scored with charring breath little clumps of trees were encouraged into new growth. There were beech and ribbonwood, *kauri* and *rimu* and many others, all skirted modestly by an underfroth of lacy ferns.

As soon as the rains eased, his herds returned to the plains to nibble and grow plump on the bitter-sweet herbal growth, a legacy of the fire. As he guided Polka through the loose knots of grazing sheep, Rhys surveyed his estate with satisfaction, feeling that same queer thrill that he had experienced when first he gazed on the land. Now this feeling was overlaid with the warm knowledge of achievement.

He never regretted settling here. At the Christchurch Club there were many intelligent and educated men to talk to, including two he had known by sight at Oxford, and though the privations of his own life sometimes made him hark back to the harshness of the goldfields he was consoled by the reminder that roughing it was a temporary situation, and in the meantime he could enjoy the glories of his surroundings. When he heard talk of the terrible fighting in the North Island between Maori tribes and troops composed of British regulars and New Zealand volunteers he felt vaguely guilty. It seemed wrong that life could be so tranquil here yet in another part of the same country people were battling to the

231

death, for the Maoris, it was said, were being crushed to extinction. That bothered Rhys, too; though he had shot a Maori himself, that act was the necessary killing of an individual maurauder, not a blow struck against a whole race. If people lived close together, they would make an effort to become friends, or at least tolerant co-existers, he maintained. This theory raised hoots of laughter at the Club, so Rhys set out to prove his point. He fixed up three of the abandoned shacks in the Maori settlement and offered them rent-free to refugees from the fighting.

'Sure and your brother's crazy!' reported Charles in glee. 'Nobody's gone near them cottages, not when they hear they'd be living with the natives. Even Birdie Nevin turned her nose up when he offered her one, and she's been crammed with her brood into one room of the barracks, so she can't afford to be picky. Ay, that were a daft idea of that high and mighty brother of yours.'

'He's got a good heart,' said Gwynne placidly. 'And lots of folk are homeless. Perhaps *we* should—.'

'He can afford to be magnatimous,' grumbled Charles quickly. 'Sure and he's a jammy bogger. The Government Agent comes down to buy meat to feed the troops and who does he go to, hey? Sure and they say that brother of yours is rolling in money. No wonder he's got a heart of gold!'

The Staffords were facing a poor season, crippled at the outset by the devastating rainstorms which damaged their orchard and delayed the vegetable crops, but instead of putting in time on his land Charles was still renovating the cottage. It had now been painted white and the chimney topped off with a glazed earthenware pipe; then because his weight had fractured some of the old wooden roof-tiles he had spent a week checking them all and replacing the broken ones with new wood, giving the roof a strange scrappy look.

Gwynne showed Rhys the porch trellis where young honeysuckle was beginning to twine through the gaps. 'It'll be so bonny, won't it, when it flowers? Ah, the scent of honeysuckle . . . And Mr Stafford is going to add a parlour to the cottage just as soon as he can. It will do him good to take his mind off his money worries, poor man.'

Rhys privately thought that if Charles cultivated his fields with the same enthusiasm he put towards his creature comforts he'd have no money worries. Only half his acreage was in crops, and with summer under way the whole area should be planted out. But he smiled at his sister and said: 'Honeysuckle here, primroses in the garden for good luck, hawthorn hedges to keep the witches away – you take the Manx ways everywhere you go. Why not have flax bushes, and *kowhai* trees and the native clematis to trail over your trellis? You're in New Zealand, Gwynne; you should enjoy it to the full.'

She looked at him askance. 'But I'm Manx. I want to display our ways!'

'Like a missionary spreading the Word?'

'No, it's not that. It's a fence, Rhys. A *fence* against this barbaric place. Oh, Mr Rennie used to scoff, too; he said I should abandon all my superstitions, but to do so would mean to immerse myself in this land, and it's too fierce, too raw. I couldn't feel at home with the Maoriness – the toneless singing – not really singing, is it? – and those weird decorations they wear for jewellery. Don't you see, I need these reminders. I have to know that there are other, better places in the world.'

'By "better" you mean more civilized,' said Rhys. 'Well, you're not alone in your views. Sir Kenneth with all his trappings of the Raj – he still dresses as if he was in India – and the McFallishes with their kilts and bagpipes! Not me, Gwynne! What I love about this country is its roughness, its unformed state. There's the feeling that it could be shaped into a near-perfect civilization, given the right directions. There's no other place on earth that has started out with the opportunities that this colony has – there's a perfect opportunity to do everything as properly and fairly as human beings can make it, and the highest aspirations of everyone could be fulfilled in—'

'Ah,' said Gwynne. 'Mr Rennie used to talk like that for hours, but that's all it was. Talk.'

Rhys bridled. He was going to say something about Sir Kenneth and his plans to curb corruption in the province, but this second mention of Lawrence Rennie offended him and he shut off the subject with a tightening of his lips.

Not sensing the coolness, Gwynne began to talk about Christmas, sighing about how scratched it would be, what with money being so tight for them. Rhys scuffed his feet, restless to go, but mention of Christmas reminded him that he had not accomplished the errand that brought him here.

'We're having a Christmas tree, though. Lisabeth has painted pictures of angels and the Wise Men and cut them out, and Mr Braddock came back from town with some strings of silver ribbon to drape around the boughs.'

233

'A German custom,' disparaged Rhys. But he was teasing. He was too fond of Gwynne to be really angry with her. Or was it the mention of Lisabeth that cheered him?

'Only that one thing. The rest is pure Manx, I promise! We're having a traditional *Yn Oie'l Verry* on Christmas Eve, with mead and soda scones with buttermilk and lamb roasted with onions and sprigs of rosemary in the old way. Mr Braddock is going to tell us stories about the "buggane" and we'll sing "The Sheep under the Snow" and "The Loss of the Herring Fleet".'

'All fine cheerful stuff!'

'You will come, won't you, Rhys?'

He didn't really want to. 'I'll be in town. I'm going to midnight mass. See if the place falls down around my ears.'

'But that's splendid! We're going too. We can drive in together.'

'All right. I'll come to your *Yn Oei'l Verry*, on two conditions. That you let me provide the mead and that you help me with a problem I have.'

'A problem? You with a problem? Never!'

'It's what I came to see you about,' he said. 'A secret.'

The package was large and flat and square – heavy, too, for Gwynne had to ask Andrew to carry it in from where it was hidden in the implement-shed. 'A painting easel,' cried Lisabeth, delighted. The other had been smashed to matchwood when a gust of wind swept it over the cliffs on her last expedition to the headland.

'It's not an easel,' said Gwynne, looking timidly at Charles and wishing she had not agreed to this scheme of her brother's. It wasn't right for Rhys to buy Lisabeth a gift like this, and she was nervous about Charles's reaction.

'I'm being spoiled,' said Lisabeth as she fumbled with the scissors. 'A pretty handkerchief from Andrew, a mirror from you and Uncle Charles, sweets from Mr Braddock and Mr Morgan, and now —' Her heart stopped and breath clogged her throat as she opened the lid and saw the gown. 'For me?' she whispered in disbelief.

It was a simple summery gown, palest egg-shell blue with darker-blue flowers embroidered in garland around the scooped neckline, along the pointed edge of the basque and around the edges of the fully puffed, flounced sleeves. Touching it in wonder, Lisabeth rubbed the delicate silk material between her

234

work-reddened fingers. The thought of having that soft cloth against her skin after the harsh prickly serge seemed an incredible luxury. Tears of awe filled her eyes.

Her reaction moved Gwynne unexpectedly; she'd never had the experience of seeing Lisabeth with something pretty, and it was such delicious fun that she forgot her worry about Charles. 'There are petticoats, too – a hooped one and a ruffled one to go over the top, and enough spare material to make a pretty little bonnet if you like. We could easily—'

'A real *crinoline*!' cried Lisabeth at the mention of the hooped petticoat, just as Charles roared: 'Have you gone stark staring mad, Mrs Stafford?'

Gaping at him, she thought: *I should have told him.*

'Are you in full possession of your facilities?' he demanded. 'A dress like this would cost five guineas at least!'

'Please, Mr Stafford. Please don't shout . . . not on Christmas day,' she soothed, wishing that Rhys was here to do his own explaining. Why couldn't he have given it to her himself? 'None of this is costing you a penny.' she said, just as Rhys had coached her. 'So you needn't concern yourself about it.'

'Who did it cost, then, hey?'

'It needn't concern you, Mr Stafford,' she repeated, but with quavering resolution. He was angrier than she could have anticipated.

Dismayed by the quarrel, Lisabeth shrank back in her chair and didn't try to stop Andrew when with a whoop he lifted the gown up by the shoulders and wafted it about like a flag. It was even more beautiful seen in its entirety, with a skirt so wide it took her breath away, with a dozen more rows of embroidered flowers decorating the endless hemline. Bows of narrow dark-blue ribbon trimmed the sleeves but, best of all, the gown fastened with a long row of covered buttons – not down the front as all of Gwynne's dresses did, but down the *back*. Only ladies with maidservants to button them in had gowns that closed at the back.

But who was it from? Not from Uncle Charles – she'd have guessed that, anyway – and not from the Days; they were kindly folk, but this was too expensive for them to afford. *Mr Braddock*, she thought. It must have been from him. If there was a fairy godfather in this household, it was he.

Charles guessed so, too. 'He can take it right back!' he shouted. 'I tell you, Mrs Stafford, I've had quite enough of that grubby fellow Braddock loitering around here, supping the food

235

I've paid for with the labour of my hands!'

'But he's generous!' protested Lisabeth, unable to keep from interrupting. 'He's not a sponger, Uncle Charles. He's always bringing—'

'And he's after something!' declared Charles darkly. 'Just show me the man who isn't! That dress is going back, Mrs Stafford, and I'll see no more of that drunken old fool around here.' He glared at Lisabeth. 'And you'll keep silent when I'm speaking, lass. I'm the head of this household, sure, and I'll have no more insolvence out of you!'

'It's his worries, dear,' Gwynne consoled Lisabeth, but she was in need of consoling herself. What possible ulterior motive could Mr Braddock have for his visits? He was an old kindly man and he only wanted to talk about Home now that he was at the end of his life. She sympathized with that and she enjoyed the chats as much as he did. *Bother* Rhys and his secrets! she railed. This was not only mean, but also unjust.

To his credit Charles did feel a prickling of guilt. On his next visit to town he remembered the stricken look of disappointment in Lisabeth's eyes, so came home with a gown for her, a poorly styled thing of cheap cream muslin, limp-skirted and frayed at the cuffs, that he'd bought at the pawnbroker's on Avonside Street.

'If only it buttoned down the back, then at least I could pretend it had belonged to someone grand,' mourned Lisabeth as she and Andrew waited outside the church on the first occasion that she wore it. 'But it would have belonged to a poor woman, and it looks like a nightgown. It's so drab and it doesn't fit anywhere.'

'It looks pretty,' lied Andrew.

'At least in the dark clothes I felt inconspicuous. Now I feel like a gowk. Look at how Mr Morgan is staring at me! I wish he wouldn't. What's he doing at church anyway? He hardly ever comes.'

'Don't worry . . . He's sweet on Mrs Gammerwoth. Everybody at school says so,' said Andrew to cheer her up. 'They stand in the street and talk for *ages*! Maybe he'll marry her now that she's a widow.'

'Oh, *stop* it!' cried Lisabeth, utterly wretched. She turned away only to find herself facing Rhys again. Elegant in a light-grey cashmere suit with a crisp wing-collared shirt and glossy black boots, he was standing under a plane tree listening to Gwynne, who was talking rapidly to him in a low voice. Whatever she was saying was making him angry, for he had a ferocious expression on his face. When he saw Lisabeth looking at him he didn't smile, so preoccupied was he. He didn't even raise his grey silk top-hat to her.

Illogically, Lisabeth felt a stab of rejection. He'd have smiled if she was wearing her Christmas gown, she thought. Yes, he'd be looking at her with admiration then instead of with that odd mixture of anger and pity. In that glorious gown she'd have been every bit as beautiful as that haughty Mrs Gammerwoth, and wouldn't *that* have made him stare!

'I thought you were bothered about Uncle Rhys,' protested Andrew, indignant. 'I just wanted you to know that he doesn't mean anything. It was probably a stray glance you saw.'

'I know,' she said sourly. *And a stray kiss, too. He didn't mean that, either.* 'Where is Uncle Charles with the wagon? I do wish he'd hurry. Oh, I wish I'd just stayed home.'

With rare understanding Andrew said: 'Never mind! As soon as I can leave school and get a proper job I'll buy you a dress exactly like the one you lost.'

Lisabeth hugged him. He was almost as tall as she now. 'I don't really care about the dress,' she said untruthfully. 'Really I don't. But it would *kill* me if you gave up your chance for an education.'

When Rhys got the dress back he tucked the box under the ridge-pole of his roof. He never looked at it.

Braddock was the real loser in this unhappy episode. Not only was his friendship with Gwynne in limbo but Lisabeth avoided him, too. Resentful about the trouble he'd caused in the household and uneasy after all Charles's insinuations that Braddock was 'after something', all Lisabeth's original distaste for the old man returned. She couldn't dislike him, but at the back of her mind was Charles's sneering remark that it 'wasn't decent' for a man to buy a girl a personal gift like that, so now she never felt quite comfortable about him. Sometimes she met him by chance when he was walking with Bollan along the road: though she smiled and said good day, there was no proper conversation. He seemed very sad, which made Lisabeth feel worse. Then for weeks she didn't see him at all. They were very busy in the fields now, harvesting peas and beans, so Braddock faded from her mind. Once her resentment died she wondered whether she should have thanked him for the dress. She hadn't ever done so because it didn't seem appropriate somehow.

The season was a disappointing one for Charles. Because his crops were late they reached their peak right at high season and were offered in the market when there was a glut of fresh vegetables. Only his small harvests of radishes and the novelty tomatoes he had grown under glass (left over from the cottage windows) fetched a satisfactory price. Brooding over his misfortune, Charles was so touchy and bad-tempered that Lisabeth and Andrew avoided him whenever they could.

Late one afternoon when Lisabeth was sorting beans into trays for sale Andrew came pounding down the track beyond the cockatoo cattages and flung himself into the shed, panting, his face scarlet. 'You've got to see what I found. You've got to!' he gasped.

She picked out a scrap of leaf and arranged more beans on top of the others, discarding any that were muddy or had been bored into by caterpillars. Her fingers worked as swiftly as her eyes.

'Come *now*,' pleaded Andrew when she wanted to know what all the urgency was about. 'You should see this. Come on.'

He led her up the ridge-path and beyond the little side-track that led to Heywood Braddock's cliff-top dwelling. They crossed a gully where feathery bronze ferns plucked at their clothes and then reached the fence boundary to the sheep station.

'We can't go there,' protested Lisabeth, hanging back when Andrew parted the wires so that she could scramble between them.

'You must,' he insisted. 'Come on, we're nearly there,'

What they were nearly to was a shepherd's hut, a tiny sod structure dug so deeply into a knoll that they were almost upon it before they saw the bleached canvas roof and the three feet of wall that jutted above the surrounding tussock. It had a chimney of corrugated iron, while beyond was a small rail corral with a brush-wood shelter at one end for the horse. Two empty kennels were near the hut doorway, and an upturned tin basin lay among a scattering of gnawed bones.

'Andrew!' cried Lisabeth, when he pushed the sacking door-screen aside and disappeared into the hut. 'Andrew, come back this *instant*!'

His head stuck out, decorated with a cheeky grin. 'It's all right. Aunty Gwynne sent me up here with a fruit cake and told me to put it somewhere up high so that the dogs wouldn't get it like they did last time. I couldn't undo the meat-safe, so—'

'You mean this is—'

'Uncle Rhys's hut. Yep, sure is! Come in, it is all right. He's not expected home until morning.'

She couldn't argue with him because he'd disappeared again, so for a few moments she stood there with her back to the hut and the sun on her face, gazing across a vast wheat-field where the wind was swimming in great strokes through the stalks making them shimmer like the ocean. Nothing of Rhys Morgan's could *possibly* interest her, she thought, but then curiosity swamped reluctance and she turned to peek gingerly through the doorway.

Inside the hut was Spartan, bare and gloomy, with light entering only from the chimney and the faintly translucent roof, which gave the room a watery grey light. Lisabeth noticed how scrupulously clean it was, with a grain-sack spread neatly on the swept dirt floor and the hearth bare with a stack of chopped wood ready for use at one side. The only personal touches were some clothes hung on the ridge-rail and a shelf crammed with new-looking books, novels, volumes of poetry and practical guides to farming. Lisabeth plucked a book by Charles Dickens from the row and was flicking it open when she noticed that Andrew had climbed on to the table and was tugging something down from the rafters.

Opening her mouth to reprimand him, she instead uttered an 'Oh!' of shock as she recognized the box. 'My Christmas gown!' she said even before he raised the lid to reveal the tissue-swathed blue silk, still exactly as she had tearfully packed it away.

'Isn't it exciting?' Andrew chirped, his eyes bright in the dim light. 'Mr Braddock didn't give you this dress – Uncle Rhys did! It's *you* he's sweet on, that's why he was staring at you. Isn't it great? He probably wants to marry you, and when he does I can come and live—'

'Stop it!' hissed Lisabeth, clenching her fingers around his upper arms and shaking him until he gaped at her in bewilderment. 'Rhys Morgan *isn't* sweet on me, and he *doesn't* want to marry me, but even if he did I wouldn't marry him if my very life depended on it. So you're never to—'

'But why not?' interrupted Andrew, almost shouting to drown her voice. 'He's going to be one of the richest men in Canterbury – Uncle Charles says so! – and he's handsome and kind and lots and lots of fun, and he always smiles and says nice things and—'

'Stop it!' she cried, tears welling, for everything her brother said stung with a truth she did not want to hear. 'You're never to talk like that, do you understand? *Never!*' And before he could argue she tore away and shoved blindly out into the bright

239

afternoon sunshine, pounding across the tussocky plain until she came to the boundary fence. Only when she had wriggled through it did she feel safe, sprawling face down on the clean-smelling earth until her breath came evenly again. The sun has hot on her back. In the distance Andrew's voice called to her and from above the cliffs came the bark of seagulls squabbling over something.

He bought it because he felt sorry for me, she thought. Not from any sense of affection, but because he's noticed how ugly and patched my clothes are.

Turning that reason over in her mind, she decided it must be the truth. Of course, he'd stared at her that day at church because he was expecting her to be rigged out in his anonymous present.

Loathsome, she thought. *Loathsome!* But the sickening feeling that coursed through her was not hatred, but shame. Shame that Rhys Morgan considered her to be an object of pity.

We all owe Mr Braddock an apology, she reflected, and instead of returning immediately to her bean-sorting she impulsively veered at the ridge-top and turned towards the coast. The shadow of the cliffs lay blue and cool on the harbour, and beyond the rib of reef she could hear the ocean gurgling and belching among the rocks, licking and picking them clean as bones.

Braddock's cottage, lost in shadow, too, was ominously silent, no sign of smoke, not even the smell of a fire. His dinghy was beached on dry land at the foot of the path so he must be somewhere around. When she called there was at first no reply, but then a faint whining and scratching came to her ears and she hurried to the other side of the cottage where Bollan's kennel was wedged between the cannibal try-pot that held the lemon-tree, and the bank behind. Bollan was there, lying on the ground halfway up the bank. At first she thought he was injured but when she reached him she saw his chain was snagged on a broken root that was protruding from the scratched earth. As she freed it he whined and licked at her hands with an oddly dry tongue. He was so thin that his side resembled a liver-spotted washboard, and as soon as she turned him loose he slunk straight to the water-dish beside his kennel, gulping the water in noisy thirsty swallows until the bowl was empty, but then he kept licking at it, desperate for more. His brown eyes, strangely sunken, gazed up at her.

He's starving! she realized, and an awful premonition stole over her. Terrified of what she would find she walked away from Bollan and knocked on the door. 'Mr Braddock?' she called timidly.

When the door creaked open a thick fetid smell assaulted her and she turned away, gagging; then with a deep breath of fresh sea air in her lungs she plunged into the dark room. At first she could see nothing but Mr Braddock's rag-heaped bed, but as her eyes became accustomed to the low light (and she was cautiously breathing the stinking atmosphere) she was then able to see what a shambles the room was in. Rubbish, old newspapers, bottles and vegetable scraps littered the table and the floor, while in the centre of the ash-choked fireplace hung the source of most of the smell, a rotting joint of meat swarming with maggots and flies. Beside the fireplace, sprawled unconscious in an armchair with an empty brandy-bottle in his lap, was Braddock himself.

'Mr Braddock?' Lisabeth repeated. Bile was rising in her throat; that stench was unbearable, clinging to the insides of her mouth and nose like some vile liquid, but though her overwhelming impulse was to dash outside again she fought off the nausea while she placed one hand on Braddock's neck, feeling for a pulse. *He's dead!* she thought in giddy panic.

Bollan had followed her in. Padding silently, nosing his way hopefully through the rubbish on the floor he came now to Braddock and thrust his nose into his master's lap, whining a pleading question. He licked the leathery hands, still squeaking out his whines, and as if in response Braddock groaned.

Yes, he's dead, thought Lisabeth. *Dead drunk!* Unable to contain the sour vomit any longer, she lurched outside and was leaning against the rough sod wall, heaving helplessly into the fluffy sugar-grass that grew there, when Joe Day came up the hill behind her.

'I can't help it,' she murmured weakly, wiping her mouth with a trembling hand. 'Don't laugh at me.'

'I'm not laughing.' His wide-set eyes were dark with concern, and he combed his curly hair with his fingers in a nervous gesture as he said: 'Is Mr Braddock . . .? Is he . . .?'

'He's alive,' managed Lisabeth, still hunched over in dizzy misery. Joe, she noticed thankfully, had gallantly turned his back and remained some distance away.

'Praise the Lord for that,' said Joe. 'There's been no smoke from his chimney the last three days, and it's better'n a week since he rowed over to the hotel for supplies. Ma was worried. It's out of character for him to stay away this long.'

Lisabeth straightened. Her legs felt tottery, and her head swam with unpleasant sensations. 'I think he's drunk all his supplies,

241

judging by the number of empty bottles. Do you think an old man like that should be allowed to buy so much brandy and whisky? It must be terribly bad for him.'

Joe slanted a hard look at her, suspecting that she was criticizing his family for selling the spirits. Well, it was hardly their fault! Heywood Braddock was a free agent. If he didn't buy from the Sumner Hotel, he'd go elsewhere. Slowly he said: 'Perhaps you should ask Rhys that question. It's him putting the money into Mr Braddock's purse, you know. Before the land was sold old Braddock had only a few pence a time for supping, and if he walked down to the jetty with a bottle of brandy it were because our mother gave it him.'

'I'm sorry,' said Lisabeth. Her mouth tasted indescribably nasty. 'I didn't mean . . .'

'So long as we've plain speaking between us, there can be no misunderstandings. That's what the Captain always says, and they're wise enough words for me.' And with that Joe strode past her to the door. 'Dear Lord!' he exclaimed as the stench hit him. Lisabeth heard him fumbling around, then he strode past her with the rotten joint wrapped in a cloth and flung it away down the cliff. Dusting his hands off, he grinned at her ruefully. 'I can sympathize with your feelings entirely, but Mr Braddock is ill. I think he's taken a fall and hurt himself. One knee is badly swollen, and he seems to be in a lot of pain. Do you think that Mrs Stafford could come and look at it?'

'She can't walk up the hill, it's too steep for her, but I know enough bush medicine to tell if anything's broken.'

'That's all we need,' grinned Joe. His relief at finding Braddock alive was obviously enormous. Clowning, he bowed to permit her to go first. 'After you, Miss Nightingale.'

An hour later Lisabeth returned to the cottage carrying a jar of warm soup and some scraps for Bollan – a heel of stale bread, a large mutton bone and the scrags of a chicken that had been killed that morning. Tipping these into his dish, she added a ladleful of water from the rain-barrel to soften the bread then whistled him out to eat. Slavering over the food, he growled at her, challenging her not to touch it, so she left him and went into the cottage.

Joe had gone, and so had most of the stench and rubbish which he'd scraped out in her absence and flung away after the rotten meat. Braddock was lying on his bed, conscious now but very weak, his skin as grey as his stubbly beard.

'Have yurr brought me a drink, darrlin' gel?' he croaked, seeing the wrapped jar.

'It's soup,' Lisabeth told him. 'Chicken soup. But Aunty Gwynne put in a dash of sherry to cheer you.'

'Ah, but she's a darrlin', too,' he sighed.

Is she? thought Lisabeth, still seething after their terse conversation. When challenged about the fact that poor Heywood Braddock was allowed to be blamed for Rhys's misplaced generosity Gwynne had at first tried to deny it and then, with evasive glances and sucking of her lower lip, she explained that because Mr Braddock was an old man 'it didn't matter as much' as the good relations she wanted to foster between Charles and Rhys. 'There's been such a strain,' she confessed. 'The finance company won't extend any more credit unless Mr Stafford gives them the deeds to this land as collateral and I'm sorry to have to say this but Rhys won't help! It was such a blow to his pride when Rhys refused to lend – just a small amount, too!'

Just the first of an endless number of small amounts, thought Lisabeth, and she left quickly, disgusted with Gwynne. The revelation that she wasn't perfect shook Lisabeth. All these years she'd adored her as a saintly soul, but now she had to wonder if that blissful calm wasn't merely a lazy acceptance of things that masked an insidious selfishness. She'd snubbed a kindly old man for no better reason than that it suited her purposes to mislead Charles, and now Lisabeth suspected that Gwynne would blame Charles for the snubbings, let Mr Braddock think it was all his fault.

'Ay, but she's an angel,' waffled Braddock. 'I always knew he didn't like me much. Yurr know that?'

Lisabeth didn't trust herself to reply. 'Taste your soup,' was all she would say.

For months Rhys had made a practice of looking out for Braddock as he rode his boundary, and stopping by the cottage if there was no sign of him. It was unfortunate that in the past week he had broken routine, travelling into town most days to consult with an architect about the house he planned to build on the cliff-top, on the very spot from where he first gazed over his land.

'It was good of you to look after him,' Rhys said to Gwynne when he called in to tell her of his plans. 'Oh, and by the way, who came to deliver that fruit cake you sent yesterday?'

'That was Andrew,' Gwynne said, 'Did you like it?'

'Delicious as usual. By the way,' he said as he turned to go, 'Lisabeth wasn't with him, was she?'

'I don't think so. No, of course not! She'd never go to your hut.'

'Mmm,' said Rhys, wondering what in the world Andrew would have taken the gown-case down from the rafters for. It was all most peculiar.

Gwynne watched him go. She was glad she hadn't mentioned Lisabeth's anger of the previous evening and how guilty the girl felt about all the suffering Braddock had been through. Best that Rhys knew nothing about all that unpleasantness.

'All's well that ends well,' she said to herself.

As Braddock grew more feeble Lisabeth took to visiting him twice a day. In the mornings she helped him out to his bench beside the whale jawbone, under the *pohutukawa* tree where she set up his easel and placed paints and brushes beside him. When she came again in the afternoon he may have managed only a few strokes, but the presence of those familiar articles seemed to comfort him. All through the day he was content to gaze out over the ocean and around towards the mountains that he loved.

' "Rangi Pokekohu," ' he said to Lisabeth. 'Hine, my wife, she told me that legend many times. When the clouds come down over those mountain peaks the Maoris say it's the fairies, the goblins. They play their magic flutes and lure folks up through the mists of heaven.' He cackled. 'They say it's where the lost souls wait for their partners to join them but, if yurr ask me, I say it's a fancy way ter explain how folks wander about in fog, fall down and get killed.'

'It's a beautiful story, though,' mused Lisabeth.

One afternoon she arrived to find Bollan whining in such an agitated way that she knew at once what had happened. Dropping the bunch of primroses she had brought him for good luck, she rushed to feel the pulse in his withered neck.

The crêpey flesh was till warm. Tenderly Lisabeth closed his eyes, thinking how sad it was that he had died alone. If only she hadn't paused to pick the primroses . . .

She looked back towards the mountains. Clouds were down, obscuring the peaks, wrapping even the foothills in thick white mists. 'Rangi Pokekohu', mused Lisabeth. She wondered if his Hine was waiting there for him.

TWENTY-THREE

HEYWOOD BRADDOCK left his small tin trunk of Manx memen-
toes to Gwynne, his old dog Bollan (with five guineas for his care)
to Andrew, and his little roan and sledge to Rhys. The balance of
his estate went to Lisabeth. Seated on a bentwood chair in the
prim white offices of Valentyne & Wood, she heard herself named
as the owner of the cottage and its contents, a rowboat, a banked
sum of two hundred and eighty-nine guineas nine shillings and
fourpence, and one hundred acres of land which, Braddock
hoped, 'would continue to be leased in perpetuity to Mr Rhys
Morgan, esquire, with said Mr Morgan being offered first opportunity to purchase this land should the need for sale arise'.

'Sure and this is a slap in the face for us, Mrs Stafford, after all
that we done for him!' grumbled Charles. 'Five guineas for a
wretched damned dog and not a farthing for us! Downright
ingratiating, that's what I call it!' He glared at Lisabeth, too angry
to speak to her. There must have been something underhanded
between her and Braddock. First that flossy gown and now this.
Braddock wouldn't have left the girl this much money unless
there was a damned good reason. Ay, she was her mother's
daughter all right. Look at her preening in the wagon, a sly smile
on her face. The daughter of a slut and a slut herself, he wouldn't
be surprised.

Lisabeth was too dazed to notice the hostility. When the money
was first mentioned there was a quick vision in her mind of beautiful gowns, parasols, delectable lacy scraps of bonnets, and shoes
that were fashioned for style, not for their ability to keep out
mud, but when the enormity of her good fortune penetrated all

245

she could think of was Andrew. This would mean that he could have the best education available to a young man in the province – a place at King's College – and as a boarder, too, so that he could study uninterrupted in the evenings instead of toiling into the night trimming vegetables and nailing packing-cases for Charles by the light of home-made tallow candles. The freedom she prayed for was Andrew's at last. Best of all, she thought, he would be away from Rhys for such long periods that hopefully the ridiculous hero-worship would end.

She squeezed his hand, beaming with happiness as the plans unfolded in her mind. First King's, then perhaps a university – a college overseas, perhaps. The world was his.

He grinned back at her. 'Five guineas!' he crowed, ecstatic over his own windfall. 'Five guineas just for looking after Bollan. He's no trouble at all – I'd have looked after him for nothing!'

Charles spat a stream of tobacco juice into the water as the cart trundled over one of the numerous narrow bridges that crossed the serpentine Avon river. 'I'll be taking the money,' he informed Andrew. 'Sure and it's me who'll have to pay for his food. Dogs don't live on air, you know.'

Andrew was flabbergasted. 'They live on bones and scraps – those cost nothing! And, anyway, doesn't Uncle Rhys give us all the mutton we can eat? He wouldn't mind if some of it went to Bollan.'

'That's enough of that. I'll not tolerate insolvence from either of you. Didn't we take you in when your mother died? Don't we deserve some thanks for that? Sure and we do!' Gwynne nodded agreement. 'And as for your precious Uncle Rhys, I'll have no talk of him, either. He's had a hand in the making of this will, you can bet your boots on that.' He shot Gwynne a triumphant glance as he flicked the whip over Major's back, hurrying him past a stretch of waste ground where urchins were amusing themselves by flinging stones at the wheels of passing carts. 'Nasty little boggers!' he commented before confiding, 'And that brother of yours needn't think he can continue getting a cheap usage of Braddock's land, either. We're selling it, and I know just the buyer who'll pay top prices!'

A few days later Rhys rode through the orchard, dismounted and hitched Polka's reins over the clothes-line prop. He wore faded jodphurs and a simple twill shirt and from a distance looked exactly like one of his shepherds.

Gwynne was sitting in the latticed shade of the porch. Beside her was a pan of translucent, ice-green gooseberries to be picked over, but instead of working she was admiring some of the treasures from Braddock's tin trunk. It had contained a magpie assortment of oddments: teaspoons with the 'fylfut' or three-legged Manx symbol, a scarf woven from reddish-brown loghtan wool, a delicate handkerchief embroidered with water violets, and underneath the other things, wrapped in a rag, a dozen golden guineas. 'We'll not mention this find,' Charles had said, weighing them in his hand. 'Sure and they're ours now. Position is nine-tenths of the law, as they say!'

'Look at these!' said Gwynne to Rhys, holding out a creased palm on which lay several pearly triangular objects with hollow centres. 'Bollans! The good-luck symbol from the gullet of the bollan fish. Did you know, Rhys, that one of these given ensures a sweetheart's fidelity, or a good crop for a farmer, or a fine harvest for a fisherman? It's strong powers these possess.'

'Perhaps you'd better get Charles to sprinkle them around his fields, then,' Rhys suggested, as he bent to kiss her cheek. 'You're a superstitious old thing. Perhaps you can tell me what charm is needed to win a young lady's heart.'

'Bless you, you don't need lucky charms for that,' said Gwynne, peering up at him through her thick, ugly spectacles. 'There's half of Christchurch setting their bonnets at you. You should hear the gossip that flies around! Perhaps you shouldn't. . . . Perhaps not. Mr Stafford comes home with some outlandish tales.'

'I don't want to hear them. I prefer to leave gossiping to those who have the inclination and the leisure-time in which to practise the art.' He paused. 'I was hoping to have a word with Lisabeth about the land lease. Where is she?'

Gwynne bent her head and busied herself with wrapping the bollan charms in a piece of thin parchment paper. 'Mr Stafford took her into town.'

'Going shopping, is she? Good. I was hoping she'd spoil herself with some of that legacy. She's worked hard, caring for old Braddock. But if it's clothes she's buying, why didn't you go, too?'

Gwynne shook her head. She couldn't be disloyal to Mr Stafford but she couldn't think of a convincing lie, either. Right at this moment Charles and Lisabeth would be in the office of Valentyne & Wood where Charles intended to force Lisabeth to

247

sign her bequest over to him. Thomas Fox might be there, too, by now. Gwynne quailed inside as she wondered what Rhys would do when he found out that the hundred acres of beautiful land was to be sold to his enemy.

'What's the matter?' asked Rhys. 'You're not your usual chatty self.' Struck by a jab of premonition he squatted to his haunches and looked up into her guilty face. 'I say, that charming husband of yours hasn't got grand designs on Lisabeth's money, has he?' When she flushed and slid her eyes away he snorted: 'He has! Well, I'll be . . . My God, Gwynne, this is a despicable trick. Has he no honour?'

She was immediately defensive. 'That's not fair! We've scrimped to feed and clothe those children. As Mr Stafford says, he took them in only out of the kindness of his heart and it's the least he can expect that—'

'Rubbish,' snapped Rhys. 'Admittedly, Andrew is dressed smartly enough, but I've never seen Lisabeth in anything but rags and cast-offs. As for Charles taking them in out of kindness, I'd not be surprised if his sole motive wasn't to get a couple of unpaid workers. Come on, admit it, he's had Lisabeth toiling since the day she moved in!'

Gwynne lowered her head. 'Don't be hard on him, Rhys. He's a good man.'

'And a crafty one, to have you thinking that. Father said that you were always biddable, easily twisted but, good heavens, Gwynne, surely even for you there are limits! I can see that you know Charles is in the wrong, so can't you speak up against him once in a while?'

She sucked her lower lip. 'Don't think harshly of him.'

'Don't think *harshly*? When I've seen Lisabeth trudging through the mud behind the plough while Charles was off dallying in town – or when young Andrew was kept out of school because Charles was too mean to pay wages to one of the cockatoos or their wives to work in the fields? He's made both children work like donkeys, so fix this in your mind, Sister; they've long since discharged any debt they might have had to you.' He stood up, but she kept her head bent. After a long pause he said flatly: 'Look. It's not you; I know that. So just tell me where they've gone, will you?'

As Rhys dismounted, Charles and Thomas Fox came bursting out of the office of Valentyne & Wood, Charles in flight and Fox in pursuit. The traffic was especially heavy, swollen with carts of goods for the market nearby, and neither man saw Rhys as he tied Polka to the hitching-post and stood there listening to the blaring argument that had erupted between the two.

'You assured me she'd accept my offer! I could sue you for wasting my time. In fact I'm—'

'Sure and I guaranteed nothing, but she's a sensible lass and I thought—'

'My time is valuable, I'll have you know! I'm busy with my campaign—'

'Maybe your offer was too low, Councillor. If you'd offered a good price to begin with, she wouldn't have stormed out —'

'Downright rude and ill bred, if you ask me! If she was my daughter—'

'What then?' cooed a soft purring voice, and both men stopped in confusion as Leonie turned smiling from one to the other. 'Please don't let me interrupt. This is all most entertaining, isn't it, Rhys?'

Rhys was in no mood to be sociable. 'Leonie,' he said, taking the hand that she extended and automatically kissing her fingers. Nodding to the men, he said: 'Where is Lisabeth?'

'I don't know,' muttered Charles. Shrugging his shoulders uneasily, he said: 'She wouldn't listen. She just ran out . . . wouldn't sign anything!'

'Good for her!' declared Rhys.

'Why the hurry?' called Leonie after him. He didn't even hear her. Already he had unhitched Polka and was swinging up into the saddle.

Beyond the Ionic-columned bank offices was a small park, neat with a black iron fence on the road side but fringed with ragged willows where it melted into the Avon's silky surface. The area was grassed and criss-crossed with paths and geometrical flower-beds where English flowers grew in straight rows. English trees grew on the lawns. Under an autumn-gold oak Lisabeth sat forlornly watching the sparrows that hopped and fluttered around watching her. Rhys recognised her bonnet. She glanced up bleakly, then seemed to shrink away as he sat down beside her.

'I had quite a job finding you. Nobody knew where you had gone.'

Surely he wasn't in on it, too? No, he wouldn't want her to sell to Fox. She looked at the swans while he told her how pleased he was that she didn't bow under pressure, that she didn't allow Charles to bully her. That made her smile.

'But I did. Uncle Charles got all the money off me, every penny of the two hundred and eighty-nine guineas, nine shillings and fourpence.' She seemed resigned. 'Mind you, I had no choice there. I'm a female person, Mr Morgan. Did you know that means that I have no rights? None. I can't vote in an election, ever! I have no say in my own affairs. Uncle Charles can simply help himself to anything I own, did you know that? He'll be able to get the property, too, *and* sell it, if he can make me sign the papers.'

'You're not going to let him!'

She slid him a sly look. 'You sound horrified. Is it the prospect of having Mr Fox as a neighbour?' As she spoke she was aware that for once she felt no inferiority to him. He was dressed as roughly as she – more roughly, and he hadn't shaved, either, she noticed. Usually for town he dressed immaculately and was sprucely groomed, so beautiful that if she saw him coming up the road she would hide herself away. Recollection of her Christmas gown and the motive of pity behind it still shamed her.

'I'd top his offer,' Rhys said. 'Charles is greedy enough to hold out for every last guinea he can get.'

But greed is only the half of it, thought Lisabeth. *Can't you see that Uncle Charles is so jealous of you that it's making him ill with hatred? It's spite that's pushing him into this and he'd never offer the land to you, not at any price!*

'Anyway, I could put up with Fox. It would take a high fence and a thick hedge, but it could be done. No Lisabeth, it's not Fox, it's you. Why did you give Charles your money? Despite what you say you must have signed it away. He couldn't just take it, even from a young woman like you.'

She sighed. 'I felt obliged. It was for Aunty Gwynne's sake as much as anything . . . They are poor and they are in debt, and Uncle Charles can't raise any more loans without the deeds to the property.'

'Which he's not getting,' said Rhys. 'Damn him! He's had every opportunity . . . But I shouldn't talk like this to you. Lisabeth, you won't let him pressure you into selling. Promise me that.'

'I can't promise . . .' She stared hard at the swans on the river. Her face was cold and set. 'No, he won't make me sell. You see, I need the money from your lease. It's Andrew. I want him to go to King's College . . .' And before she realized what was happening out came the whole story. 'You see, I can manage without money, but not Andrew! And I thought that if I gave Uncle

Charles Mr Braddock's bank account, then . . .'

'Then he'd agree to a college education for Andrew,' finished Rhys.

'Yes, that's right. I'm responsible for him.'

'So is Charles, damn it all! Lisabeth, you are responsible to you. I can't bear to see you putting yourself last all the time. You're a beautiful young woman. You shouldn't be—' He could see that he was frightening her; the hands he had impulsively clasped were trembling in his, and she stared at him apprehensively. Frustration choked him. Why did he always have to be the enemy?

'Lisabeth,' he said. 'I want to marry you. No,' he added hastily when a look of pure terror blazed in her blue-black eyes. 'Just listen to me. For some reason that escapes me, you seem to be afraid. Whether it's of me or of life in general I don't know; but, Lisabeth, I'd like you to let me show you that there is nothing to fear. Nothing! Life is marvellous, it's a celebration, an endless glorying of existence. The way you live now, as an unpaid serf, is appalling, but things needn't be like that. Marry me, Lisabeth! I'm building a big house up on the cliff-top, and when you go from the Staffords' I'll hire someone at my expense to look after Gwynne as a companion, so you won't need to feel guilty about—'

'No! No, never.' She started to rise.

Tightening his grip on her hands, he forced her to sit back down again. Damn his clumsiness! He'd made the proposal sound like a business arrangement or, worse, as if he was doing her a favour. No wonder she refused. But how could he tell her that she haunted his days and how his nights were permeated with her unless she gave him some small sign of encouragement?

'Lisabeth, you must tell me. What is this . . . this barrier between us? Sometimes you almost seem to hate me.'

A great swelling of emotion blocked Lisabeth's throat. Hate. That was it. She hated Rhys Morgan. Of course she did. He was loathsome, wasn't he? Look at the way he was leaning over her, pressing her against the back of the bench with his stong rough hands. He smelt of sheep and clean sweat without a trace of his usual bay rum, and the way he was staring aggressively at her – was anything more obnoxious than that?

Go on, prompted an inner voice. *Tell him that you hate him! Rub his nose in it!* Bur she was dumb, and weak pathetic tears pricked under her eyelids.

'Talk to me, Lisabeth,' he said, not pleading, but asking as of

251

right. When she didn't speak he said: 'It's something to do with your mother, isn't it?'

The swelling pressure in her throat burst, and poison flooded out, gushing through her. 'Of course it is!' she flung at him. 'You ruined our lives! We were happy until you came along, but then everything went sour and it was all your fault! You killed our happiness! You destroyed our family, our life together! We—'

'Lisabeth!' Shifting his grip to her shoulders, he shook her, hard, so that her face swung around and she glared back at him in the slanting sunlight. 'This is incredible! *You* may have been happy, but Mary wasn't! She told me so herself, over and over, how wretchedly miserable she was stuck there in the bush. No! Listen to me, will you? If you think I stole into your lives and wrecked everything, then you couldn't be more wrong. What happened between Mary and me isn't something I'm proud of, but I needn't apologize for it, either, especially not to you. You should be glad that she had a little happiness when her life was at such a low ebb.'

His effrontery outraged her. All she could see was the image of her mother sitting sadly beside the window in that shabby hotel room, gazing, always gazing out to sea and growing more melancholy as her hopes withered. 'If you gave her any happiness, you took it all back afterwards! She wrote to you and you never even sent her a single word of comfort! You just used—'

'She never wrote to me!'

'She did!' cried Lisabeth. 'She told me that she'd given the letter to Uncle Charles to post. He wouldn't tell her your address, you see, but he offered . . . ' Her voice faltered as a sickening suspicion rose in her mind. Rallying, she said: 'If you had heard from her, would you have come back?'

Bloody Charles! thought Rhys. He decided to be honest. 'I would have replied, but not come back. I was very young then and, though I was extremely fond of Mary, once I left everything faded behind me and there were other things, other people . . . Lisabeth, you're naive and inexperienced, but I'm trying to pay you the compliment of being as frank as I can. Mary was an episode in my life, and I know that's all I was in hers. Life moves strongly, Lisabeth. It flows in one direction only and, even if you want to, you can't swim against that flow. As you grow older you'll come to realize—'

But she couldn't bear to listen to his reasonable argument. Mamma was an 'episode', Andrew was born of an 'episode', and to

252

hear Rhys speak all the attendant misery and unhappiness meant nothing to him. Into her mind, unbidden, sneaked a respect, an admiration for the way Rhys was being so direct and open with her, but she stamped on those feelings hard. To admit that he might be right would be to negate all these years of harboured resentment, and she couldn't face up to the possibility that she might be wrong. Her conviction was too frail to endure that.

'Please . . . please let me go!' she cried.

Immediately he was remorseful. Here he was battering her with arguments, when she'd already endured a double dose of badgering from Charles and Fox. But in his mind Rhys was satisfied now. The air was cleared between them; resentment would end. His heart flooded with love and joy as he raised her hands to his lips so that he could kiss her fingers.

'I want to marry you, Lisabeth,' he whispered against her skin. 'There's always been a distance between us, but because of Gwynne I feel that I know you better than anybody in the world. You're a good person, sweet and kind and worthy of far more than I can offer, but if you accept me I promise that I'll—'

'No!' She snatched her fingers away and again tried to escape, but he held her wrists so that her hands beat uselessly in her lap. He didn't know the half of it! This was her worst nightmare coming true.

He searched her face with his intense blue eyes and, seeing the genuine concern in them, she had to drop hers, ashamed. He said: 'This isn't the time or place to ask you, Lisabeth, but will you promise me that when you feel better you'll think about it?'

She shook her head. Those stupid weak tears were nudging out from under her eyelids, but she mustn't cry in front of him! 'Please go away,' she whispered.

And after a moment he did. The crisp tread of his boots moved past her, and he snapped his hat up from the bench-back where it hung, and then he was gone.

Lisabeth stared unseeingly at the swans. Inside her was a vast unsatisfied emptiness, an ache she could not fathom. When footsteps approached behind her she turned quickly, but it was not him and illogically a sharp disappointment stabbed her. This made her irritated; it was all wrong! She would be happy, she was sure, if she never had to set eyes on Rhys Morgan again.

TWENTY-FOUR

CHARLES COULDN'T GIVE UP. The bank account had cleared his debts with over eighty guineas to spare, but the lure of what Fox was prepared to pay was irresistable. At night he whispered to Gwynne describing the improvements he could make to the cottage, the furniture they could buy, the smart carriage they could have.

'A piano, Mrs Stafford, we could put a piano in the new parlour,' he murmured, his voice disembodied in the darkness. 'You've always wanted a piano.'

'Perhaps when I was younger . . . I could never coax my fingers to play now. But the carriage would be lovely,' she sighed, picturing herself alighting at the grand homes of Christchurch and leaving her visiting-cards on the silver salver in the hall. She'd have callers in return, too, once Rhys had finished building his mansion. The very cream of society would trickle out to call on him.

Lisabeth, however, remained stubborn. Charles had brought the papers home, but they remained on the dresser, tucked behind Gwynne's green salmon-dish. Thomas Fox's offer climbed from five hundred guineas to seven hundred and fifty guineas, but still she refused to budge.

'Why don't you just give in?' asked Andrew. 'He's in such a foul mood all the time it hardly seems worth it. Besides, I don't want to go to that school. Mr Smale says they're terribly strict at King's College and the boys have to swot all the time. I'd hate it.'

'No, you wouldn't,' she insisted, gazing earnestly into his clear green eyes. Thank goodness for those eyes; they neutralized his strong and growing resemblance to Rhys. 'You'd love it. You'd eat it up. Andrew, I envy you, the opportunities you'll have! The only education I can hope for is the scraps I can glean from Uncle Charles's newspapers and from those few books of Mr Rennie's that I managed to hide when his things were being bundled up, but you – you'll have it all given to you!'

A cart loaded with white stone was trundling past along the road. Turning his head to watch it, Andrew said: 'That's the fourteenth delivery this morning! Uncle Rhys's house is really coming along now.'

Lisabeth felt like snatching the push-hoe from his grasp and hitting him with it.

'This is magnificent, Rhys,' approved Leonie. She had ridden out on a speckled grey mare to inspect his house. Since her bereavement she had taken to riding everywhere in her elegant black riding habit. It conformed with society's decree that a widow wear black, but at the same time didn't feel like mourning garb. A neat solution, she thought, and, since she had no tears to shed for her bloated over-sexed husband, an appropriate solution, too.

'Let me see if I can remember where everything goes,' said Leonie as she and Rhys strolled along the cliff-top beside the looming white walls. 'The stables will be there beyond the kitchen yards, the entrance hall is here at the top of a double flight of stone steps, and along that way your library and study will overlook an orangery and lily-pond. There are reception rooms through here beyond the hall, while the dining-room is within twenty yards of the kitchens and the wine-cellars are below, with stairs down through the butler's pantry.'

'You know the place as well as I do!'

'It is my third visit. But what about the ballroom, Rhys?'

'There won't be a ballroom.' He patted the gloved fingers that twined through the crook of his elbow. 'Didn't you know? I can't dance!'

Leonie tightened her grip; from experience she knew that a friendly pat on the hand always preceded his pulling away from her. 'You can't dance?' she repeated. 'You play the harpsichord like a poet but you don't *dance*? Then, I shall take it upon myself to teach you! I shall come here every evening and give you lessons.'

He had been joking – of course he danced – but she was

255

studying him with her glittering toffee-brown eyes, and he realized that his light-heartedness had evaded her. Gently he said: 'I couldn't accept that generous offer, tempting though it is. It wouldn't be fair to you. You're in mourning, Leonie.'

'I've never mourned anything less in my life,' she told him as he winced, wishing she wouldn't be so blunt. 'Rhys, I—'

'Excuse me, please, Leonie,' he interrupted hastily, detaching her hand from his arm as he spoke. Walking across to where the closest group of stonemasons were fitting a row of blocks together, he talked to them in a quiet voice, filling in time while he pondered on how to deal tactfully with the beautiful Mrs Gammerwoth. If she kept on coming here, it wouldn't be long before a full-blown scandal erupted and that would be destructive to everybody.

When he turned back she was shading her eyes as she stared along the ridge-path. Voice sharpened with exasperation, she said: 'It's that lad again, the one who looks like you. I do declare, Rhys, every time I come here he follows me up the hill. I wonder if that sister of his puts him up to it.'

'She's really sweet on him,' reported Andrew at dinner. 'She calls him "Rhys" all the time and once she said, "Darling Rhys".' He almost choked on a mouthful of mashed potato at the recollection. 'Poor Uncle Rhys looked just like Bollan does when he's being scolded for digging up the garden.'

'Eat your food properly,' said Lisabeth.

'Sure and she's sweet on him, all right. He were talking to her in town yesterday, too. Right outside Fox's office, it were. If you ask me, I'm confluent that there'll be an end to that feud soon.' Wiping his damp beard with a white square hand, he shot Lisabeth a calculating glance. 'One thousand guineas, Fox said.'

The food tasted like cardboard in Lisabeth's mouth. 'I can't sell. I'm sorry, Uncle Charles, but I really can't.'

Gwynne shook her head. While they talked she had been preoccupied with her own worry. 'I do wish Rhys would listen to me. I tried to persuade him, but he took no notice. White stone is for grave-markers, nothing else, and Rhys is building his whole house out of it. It's the most fearful bad luck!'

Charles snorted. 'You and your silly suppositions! Of course it's not unlucky. Look at the Tower in London. That's made of white stone, isn't it?'

'Yes,' agreed Gwynne.

'There you are, then!'

'But think of all the things that have happened there! All bad, Mr Stafford, all bad terrible things!'

Charles's face was inscrutable in the bronze lamplight. Yes, he'd wish Rhys bad luck, thought Lisabeth in the silence that followed. She repressed a shiver. It was impossible seriously to imagine anything unlucky happening to Rhys. He was so healthy, so handsome and smiling that it was almost as if he was made out of sunshine.

If only I didn't hate him so much, she thought wistfully.

On the last day of the month Rhys deposited the land rent for the second quarter of the year in a special account at the bank and on the way home sought Lisabeth out to give her the papers for it. He found her shucking ears of maize and tossing them into the corn-rick for storage. Absorbed in the task, she didn't see him.

It was a cold grey day, low with the threat of rain. She wore an old wrap of Gwynne's around her shoulders and a man's woollen scarf tied around her head, but despite the extra layers of clothing her face had a blue tinge. He noticed that she worked mechanically, shoulders sloping with fatigue, and as he watched her he grew more and more angry. Eventually, without attracting attention to his presence, he marched inside and confronted Gwynne.

'You have to help me,' he said without preamble. 'I want to rescue Lisabeth. I'm going to take her away from this virtual slavery, and you're to help me do it.'

Gwynne was startled. She had been polishing her dozen silver knives and forks and daydreaming of a finer life. 'We couldn't do without her,' she blurted without thinking, then the word 'slavery' impinged on her consciousness and she flushed. 'Mr Stafford has been a bit hard on her lately,' she admitted. 'But it's only because she's being so stubborn. If only she'd listen . . .'

'Do you mean he's overworking her because she won't agree to sell Fox her land?'

Gwynne's flush deepened, and she looked away.

Rhys sat in a ladder-backed chair opposite. 'There is one thing everybody has overlooked. Lisabeth couldn't sell to Fox even if she wanted to. I have first option on the land according to the terms of Braddock's will. I should have spoken up earlier, but it's been entertaining watching Fox and Charles circling around each other. However, the joke's well and truly gone stale now, so would you please tell your noble husband to ease off Lisabeth? She's an innocent victim in this.'

257

Dipping the rag into her pot of cleaning paste, Gwynne said: 'Then, you'll buy the land? You will, won't you, Rhys? It would mean so much to—'

'Not on your life,' Rhys cut in. 'That charming husband of yours would have the money off Lisabeth in five minutes if I bought it. This way she has an asset, and an income.'

'You're far too harsh on—'

'Shush.' Rhys reached over and plucked the knife from her grasp. 'Go and fetch your bonnet, and Lisabeth's too. I've a cab waiting down at the corner. We're going into town on an errand. Hurry up. I've an appointment with the headmaster of King's College in an hour.'

On the drive home Lisabeth was silent as she had been on the way in, but this time instead of staring fixedly out of the cab windows she kept sneaking surreptitious glances at Rhys. The main difference between him and the Staffords, she now realized, was that, though they all dreamed the same dreams, Rhys plunged in and made things happen. He wanted a place at King's College, so he went in and demanded one. There were no free places – gentry from as far away as Sydney were sending their sons here for an education – and the fact that, though Andrew was born into the Church of England, he had been raised a Catholic counted heavily against him. Lisabeth realized early in the interview that she would never have been able to enrol Andrew, but Rhys managed the impossible. For the first time she understood just how respected Rhys was in the province. He was already a man of substance and influence; people bowed to his will.

Lisabeth kept her eyes averted from him for fear their glances would meet, and only on the way home did she permit herself to look at him. *Marry me, Lisabeth!* he had said. Every time she looked at him she heard the words again and a sharp thrilling jolt went through her. This was her revenge for Mary, that she would refuse him no matter how he begged her, and in spurning him she would find satisfaction.

But to her disappointment he ignored her and addressed himself to Gwynne, who had seized the opportunity to bleat out her fears about the white stone, how terrified she was that it would bring him bad luck.

'You're precious, you are!' he remarked, patting her hands. 'I'll never have bad luck, surely you've realized that by now. The house will be all white stone with high-peaked roofs to echo the shapes of the mountains, and I'm calling the station "Mists of Heaven" after the mountain legend. Old Braddock regaled me with it many times. "Rangi Pokekohu" it is in Maori. I'd prefer to call the station that, but I have to be practical and choose something the wool-buyers can pronounce, so "Mists of Heaven" it is.'

'That's a right bonny name,' sighed Gwynne.

Lisabeth thought so, too, but nobody was canvassing for her opinion. *Marry me, Lisabeth!* he had said, but today she might not even have existed. When they arrived back at the cottage he made a flourish of helping Gwynne out – smiling at her with that dazzling dimpled grin and kissing cheek – but Lisabeth had to help herself down. She began to wonder if she had dreamed the entire episode.

The rejection had hurt Rhys, but if anything, his interest in Lisabeth was sharpened. She was the woman he wanted to marry, and he was determined to have her, but pride stood tall in his personality and he was not going to grovel at her feet.

While he rode the boundaries he turned the matter over in his mind. He wanted her soon, now, so that together they could choose the furnishings for the mansion that was rapidly taking shape on the cliffs. Building a house was a lonely business, the proper occupation for lovers, not for a solitary bachelor, and Rhys needed the colour of Lisabeth's opinions so that the house would be equally hers. It wasn't right that Leonie's ideas were being woven into the fabric of the place, but it was she who was always there making helpful suggestions, and her presence was both a relief and an irritant to Rhys, who needed the feminine opinion. Damn it, Lisabeth was the one who should be there, but Rhys wondered if she had so much as laid eyes on the place, for she never offered a single comment about it.

But he was determined not to grovel to her.

He turned to Gwynne. She listened to his dreams in a kind of frightened joy, blinking back tears and twisting her top apron between her hands as he described how he loved Lisabeth and wanted to marry her but there was some obstinate blockage there. Perhaps a sense of loyalty and obligation to Gwynne?

'But this would be marvellous!' quavered Gwynne. 'If you would engage a companion for me, as you promise, then Lisabeth would be free to go, and this way I wouldn't lose her at all, for she'd come and visit me every day, I know she would! It's been my greatest fear that she might marry someone who lives a long way away, you know. I so dread the loss of her!'

259

Which is why you've conspired to keep her looking dowdy, thought Rhys, but he shoved aside uncharitable thoughts and said: 'See what you can do . . . Play the Cupid, eh?'

'I'd be delighted,' she said.

Gwynne's talents were not in the field of negotiation or diplomacy, however. She dropped a few clumsy hints to Lisabeth, who reared back in alarm, and when she saw that Lisabeth was not going to reveal anything of her own feelings she appealed to Charles for help.

'Someone wants to marry Lisabeth. Someone extremely eligible,' she began nervously. His reaction made her wince. He bellowed.

'Sure and he can come to me, whoever he is, and I'll give him a short shrift, I promise you that. She's not marrying anybody, the obstetric little hussy! Sure, and if someone's asked her he's only after her land, you can be sure of that, Mrs Stafford. So you—'

'It's Rhys,' she said.

'What?'

'Rhys wants to marry her.'

'Well, why didn't you say so?' blustered Charles. 'This puts a very different complexity on the matter.' Squinting at her, he lowered his voice so that it would be contained by the packing-shed walls. 'Sure and I don't mind admitting that I could look with favour on that brother of yours. We've had our differences, true, but there is some good in him, and I don't mind being the first to come out and say so.'

'I'm so pleased,' said Gwynne. 'Mr Stafford, I can't say what joy this brings me. Oh, if you two could be friends . . . '

As he watched her hobble back towards the cottage he absently tore off a plug of tobacco and tucked it into his cheek. So Rhys wanted Lisabeth, eh? When all of Christchurch was certain that he had tickets on the beautiful widow Gammerwoth, all the time he had a secret fancying for plain little Lisabeth. There was no accounting for taste, that's for sure! Charles spat a jet of tobacco juice into the rusty tin he used as a spittoon and smiled to himself as he began to calculate how he could turn this situation to his advantage.

Rhys was down at his sprawling wooden stockyards drafting sheep when Charles sought him out. It was a biting-cold day, stinging with an icy wind that howled off the mountains.

'I envy them their thick woolly coats,' said Rhys, who always tried to open their conversations with a pleasant remark. Charles as usual just grumped – probably didn't even hear the words, thought Rhys, wondering why he bothered.

'So you want Lisabeth's hand, do you?' Charles said.

'I wouldn't mind the rest of her as well,' joked Rhys. 'But, yes, I think she's worked off any debt she owes you. Wouldn't you agree?'

Charles wasn't prepared to discuss that. Besides, hadn't Rhys promised a paid servant to replace her? Cannily he left that topic aside and came straight to the point. As Rhys swung the little wooden gate that drafted the sheep into one pen or the other Charles shouted into the wind and over the noise of baaing and barking: 'I have to give permission afore she can marry you, right? I'm her guardian, right?'

'Right,' said Rhys over his shoulder. He stopped the next sheep that came hurtling down the race, twisted its head in both hands to force its jaw open and examined its teeth, then sent it into the right-hand pen. 'Whew!' he said, straightening and flexing his tired back. 'I don't know which is worse, the stooping or the smell. Sheepy odour seems pleasant enough out on the tussock land, but here in the yards . . .' He grimaced. This was a task that had to be done before the autumn shearing; it made sorting and baling the fleeces a much easier task.

Charles was saying: 'If I'm to give permission, I think I should have some small commiseration for doing it.'

Rhys glanced around at him, puzzled. 'Commiseration?' he repeated, then belatedly guessed that Charles meant 'compensation'.

'Yes!' roared Charles into the hollow sound of the wind. 'A dowry! A bride-price! That be the custom, don't it?'

Rhys shook with laughter and had to signal the dogs to ease off their barking for a spell so that he could rest. 'Yes, that's right,' he gasped when he could speak. 'You're supposed to give me a present for taking her off your hands. What do you think would be a fair sum, eh, Charles? What about twelve hundred and fifty guineas? Isn't that what Fox's offer is up to now?'

Charles glared at him. 'That weren't what I meant!'

He glowered so ferociously that Rhys was provoked. Grabbing a bunch of Charles's coat-front, he jerked him closer, off balance, and hissed into his face. 'I know what you meant. You were out to look for a profit for yourself, weren't you? It isn't enough for you to have worked Lisabeth like a slave, you want to sell her like one as well. I love Lisabeth and I want to marry her, but you're to keep your greedy sticky paws right out of this whole affair!' In disgust he pushed Charles away so that he thumped up against the post-railing. Sickened, he was about to resume his work when something ugly in Charles's expression made him pause.

'There is one more thing,' he said. 'I want Lisabeth to marry me of her own free will, but if you interfere and try to influence her against me, then I swear that you'll rue this day . . . by God you will!' And with a harsh whistle he started up the dogs' barking and again the sheep came pelting down the ramp.

'When Lisabeth's betrothed to him he'll be generous to us both, you'll see,' consoled Gwynne. 'He's only irritable now because Lisabeth's keeping him dangling. Once she agrees to marry him he'll be all sweetness and light. I promise you, Mr Stafford, so don't be downcast!'

Charles was not one to allow a matter to lie fallow. He was so edgy and impatient that Rhys often chaffed him by saying that it was a wonder he left the seed in the ground without digging it up to see if it was germinating – a joke that caused Andrew much mirth because that's exactly what Charles did do, each day digging up a few seeds to see how they were coming along.

Now he was impatient to see the stalemate between Rhys and Lisabeth resolved. Ignoring Gwynne's pleas that such a sensitive and delicate issue would be best left to her, Charles began to bully Lisabeth into agreeing to the proposal.

'It's time you married,' he told her bluntly. 'Sure and you're an adult now. Time you were making your own life, out in the world. You can't expect Mrs Stafford and me to feed you for ever, you know.'

'Mr Stafford, please! I beg—' began Gwynne.

'Stay out of this!' he ordered curtly, and she was silent.

Lisabeth despaired. If only she had Andrew to talk to, everything would be all right. He knew how to josh her into an optimistic frame of mind, but without him to buoy her spirits up she felt helpless, trapped and depressed. Life was becoming intolerable. Gwynne was too frightened to take her side, and all day out in the fields Charles subjected her to a continuous spate of harassment. Exhausted and defenceless, Lisabeth began to weaken under the pressure.

One day Joe Day rowed his mother across the harbour for a visit with her friend Gwynne, and when the two women were comfortably settled and gossiping over tea-cups in front of the fire he went in search of Lisabeth. He found her out by the pig-sties chopping up pumpkins for the six large white pigs. Because of the squealing she didn't hear him approach and looked up, startled. She was crying.

'It's just the wind,' she apologized in response to his immediate concern. 'It affects my eyes . . . makes them water.'

Taking the tomahawk from her grasp, he said: 'You could cut yourself. Andrew should be doing this for you.'

'He's in school. He comes home only once a month and then just for the day. I miss him so . . . so. . . .'

'Hey!' cried Joe in alarm. Seating her on the chopping-block, he knelt in front of her, his merry hazel eyes peering up into her downcast face. 'There's more to it than that. Come on, Lisabeth, you can tell me. There's only plain speaking between us, remember?'

She tried to smile back at him. Yes, he was a dear and trusted friend; all the Days had proved their worth. She could confide in any of them. 'Uncle Charles wants me to marry someone I detest,' she said. 'He's badgering me, and I can't take much more,'

Joe whistled between his uneven teeth. 'That's bad. That could be terrible in fact. Is it Thomas Fox? I've seen him once or twice talking to Mr Stafford, and I wondered what business those two might—'

'It's not him.'

'That's a relief! I'd hate to think of you being forced—'

'It's Rhys Morgan,' she blurted out.

'Rhys?' Joe looked so incredulous that Lisabeth wondered if she had uttered the wrong name by mistake. 'Rhys? He wants to marry you and you've refused?'

'I told you! I detest him.'

But Joe was no longer taking her seriously. 'Wow,' he sighed. 'If I had even a quarter of the advantages that Rhys Morgan has to offer, I'd be the happiest man in the province!'

Indignant and annoyed, Lisabeth said: 'I mean it, Joe! I hate the man. I couldn't endure the prospect of having anything to do with him in that way—'

Joe wasn't listening. 'He's got everything,' he murmured.

Lisabeth bit back an exclamation as she noticed a dreamy expression in Joe's eyes. He was a handsome lad, a riot of dark curls pushing from under his frayed tweed fisherman's cap and a bluish shadow on his chin. Thinking how unlike Rhys he was, she decided he was extremely attractive, and that expression in his eyes encouraged her to say: 'Joe . . . what do you think of me'

'You're not well,' he said bluntly. 'And you're not thinking straight. If you honestly think that you hate Rhys Morgan enough to make yourself ill over him, then . . .' He shrugged helplessly.

'You don't believe me, do you?' said Lisabeth.

'No, I don't. How could you hate him?'

Joe's attractiveness evaporated. He was laughing at her. 'I do,' she burst out angrily. 'I detest him. He's loathsome and . . . and . . .' Tears burned her eyes, and her throat choked with sobs. 'He's . . . Oh, what's the use?'

'You really are sick,' cried Joe in alarm, recognizing that Lisabeth was teetering on the brink of a full breakdown just as his tragic sister-in-law Sarah had been before she drowned herself in the Avon. 'Lisabeth, you need a rest. Proper care . . .'

Her shoulders quaked. 'Don't be ridiculous! How . . . how can I poss—'

'Come back to the house. I'll feed the pigs later, but first I'll see what Ma says. Maybe you and Mrs Stafford could come over to the hotel for a few days.'

Lisabeth sighed. The pigs were still squealing, clamouring for food. There were late beans to be packed and the first of the new season's cauliflowers to be harvested. One of the drains beyond the shed had blocked, and it would take half a day to clear the conglomeration of dead vegetation so that the water could flow again. The lettuce-field needed ploughing over, and Uncle Charles was talking about putting in a crop of onions.

'You look absolutely done in.'

The concern in his voice was like a balm. 'You're a good friend, Joe,' *If only you were older and ready to settle down*, she thought. 'I'd love to rest, but what I really need is to get away from here. Permanently.'

TWENTY-FIVE

THE HOTEL WAS QUIET; the trek to the goldfields had finished for the season and it was still too early for the incoming tide of exhausted prospectors returning, so apart from an elderly Yorkshire botanist who was studying native flaxes and lacewoods for their fibres the rooms were empty and the corridors silent. The Captain was in Wellington fetching a cargo of Canadian clover-seed with the *Flirt*, and Joe and Alf were gone for every daylight hour salvaging the cargo of a freighter that had run aground on the bar in a freak on-shore wind. Gwynne and Mrs Day fell comfortably into all-day chat sessions, while Lisabeth was left alone.

On the first day she slept until almost noon when she was woken by Mabs, who rattled a tin bath on to the bare floor beside the bed and sluiced two pails of steaming water into it. Arms akimbo, she sniffed; 'Oi don't see why oi should wait on young 'ealthy madams. Oi got other thinks ter do.'

A bath! Lisabeth flopped back on to the pillow, weak with delight at the prospect of the luxury. A bath just for her to soak in as long as she liked. What an angel Mrs Day was to think of such a thing.

They stayed three nights, which was the maximum Charles grudgingly permitted, and in the soft glorious days Lisabeth strolled along the driftwood-scarred beach with the cold wind on her face, gathered velvety sugar-grass balls and rolled them in her work-stiffened hands, and climbed the zig-zag road from where she could watch Joe and Alf manoeuvring packing-crates from the surf-washed deck of the broken cutter into their leashed tossing rowboat.

Over on this side of the harbour she felt safe from Rhys. She thought about him often – it was impossible not to when every time she glanced out across the beach his mansion caught her eye. Odd how when all that time it was being built she had never once seen it even though the rise on which it stood was less than half a mile from the Staffords' cottage. The white walls caught the sunlight and blazed like new snow. Even from this distance the building was huge and impressive.

'It's almost finished, too,' Gwynne told Mrs Day at dinner. 'Eight bedrooms it's got, not counting the servants' quarters. He took me up in the trap one day to look at it. The magnificence quite snatched my breath away.'

Lisabeth wished she wouldn't talk about Rhys all the time; every mention carried the distinct pressure of a hint.

'Is it true that he's planning to marry soon?' asked Mrs Day. 'He's been choosing furniture and curtains with the Gammerwoth widow, and everybody seems to think—'

'Excuse me, please,' said Lisabeth, pushing back her chair. 'I'll go and see if Joe and Alf are coming in yet.'

On the last evening a caller came to see Lisabeth. Mabs showed the tall paper-skinned man into the parlour and dashed upstairs where Lisabeth was laboriously poring over one of Mrs Day's penny novelettes in the last of the fading daylight. Bemused by Mab's excitement, Lisabeth followed her down and entered the parlour to an accompaniment of nudges and winks as Mabs closed the door with a flourish behind her.

Sure that Rhys was waiting to see her, Lisabeth had rehearsed a curt crisp speech. When Athol Nye unfolded his lanky limbs from a prim wing-chair and stood with both hands extended to greet her she experienced a flat sensation of disappointment.

'Mr Nye, what a pleasant surprise,' she said, managing to smile.

He had heard she was at the hotel and came to visit her – not on any particular errand, she soon decided, but to talk about himself, his job and the exhibition of paintings he planned to hold in the late winter. He was exactly as she remembered; rigid, shy and faintly aloof – all qualities she told herself she approved after Rhys's impetuous suffocating demands. Athol's company was restful, cool and light as water.

Mabs brought them tea on a tray, which she set down on a knick-knack table, treading meaningfully on Lisabeth's foot as she offered to pour.

'No, thank you,' declined Lisabeth.

'Prefer ter be alone, then, does yer?'

Lisabeth could have kicked her. Couldn't she even have a calm and civilized chat with a man without insinuations being made?

But Mabs must have had a sixth sense about men with courting on their minds because, when at length Lisabeth thought to ask after Mrs Nye, Athol suddenly seemed to remember something. Gulping down the last crumbs of his third piece of chocolate cake, he dabbed at his lips with the serviette and whispered; 'Miss Stafford, if you've no important plans for the future, would you care to consider the prospect of becoming my wife?'

Lisabeth stared at him blankly. The proposal had been uttered in the same thin tones with which he had accepted an extra wedge of cake. Now he was biting into a fourth without any apparent interest in her reply. She watched him, her mind seething with a conflict of chaotic thoughts while he nipped at the cake with his small grey teeth and pursed his lips as he chewed. He did not look at her.

Presently the serviette dabbed his mouth again and he focused his attention on her. He was a man of exquisitely precise habits. 'You are thinking it over,' he said.

'Yes . . . I suppose so.'

'I'll say goodnight, then.'

Again he took both her hands in his, but this time he stooped to paint a dry kiss on her cheek. She liked the feel of him. He had a poor smell, the aroma of home-made lye-and-muttonfat soap, but there was something healing in his manner that eased and rested her. She stood on the lamplit veranda and watched him stride out into the blustery darkness. He did not look back.

That same day Rhys arrived at the Staffords' cottage in fine high spirits. On the previous evening he and two of the sepoys, all three swathed in a disguise of low-pulled bushranger hats and loose farm smocks, had attacked Fox's offices with posters and pots of paste. Under cover of the moonless night they had slapped more than five hundred copies of Sir Kenneth's campaign poster all over the outside walls and windows of the Barnaby Street building.

When Rhys rode by on his way home from a meeting with Sir Kenneth a team of men were still scrubbing and soaking the shreds of paper from the paintwork.

'I'll have your hide for this.' promised Fox, who ran shouting along the street after Rhys.

Reining Polka in, Rhys feigned polite ignorance. 'I beg your

267

pardon? Oh . . . the posters! Really? I thought you'd hired those men to improve the appearance of your office. Why not keep the slogans there, Mr Fox? It could do wonders for your business – add a touch of respectability, perhaps!' As he rode away, a banner of laughter billowed behind him.

'Lisabeth's not here,' scowled Charles when he called in. The few days had gone poorly for him, and he was nursing indigestion from his own ill-cooked meals and a scalded wrist where he had splashed boiling water on to himself while brewing tea. He glared at Rhys belligerently, daring him to cause trouble.

Rhys smiled, his high spirits undimmed by this surly reception. 'Then, I'll call in again later,' he said and strolled out whistling.

Charles propped his elbows on the table and blew on his mug of thin soup to cool it, while he reflected on the advantages there could be in having Rhys for a friend. An ally, he thought, projecting ahead, and then even a business partner. Who could foretell what impressive heights they could reach together, with Rhys's money and Charles providing the business acumen? People would make way for his gleaming landau as he was chauffeured through town instead of jostling his spring-cart and yelling at him to watch where he was going. He could be rich, he could command respect.

When Gwynne and Lisabeth arrived home next morning he set to work on the girl at once. 'You'll get yourself up there and you'll accept his proposal at once, before he has second thoughts. Show a bit of gratitude for all we done for you and your brother. Where would you be now without us, hey? Sure and it's time for a bit of retaliation, missy, so get yourself up to the new house and tell Rhys you'll be honoured to have him.'

Lisabeth froze midway through the act of untying her faded bonnet-ribbons. As Charles ranted on her eyes grew enormous and dark. *Terrified*, Gwynne thought as she watched, not daring to interfere, for Mr Stafford was in a far worse mood than she might have anticipated. When he had finished there was a moment's silence with no sound but the rattle of the wind lifting a loose tile on the roof.

'I can't,' said Lisabeth at last. 'Please don't ask me that any more, Uncle Charles, because I simply can't do it.'

'Why not?' he said, flinging down the newspaper and shoving himself out of his fireside chair. 'All right, lass, there's been weeks of shilly-shallying from you. Now let's have some blunt talking, shall we? What's your objection to Rhys, then? Come on, let's be having it.'

'I just don't like him,' said Lisabeth as she removed her bonnet and hung it on a peg. 'I'm sorry Aunty Gwynne. I don't want to hurt your feelings, but he doesn't appeal to me at all.'

'Codswallop!' thundered Charles. 'I never heard such rubbish in all my born days.' There's more to it than that and, by heaven, Lisabeth, you'll not move from that spot until you've told me the real reason for your obesity!'

Looking into his rheumy, shrewd eyes Lisabeth thought: *He knows! He knows about Rhys and Mamma.* She felt ill, and for a moment her gaze faltered under his stubborn stare. He wanted her to spit it out, rake over the sorry story of Rhys and his long-ago treacherous use of her mother. Perhaps he even knew about Andrew . . . Her scalp chilled, and she swayed giddily. Surely not, oh, surely not!

'Yes, there is another reason,' she heard herself say. 'I want to marry someone else. A Mr Athol Nye, a schoolmaster.'

Charles gaped at her. The loose tile tapped away unseen. 'That arrogant fellow who—' he began, but was interrupted by a shriek from Gwynne.

'Mr Stafford, your newspaper!' she cried and, looking beyond Charles, Lisabeth saw the yellow glow of flames flapping against the wall above his chair. Pushing past him, she rushed to help Gwynne to beat the fire out.

Until she declared her intention Lisabeth had had no thought of seriously considering Athol Nye's proposal, but once the words had been uttered the idea seemed to form positive advantages around itself like a shell developing around a kernel of truth. She liked Athol, she respected his views and, though she could not admire his paintings, she appreciated his style and perception of the world. He had soul, she decided as she leaned her cheek against Bella's warm flank. He wasn't interested in vulgar aims like amassing a fortune or being a grand station-owner or building a grotesquely large mansion. Money probably never entered his head! While she milked and mused, she recalled things Gwynne had told her about Rhys – how cultured he was and how knowledgeable in the fields of art and literature and music – but she shoved those thoughts aside impatiently, choosing her own disparaging image of Rhys. That image suited her purposes much better.

Charles was furious, and Gwynne ached with dismay, but she put her disappointment aside and reassured her husband by saying that Rhys would understand and that the situation would heal in time. Privately she dreaded the day he would find out. Lisabeth wrote Athol a brief note saying that they could be married as soon as formal arrangements were made. He replied immediately, setting a date less than two weeks away. Crumpling the note in her fist, Lisabeth wept. She was making a mistake, she knew it, but there was no turning back now. She had never felt so alone and so miserable in her entire life.

Sensing her deep inner turmoil, Gwynne yearned for a means to bridge the gulf between them; but, realising that she had let Gwynne down by rejecting her beloved brother, Lisabeth retreated behind her decision. An uneasy calm lulled the household, and Lisabeth went about her tasks mechanically, as if she was drifting in a paralysing dream.

Because Charles refused to pay for a trousseau and the school fees absorbed all of the land rent, Lisabeth could do no shopping. This made her feel wistful; in her imagination brides and pretty things went together, and it would have injected some enjoyment into the proceedings to have even one new dress to wear. Glumly she inspected her tattered bonnet. Gwynne offered to sacrifice a second-best table-cloth to re-cover it, but when Lisabeth saw that the proffered cloth was Gwynne's sickly yellowish-green velvet she shook her head sadly. It was better to be anonymous in ugly dark clothes than conspicuous in ugly bright ones.

'Have you told Andrew yet, dear?' asked Gwynne a few days before the wedding, though she knew Lisabeth hadn't. 'I do think he'd like to be told in advance.' Sucking her lip nervously, she reflected that Rhys should be told, too, but she hadn't the heart or the courage to tell him. Always in her mind was the image of his dear intelligent face when he described how he loved Lisabeth and hoped to marry her. At that stage he believed he had all the time in the world, that there was no hurry and that it was best to wait and allow her love to develop all by itself. *It's Mr Stafford's fault*, she mourned with a rare flash of disloyalty. *If he hadn't forced the lass, she'd never have dug her heels in like this. Oh, but I shall miss her!*

'I'll write Andrew a letter today,' Lisabeth promised.

The Provincial Government elections were now less than a month away, and Rhys was busy every day assisting Sir Kenneth. For the most part he was merely a 'presence', someone to add personality and colour to the campaign, but occasionally – if the audience wanted an outline of Sir Kenneth's views on separatism – Rhys would step forward on the beribboned podium and speak, for this was an issue near to his heart.

'A war is being fought in this country,' he would say quietly when the heckling and jeering that always greeted new speakers had lulled. 'The war is not between enemies but between people with a common bond! It is not between settlers and Maoris but between two factions of people who inhabit this, the greatest of God's own countries! All of us are immigrants, for even the Maoris have been here but a few generations. We *will* be friends, we *shall* work together when this squabbling is over, but in the mean time and more urgently the fighting must be stopped. The only way to do that, friends, is for all of us to be seen to be pulling together. True, the war is not on our doorstep but it is in our land and, like it or not, we are responsible for what happens in another part of our country. Some resent the taxes we pay to finance the war; their cry is that we should break away, abandon our fellow-colonialists, present a show of weakness to the troublemakers and those who seek to disrupt the peaceful settlement of this fair land. I say "No." We must be strong. We must stand together. In comradeship and in unity this country will rise above the squabbles to become a truly great nation.'

Once, when the applause was dying down Sir Kenneth leaned towards Rhys and muttered: 'You speak well, lad. You make it sound as if you really mean it.'

'But I do,' responded Rhys in surprise. 'And aren't they your views too?'

Sir Kenneth snorted. 'Don't care a fig one way or the other. Let the stupid bastards all kill each other if they want to.'

'But you told me—'

He patted his snowy whiskers and winked . 'I just take the opposite tack to Fox on every issue, that's all. It's politics, my boy.'

Rhys had to laugh at the unashamed duplicity. Who was the rogue here, Fox or Sir Kenneth? he asked himself.

On the first Thursday in April, Rhys had dinner at Benares before going on to a campaign meeting at the Masons' Hall. It was to be one of the most important rallies of the campaign, but Sir Kenneth showed no nervousness. All through dinner his only conversation was about Azura, his god-daughter, who was due to arrive next week in the *Pride of India*. 'Appropriate, wouldn't you say, hey?' he chuckled as he dissected his lobster vol-au-vent. 'She loves Indian things above all else – bar some of the food, mind you, but you can't blame her for that. All flour and flatulence, hey?'

'Kiki, please!' fluttered Lady Launcenolt. To Rhys she said: 'The dear girl thinks it's fate that after all these delays she's finally making the journey in a ship by that name. Oh, Rhys, I can't wait for you to meet her.'

'Well, actually,' began Rhys. 'It's very premature of me to say anything, but—' He stopped. How could he make an announcement about Lisabeth when absolutely nothing was settled? That was ludicrous. On the other hand, he felt vaguely guilty that these two warm-hearted folk were being allowed to nourish a false hope that a romance might blossom between him and Azura. He shrugged, then suddenly aware that both were looking at him expectantly, waiting for him to finish his sentence, he raised his glass and said: 'It may be premature but call it a premonition, if you like! Here's to *Councillor* Sir Kenneth and to victory!'

'Bravo!' cried Lady Launcenolt, clinking her glass to his. 'What is it, Albert?' she said to the sepoy who materialized at her side.

He whispered in her ear. She frowned at Rhys. 'Albert says there's someone to see you. Young Andrew Stafford. Apparently he's run away from school. Perhaps you'd better go out and talk to him – he's in the kitchen, soaked through in this rain. They're drying him out by the fire. Albert says he's incoherent, frightfully distressed about something.'

TWENTY-SIX

LISABETH WAS PLAITING HER HAIR and listening to the soothing drum of rain on the roof when she was alerted by the whinny of a horse seemingly from just outside her window. Lifting one edge of the curtain, she peered out into the lashing darkness, but the rain was thudding against the glass with such force that if there was anything out there it was lost in the downpour. Shivering, she let the curtain fall and padded across to the bureau to blow out the candle.

A tumult of pounding on the door stopped her. Tossing the plait over her shoulder, she pulled a blanket from the bed and wrapped it around herself to cover her nightgown and hurried to see who might be calling at this hour. Gwynne and Charles had gone to bed over an hour ago, but Lisabeth, unable to summon the slightest drowsiness, had elected to stay up reading and toasting her toes by the fire's fading embers.

'All right, all right!' she called as the thumping continued. 'There's no need to wake every—' The rest of her words died on her lips as she flung the unbolted door wide and Rhys lurched into the room. 'It's you . . .' she said foolishly. 'I thought that one of the cockatoos—'

'It's me,' he said tersely. He was sodden. Rain blackened his boots and ran in rivulets from his oiled-cloth coat but he was hatless, his hair plastered in putty-coloured chunks over his wet forehead and his eyelashes sticking together in bunches. Even his moustache dripped water as he spoke. 'Yes, Lisabeth, it's me, and I've come to see you.'

He was furious, she realized with inward dismay. 'Now?' she

asked stupidly, as from their bedroom Gwynne called out to ask who was there.

'It's me – Rhys!' he replied then turned to Lisabeth, 'Tell her not to come out. I want to talk to you alone.'

Lisabeth just stared at his angry face. She wished she hadn't answered the door. She wished she had the courage to tell him to go away – that she didn't want to talk to him. Hugging the blanket tightly around her, she shivered.

'Go on,' he hissed urgently. A soft glow of light appeared beyond the open doorway that led to the bedrooms beyond. 'Stop her. She's getting up.'

'No,' said Lisabeth, dragging out her courage and holding tightly lest it slip away again. 'If you've anything to say, you can say it to Aunty Gwynne. I'm going back to bed!'

He had begun to shuck off his saturated coat, but her reply stopped him and he reached out swiftly to seize her wrist as she turned away, jerking on it hard and spinning her around to face him again. 'I'm going to talk to you and you're going to listen!' he informed her. When she struggled silently to pull her wrist free his eyes narrowed and he called out to Gwynne: 'Don't bother to come out, sister! I'm leaving now!'

'Good,' spat Lisabeth, annoyed that he was hurting her, and even more annoyed that he should come bursting in just when she had begun to come to terms with her decision and her future. The last thing she needed was for him to disrupt everything. Rhys Morgan had been banished from her mind and her life. To do that had meant taking a drastic and unpalatable step, but she was prepared to marry Athol Nye in order to gain her freedom and only hated Rhys all the more intensely for forcing her into the match. It *was* all his fault. She had never wanted him, never consciously encouraged him, so why did he insist on meddling in her life?

To her astonishment he did not let her go as she expected but scooped her up in his arms and strode out into the rainy night, holding her hard against his chest. By the time she had recovered from the shock enough to scream and struggle he was striding past the furthermost apple trees, and behind them the open door of the cottage was a pale blurry oblong in the distant darkness.

Still clutching her, he swung up into Polka's saddle as easily as if he had been cradling a sick sheep. As his weight settled the tired horse plunged forward, eager to be home in the dry warm stable with oats and chaff in the feeding-box.

274

Lisabeth struggled furiously, but Rhys wrapped his arms around her, pinning her flailing arms and restricting her kicking legs. 'It won't do you a bit of good,' he assured her in a voice that was cheery resolution. 'You're going to listen to me, Lisabeth, so make up your mind up to it.'

Loathing him with every scrap of strength she could summon, she wondered viciously if he was deliberately making the journey as uncomfortable for her as he could. Rain was beating with such force in her face that she had to close her eyes, and with every breath she took splashes were inhaled, causing her to splutter and cough, but she could not even twist her head because to do so would mean that her face would be resting against his chest. *I'd rather drown than shelter my face against him*, she told herself, so drown she almost did. Her body was held in such a rigid, locked position that every stumbling step of the horse's hoofs jarred right through her. Occasionally her body sagged with pain, and as soon as that happened Rhys relaxed his grip, but when she felt a loosening of the bonds that held her Lisabeth immediately began to kick and lash out again, and again he imprisoned her tightly.

'I'm not hurting you, am I?' he asked her once. The question inflamed her rage so acutely that she couldn't reply. Not hurting her? As if he cared what pain he inflicted!

The rain that had poured down in torrents all evening was now faltering, all wrung out. By the time Polka reached the top of the ridge-path it had stopped completely and the clouds were scudding away like curtains drawing from a freshly washed stage. From a gap a half-moon shone, thin and pale as an opaque honesty seed, and as Polka's gait quickened against the crunch of the gravelled driveway Lisabeth opened her eyes to see the looming white walls and steeply gabled roofs. Oriel windows glinted in the moonlight, and puddles like swatches of silk were strewn on the courtyard. From the distance came a slow roll of surf, and beyond the cluster of tombstone-like rocks on the headland spread the oily dark ocean.

On the entire ride Lisabeth had said nothing, but now when Rhys set her down and without letting go of her wrist dismounted, too, she clutched the now-loose rug up to the front of her nightgown with her free hand and pleaded: 'Please, Rhys, let me go home.'

His face was set, hard-edged by the faint silver light, his eyes unfathomable shadows. His voice was toneless as he said: 'Go home? Lisabeth, you are home.' And he laughed.

275

Before she could utter a stinging retort a figure emerged from one of the many doorways that encircled the courtyard. It was Tommy Nevin, Birdie's oldest son, she saw in surprise. He did not glance at her but rushed to take Polka's reins and lead him away.

'Is there a fire anywhere?' asked Rhys, still gripping her wrist.

'Ooh, ay, sir. There be a foyer in your room sir . . . your budroom, sir,' he said as he scuttled towards the stables.

'Tommy!' called Rhys. 'As soon as you've seen to Polka go and wake your mother, would you? Ask her if we can borrow one of her dresses, please – oh, and a petticoat, too. Miss Stafford is soaked right through.'

'No!' hissed Lisabeth, imagining the gossip that would spread through the district as soon as Birdie Nevin had savoured this piece of news. 'Rhys, this is ludicrous . . . insane! Please let me go.'

'The only insane thing is your proposed marriage,' snapped Rhys, and with this, the confirmation of her frightened suspicions, all the fight went out of Lisabeth and her spirits plummeted. How in the world had he found out?

'You weren't supposed to know,' she accused him as he flung her into a spacious upstairs room and turned the key in the lock behind them. Hunching over, she rubbed her shins where they had bumped and barked against items of furniture on the half-dragging flight up an unlit staircase and along gloomy corridors. When she glanced up he was looking at her with what she interpreted as amusement so she straightened, tugged the blanket around her shoulders and loftily ignored him while she gazed around the room instead.

It was a mellow, warm room, lined with honey-coloured panelling that seemed to reflect the flames in the wide marble-tiled fireplace. The honey-wood floor was spread with large square carpets patterned with entwining flowers and leaves, a theme that was repeated in the richly embroidered hangings around the magnificent four-poster bed that dominated the room, standing as it did on a carpeted platform, spread with a brocade coverlet and heaped with velvet cushions in soft autumn colours. Not in all her life, not even in pictures, had Lisabeth seen anything as splendid as this room.

Some of the awe it inspired must have shown in her face, for when she turned at last to the nearest wall and saw herself bedraggled, sodden and reflected in a row of tall matching pier-glasses she saw, too, that Rhys was watching her, had been watching her reflection all along, smiling openly at her reactions to the opulence.

Jerking her chin high, she blanked her face. 'I want to leave,' she announced, sneaking another glance at herself. Dear Lord, did she really look so dreadful? A wet chook had more charm than she did right now with her wild, bloodshot eyes and her snakes of dripping hair. She was freezing, blue and tight-faced.

Rhys said: 'I never thought I'd ever have cause to accuse you of being boring, Lisabeth. Tell me what you think of this, mmm?'

To her horror Lisabeth said the first thing that popped into her head. Teeth chattering, she remarked, 'That doesn't look like the kind of bed one would put a chamberpot under!' and when he roared with laughter and said, 'That's better!' she could cheerfully have killed him.

He had lowered a wheel-shaped, swagged chandelier and was reaching amongst the crystal droplets to touch a taper to each of the candles. His laughter set the whole thing wobbling, and the crystals chimed softly in accord. Over his shoulder he said: 'There's a tea-tray on the hearth and a kettle on the hob. Be a good girl and brew the tea, would you? Ah, that must be Tommy with the dry clothes,' he added as he hoisted the chandelier again and anchored it to the ornate bracket on the wall near the marble mantelpiece.

With the steaming kettle in her hand Lisabeth pondered for a moment the possibility of flinging it at Rhys and, while he was distracted, dashing to freedom through the door, but almost as soon as she had considered the feasibility of escape the opportunity had gone. She poured the water into the teapot instead and allowed the warmth of the fire to thaw her numb face and hands. She was so cold her bones ached.

'Here,' said Rhys, bringing over a fluffy towel from the inlaid marble washstand and placing it around her neck; it was as thick and soft as whipped cream, nothing like the stringy, hard cloths the Staffords used to dry themselves with. 'Here, dry your hair, and put these on. I'll go into the garderobe to give you some privacy.'

She wanted to refuse. She wanted to fling Birdie Nevin's garments at him – what was this, a housekeeper's uniform? – but against her will she was intrigued. This atmosphere of blatant luxury intoxicated her, she was tempted by the delicate chocolate cakes on the tray (now supplemented with an extra cup, saucer and plate thoughtfully provided by Tommy Nevin) and, above all, she found herself wondering what Rhys intended to say to her

277

that needed such enormous trouble in which to do it. Though she would never have admitted it, Rhys's impulsive kidnapping had thrilled her, made her feel important.

Marry me, Lisabeth, he had said. Afterwards he was so off-handedly cool that she wondered if the proposal had been a regretted aberration. Now this – she gazed around the elegant room again, thinking how far he had come since he bunked down in that primitive shepherd's hut. *That* was what she had pictured when he asked her to share his life.

Not that his mansion made any difference, she told herself sternly. He was what he had always been – Rhys Morgan, Enemy – stuck into a compartment from which he could never be moved. After all, the past could never be changed, and because of that he must never be forgiven. Having thus reassured herself of the rigidness of her position, Lisabeth relaxed, knowing that nothing he could do or say could possibly affect her as long as she stood firm behind her protective wall.

Pulling up the petticoat under her sodden nightgown, she stripped off the soaked garment then donned Mrs Nevin's baggy black dress before rubbing her wet hair with the divine, soft towel. By now the fire's warmth had seeped through her, melting away the painful cold and replacing it with a sense of delicious well-being that was only slightly marred when she glanced again at the mirror and saw what a fright she looked in the elephantine garment, with her hair scragged in all directions like a witch's broom. Even though she hated Rhys she wanted to look her best in front of him, didn't she? so automatically she smoothed and patted with her hands to shape the damp locks down to the shape of her head.

I still look a gowk, but it will have to do, she told herself, turning back to the hearth. Mmm but those cakes looked delectable.

Rhys returned without knocking. Ten minutes ago she would have indignantly commented on this breach of manners, but she was sitting on a hassock while her hair steamed gently and was too relaxed to care. He had towelled and brushed his hair and had changed out of his own soaked clothes into something elegantly casual, she noticed, but when he saw her dress he laughed. 'That gown doesn't suit, does it? We should be thankful that it's Gwynne you get your hand-me-downs from and not Mrs Nevin.'

At once Lisabeth stiffened. All the sweet comfort fled and was replaced immediately by a flood of hot shame as she recalled the Christmas gown and the despicable feelings of pity that motivated it. Standing up, she blurted: 'If you've brought me here to laugh at me and mock my clothes, then—'

'Sit down and pour the tea,' he cut in, annoyed with himself for beginning so badly. She'd looked like a contented kitten sprawled by the fire when he came in, and now she was far more like a cat that had been provoked by a large ugly dog. Why did he handle her so clumsily?

'I'm not thirsty.'

'Please, Lisabeth.'

She relented and settled back on the hassock. Drawing up a chair, he watched her as she gracefully prepared the cups of tea, adding spoonful after spoonful of sugar to her own until she'd stirred up a brew that in Rhys's opinion would have been undrinkable. He was about to comment tactlessly, then remembered the hard physical labour she did and decided that she must need all the energy she could get. Once she was ensconced in a more leisurely life, lightly sweetened tea could be just another of the pleasures to which he would introduce her.

If he had the opportunity.

'Lisabeth, I brought you here because something alarming – something distressing – happened this evening. Andrew ran away from school.'

'He didn't!' Cup dithered on saucer, and she gaped at him. 'But why? And why couldn't you talk to me about that back at the cottage? None of this makes—' He began to interrupt her. Both stopped talking, then in the silence Lisabeth said: 'Why did he run away? He seems so happy there.'

'He is happy. I took him back and squared things away with the headmaster, who assured me that Andrew would be punished but, in view of the provocation, not very severely.'

'Provocation? You mean they're bullying—' Her eyes grew huge and worried. Leaning forward in her shiny black bubble, she set the cup down on the tray.

'He ran away because he's upset on account of you, Lisabeth.'

'Oh.' Hands knotted in her billowing lap. The letter. The news that she was soon to marry Athol Nye. Jutting her chin, she said: 'Then, he shouldn't be worried. He should be joyful for me.'

'On the grounds that someone at least should be joyful?' he asked sarcastically. 'Come on, Lisabeth, is *anybody* pleased about this ridiculous union? Even Mr Nye seems lukewarm, wouldn't you say? I mean, he's hardly given you an ardent courtship, has he?'

Lisabeth's eyes swung to his face in astonishment. 'Have you been spying on me? How do you—' Belatedly she realized that not denying what he said was tantamount to admitting the truth.

'I haven't been spying. I don't need to. Young Andrew came dashing into Benares early this evening in a fine state, absolutely heartbroken and clutching a crumpled soaked letter in his fist. He pleaded with me to try to stop your marriage. Apparently the boys at the school filled with his head with all kinds of nasty scraps of nonsense about Mr Nye – he teaches advanced literature studies there three afternoons a week and he's made himself so unpopular that when Andrew heard—'

'I see,' cut in Lisabeth coldly. 'But I *don't* see what business it is of yours to—'

'Listen to me, will you?' He thrust the plate of cakes at her with a 'Here, eat one of these and be quiet' kind of gesture, so she took one and picked at the frilled paper case, intrigued by what he was saying but boiling with resentment that he should be taking Andrew's side. That was her place! Andrew should have come to her if he was upset, not gone running to Rhys. The treachery of it dumbfounded her. It was a good thing she was marrying Athol and removing herself completely from this district. From the wedding day on Andrew would come to her for his holidays from school and neither of them would ever have to see Rhys Morgan again. *The absolute arrogance of the man!* she thought as she studied his strong intelligent face. Look at the deep concern in those blue eyes! Yes, he'd probably looked at Mary once with that same 'deep' concern, but how quickly he had turned his back and forgotten her as soon as it suited his purposes. Sick emotion – a vile mixture of self-pity and loathing – rose in her throat, and she flung the pretty little chocolate cake into the fire where its dainty crown of crystallized violets and angelica leaves immediately began to melt.

He ignored her rudeness, knowing how distressed she must be by his unwanted interference yet determined to make her see how foolish and unsuitable her proposed marriage was. 'I know how hurtful and silly young boys can be, so I told Andrew to take no notice of anything they said, but at the same time I was more than a little disturbed by the news, so I rode out to Sumner to ask the Days if they knew anything about Mr Nye and about the arrangements he might have made.'

'And they told you nothing, of course!'

'At first, no. They said that you wanted privacy and they'd respect your wishes. . . . —'

'. . . But as I was leaving Joe followed me out and told me that I had a good reason to worry.'

'Joe did?' She felt crushed. Surely Joe wouldn't betray her.

'He said . . .,' Rhys began and stopped. Instinct told him that he had already said more than enough and, though he usually ignored that instinct, this time a glance at Lisabeth's stricken face was sufficient to dry up his argument. What would be the point of dragging out all the unpalatable things Joe had said about the Nyes? His task now was to persuade Lisabeth to marry him instead, and no advantage could be gained by antagonizing her still further.

'Joe cares about you,' he said quietly. 'I wouldn't be surprised if he wasn't even a little bit in love with you himself. He wants what's best for you, Lisabeth. We all do.'

Averting her face, Lisabeth stared into the flames, at the sticky mess of chocolate cake. It seemed to her that she was contemplating the ruins of her own life. *If only it hadn't happened!* she cried inwardly, aching with a queer pain she did not understand. What a mess this all was, yet there was no going back, no possible way to alter the course she had set for herself. Treacherous tears born of weak self-pity burned behind her eyelids, and she concentrated fiercely on repressing them. He mustn't see her cry! With dignity she must extricate herself from here, and once home in her cold little room she could permit herself the luxury of an unashamed wallow in tears, but not until then . . .

'Joe wants to see you happy. So does Andrew, and so do I, Lisabeth,' Rhys was saying. He was still leaning towards her, almost touching her, his voice low and earnest. She could smell his spicy-sharp cologne and occasionally in the lull of the flames hear a rustle of his cream silk shirt as he moved. All these details impressed themselves upon her and heightened her misery and sense of hopelessness.

'I vowed I wouldn't ask you again, so this time I'm telling you,' he said. 'You're going to marry me. Everyone else can see that I'm the right one for you, and I think that you know it, too, but you're too stubborn and—'

'No!' cried Lisabeth with a vehemence that surprised even her. How *dare* he order her to marry him! 'I said "No" before and I mean it . . .' She shivered despite the fire's warmth. 'You've no idea how much I meant it! So don't you see, bringing me here was a waste of time! An absolute waste of time because I'll never—'

She had twisted her head to face him now and was flinging the

281

words at him in a blind desperation, her face tight with pain and her eyes very bright and trembling with unshed tears.

In one fluid movement Rhys moved out of his chair, knelt before her and cupped her face in his hands, stilling her words with a simple kiss. She crumpled at once.

If only he hadn't touched her! She was weak and vulnerable, her defences awry, and his kiss probed through the confusion in her mind, lulling the chaos, quieting the storm of angry protest that raged through her brain. She was so still she was not even breathing – like a hurt dove, thought Rhys, who had once cradled one in his hands and marvelled at the frantic heartbeat though the bird stayed perfectly quiet.

He kissed her with an extreme of gentleness – a thistledown touch – and his palms were so light on either side of her jaw that she could have pulled away with the slightest movement. She did not, but her eyes were snapped wide open, staring in terror at his face. With utter delicacy he moved his lips on hers in a subtle circular motion and at the same time slid his hands back over the faintly moist hair to caress the slender hollows of her neck, behind her ears. At this touch she sighed, and her eyelashes fluttered, drooping to screen her eyes.

Only then did he move, not taking his mouth from hers but drawing her up with him as he stood and then wrapping his arms around her. She quailed then, flinched against the feeling of his lean hard body against hers, but he kissed her more, with greater tenderness, and with another tiny sigh she relaxed against him.

Now he would risk everything. With his mouth away from hers and his cheek resting on her cool white brow he murmured: 'I love you, Lisabeth.'

In the warm darkness of his neck's curve her eyes squeezed tight in pain as she registered the declaration and her own unspoken but irrefutable response. *If only*, her heart cried. *If only the past could be wiped away. If only none of it had ever happened!* But it had, and soon, in a minute, the moment she had summoned up the will to push him away, she would . . .

Kissing her again he murmured against her mouth and pressed her shoulders and waist tighter against his body.

She wanted to resist, she *had* to resist, but her body was boneless, her muscles melted and her heart flowed into his as he scooped her up in his arms and, still kissing her, carried her across the room, up on to the platform and laid her on the bed. When she opened her eyes she was gazing up at the tented tapestry

282

canopy with its pattern of golden flowers and dark green leaves twining on a velvety russet background. Then his face hung over hers, his eyes soft with incredible tenderness and his voice hushed as if he was in church. 'Lisabeth, I love you,' he repeated, and this time she was able to meet his eyes, though her response echoed so faintly in her subconscious that neither of them heard it. Instead her hands rose up as if of their own accord and placed themselves around the back of his head, the fingers lacing in the thick, damp hair.

To Rhys this was response enough. With a groan of joy he began kissing her again, this time with an urgency that at first unsettled and stiffened her but then relaxed her until she was shivering with a wild and delicious excitement that rippled through her like a chill. She forgot that she hated him, forgot that this was the loathsome Rhys Morgan, forgot Athol Nye and that she was to be married tomorrow, forgot where she was. All she knew was that this was what she wanted – no, *needed*: Rhys kissing her and enfolding her in his arms, caressing her in a way that she refused to think about but absolutely gloried in.

He did not speak. She did not realize it, and would not have understood, but he was far more terrified than she, almost paralysed with nervousness that she might push him away and run shrieking from the bed, for then he would have lost her for ever. This was no mere seduction, it was a *de facto* wedding night, and he was out to claim her, make her his so that all her other plans would become tainted and impossible. She belonged with him, and by making love to her he had to show her where her heart and mind, not just her body, lay.

Hardly daring to breathe, he propped himself up on one elbow, leaning over her to kiss her still, for the sweetness there was such that he knew he could never have enough of her. That one hand caressed her neck but the other he sent on a bolder journey, down to the hem of the ugly black gown and up underneath, his fingers trailing a thrilling path over her satiny skin again and again until he had bunched the material up to her chest and her breasts were cupped one at a time in his daring hand. Breathless, he kissed her harder, praying she would not stir, but her fingers spasmed in his hair and she moaned deep in her throat as he traced another line down over her warm belly where his fingers encountered the coarse fabric of the brief garment she had worn under her night-gown. Slowly, slowly, he tucked his thumb under the band and slid it downwards, easing it over her hips.

Now she did balk. When she realized that he was tugging away the garment ladies always wore to protect their modesty she was outraged. Her head twisted away from his kisses, and her hands jerked down as she thrust at his shoulders with all her strength trying to wriggle out from under him, but the mattress was deep and soft and enveloping and the weight of his body bore down on her, rendering her helpless.

With ease his hand pulled her garment down and his booted foot hooked in it and kicked it free of her ankles; then he was fumbling with his own clothing for what seemed an eternity while she never stopped struggling against the force of the one arm and shoulder with which he kept her pinned.

'Please, Rhys, please let me go!' she cried, and at the sound of her voice he was kissing her again but this time she felt the warm smooth length of his body close against hers and it felt so incredibly wonderful that the protests died in her throat. With a whimper she subsided – what could she do anyway? – and she nibbled his lips and returned his kisses and stroked the wondrous planes of his face while he moved sensuously against her, one hand caressing the secret place between her legs so that her body relaxed and opened under his touch.

For an instant he turned his head away and brought his fingers up to his mouth then stroked her again, and this time his touch was wet and sticky and a moment later he slid his body over hers so that the entire length of him was pinning her down, his legs pushing hers apart, his belly smooth and warm against hers and his chest insistently pressing her breasts.

'Lisabeth' he gasped, then took a long, shuddering breath as he raised himself up on his elbows. As he did so, she felt the shaft of hardness enter her, silkily at first, pleasantly so, then with a burning force that made her cry out in shock and pain.

'Lisabeth' he gasped again, an urgent message with no substance, but it did not matter, for she couldn't hear him now; she was hurting and confused and battered, as if she was caught in the teeth of a screaming gale that was tossing and knocking her about. Her body tensed, the pain continued and then quite suddenly she gave herself up to the inevitability of it and something magical happened. Rhys continued to thrust into her but it no longer hurt, it was quieter somehow, soothing, nuzzling, caressing and very exciting, lifting her a fraction higher with each stroke to a new and more intense plateau of pleasure. She was sobbing in the aftermath of the hurt, but now the sobs were of delight and she cried and murmured against his neck as her body quivered and quickened under him until finally with a pure cry of ecstatic surprise she tightened her arms around his perspiration-slicked back and her body slumped with the strangest and most intense sensation of joy that she had ever known.

For a long time they lay together, their bodies entwined but faces not touching. Lisabeth looked up at the awning, memorizing the design, and at Rhys's contented face, the thick curve of dark eyelashes all tipped with gold above the downy upper cheek. She knew enough of life to guess what had just taken place between them and at first was too numbed with drowsy ecstasy to care, but gradually a small cold voice of reason began to echo in her head.

Look at you! she told herself in disgust. *You're as weak and pathetic as your wretched mother, succumbing to this man, letting him have his way with you. Have you forgotten who he is and what harm he's done you?*

She shivered, and, misunderstanding the cause, Rhys tucked the coverlet around her shoulders. 'I'll take you home now,' he said. 'We'll wake Charles and Gwynne and tell them that you're marrying me, instead . . . It's going to be marvellous, Lisabeth, I promise! Don't look at me like that! It gives me the shivers, too, because you're so exactly like your mother that I—'

Lisabeth sat up in one swift horrified reflex. Tugging the black skirts down, she scrambled off the bed away from Rhys. He glanced at her, bemused, not realizing the damage his careless words had inflicted, not knowing that the very mention of Mary was enough to bring down on Lisabeth's head the guilt of torn resolutions and broken vows. Not until she scooped up first the undergarment and then her nightgown and rug did he understand that she was fleeing from him and from what had happened between them.

'Lisabeth, don't do this!' he cried, scrambling from the bed and clutching his shirt around his waist to screen his nakedness. 'We've got to talk. We've plans to make . . .' She had taken the key from the mantelpiece and was already twisting it in the lock, swinging the door open. 'Lisabeth, please . . .,' he called after her. 'Wait . . . You can't run off. . . . I need to see you safely home. You might —'

The remainder of his words were cut off as Lisabeth snipped the door shut, jabbed the key in the lock and gave it a quick turn.

For a moment she leaned her shuddering back against the door, her eyes clenched shut in the darkness as she fought down the feelings of revulsion and dismay. For a short time there she had lost herself completely, but she might have known that the past would always intrude. Bitterly she reminded herself that this was all her own fault. She had succumbed to his lovemaking just as her poor stupid mother had done, and now the shame of her weakness sickened her.

Beside her hip the doorknob twisted, and Lisabeth jumped away and lurched down the dark corridor until she came to the stairwell where tall windows were lit by a pale sky. Here she left the key, placing it on the extended palm of a suit of bronze armour that stood guard over the landing.

With the rug around her shoulders and her garments in her hands she plunged out into the moonlight. By the time she reached the cottage and crept into her room under the screen of Charles's snoring the sky was blushing with the first light of dawn.

TWENTY-SEVEN

KNOWING THAT HE HAD NO HOPE of catching her now, and that the wedding was not set until five the next afternoon, Rhys went back to bed unworried, his mind occupied with the problem of redesigning the suite of rooms so that no matter what the provocation he couldn't be locked in ever again. By the time Birdie Nevin freed him next morning he had already washed, shaved and rehearsed what he would say to Lisabeth. After grabbing a heel of bread from the kitchen for breakfast, gulping a mug of fresh water and picking up an apple from a barrel in the cool-room he hurried out to the stables where Tommy had Polka ready for him.

There was nobody at the Staffords' cottage and the cart was gone. Walking through, he noted that the ashes were still warm, that there was a fresh, still frothy pan of milk in the buttery, and that the butter-churn and butter-pats were still damp from use, but when he walked through the cottage a second time, this time going into the bedrooms, he saw that all Lisabeth's things – her clothes, boots, hair-brush and pin-tray and even the miniature portraits of Mary and Andrew Maitland – had been removed. *Mary*, he thought. *Yes, Mary*. . . . Was that why . . .?

For a second he stood in dumbfounded silence, unable to believe the implications of this evidence. When he had made love to her he had known with an absolute certainty that she was responding with a passion to equal his. Sure, she had fled, and that was perturbing, but Rhys was confident that Lisabeth would calm down and listen to the clamour of her inner feelings. He'd planned that by the time he arrived this morning she would have had an ample period in which to reflect and contemplate her future.

Instead he had given her ample chance to escape.

Grimly Rhys swung into the saddle and rode at a furious gallop to the tiny sickle of beach below the cliffs where the rowboat was kept. Tethering Polka to a low branch of an overhanging *pohutukawa* tree, he dragged the boat down to the water, took the oars from their separate hiding-place behind a flax clump a few yards away, and with a flailing and splashing launched out through the shallow water until the harbour floor dropped away and the oars bit deeply.

When he arrived at the Days' boatshed it was almost noon, the pale sun overhead and a cold wind burring the damp sand. In reply to his shout Joe Day emerged from the maw of the shed while Alf stood in the weak shadows behind him, a planing-tool in his hands.

Looking at his face, Joe had no need to ask the nature of his errand. Shrugging apologetically, he said: 'Sorry, mate, I really am. She married Athol Nye at ten o'clock at the Ferrymead church. News is that it was planned for ten all along but she told everybody afternoon so that—'

'So that I couldn't interrupt the proceedings,' Rhys finished viciously. 'Damn! Oh, damnation!' He stopped. Swearing was so pathetically ineffectual against the enormity of his disappointment.

'I am sorry,' said Joe. 'Word came to Ma only half an hour before, and of course that wasn't enough time to alert you, so I figured if her heart was set on it that strongly what could we do anyway?' He smiled hopefully at Rhys's bleak face. 'Tell you what – why don't you come fishing with us, eh? We've got some clobber here you can change into, and Ma will fix us a slap-up picnic lunch. We'll try the *hapuka* grounds out past the headland. What do you say, eh?'

'No, thanks . . . Another time . . . What did Mrs Day say about the wedding? Did she make any comment afterwards?'

Joe looked uncomfortable. His fingers plucked at the peak of his fisherman's cap. 'It was . . . What did Ma say? Depressing, that's it. Old widow Nye cried all the way through. Word is she found out Lisabeth handed over Braddock's money to Mr Stafford, and because of that she wanted Athol to call the wedding off. Forgive my frankness, but she's a grasping old Tartar if ever there was one.'

Rhys said nothing. So on top of everything else Lisabeth was being married for her nonexistent inheritance. Though there was

288

the land, of course. Lord help him if the Nyes all decided to move over there to live on it, right next door to him. He'd accept that she'd married someone else – he had no choice – but it would be unendurable to have her on his doorstep but still unattainable.

He shook his head. It was all too new to comprehend fully. 'I really didn't think she'd do it,' he told Joe. 'I was so positive.'

'Sure, mate,' said Joe.

For two months Rhys did nothing. On that first terrible afternoon he rowed back across the harbour under a white whirling sky, his mind seething with ugly and persistent images. Back home he cleared his clothing from the garderobe, making trip after trip through the room without once glancing at the platform which held the magnificent bed. She loved him. He knew it . . . he was so *sure*.

As soon as all of his personal effects had been moved and dumped in a heap in the wide corridor he locked his room and, straining with the effort, inched a huge wooden dresser out of the room next door and along until it completely blocked and hid the doorway. Leaving a bewildered Birdie Nevin to resettle his things in one of the other bedchambers, he trudged down to the library where he sat dejectedly at the dainty maplewood harpsichord, his hands slumped on the keys.

Absently he began to play a softly haunting sonata by Haydn. It was as if the keys had taken his fingers and led them into the first few notes then the rest of the music flowed by itself. Rhys was not aware of consciously playing, only of the music lapping around the edges of his sensibility. Inside him was a cold, hard core of numb disbelief. He had been so *sure*.

Upstairs Birdie Nevin was hanging up his clothes and setting out his silver-backed hair brushes when she heard the first vibrating chords, and she nodded her round grey head in relief and appreciation of the music. You'd never think that a man with work-rough hands like his could coax such sweetness from an instrument, she thought. That was Mr Morgan, nine parts man but one part angel, and again she wondered whether he had Irish blood flowing in his veins. Such a man as he deserved to be Irish.

She was untangling the confusion of razors, strops and barber's towels from where Rhys had swept them all into the blue china water-ewer when abruptly in mid-phrase the music stopped. Thinking that a visitor had interrupted him, Birdie stopped, too, for it was part of her duties to greet visitors, but before she could ease herself up from her plump knees there was a cry, a terrible cry bursting with pain and anguish that reverberated up the stairwell and along the upper storey of the mansion.

'Sweet Virgin, sumbudy's culled the muster!' she gabbled as she waddled towards the sound, puffing down the stairs as speedily as her ridiculously tiny feet could convey her. More shouts, crashings and the sharp ripping sound of splintering wood hastened her on until when she reached the open library door she halted, one chubby hand clutching the frame for support as the babble of prayer died in her throat. The master had gone crazy!

Rhys was crying, and every few moments another shout of pain roared from him as in an orgy of anger and misery he lashed out with an ornamental Japanese sword that had rested on brackets above the fireplace. The harpsichord was in shattered ruins, and with every blow that landed on its broken frame more wires snapped and keys scattered across the oriental carpet like broken teeth.

Birdie Nevin was a simple woman but she understood male rage sufficiently to know that Rhys was railing against fate and not against any particular person. This was a harmless anger. Without hesitation she stepped into the room, saying: 'Mr Morgan, please! I'm surprised at you!'

Swinging around, he stared at her uncomprehendingly, then the sword dropped from his hands and without a word he slumped to his knees. 'Oh, Birdie, I'm in such pain!' he said as she rushed to his side. 'I can't—'

'Hush, now,' she soothed, taking his head against her lap. 'Hush . . .'

There was a sudden sharp rapping at the nearby front door, and a high feminine voice called: 'Rhys? Are you in there? What in the world is going on?'

'It's Missus Gammerwoth,' Birdie said.

Rhys started to laugh, a hopeless, ironical sound. 'It would be. Who else would it be?'

'Rhys, are you there?' rose the voice.

'Get rid of her,' sighed Rhys. 'Tell her anything you like, just send her away.'

For two months Rhys concentrated on putting Lisabeth out of his mind – or so it seemed to Gwynne, who watched him anxiously. Now that the road up to Mists of Heaven was finished she visited the house as often as she could, begging Charles to drive her up there before leaving on his excursions to town and collecting her when he returned. Though she could not walk far, she passed the hours contentedly sitting in a wicker armchair in the huge warm kitchen, resting her feet on the log-box and chatting to Birdie Nevin while she rolled out pastry for pies, mended shirts or ironed table-cloths and sheets with the brace of flat-irons that kept hot on the top of the stove. From her Gwynne learned that Rhys lived a sober quiet life, that he worked long hours out on the station and despite her efforts to tempt his appetite he ate sparingly. Seldom going to town these days, he ignored the invitations and visiting-cards that collected in drifts on the receptacle that rested inside the front door. He was popular, Gwynne noticed with pride. Every visit with Birdie was interrupted several times by hopeful callers, all of whom were turned away.

Birdie told Gwynne that the Gammerwoth widow called most often and, she suspected, tracked him down where he was working in the paddocks, for sometimes there was a note or an invitation in her elegant script left in his pockets when his garments were put out for the laundry. But Birdie never mentioned that terrible day when Rhys had smashed the beautiful harpsichord. On the whole subject of Lisabeth, Birdie's lips were stilled. As someone who had suffered a deep personal tragedy of her own Birdie recognized it in another and, though she adored gossip, that episode was allowed to lapse without comment, but Birdie's heart ached for her master and it was a long time before she could hear Gwynne sigh the name 'Lisabeth' without experiencing a pang of protective rage.

Eight weeks after the wedding Rhys rode over to Sumner and had a talk with Joe, who told him where Lisabeth lived but warned him not to go there.

'You'll only cause trouble for her,' he pointed out. 'They'll be wanting to know why a young man is calling on her, won't they?'

'I'm bringing a message from Gwynne,' said Rhys.

'Sure you are!' Joe bent his head over the ropes he was knotting. 'Maybe you don't know that Charles has cut her off. Right up until the last he thought she'd sign the land over to him. Even outside the church . . . I've never seen him so angry. No, there'll be no messages from the Staffords. I'm sorry, Rhys,' he said, glancing up. 'I offered to row Mrs Stafford over to visit Lisabeth one day, but she refused, said her husband wouldn't like it.'

'That's Gwynne,' agreed Rhys sourly. 'Always taking the easy way.' Then he thought: *What about me? I knew I wanted*

Lisabeth but I paid scant attention to her. Because she was unencouraging, I kept away when I should have been there every evening and to hell with Charles and his sour face! My dramatic, romantic gestures weren't enough, weren't nearly enough.

'I must see her,' he told Joe. 'Will you help me?'

Joe looked unhappy. 'Old Mrs Nye takes the eggs to Ferrymead on Thursday mornings,' he said.

The Nyes' cottage was tucked into a valley in the Port Hills behind Ferrymead a little more than two miles from the crossing along a track that wended over fern-tufted ground. The farmlet itself was cleared and sown with grass – an inferior strain of cocksfoot, noticed Rhys who had developed an appraising eye for pastures. It was one large paddock dotted with burned tree-stumps and littered with a few large logs, one of which was half cut-up for firewood.

'They sell it,' explained Joe as they edged along the ridge overlooking the property. 'Athol brings home driftwood every afternoon on his walk back from the ferry, and they use that for themselves, while this good stuff gets tied into bundles and sold at the market. Alf used to cart it in for them, but they argued over his fees so now Athol delivers it himself on his way to school.' He snorted his contempt. 'He uses a hand-cart to carry it. Horses eat feed, you see, and they don't produce owt but manure, though no doubt the Nyes would find a market for that, too, if they had a horse!'

Rhys wished he could be amused.

On the land were sheep and a couple of cows wandering free, while dozens and dozens of hens were all fenced into yards walled and roofed with chickenwire. Beyond the fowl-houses squatted an unpainted shack with a roof thatched native-style. Lisabeth was outside the shack pounding something in a large wooden tray, but before Rhys could decide what she was doing the door behind her swung open and a small spare figure dressed in black with a black bonnet emerged and without a nod or a word to Lisabeth marched past her and down across the meadow towards the farm gate. On her arm was a large basket covered with a fresh white cloth. Lisabeth paused to watch her, and the sound of pounding stopped. As soon as that happened the older Mrs Nye stopped, too, and turned to glance at her in such a reproving way that at once Lisabeth resumed thumping with a fury.

Rhys smiled thinly and laughed out loud when, as the thin black figure disappeared, Lisabeth sank down immediately on to an upturned barrel, her shoulders sloping with fatigue.

'Wait here,' he ordered, pressing a small bronze pistol into Joe's hand. 'Fire this if the old biddy returns. Up in the air, eh? And away. If a shot landed in the fowl-yard, there'd be pandemonium.'

'Good luck!' said Joe, but Rhys had already gone, vaulting the split-rail fence with ease and loping across the rough ground.

Lisabeth saw him coming and stood up, her face draining of colour. 'Rhys!' she whispered, and he knew that whatever had happened to her she still loved him.

By the time he reached her side her defences were up, her spine stiff with resolution. 'What are you doing here?' she demanded as she gave the pestle a few more thumps. She was, he saw, bashing kernels off dried corn-cobs to feed the hens.

'There's a machine that does that,' he said without thinking, then cursed himself immediately for getting off to yet another bad start. Why did he do this? He should have run right up to her without stopping and swept her up in his arms, but now she was cool and prickly, both hands clutching that stick as if it was a weapon.

'Machines cost money,' she informed him. 'And speaking of money have you come to see me about the lease? I thought we'd arranged to have the income paid straight to the school for Andrew's—'

'So the Nyes don't know about the land?' guessed Rhys.

Her face tightened. She was very thin and pale – not well, thought Rhys who was studying her closely with intense interest. No, not at all well.

She shivered and pulled the piece of tattered blanket that served as a shawl up around her shoulders and neck. Wisps of dull hair escaped from below the faded cloth that was tied, gypsy fashion around her head. 'You wouldn't tell them, would you?' she pleaded. 'Only . . . Athol thinks that all the property went to Uncle Charles and believes that *he* pays the fees. Only . . . if he found out—'

'He'd have it off you. I understand.'

He was looking at her, unsmiling, in such a way that she was acutely conscious of her grubby clothes and unwashed face and hair. His steady gaze made her squirm, but she was not going to offer excuses. The fact that the rainwater from this roof was useless for any purpose, and that all their water had to be carted laboriously from the spring over a mile away in the hills was her misfortune, but certainly none of his business. Twice a week she trudged up there and braved the freezing water to give herself a thorough scrubbing with Mrs Nye's ashy, caustic, home-made soap, and twice a week she endured the complaints that she was 'extravagantly wasting it', but still she never felt properly clean.

'You *don't* understand,' she corrected him. 'Athol is a kind man, but under the law he can make me give it to him, and that land represents Andrew's education. I couldn't risk losing it.'

'If he's as kind as you say, he'd be happy to pay for the lad's education,' said Rhys, and again, when a seeping of dark colour crept up over her thin face, he could have bitten his clumsy tongue.

Lisabeth attempted a laugh. 'They say that a cobbler always wears the holey boots! Athol says it's a pity Charles can't coach Andrew at home and save the money from the fees!' she told him. 'It's just as well that the matter is out of Uncle Charles's hands!'

'Do they get on well, then? Young Andrew and your husband?' Rhys spoke with care this time, hiding the resentment he felt. Since the wedding he'd even stopped visiting Andrew at the college. There was no point now in fostering a relationship with him and, besides, for all his efforts he had never been able to overcome that aversion he felt towards the boy, though by now he had decided that it was a mixture of animosities: revulsion because of Mary and jealousy for the unstinting affection Lisabeth lavished on him.

'Like a house on fire!' chirped Lisabeth, lie-bright. She longed to tell him the truth; that Athol refused to have the boy here for even a day's visit; that she fretted about him and missed him acutely. She added: 'But you know schoolmasters; they have so much to do with children through the week, they're tired of young voices by Sunday.'

Rhys was sorry the subject had arisen. It was her he had come to talk about. He tried to reach for her hands, but she flinched away, so he said: 'I've been thinking about you, and about us . . . What happened between us.' She dropped her eyes, so he asked the top of her head: 'Lisabeth, are you pregnant? You should know by now, and I was wondering . . . I *hoped* that perhaps you—'

'No, I'm not,' she said with harsh bitterness, adding silently: *And there's no chance I ever will be, either.*

'Oh.' He turned away, but not before she saw the look of keen disappointment in his eyes.

*   *   *

Long after he had gone that look haunted her, and over and over she pondered the way he'd said: 'I *hoped* that perhaps you—'

Had he come to kidnap her again, and would he have carried her off if she had confessed to being pregnant with his child? He'd really wanted her to be – she'd seen the evidence plainly in his face.

That would have been a pretty pickle! she mused as she scattered corn for the hens. *First Mamma and then me! Rhys Morgan's follies! No, thank you! This is what I want - a husband of my own and a cosy little home . . .* Then she crumpled inwardly, her blossoming of bravado shrinking into a cold hard knot of despair. *What have I done?* she thought. *Oh, what a mess!*

She'd brought it all on herself, and that was her shame. Shame kept her on the farm – not that she'd want to venture far in her shabby old clothes. Shame kept her from visiting Gwynne for fear that her aunt's shrewd eyes should spot her unhappiness, and shame kept her from repeating the one visit she made to Mrs Day. They had sat on the veranda chatting over morning tea when she noticed that the older woman was eyeing her in a peculiar manner, and only then did she realize to her horror that she had methodically eaten every one of the dozen scones from the platter. When Joe and Alf came up for a cup of tea there were only crumbs left, and Lisabeth was scorching with embarrassment. How could she explain that she was almost starving, that meals at the Nyes' place were the bleakest fare – a meagre bowl of porridge with salt but no milk for breakfast, and thin soup made of chicken scraggings and sow-thistle for dinner? Shame kept her silent.

Once she complained. Mrs Nye sniffed haughtily. 'We eat excellent fare compared to the average Indian family,' she declared. Having heard fabled reports of wonderful meals at Benares, Lisabeth wondered at the truth of that. She did know that Athol supplemented his diet while away at school, because occasionally he brought her home a cream bun or a slice of custard-cake which he hid at the gate and gave to her when they went for a walk after dinner. It gave him pleasure to watch her eat, he said.

When she had been there a few weeks she began to suspect Mrs Nye of supplementing her own diet, too. Lisabeth noticed that the pats of butter were often different from the way she had left them, and when she raked the ashes out of the hearth there were invariably pieces of crushed egg-shell amongst the dead embers.

As soon as she was certain about her suspicions Lisabeth began to steal, too. Every time she collected the eggs she put two warm brown ones in a hollow by the cow-bail and as she was milking the cows she squirted some milk into the tin dipping-ladle, broke the eggs into it and whipped them up with a stick before gulping the sweetish thick liquid. The first few times this drink made her gag, but from the moment she was accustomed to the taste she looked forward to morning milking. Mrs Nye's meanness drove them to bed at dusk because lamp oil cost money, and often there were no squares of old newspaper for use in the privy so Lisabeth had to use dock leaves, but it gave her a grim satisfaction to know that in some small way she was getting the better of her mother-in-law.

Lisabeth was a generous-hearted girl and would have made every effort to be friendly to Mrs Nye, but the woman was as stingy with her own self as she was with food, never making conversation and uttering the few necessary words grudgingly. Soon Lisabeth disliked her with heartfelt sincerity, and her life on the farmlet would have been unendurable if not for Athol's shy kindness.

'Forgive Mother,' he said on one of their evening walks, the only chance they had for a semblance of privacy. 'She was keen on the idea of my courting Mrs Gammerwoth.'

For her money, I suppose, thought Lisabeth, smiling to think of the elegant Leonie enduring the living conditions in this tiny, cramped hovel. On rainy evenings when they couldn't get out Lisabeth felt like screaming with frustration.

Living as they did in the one room with only flimsy curtain screens in front of the beds, sex was out of the question, for every cough, every deep breath was clearly audible to all. Athol had made love to her three times in the two months, always in the open fields under cover of darkness and, because he didn't want children, always in a perfunctory abbreviated manner that left her with her clothing barely rumpled and with all her feelings untouched. That one night of passion in Rhys's arms seemed less real and more dreamlike with every passing day, until something happened to swing it back into sharp cruel focus for her.

It was on a Saturday afternoon. Athol's custom was to go painting on Saturday afternoons, and Lisabeth always went with him, taking her watercolours and his spare easel. Though he adopted a patronizing attitude towards her from the first and treated her like one of his pupils, even scolding her if she ignored his suggestions for improvement, she enjoyed their outings to the isolated vantage-points he chose. The long walks were refreshing on the bracing winter afternoons, and the mountains (not visible from the Nyes' shack) looked breathtaking with the crisp snow draped like textured muslin curtains right down over the foothills behind Mists of Heaven.

One afternoon Athol chose the mansion atop the cliffs as his subject and chatted away to Lisabeth in his spinsterish manner about the architectural details and the way the gable peaks perfectly echoed the mountain range behind it. Lisabeth could have done without the lecture – why did *everything* have to be a lecture? – but she pretended to listen while shutting her ears as she dashed off a quick pen-and-wash sketch of the harbour entrance and the latest ship that was breaking up on the Sumner Bar. She was pondering the fate of the crew and cargo when suddenly something Athol said snapped her attention to him.

'I heard a bit of gossip about Morgan the other day. He's getting married soon.'

A void opened under Lisabeth's heart. 'When?' she croaked.

'Could be married already,' said Athol, frowning over a perspective he was not happy with. 'A lass fresh off the boat from England, apparently. Someone Sir Kenneth and Lady Launcenolt know. She's residing with them, the story goes. Didn't Rhys Morgan help Sir Kenneth win the provincial elections?'

Lisabeth's throat was so dry she couldn't speak.

'A double blow for ex-Councillor Fox if you ask me,' continued Athol. 'He lost the election because of Morgan and now, when half the town was expecting Morgan to marry his daughter – that's Mrs Gammerwoth, you know – he up and marries someone else. I say, are you all right? You look pale.'

'Just a headache,' she whispered.

'A headache,' repeated Athol, too interested in his story to take time out for sympathy. 'And what a coincidence,' he crowed. 'Poor Mrs Gammerwoth! First I reject her and then Morgan does. I'll bet that's one in the eye for Fox.'

'She'd never have looked at you!' cried Lisabeth with a venom that shocked her as she heard her spiteful voice. Immediately she was all aghast apology. 'I didn't mean it, Athol, truly. It's just that your news . . . I'm surprised, and nobody *told* me . . .'

'Told you? Oh, of course, Morgan's a relative of yours.' Athol was mollified by the swiftness of her apology. Women could be touchy at times; he knew that and was glad he'd been born a man. 'Never mind, Lisabeth. It's not as if he's a *close* relative.'

Closer than you could imagine, thought Lisabeth wretchedly.

TWENTY-EIGHT

WINTER CAME HOWLING DOWN FROM THE MOUNTAINS freezing everything with its glacial breath, and when the plains were numbed and defenceless it began battering, first playfully then maliciously, giving the young colony the worst beating it had so far experienced. For weeks on end gales raced shrieking across the tussock land towards Christchurch, the harbour and the Port Hills. Trees were torn out by the roots, barns scalped and gardens plucked naked.

The coast was at its most treacherous. The Days kept their shipping signals displayed, tying the flags down against the balcony-rail against the tearing wind, but still ships risked the bar, desperate for safe anchorage from the buffeting ocean. In one week alone two ships were wrecked and three more had to ditch their entire cargoes. Athol came home with stirring stories of Joe's bravery. In the teeth of a hurricane-force wind he had rowed his little boat out one night to rescue the crew of four from one ship that was being pounded into matchwood by gigantic waves.

Tucked into their hollow in the hills the Nyes were safe from the worst of the gales, though one afternoon a rogue gust snatched at the edge of their thatched roof and wrenched a great ragged piece out in a single blow, leaving the roof looking like the back of a moulting chook, Lisabeth thought. Afraid that the whole roof would go next, Mrs Nye insisted that Lisabeth climb up on the thatch and spread part of an old canvas tent over the hole, tying it in place with strips of flax from the swamp beyond the gate. Knowing that if the wind was determined there was nothing they could do to prevent it, Lisabeth nevertheless obliged and spent a bone-chilling three hours struggling with the flapping canvas, the awl and the strips of flax. Task completed, she slid gingerly to the ground and hurried inside to find her mother-in-law huddled over the meagre fire hastily scraping up the last of something out of a bowl.

'Oh, good!' said Lisabeth through chattering teeth. 'I'm starving! What are we eating?'

Mrs Nye didn't look at her. 'I need to keep my strength up,' she replied primly, shuffling over to the bench and wiping the dish out with a damp cloth. 'You're young and strong. You don't need as much nourishment as—' She broke off, and before the flabbergasted Lisabeth could protest she uttered a cry of horror. 'Just *look* at your lovely gown! You careless child, you've utterly ruined it!'

Glancing down, Lisabeth saw that the tired old fabric in Gwynne's hand-me-down dress had finally disintegrated and long ragged splits had opened from waist to knees all around the skirt. When she raised her arms to see better, gaping splits appeared under her arms, too. The sight cheered her enormously. 'I'll have to have a new dress, won't I?' she announced happily, and when Mrs Nye's face twitched in dismay she added: 'And I'm having something to eat, right now.'

This uncharacteristic lapse in her daughter-in-law's behaviour distressed Mrs Nye so much that when she volunteered to feed the hens at dusk Lisabeth glanced at her oddly. True, Lisabeth was fully occupied cleaning and dressing the half-dozen hens which would go to tomorrow's market, and she was running late because of the time taken to patch the roof, but it was also true that since her arrival there had been a definite division of duties: Mrs Nye cooked the meals (a task which admittedly took very little time) and Lisabeth did everything else.

'Athol's due home,' observed Mrs Nye, unusually chatty for once. 'You know how he likes to see that everything's done and tidied away.'

Amazing, thought Lisabeth. *Next she'll be telling me to pop one of these into the pot instead of just the necks and feet.* Swiftly she completed her task, sorted the innards out – some for the pot, some for burial – and fed the last of the feathers to the fire, wrinking her nose against the acrid smell as they curled and blackened. Inside the cottage it was beginning to grow dark, and outside the wind was keening like a mourner high above their valley.

Lisabeth was listening to it, feeling warm and safe, when the door flapped open and Athol entered, unwrapping a muffler from around his neck and shucking off his coat.

'Where's Mother?' he asked in response to her greeting.

'Feeding the hens.' Lisabeth tucked a white cloth over the heaped chicken carcasses and picked up the bucket of offal.

He frowned. 'Did you let her go out to tend them in this weather?'

'Why not? It's died down a lot now and, besides, it was her—' She stopped. Mrs Nye had been gone for a far longer time than was ever needed to carry out that simple chore.

She followed Athol outside. Dusk was thickening and, though some of the hens picked and walked in their yards, most had retired to roost. Just outside the gate of the nearest pen Mrs Nye's slumped form was propped like a log against a stump. Lisabeth watched as Athol, with a bleat of alarm, stumbled to pick her up and carry her inside.

'My ankle,' moaned Mrs Nye beside the fire.

'Why didn't you call out?' asked Lisabeth.

'I did, I did!'

'But Athol must have passed within a few yards of you as he came up the hill.'

'I think I blacked out,' sighed Mrs Nye. Athol shot Lisabeth a withering glance so she went back outside and instead of burying the innards in the garden for fertilizer she dumped the contents of the pail down the privy instead.

In what was left of that evening Athol danced attendance on his mother and next day hurried home from school with a gift for her: a single chocolate twisted in a square of paper. He bathed his mother's ankle while she uttered feeble martyrish moans. Glancing over her shoulder, Lisabeth noticed that the injured ankle was thin and white and perfect, with no sign of either swelling or bruising. She got the message. Any hint of rebellion on her part would be resisted, and Mrs Nye had powerful weapons with which to dragoon Athol on to her side.

I'm nasty-minded to be so suspicious, thought Lisabeth, but when she innocently remarked that there was not so much as a limp when Mrs Nye (thinking she was unobserved) hurried to the privy, the swift way Athol reprimanded her left her in no doubt as to her situation – A daughter-in-law must be respectful, obedient and considerate at all times.

It is my fault, reflected Lisabeth. Since the news of Rhys's marriage she had been so unutterably depressed that she was constantly antagonizing both Athol and his mother. Unable to flood out the bitterness of her regrets with a wallowing good cry, she chafed and irritated instead, only able to relieve her feelings with outbursts of energy when she attacked the woodpile each morning and chopped up the log segments that Athol had split for her the night before.

When the weather closed in she and Mrs Nye were forced to spend nearly all their day inside. By now the cows were dry and the hens had gone off the lay, so outside tasks were reduced to a minimum. Mrs Nye sat staring at the fire's embers and picking at her teeth with a sharpened quill cut from a tough wing-feather, while Lisabeth, bored and restless, took out her watercolours.

'It's not Saturday,' said Mrs Nye.

'We've not been out for weeks. I miss my painting.'

'I could understand that if you had a gift for it,' said Mrs Nye. 'If you've nothing better to do, perhaps you should mend your dress.'

Lisabeth laughed.

'What is amusing in that suggestion?' she asked, and instead of replying Lisabeth rummaged in the box at the foot of her bed and brought the shredded garment to show her that the fabric was rotten, hopelessly beyond repair. Even Athol agreed that she would have to have a new dress, and came home one day with a bundle of soft cashmere material in a deep midnight blue that enhanced the colour of her eyes. Holding it up against herself, Lisabeth danced around the bare earth floor, revelling in the luxurious feel of the cloth.

'How much did it cost?' harped Mrs Nye.

'Oh . . . I forget. But not more than two shillings and sixpence a yard, as you said,' he added hastily, his papery skin flushing.

Lisabeth laughed; she knew he lied. 'It doesn't matter if it was cheap – it's so pretty!' she said.

For the next week she was in heaven, unpicking her old dress (rescuing the stiffenings and buttons) and using it for a pattern as she carefully snipped out the precious soft cloth. She sewed meticulously and slowly but crawled out of bed at first light and, blowing frequently on her fingers to warm them, began stitching as soon as she could see. Nine days later, red-eyed and sore-backed from the hours of sitting in the one position, she was triumphantly examining her creation. It was as perfect as her skills allowed, each button neatly re-covered in blue fabric, each button-loop precisely measured. After hastily trying it for a final fitting behind the curtain screen she pressed it with a flat-iron and folded it carefully in the clothes press, ready for the morning.

It was now mid-afternoon, and thick frost still lay on the south slopes of the hills. Taking a stringy grey towel and the soap-dish, Lisabeth went up to the spring where she forced herself to strip then braced herself against the sting of the icy water. She was thorough, because the new dress deserved a clean fresh-smelling body, so this time she even shampooed her hair with a lathering of the hard soap, rinsing again and again so that the dark tresses would dry with a healthy shine.

'You'll catch your death,' sniffed Mrs Nye when she returned.

'I feel marvellous!' Lisabeth told her. 'I hate bathing in that freezing water, but afterwards, oh, but it feels so incredibly good! Really, Mrs Nye, you should try it some time.' She definitely needed it, Lisabeth thought privately, for a piercing sour odour accompanied the older woman everywhere.

'My mother taught me that washing is dangerous and debilitating,' she retorted. 'And my mother was a sagacious woman.'

'I'm sure she was,' said Lisabeth. '*Strong*, too, no doubt.'

Next morning, while Athol was brushing his jacket and polishing his boots, Lisabeth unpacked her new dress and slipped it over her head, smoothing the close-fitting sleeves and settling the fully gathered skirt over her hips. Pushing the curtain aside, she strolled out to where Athol was combing his beard and peering into a tiny rust-bloomed mirror.

'Would you like to button me up?' she asked.

Athol glanced at her, startled. 'Button you – oh, I see. Very nice, Lisabeth,' he said, inclining his head and pursing his lips in critical approval. When she twirled around and he saw that down the back from the high collar to the base of her spine was a row of buttons and a row of empty button-loops he said: 'But you really meant it! I thought the front of your gown looked different somehow.'

'Far more elegant, don't you think?' said Lisabeth. 'And you don't mind hooking up a few buttons, do you?'

'Well . . . I am a busy man,' he told her primly, but with a smile. 'But why couldn't you put the buttons at the front, so you could reach them?' he asked as he twisted them each into place

'You wouldn't understand,' she assured him. 'You do realize that I'm going to have to go out, now that I have something to wear? I want to go and visit Andrew, first of all . . . Why, Athol, what's the matter? You don't mind, do you?'

302

'No . . . of course not,' he said, but in such a tone that she knew something was wrong. 'I have an idea,' he said swiftly. 'There's to be an exhibition of my paintings in the King's College Hall in the first week of the winter vacation. There's some space free on one wall. Would you like to display a few of your water-colours, too? Then you can come in with me every day and perhaps your relatives could visit you there.'

'That would be wonderful!' she breathed. 'Do you realize that since I've been here the only contact I've had with them all is by letter? They're good about writing, but I miss everyone so much, especially Andrew.' Again she caught an odd expression on his face. 'Athol, please tell me. What *is* wrong?'

Athol looked down at her from his great height, considering, then he said: 'Your brother is causing disruptions in his classes at school, I'm afraid. There's talk of expelling him.'

'Athol – no!' Instantly she rallied. 'But you'll intercede for him, won't you? As a tutor there, you must have considerable influence—'

'An influence I would never dream of exploiting,' he rebuked her, 'If the boy misbehaves, he must be punished. If the boy is an undesirable influence, he must be removed.'

'I can't believe I'm hearing this. I know you don't want him here upsetting your mother, but this is important, Athol! Surely you can help him now, when he needs it.' Even as she spoke a small cold voice inside her head was reminding her that it was at least partly her fault that poor Andrew felt abandoned. She should have ascertained Athol's attitude before she married him, but even without talking to Andrew she guessed that a lot of the problem would be to do with Rhys. The loss of his idol would have hit Andrew a cruel blow, and Rhys had dropped from his world without a word of explanation. Why should it be any other way? Rhys owed them nothing and, anyway, wasn't all this misery and sacrificing on her part a master-plan to remove Andrew from Rhys's influence for ever?

Only it hadn't worked according to plan, reflected Lisabeth bitterly. Now nobody but her wanted Andrew, and she wasn't allowed to have him. He was a poor pawn in a game with no winners, only losers. All because of Rhys.

When Athol spoke she jumped and flushed scarlet. It was uncanny – as if he was reading her mind.

'I've heard more gossip about Morgan,' Athol told her in an effort to cheer her up. She looked so glum, but she could pout all she liked; he'd not change his mind. That was better; he had her attention now. 'Mr Morgan and his wife have engaged a *nurse*, a Miss Merryman, the sister of one of my fellow-tutors,' he told her, nodding significantly.

Lisabeth's heart shrank to a small, hard knot. *A baby*, she thought dully. *A baby already*. With masochistic vividness she pictured Rhys in that magnificent four-poster bed with his wife (whom Gwynne, with unthinking cruelty, had described as fair, very pretty and pleasantly plump), and now as Lisabeth tortured herself with the image the pain was so intense she had to turn away.

You could have had it all, the cold little voice reminded her. But she couldn't. Not with Mary and the past looming up at her. *It could never be*, she argued. *Never!* But still the voice mocked her.

Only Andrew mattered now, she told herself as the painting exhibition was readied for viewing. He was home with the Staffords for vacation, and soon they would all be coming in together. Lisabeth's heart was in a panic of excitement; she longed to see them yet dreaded having to smile at the news they would bear. *I'll keep the conversation firmly on Andrew*, she resolved. *I'll talk about my interview with the principal, and urge them to encourage Andrew so that he keeps trying to do better.*

Attendance at the exhibition was disappointingly light. The college hall was a vast gloomy room with high windows and echoing floors, and in an attempt to give some intimacy to the display Athol had arranged his best works on screens grouped around the doorway, while the remainder hung on the walls. Lisabeth's dozen watercolours looked insignificant where he had put them – away from the other work in a rather dim corner – and she was also disappointed when she saw the prices he had set on her pictures: a mere five shillings each when three guineas was the lowest price for one of his. 'A high price commands respect,' he told her. 'You must learn to set a high value on yourself, Lisabeth.'

She bit her tongue, but after the first hour it was one of hers that bore a red 'sold' label, and after the second hour three of hers had been sold, while none of Athol's found buyers. Clearly annoyed by the attention hers were receiving, Athol removed all the price labels and replaced them with a sign reading 'Watercolours by a local amateur, two guineas each'.

'Athol, that's hardly —' she began, but he shushed her and strode past to greet a plump, parsonish-looking man who was introduced to her as Mr Brecon, the arts critic from the *Lyttelton Times*. Guiding him round the exhibition, he left Lisabeth standing disconsolately by the door, reflecting that now she had no chance at all of adding to the fifteen shillings in her purse, and it would have been lovely to have enough money to buy herself a pair of new boots to go with her beautiful new gown. These old ones were so scuffed that she minced along with minute steps to keep them hidden below the hem of her gown; they were cracked with age and, though the toes were stuffed with rags, still the damp soaked through. It was unfair of Athol to sabotage her chances of making a little money, she thought, glancing over to where he and the arts critic were engaged in agitated conversation near her modest display. Who in the whole of the province would pay two guineas for watercolours 'by a local amateur' when Athol's far more elaborate and ornately framed paintings were available at only a slightly greater cost?

A throng of people entered, accepted the brochures Lisabeth handed out and in groups of two and three wandered about the hall; but one, a well-dressed man of about thirty, entered and without a word to her or a glance at the sheaf of brochures strolled until he reached the dim corner where her pictures hung. He stood in contemplation for only a minutes then walked back to where Lisabeth stood. 'I've chosen five,' he announced, placing two gold coins on the table beside her. 'The two remaining on the top row and the three in the lowest row.' Before Lisabeth could utter a word he opened a mother-of-pearl inlaid box and withdrew his card which he dropped on to the coins and with an unsmiling nod at her walked from the room. Mr Brecon bustled over in time to hear this. 'My dear!' he exclaimed in hushed tones. 'What an honour! Do you have any idea who that was?'

'A Mr Arch . . . Archibal . . .' attempted Lisabeth, frowning over the name as she studied the Gothic script in which the card was engraved. 'I can't read this. It's—'

'Give it to me,' said Athol, taking it.

Mr Brecon was squirming with excitement. That was Mr James Archibaldiston, the buyer for the Southern Cross Galleries in Sydney, that's who! Five paintings! What an honour! He must have been immeasurably impressed by your work.'

Lisabeth was too stunned to care. Ten guineas! she thought, weighing them in her palm, but at the same time she was puzzled.

The art-buyer had been here but a few moments and he'd not so much as glanced at Athol's display. Surely there was more to art appraisal than such a perfunctory examination.

Athol thought so, too. His smile was thin and bitter as a strip of green lemon peel as he held out his hand for the money. '*If* you please, Lisabeth,' he demanded silkily.

Her fingers tightened around it.

'Please, Lisabeth,' he repeated, smiling but gripping her hand in a crushing squeeze to try to make her free the coins.

'If you two will kindly excuse me,' murmured Mr Brecon, glancing with a certain sympathy at Athol. The fellow had protested vehemently that his wife had no talent whatsoever, and the purchase of so much of her collection must have been quite a slap in the face for him. The *Lyttelton Times* review would be a second blow, he feared, and was glad of the diversion provided by the arrival of a group of Mrs Nye's friends. It allowed him to make his escape without having to offer insincere congratulations to Mr Nye.

As the Staffords rushed to greet them Athol had to drop his grip, moneyless, while Lisabeth turned thankfully, tense and shaking with pain. Her heart swelled with love as she hugged Gwynne, pecked the air beside Charles's tobacco-scented beard and then with a sob of pure joy flung her arms around the bashful-looking Andrew. 'You look so handsome!' she cried, 'So tall and healthy and so handsome!' And to his extreme discomfiture (exacerbated by the sight of one of his schoolmates wandering in) Lisabeth kissed him exuberantly on both cheeks.

'I've missed you so *much* – all of you. Oh, please, Aunty Gwynne, don't cry! You'll start me off, too. Seeing you all like this makes me feel so homesick.'

She gazed at them hungrily. Andrew was smart in his prim college uniform, and Gwynne so dear as she dabbed away tears with a handkerchief Lisabeth remembered hemming last winter. In her faded grey serge she looked older and smaller than Lisabeth remembered, as if her body was folding up on itself like a withering flower. Lisabeth guessed that her rheumatism must be bothering her badly this harsh winter. 'Who is looking after you now?' she asked, for Gwynne's brave little notes never mentioned the trials of day-to-day living, only recitations of the meals they had eaten and glowing praises of Charles. Every deed of his, it seemed, merited favourable comment.

He was scowling at her. Ever since her letter inviting them along had arrived he had been practising a sharp little speech to blast at her, and now, before Gwynne could reply, he cleared his throat and spoke up, loudly so that Athol wouldn't miss a single damning word. He had never forgiven her for her stubbornness nor for the way she had made him look foolish in front of Fox by refusing to sign over the land and now was his opportunity to punish her. 'About your land, Lisabeth . . . Mr Fox and I met the other day. His offer now stands at fourteen hundred guineas. I told him sure I'd pass the infiltration on, and see whether your husband were interested.'

Lisabeth swallowed. Stricken by this betrayal, she dared not look at Athol, and his leaden words fell on her heavily, making her sick with apprehension,

'Her husband is extremely interested,' he said. 'Do tell me more, Mr Stafford.'

Lisabeth quailed inwardly. How could Uncle Charles be so callously destructive? He knew that the money from the lease was financing Andrew's education, thus relieving him of any obligations in that direction, so why did he do this? What had he to gain but the pettiest spiteful revenge?

To cover the awkward silence Gwynne said brightly: 'How are you doing, Mr Nye? Have you sold many paintings?'

How like her, thought Lisabeth wryly. 'I don't know about Athol, but I've sold eight out of twelve!' she said, deliberately boasting. As she spoke she could almost feel Athol's resentment, but she hurried on with ersatz brightness. 'Five of them were to an important art-buyer. Isn't that splendid? Come on, Andrew, and help me with the red labels.'

'I'll come, too,' offered Gwynne.

'We'll manage!' Lisabeth told her, and hustled Andrew away.

'What in the world is wrong?' he hissed at her. 'You look as white as Ophelia. Sorry, you wouldn't know who she is. We're studying *Hamlet* at — I say, Lisabeth. You're shaking to pieces. What's wrong?'

'Just a cold,' she told him. What was the use of burdening him with her problems until she absolutely had to? 'Are you enjoying school now?'

'I'm trying,' he admitted reluctantly, then burst out: 'Studying is much more fun when you put lots of effort into it. Funny: it should work the opposite way, don't you think?' Slanting a sideways glance at her, he said: 'You look pretty, you know that? That colour's lovely.'

'Thank you,' she beamed. 'I made it myself.'

'I still haven't forgotten my promise to buy you the most elegant gown in the whole of the colony just as soon as I'm earning money of my own.' He frowned. 'It might take time, though. I've decided, Sis . . . I want to be a doctor.'

'A doctor! Andrew, that's marvellous! A fine and noble profession!'

'Yes, but years of study, *and* possibly university in England.'

I'll never manage that, she thought hopelessly. *Especially not now, when I'll very likely lose the land to Athol and his mother.* But shoving that nasty speculation aside she said: 'What caused your change of heart, darling? Only a short time ago I was so worried that you hated school.'

'It was because of Uncle Rhys,' he told her eagerly. 'The doctor goes up to Mists of Heaven a lot, to see Mrs Morgan. She's poorly, though Uncle Charles reckons she's a hydrophobiac, and if he means hypochondriac, then he might be right!' Oblivious of the dismay mention of the Morgans was causing Lisabeth, he forged on brightly. 'Uncle Rhys said that doctors are the most important people in the world, and he said that I have the perfect temperament for it, so I asked Doctor Meakings all about how to become one, and it sounded interesting! I say, it is alright by you, isn't it?'

'It's marvellous.' She gave him a quick hug, but turned her face away so that he wouldn't glimpse her expression. As she pinned up the scraps of ribbon beside her pictures she reflected on the irony of events. If her hope had been to keep Andrew for herself, then marrying Athol was the worst thing she could have done. Now it seemed that Rhys was influencing Andrew's future, choosing a career for him. That was what fathers were supposed to do for their sons, she thought soberly. Is this what Fate was determined to do, bring the two together at every opportunity, no matter how she schemed and planned and contrived to keep them apart? Was this, in fact, the essence of Fate, a triumphing of natural progression over the machinations of Man?

She sighed. Far more immediate problems loomed in front of her now. Somehow she had to persuade Athol to allow her to keep her land. Feeling the ache in her knuckles where he had ground the bones together trying to force her to give her ten guineas, she doubted that she would succeed.

'What wounds me most is your wanton deceit,' Athol informed her as they waited in the gusty evening for the stagecoach back to

Ferrymead. He gazed crossly along the deserted street and tugged out his cheap metal fob-watch to squint at the time. Snapping the cover shut, he replaced it in his waistcoat pocket. 'They're ten minutes late. Really, the time I've wasted through their inefficiency is staggering.' Then without a change of tone, he continued berating her. 'It was utterly deceitful of you, Lisabeth. To take advantage of my offer of marriage yet deliberately to conceal your own assets—'

'I didn't look upon them as mine. The land was for Andrew, for his—'

'If Mr Braddock had wanted Andrew to have the property, he would have deeded it to him, don't you think? No, Lisabeth, there can be no argument here. You have been abysmally lacking in your proper duties as a wife, and —'   .

Lisabeth stopped listening. It occurred to her that Athol was actually pleased to have the opportunity to chide her as if she was one of his pupils. That was exactly how he was making her feel: small, guilty and wretched, utterly without redemption. Certainly he was too much of a gentleman to vent his jealousy over her triumphant sale openly, but what he did instead was nag at her, pouring out bileful accusations until she felt beaten and defeated.

She would lose the land, nothing was more certain, she mourned in despair as she stood back from the puddles as the coach, drawn by four muscular horses, rolled to a stop. It was a relief to see that the inside was almost full, for that meant Athol had to climb to the roof and she had a respite from his barrage of lofty disapproval. It would be a brief respite; with a shudder she contemplated the evening, when Mrs Nye would begin scolding her, too. She could picture the gloating expression on the old woman's face. All along she'd hated Lisabeth, and this would prove what an accurate judge of character she was.

Wedged into one corner of the hard seat, right against the coach-frame, Lisabeth tucked her threadbare coat over her dress to keep out the draught that whistled under the door and around her ankles. As the rattling motion jolted along under her she wondered about Andrew. His future looked bleak. Charles would never agree to pay the college fees – pity help Andrew in fact if he had to fall back on Charles's tender mercies. She had nobody to turn to, for Athol had made it plain that under law he was able to claim all her property and dispose of it however he liked. Even Rhys was unable to help her now, she thought dismally. (If he wanted to, which she doubted.) She was powerless.

Months ago she might have derived some alleviating comfort by dwelling on the disruptions having Fox as a neighbour might cause to Rhys's life, but now there was no cheer in that. And then, as the coach rattled past the first of the new gas-lights on the street corner by St Barnabas Church, Lisabeth suddenly realized that she no longer hated Rhys. She no longer wanted to hurt him; he no longer seemed loathsome to her. The sensation was depressing; it was a curious flavourless emptiness, like probing a sensitive molar and discovering that the toothache had gone. Through the smeared window she stared at the lamplit church spire and the whirl of the Milky Way in the blackness beyond and thought: *I stopped hating him long ago. It's been a habit for months and I didn't even realize it.*

At Ferrymead, Athol was off the coach and buying the ferry tickets when Lisabeth climbed down. He did not speak to her while the ferry inched across the river on its sagging steel cable (pushing upstream with the incoming tide), nor did he help her off the other side, so she had to jump down the short drop to the jetty by herself. Clutching her little cloth purse in both hands, she hurried after him, picking her way through the throng of drunken revellers returning home.

As soon as they were out of earshot of the other disembarking passengers Athol began again. 'The first thing that impressed me about you was your air of honesty, your open-faced expression,' he complained in aggrieved tones. 'It was all deceit, wasn't it, Lisabeth?' And he rounded on her, blocking her way, suddenly menacing.

She stopped, quaking with apprehension. Normally she would not have been afraid of him, but worry about Andrew heightened her nervousness, making her vulnerable. She said nothing. He glared at her, his face pale and his form hunching at the shoulders like a huge black bird, a species of eagle or vulture. Even his words were a threatening hiss.

I don't have to stand for this: she thought defiantly as he turned away again. *I've got eleven pounds five shillings in my purse, and if I run away Athol won't be able to take the property from me. Yes, why don't I just run away?*

There under the peppered silver sky the solution seemed ludicrously simple, just as plans wrought in darkness often do until daylight illuminates the flaws that make them impossible in practice. Run away! Of course! It would be so easy it was a wonder she hadn't thought of it before. All she had to do was turn around now and walk back the way she had come.

She took a few steps, paused, and looked around. Athol's tall black form was striding away, but his pompous voice was still audible above the distant murmurings of the sea. All around spread a feathery ocean of *manuka* brush, silver- topped and featureless.

Lisabeth's resolution stiffened. The eleven pounds five shillings in her purse would buy her somewhere to hide, somewhere to sleep. She need not be afraid of the wilderness. Picking her way over the uneven ground, following the worn thread of track, she quickened her pace. When she rounded the slope of a hill where the track forked towards Sumner she went that way. Soon she was descending to the Sumner- Ferrymead road, with the harbour a spread of rippled silk before her, and directly across, below the silver mountains, the faint yellow glow where the windows of Mists of Heaven were lit against the night. Lisabeth wondered what Rhys was doing.

By now Athol was so far behind her that when he turned to discover her gone and bellowed out an angry shout to her, it was so weakened by distance that Lisabeth barely heard it. She broke into a run and was still running when Mr Berry the butcher overtook her in his little cart.

Reining Strawberry in, he peered through the darkness. 'Why, it's Miss Stafford!' he exclaimed. 'Are you going to the Sumner Hotel, dearie? Would you like a lift, then?'

'Yes, please.' He had probably been out carousing, but she knew him so felt safe.

As she climbed up beside him he said: 'What brings you out on the road at this time of night?'

'It's a long story, Mr Berry,' said Lisabeth. 'A very long story indeed.'

TWENTY-NINE

THE HARSH LIGHT OF NEXT MORNING brought home some unpalatable facts to Lisabeth. Mrs Day had made up a bed for her last night without comment, but when at breakfast Lisabeth confessed that she had left Athol the older woman's kind face tightened with blank dismay. 'You've taken solemn vows in the eyes of God, my dear,' she reminded Lisabeth sternly. 'You belong to your husband now. Take heed of the Good Book's words,' she added in a coaxing tone. 'Go home and tell him you're sorry. Be a good wife and be prized above rubies!'

Lisabeth's appetite withered, and she pushed her plate of scrambled eggs and bacon away. 'It's my land he prizes,' she said bitterly. 'He wants to take it off me.'

Mrs Day didn't understand. 'But it belongs to him,' she pointed out. 'When a woman marries she brings all her worldly goods and gives them up to her husband's care. It's the way of the world, my dear.' And she took Lisabeth's untouched breakfast out to Mabs in the kitchen.

'I'll go into service,' Lisabeth told Mabs when she was helping her wash the dishes. 'Yes, that's what I'll do. I'm healthy and strong, I can't cook, but I know how to do most other things. Surely I'll have no trouble finding a situation where I can earn my keep.'

Mabs laughed shortly. 'Oi can tell yer now, yer ain't got not an 'ope of findin' a place in service, not with an 'usband oo's still breathin'. Trouble, that's what an 'usband means,' she added darkly, shaking a soapy ladle at Lisabeth.

Later, on the sunny veranda with its view over the harbour, Mrs

Day concurred with this. She paused over the heaped basket of thick-knit fishermen's socks she was darning and warned: 'A respectable family would not employ you, not when there are so many decent young women looking for positions. And would you want to toil in some sleazy tavern, cleaning up after the intoxicated dregs of society? I think not, my dear.' Leaning over to pat Lisabeth's hand, she urged: 'Go home and make peace. It's the only choice open to you, and it is the proper one.'

Proper! Decent! Respectable! She couldn't have spelled it out more plainly for me if she had a Bible in one hand and a Society Register in the other, thought Lisabeth grimly as she stared from her upstairs window along the bleak windy road. Because the winter storms had dashed salt spray right up to the cliffs there was not a scrap of green vegetation to be seen, just bare rocks, sand and the scrape of gravelly road dotted with a few travellers, some on horseback, one group in a spring-cart and some walking, like those two black-clad figures, the tall thin man and the straight-backed spare woman with the unfashionable slim skirts and the walking-cane . . . Her throat dried, and she swallowed with difficulty. Athol and Mrs Nye. They had come for her. There was no where to run to now.

Tiptoeing downstairs, she padded through the morning room and stood just inside the door. Through the partly opened sash window beside her she could hear Mrs Day's hearty voice boom out a greeting. 'It's a fine bracing day for a walk,' she was saying amicably. 'I suppose you've strolled over to see Lisabeth.'

'Six miles is hardly a stroll on this stony road,' quibbled Mrs Nye. 'But, yes, we have come on account of my daughter-in-law. The poor child seems to have lost her wits.'

'Indeed?'

'Must unfortunate,' put in Athol in his rustly voice. 'But thank you for taking care of her for us. We've come to take her home now.'

Lisabeth stepped out on to the verandah's worn wooden floor. 'Then, I'm very sorry, but you've come in vain,' she told them. 'I've left you, Athol, and I'm not coming back, so make up your mind to accept it. I don't know what's going to happen to me, but I'll find something, of that I'm sure. All I do know is that nothing could possibly induce me to return. So I'm sorry if you've wasted your morning, but there it is.'

Athol's papery skin reddened and his eyes narrowed as he drew himself up to his maximum height. She had a sudden image of

313

him adopting this very stance when he was about to reprimand a recalcitrant pupil, and swiftly had to smother a giggle, but her amusement died when he said: 'I can tell you exactly what will happen to you, Lisabeth. We shall send two doctors to examine you, and because of your stubborn unco-operation you will duly be declared not of sound mind and committed to a . . . to, ah . . . a nursing home.'

'Nursing home?' snorted Lisabeth. 'Come on, Athol. You're a schoolmaster, and schoolmasters are precise, aren't they? So why can't you come right out and say 'lunatic asylum?' That is what you mean, isn't it?'

'I told you she'd try to cause a nasty scene,' carped Mrs Nye. 'I told you all along she was—'

'And I'd like to hear what *you'd* say if your son informed you that he was having you committed!' snapped Lisabeth. 'I wonder which is the more certifiable – wanting to hold on to what is rightfully one's own or scrimping and hoarding and starving your family and living like beggars when you have ample income from Athol's salary and from the sale of eggs and firewood and dressed chickens to lead a very comfortable life? If I thought that the money from my land would go to a good cause, then I might consider coming back, but I know without doubt that things would go on as usual, with gruel for breakfast and soup made out of weeds and chicken-feet for dinner. After months of your food I'm like a starving person, and even a plate of eggs and bacon is too rich for my stomach!'

'Stop her, Athol! I've never heard such barefaced lies,' hissed Mrs Nye, her face rigid, hard as her close-set eyes.

'Lies! Is it a lie to say I've never been without a feeling of hunger since I arrived at your place? Is it a lie to say that while I'm outside labouring at the farm tasks you're inside cooking eggs and secretly eating them? Yes, I know because every day I found scraps of pulverized egg-shell in the ashes. Is it a lie to say—?'

'Lisabeth, that's quite enough!' interrupted Athol. 'Mrs Day isn't interested in all our dirty laundry, are you, Mrs Day? As for you, Lisabeth, what I said still stands. Despite this ill-mannered outburst we are prepared to take you home with us, but if you don't come we shall send the doctors to see you!'

'Can they do that?' she asked Mrs Day when they had gone. 'Athol sounded so positive. He can't really have me put away in a lunatic asylum, can he?'

'I'm afraid he can, especially after the way you shouted at him.

That display of bad temper won't look encouraging on the doctor's reports, you know.' Mrs Day was regarding her with such distaste that Lisabeth understood exactly what Mabs meant about a husband meaning trouble. It was also clear that she had worn out her welcome; with the doctors coming at any time it would be prudent to move anyway.

Standing up from where she had hunkered down on the steps, Lisabeth said: 'I'm truly sorry to have caused a scene, Mrs Day. I promise that it won't happen again.'

'Won't it?' asked Ann Day, looking at her searchingly.

Lisabeth knew that she had to leave, and now.

Joe rowed her across the harbour and insisted on waiting to make sure everything was all right. She smiled a reassurance. 'Don't worry! They'll be delighted to have me back!' For in her mind the only problems might be with Charles. She would sweeten his welcome when she plunked her eleven pounds five shillings painting money down on the table, but would she be able to live happily in the same house after the petty spite he'd displayed against her?

He was in the orchard, muffled in netting with a smoking funnel-can in his hand, sorting out some of his bees into new hives for spring. A task that should have been done in late summer, thought Lisabeth as she called out a cheerful greeting and asked if Aunty Gwynne was inside.

'Where do you think you're going?' he demanded, lumbering over to block her way. Wafts of smoke blew in her face as he shooed his hands at her. 'We don't want you here.'

'I've come to see Aunty Gwynne,' said Lisabeth, glancing at the parlour windows where there was a twitching at the curtains.

'You've left your husband, that's what you've done!' roared Charles. 'Don't you think it's bad enough, treating us with ingratiating disrespect, so you do it to your husband's family, too! Well, you needn't think you'll be taken in here as if nothing had happened.'

'How do you know I've left Athol?' Lisabeth asked, astounded.

'Because they came looking for you, that's how! That damned impermanent woman, you should have heard the way she spoke to Mrs Stafford! Sure and I sent her packing with a flea in her ear. And you, too, Missy. You'll go the same way, and now.'

Lisabeth stared at the hostile face behind the gauzy cloud. He'd get over it; Charles's tempers never lasted long, but she'd have to

315

go away until he simmered right down. 'Very well, I'll leave. But please give my love to Aunty Gwynne, will you?'

Instead of returning to the road the way she had come Lisabeth walked towards the back gate, down the path that lay alongside the house. As she passed the parlour she waved at Gwynne, who was now visible in a gap between the curtains. Gwynne raised her hand to wave, glanced in Charles's direction and dropped her hand again. *As blindly loyal as ever*, thought Lisabeth, saddened and dismayed. She hoped that hostility of Charles's was indeed temporary, but Gwynne's frightened attitude just now gave her ample cause for worry. She was counting on a refuge here; now she wondered how was she going to manage without a roof over her head?

Thankfully, Joe was as good as his word, waiting by the boat. 'I saw the Nyes being rowed over from Ferrymead this morning,' he explained when she praised him for his thoughtfulness. 'Guessed that they might have fouled the nest for you, so to speak.'

Apart from that comment he rowed in silence, not the chatty jovial Joe she was used to. *I'll find this everywhere*, thought Lisabeth with a cold premonition. Nobody approved of what she had done. The reasons didn't count; it probably wouldn't matter if Athol had beaten her senseless, because the only significant fact in everyone's eyes was that she had run out, and everybody without exception so far thought that she should not only go back, but also go back and apologize.

Never, thought Lisabeth, her chin raised proudly, her blue-black eyes clear with resolution. *I'll never go back! I'll find a job, and I'll sell more of my paintings. Somehow I'll get by.*

Joe's sure powerful strokes had them out in the harbour and beyond the shadow of the looming cliffs in only a few minutes. Lisabeth turned her head to admire the graceful *pohutukawa* trees that clung with gnarled roots to impossibly steep sections of the rock. The foliage was hazed with red; it was almost springtime, and buds were fattening ready to burst and set the whole cliff-face ablaze with scarlet blossom. She was gazing at the trees, imagining how it would look, when her eyes lit on Braddock's old cottage crouching in its hollow on the cliff-top.

'I could live there!' she cried aloud. Twisting back, she said to Joe: 'I've just had a marvellous idea! Nobody wants to take me in, but what's to stop me from living alone? I own that cottage, don't I, Joe? I could live there! It would be perfect.'

Joe looked troubled. 'No, it wouldn't, Lisabeth,' he said after a time.

316

'Why not?'

'Because of Rhys, that's why not,' he said frankly. 'He was desperate to marry you, Lisabeth, desperate even after you were married just to see you. It wouldn't be fair of you to move in right next door to him. It wouldn't give his marriage a chance.'

'Wouldn't it?' asked Lisabeth, intrigued by Joe's concern and thrilled to think that she still had power over Rhys. But common sense swiftly took over and she said, 'That's nonsense. Aunty Gwynne writes that Rhys is very happy with his new wife.' As she spoke she was aware of the familiar stirrings of envy and, feeling her cheeks grow warm, she hoped that Joe wasn't gazing too observantly at her face. 'Besides, I don't think I have much choice. If nobody else will take me in, and I can't get a job, that's the only place left to me.'

'You could go back to your husband.'

'And let him take the land? And have Andrew's education ruined?'

'He can read and write now, can't he? What more does a man need?' Joe dipped his oars a few more times in the water then said: 'Your whole life revolves around Andrew, doesn't it? I think there's a lot more to it than meets the eye.'

'You're wrong,' snapped Lisabeth. 'He's my brother and I'm responsible for him. Athol wouldn't help him. Do you know that he never once let Andrew come to visit me at home?'

'Probably was afraid the boys at school would all hear about how shabby the Nyes live, if you ask me,' said Joe, blunt speaking on every subject. 'Ah, who knows, Lisabeth? To me it's wrong for you to leave your husband, but I wouldn't fancy that as a life, so I can't honestly blame you.'

'Then, you'll row me back to the beach again, after I've bought a few things – blankets and sheets and some food?'

Joe grinned. 'You'd better lash out on some tins of carbolic powder, too. That cottage has been empty for ages. It'll be absolutely thick with fleas.'

It was more than thick, it was seething, Lisabeth discovered to her disgust. She took only one step into the dim room before a tickling on her bare shins up under her petticoat alerted her and, raising her hems, she saw that her legs were speckled with dozens and dozens of fleas. After hurrying outside and beating at her legs with bunched skirts she levered the top off the first tin and re-entered, this time sprinkling the stinking powder as she went.

317

Even then she collected a raft of fleas, for when she closed the door, leaving the cottage to fumigate, and sat on the ancient wooden bench where Braddock had died she lifted her skirts again and saw dozens more black specks plus ugly red swellings from her boot-tops to her knees. Revolting things, she thought, licking her handkerchief and scrubbing angrily at her skin to relieve the itching. She hoped that carbolic would indeed get rid of them; if not, she was in for a very uncomfortable life.

After an hour she ventured in again and this time was able to sweep the floor and drag out the worst of the rubbish including all Braddock's bedding, which she heaped with the litter at the edge of the cliff-top, and then, with the aid of an old Lucifer and a striking-tin from near the fireplace she set fire to it all, and stood watching and wondering what old Heywood Braddock would think if he knew that she was moving into the cottage he had built, in which he and his wife Hine had lived for so many years.

It seemed like a happy place, she decided after she had laid another, lighter dusting of powder over the floor and had brushed it into every surface of the drawers, cupboards and ledges of the single heavy bureau the cottage contained. The cottage was tiny – one cosy room with an iron bedstead, a wooden table with two chairs and a large home-made armchair upholstered in hide. This, once thoroughly debugged, would make a comfortable enough bed for Andrew when he came to visit, she decided, for already in her mind's eye it was Andrew's home, too.

There were no cooking utensils, no plates or knives and forks, and neither a lamp nor a mattress, for the shepherds had swiped all those, but Lisabeth still had six pounds of her money and a hope that Gwynne might lend her a few things as well as give her the milk and vegetables she was planning to scrounge. Perhaps if she offered to milk the cow and churn the butter Charles might let her trade labour for goods. It was worth asking.

Deep in thought as her mind twitched with plans, she was startled by a tapping at the door. It was young Tommy Nevin, open-mouthed with astonishment when he recognized her.

'I were sunt dine ter check on't fire,' he stammered.

'You may tell whoever sent you that I'm here to stay, and that there'll be smoke from the chimney every day,' she told him happily. 'This is my cottage and I'm settling in.'

Shortly afterwards, just on dark, there was another knock. Lisabeth turned from where she was spreading her new blankets over the wire-mesh bed-base to see Rhys standing arms akimbo in the doorway with an angry expression on his face. His chin was unshaven, he was still dressed in the day's rough work-clothes: a farm-smock, twill trousers and high scuffed boots. Before Lisabeth could speak he advanced into the room and slapped the door shut behind him.

She noticed that he smelt of sheep-dip, but all he could smell was the irritating odour of carbolic. That he noted in passing without registering it, for all his attention was on her as she gazed back at him, those enormous eyes bright in the flickering gold from the hearth. He didn't speak, but paused, waiting.

'I've left Athol,' she told him in an expressionless voice. 'I've left and I'm never going back. I hope you don't mind me living here,' she babbled on when he offered no comment, just stared grimly at her. 'I know you're leasing the land itself, but I didn't think you'd mind —'

'It's too damned bad if I do, isn't it?' he said. 'You married Athol Nye to get away from me and not for any other reason I could fathom. So why come back, Lisabeth? You left me, so why not stay right away? Why come back here and start living almost in the shadow of my own house?'

Her spine stiffened as his cold, measured words dropped into her mind like stones. Had she expected a welcome? 'You'll hardly ever see me,' she told him. 'If you're worried that I'll be underfoot all the time, wandering about your property —'

He laughed. It was an ugly angry sound. 'I'll *know* you're here, won't I, Lisabeth? Whether I see you or not, I'll always be aware that you're right here. When I go to bed at night I'll know that you're lying there, only a few yards away, and when I eat my meals I'll be able to picture you there at that little table —'

The violence in his voice stunned her. 'You seem very displeased,' she whispered.

'Displeased?' He grabbed her by the elbows, and shocks radiated up her arms from his touch. 'Displeased? Lisabeth, I assure you, I detest the very thought of your being here.'

Dismay struck into her. Now that she had lost all feelings of hatred towards Rhys she had even allowed herself to hope that they might be friends – not real friends of course, but people who shared warm feelings towards each other and wished each other well. 'But why?' she pleaded. 'I'd never hurt you.'

He laughed again. This time, full in her face with his eyes glaring at her, the laugh seemed uglier and filled with a deeper anger. There was something else there, too. Pain. 'Never hurt me?' he repeated. 'Lisabeth, do you know how much you've already hurt me? I thought I'd escaped you, but now—' He broke off and stared down into her face, which was suffused with a fragile tender expression while her eyes gazed unblinkingly into his, radiating a gentle warmth. Her lips trembled. With a groan Rhys let go of her elbows and swiftly knotted his arms around her, crushing her against his chest and pressing his mouth down on hers with a sudden furious explosion of passion that sent tremors of emotion shuddering through her body. She was gasping, unable to breathe, and his bristly skin was grinding cruelly against her face; but, oh, being in his arms again was glorious. Tentatively she slid her hands up over his wide shoulders until her fingers were entwining in the crisp hair at the back of his neck.

Her response brought him abruptly to his senses. Thrusting her roughly away, he strode to the door, opened it and was going to walk right on out, but hesitated for a moment instead as though gathering his composure, then he half-turned to face her and said: 'That shouldn't have happened. Believe me, Lisabeth. I wish it hadn't.'

Then he was gone.

Shaken to the core, Lisabeth sat on the edge of the hard bed, her hands twitching and trembling like live things in her lap. He still loved her. No matter how happy he was with his wife, it was her he loved. A wild, singing happiness rose in her heart. Rhys still loved her! Hugging herself, she laughed aloud with nervous joy.

Inevitably her elated mood faded, and when it did cold reality had room to encroach into her mind. Rhys hadn't kissed her with love but with a brutal hunger, uncaring, demanding. Her mouth and face were still stinging from the careless force he used. He hadn't been pleased to see her, nor had he said one warm or pleasant thing. Instead he had made it quite plain that he had preferred to have her still living with her husband. That was hardly an attitude of someone madly in love.

He does love me, Lisabeth whispered in desperation as she hunched by the fire. *He does, I know he does!* But even as the words echoed mockingly in her mind she was thinking that she only believed that because she wanted to: because now, unpalatable as the truth might be, she had to accept the fact that she was in love with Rhys.

I probably have been for years, she reflected as she poked listlessly at the embers with Braddock's old iron toasting-fork. *All that hatred of him was probably based on fear. I was already half*

in love with him – had been from the moment I saw him – but
because of what had happened to poor Mamma I was terrified that
the same thing was going to happen to me, that history would
repeat itself and this time I would be the victim.

She smiled bitterly and stabbed at a scrap of burning wood.
What a waste of her life! If only she could have realized this ages
ago, then none of this misery would have happened. Only she
never would have been able to see the truth any sooner, she
realized. Andrew always came first, and it was worry about him
that had tainted her motives and caused her to make all the
mistakes she did.

Even if she could wipe the slate clean and begin again she
would have all the same choices, done all the wrong things for the
wrong reasons and ended up like this, with herself in a hopeless
bind, and with Rhys hating her as she now feared he may.

What a mess! she thought as she tossed and turned on the
uncomfortable mattress-less bed. *What a convoluted mess!*

Lisabeth knew that one of her most urgent errands should be to go
and see Andrew and explain her domestic situation to him, but
because he was a prudish and conservative boy in many ways she
dreaded what he might say so put off going to town for a few days,
spending the time instead sorting through a box of painting
equipment she found behind the bureau, seeing what she could
salvage. She needed to begin turning out work as soon as possible
if she hoped to buy food, so, unable to postpone the chore any
longer, she walked down to the road on Friday and caught the
midday stagecoach into town.

It was a rainy dreary day, the kind of day in which the cottages
tucked behind their hedges looked warm and inviting with smoking chimneys and lit windows. Puddles lay in the mud-churned
streets, and horses splashed along with heads down, looking more
miserable than their wrapped-up riders. Lisabeth wished that it
had been rainy on that day she had come to the exhibition with
Athol, because then she would have an umbrella, but as it was she
would have to let the rain beat down on her and worry about how
to dry herself off afterwards.

In the centre of town the shops all had their verandas decked
with bunting to celebrate the wedding of the Prince of Wales in
England. How sad it looked, all sagging and dripping, the paint
running and the bright colours dulled. To fill in time before
school lessons were over for the day Lisabeth shopped, purchasing

new paint-brushes and paper which the storekeeper tied with a long string so that she could hang them under her coat, out of the wet. In the stores the talk was all about some particularly brutal fighting in the North Island, near a place called Waitamanui. The name was so mangled in the pronunciation that Lisabeth heard it several times before she started with recognition. Waitamanui! That was their town. And, by the sound of the reports, it was fighting at the *pah* inland and up-river, which was right near their old home. She shuddered as she listened to the details of the clash between Queen's soldiers and Maori insurgents. Several soldiers had been beheaded, and their heads stuck up on pikes around the *pah*'s palisades. Lisabeth wondered if some of the insurgents were related to that Maori thug whose body lay at the bottom of their old well.

Charles often bemoaned the splendid life he had been forced to leave behind, but he'd never be able to go back now, she thought as she purchased a newspaper carrying an account of the fighting. This story would be of great interest to him, so she hoped the small gift of the newspaper might break the ice between them. If she was going to live there, somehow she had to smooth over the rift so that she could visit Aunty Gwynne.

'There's fireworks to celebrate the prince's wedding tonight,' the man who sold her the newspaper said as he pressed the change into her mittened hand. 'It'll be a right fizzer if this weather keeps up.'

But it *was* spring, she reminded herself as she stood under a dripping *kauri* tree and waited for the prefect to come along with the huge brass bell to clang out the signal that classes were over for the week. Yes, spring despite the freezing water down her neck and her feet turning to ice. All around her were sodden daffodils and jonquils, ugly in the rain as blobs of stale custard, their frilly trumpets mashed.

Out rang the bell. Doors flung open, and out poured the boys, surging along the wet paths, shouting and jostling each other. It was always the same – they all seemed to be tall and fair-haired – but then she saw her one with the familiar slanting clear-green eyes and waved. He saw her and ran over, grabbing her arm and hustling her back into the echoing corridor. It was dim and cold and smelt of wet boots.

'What are you doing here?' he demanded.

'Andrew!' she tried to laugh. 'Don't I get a kiss? A hug?'

He scowled. 'Is it true?'

'Is what true? Andrew, this is no way to greet—'

'Is it true that you've run off and left Mr Nye? The school's riddled with gossip about it.'

A cold thread of fear looped around her and tightened. Andrew seemed so hostile and disapproving . . . She had assumed he would understand, she had hoped he would not even be particularly interested, but it seemed he was more prudish and conservative than she had feared. After a pause she said lightly: 'You know what gossip is, dear! Pay no mind to it.'

'When it's about my *own sister*? And it's terrible things they're saying.' She could see from the hurt in his eyes that he had suffered many taunts. 'Tell me it's not true that it was all Rhys Morgan's idea that you leave Mr Nye.'

She was aghast. 'Is that what they're saying?'

'Among other things. But it's not true, is it? Uncle Rhys would never do anything dishonourable . . . Only, it looks so bad because you're not with Aunty Gwynne. Did they chase you away?'

'I wanted to live alone,' she lied.

'That's so *wrong*! I mean, you got married to Mr Nye, so you should stay with him!'

'I thought you'd be pleased! You don't even *like* Mr Nye, and he never lets you visit. Andrew, don't you see—?'

'He was decent enough to me before, but now he hates me. At first I didn't believe the gossip, but when Mr Nye started to pick on me I knew it must be true. He caned me yesterday.' And Andrew glared at her as if it was her fault.

She shivered. Perhaps it was. A group of boys hustled past, muttering. They glared sideways at Andrew and sniggered. Lisabeth felt helpless. She'd only left Athol so that Andrew could continue here at school, and now the place was becoming intolerable for him. It wouldn't be long, she guessed, before he was so miserable that he ran away, too, and what advice could she give him then? Her life was spinning in circles because she ran away from one problem after another, yet when she examined her problems was there really any other solution? If she was a man, she could stand up and fight for herself, but a woman had no rights. Her father or her guardian and then her husband and later her sons could all make decisions and force her to abide by them. In this society a woman was as defenceless as a rabbit among the wolves – to survive she needed to use all her wits and she also needed to be able to run.

Andrew waited until his classmates had jostled away out of earshot, then continued furiously: 'As soon as I get a chance I'm going to see Mr Nye and I'm going to ask him why he drove you away! Look, maybe if we begged him he'd take you back again.'

'No, Andrew, no! Promise me you won't do that!'

He shook off her clinging hands and backed away. His eyes were as angry and filled with hatred as they had been at the beginning of their interview. She had made no progress at all. 'I've got to go. I'm on detention, again.' He smiled thinly. 'I suppose I could thank you for that.'

Hurrying after him down the flagstone path, she plucked uselessly at his sleeve. 'Please don't be so bitter.'

He glared at her, his soft immature face contorted with disgust. 'If you don't like him, why did you marry him?'

'Partly because of you,' she said helplessly.

He was striding away, but now he turned to wither her with another glare. 'I wanted you to marry Uncle Rhys! If you'd hoped to please me, that's what you should have done.'

'Andrew, you don't understand . . .'

'You're right at that!' he snorted, and before she could protest further he was gone.

Too sick at heart to attempt another visit with Charles and Gwynne, Lisabeth trudged home from the coach-stop and used the newspaper to light a fire, brewing herself a lemon drink to fight off the chills. While her clothes steamed dry over a chair she wrapped herself in a blanket and huddled close to the warmth, listening to the rain drumming on the slate roof. When she had thawed out she used a piece of her precious drawing-paper to write Andrew a letter – not a long involved explanation, for spoken words were needed for that, but a simple note saying that she loved him and would like to see him again one day soon. She hoped that the message would touch his heart.

THIRTY

AZURA DIPPED HER SILVER SPOON into her bowl of asparagus soup and said: 'I hear that Rhys has a concubine! Miss Merryman's brother tells her that Christchurch is agog about this Mrs Nye being lured away from her husband by Rhys. Tell me, Bea, is this true?'

In the stunned silence Rhys and their guests stared at her while, unconcerned, she dipped up another spoonful of soup and another.

The four were partaking of their weekly dinner-party at Mists of Heaven and were seated in sumptuous comfort in the high-ceilinged, maple-panelled dining-room, their chairs geometrically placed around an oblong table which would seat twelve with ease. Heavy silver candelabra graced the table, and summer roses bloomed from bowls on the sideboard. From the ceiling hung banners from the college Rhys had attended at Oxford, while the high oriel windows bore the three-legged 'fylfut' emblem, Rhys's one concession to his Manx heritage.

These dinners were always formal because Azura preferred it that way. She could wear her diamond tiara (a wedding gift from Rhys) and one of her extremely tight watered-silk ball-gowns, but best of all she could command a great many courses from the kitchen. Even with only two helpings of each course she was able to enjoy an enormously satisfying meal that way. In her fifth month of pregnancy Azura was already very fat.

'But I'm not being silly,' she rebuked Rhys, swallowing the last of her soup and smiling. Azura's smile was her best feature, a pink healthy revelation of large even teeth and neat scalloped gums.

She smiled often. Though obesity was distending the graceful lines of her face, trebling her chins and inflating her cheeks, she was still pretty with very white skin and tepid grey eyes framed with long curling lashes the same light gold colour as her thin upswept hair. As she rang the bell for service she laughed at the other three. Rhys looked angry, Sir Kenneth disturbed and Lady Launcenolt thunderstruck.

Siobhan Nevin trotted in with the tureen. The others waved her away, but Azura helped herself to more and stirred in some fresh cream from a silver moisture-beaded jug. 'There, that made you all jump, didn't it! There's nothing like a concubine to stop the conversation!' She nodded at the girl's slender back as the white-ribboned cap and prim starched bow were vanishing into the hallway. 'I should be careful in front of the servants, though, I suppose. All the Nevins have tongues that wag at both ends.'

'And Siobhan is only twelve,' said Rhys in a controlled voice.

'Then, she wouldn't understand, would she?' pouted Azura.

'Why say such things at all?' asked Rhys.

'Because I'm bored,' she replied, concentrating on her full spoon. 'I'm sure Bea is, too! Whenever you and Kiki get together you talk of nothing but politics! Honestly, I think I'd prefer a gripping narrative about shearing or sowing wheat or the price of wool. Anything would be more interesting than politics! I mean, who cares whether the capital of the colony is Auckland or Wellington and whether Canterbury has a separate government? Do you care, Bea?'

Lady Launcenolt shrugged unhappily. In her lap and hidden by the table her fingers were nervously plucking at her serviette hem with such persistence that already the stitching had unravelled all along one side, but even while she tugged and picked at it she was unaware of what she was doing. This terrible gossip, where *had* Azura heard it? Suddenly she burst out: 'It's all nonsense! Utter nonsense!'

'What? Politics?' rumbled Sir Kenneth, baffled.

'No . . .' Bea glanced towards the door. Siobhan was staggering back in with an immense platter of fish dumplings. 'No . . . this other business is nonsense.'

'Oh, Rhys and his concubine!' said Azura gaily. 'What a pity! I was going to ask him to entertain us later with an account of his scarlet woman, but we shall have to settle for a little *Scarlatti* instead!'

'I could slit his throat,' muttered Lady Launcenolt in the brougham on the way home. 'I could strangle whoever passed on that

326

poisonous story, but one must face up to it, Kiki – Rhys is the villain of the piece. Fancy upsetting darling Azura when she's in *her* condition!'

'Mmmm,' said Sir Kenneth, more disturbed by the mention of pregnancy than by his wife's uncharacteristic violence. Because Rhys was being attacked he felt bound to comment. 'You fret too much, dear. Azura didn't seem in the least upset. It didn't dint her appetite, did it, h'm, this gossip? I say, Bea, if you look up here there's a perfect view of Orion. The stars always seem so much brighter in this hemisphere. I wonder if the atmosphere is thinner down here?'

'Yes, he's the villain,' mused Bea as if he hadn't spoken. 'If he hadn't encouraged Thomas Fox's daughter, there never would have been a scandal! You mark my words, Kiki, the Foxes are behind these whispering campaigns. That Gammerwoth woman is beside herself with jealousy because Rhys jilted her to marry Azura. Did you know there was a rumour that Mr Fox was going to call Rhys out over that? Concubine, indeed! I suppose they mean that wretched Stafford lass – married a schoolmaster who beat her, didn't she? Very peculiar habits some of these school-masters . . . But I suppose you hear all the gossip, too.'

'All of it,' sighed Sir Kenneth, gazing out towards the sprin-kling of town lights. Odd how distance bleached all the warmth out of them. Yes, he'd heard the gossip. Everybody in the prov-ince now knew that, though Rhys first courted Councillor Fox's daughter, he switched affections after Fox lost the election and set his sights on Councillor Launcenolt's ward, a naïve lass fresh out from Home. The story was slick nonsense of course, but was plausible because councillors carried so much power and influence in the province that to get on in business and social circles one could do no better than cultivate one as a patron – the giver of contracts, the buyer of goods and the opener of doors. No wonder there was gossip. Also, Sir Kenneth had to admit, there was the abruptness of Rhys's engagement to Azura. Certainly he and Bea were delighted, but Rhys was so perfunctory, so lacklustre about the courting that Sir Kenneth could see his heart wasn't in it. It was a bit of a pity really, but Sir Kenneth had lived enough years on this earth to know that compromise is often the only answer. He doubted even now that Rhys loved Azura, but did that matter, as long as he treated her well?

'Rhys is rich and successful, and nice to look at. People always gossip about men like him. Would you rather she had married someone ugly and insignificant?'

'You must know something else,' persisted Bea. 'Do you think the Stafford lass is his mistress?'

Sir Kenneth decided to end the conversation. 'If she is, then she must be a very tolerant woman! Not one of my mistresses would have agreed to be tucked out of sight in a tumbledown shack on a isolated cliff-top. Every one of *my* concubines insisted on a smart town house, a carriage of her —'

'Kiki, stop it! You are naughty!' She flicked his beard with her gloves, fluffing the long strands upwards and outwards as she often did to puncture his dignity when he annoyed her. Both of them were laughing.

Lisabeth was as good as her word to Rhys and remained out of sight for the next few weeks. Athol's threat to have her committed was very much on her mind, so most of the time she remained inside the cottage re-creating the watercolour paintings she had executed on her outings with him over the Port Hills last winter. Because they were fresh in her mind she had no difficulty, only enjoyment, in playing them out again; and as she worked she experienced a few quiet twinges for the pure simplicity of that life. If only Uncle Charles hadn't given vent to his petty spite and told Athol about the land.

Now she felt tainted. She heard no more gossip, but sensed it in the way Charles roared at her to keep away whenever she walked past the cottage as she did twice a week to wait for the stagecoach so that she could send Andrew a letter. His enduring resentment was a disappointment to her, but she did understand. Not only had he lost her labour but his chance for riches, too, and now that his revenge had backfired he was surrounded by scandal. As an insatiable gossip himself, Charles feared the smears of scandal and the cutting tongues of mischief-makers.

Lisabeth did notice that he was always working alone. She guessed that his gardens were still earning poorly, that he could not afford to pay for labour. This gave her encouragement. If the breach hadn't been healed by harvest-time, she would offer to help and that would certainly smooth things over.

Conditioned by her months of appalling food at the Nyes', Lisabeth was able to eat sparingly and still feel satisfied. Her tiny hoard of money was dwindling but very slowly, thanks to Joe Day who brought her not only an old mattress from the hotel and a treasure trove of pots and utensils and clothing he had salvaged from shipwrecks but also a regular supply of fresh fish – flounder,

328

thick juicy snapper and an occasional billyful of succulent prawns.

'You're my only friend, and I can't thank you enough,' she said when he arrived one day with a smoked gurnard and the news that the Nyes had decided simply to cut Lisabeth from their lives and not proceed with the plans to have her certified insane.

'Don't thank me,' he said. 'Word is that they'd never have succeeded anyway.' He paused, then added bluntly, his merry eyes suddenly serious: 'Though most folk would say you *are* mad, you know. It's not done for a woman to live on her own. Not done at all. If you keep it up, people will begin to whisper that you're a witch and children will throw stones at you in the streets.'

'Then, I'll have to learn to run fast, won't I?'

'It's not a joke, Lisabeth. Make peace with Mrs Stafford, eh? Go back to live with them. It's the only way.'

'I would if I could,' said Lisabeth. She missed Gwynne, missed the security of having other people around but, most of all, longed to have someone to talk to. Gwynne she had not seen at all apart from once when she was walking down the ridge-track and saw Gwynne out by the gooseberry canes. Though Lisabeth hurried to speak to her, by the time she reached the orchard Gwynne had retreated inside and shut the door. Reluctantly she acknowledged that Gwynne had seen her coming.

Andrew's silence saddened her even more. When he never replied to her letters she began to wonder if in fact they reached him, so on the day that she took her first batch of paintings into the local gallery on Cashel Street she walked down the long road past the Canterbury Club and the Provincial Council offices to the grey stone buildings that housed King's College. There, in the same place, she lay in wait for him after classes, but this time he dashed past with the other boys, and the wincing hurt look he flung in her direction was message enough. He did not want her, either.

The headmaster was unsympathetic and mortifyingly direct. Andrew was continuing to achieve brilliantly academically, despite the disruptive influence her domestic instability had caused on the school. 'Mr Nye is leaving us soon,' he informed her accusingly. 'A small school is opening in Ferrymead and Mr Nye has been granted a modest position there. In the normal run of circumstances he could have been appointed headmaster, but as things stand . . .'

'I see,' whispered Lisabeth. 'But what about Andrew? it's nearly vacation-time, and—'

'Master Stafford has requested to be allowed to board with the caretaker for the holidays, helping him with the grounds work in return for his food, but for the most part spending his time studying. It's not unusual. Other boys who have had nowhere to go have done this in the past,' he commented crisply.

But he does have somewhere to go! She attempted a smile, managed a grimace of pain. 'Thank you for your time,' she said.

Thanks to her certain notoriety, her paintings sold well. Lisabeth told herself that this success was owed to Mr Brecon's article, where a torrent of criticism describing Athol's work as 'pedestrian and uninspired' had been followed by a few warm remarks about her 'fresh, lively' work. In truth, few people ever bothered to read Mr Brecon's reviews, but everybody avidly enjoyed gossip and her name on a card in the gallery window attracted brisk interest. Her first dozen paintings sold so fast that the elderly couple who owned the gallery sent the delivery boy out to collect more from her. Pleased and surprised, Lisabeth bundled up another batch and hesitated only a moment before scribbling out a note to accompany them.

'You've doubled your price?' frowned William Buck, a lanky youth who also performed housekeeping errands at the gallery and helped with framing. 'Ah, Mr Watson, 'e won't like that!'

'Then, he can send them back again,' she said, shocked by her own daring. 'I have to support myself, you know.'

None of the pictures came back.

Lady Launcenolt revelled in the glory of being a councillor's wife and often attended the Provincial Council meetings, sitting in the ladies' gallery with the other wives and nodding and smiling when Sir Kenneth rose to address the House. She wore her best hats and secreted a bag of peppermints in her muff to suck at during the many tedious stretches. It reminded her of the Indian Raj days, when Sir Kenneth sat on the bench meting out stiff sentences to wrongdoers.

Life was sweet for her, for when Sir Kenneth was away on one of his visits to Parliament in Wellington she was able to spend all day with Azura, and Azura was the light of her own childless existence. Everything had worked out splendidly, Azura coming out from Home alone in the end, Rhys marrying her, and now there was all the pleasure of seeing her ensconced in luxury. The only bug in the brew was this nasty gossip, which was as virulent as a disease with new twists and strains constantly surfacing. If Lady

Launcenolt could have cheerfully slit Rhys's throat, then there were quite a few other things she could have inflicted on that miserable Stafford lass. By now Lady Launcenolt had decided that it was all her fault.

Her dismay was severe then, when one day having emerged early from the Council Chambers she decided to stroll through town while waiting for Leopold to collect her. She chanced by the gallery and saw a display of Lisabeth's work, her name prominently featured in the window and the tastefully framed pictures arranged on artist's easels draped with sky-blue silk. The osprey feathers on Lady Launcenolt's bonnet quivered, and she had to take in several deep breaths to settle her agitation. Only when she was sufficiently composed did she step into the shop to demand that the offending paintings be removed at once.

Mr Watson was equally dismayed, but remained politely uncooperative, even when she hinted that should the gallery become a public nuisance Councillor Launcenolt could exert influence to have it closed down. 'Her paintings command high prices, and people want to buy them,' he apologized.

'But she's a wanton, a . . . a hussy, a threat to the fabric of society!' flustered Lady Launcenolt.

'I am sorry, but it could be that someone has misled you,' he offered tactfully. 'Mrs Watson and I have visited the lady in her cottage. She does lead an unconventional life, that's true, but many artistic people do, you know.'

'*Unconventional!*' Not daring to trust herself further, Lady Launcenolt left.

Sir Kenneth was disturbed when she broached the subject. 'I can't interfere, Bea. This is the kind of thing I accused Thomas Fox of doing. Can you imagine the political capital he'd make out of it if I meddled? Besides, we don't know if there is any truth to these rumours about Mrs Nye. All we know is —'

'I'm sure Rhys is in love with her,' blurted out his wife. 'You should have seen his face when I mentioned her name at luncheon on Saturday!'

'You *what?*'

'Oh, it was nothing . . . All I said was that the cottage was such a primitive place it must be frightfully inconvenient for her living here alone.'

'You shouldn't have said anything,' said Sir Kenneth, but mildly, for he never deliberately upset his wife. 'By the way, what did Azura say?'

'Oh, she said I had a "Bea" in my bonnet. She made a joke of it, you know her, so brave. She's not well, though . . . The doctor had been there again most of the morning. I fear for her, Kiki, I really do.'

'Nonsense,' said Sir Kenneth. 'She's as strong as a horse.'

Knowing that only she could see the danger, Lady Launcenolt brooded even more. Azura was in a delicate state, Azura needed protection. The trouble was that nobody could see it but her.

Andrew's twelfth birthday fell in the first week of summer vacation. Not having any idea of what he might like, Lisabeth spent a whole guinea of her precious money on a gift chosen by the man in the toy-shop, a set of lead soldiers attired in the uniforms of the Duke of Wellington's men. Instead of delivering them to the college she took them home with her, still hoping that he would come and stay. Every time she wrote she told him of small improvements she was making to the cottage in the hope that he might spend his holiday with her.

He did not respond. Finally, on the birthday itself Lisabeth wrapped and labelled the gift, found fourpence for the coachman, tucked her hair up under her bonnet and walked with the package down to the coach-stop. It was a glorious morning, ripe and drowsy with the promise of a lazy afternoon. From the butter-yellow gorse around her cottage came the indolent hum of bees, while ducks quacked on the lagoon and gulls swooped like kites on strings above the tug of the surf. Three ships waited on the glittering ocean for the tide to lift them or Joe to guide them over the Sumner Bar. One was a steamer with a stubby stick of funnel dragging a limp grey banner along the horizon behind it.

The cockatoos' cottages stood open to the sunshine, and bedding aired on the fences. Old Bollan was tethered outside his kennel in the orchard, scratching behind one liver- spotted ear, his lips drawn back in a grin. He stood up and whined, lashing his tail as she passed. *I should ask if I can have him,* she mused. *A dog would be company, and I can afford to feed him now. Perhaps if I offered to buy him* . . . The thought made her smile. Uncle Charles had chased her away at first when she approached him wanting to buy milk and meat, but when he saw her taking her money to the cockatoos' cottages next door he had changed his tune, and had appeared at her door one evening with a battered enamel billy-can, telling her that if she left it at his gate of an evening he'd fill it with fresh milk for a penny. Delighted, she had done so, only to find that the milk was thin and bluish, skimmed of every drop of cream. *Miserable sod!* she thought, silently vowing that if she ever did get Bollan she'd buy meat in town or beg scraps from one of the McFallishes rather than rely on Charles to sort her out a few choice cuts. He'd toss her the hoofs, ears and tail and then charge prime beefsteak prices, no doubt.

Humming to herself, she swung along the scrape of side-road towards the junction where it joined the north–south coach route, and as she rounded the corner by the thickest of *kahikatea* trees she saw the Launcenolts' wine-coloured brougham moving very slowly towards her. One of the sepoys was driving the matched black horses, and on either side of the road, quite some distance ahead, two other sepoys walked, scratching at patches of bare earth with short rakes as they came.

Dawdling, Lisabeth watched them with interest. They were striking figures in their scarlet tunics and tall turbans pinned with enamelled brooches. At first she thought they were searching for some lost object but then as she drew closer she noticed that they were sprinkling a dark fine substance into the scratches they made.

'You look busy,' she remarked as she came level with the sepoy on her side of the road.

His black eyes flashed at her with a rolling of white. 'We are about cultivating the roadsides, ma'am. We are planting the wilderness flowers to make all pretty for Miss Azura.' Reaching into the bag at his waist he extended a pink-palmed hand to show her the mixture of different-shaped seeds.

'What an enchanting idea!' sighed Lisabeth, imagining how transformed the roadsides would be when they were carpeted by a profusion of multi-hued wild flowers. 'What? For me? Oh, thank you!' And she opened her hand so that the sepoy could funnel the seed into it. 'I'll plant these by my door.'

'You are about welcome, ma'am,' he said, inclining his finely shaped head. His skin was dusky as a Black Hermitage grape. When he smiled his teeth were startling.

Lisabeth paused, turning to watch him go by, and when she turned again with a little sigh of happiness she noticed that the carriage had rolled much closer. Sitting in it, alone, and glaring at her with a frosty expression was a handsome woman who must be Lady Launcenolt, Lisabeth decided.

'Good morning!' Lisabeth smiled, puzzled by the elderly lady's cold demeanour, for she had heard only pleasant things about this woman who was one of Rhys's oldest friends. Besides, out here in the country a chance meeting almost guaranteed a smile, but this woman looked positively ferocious.

'Young lady, what is your name?'

The question was so coldly asked that Lisabeth understood at once. Lady Launcenolt was Azura's godmother, and her hostility meant that she had heard the gossip and believed that Lisabeth was out to make trouble. Thinking quickly, Lisabeth decided to avoid a confrontation. 'My name is Miss Maitland. What's yours?' she said.

'I see.' There was a moment's hesitation, then the woman burst out angrily; 'I thought you were that dreadful Mrs Nye, and I'd like to give her a piece of my mind!'

'I've never heard of her,' replied Lisabeth, but when she walked on quickly her legs were shaking. This was terrible. Everybody – even people she'd never met – thought ill of her.

But as she waited for the coach her native common sense rescued her plummeting spirits. *If I can survive Andrew's rejection, then I can cope with anything,* she told herself grimly. *Things can only hurt me if I allow them to, and I won't be wounded!*

Feeling a grittiness in her palm, she unfolded her fingers to reveal the seeds, and immediately lightness crept into her mind. There was kindness for her; good things did happen.

'I've made terrible mistakes but I'll not mourn over them,' she resolved aloud. 'I'm envious of Azura but I'll only make myself unhappy if I sigh over Rhys and dwell on what might have been.' And with determined cheerfulness she lifted her chin and smiled. Nobody saw her but half a dozen dusty sheep in the meadow opposite, but she felt better in her heart and that was all that mattered.

THIRTY-ONE

LISABETH WAS WAKENED AS USUAL by Bollan's whining and scratching to be let out, and as usual she muttered darkly about her folly in buying him. Bollan was good company, impeccably house-trained, and with him around she lost her nervousness about being alone, but while she liked to lie abed in the mornings he insisted on being let out to nose around and chase rabbits in the early dawn light.

'It's Christmas Day, for heaven's sake,' she protested as she padded through the darkness of the windowless cottage and opened the door a few inches to the cool grey morning. Bollan flowed out, his tail rapping the door as he eased through. It was then Lisabeth heard a horse galloping away – from very close by, it seemed. Thinking nothing of it, she yawned and fumbled her way back to bed.

Christmas Day, she thought, *Church. A visit to Andrew. A long, long walk into town because there will be no coach service today. No time to lie in this morning.*

Groping around, she splashed some spring water from a billy into her battered tin washbasin and scrubbed her face with a square of rag, swabbing under her arms and around her belly then rubbing the wrung-out cloth between her toes. Refreshed, she pulled on her long-legged split-crotch undergarment and tied the drawstring at the waist, then slipped a petticoat over her head. Opening the door a few inches to give herself some light, she hesitated over Joe's salvaged garments before choosing the blue cashmere gown instead. It was far prettier than the others, but she seldom wore it these days because of the contortions and strains

335

she needed to fasten those wretched buttons. As it was, there were still four she never could reach, and a shawl was essential to cover that gap between her shoulder-blades.

'You'll be sorry,' she warned herself. It promised to be a hot day, this was a winter-weight gown, and that walk would be perishing under the sun.

Wondering if she had time to prepare something to eat, she went outside to tie Bollan up. If she left it too late to call him, he wandered back to the Staffords' and then he couldn't hear her yelling his name. But he hadn't strayed far this morning and came loping through the flax thicket to meet her. Holding his collar, she led him to where his chain was fastened near the lemon tree, snigged him captive and then topped up his water-dish. As she turned to go back inside she noticed a wicker Moses basket propped up on the top of the woodpile against the house.

Lisabeth tried to lift it down, but it was so heavy she had to drag it lower in a series of bumps down the stacked logs. Removing the white cloth that covered it, Lisabeth gasped. 'Christmas!' she exclaimed aloud, for that's what the basket contained – a complete Christmas feast. There were oranges, apples, fresh sweet rolls, a pat of butter in a glass jar, a pot of jam, a wedge of Cheddar cheese wrapped in muslin, a large chunk of pink ham, a block of fruitcake . . . By now Lisabeth's arms were heaped full, and there were still more treasures, the bottom of the basket not yet visible.

'Aunty Gwynne,' whispered Lisabeth, her eyes brimming with tears of gratitude. Guilt, too, for she had been furious with both her and Charles on the day she collected Bollan. After listening implacably to her pleas to be allowed to share Christmas Day with them Charles had taken her money and shut the door in her face. As she led Bollan away she could hear Gwynne crying and she thought: *Why is she so spineless? Why doesn't she stand up to him once in a while?* And most of her anger had been directed at Gwynne.

And now Gwynne had given her a Christmas. How she had accomplished it Lisabeth couldn't imagine – assembling the treats without Charles suspecting and having one of the cockatoos deliver it – or one of the McFallishes, more likely. That was it; she'd dragooned them into being her accomplices!

Now it really *was* Christmas! Lisabeth set aside a beribboned jar of boiled sweets to add to the shirt she was giving Andrew and arranged the remainder of the delicacies in a pyramid on her table. *I'll approach them after the services,* she resolved. *Charles is always in a benevolent mood after church. I'll thank Gwynne then, if I can sneak a quiet word;*

But the Staffords, for the first time in all the years Lisabeth had known them, were not at the Christmas Day devotions. Nor was Andrew.

The caretaker's cottage was a stone box built like a bulge on the inside of the wall near the main gates. Children wailed inside, and there was the smell of roast meat charring – a sour burned smell. The caretaker's wife was obviously not a very good cook.

In reply to her rapping the caretaker came, an enormous grease-spotted napkin tucked at his throat and several children clinging like barnacles to his legs, peering around at her with blank expressions. *Like fish,* she thought, as more pale faces emerged from the gloom.

'The wife died a year ago, and the housekeeper's gone home for Christmas,' he explained. 'Got to cope the best way I can. No sense moping, right?'

Lisabeth nodded. 'Is Andrew there?'

'Gone home, too. Mr Stafford fetched him last night, late. His wife's taken poorly, too. Bad thing. Y'know what? I reckon women ain't got the constitution men has. The slightest little thing knocks them right off. Not builded as strong as we are, o'course, and—'

Lisabeth fled.

By the time she had marched the whole way back Lisabeth had built up a steaming temper. She was panting, scarlet-faced, and so angry that a red mist danced before her eyes as she flung into the house without knocking, plunked down Andrew's gifts on the workbench and shoved both hands on her hips, confronting Charles who heaved himself out of his comfortable chair in a bewildered indignation at her precipitous entry.

Too angry at first to speak, she surveyed the room in disgust. By the looks of it not a tap of work had been done for weeks. The grate was cold. Dust lay thickly on the floor, the table and all along the dresser shelves. Opened biscuit-tins lay scattered around, and drinking-mugs stood in crusted circles of milk. By the look of things Charles had been living on luxury rations that needed no preparation. What about Gwynne? Had he been feeding her the same rubbish?

337

'Why didn't you send for me?' she demanded, staggered that his selfishness would have plumbed such depths. 'You know I'd come and look after Aunty Gwynne. Where is she? Has the doctor been?'

'Get out! Get out!' Charles shouted, flapping his newspaper at her. 'You're not welcome here!'

'I never have been welcome, I know that now,' said Lisabeth bluntly. 'But I'm here, and you're not getting rid of me. Tell me, has the doctor been? What did he say?'

She tried to push past him, but he blocked the way to the bedroom. 'You know Mrs Stafford . . . She doesn't want fuss! And she doesn't want you, either. You needn't think you're going in there and upsetting her with all your nonsensical crapulence! Go back to your husband, young lady. You've brought down enough scandalous aspirations on this household. We're decent people!'

There was a silence, so thick with hostility that Lisabeth could have punched a fist through it. Then, from up the corridor, came a feeble wavering voice. 'Lisabeth . . . Is that you?'

'Get . . . out . . . of . . . my . . . way!' said Lisabeth between her teeth.

The room stank. Stumbling to the window, Lisabeth jerked back the curtains and flung open the windows before turning to face Gwynne. She was a frail pale wraith, thin and wasted, her eyes dull and her features more birdlike, sharp and bony. Andrew was sitting on a chair beside her, crying, holding her skeletal hands in both of his. When Lisabeth burst in he wiped his eyes and stood up, obviously ill at ease. Before he could wriggle away she gave him a quick hug and said: 'Go and fetch Rhys, quickly. Tell him his sister needs urgent medical attention.'

'I already wanted to do that, but Uncle Charles said—'

'Good for you. That was the right thing!' she cut in, praising him to forestall further argument. 'Never mind what Uncle Charles says. Just go and fetch Rhys.'

'Rhys . . .,' murmured Gwynne from the bed.

Andrew turned away so that she wouldn't hear, and murmured: 'He might refuse to come. He arrived first thing this morning with a big hamper of food. Uncle Charles was rude to him – really rude – and threw things at him, then slung the hamper so that everything rolled out all over the ground. Uncle Rhys never said anything but he looked disgusted.'

'What happened to the food?' asked Lisabeth faintly.

'I rescued that! It's all stowed in the implement-shed.' In his glee he had forgotten his own resentments, Lisabeth was glad to see. Inwardly she prayed that this morning would be the turn of the tide for all of them, but she would have to tread carefully, go gently and not inflame old antagonisms.

'Tell Rhys that Gwynne needs him,' she said. 'He won't let her down.'

'Rhys . . .,' murmured Gwynne.

Lisabeth bent to kiss the cold white brow. The skin felt dead already, she noticed with a stab of panic. 'Rhys will be here soon,' she said. 'I'll tidy you up so that you look nice for him, shall I?'

Later that afternoon Rhys found Lisabeth by the big drain behind the orchard. She had been sluicing and scrubbing Gwynne's soiled bedding and was now spreading the blankets out over the flax bushes to dry.

'What a way to spend Christmas,' she joked. He had walked right up to her and was standing as close as possible without actually touching her. A joke was her last defence. She was so glad to see him that she wanted to cry, yet she dared not look into his face. He was dressed in jodhpurs and tall shiny boots, and a summery silk shirt, while at his throat a light cravat was pinned with an elegant cameo of Athena. Lisabeth wondered if it was a gift from his wife. *That's it! Think about his wife*, she reminded herself. *Don't think about him riding up to my cottage while I lay in bed this morning, leaving me gifts heaped outside my door.*

'You shouldn't be doing that.' It was the first time she had heard his voice since the day she moved in. 'You don't have to be a drudge, Lisabeth. It's not right. I'll send Birdie Nevin or one of the other —'

'No!' she insisted, then modulated her voice. 'I want to look after her, Rhys. I need to establish a friendship with her again. I need to be close to someone.' She paused, wishing she could have bitten her tongue to stop that from slipping out. She didn't want Rhys to guess how lonely she was. Hurrying on, she said: 'What did the doctor say? Is it bad news? Oh, I pray it's not!'

'She'll be all right.' He stooped down and picked up a pebble which he tossed into the drain. It was an irrelevant boyish thing to do, and she guessed that he was as nervous as she. 'Her rheumatism confined her completely to bed, and if Charles had been up to looking after her that wouldn't have mattered. Unfortunately . . .' He paused to toss another pebble. 'Unfortunately, Charles is sicker than she is.'

'Uncle Charles?' She, too, had been fidgeting, wringing out an already wrung-out pillow-sham. Now she gaped at his cravat pin. 'Uncle Charles is ill?'

'Doctor Meakings is seriously worried . . . He's got a growth in his stomach, a bad one. He can't eat properly and he's suffering considerable pain . . .'

'So he's lashing out at everyone within reach like a wounded bear,' finished Lisabeth. 'And I've been thinking uncharitable things about him. All these weeks. . . . I should have guessed he wasn't himself.'

'Don't blame yourself. I should have noticed his greenish colour, too. And the fact that he's lost weight.' He laughed mirthlessly. 'Even if that escaped me, I should have twigged something was badly wrong when he pelted me with food this morning – all the things he used to like most, and now he can't face any of it. The only nourishment he can take is milk and dry biscuits.'

'Poor Uncle Charles . . .' Staring at the pillow-sham as she twisted it between her hands, she murmured: 'Thank you for the gifts you left me.'

He placed one hand on her arm. One hand. She stared at the strong brown fingers. She closed her eyes. He was saying: 'I had to leave them there. I was afraid you'd take umbrage and pelt me, too.'

'I wouldn't. I—'

'Then, you should.' He was no longer taking refuge in jokes. 'Damn you, Lisabeth. Why *did* you come back here? Was it because of me? Was it?'

She turned away, towards the mountains. They were soft and blue, hazed in the summer heat, melting into the sky. She had to be honest even though she was no longer sure of her reasons. Once her mind had been as sharp and hard as ice, but now it was all water. Nothing was definite any more. 'I left Athol because of Andrew. It was something I had to —'

'I don't believe you,' he said harshly. 'Look at me, Lisabeth. Look me in the face and tell me. Go on.'

She couldn't. The events of the day overwhelmed her, and she shook her head, saying: 'Does it matter?'

'Of course it—' He bit back the rest of it and said: 'No. I suppose not. My life is settled and even if you persist in getting yourself talked about I imagine you're happy enough there. I say . . . there's nothing between you and young Joe Day, is there?'

'Of course not!' Where all else had failed, that brought her head up with a snap and she glared into his eyes, seeing jealousy and something else – protectiveness? possessiveness? – there.

Rhys sighed, a long frustrated exhalation of controlled breath. She had done it again. Once more he had revealed everything, and her thoughts were maddeningly secret, screened behind those unfathomable blue-black eyes.

In the first days of the New Year, Azura was delivered of a baby girl, seven months to the day after her marriage to Rhys. The province was agog; anonymous pamphlets flourished on every hoarding, every shop-front, accusing the pair of immoral pre-marital conduct. Gloating Charles brought one back from town and flourished it under Gwynne's nose. 'I knew there was indecency in the haste of those nuptuals. Here's proof of it!' he said.

'Please, Uncle Charles,' cautioned Lisabeth; but Birdie, who was there visiting again, said: 'A suven-munth bebbie? Ah, thut's naught ter be surpraised abaht. Two of mine was early by more thun thut, Muster Stafford! Nine munths is notral, but there's naught surpraisin' in suven, neither!'

'Is that right?' said Charles, his gaze sliding around to Lisabeth who sat quietly in a corner with her embroidery.

'Right as I'm suttin' here!' repeated Birdie emphatically, tak-ing Charles's lead as an encouragement to launch into her own favourite topic, her numerous pregnancies, regaling them with details that made Lisabeth wince and Charles flee the room.

Gwynne smiled. She was so much stronger now it was heart-ening to see her. 'Poor Mr Stafford,' she said in her lilting voice. 'Men are such tender creatures, aren't they? For myself I enjoy hearing about babies; it makes me thankful to have escaped the process, *and* compensates for my never having had any. I would so have loved . . . Ah, never mind! Lisabeth has been my comfort, haven't you, dear?'

The truth had been kept from the Staffords. Doctor Meakings had prescribed massive doses of laudanum under the guise of a 'tonic', but Lisabeth dreaded the day Gwynne would look at Charles and see the inescapable facts for herself. Though the laudanum had blunted the edge of his temper, he was becoming weaker and greyer with each day. He no longer pretended to work in the fields, and the weeds grew, choking the stumps of last season's rotted cabbages, blanketing all the fields in ragged green.

With Lisabeth he shared an uneasy truce. She spoke to him, but

341

his only reply was to grunt and turn his back. Lisabeth didn't care. Andrew had forgiven her for leaving Mr Nye; the gossip at school had long since been overtaken by more interesting topics, and her frequent presence at the Staffords' place lent her back some respectability. There was still a guarded quality to their friendship, but Andrew shared things that had happened at school, and when he brought home his report card one Saturday and walked up the hill to her cottage to show it to her first she hugged him and cried tears of pride and relief. It did not matter that he pushed her away, embarrassed. At long last he was really home.

That next year was the slowest and in many ways the most painful of Lisabeth's life. By the end of summer Gwynne was mobile again, fit enough to ride in the trap up to Mists of Heaven to see the baby, and to report all the details back to Lisabeth. She was even able to ride over to the tiny Maori church on the coast where, on a whim, Azura had the baby christened Vashti, an Indian name that meant *'Thread of Life'*. 'Rhys tried to put his foot down,' she whispered to Lisabeth. 'They quarrelled, inside the church! Rhys said Vashṭi was an outlandish name and, though he relented there, he announced at tea later that he never intended calling the girl anything but Daisy. She's such a pretty little mite, too! The image of her mother, with—'

'Yes, yes, you've told me,' interrupted Lisabeth, who was rolling out pastry for an apple pie. 'And Uncle Charles? Did he enjoy the tea?'

'He didn't eat much,' said Gwynne with a frown. 'He's gone off his food lately.' Then she brightened and added: 'Oh, and wonderful news! Azura and Rhys are to be parents again! Yes, so soon! Isn't it lovely? Before Christmas, Miss Merryman said.'

Lisabeth whacked the rolling-pin down hard and rubbed it back and forth. 'Yes. That's lovely,' she said tonelessly.

The baby, a boy, was born in early December. This time Azura chose Darius, and this time Rhys did not argue.

'If you ask me, there's something wrong with Azura,' fretted Gwynne as she unpinned her bonnet after making a visit to greet the new arrival. 'She lost weight after Daisy was born, but now she's so bloated that she looks terrible. Her skin is all blotchy, and she wheezes when she breathes. I don't know how she can get up out of her chair. I watched her eating a dish of blancmange, and she could barely bend her fingers to hold the spoon.'

'It might be best if she couldn't hold a spoon,' retorted Lisabeh tartly, marvelling that Gwynne could be so observant about

Azura's health yet so completely obtuse about what was happening right in her own household. Charles was dying by inches, and it was terrible to witness.

On Christmas Day he rallied. Rhys had given him a bottle of whisky and, in an echo of the way Lawrence Rennie had celebrated Christmases long ago, he sat outside in the leafy shade of the orchard and drank it steadily, looking into his glass from time to time as if the liquid contained some secret he sought.

From where she worked peeling potatoes to tuck around their roast-chicken dinner Lisabeth watched him. He was drawn and trembly now, a palsied old man, not the blustering obnoxious Charles she had so rigorously battled against. It made her sad to see him shrunken inside the shroud of his pugnacity.

So absorbed was she in observing him that she didn't realize that Gwynne had walked up beside her and was watching, too, until she suddenly said: 'I'll miss him terribly, you know.'

Lisabeth swung round, shocked. Gwynne looked at her sadly and nodded. 'Yes, I know, dear. I try to pretend it isn't going to happen, but that won't help. He's going to leave us, and soon.'

'Oh, Aunty . . .,' said Lisabeth, too stricken to deny it. 'Oh, I'm so sorry!' And she put her hands on Gwynne's shoulders in a helpless gesture of comfort.

'Don't cry,' chided Gwynne. 'Andrew will be back from Mists of Heaven soon, and we're supposed to be having a happy day.'

Lisabeth was basting the chicken when Andrew came pounding through the door, gasping: 'It's Uncle Charles . . . he's raving, blathering on about Uncle Rhys and seven-month babies of all things. I think he's gone mad!'

Wiping her hands on her apron, Lisabeth dashed outside, with Gwynne limping painfully after her, but by the time she reached the wooden bench under the pear tree Charles had lapsed into a stupor with his chin resting on his chest, breathing raspingly. Lisabeth picked up the empty bottle. 'Let's get him inside,' she said.

He woke that evening, when his bellows roused Gwynne, Lisabeth and Andrew who were whiling away the time with a pleasant game of Royal Parcheesi. 'Send the boy in here!' he roared. 'It's time he knew the truth!'

'What 'truth'?' asked Andrew, shaking the dice in their tiny ivory cup.

Lisabeth's face was white in the golden lamplight. 'I think he's got a bad head from the whisky,' she explained and, urging

Gwynne to stay where she was, she hurried into the bedroom where Charles was sitting up in bed, shouting. She stooped to light the candle beside him and when she stood up saw that a ribbon of vomit and blood had made a running wound of his mouth. 'I'll fetch a sponge,' she said.

'You'll fetch Andrew,' he told her, his eyes hard with determination. 'There's things he should know and, by the powers, I'm going to ascertain him of the facts!'

Lisabeth shut the door quickly, then walked over to the washstand. 'What facts are those, Uncle Charles?' she said lightly, though it was an effort to keep her voice steady.

When she reached out to dab at his beard he dashed her hand with the wash-cloth away. 'Ay, but you've a devious one, aren't you?' he said nastily. 'A slattern and the daughter of a slattern, too. Ay, you know what I'm on about. Rhys! Rhys Morgan, that's what!' His voice climbed until he was shrieking into her terrified face. 'It's time the lad knew all there is to know about Rhys bloody Morgan!'

'Be quiet!' hissed Lisabeth desperately, still trying to dab the wash-cloth at his mouth.

Charles fell back on to the pillows, gasping with exhaustion. His rheumy eyes had retracted so far back into their sockets that he seemed to be glaring at her from the inner recesses of his skull. He was weakened, enfeebled, but when he spoke it was in a blasting shout, with every vibration of energy he could strum together. 'Come in here, lad!' he bellowed past her, and as he recovered from that effort he panted: 'You're a dirty slut, and don't deny it. That land of Braddock's – don't tell me he gave it to you out of kindness! Then there's Rhys . . . What are you doing for him, lass? The same as your slut of a mother did?' 'His fingers knotted in the bedcover as he crowed: 'It's time young Andrew knew the truth about you, and about Mary, sure, and about who his father—'

Lisabeth couldn't endure his taunts. Dimly she wondered why he hadn't flaunted all this at her before, but perhaps he had been waiting for the truth to come out of its own accord, and now with the combination of a monumental hangover and the knowledge of his own impending death all his spite and poison bubbled over, until he was driven by his own private devils into spitting it out.

'Stop it!' she cried, grabbing at his hands and shaking him. 'They're vile lies! None of this is true!'

'It's the truth, and you know it. Sure and it's time the lad were told that Rhys—'

344

'Stop it!' shrieked Lisabeth, thrusting the wet wash-cloth over Charles's mouth and holding it there. 'Stop it at once, you vicious old man! Haven't you poisoned my life enough with your—' She broke off and lifted her hand away from Charles's still slack mouth. His eyes were still staring at her, but there was something vacant in them now. His breathing had stopped.

'Oh, no!' she cried, and her voice soared in horror. 'Oh, no! *No!*' Grabbing his shoulders, she shook him. His head flopped forward.

'What's the matter? Why all the shouting about Uncle Rhys?' asked Andrew, and wheeling around Lisabeth saw that he stood in the doorway with Gwynne peering around his shoulder.

'I'm sorry,' Lisabeth said, stupid with disbelief. 'One moment we were roaring at each other and the next . . .' She shrugged. There was nothing to say. Nothing but the terrible possibility that she might have killed him, and how could she say that? How could she possibly explain what had happened? 'Aunty Gwynne, he's . . . he's dead!'

Gwynne hobbled past her. 'I'll be all right, dear. Just leave me alone with him,' she said when Lisabeth reached out a hand to her. So Lisabeth and Andrew went out to the orchard.

'We'd better send for Rhys, I suppose,' said Lisabeth, thinking that last year they had disrupted his Christmas Day with the discovery of Gwynne's illness. Now, one year to the day later, it was Charles who had died.

'What was he saying?'

'What?' Lisabeth was slumped on the bench where Charles had been most of the day. She was staring at her hands in the light from the cottage windows. *Did I do it?* she wondered.

'We could hear Uncle Charles from the other room, you know. Aunty Gwynne was trying to talk loud so that I couldn't hear, but I still caught most of it. He wanted to tell me something, didn't he? Something about Uncle Rhys.'

'No,' said Lisabeth quickly. Raising her head, she appealed: 'Please understand, people sometimes do say things . . . It was the whisky talking. He was ill, Andrew, and he had to take very strong medicine. Mixed with the whisky it made him imagine things.'

There was a long silence. The night was filled with the scratchings of insects and the faint unpleasant odour of rotting weeds from the neglected gardens. A ripple of laughter erupted from one of the cockatoos' cottages.

'You're lying,' Andrew burst out suddenly. 'There's something to do with Uncle Rhys going on and you don't want me to know what it is. You just think I'm a baby, don't you? Well, I'm not!' he shouted at her, and in the patchy light his face looked furious, and so like his helpless-baby rages of long ago that she had an inappropriate desire to smile. But she couldn't; this was no smiling matter.

'Your age has nothing to do with it,' she told him.

'I have a right to know!'

'Andrew, please believe me. . . .'

'I don't believe you!' He was glaring.

'Then, please listen at least,' she said helplessly.

'No, I won't listen! You're lying to me! I know you are. Uncle Charles wanted to tell me something and you . . . you stopped him!' Too angry to continue, he flung away indoors and banged the door shut behind him, leaving Lisabeth still sitting on the bench.

Yes, I stopped him, she thought.

THIRTY-TWO

Now THAT CHARLES WAS DEAD everybody expected Lisabeth to go back and live with Gwynne. Lisabeth herself expected it, too, but to her horror she discovered that the accident or deliberate act that had precipitated Charles's death was ground into her consciousness so deeply that she was unable to rid herself of the guilt. Again and again she relived that moment when she pressed the cloth over his mouth to stop the torrent of accusations. Had she used too much force? Would Charles be alive still if she hadn't tried to stop him shouting out the truth about Rhys and Andrew? Or had she simply been unlucky and chosen the very moment to smother his words when his heart was jolting on the very brink of stopping for ever?

Whatever the answer, the question haunted her. She was unable at first to go to sleep in the cottage, and then when the nightmares intensified she was unable even to lie down. It was as if Charles was driving her out of his home just as he had done when he was alive. Without sleep Lisabeth grew haggard and tormented by exhaustion. Everything, even a simple act of brewing a cup of tea, became an ordeal filled with the hazards of scalds and burns.

One day shortly after the funeral Rhys came in and found her dabbing butter on a blistered wrist. When she raised her head to tell him that Gwynne was in the other room, he was shocked by the desolation in her face. Her eyes, usually so bright that the whole world reflected in them, were listless and dull with fatigue.

'Lisabeth!' His own smile faded, and he instinctively put his arms out to gather her against his chest, but stopped just in time and stepped back a pace. 'Lisabeth, you look terrible.'

'Thank you.' She twisted her mouth wryly.

'This is too much for you, isn't it?' he asked her.

She nodded, then raised her face again. 'Rhys, I don't know what to do. I can't . . . I can't stay here. I'm sorry, I can't explain it . . .' Her voice faltered as if every word was a separate effort.

'Then, don't,' he said quickly. 'Birdie Nevin gets on splendidly with Gwynne. She'd leap at the chance to come and live with her. Look, Gwynne is my responsibility as much as she is yours. Let me do this for both of you.'

'Would you? Oh, would you? I'd be so grateful . . .'

'Don't be.' It was deliberately brusque, as he turned away.

She stopped him with one hand on his sleeve, her fingers plucking tentatively at the cloth. He turned back so quickly that he hated himself. 'Thank you,' she whispered. That was all. Even as worn and bedraggled as she was she was capable of teasing him.

He took a deep breath and said with deliberate coldness: 'I must go. I only have a few minutes to spend with Gwynne. I promised to take Azura and the babies to visit at Benares.'

With satisfaction he noticed the hurt in her eyes. She shrank away at once. 'Don't let me keep you,' she said.

'I won't,' he promised.

Gwynne accepted Lisabeth's decision to go with the same equanimity with which she accepted everything else, but Andrew was bitterly resentful and badgered her to stay, refusing to listen to her pleas that it was impossible.

'I try to explain, but he won't be persuaded,' she sighed to Joe Day as he sat on the grass nearby with Bollan, watching as she painted a view of the harbour. Joe often stopped by when he had ferried his mother over for a visit with Gwynne. 'Nothing I do seems right any more.'

'He doesn't want you to be talked about,' said Joe frankly. 'He's a young man and he's sensitive about things like that. Besides, you must admit your reasons for wanting to live alone are pretty flimsy.'

And they're the only reasons I'm giving, thought Lisabeth as she felt the warmth staining her skin. 'I thought the gossips had tired of me ages ago,' she said.

'Don't you believe it!' laughed Joe. 'Seriously, though, Lisabeth—'

'If it's serious, then I don't want to listen,' she told him.

Perhaps it was because of the mystery surrounding the events of

Charles's death, but Andrew now began to spend more and more time at Mists of Heaven. Rhys encouraged him, for despite that lingering antipathy there were lots of qualities about the lad that he liked, subtle things that reminded him of Lisabeth. He had a fine mind, too, and Rhys was quick to appreciate what an enriching experience education was for him. Andrew had always idolized Rhys, but now he transferred that feeling to the environment in which Rhys lived, the map room where Andrew pored for hours over the collections of fascinating old documents and the library with its bookshelves so tall that a ladder on wheels was needed to reach the upper rows of leather-bound volumes. For Andrew, this was Paradise.

Rhys made him welcome. 'It's a pleasure to have the rooms used,' he said. 'I don't utilize them as fully as I should, and rooms like these should be appreciated.'

Azura, however, disliked Andrew from the moment she first saw him, when the likeness to Rhys startled her. Normally neither observant nor perceptive, Azura instinctively sensed that here was a ghost from the past.

'He reminds me of you,' she said, watching for a reaction.

It was not what she expected. 'Leonie used to say that, and it annoyed me unutterably,' he snapped. Azura retreated at once; comparisons with Leonie were both odious and threatening. She had seen Leonie often, in town, seen her laughing and flirting with Rhys, felt the sting of her patronizing glance, her expression that said: 'What a fat, ugly wife Rhys has!' Even a mention of Leonie was enough to shut Azura in her boudoir for the afternoon with a huge box of chocolates for comfort.

What annoyed Azura even more was the way Daisy developed an instant affection for Andrew and toddled after him, calling his name as soon as his voice was heard in the hall whenever he arrived and gave his cap to Siobhan. 'I want her kept away from the boy,' she instructed Lena Merryman, but the nurse was as lazy as her mistress. In the afternoons while Azura dozed or nibbled sweets Miss Merryman read penny novelettes while with one foot she rocked the cradle in which Darius slept. He was the child she liked. From the first he was a placid baby, while Daisy argued with everything, questioned everything and shrieked to the rafters if she didn't immediately get her own way. How much easier it was for Miss Merryman to ignore the girl and allow her to roam all over the house if she wished, so she ignored Azura's directives, too, and now, when Andrew visited Mists of Heaven at weekends and in holiday times, invariably Daisy came to sit at his feet, watching him with her pale eyes, copying everything he did, pretending to read and turning the page of her book whenever he turned one of his.

'Do you think it's wise, dear, allowing Daisy to spend time alone with that boy?' asked Lady Launcenolt when she arrived one day to visit and, hearing giggles from the Library, found Daisy combing Andrew's hair while he was copying a page of verse from an old collection of poetry. 'There's something covertly *intimate* about their friendship that seems vaguely wrong to me,' she fretted, wringing her large hands. 'I mean to say, one should be so careful.'

Alarmed, Azura decided to dismiss Miss Merryman, but then thought about the time and effort involved in hiring another nurse so simply reprimanded her instead. 'Instruct Siobhan to let you know the minute he arrives, then take Daisy out for a walk or, better still, teach her to ride that wretched pony that Rhys insisted on buying for her. And, Miss Merryman,' she added as the nurse turned to go, 'don't let Daisy see your sour face. I'm having enough trouble with her as it is!'

Andrew was relieved. 'Now that I see less of Daisy I enjoy my study periods up there more,' he confided to Lisabeth. 'She's a nice little girl but such a pest, and what I like most about Mists of Heaven is the feeling that I've got those huge serious rooms all to myself. I really feel at home up here, at peace, somehow. It's as if, in some weird way, I actually belong there.'

Lisabeth frowned. At heart she envied Andrew and his access to such marvellous books and the riches they contained, but now she worried. A shiver of apprehension rippled over her. Andrew felt at home in Rhys's house. He was at peace there. And Daisy, poor lass, who was neglected by her mother in favour of the boy, sensed somehow the bond between herself and Andrew and responded to its pull. Lisabeth sank into worried thought as she gazed unseeingly out towards the far rim of the peninsula, towards the huddle of square-shouldered rocks. On the sunlit slope of the crater bowl a scattering of sheep straggled upwards, their many-toned bleats drifting in chords on the wind. Life was as usual, it was a ripe autumn day, but Lisabeth felt uneasy.

'Perhaps some day I could live there,' mused Andrew.

'Perhaps some day you'll have an even grander house of your own,' said Lisabeth, ruffling his hair to mask her own disquiet. 'All you'll have to do is work hard and be extremely charming to your rich patients! Now tell me, are we going together on the celebration ride when the steam train goes through the tunnel on the opening of the new Ferrymead-to-Lyttelton line?'

'Rather!' he exclaimed, his eyes alight. 'And could we go to the luncheon first? They say that thousands of people are going to dine inside the tunnel itself, and tens of thousands of candles will be standing on rock shelves along the walls to give light. Do say we can go!'

Lisabeth looked perturbed. 'I'd like to, but I can't afford that, dear. My paintings aren't doing as well as I'd hoped, and everything is so frightfully expensive –' She broke off, dismayed by the downcast expression. 'I do try, Andrew,' she said gently.

He shrugged away. 'I hate being poor!' he snapped at her suddenly. 'It's all your fault. If you'd married Rhys instead of Mr Nye, then we'd have plenty of money, wouldn't we?' And before she could reply he stormed away, running up the hill in the direction of Mists of Heaven, knowing that she would never follow him there.

But his words hurt, and when next day he told her that Rhys had invited him along to the luncheon and that he had accepted she found it difficult to smile.

'It was Daisy's idea,' he reported. 'Uncle Rhys has to go to be in the official party with Sir Kenneth, and Mrs Morgan doesn't want to go – she gets claustrophobia – so Uncle Rhys said nobody would mind if I went along instead. You don't mind, do you?' he added artlessly, selecting a plum from the bowl on her table and sinking his teeth into it. 'It'll save you the money from our train tickets.'

Lisabeth's temper inflamed. Whisking the bowl out of reach before he could take another, she said: 'I'll take Aunty Gwynne instead.' Even as she spoke she knew she wouldn't go. She really couldn't afford it.

Money was short all winter. Andrew had grown so tall that his entire winter wardrobe needed replacing, and Lisabeth had to scrimp and almost starve herself, cutting down on everything to pay the bills at the drapers who supplied the King's College uniforms. It was no use asking Gwynne for help; though Rhys was paying her an allowance to meet expenses, he was unaware that Charles had died leaving debts all over town, debts that Gwynne would be scraping a long time to discharge, but when Lisabeth asked why she didn't tell Rhys about her financial difficulties

Gwynne was horrified. 'I want Rhys to think well of Mr Stafford, you know that,' she chided. 'Besides, this is the worst year for sheep stations in the history of the colony.'

'I'm sure he's not wondering where his next meal is coming from,' retorted Lisabeth tartly.

Her comment was equally sharp when, after Christmas, Andrew asked her for two guineas to buy a birthday gift for Daisy. After saying *No* in the bluntest terms and adding a few observations about the material wealth that surrounded the girl, Lisabeth relented. 'Why don't you make her something absolutely magnificent?' she suggested. 'A doll's house, or a snow-sled, or even a wagon to be towed behind her pony. She'd appreciate something you'd made yourself.'

'A kite!' he said, already fired with enthusiasm. 'These hill-tops will be the perfect place for flying kites, and I have the pattern for making the hugest, most splendiferous kite you could possibly imagine! Unless,' he pondered, frowning, 'unless a hot-air balloon might be better. I know how to make one of wicker-work with a paper skin, and a burner underneath. Yes, that would—'

'No,' said Lisabeth quickly. 'A kite would be much more suitable for a four-year-old girl. Nobody could possibly be hurt by a kite.'

He constructed it of tissue paper, string and split bamboo over several rainy evenings and in a fever of excitement. Lisabeth watched him fondly, thinking that these evenings could almost be counted now, that in two or three years he would be leaving to study overseas. It was as if he knew how close to maturity he was and with this kite was relishing the few remnants of childhood that remained.

When finished, the kite was as 'splendiferous' as promised, a gigantic red and orange creature painted with a Chinese lion's face and body and with a long red tail made of elegant bow-ties. Andrew hung it from the rafters to dry in the fire's warmth and then peered out into the night. 'It's stopped raining and the wind's up! If it's like this tomorrow, it will be perfect kite weather.'

'Birthdays should always be fine,' mused Lisabeth, bent over knitting-needles beside the fire. 'I don't know why, but if it's sunny on my birthday I am in the best of spirits, but if it rains I brood about dying. I wonder why that is.'

'Dying!' Andrew bolted the door.

'Only on my birthday, for some reason.' She smiled reassuringly at him. 'Honestly, Andrew. I'm only nine years older than you, but sometimes I feel more like your grandmother than your sister. Still, I'm glad you're going up there to celebrate with Daisy tomorrow. Only . . .'

'Only what?'

She frowned. 'I was going to say "Only be careful". Stupid of me . . .'

'Yes, Granny,' said Andrew, smiling.

When Andrew arrived at Mists of Heaven carrying the kite above his head both the children were down in the courtyard with Miss Merryman. Daisy shrieked with delight when she saw it, and Darius immediately gurgled gleefully and toddled after the long, dragging tail, flopping on to his cushioned bottom to snatch at the bow-ties.

'Leave it alone! It's mine! Miss Merryman, make him leave my kite alone!' screamed Daisy, stamping her foot so hard that her yellow ringlets jiggled. Her pale eyes distended with the threat of tears.

'Hush, you'll disturb your mother,' scolded Miss Merryman, a plump middle-aged woman with curly black hair and a severe grey gown. She hesitated. She should whisk Daisy away, but it was the child's birthday after all. 'Take the kite around to the lawn, Andrew. You and Daisy can play with it there. But do be quiet, will you?' And, scooping up Darius, she meandered off towards the kitchen, where she found a sugar-tit for him and put him down beside a basket of kittens while she settled to have a cup of tea and a gossip with the cook, a woman from her own home county of Sussex.

Today the kittens had lost their usual fascination for Darius. He was thinking about the splendid kite, of the bright swirling colours in the design and that jaunty, bouncing, sinuous tail. While Miss Merryman and the cook chatted he climbed to his feet and tottered, unnoticed, out of the room.

On the south side of the mansion was a broad apron of lawn with a spectacular view of ocean, plains and mountains. Sheltered on two sides by a walled orangery, the lawn was fringed by geometrically exact beds of roses swelling into flower and thick mats of velvet pansies. In the centre of the grassy sward, set in glazed tiles, lay a large octagonal fish-pond where faint pink shapes glided under fleshy heart-shaped lily-pads. After all the rain the grass was sodden and the glazed tiles were littered with wadded petals, but there was a sharp perfect breeze buffeting in from the ocean and plenty of room here to run.

'I'll show you what to do first,' said Andrew, darting into the wind and unwinding the kite-string as he went.

The kite soared, dipping and curtsying from side to side, its tail swimming behind it.

Daisy skipped along, laughing. 'It's so beautiful! Oh, please, Andwew, let me hold it!'

'Are you strong enough?' he teased. 'It's pulling like a big snapper on the fishing-line, you know.'

' 'Course I'm strong enough!' Daisy stamped her elegantly booted foot and smacked at the front of her blue and white spotted, ruffled gown. 'Let me! It's mine now!'

The kite was well aloft now, so Andrew put the winding-stick into Daisy's hands. Whooping joyfully, she ran along, jerking on the string so that the kite dipped into a wide, looping spiral. To her it looked like a giant butterfly and a whole flock of baby butterflies circling against the sun, so bright that it made her dizzy. She stopped, and as soon as she did so the kite flagged and began to drop in the sky.

'Andwew, help me! It's going wrong!' she cried, tugging at the string harder but failing to stop the downward plunge. By the time Andrew reached her the kite was fluttering, sighing, to rest on the grass, and Daisy was flinging a fit of screaming exasperation. At that moment, too, Darius was toddling earnestly around the edge of the rose-beds, but neither Andrew nor Daisy saw him.

There it was! The magical kite, lying on the lawn like a resting bird with its tail curved in a gigantic S on the tiles that edged the lily-pond. Hurrying as fast as his kid- leather bootees would carry him Darius pounded purposefully towards it.

Andrew was laughing, making Daisy laugh, too. 'Let's run together and make it dive upwards into the sky,' he said. 'Come on, are you ready? One, two, three, *go!*'

The string of beautiful bow-ties twitched. Darius was almost there; his chubby starfish hands opened and closed and he tottered faster. The tail skidded away along the tiles. Darius opened his mouth to call to it. His legs beat fast across the last of the lawn and he stepped on to the smooth glazed tiles. They were slippery, splattered with wet petals, and Darius' little boots were slicked underneath with moisture from the grass. His feet slipped together, he slid a few inches, then jolted over backwards with full

354

force, striking the back of his head on the stone edging before rolling, unconscious, into the pool.

There was no splash. The lily-pads parted and gave way under his weight, then floated up around him while the whole quilted surface of the pool swelled and sagged a few times as if an enormous heart had pulsed for several seconds, then stopped. There was no sound. Andrew and Daisy, laughing together as they launched the kite, were not even aware of what had happened. It was not until Miss Merryman tardily shifted herself to come looking for him that his body was discovered.

From where she was spreading damp laundry out over flax bushes around the cottage Lisabeth heard the screaming and knew at once that something terrible had occurred. There had been those vague feelings of unease, that sharp premonition last night when she wanted to warn Andrew to be careful, and now . . . It seemed he'd only been gone five minutes . . . Her heart shrank with dread.

Without even pausing to untie her apron Lisabeth fled up the hill. Except for that one night before her wedding she had kept right away from Mists of Heaven, vowing never to go near the place again; but this was different, there was trouble and all her instincts warned her that Andrew was involved.

At the top of the hill she skimmed a stile over a stock-fence and threaded her way through a thicket of ornamental shrubs before bursting out on to the edge of the lawn, calling his name as she ran.

He came to meet her, staggering across the bright grass, his face grey. 'It's terrible . . . terrible!' he babbled, and she could see that he was struggling not to cry. Behind him in a grim tableau near the pond horror itself was being enacted. Several of the Nevin youngsters had clustered there and the nurse, all of whom were in uniform. There was also a blowzy fair woman in a wide cream lace crinoline and lace house-cap – Azura, guessed Lisabeth, for she had glimpsed her sometimes in her carriage. Rhys was there, too, on his knees, on the grass, working on the sodden corpse of his son, and therein lay the horror. The Nevins and the other servants could see the boy was dead, for all were sobbing in frightened abbreviated gasps, and Azura could see it, too, and shouted at him to stop, to leave the child in peace. Even at this distance the hopelessness was immediately obvious to Lisabeth; she had seen enough dead animals to recognize that

355

sagging inertia, but though the boy's face was already turning blue under its slimy caul of pond mucus Rhys refused to accept that he had gone. He was desperately trying to resuscitate him, flexing the tiny arms and pumping the diminutive chest, and while he worked he was talking to Darius as if he was alive, telling him that he loved him, that he had made plans for him – such wonderful plans! – that he must try to breathe, try harder. Ignoring his wife's shouted commands to leave the child be, he worked frantically, as if he was alone with his son. 'Come on, Darrie!' he repeated over and over again. 'Come on, Darrie! I know you can do it!'

There was such love and such vain hope throbbing in his voice that hearing it Lisabeth's heart swelled with compassion. She wanted to reach out to him, for she understood exactly what torment he was undergoing, and to witness it was to share his pain. This is how it had been for her when Mary died. She had been convinced that if only she could keep clinging to her mother, somehow keep the lines of communication open, then Mary could not slip away from her.

She stood a distance away in silence, leaning against Andrew. Once Rhys raised his head and gazed in her direction, but his face was bleak, his eyes empty, and she knew that he had not seen her. In his world there was nobody but his son.

The doctor arrived, a stocky hearty-looking man with large gingery mutton-chop whiskers. Lisabeth thought that he looked more like a publican than a distinguished doctor but she soon saw how efficient he was. Within a few seconds he had checked for a pulse, listened for a heartbeat and flipped the eyelids in turn to examine beneath them, and all the while Rhys tried to push him away.

'I'm sorry, Mr Morgan, you tried your best, but there's nothing more to be done,' he said.

Azura screamed. Rhys raised a haggard face to the doctor, who was standing up now, folding his stethoscope. 'Do something, damn you!' he demanded. 'Purge him! Bleed him! Do anything . . . anything. Don't just stand there making pronouncements. You're the *doctor*, damn you!'

'That's absolutely true. I'm a doctor, not a magician. The boy's been dead for some time. I'm truly sorry, sir, but it's over. 'He turned to Azura, who was dabbing at her swollen eyes. 'My condolences, madam. I do sympathize, my dear. The loss of a son is a cruel blow, especially a first son as this lad was . . . But please take heart. You'll have other sons. God in his wisdom will comfort you. . . .'

Azura bunched the handkerchief in her fist. 'Not with more sons, He won't!' she hissed. 'There'll be no more children for me, I can tell you that right now. This is his fault! This would never have happened if he hadn't encouraged that . . . that . . . smarmy irresponsible guttersnipe over there to come into our home!'

Rhys showed no sign of having heard the outburst, but the doctor was aghast. 'Mrs Morgan, please!' And he muttered to Miss Merryman to fetch a vinaigrette and quickly.

'She's not to fetch anything! She's dismissed, as from this moment. Go and pack your bags, Miss Merryman. And I'll thank you not to have the impudence to ask me for a reference. I don't want anything to delay your departure. You, too,' she called, raising her voice in Lisabeth's direction. 'It's your fault, too, spreading poison into our lives. Just look at this, both of you! See what you've done!'

She doesn't really care, thought Lisabeth, regarding Azura with pity. *She's lashing out, blaming everybody because if it's anybody's fault it's hers. She probably neglected that poor little wretch, too, and by screaming accusations now she's trying to hide her own guilt. But did she really love the baby? I doubt it.*

'You!' Azura was rasping at Andrew now. 'I never want to see you again! You're not to set foot on this property, ever. Is that clear?'

Lisabeth glanced at Andrew. His face was ashen, and his lips parted as if he had been struck. Being banned from Mists of Heaven was obviously a cruel blow to him.

And to Daisy. She had been hanging back fearfully, too young to comprehend the severity of what had happened yet fully conscious that Darius was dead and in some roundabout way it all had to do with Andrew and the birthday kite. When her mother issued the edict against him that was crisp and plain enough for her to understand immediately. If Andrew was unable to visit Mists of Heaven, she would never see him again. Pushing forward between the servants' skirts, she flung herself at her mother, shrieking.

'No, Mamma, no! Andwew's my special fwend! You can't send him away!' she wailed. As she bellowed she grabbed the cream lace skirts in both fists, rocking Azura's crinoline so that intermittent glimpses of fat cream-stockinged ankles showed.

'Stop it,' said Azura, but when Daisy continued to wail she drew back a cushiony beringed hand and slapped the child so hard that Daisy rocked back and would have fallen if Siobhan Nevin hadn't been there to catch her.

Sickened, Lisabeth turned away. 'Come,' she urged Andrew, tugging at his arm. 'Come on, there's nothing we can do.'

He shook her hand off. 'The *witch!* . . . It wasn't my fault at all! I'll have it out with her. I'll—'

'Please, Andrew. Don't . . .'

His face was tense. 'Uncle Rhys must know it isn't my fault. Why doesn't he stand up for me?'

Still tugging at his arm, Lisabeth glanced back to where Rhys knelt, head bent over the body he cradled tenderly in his arms. She ached to go to him. If only she could walk over there and kneel beside him, put her arms around him and let the love that was welling up inside her spill over on to him, she could soothe his grief, she could ease his torment. But she had no right to go near him, no right even to be here, for that matter.

'Why didn't he stand up for me?' repeated Andrew bitterly.

Lisabeth said: 'Rhys didn't even see you, dear. He didn't hear a word of what his wife said.' Privately she was thankful for that.

THIRTY-THREE

'**I**'M WORRIED ABOUT RHYS,' fretted Gwynne when Lisabeth arrived for her usual morning visit. 'Three times now I've gone up there of an afternoon only to be virtually shown the door. Birdie tells me that Mrs Morgan keeps to her room all the time now, and she's got that Lady What's-her-name there and two of the darkies looking after her.'

'And how does that connect to worries about Rhys?' asked Lisabeth lightly as she hung up her bonnet, donned an apron and took up the long poker to stir the fire.

'There's been quarrels, Birdie says. She's hinted in the past that Rhys and his wife don't get on, and I've seen the evidence with my own eyes. I mean to say, what kind of a woman would quarrel with her husband at their first child's *christening*, I ask you! But now there's open warfare, shouting and doors slamming, and Lady What's it galloping downstairs in a tizz for pots of camomile tea to calm Mrs Morgan's poor nerves. Birdie says it's all taking a burden on Rhys. He spends all his day away from the house and every evening takes his dinner in the map room alone and then goes for long walks until the early hours. They're even keeping Daisy away from him. If you ask me, that boy's death has wreaked havoc on him.'

Lisabeth kept her back turned so that Gwynne would not see her face. Straining to keep her voice casual, she said; 'If you ask *me*, Aunty Gwynne, you're as much of a gossip as Uncle Charles ever was!'

'Listen to me, young lady,' responded Gwynne. 'If married couples were as happy – as blissfully happy – and as devoted, as me and Mr Stafford were, then this poor old world would have a sight fewer problems.'

Distance lends enchantment even to sour Uncle Charles, thought Lisabeth wryly. She still felt as if his wraith was hovering near her, but towards Charles himself she now felt no animosity. His bullying antagonism had shaped her life, often exerting pressure in the wrong place and causing her to veer off in disastrous tangents as in her marriage to Athol, but most of her resentment had been over his selfish behaviour towards Gwynne, and if Gwynne now wanted to remember him as an angel who was she to contradict?

That evening she saw Rhys when she was outside gathering herbs for the mussel stew she was preparing for her dinner. He was walking away in the distance, towards the headland where the circle of stones stood pale in the dying sunlight against the dark ocean beyond. At first she did not recognize him, for he was walking with head down and shoulders hunched, but he paused for a moment to glance out towards the Sumner Bar and she saw that it was him, so solitary and beaten-looking that her heart wrung with pity for him.

She watched him for some time then with the sensation of being wrenched away turned resolutely and entered her cottage, shutting the door and closing off her view of the peninsula. As she chopped the herbs and stirred them into the fragrant fish broth she thought about him, and when she tipped the basin of scrubbed mussels in and covered the pot she stood staring at the empty tin basin for a long time. Her heart was so heavy that she knew she would be unable to eat anything.

Lisabeth wished she had not seen him. She walked to the door, then took her hand from the bolt and walked back to the fire. The stew was bubbling; she took it off the fire and placed the pot on a cool part of the hearth. Again she went to the door, again she walked away from it. On the third journey she plucked her cloak and bonnet from their pegs behind the door and slipped outside quickly, before she could change her mind again.

Darkness was already blotting the landscape. When Lisabeth stepped out into the open a sharp wind sliced in from the sea, stinging her eyes, hurrying her fingers as they fumbled with her cloak-buttons. A scum of sudsy cloud was thickening over the horizon, warning that another spring storm was on its way. Shivering, Lisabeth thrust her hands into her cloak-sleeves and strode out across the rough ground.

She was crazy, she knew that. Rhys would tell her to go away, tell her to tend to her own affairs, for what did he want of her condolences? She could hear Bollan whining from where he was still chained up behind the cottage and hesitated before deciding not to take him. 'I'll be back to feed you soon, boy,' she called over her shoulder.

The ridges and craters of this headland were a source of endless fascination to Andrew, who had described to her in detail how millions of years ago molten rock had forced its way through fissures in the volcano walls and, hardening on exposure to the air, formed ridges, dikes and these mossy Stonehenge-like structures that loomed up out of the ground at her as she hurried past. Knowing how they evolved did not lessen her trepidation and she tried not to look down into the yawning blackness of the crater. It was like a vast mouth with these rotten teeth protruding up all around.

Before climbing the far hill-top the path dipped into a trough of shade. Hugging her cloak around her, Lisabeth scurried through it, biting back a cry of fright when she turned her ankle on a loose stone and lurched, almost falling. She ran the last few yards to the crest of the hill.

Rhys was sitting on a flat stone, shoulders hunched, his fair hair ruffling. He was wearing working clothes and was smoking a thin cigar. Lisabeth came to a halt a pace behind him, her face warm under the smack of the wind. He was not aware of her presence.

Below and beyond lay a darkening world, the restless shadowy sea that boomed and sighed, smothering the silence with a blanket of sound. To the east stretched a vague tumble of cliffs and black rocky slopes, diminishing into the distance where, on the furthermost point, a tiny stone lighthouse stood, its swivelling eye winking a light into the gathering dusk.

Lisabeth said: 'I've never been out here before. It's beautiful.'

He turned part of the way towards her then away again. When he did that she braced herself, expecting to be told to go back, but he said: 'The Maoris say that these hill-tops are inhabited by the *turehu*, the fairies who play flutes and sing in the mists. I wonder if it's true.' His voice was low and weary, as if he was reading something aloud without understanding, nor caring what it was. 'In the winter the mists come right up to the house.'

'Yes,' said Lisabeth quickly. 'I look out in the mornings and think I'm in the clouds. Mists of Heaven . . . perhaps it is true.'

'Mists of Heaven is a joke,' he said harshly, and lifted a bottle to his lips before putting it back out of sight below the stone on which he sat.

Lisabeth's scalp crawled when she saw that. This was no place

361

for Rhys to be drinking, out here where the cliffs dropped a sheer three hundred feet into the surf. She bit her lip nervously. He said: 'My favourite place, this. It reminds me of Home.'

'The Ballakelly Circle.'

'You . . . how do you know that?'

'Aunty Gwynne said that the first day we rowed over here to look at the land. That's why I've never come out here before. I imagined the "Buggane" lurking here.'

'Ah, the "Buggane",' he said without interest, and again the bottle rippled gold as he tipped it up. 'The frightful one who can tear trees up by the roots and crush cottages and scatter the timbers like breadcrumbs. He can't hurt you, Lisabeth. Save your fears for the real demons in life, the ones we invent ourselves. They are the ones to beware of, Lisabeth. They wield the power, and do you know why?' He waggled his cigar at her. 'Because *we* give them the power. We invent demons, we breathe life into them and invest in them power to hurt us. And, my God, they do!'

How true that is, thought Lisabeth, reflecting on her failed marriage, on the guilt over Charles's death, on all the useless wasted pain she had inflicted on herself in hating Rhys. *I made my own demon and, my God, it hurt me beyond endurance.*

He tipped the bottle up, drained it and hurled it high in an arc over the cliff's edge. The sun flecked it with light before it dropped away into the darkness.

'I didn't know you drank,' said Lisabeth without thinking.

'Didn't you?' He flung the cigar butt after the bottle and watched the trail of red sparks before turning to her with a crooked smile. 'All men drink, Lisabeth. Men drink and women take to the couch. It's the way of the world. But what about you, Lisabeth? What do you do?'

She wished she hadn't come. She had nothing to offer him, no way of reaching him. 'I only wanted to say how very sorry—' she began.

He stopped her. 'Don't say you're sorry, Lisabeth. I'm sick of the word. What does it mean anyway? Nothing! We're all sorry, sorry we did this, or sorry about that, but what good do our regrets achieve? Nothing! All the regrets in the history of the world heaped up together mean less than one miserable little heap of sh—I mean, one miserable worm-cast. Life goes on, crushing us under our own misfortunes.' He waved one hand in a sweeping gesture towards the ocean. 'What does it matter? We can't go back to pick up the pieces.'

Suddenly she was angry. 'Will you listen to yourself, Rhys Morgan? That's not you talking. That's a beaten pathetic wretch and you're young and strong and – yes – wealthy with a glittering life in front of you. The whole province envies you, yet here you are practically snivelling and feeling sorry for yourself. It doesn't matter that we can't go back, but we can go forward. We can turn our backs on the past and—'

He was on his feet, grabbing her shoulders, shaking her. 'You don't understand, do you? I've lost my son, Lisabeth! My *son*. I lost him when he was still in the nursery. I never got to take him on a horse with me, or show him the station, or teach him to play cricket or how to fish or sail a boat. I wanted to be there every step of the way when he was learning about the world, to share his wonder, to . . . to . . .' He bowed his head, unable to continue.

Lisabeth was stricken. His hair was brushing her face, his fingers were cruel on her shoulders; his pain was her pain. Gently she said: 'Rhys, lots of people lose their sons. You'll have another.'

He shook his head, *no*, and she remembered Azura's angry words, but surely Azura was distraught, she didn't mean it. 'She'll change her mind, Rhys.'

'What?' He raised his head, laughed. 'No, Lisabeth. That wouldn't make any difference. I won't go into details but, believe me, it's final. I had a son, and now he's dead, and I'll never have another. It's a terrible feeling, Lisabeth. Like being condemned to eternal solitude. A man needs a son, someone he can reach out to in the next generation. All that I've worked for here, everything I've built up, was in preparation for that link with the future. Now the link is broken, and I lost my son before I even got a chance to know him. Oh, Lisabeth, if only you could understand . . .'

'I think I do,' she said slowly. Her mind was pelting with a confusion of thoughts. Should she tell him? Should she come up with it now? *You do have a son! You are not alone! Andrew is your son!* Should she? Was it fair to Andrew? Surely if the truth was to come out he should be the first to be told. Besides, it shouldn't be done like this, dragged out on the moment's whim; and Rhys had been drinking, she didn't know how befuddled he might be. Yes, he'd want to be sober when news like this was broken to him.

Yes, I'll tell them, but Andrew first, she decided, her spirits lifting as she contemplated the gift she would bestow on them both. Andrew would be overjoyed. All his life he'd idolized Rhys, and the banning from Mists of Heaven had been a bitter blow. That would be the first thing to be revoked, of course! Perhaps Rhys would invite him to come and live—She stopped herself. There was no point in racing ahead with her imaginings, but it was all such an exciting prospect. When she met Andrew at the coach-stop in the morning she would tell him the whole story, every-thing from the beginning while they walked home together.

Warmed by the resolution Lisabeth sank down on to the rocky ground, closing her eyes and letting the ocean breeze cut cleanly into the rim of her bonnet. *Oh, Rhys, what will you say?* she wondered, hugging herself with anticipation.

There was a faint scraping sound across the surf, and amongst the salt the whiff of cigar smoke. Rhys said: 'I think you do understand, Lisabeth. After all, you lost both your parents and that must have been very distressing, especially . . .' He stopped, contemplated his cigar for a few seconds, then abruptly began on a different tack. 'I was at Oxford when my parents were killed. Gwynne was here, and I never really knew her, but she was family even unknown and such a distance away. At Oxford I was among friends when the news came, but even so it was a terrible shock. Suddenly I was completely alone, adrift in the world. That's how I feel again now.'

'But you're not alone,' said Lisabeth, opening her eyes. Now the darkness was spreading like liquid and the clouds curdled dark, thick and grey, closing in.

'Aren't I?' He was leaning towards her now, the only way he could see her face in the gathering dusk.

'No, you're not alone!' she repeated, her eyes enormous with repressed emotion. 'Oh, Rhys, I've made so many terrible mis-takes . . . I've caused us both such unnecessary pain!'

'Hush, don't say that.' He was bemused, not understanding. She raised one hand to her throat, and he took it in his, lifting it to his face and pressing his mouth into her palm.

Her heart spasmed as the sweetest feelings trickled through her, but still she was absorbed in the enormity of what she would soon tell him. 'Oh, Rhys,' she whispered in joy and placed her other hand against his cheek. It was going to be so wonderful!

It happened by itself, or so it seemed to him, fuzzy as he was from the mixture of grief, fatigue, alcohol and her apparent will-ingness. There had never been a moment since he married that he could feel free of Lisabeth, but he had never once consciously planned to seduce her, either. Now he was suddenly overwhelmed.

He kissed her palm and felt her tremulous response, and the next thing her lips had replaced her hands and he was devouring her with a hunger that tore at him, demanding to be satiated.

For Lisabeth there was a tiny shock when his arms clamped around her and his mouth fastened over hers. It was only the smallest cold hiss of awareness, no more than a little dash of cold water splashed into a fire. For an instant it cleared a space in her mind, a space when she could have – should have – pulled away, but then the flames engulfed her and she was lost in the sensations of his mouth over hers, of his skin burning under the coolness of her fingers. Closing her eyes to the tumultuous darkness, she was lost and it was as if nothing terrible had ever happened to her, not Mary or the pain or her marriage or the shameful taint of gossip. All was swept away in the golden haze of a new and glorious beginning. His arms pulled her hard against him and then relaxed, but still she clung to him and now he was kissing her with a slow and marvellous wonder, with gratitude and tenderness, one hand stroking the smooth column of her throat and the other lifting her skirts, easing her, arranging her, lowering her to the cold bed of rock.

When he took her it was swift and hard and desperate. He tried to hold back, but all his being raced towards her with an energy that he had no hope of restraining. She cried out and clung to him as they meshed together, and it seemed to her that their very blood mingled and their hearts pounded with a single rhythm. Afterwards she stared up at the sky, feeling the warmth of his cheek against hers and the languor of his body damply entwined with her body, and wished that somehow all the complications of their lives could melt away and they could just go forward together from here.

When he pulled away she wanted to reach out, to draw him down to her again, but instinctively she let him go and turned on to her side, drawing her knees up under her skirts, comforting the bereft feeling of emptiness that suddenly invaded her body. It was a feeling as much spiritual as physical, for in the instant he withdrew she was reminded that she had no rights to him, that this was a stolen interlude, no more. A poignant sadness crept over her, but she pushed it away, determined that nothing should sour their meeting, especially not her futile regrets. 'The ocean is such a vast distance below us, but I can feel the drumming of the waves right up here, through the rock,' she said, her voice resolutely light. If there was going to be emotional talk between them, she had decided that it must come first from him.

He was on his feet, staring towards the cottage. She could not see his face and only sensed the tension as he said: 'Lisabeth . . . That's not the waves, it's footsteps . . . Somebody's coming. It's Andrew, I think.'

Before he finished speaking she heard Bollan barking and raised her head to see a wavering light splash over the looming pillars of rock around them. 'Lisabeth!' came Andrew's voice, still a way off. 'Lisabeth, are you all right?'

She tried to scramble up, but Bollan was there before she was even on her knees, jumping up over her, slurping at her face, delaying her so that when Andrew reached them she was still dusting her skirts, her bonnet awry and her cloak unbuttoned.

'I don't believe this,' said Andrew. Lisabeth glanced up at his face, yellow and malevolent above the kerosene-lantern. He was panting, breathless, and he heaved the words out at her. 'I was worried. You weren't there, so I let Bollan go and followed him. He knew where to come. I don't believe this. I just don't . . .'

Lisabeth said: 'Don't be dramatic, Andrew! Rhys and I were just—'

'I know what you were just doing!' He burst out at her in a fury, his breath recovered. 'I'm not a fool. Even if I couldn't see with my own eyes, it doesn't take much imagination to guess what the two of you would be up to out here in the darkness. Not star-gazing, that's for sure! Not on a night like this!'

'That's quite enough, Andrew,' Rhys cut in sternly. 'You've absolutely no right to speak to your sister like that.'

'You keep out of this, you sanctimonious bastard!' cried Andrew. He was so angry he was almost sobbing. 'This is what Uncle Charles was trying to warn me about when he died, wasn't it, Lisabeth? He knew all about you and Rhys and what was going on. That's why you stopped him. You didn't want the truth to come out, and it's no wonder!' His gaze swung accusingly from one to the other, and he was crying now with rage, his face contorted, grotesque in the lamplight. 'Do you want to know something really stupid? When there was gossip about you two, after you left Mr Nye, I stood up for you both! I got in fights, and I was caned, because I dared to punch out anybody who repeated sordid stories about my sister and the man who paid my tuition at school.'

'Andrew, you've got it wrong,' pleaded Lisabeth.

'No, don't try to argue with him, Lisabeth,' said Rhys. 'The rights and wrongs of this don't come into it. The fact is that Andrew has no right to condemn you, or dictate to you. He's—'

'You bastard!' shrieked Andrew, dropping the lamp and hurling himself at Rhys, swinging his fists at him. 'You keep me away from your home over something that wasn't even my fault and now you're telling Lisabeth that her immoral behaviour doesn't matter!' As he spoke he pummelled Rhys, sobbing the words out, punching them home.

Lisabeth was horrified. Snatching the lamp up to save it from tipping over, she retreated until her back bumped against one of the tall standing stones. Slicked in yellow light the two figures struggled, locked in combat, against the perilous background of that precipitous drop only a few feet away. Though Andrew was the smaller and lighter of the two, he had the power of fury on his side, while Rhys was slowed, handicapped by the effects of the whisky he had drunk. Rather than retaliate, he was trying to grasp Andrew's wrists simply to stop him, but the lad was too swift and punches were thumping home on Rhys's chest, neck and face. Rhys cursed, lunged, and the two swayed on the edge of the cliff, while Lisabeth watched and held her breath.

Finally Rhys realized that unless he did something drastic he was going to be quite seriously battered, so with a feeling of resignation and the knowledge that this had to be done convincingly, just once, he drew back his fist and punched Andrew squarely between the eyes with a blow that sent him reeling then staggering to a skidding heap on the rock at Lisabeth's feet, where he flopped on to his side, his arms limp.

Rhys shook his hand, wincing wryly . 'It's a long time since I did that,' he said.

'You've killed him!' whispered Lisabeth, stunned. Setting the light down, she knelt beside her brother's inert form.

'He'll be all right,' Rhys assured her. 'Just a tap to bring him to his senses. He'll come round in a few minutes.'

To Lisabeth this seemed the height of callousness. 'You call that a tap? You utter bully! He's only a young boy, and you —'

'Easy on there, Lisabeth. He was hurting me and I tried to stop him. What would you have done?'

'Not that. Certainly not that!' She turned Andrew on to his back and placed a hand on his brow. 'That was brutal, Rhys. Brutal and uncalled for. Andrew was only trying to defend me, you know he was! You had no right to turn on him so viciously.'

Shaking his head, Rhys stared at her, bemused. 'Have it your way, then,' he said at last. 'I'm a brute and a bully.'

'Right!' she snapped.

'Right,' he agreed. 'Now that's settled, if you'll kindly walk ahead with the lantern I'll carry him home for you so that you can tend his wounds.'

'There's no need to—'

'Oh, be quiet, Lisabeth,' he said, exasperated, and pushed her aside to heft Andrew over his shoulder.

She marched ahead, quivering with indignation yet more miserable than she had felt for a long, long time. She was right to turn on Rhys, she was right to defend Andrew, but the victory Rhys had handed her was a hollow one. None of this showed, however. With back rigid and head held high she opened the cottage door for him so that he could bring Andrew inside and sprawl him on to the chair. Her cold dignity was immaculate.

'Thank you very much,' she said, stiff-lipped. She didn't dare look into his face.

Nor did he look at her. 'Any time,' he said sarcastically. 'It's been a pleasure.'

When he had gone she held the door shut and leaned her brow against it, her body slumped with unhappiness. *I won't cry*, she vowed. *I won't.*

There was a noise at the door and her mind leaped with hope that it might be him, come back to make peace with her, but it was only Bollan scratching to come in for his dinner.

'A great help you were,' Lisabeth scolded as he plunked his hindquarters in front of the fire and, grinning at her, scratched under his chin. 'Why did you have to lead Andrew straight to me? Why didn't you go and chase a rabbit instead?'

Andrew woke an hour later with a ferocious headache, a foul temper and the beginnings of two monstrous black eyes. He dashed away the damp cloth Lisabeth was holding on his forehead. 'Don't touch me,' he said furiously. 'Don't ever touch me again.'

Her heart contracted when she saw the hatred in his eyes. 'Please, Andrew, don't be like this. Please at least listen,' she begged.

'Listen to what? You're both married to other people. It's disgusting! Why didn't you marry Rhys if this is what you wanted? Or would that have been too easy for you? Too respectable, is that it?' He sneered as she drew back her hand and her eyes narrowed. 'Go on, slap me. You might as well have a go, too.'

368

She lowered her hand, defeated. 'I don't want to hurt you. I never wanted to hurt you. Andrew, please believe me, but everything I've done has been for you.'

'Oh, really? Like leaving Mr Nye and making me a laughing-stock at school, and coming to live close to Uncle Rhys so that you can be his mistress, and taking money off him, too, I suppose. Is that what you do for him in return for him paying my school fees? Well, you don't need to worry about that any longer. I wouldn't stay at school another minute knowing it was my sister's immoral earnings that were paying my fees!'

Lisabeth listened to him, sick with the realization that Andrew was repeating things that had been slyly put to him by some of the nastier boys at the school. The worst of it was that there was no answer to any of it, except wearily to repeat that he was mistaken, that it was all lies; but even that was a lie in itself, and she no longer had the appetite for more dishonesty. With a twinge of wry irony she recalled her joyful resolve of only a few hours before, that she would share with Andrew the information that Rhys was his father. There was no possibility of that now. Even if she tried to broach the subject Andrew would fling it back at her. Perhaps, if she remained calm, waited until he was over the worst of his rages . . .

'What are you doing?' she asked as he stood up and walked over to where his carpet bag stood at the foot of her bed. He was putting on his coat and winding his scarf around his neck. 'Andrew, you're not leaving. You can't . . . not like this.'

He picked up his cap. 'I'm leaving you, I'm leaving school and I'm leaving Christchurch,' he informed her crisply.

'But your education, your career!'

'If I study, it'll be at my own expense from now on,' he retorted. 'Goodbye.' And without a further word he was gone, before she could protest more, before she had time to get up. She dashed after him and flung the door open, racing after him in the darkness, calling his name. There was no reply. He had vanished.

THIRTY-FOUR

On HIS WAY INTO TOWN WITH THE WAGON to collect an order of kitchen and stable supplies for Mists of Heaven, Tommy Nevin overtook Andrew trudging along the dusty stretch of road where the river-flats bogged down into a desolate spread of swamp. It was a cold, oppressive morning, the sky heaped with billows of dirty cloud, and in the distance a wind corrugated the harbour and chased the gulls ashore. Tommy noticed that Andrew's overcoat was flecked with sprigs of hay – tumbling a girl, no doubt, he thought sourly. He was sixteen, the same age as Andrew, and disliked him with a contempt born of envy. As the wagon drew past him Tommy slid another glance at him and saw the purpling that bloomed around both eyes. He pulled on the reins at once, his broad freckled face suddenly crafty with interest.

'Goin' ter the suttee? Hop in, thun!' When Andrew didn't respond, he added: 'A bug storm brewin'. I'm tullyin' yer, it's going ter be pultin' dine with rine in a munnit.' As he spoke a scattering of drops appeared, large as pennies, in the roadway between them.

Andrew climbed in and settled on the sacks in the wagon, pulling his cap down and his collar up around his face. Tommy chattered to him. He was a persuasive lad, brimming with Irish charm; and, though Andrew had no intention of telling him a thing, by the time Tommy had set him down outside the stagecoach station he had revealed that he had slept rough last night after a quarrel with Lisabeth and now he was running away up north to look for work. He had also let slip that it was Rhys Morgan who had inflicted the damage to his face. 'But you should see

370

him!' added Andrew with a surge of bravado.

After commiserating and wishing him luck, Tommy drove off, whistling. The roman-numeralled clock above the brand-new post office informed him that it was not yet nine o'clock. A pity. It was quite some time before Mr Fox was likely to be in his office, and Mr Fox would be especially grateful for this piece of news. Tommy could hear the jingle of siver coins already.

For Thomas Fox, money paved the way to almost anything. Now that it might be a fruitful time to talk directly to Lisabeth herself, he and his purse had no trouble convincing Mr and Mrs Watson that they should call her in to the gallery to discuss the framing, the presentation and the pricing of her work.

Lisabeth came next afternoon after visiting first the school to talk to the headmaster about Andrew and then the police, who were sympathetic but unhelpful. With the whole colony in a turmoil and fresh gold-strikes being made every few months there were so many young men running away from home that there was no longer any point in keeping tabulations of their parents' complaints. When she reached the gallery she was an hour later than the time arranged and was flustered and distressed, her ears still humming with the cross words she'd had with the young constable.

'You'd think they'd make some effort, at least,' she complained to Mrs Watson as she shook the rain from her umbrella at the door and propped it inside on the brass draining-rack. 'I mean to say, if one is compelled to go to the police to seek help, they should at least perform the courtesy of offering a *token* assistance.'

'Not necessarily,' chirped Mrs Watson, who never agreed with anything that was ever put to her. 'They are so busy these days. It's this wretched gold . . . makes men greedy, my dear. All these brutal murders . . . It turns my blood to junket! I won't step outside my door at night, you know.'

'It's safe here in the town, surely?' said Lisabeth, wondering unhappily if Andrew had set off for the goldfields himself

'*Ladies* aren't *safe* in towns,' Mrs Watson assured her, lowering her voice meaningfully, then adding in a normal tone: 'Mind you, most of these murder victims are young men going about minding their own business. Makes one wonder . . . Oh dear, you do look pale. Come out the back; there's a fresh pot of tea brewed.'

Lisabeth noticed that five of her latest batch of pictures were still unsold, as were a great many paintings she recognized from her previous visits. Times were, it seemed, tight for everybody

371

now, after a particularly harsh winter. Nobody was buying.

The gallery consisted of three rooms: the front high-ceilinged silk-walled area where not only paintings but also nude statuettes (which Mrs Watson described as either 'romantic' or 'classical' depending on whether they had a draping at the hips) were displayed along with a selection of antique oriental vases; behind this a cluttered room where William Buck stained or gilded the ornate frames; and at the rear of the building, overlooking a littered yard, a tiny room with a scratched table, three green velvet chairs and in the corner an oil-burner with a brown enamelled kettle at the boil.

On one of the chairs sat Thomas Fox, his top-hat on his knees. He was staring at the yard as if there was something of interest there, and tugging at his long grey side-whiskers, and only when Mrs Watson said, 'Councillor Fox,' did he turn, and nod forward from the waist, not rising.

Lisabeth stepped back a pace, knowing at once that she had been summoned at his bidding.

'Plain ''Mister'' for the moment, but only for the moment, hey, Mrs Watson?' he said, though it was Lisabeth on whom his hard pebbly eyes were fixed. 'Mrs Nye, is it? Permit me to offer you condolences about your mother-in-law.'

Mother-in-law? Lisabeth had been about to walk back down the narrow passage and away but this stopped her. 'Thank you,' she said. *Mother-in-law?*

'Tragic,' continued Fox. To Mrs Watson he said: 'Only yesterday it happened. Mr Nye went home from his school and found her lying out in the fields, soaking wet. She'd broken her leg in a fall and been unable to drag herself back inside. Died of exposure in the rain and cold. Tragic.'

Mrs Watson cluck-clucked as she poured some tea.

'How do you know all this?' Lisabeth heard herself ask.

'All kinds of information come to me.' When he parted his lips Lisabeth saw he had small yellow teeth. 'Information about your brother, for example. Yes, you seem astonished, but I even know that you are worried about him. Then, put your mind at rest, Mrs Nye. Andrew Stafford is in Nelson. He is employed in the offices of the Kauri Timber Company and has lodgings at this address. With a respectable family,' he added as he passed the folded slip of paper to her.

Lisabeth noticed the subtle accentuation of the word 'respectable' and wondered fleetingly whether Mr Fox was jibing at her, but the news of Andrew was such an overwhelming relief that she didn't care. Subsiding into a chair opposite him, she said: 'How did you come by this information? Why did you go to all this trouble to set my mind at rest?'

He smiled. He had a peculiar smile that twisted only the lower lip while the long monkeyish upper lip remained still. 'The information was easy to come by. Coach-drivers are amenable to small supplements of their wages. But trouble? It is no trouble to set your mind at rest. It is a pleasure.'

Lisabeth tucked the folded note up the sleeve of her blue cashmere gown and pulled the shawl tight around her shoulders. He wasn't being kind at all. He'd heard that Andrew had gone, that the rent money for the land was no longer needed for his education, so now he had contrived this meeting in order to approach her directly about selling. No, kindness had nothing to do with this!

Without preamble she said: 'What makes you think I would sell to you, Mr Fox?'

The eyes hardened again. He had wrinkled eyelids with no lashes. *A most unpleasant man*, she decided. 'You wouldn't want to sell to Mr Morgan, would you?' he said smoothly. 'Not after what's happened.' She stared him right in the face, revealing nothing, so he added patiently: 'You may not be aware of this, Mrs Nye, but it was Mr Morgan who drove your brother away. I can't imagine that you'd want to go on living next door to him after that. I mean, what would people say?'

She lowered her eyes. What people might say was beginning to rankle. It was all very well to toss her head and tell herself that she didn't care what gossip-mongers invented, but Andrew had been hurt by the slanders, so badly that when she tried to talk to him he was too wounded to listen. It was gossip, not Rhys, that had really driven him off. Gossip that she, uncaring and indiscreet, had brought down on herself.

'I'm offering two thousand guineas,' he added casually. Mrs Watson gasped at the figure, and Fox smiled, nodding at her as if to approve her awe. In contrast Lisabeth merely stared at the pages of the *Illustrated London News* with which the room was papered, focusing on a portrait of Prince Albert's funeral. *Mrs Nye is dead, Andrew is gone, Mr Fox is offering me more money than I have ever dreamed of, and I'm past caring about anything*, she thought.

Turning her face back to Fox, she said: 'Why *this* land? What's so special about it? There are places on the Port Hills that are equally pretty and are more convenient for someone like yourself who has business in both Lyttelton and Christchurch, and the land itself isn't so unique – unless there's gold on it! So—'

'Mrs Nye!' cried Mrs Watson, cutting in, he thin yellowish face shocked at what Lisabeth was doing. 'This gentleman is offering you generous terms for your property and you are trying to *dissuade* him. I'm sure—'

'It's all right,' said Thomas Fox. To Lisabeth he said: 'I've asked myself the same question many times. Why that land? Why am I driven to that particular place? There's really no answer, except to refute what you say, because nowhere in the Port Hills is half as pretty. It's like women, Mrs Nye. When a man's heart and mind are fixed on a certain woman no other will do, and even when she dies no other can take her place. I'm a man of powerful desires. Compulsive desires! Sometimes I think that's a blessing, sometimes I know it's a curse. That's the place I want to be, nowhere else, and it's my earnest hope, Mrs Nye, that you will sell to me.'

His hands rested on the table, clutching his gloves. As he spoke his fingers plucked at the fawn leather. He had old hands, the flesh bunching over the joints, the skin transparent. His voice was steady, but his hands were restless. Lisabeth wanted to be repelled by him – she didn't like him at all – but instead a strange sympathy entered her heart.

When he had gone Mrs Watson fussed, pouring them both cups of tea, pursing her lips as if to hold her opinion in her mouth, savouring it, before letting it out so that Lisabeth could benefit, too. 'I thought that was disgusting . . . To speak to a lady like that! Really, Mrs Nye, you should have excused yourself and not listened to him.'

'Because he told me honestly how he felt?'

'There are certain standards . . . Certain standards.' Lisabeth could see that she didn't meet them. 'Any respectable lady . . .'

Putting the pink porcelain cup down, Lisabeth stood up.

'Oh, you mustn't go! I haven't . . . . You haven't told me whether you'll sell! You will, won't you? Two thousand guineas! That's a for—'

'Excuse me,' said Lisabeth. 'Other errands need to be attended to.'

Any respectable lady . . . The words sounded in her head all the way home, buzzing above the squeak of the coach-wheels and jouncing as she hurried on foot to Gwynne's cottage. *Any respectable lady, that's what I'm not*, she thought bitterly. *The whole world's trying to tell me that now.*

Birdie Nevin was there. These days she divided her time between the cottage, where she slept in Lisabeth's old room, and Mists of Heaven. Lisabeth had forgotten that this would be her free afternoon and was disappointed to find her there. Gwynne had a towel around her shoulders, and Birdie was combing her damp hair, her large capable hands gently holding the ivory comb.

Knowing that Gwynne would be interested, Lisabeth began to tell her about Athol's mother, but stopped suddenly and looked at Birdie with speculative eyes, reasoning that *she* could be even more interested, that someone in her situation was ideally situated for ferreting out information and passing it on. If Andrew had told Gwynne why he was leaving, she was likely to have discussed it with Birdie. Fox had to be obtaining his intelligence from someone close to the source, so why not the Nevins? They had been treacherous and in his pay before. Perhaps even now Birdie was not to be trusted.

Lisabeth turned cold as she recalled exactly how much Birdie did know. The night before her wedding, Tommy had seen Rhys carry her there and Birdie knew that she was there all night in his room. Her stomach iced over as she thought: *That's why he didn't stand up for me when I entered the room. That's why he was franker than he should have been. He thinks I'm a slut, not worthy of the smallest gesture of respect.*

He knows all about me.

Every Sunday since Charles died Lisabeth had caught and harnessed Major then driven Gwynne to church in the wagon. Afterwards they usually went straight home, but today Lisabeth pointed Major in the other direction, saying that since it was a lovely day they might as well go to admire the primroses in the park.

Gwynne was looking forward to putting her aching feet up on a hassock and to supping three or four cups of her hot strong tea, but the mention of primroses brightened her.

'Ah, the flowers of Home,' sighed Gwynne. As she aged the tide of her memories receded, leaving the childhood images exposed like rocks when the ocean has pulled away. The Isle of Man was fresh for her, its contours clearly remembered.

Lisabeth stopped the wagon under a huge chestnut tree that was tender with new leaf. Sunlight slanted through the branches, and beyond the park's black iron railings was a spread of gentle gold. 'There,' said Lisabeth. 'Doesn't that take you back?'

'Indeed it does, lass!'

As Lisabeth helped her down she thought how much better Gwynne was looking these days. Her face had filled out into its old comfortable contours, and her hair had a healthy silver sheen. It was odd, thought Lisabeth, that though Charles was still very much the centre of her life she didn't pine for him in the least. Her fictional image of him as the wonderful husband and good provider had always seemed a little ridiculous when compared to reality; perhaps she saw that, too, and now he was gone she could maintain the pretence without the fear of Charles contradicting her with some selfish or stupid action.

'Aunty, you're looking well,' she said, placing an impulsive kiss on a downy cheek. 'Come, let's sit on that bench where we can admire the flowers. I need to ask your advice.'

Gwynne sat in bemused silence, listening, then broke in to say: 'Oh, no, dear! You're mistaken. There's no gossip—'

'Please hear me out,' begged Lisabeth. 'This is difficult for me.' Choosing her words with care, she told Gwynne of the anguish she had been suffering since she left Athol and was made to endure the isolation of an outcast. People shrank away from her overtures of friendship, clubs closed their membership when she approached – even the church fellowship groups – and when she offered to give painting lessons, or to arrange the flowers at the church or help visit the parish sick, the priest discouraged her. 'None of this mattered when I had Andrew here at school. I had hoped that sooner or later we would be friends again, and I was right. I could turn my back on society, tell myself I didn't need companionship and look to the future, but now that Andrew's gone the world seems an empty place. I wonder, Aunty, if I should simply sell the land and go right away, start over again somewhere else.'

There was a silence. Gwynne watched the bees working in the flowers, stumbling their way from one throat to another. She was silent for so long that Lisabeth wondered if she had heard a single word. Then she said: 'You want to know what I think, lass?'

'I'd be grateful. I'm so confused, and there is nobody else I can talk to.' Not even Rhys, she thought. He'd kept well away since that night on the cliff-top. Not that she wanted to see him anyway.

He should have been more understanding, instead of treating Andrew like a truculent child in need of a thrashing.

Gwynne said slowly: 'Mr Stafford always said that when a situation grew too difficult to cope with any longer the only thing to do was to leave. A fresh start! That was his remedy. New faces, a new situation, new opportunities. Yes, that's what he would have done.'

'I see,' said Lisabeth. That solution no longer seemed attractive to her. Charles had run away from everything, and look at what a mess denial had made of his life. Hers, too. If she had faced up honestly to her feelings about Rhys instead of always harking back to her sense of betrayal when Mary had died, she would not be caught up in this web of gossip now. She would have married Rhys and *she* would be the one living at Mists of Heaven. *She* would be occupying that magnificent room with the enormous bed and the fireplace, the mirrored wall and the wheel-shaped chandeliers.

She would be occupying her rightful place.

But if she sold up and left the district she would have the chance to forget Rhys, forget her self-inflicted injuries and her jealousy of Azura. 'Aunty, I'm so terribly confused,' she said. 'Thank you, but I still don't know what to do.'

Gwynne patted her hand. 'It will come to you,' she assured her.

What did arrive was a letter from Athol. Lisabeth sat outside on the bench with Bollan's head resting in her lap, fondling his ears with one hand while with the other she held the single page.

Dear Lisabeth, wrote Athol in his impeccable, angular, upright script. *Thank you for your letter and the sympathy expressed therein. I understand your reluctance to attend the services, but Mother is now reunited with Father and is enjoying her Reward at last. I would like to see you soon at a time convenient to you, to discuss an important matter of some delicacy. Yours sincerely, Athol James Nye.*

A divorce, thought Lisabeth. What else could be a matter of delicacy and importance? Athol was heartily sick of the gossips, too.

She rowed over to Ferrymead, tied the boat to the pilings of the jetty and asked instructions from the Customs officer at the cargo-shed. The school was half a mile back on the main road towards Christchurch, and Lisabeth walked there along the road-verge because the road itself was churned and muddy. Bullock teams were dragging logs down to where extensions to the wharf were

377

under way. Because she had plenty of time and it was an oppressive overcast day, too warm for brisk walking, she paused to watch the huge beasts lumbering along with the gigantic logs skidding through the slush behind them. Where would there have been trees that size on the plains? she wondered. They must have been dragged uncountable miles.

The school was a grim two-storey building with a formal-looking slate roof and grey masonry trim around the many windows. From a distance it appeared to be floating in a sea of white-blossomed *manuka* scrub, but when she reached the entrance she found a banner of lawn stitched along both edges with rows of young English trees. No wonder the nurserymen prospered in Canterbury, thought Lisabeth. Everybody, even schoolmasters, yearned for the atmosphere of the Old Country. Lisabeth wondered if this was anything like England, the jagged white and blue mountains, the vast plains, the shimmering summer heat and the fresh smell of the sea.

Athol saw her standing alone outside the gate after the school had emptied. He recognized the cashmere dress at once, for since she left he had been sensitive to blue dresses and never let one go by without a leap of the heart followed by a deflating feeling of disappointment. But this time it was definitely her.

He approached unnoticed. She was turned away, following with her eyes the fraying ribbon of smoke towed by the distant train engine as it racketed towards Christchurch. Athol wondered who buttoned the gown for her now that she lived alone, and the speculation burned an acid blemish into his mind.

His greeting was therefore cool, and her response uncertain. She craned her neck to read his tight papery- skinned face. He was as fine-looking as ever, but thinner and more aloof in his bearing than she remembered. His expression was inscrutable.

'You still have the dress I gave you.'

'Yes,' she said, grateful for the neutral topic. 'It's my only good one, and I seldom wear it. I never can fasten all the buttons, you see, that's why I have to wear a shawl even on a hot day like this.'

He noticed the blisters of perspiration across her brow. 'Permit me,' he said, and after a second's hesitation she turned and dropped her chin forward to her chest, but moved away a pace as soon as he said: 'There.' The intimacy had flustered her.

'So this is where you teach?' she said brightly.

'Lisabeth, you look well,' he said. He had forgotten so many things about her – the tiny bump halfway along her nose, the thread-like scar on her chin where a piece of splintery wood had flown up from her tomahawk one morning, the incredible colour of her eyes, the irises so cobalt, the whites so pure that she was like a picture sketched on to a pristine sheet of paper. She looked so innocent yet he had heard such rumours about her. Not that any of that mattered, he reminded himself. When he welcomed her back he would be seen as the benevolent husband, a biblical figure, and she the repentant lowly wife.

He was careful. It was in Athol's nature to proceed with utmost caution when the way was uncertain, so as he walked back with her to Ferrymead he talked only of the few happy times they had shared in their marriage. He was conversational, friendly, and there was not a hint of pleading in his voice.

She wondered how he was managing without his mother, but she refrained from asking outright, though she noticed his unpressed trousers, the inground slate-dust on the sleeves of his jacket and the stripes of grime worn into the creases on his shirt-cuffs. Athol had always been so immaculate.

When he helped her into the rowboat she looked up at him, puzzled. There had been no mention of anything important between them. 'Athol, you said you wanted to see me on a matter of delicacy.'

'Ah, did I? Oh, yes.' He'd clearly forgotten penning those words. 'Perhaps I could come calling on you? Would Saturday afternoon suit?'

'Saturday would be perfect.' She pictured Athol arriving at her cottage, intruding on her territory. She wasn't ready for that. 'I'll be at the Staffords',' she told him. 'The blue and white house at the foot of the hill. Look for the jasmine trellises.'

He wants me back, she realized as she rowed away and his hand was raised in farewell. There was a small warm feeling inside her, nourished by the knowledge that for the first time since she left she was doing something that would meet with society's approval. *Athol actually wants me back!*

Halfway across the estuary she leaned on the oars, panting, the sound of her blood beating in her ears. Her arms and legs were prickling with sweat. She promised herself a warm sponge-down when she arrived home, or perhaps she could go down to Gwynne's, beg the use of the portable tin bath and boil up Gwynne's big black pot for a proper luxurious soak.

As she dragged on the oars again she thought about Athol and the marriage they'd shared. He'd been kind to her, smuggling little treats home, paying far more than his mother decreed for this beautiful cloth for her dress. No, it was his mother who had ruined things. Life there would be a very different prospect now that she had gone. She rested again, watching a cutter tacking close by on its way to the Ferrymead wharf. Its deck was heaped with sacks of coal, and its sails were smudged with great blooms of coal-dust.

'Lisabeth!'

She shaded her eyes against the water's glare. When her name came again she dug one oar into the surface and turned the rowboat to see Joe Day grinning at her from his own dinghy. A silver-flecked net was heaped behind him in the prow.

He gutted a couple of fish and tossed them into her boat as they bumped together on the current. 'You been to visit Ma?' he wanted to know.

'No . . . Athol, actually. We've had an extremely pleasant chat.'

'Really?' He looked so pleased for her that the warm feeling grew. 'I thought he wanted you back. He was at the hotel the day after Mrs Nye's funeral and he asked lots of questions about you.'

'What sort of questions?'

Joe looked uncomfortable. His merry eyes sobered. 'He wanted to know whether you'd sold that land of yours. I told him I didn't know anything about it. He seems a nice fellow, though, Lisabeth. His mother's death had really rocked him.'

'He is a nice fellow,' she said, but as she rowed on another memory insinuated itself into her mind and she recalled Athol's reaction when Charles told him about the land, his strident demands, his anger. She shrugged, putting the memory aside. Of course Athol would be interested in her property; it was only natural, it meant nothing sinister.

The tide was right out when she reached the shore, wet slicks of seaweed were sprawled over the finely ribbed sand. Further towards the headland a small group of Maoris from the settlement over the isthmus were stooping, wrists and ankles in the water as they dug for *pipis*, the succulent native clams, which they tossed into open-mouthed flax baskets. One of the children broke away and dashed over to help her drag the rowboat up to where she kept it tethered under the arching roots of a *pohutukawa* tree.

It was Henare, a boy of about ten with a tangle of shoulder-length black curls and a broad-nosed thick-lipped face impudent and irresistible in its charm. He wore the uniform of poor children everywhere; baggy adult hand-me-downs, the jacket sleeves turned back and smeared with sand, the trousers rolled up until the turn-ups were wadded wheels of fabric. No shirt, of course. These were probably the only garment he owned.

He thrust a basket of *pipis* at her. 'Here, Missus Nye! *Hakari.** Pipi* for you.'

'*E tika hoki*, – thank you, Henare,' she said. One rainy day in winter when Henare and his older sister had knocked at the door selling crayfish she had invited them in, given them steaming bowls of soup which they slurped from the rim and bread that they tore into chunks with their teeth. While they thawed by the fire she had painted portraits of them both, not good likenesses because landscapes were her speciality, but they must have been satisfied with them because ever since Henare had treated her with touching generosity.

Yet Charles was terrified of these people, and once I was, too, she thought. Healed by the exposure to the open landscape, all her own terrors of the unquiet dark bush had long vanished, while acquaintance with these gentle-mannered people made the recurrent tales of atrocities in the north seem fiction and even her personal nightmares of the tattooed thug brandishing that axe had faded into uncertainty.

She smiled as Henare scampered back to join his brothers, sisters and cousins, and as she straightened with the basket of seafood something on the cliff-top caught her eye. A man on horseback silhouetted against the lowering sky. Rhys. There was a stillness about him that suggested he had been there for some time watching her.

Lisabeth faltered, then stiffened her shoulders, and with the basket swinging in one hand she turned towards the foot of the steep path. By the time she reached the lap of land in which the cottage crouched she felt hot and tired and irritable. Rhys was watching her. That warm, carefully nourished bud of self-approval had disappeared, and in its place was a sensation of sour emptiness. *Damn you, Rhys,* she thought.

Hakari = a gift

381

THIRTY-FIVE

RHYS WAS UNAWARE that Lisabeth had seen him. He had watched her since she and the rowboat were a single dark flaw in the rippled silk of the harbour, and as she glided closer to shore he abandoned his task of rounding up a few stray ewes to be mustered into the lambing paddocks, fastening his attention on her instead.

This was the first time he had seen her since the quarrel of almost three weeks before, and the residual ache from her angry words still lingered. Andrew's bruises on his face had gone; after telling Azura that he had fallen down a bank he rode out into the foothills acres and stayed there in a shepherd's hut until the swelling subsided. When on his return he learned that Andrew had run away he went straight to Gwynne offering help. It piqued him to hear that Lisabeth already knew his fate. His plan had been to win back Lisabeth's regard by discovering Andrew's whereabouts for her. Not that he regretted hitting the lad; in his opinion Andrew was an obstreperous young bugger who deserved more than the single punch Rhys gave him. It was Lisabeth he mourned. Terrible though it was to admit, the final loss of her would be worse than the grief he had endured over his son's drowning. He needed her regard.

I have no right to think this way, he told himself as her figure disappeared between the thickets of *toe-toe* bushes at the base of the cliff-path. I have no right to dream of her in the grey hours of morning or to picture her as I go about my work. I have a wife, freely chosen, and a daughter I adore, and, as Lisabeth pointed out, I'm one of the most envied men in the province. Jerking on

Polka's reins, he snorted aloud. 'Then, how come I'm so bloody miserable, hey, Polka?' he said.

The sound of Azura's laughter greeted him as he loped up the marble stairs towards the nursery. 'Where's my girl?' he called heartily, his mood lightening at the prospect of a romp before dinner. 'Daisy, where are you?'

'She's in here,' called Azura from her boudoir. 'Do come in and listen to this, Rhys.'

Her voice sounded blurred but there was an edge to it, a gloating nasty edge that made him pause, hand on the doorknob, before going in.

This was a room he rarely entered. It was a crammed untidy place littered with glove-stretchers and wig-stands and overstuffed cushions and dishes of sweets and sugared fruits and toffee almonds. It smelt of powder, perfume and Azura's body, for though she dusted and sprayed herself generously she seldom bathed. The walls and ceiling were covered with a floral printed fabric, tiny roses and bluebells on a dark background; and as Rhys stepped reluctantly through the door he had the sensation of being wrapped in a stale bouquet.

Azura and Daisy were sitting on a chaise-longue that was covered in the same busy fabric. Azura wore a sateen housedress in soft pink, lace-trimmed, while Daisy wore riding habit, the miniaturized version of one her mother used to wear, a black full skirt and severe little jacket. Daisy had a glass of lemonade in her hands, while Azura was balancing a dinner-plate heaped with sandwiches, cream cakes and jam tarts from the three-tiered silver stand on the tea-trolley where a silver tea-pot and hotwater jug on a spirit-burner awaited.

'Pour the tea, will you?' said Azura, using the same tone in which she issued orders to the servants.

Rhys didn't move. 'What did you want me to hear?'

'Oh, tell him,' said Azura, seeing that Rhys was going to turn on his heel and leave. 'Go on, Daisy, tell Papa what you heard Tommy Nevin saying to Birdie.'

'She was *eavesdropping* and you encouraged—'

'Oh, don't be fussy, Rhys. It's about those sordid relatives of yours, the ones Bea calls the Immigrants. *And* it's about you,' she added malevolently, her eyes fastening on to a forkful of golden spongecake as she lifted it to her mouth.

Rhys bristled at the contempt in his wife's voice. She was beginning to sound like Bea. If Lady Launcenolt looked upon the

383

Staffords with scorn before, she had always taken care to hide her opinion, but since Azura arrived there had been a constant surfacing of snide remarks, sidelong glances and hints that Gwynne and the family should be tolerated at a distance, not suffered at close quarters. Rhys knew that Gwynne had tried to be both sisterly and neighbourly to Azura, but her every approach had been blocked by a rebuff. Rhys blamed Bea for this snobbery, though many times he'd explained to his wife that the colonies were an open society, not stratified like India or England, and by looking down on his family she was in a sense looking down on him, but whenever he talked like that she would say nothing, simply smile blandly and pop another sugared fig into her mouth.

Now Rhys could feel his anger boiling. 'I'll not have you talk like that in front of Daisy,' he said. Daisy puffed her cheeks out with a mouthful of lemonade, swallowed and smiled. 'Look at her manners, will you? She needs a governess, someone who'll teach her to be a lady. Those Nevin youngsters are letting her run wild.'

'Very well, dear. If you don't like the Nevins, I'll dismiss them all,' Azura said blithely, biting into another slab of cake.

'I didn't mean that.' Why did she always twist everything around so that the tail of his own remarks lashed back at him? 'At least, not until I've heard what Tommy Nevin was saying about me. What did he say, Daisy?'

Daisy pouted. 'Go on, tell Papa,' prodded Azura through a mouthful of pastry.

'Well,' said Daisy, throwing out her small chest in importance. 'I went out to the stable to see if Tommy would take me for a wide, and he was talking to Birdie and he didn't see me, and he was saying that Andrew wan away because you hit him in the face and blacked his eyes and that Andrew hit you, too, and that's why your face was all hurt before and that it was because Lisabeth—' She broke off to take a breath. 'Who *is* Lisabeth, Mamma?'

'Go on, tell her who Lisabeth is. Rhys. Go on, I dare you,' hissed Azura. 'Fell down a bank, did you? Oh, dear, how unoriginal! A child beat you, Rhys! A child!'

Rhys shot her a glance filled with disgust and turned, jerking the door open. Behind him Azura began to laugh. He glanced back at her as he slammed out. She was reclining on the chaise-longue, helpless with mirth, the plate of ravaged delicacies shuddering in her hands, her whole body convulsed, quivering, and her face contorted, pretty eyes screwed up, mouth wide open showing a spluttering stuffing of half-chewed cake. *Revolting*, thought Rhys.

As her laughter had accompanied him up the stairs, now it beat behind him as he stamped his descent, furious. He had reached the bottom before he realized that the noise had stopped, and was halfway across the entrance-hall when Daisy's scream halted him so abruptly that his boots swivelled where he stood on the mosaic floor with its design of ferns, bellbirds and native *tuis**.

He glanced back up the stairwell.

'Papa, come quickly!' shrieked Daisy's voice, high and shrill with terror. 'Something tewwible's happened to Mamma!'

His boots skimmed over the marble rises, his hand barely touched the ornate oakwood banister. Daisy was stumbling out of the room when he reached the door; she jumped into his arms, wrapping her arms and legs about him as if the hounds of Hell were after her.

The door had swung shut. Rhys kicked it open. Azura was lying as he had last seen her, head back, mouth agape, but now the plate lay shattered on the floor and her eyes were open, staring at the floral ceiling. In the light filtering through the lace curtains at the Palladian windows Rhys could see at once that she was dead, for her face had a throttled look and her skin was an unnatural bluish grey.

Daisy's screaming was deafening, but Rhys could hear a chime of voices and a clatter of the loud-soled shoes that Azura made her servants wear. 'Holy Virgin, whut's happened?' cried Birdie. She pushed past Rhys then stood aghast, crossing herself, while Siobhan peered in and dashed away shouting: 'It's the mustruss! She's daid! She's done choked herself ter death!'

Rhys was dazed. Still bound about by the shrieking, clinging Daisy, he instructed Birdie to send for the doctor then walked downstairs and out into the rose garden where he sat on a mossy stone bench and stared into the lily-pond where Darius had died. Absently, he stroked Daisy's back. A sour-skinned emptiness swelled like an enormous bubble inside him. 'Hush, darling girl,' he murmured. 'Hush, darling. Your Papa's here. He'll look after you.'

Lisabeth kept away. Last time she offered condolences to Rhys disaster had followed; uneasily she dwelt on the passion they had shared that night and wondered if she had brought misfortune on

---

*tuis – parson birds

Rhys. They had sinned, and that was often the way of God, to punish the innocent to bring guilt to crush the wrongdoers. She was haunted.

Gwynne's pronouncement was simple. 'Sure and that house has brought bad luck down on their heads,' she declared, shaking hers sagely. 'White stone is the height of ill fortune for us Manx folk. I tried to warn Rhys – by heaven, I did – but he wouldn't listen.'

'He wanted his house to echo the spirit of the mountains,' mused Lisabeth, who had moved back with Gwynne because Birdie was needed at Mists of Heaven now to look after Daisy until a new governess could be hired. She came unwillingly but found to her relief that the spectre of Charles bothered her much less than before. It was Andrew who occupied her troubled dreams until, on receipt of the news about Azura, he finally penned a letter which arrived on the coach less than a week after it was written. Gwynne hobbled in from the road waving it and gurgling with delight, and Lisabeth fell on it and read it hungrily. It was a bare five sentences, it was terse but it was a new beginning.

Out and about more now, Gwynne brought scraps of news for them to pick over. It was she who went to the funeral and reported back what a dismal affair it had been. Rhys looked exhausted, Sir Kenneth and his wife frail and distraught. It was to them that Daisy clung, wailing all through the service, poor motherless waif. The coffin was as broad as a piano-case; this Gwynne reported in an undertone as if it was wicked somehow to have noticed. It was so big that when they took it to the grave it was immediately obvious that it would not fit into the narrow trench which the sexton had hastily to widen. And all the afternoon it rained.

It was the worst summer on record. Birdie splashed in regularly, scraping thick peelings of mud from her boots on the jack then shucking them off at the step. She brought news, too, of the frustrations Rhys was having in finding a suitable governess for his daughter. One likely-looking lass arrived but before she could begin her duties Lady Launcenolt examined her, sniffing with a vinegar face over her references, poking about in her luggage, inspecting her fingernails and the rim of her collar and behaving so overbearingly that the girl fled in tears.

Birdie laughed over that, and Gwynne flung her own top apron over her head, but neither was amused when Birdie described how Tommy had been issued with marching orders. 'Jest a wee disagraiment over whuther his horse were rubbed dine properly, too!

Jest a *wee* disagraiment!' But she added that Tommy had never intended to stay. Ever since he was a 'wee lud' he'd wanted to go to sea, she told them, but her eyes were unutterably sad in her defiant face.

Gwynne was shocked that Rhys could be so harsh, but Lisabeth, now cautious of the Nevins, reserved judgement, guessing that a far deeper reason lay behind the dismissal.

Other gossip came from an unexpected source, Athol Nye. He called regularly after classes on Tuesdays and Thursdays and came for luncheon on Saturday, staying all afternoon. Lisabeth was glad that she was living with Gwynne now, for she was not ready to be alone with her husband again, nor was she ready to think of him as such. She ignored his plaintive expression and encouraged his gossip, for he knew such diverse things as how the city's cathedral plans were coming, that *Othello* was playing to appreciative audiences at the Grand Theatre, and that salmon and trout spawn were being liberated in rivers all up and down the country. He was also a messenger for Lisabeth, delivering paintings to the Watsons' gallery and twice bringing back a number of coins folded up in a paper.

He also told them about Leonie Gammerwoth. As soon as Azura's grave was filled in she set her cap once again at Rhys, and Athol took delight in relating this because he had always fancied himself as one of her suitors and liked to believe that she had never recovered from her 'passion' for him. In the past years she had kept close company with a concert pianist, a much younger man, who came originally to the colony with a theatre group then stayed on after the concerts, discovering an idyllic existence as a rather active social butterfly, gadding about everywhere and paying for accommodation and dinner-parties by entertaining his fellow-guests with magically performed Chopin and Liszt sonatas afterwards. Athol was carefully vague about the rumoured nature of their relationship; it was Birdie who made that explicit when she recounted delicious scandal about the scene Paul Hammond threw at the Four Ships Ball, threatening to commit suicide if Leonie abandoned him. There was only one possible interpretation: Leonie was the musician's *mistress*. Perhaps she was planning to abandon him for Rhys, hinted Birdie.

'She visits Mists of Heaven frequently, I believe, and alone,' mused Athol. 'Have you noticed her dark green carriage pulled by matched bays? It's very distinctive.'

Because she had, and often, Lisabeth changed the subject to

387

Andrew, partly out of spite because she knew that his name irritated Athol as much as Leonie's name irritated her. Andrew had written several letters to Gwynne, letters Lisabeth pounced on and devoured eagerly as if they had been meant for her. For surely they *were* meant for her. Why else would he elaborate about his well-paid mill job and the ease with which he was studying in the evenings if not to show her how well he was managing without her? They were a shout of independence, and she read them with a mingling of pride and regret that he no longer needed her.

'He's looking after his health, too,' she reported. 'Even though he works long hours to support himself he makes sure he gets enough sleep so that his brain is keen for studying.'

'So you no longer provide for him?' said Athol quickly.

She gave him a sharp sideways glance. 'I'm saving every penny of the rent money for his future. Andrew hopes to study at the Royal College of Physicians in Edinburgh, and if he is accepted I want to be sure he'll be able to afford to go. He's sitting the entrance examinations in Dunedin in the New Year and I'm hoping – we're *all* hoping – that he'll stop by for a visit on his way through.'

Athol fiddled with the harness on his horse, a cream mare borrowed from one of the other schoolmasters. 'Why wouldn't he?' asked Athol.

Lisabeth flushed. She plucked an overlooked over-ripe gooseberry from the hedge and picked at its dried calyx. All the trees were withering now, blighted by the first damp cold. The summer seemed to have danced past in a series of rainstorms.

'Young Andrew. The boy means a lot to you, doesn't he?' asked Athol cautiously.

'You should know that,' Lisabeth replied, her voice frank with an edge of bitterness. 'I used to beg you to permit him to visit me. Surely you remember?'

He winced again. Lisabeth didn't care that she hurt him. She gazed beyond the purple foothills to the mountains, white already to their hems and slicked with the gold sheen of afternoon light. The sky was flecked with a sheet of birds flying inland in ragged formation; they cried out to each other, and the sound filled the afternoon. Athol said: 'I know I treated you badly in many ways, Lisabeth. I want to assure you that when you come back this time—'

'*If*, Athol, not when.' Craning her neck, she looked steadily into his face. 'I'm not ready to talk to you about that,' she told him.

'But I've been here eight times now,' he informed her stiffly, a

388

flush of colour seeping under his papery skin. 'Don't you think it's high time you considered —'

She said: 'It's for the rest of my life, Athol. It's final. I rushed into marriage with you and it was a disaster, so this time—'

'You are my *wife*, Lisabeth,' he reminded her. 'Leaving me didn't change that. In the eyes of the law and in the eyes of God you are still my wife. Sometimes I wonder if you've forgotten your vows.'

'No, Athol, I haven't forgotten.' She was rolling the gooseberry between her fingers when it suddenly ruptured, gushing pulp and juice on to her slate-green skirt. Dropping the fruit, she bent to wipe her fingers on a tuft of grass before continuing. 'Perhaps you'd prefer to stay away for the moment. You could come again in spring if—'

'No,' he cut in firmly. 'I'll keep coming. I enjoy the visits. But bear this in mind, Lisabeth. I am your husband, and your rightful place is in my home.' He swung up into the saddle, looking odd and awkward, his head too high and his feet hanging too low. Before he rode off he looked at her grimly. 'Decide soon, Lisabeth,' he said.

Lisabeth shivered and turned away, hugging her shoulders as she trudged back indoors. Gwynne looked up from where she was brewing another pot of tea. After Athol had gone she liked to sit and mull over his visits. 'What a gentleman he is!' she enthused. 'There's something so distinguished and yet so approachable about a schoolmaster, don't you think?'

'You didn't like him before,' teased Lisabeth, though she was not in the mood for levity. A vague feeling, an apprehension, was gnawing at her.

'Oh, I've always admired Mr Nye. So fond of his mother, he was. I like that in a man. No, it was Mr Stafford, bless his soul. He had a fixation about schoolmasters. In his opinion they were all arrogant.'

Arrogate, corrected Lisabeth, but she did it silently. 'Don't get your heart set on Mr Nye . . . I haven't decided yet whether I'll go back to him.'

Gwynne looked bewildered. 'But you will, dear, won't you?' she asked anxiously. 'I mean, it is the right thing to do.'

Lady Launcenolt vibrated the tiny elephant-shaped silver bell that rested on the luncheon-table beside her tea-cup. When Leopold came padding silently in his crimson embroidered slippers

389

she said: 'You may send Miss Bridewell in now, so that Mr Morgan can cross-examine her.'

'I say,' protested Rhys in a murmur. 'I want to offer her employment, not charge her with a crime.'

Sir Kenneth frowned. He had aged in the weeks since Azura's death, or perhaps he had been gradually ageing all along and Rhys was too preoccupied to notice. Now his face was so thin and wasted that his vast white beard seemed to be rooted in the bones of his jaw and cheeks. This frailness alarmed Rhys, who reacted by being especially deferential to him. Sir Kenneth thumped the table with a freckled hand and declared: 'You're too soft, my boy. That was the problem with Miss Merryman – you treated her like a guest instead of a servant. Start out tough and you'll have no problems later, eh?'

'I'll remember that, sir.'

Miss Bridewell was short and stocky, this squatness being emphasized by the wide, swaying crinoline that she wore under her yellow tailored costume. Her hair was brown, plainly styled with a centre parting and a huge chignon low on the nape of her neck. She had a square face with an aggressive jaw and thin-lipped mouth, but her eyes in contrast were weak-looking, small and watery with untidy straggling brows. When Rhys saw her he knew at once why Lady Launcenolt had driven off the other girl, the one he had chosen. *She* had been much too attractive; Lady Launcenolt wanted to make quite certain that there would be no gossip about Rhys and the governess. Stroking his moustache to hide a smile, he nodded. This one would do as well as any.

'Don't you want to ask her anything?'

'All right,' said Rhys. 'Tell me, Miss Bridewell, what is your philosophy in bringing up children?'

'A firm hand is what's required, sir,' she responded immediately. She had a flat hard voice that reminded him of ducks quacking.

'Not too firm, nor too literally,' warned Lady Launcenolt. 'And while you are in Mr Morgan's employ you can dispense with the crinoline, please. A crinoline is not an appropriate garment for the nursery.'

Miss Bridewell's jaw jutted, and an impenetrable glaze masked her eyes, but her voice betrayed resentment. 'And why not, ma'am? How does my manner of dress affect—'

'A governess's job involves a great deal of bending, and crinoliness sway upwards,' said Lady Launcenolt, flustered but crisp. 'Remember that children have eyes, Miss Bridewell.'

The girl fixed her gaze on Lady Launcenolt for one dismissive moment before turning to Rhys, who was leaning back in his chair and trying not to laugh aloud. She said: 'It's you I'll be working for, sir? Are you Mr Morgan from Mists of Heaven by any chance?'

'Yes, he is and you may go now,' said Lady Launcenolt. When Miss Bridewell had manoeuvred herself and her skirts out of the room she heaved a bosom-quivering sigh and rolled her eyes at Rhys. 'I fear you'll need to be extremely positive with her. Oh, what a simple life it would be if we had no servants to worry about! You're very quiet, Kiki. What did you think of her?'

'I prefer to leave it to you, my dear.' Pushing his chair back, he stood up. 'Come into the study, Rhys. I'd like to discuss strategy for the upcoming election, hey? Do you feel up to being my campaign manager again?'

'Certainly. If you feel up to running.' Rhys spoke lightly, but there was a thread of concern in his voice.

Sir Kenneth picked it out. 'I'm a young pup yet when it comes to politics.' He stood at the dining-room French doors that overlooked the azalea beds. 'Got to keep Fox on the trot, eh? Ah, don't mind me, boy. Losing Azura, that was a tough one. She meant the world to us, my boy. But you know that, don't you?'

Rhys was swamped with guilt so acute that he could not meet the old man's eyes and looked instead at the ornate red and bronze pattern on the Indian carpet. His lack of grief was a disappointment, he knew. This childless couple had doted on 'their' Azura all her life. It had been a coup for them to have her come to New Zealand alone and a supreme triumph when she married Rhys, thus severing herself from the ties of family and becoming theirs for ever.

And Rhys had not valued their treasure. If they saw it when she was alive, they had hope, but now she was dead the contrast between their desolation and his indifference was an embarrassment. Rhys regretted the cooling between them, but what could he do? The only consolation was their obsession with Daisy, so Rhys reluctantly let them smother her as once Azura had been cosseted. Lady Launcenolt's ideas were hopelessly out of date – surely a child of four need not wear a chemise while bathing to prevent accidental glimpses of her own body! – she was dictatorial and rigid and unfortunately age had sharpened her appetite for combat and she delighted in clashes of wills with the servants at Mists of Heaven. Each encounter with her eroded

391

the esteem Rhys held for her, but he let her rip; with the guilt holding him back there was nothing he could do but indulge her.

Towards Sir Kenneth his feelings were more complex – mateship, respect and warmth mingled with a filial bond he valued. Lifting his eyes from the carpet he said directly: 'I'm numb, sir. Azura's death hasn't really hit me yet, but I'm still grieving the loss of my son. I don't know if you understand, but—'

'Of course, my boy, of course,' Sir Kenneth said at once, with such a generosity of forgiveness that Rhys hated himself for using the old gentleman's childlessness as a shield for his own barrenness of feeling. His only consolation was the suspicion that Sir Kenneth would prefer it this way.

Rhys had no time to brood, for the old man took his elbow, holding it as they walked together and using Rhys to take some of the weight a walking-cane might. 'I've not stopped trying to get you right into politics, too,' he warned. 'Though once you've tasted it you'll need no persuading. The charge of power beats everything, even' – and he winked – 'the flesh! And so many changes are sweeping across the land. This is not just going to be a fine brave country but a rich one, too! If this fellow Vogel has his way, the whole colony will be linked together with railways and roads and bridges spanning the mighty rivers. Sailing ships will be outdated, and folk will travel everywhere in railway trains. Can you imagine such a thing?'

Rhys smiled down at his friend, relieved to be on to a safer subject and in the ease of his company. 'I know we'll be the greatest country in the world. Haven't we been the first in the Empire to give our natives the vote? Where else have they done that? And they're electing four Maoris to Parliament to discuss the fair and rightful treatment of their fellows. I say that's a marvellous thing!'

Sir Kenneth frowned. 'What about all this land the Crown has confiscated to punish the tribes that waged war on us? D'you think that was uncalled for?'

'Not at all. In Maori law the loser forfeits every inch of his land to the victor. We're only taking a small part of it, aren't we? Wouldn't you say that was more than fair?'

Sir Kenneth's face cleared. 'Never knew that. Maori law, hey?'

'It's called *Utu*. An eye for an eye.' Rhys shivered. Memories of that tattooed warrior in the well always made him feel uneasy.

'Yes, an eye for an eye, that's their way. You can tell your colleagues in Wellington that.'

When Gwynne fell ill with a severe cold that autumn Lisabeth put her to bed and nursed her devotedly, though too enthusiastically, according to the suffering Gwynne. Lisabeth bound hot poultices to her chest and coaxed her with sugar lumps sprinkled with spirit of camphor. She gathered leaves from the blue gum trees along the roadside by whacking at the lower branches with a long stick, then crushed the leaves with boiling water, set the brew beside Gwynne's bed and stuffed up the gaps under the door with paper so that the fumes could not escape. All this Gwynne suffered with gasping red-faced resignation, but when Athol produced a bottle of ipecacuanha and vowed that the apothecary in Christchurch swore by it Gwynne rebelled.

'Ipecacuanha!' she croaked. 'They haven't even changed the ghastly purple label! The very sight of it makes my stomach heave. I was dosed on that vile tack more than thirty years ago, and the taste will never leave me. I tell you, lass, I'd die before I let another spoonful past my lips!'

'I believe you,' laughed Lisabeth as Gwynne flung the blankets over her head. 'Never mind. First thing in the morning I'll pop up to the cottage and see if there are any more lemons ripe. A drink of lemon juice, whisky and honey . . . would you prefer that?'

The blankets folded back. 'You could tempt me, lass,' she joked hoarsely.

Lisabeth slipped out early, hoping to prepare the drink before Gwynne woke after a tortured night of cough-fragmented sleep. Donning her stout boots and tossing a frayed black shawl around the shoulders of her drab fawn 'salvage' dress, she squelched across the orchard to free Bollan, and with him running and nosing ahead of her she strolled along the ridge-path.

A quilt of autumn mist lay over the plains. When she looked back towards town Lisabeth could see faint golden smudges of willow trees blooming on the white and the gables of occasional buildings. She recognized the spire of their church. The sun was melting a crust of cloud above the horizon, and already the harbour looked bright as chain mail, textured by millions of scalloped ripples. Smoke frittered from the chimney of the Days' hotel across the bay. Lisabeth paused for a moment to try to pick out knolls in the Port Hills where she had been painting with

Athol. Since Charles died there had been little time for painting, and she missed the warm glow of accomplishment that she derived from completing an attractive little scene. Memories of those carefree days spent tramping over the heath with Athol acquired the patina of nostalgia.

What will I do? she wondered as she turned and tramped up the steeper part of the track. Ahead of her Bollan barked. Excited, she guessed, over seeing their old home. He continued to bark, and as the noise quickened, undimmed by her called commands, she wondered what was wrong. As she broke through the patch of *manuka* scrub that overhung the track there was a timid cry and Lisabeth covered the last few yards to find, huddled on the seat beside the huge whale jaws, a very small, very frightened little girl.

'Stop it, Bollan!' repeated Lisabeth, reaching to cuff him and switching off his barking mid-swipe. He retreated, wagging his tail, whining with squeaking eager sounds.

Lisabeth guessed at once who the girl was. The quality of fine linen and the intricate embroidery of her nightgown were enough of a clue even if Lisabeth hadn't recognized the large baby-blue eyes Daisy had inherited from her mother. Today there was no trace of the hysterical little girl who had screamed for 'Andwew' on that terrible afternoon at Mists of Heaven when Darius had died. Daisy's lip trembled, but she composed herself swiftly and gave Lisabeth a haughty look. 'Who are you?' she asked.

Lisabeth discarded 'Mrs Nye' as being too formal. She sat beside the girl, noticing that the child's bare hands and feet were blue with the cold. 'I'm Lisabeth and you're Daisy,' she said, shrugging out of her shawl and draping it around the bird-thin shoulders.

'I'm Vashti,' came the piping response. 'Miss Bwidewell said that I have to have my wight name. I hate Miss Bwidewell.'

'Who is she?' Rich children have curling-ribbons, not rags in their hair, Lisabeth observed.

Daisy snuggled into the shawl. 'Why are those ships always stopping out there?'

'They wait for Pilot Joseph Day to bring them in. He's a brave man who sometimes saves people from drowning if their ships bang into the sand bar.' Lisabeth suddenly realized that ship-wrecks and drowning were inappropriate topics, so she said: 'What are you doing out here, Daisy? It's not even properly morning yet.'

'I'm *Vashti*,' she insisted in a voice so reminiscent of Andrew that Lisabeth's heart turned over. This child's face was more elfin and pointed than Andrew's had ever been, but she had the same broad brow and high cheekbones, and his manner, defiant and vulnerable. Lisabeth wanted to hug her.

'I ran away once, when I was very, very little. We lived in a town in England, near the sea like this. I was cross with my mother – she'd promised to make Apple Cobbler for pudding but when I'd eaten all my vegetables she told me she'd forgotten, and I was so cross that I stamped my foot at her. I knew she'd smack me then, so I ran away before she could catch me, and I hid in the forest on the sea-shore. I suppose it was a park, really. Then I was even more afraid because I thought there might be a wolf come along and eat me.'

'Me, too!' cried Daisy, clapping her hands in delight. 'And then Andwew's dog came and it barked! I was fwightened, too!' She shoved a fist into her mouth, giggling, then said: 'I haven't got a mother . . . only Miss Bwidewell and I hate *her*.'

'I'm so sorry!'

'I used to have one, but she died,' announced Daisy with all the callous frankness of the young. 'Mamma said that Lisabeth was a tewwible person,' she added, staring doubtfully at her.

Lisabeth's lip twitched. She gazed out across the harbour, where a pucker in the chain mail told that Joe Day was already about his pilot's duties, rowing out to lead the first of the ships up the channel. 'Perhaps I am.'

'Miss Bwidewell is a tewwible person!'

Both turned as Bollan barked again and the sound of galloping hoofs thrummed through the ground, so cloe that they could feel the vibrations. Rhys, angry and dishevelled, rode into view, dismounting when he saw his daughter huddled there under the shawl. He was unshaven but wearing evening clothes, rumpled velvet trousers and a silk shirt only half tucked in. Either he had just returned from a night of roistering or he had leaped out of bed and flung on the first garments to hand. Had Leonie been visiting him again?

'Daisy, are you all right?' he demanded, brushing Lisabeth's reassurances aside and scooping his daughter up. 'Darling, it was very naughty of you to lock Miss Bridewell in her room.'

'I hate Miss Bwidewell!'

'Darling, please . . .' He looked baffled and defeated. 'I don't know what I'm going to do with you.'

She giggled and tucked her head under his chin so that the curling-ribbons tickled his neck. Then Rhys looked at Lisabeth and forgot he was holding the child. She was gazing up with an unguarded expression, obviously moved by the sight of him with the child twined in his arms. Already it seemed forever since that night on the cliffs, and in the time between he had booted her out of his dreams and squashed every intrusion she made into his mind, fighting her so doggedly that he had forgotten how beautiful she was.

His face tightened as he closed his mind. Daisy was the shield between them. *Lisabeth, I could die . . . I ache for you! Lisabeth, I*—But he said coldly: 'She ran away and I was worried.'

'I'm not surprised. She's a lovely child.'

'Not lovely at the moment, I'm afraid. Poor Miss Bridewell had hysterics.'

Her eyes transposed the texture of his skin to her fingertips so vividly that she could feel the stubble, prickly and warm. Clenching her hands, she turned away. Both dinghy and ship were already in the stream.

'Let me stay with Lisabeth, Papa!' cried Daisy. 'Please, Papa! She's my fwend! *Please!*' And she wriggled beseechingly, thrusting her face up to his.

'But you're not dressed, dear,' said Lisabeth, coming to his rescue. 'Perhaps another time . . .'

'I'm afraid that's up to Miss Bridewell.'

'On her day off, then?' suggested Lisabeth. 'Birdie could bring her down to visit at the cottage . . . Aunty Gwynne would be thrilled. She *is* her aunt, Rhys.'

'I'll see.' He was still staring at her, but brutally now. 'So you're staying on? I thought you were leaving soon.'

'Birdie's been gossiping again,' she said.

'Are you?' But she wouldn't reply. Wouldn't even look at him. 'I do hear that he's come courting again.'

You're a fine one to talk! 'So are you, I hear,' she retorted.

'What's "courting", Papa?'

'I'd better get you back to the house.' said Rhys. 'You're freezing . . . Gracious, where did you find this tatty old thing? It looks as if—' He spoke without thinking and would have gulped back the words if he could when Lisabeth silently held out her hand for the shawl.

Wrapping it around her in one graceful gesture with an end flung back over her shoulder, she walked away. Bollan lifted his head from where he had been sniffing out old bones in the overgrown flower-bed beside the door and loped after her, tail lashing.

'Lisabeth!' called Rhys.

'She doesn't like you, Papa, but she likes me,' said Daisy.

'If only it was that simple,' murmured Rhys.

THIRTY-SIX

AFTER AN OPPRESSIVELY SOGGY SUMMER and an autumn striped with rainstorms the winter set in cold, windy and abrasively dry. As the water absorbed by the land rose back to the surface the wind dashed shrieking from the mountains and whisked it away. All across the plains the tussock dried to a brittle crisp, and when the station-owners congregated at the Christchurch Club they grumbled about scant feed and the ominous signs that a drought might be coming.

'I don't know what it is about farmers, we all seem to grumble all the time. It's too wet or too dry or too hot or too cold. No, sorry, it's always the *wettest* winter in living memory or the hottest summer.'

'Most of us who stay indoors never notice the weather at all,' chuckled Sir Kenneth, who with his back to the fire was lifting his coat-tails to the warmth.

'It is very dry,' agreed Lady Launcenolt from the sofa. She was bending forward watching Daisy, who sat on the floor with pieces of a jig-saw puzzle spread around her. 'I've left all sorts of instructions with the gardener about keeping the shrubs watered. Once they start to brown off it's usually too late.' She fiddled with her pearl choker, sighing. 'Oh, Kiki, I so wish that we didn't have to go. Eight months in Wellington! Our darling will be quite grown up when we get back. My, but we'll miss her!'

'We'll miss you, too,' Rhys told her, though privately he was relieved she was going. It would give him some respite from the constant meddling in Daisy's upbringing. She meant well, but she was ruining the child before his eyes.

* * *

Arriving home in December at the end of a protracted rainless spring, Andrew found the cottage decorated with Welcome signs, plaited straw wreaths and paper angels all crafted by Lisabeth in a fever of nervous anticipation. She hung back watching as Andrew hugged Gwynne's frail form against his strong body.

'You're so thin!' crowed Gwynne, poking him in the ribs. 'Ah, but we've all sorts of good things to put fat on those bones, plump you out before you face the bleak Scots fare. But you're so handsome, lad! The girls in Edinburgh will be running after you calling "Och, ay! There's a bonny braw lad!" '

'I have to pass that examination first. Not just pass it, but pass with distinction. There's a scholarship, you see, and without it I couldn't afford to go. Even with it there's going to be a grim period of budgeting unless I can find well-paying part-time work.'

'No need for that,' blurted out Lisabeth, twisting her hands together in her apron. 'I've not spent a farthing of the rent money, and it's piling up steadily in the bank. It's all for you to use as—'

'No, thanks,' he said curtly. 'I'll not touch a penny of his money.'

'It's not his money, it's mine!' cried Lisabeth. She'd been anticipating this argument. 'I get a fair market rent for the property, no more, and I look on it as being Mr Braddock's money if it was anybody's. Besides, Andrew, you're wrong about Rhys. Very, very wrong.'

'Wrong about what?' asked Gwynne, who was at the table fussing with the plate of scones and the dishes of jam and whipped cream. 'Look, Andrew! I made your favourite. Devonshire tea.'

But Andrew was looking at Lisabeth, at her still white face, her wide dark eyes. 'Maybe I am,' he said at length. 'I expect he just took advantage. We'll say no more about it. All right?'

All right? Lisabeth flew into his arms with a sob. 'Oh, Andrew, I'm so happy!' she cried.

'What is going on?' asked Gwynne.

'Nothing,' Andrew told her. They looked into her baffled face and laughed.

While Gwynne plied Andrew with jam and cream-topped scones Lisabeth sat opposite, too excited to eat. He had changed so much this past year, she noticed. Now he was so tall that even sitting down he was higher than diminutive Gwynne, and his bones had grown thicker, too, broadening his hands, strengthening his long fingers and broadening the planes of his face subtly erasing the force of his resemblance to Rhys. The long time spent indoors had kept his hair dark, too, and there was none of that Morgan bleached blondness. But the resemblance was still there in a dozen ways – in the suddenness of his grin, the crinkling at the corners of his eyes, the lilt in his laughter, the way he drew a quick breath, while when he was in repose, listening to Gwynne's prattle, the likeness to his father intensified.

'Bollan!' Andrew exclaimed abruptly, beaming at her and quite unaware of the tumult of her thoughts. 'That bark . . . that has to be old Bollan.'

Lisabeth jumped up. 'I decorated him to greet you, then quite forgot . . .' She opened the door to let him in. 'Oh, Bollan! Your pretty bow-tie is all muddy. How did . . .?' She stopped. Athol Nye was strolling up the path looking very pleased with himself.

'I've come to welcome the lad,' he said, extending a package wrapped in newspaper. 'It's a book,' he explained when her hands sagged under its weight. *The Encyclopaedia of Anatomy.* You may like to put it away somewhere so I can give it to him later, privately. He may open it, and some of the illustrations are – well, not suitable for a lady's gaze. It's a medical volume, you see.' Sauntering inside, he hung up his boater as if he owned the place, leaving Lisabeth staring after him.

'How did you know Andrew would be here?' she asked later when her annoyance had ebbed. This was to be *their* day. How dare he intrude when they wanted Andrew all to themselves?

'I told him, Sis,' said Andrew blandly. 'Mr Nye has written to me several times. It was he who told me about the scholarship.'

Well, thought Lisabeth, gaping from one to the other. *This is a switch!*

To her dismay Athol visited every day during Andrew's stay. He had appointed himself the lad's tutor and spent his prolonged visits closeted in the parlour with him, earnestly coaching him for the examination while Lisabeth, pointedly excluded, went resentfully about her chores.

Gwynne was delighted to have two men to bake for. 'Don't fret about the way of the world, dear,' she counselled as she watched Lisabeth splash water into the scalding-pail and dunking a decapitated chook before plucking it.

'I can't help it,' muttered Lisabeth, savage with frustration. 'I feel so inadequate, so . . . shut out. Because he's a man Andrew can enrich his life with all this learning, but those doors will never open for me. Do you ever listen to their conversations, Aunty Gwynne? Rossetti and Byron, Eliot and Thackeray and Trollope, people and places I've never heard of. Never will, either. And I've got no rights, no opinions that will ever count. Doesn't it ever bother you that you can never vote in an election? That brute who tried to kill us in the well, *he* could if he was alive. All the native men can, even the worst savages, but *we* can't because we're women. Is that fair? Is that just? It's as if the world has decided that we're dullards, that women have no brain and can't think. They're wrong! Look at me, I practically taught myself to read and write, and look at you, too . . . In lots of ways you're far smarter than Uncle Charles ever was.'

Gwynne was nonplussed. To her this made no more sense than railing against the sky being blue. 'Aren't you pleased that Andrew and Mr Nye rub along so well together? I thought you'd be overjoyed that he's taking Andrew to Dunedin.'

'What?' Lisabeth wrinkled her nose against the odour of hot wet feathers and warm innards.

'It's good of Mr Nye. He has relatives there, so it won't cost Andrew anything for lodgings, either. What's the matter, dear? Didn't you know?'

'Not a word,' said Lisabeth, pulling savagely at the sodden feathers, mindless of the hot water seeping through her apron. 'Not one word. Nobody thinks to tell me anything. I'm only a woman. It doesn't matter that I was hoping to go to Dunedin with Andrew. My wishes don't count.'

But when Andrew came out into the balmy evening to talk to her while she milked the cow she broached the subject mildly, hiding the fury that writhed like an animal inside her.

'Oh, good, you don't mind!' Relief was shining from Andrew's eyes. 'As Mr Nye says, it's not a social occasion, and he can help me with last-minute cramming. You know, Sis, I think he's trying to ingratiate himself with me to help win you over. He really wants you back, you know. It's touching.'

'It doesn't move me,' said Lisabeth tartly.

'You don't mean that, do you? I never liked Mr Nye, but he seems so different now I'm not one of the pupils at his school. I'm quite warming to him.'

'I'd noticed,' she muttered against the warm flank.

'I can even see why you married him. And he needs a wife.

401

Have you noticed how scruffy, how shabby he is now he has nobody to take care of him?'

Almost shuddering with rage, Lisabeth marvelled that her voice was so calm. 'Don't agonize over him, dear. Mr Nye could employ a housekeeper if he wanted. Or he could send his scruffy clothes to the laundry in Ferrymead to be cleaned and mended.'

'He tried a housekeeper once, but it didn't work out,' said Andrew as he plucked a paspalum stalk and bit into the milky stem-end. 'She ate all the food he provided for both of them and demanded a fortune in wages.'

Ah, there's the snag, thought Lisabeth, unsurprised. Once a Nye always a Nye, it would seem.

By an effort of will over inclination Lisabeth remained pleasant to Athol, too, assuaging her jealously by telling herself that he was not intentionally monopolizing Andrew, but was helping him in a way that she was unable to. After all, open resentment would cause conflict and nothing must distract Andrew or stand between him and the scholarship. He *mustn't* fail.

Athol agreed. Early in the New Year when Lisabeth walked out to the gate with him on the afternoon of his final visit he said: 'I'll take care of him so that he's in top form for the big day. I'm confident he'll win, Lisabeth, and won't that be a boon for you? After all these years of sacrifice you'll no longer have to support him. He can stand on his own feet now.'

'I've never considered it sacrifice,' said Lisabeth, pushing an unworthy suspicion from her mind. Was Athol merely pandering to selfish avaricious motives in the attention he paid Andrew? Was he hoping to reap the financial gain when the lad no longer needed her?

At that moment an open landau rolled down the hill and Birdie carolled: 'Yoo-hoo! Lisabaith, look at me!' Birdie, gaudily plumed in her Sunday best, sat beside the coachman as Rhys, in topper and morning suit, rode in the back. 'We're uff ter the raices!' Birdie shrilled as they rumbled past. Rhys waved sedately, gaze fixed on Athol, his face inscrutable. Lisabeth had only the briefest glimpse of him before the landau passed, swirling them in its great choking wake of yellow dust.

'You'd think they owned the road,' coughed Athol, peeved.

'He does,' said Lisabeth. That glimpse of him slid a cold layer of despair over her already depressed spirits. While she was struggling against gloom at the prospect of losing Andrew again, *he* was enjoying this glorious afternoon by disporting himself at a race meeting. With Leonie Gammerwoth, no doubt.

Brushing dust from her skirt, she left Athol to see himself off and wandered back to where Gwynne sat on a bench under a pear tree.

'Have you made your decision yet, dear?' Gwynne wanted to know. 'It would be lovely to be able to share the news with Andrew before he leaves.'

'No,' Lisabeth said without elaboration. The very thought of that on top of images of Rhys and Leonie soured her stomach. Not pausing in her stride, she carried on to the other end of the orchard and continued the half-finished task of propping laden apple-boughs with supporting stakes. The sun beat on her bare head, there was a drifting summery scent of jasmine and the steady whine of bees working the clover. Lisabeth's spirits lightened a fraction. Of course it would be more fun to dress up and go to the races, but this mild outdoors activity was acceptable as a substitute, she told herself, but without much conviction.

The sun intensified, drawing to its late-afternoon peak of intense heat. Lisabeth walked back to Gwynne with a withered twig in her hands. 'The ground's drying out alarmingly fast. We'll have to water these trees next week if there's no rain. Ugh, what a job that will be. Remember how in the last drought we all had to tote barrels from the spring? It was back-breaking work.'

'Terrible,' agreed Gwynne, examining the crisp leaves. 'And it was all for nothing. That was the year the caterpillars came in their millions, wasn't it, and we had to make a fire-ditch to keep them off the gardens?'

Lisabeth laughed, though at the time it *had* been terrible, a nightmare of fatigue and panic. In her sleep for weeks afterwards the crunching sound of millions of voracious mouths haunted Lisabeth. 'Remember how loud—' she began, then paused. 'I can hear crying, a child.' She frowned. 'There's a little girl in a night-gown screaming blue murder along the road there. Who is she? She's not one of the Gullicks, nor—'

'It's Daisy! cried Gwynne, squinting through her thick lenses, though by now Lisabeth had run to intercept the child.

Daisy was in a dreadful state, her face purpled with the effort of screaming, her nightgown ragged at the hem and smeared with dust from the time she'd tripped in the dirt. Her hands were grazed, her face smeared with the mud of tears and grime. 'Andwew! Andwew!' she wailed.

Stopping, Lisabeth put an arm around Daisy, pulling her close.

403

Through the winter she had seen the girl half a dozen times; when Rhys took her into town with him he made an occasion out of stopping by to visit Gwynne. Lisabeth noticed that though Daisy often was dull and listless she never seemed very happy, not carefree and laughing as a child should be.

Now her distress alarmed Lisabeth. 'What's the *matter*, darling? Why do you want Andrew?'

'Miss Bwidewell said . . . said Andwew was here and . . . and I'm not allowed to see him!' she wailed. 'When I cwied she whipped me and . . . and made me go to bed!'

'So you ran away,' said Lisabeth lightly. 'That was very clever of you. Come on inside and you can see Andrew. He'll be so pleased to have a pretty visitor like you.' The gentle words soothed Daisy, and she allowed herself to be led inside, where Gwynne was squeezing a lemon to make her a glass of lemonade.

Andrew was coming out from his bedroom with a pair of stout boots in his hand. 'Daisy!' he called, picking her up and swooping her up towards the ceiling so that she gurgled with joy, her nightgown skirt flying out from her legs. 'Daisy, you beautiful lass! You just came in time. I was off for a last tramp around the cliffs. Don't know when I'll be back this way again, and I wouldn't want to leave without saying goodbye to you.'

'Miss Bwidewell wouldn't let me see you!' She patted his face shyly, and Lisabeth wished she could sketch them together, just like that.

'Well, here I am, and you *are* seeing me!' he crowed, tossing her up at arm's length again, his hands under her armpits, her hair puffing out from her head, her laughter bouncing around the room. Gwynne laughed, too, joining in, but Lisabeth was silent and when Andrew set Daisy down she asked him to do it again.

'Go on, one more time! See how high you can swing her,' she urged in a tense little voice. This time she plucked at Gwynne's sleeve and showed her what she had noticed when Daisy's ankle-length gown billowed out. All along the thin white legs from the back of the knees to just above the heels, blue stripes indented the skin. Gwynne gasped, and Lisabeth shook her head, warning her not to say anything. 'That was splendid!' approved Lisabeth. 'Come and sit down, Daisy. Have some lemonade with Andrew, and I'll cut you each a piece of cake. Would you like that?'

'Do you think Rhys did that?' whispered Gwynne when Andrew was teasing Daisy by pretending to eat her cake and Daisy was squealing in appreciation.

Lisabeth shook her head. 'But surely he must know if the governess whips the child . . . Oh, Aunty Gwynne, what shall we do?'

Gwynne sucked her lip. 'It's nowt to do with us, lass. Interfering only stirs up muck, you know that.'

'Then, there's going to be muck stirred, I promise you that,' said Lisabeth.

They did not have long to wait. Before the glasses were empty and the plates bare there was a rapping on the door and a flat hard voice called: 'Vashti Morgan, will you come right out here at once.'

Daisy's laugh tripped off; she stared nervously at Andrew.

Lisabeth went to the door and stepped out, closing it behind her. 'Miss Bridewell?' she said.

The woman was red-faced and stout but no older than Lisabeth. Her small eyes narrowed still further. Though Lisabeth had said nothing provocative, Miss Bridewell seemed ready for a fight. 'I have come here to fetch Vashti home,' she announced. 'Don't bother denying that you have her. A woman at the house over there heard her screaming and saw you dragging the girl into this house.'

'It wasn't like that at all,' said Lisabeth. 'And I doubt that Mrs Gullick would have said so. Yes, Daisy is here. She's visiting Andrew.'

Miss Bridewell's jaw set. 'The child's name, *bestowed in church*, is Vashti. Mrs Gullick *did* say so, and Vashti is *not allowed* to see Andrew.'

'By whose orders?'

'Her father's,' snapped the governess. Seeing that she had the advantage and that Lisabeth was rocked by this, she added for emphasis: 'Vashti heard the boy was here and begged to visit, but her father expressly forbade it.'

'And did he order you to whip the child? To beat her black and blue?' When the governess clamped her lips shut rather than reply Lisabeth hissed: 'You thought it was safe to do that because Rhys was going out, didn't you? You didn't think anybody would ever find out.'

'Mr Morgan permits me a free hand with the child.'

'If you used your hand, it wouldn't be quite so bad,' retorted Lisabeth. 'But you've used a crop on her. How could you be so vicious to a helpless little girl? I'm sorry, Miss Bridewell, but I don't believe that Rhys would encourage you to beat his daughter, and when I next see him I'm going to ask him what he's thinking of.'

Miss Bridewell's mouth opened and shut, like a fish gasping for oxygen. Finally she found her voice. 'There's no call to do that, ma'am.'

'You mean it won't happen again?'

'No, ma'am. It won't.' There was resentment in the tone but also respect. Lisabeth was inclined to believe her.

'Very well. You may take Daisy home, but you may also be sure that I will come and visit her. Regularly. I don't need to say why, do I?'

'No, ma'am.' This time there was no argument about the name, but Lisabeth had misgivings about everything else as she watched Miss Bridewell lead the tearful Daisy away.

Daisy hated the taste of laudanum. It was syrupy and dark with a bitter slimy aftertaste that clung to the inside of her mouth so that for hours after, even when the drowsiness wore off, a flick of her tongue in the wrong place could swamp her with the peculiar gagging flavour. Usually Miss Bridewell stood sternly tapping the spoon against the side of the iodine-coloured bottle until Daisy had swallowed and opened her mouth to show that it was empty, but after the long walk she was so tired, hot and angry that she shoved the spoon into Daisy's mouth, held her nose until she stopped kicking, then marched out of the room, slamming the door behind her.

Daisy rolled over and pressed her face against the mattress, opening her mouth and letting the black liquid flow, then she swung out of bed, tiptoed across the braid rug to the Italian-tiled washstand where she cautiously dipped some water from the ewer with her pink porcelain tooth-mug, rinsed her mouth and swilled out into the slop-basin. Quite a lot of the laudanum had been swallowed; she could feel the burning trail of it right down into her chest, but she also felt that expanding sensation of victory. Again she had outsmarted horrid Miss Bridewell.

The laudanum had made a big dark stain on the mattress. Daisy tugged the sheet over it and tiptoed to the window, gazing out across the headland. Andrew would be out there. He said he was going for one last tramp around the cliffs because tomorrow he was going away in a sailing ship to some place with a long name that Daisy had never heard of before.

Her door was not locked. Laudanum acted swiftly to overtake

406

its recipients, and already Daisy could feel the first giddy tingle of preliminary light-headedness. Silently she twisted the large silver door-handle and drew the door open. A few minutes later she was running across the rose-garden lawn towards the shrubbery, the stile, the cliff-path – and Andrew.

The sun seemed very, very hot to Daisy. Her feet hurt on the stony track, and she kept stumbling and bruising her already grazed hands. Along the way grew thorny bushes that reached out as she passed, scratching her arms and plucking at the thin fabric of her nightgown so that soon it was as dirty and ragged as the other had been. As she trudged along she gazed towards the shore, wondering if that's where Andrew was, down where the foam of the dark ocean dashed like spittle over the rocks. It seemed a very, very long way. Daisy's head swayed with giddiness and her mind began to thicken until it was a great fuzzy mass with only Andrew clear and sharp in the centre.

When she reached a place where the path had dropped away in a rock-slide she sat down blankly, staring at the sprawling *pohutukawa* trees that spread their scarlet blossoms in a canopy above the rolling surf. She turned her head and looked back at the steep white gables of Mists of Heaven far in the distance. The leaded windows twinkled like jewels in the late sunlight. Daisy felt very tired. Pushing herself to her feet, she trudged back the way she had come.

She saw Andrew when she was traversing a steep narrow portion of the track where on one side the walls rose sheet to the crown of the headland and on the other they dropped away in a series of jutting ledges to the sea some two hundred feet below. Andrew was ahead of her and on a lower section of the track where it had zigged then zagged. He was swinging along easily, planting his boots with the surefootedness of someone thoroughly familiar with the landscape. He was walking away from her, following Bollan who loped on ahead.

'Andwew!' she screamed. 'Andwew!' But the drone of the ocean swamped her words and washed them away. Daisy hurried, her soft bare feet dancing and scrambling as she winced her way over the sharp rocks. It was no use. She could never hope to catch up to him and no matter how loud she shouted he was wrapped in the much closer noise of the sea. He would never hear her.

Daisy pouted, tears of frustration prickling her eyelids. Then she noticed that the track had zigged again, Andrew had negotiated that corner and was striding back towards her. Daisy picked up a stone and threw it so that it skittered down the cliff-face ahead of Andrew. He stopped and glanced up. 'Andwew!' cried Daisy, stepping forward and waving.

The path was firm but her feet wavered, confused by her laudanum-fogged co-ordination. Suddenly she was suspended in air as the cliffs slowly tilted around her, and the next moment she was being whacked all over by rocks, battered and tossed as she rolled down the slope. She screamed and grabbed protruding thorn bushes in a desperate attempt to slow herself down, while Andrew, transfixed with horror, watched her fall.

'All right, where is she?' demanded Miss Bridewell when Lisabeth opened the door an hour later. 'I'll have you know, Mrs Nye, that it's an offence to lure a child away from its home.'

'Go away, please,' said Lisabeth wearily. 'Daisy isn't here.'

Miss Bridewell knocked again. When Lisabeth swung the door wide this time the governess's arrogant demeanour had gone and in its place was a look of genuine concern. 'Are you sure?' she said in a frightened voice. 'Vashti isn't here? But one of the stable-boys saw her running along the cliff-path ages ago.'

'Oh, dear Lord,' whispered Lisabeth. 'Andrew. She heard Andrew say he was going out there.' Pushing past the governess, she ran towards the shore.

She heard Andrew's shouts before she saw either of them and when she stepped to the edge of the path and peered over her heart shrivelled with dismay. Andrew was clutching Daisy against him on a ledge some ten feet below, and beyond them stretched a bleak scarred expanse of rock-face, plunging in rough steps to the water-slicked and waiting rocks far below.

Andrew looked up and saw her. His face cleared; in that first second she could see how desperately worried he had been, then relief softened his features. 'Daisy's hurt – nothing broken, just shaken up – but I've twisted my ankle and there doesn't seem to be any way of getting back up,' he told his sister. Then he grinned. 'I suppose we could jump . . .'

'Don't you dare even to talk like that! I'll go and get Bollan's old rope from the cottage. You just stay there; I won't be long.'

'I won't go far. Just call out for me,' said Andrew.

'Oh, *Andrew* . . . How can you make jokes . . .?'

'Sure beats crying,' he told her. He glanced over the ledge-rim, and immediately his head swam with a sick, hopeless feeling. 'Hurry, will you, Sis?' he called up to her. 'I've had about as

408

much of this view as I can stand.' He stroked Daisy's hair. It was soft and wispy, like cornsilk. 'We'll be out of here soon, Daisy, I promise you.'

'I want my papa,' sobbed Daisy.

'I think you may have mentioned that,' Andrew teased, but with the utter abandon of her five-year-old's emotions she refused to be comforted. She was bruised and bleeding all over, her head pounded and she was terrified.

There was nothing to secure the rope to. Lisabeth tried one of the wiry little thorn bushes, but when she tested it a rattle of pebbles dislodged from around it. Any real weight and the whole plant would jerk out by the roots.

'Hey,' called Andrew as the gravel rained around him. 'What are you trying to do, stone us?'

'I'll have to take the weight myself,' Lisabeth told him worriedly. 'Should I try, or would you like to wait there while I go for more help?'

Andrew closed his eyes. 'Please try . . . see what you can do. This view is getting very, very tedious.'

Persuading Daisy to let go of Andrew was the most difficult part. She clung to him with the desperation of one drowning, and he had to unclench each hand several times before she could be coaxed into facing the ascent, and even then when Lisabeth pulled on the rope which was now fastened around her waist and shoulders Daisy lashed out, screaming, kicking Andrew in the shoulder, blindly convulsing, scraping her hands and feet on every rough patch on the way.

'Daisy, please try!' shouted Lisabeth as she strained on the rope. The way the child was kicking out at Andrew terrified her. If she should catch him off balance . . . The thought made her dizzy with horror. Anxious to get her out of his range as quickly as possible Lisabeth dragged on the rope with every fibre of her strength, ignoring Daisy's shrieks as she was scraped over the rocks. As soon as the child was close enough Lisabeth lunged out and snatched at one of her wrists, lumping her without ceremony to the path beside her where she checked the child swiftly for broken bones before turning her attention to Andrew.

He scarcely needed her. Using the rope only for balance he scrambled up easily with only one bad moment when his boot skidded on a crumbling section of rock and a cacophony of gravel chattered away down the cliff below him. For a second both he and Lisabeth froze, but then his scrabbling boot found a firmer foothold and he thrust himself upwards again.

'Are you all right?' he wanted to know, patting Daisy's head as she clung to him sobbing noisily.

'What about you? What about your ankle?' asked Lisabeth.

With difficulty he reached over Daisy's grasping hands and tested his ankle. 'It's all right. I'd banged it in the fall and didn't want to risk the possibility that it might be damaged.' He grimaced, testing it. 'Daisy was so violently upset . . . so boisterous that I thought it best to stay put and try to keep her calm.'

Lisabeth felt mushy with relief, but Daisy's high, keening sobs were scratching at her already frayed nerves. 'Hush, Daisy, *please*,' she begged. 'Stop crying, dear. We'll take you home to your papa now . . . He'll be home by now and he'll be so worried about you.'

Though her touch was gently coaxing, Daisy pulled away with violent recoil and clung even more desperately to Andrew. 'No!' she shrieked. 'I want Andwew!'

For a fleeting second Lisabeth understood something of the frustration that might have driven Miss Bridewell to chastise the child. That hysterical screaming was almost unbearable.

Birdie came hurrying to answer their battering on the door. She was flushed – from the sun, Lisabeth guessed – and had an unusually bright glow in her eyes. The master was still out, she told them, adding slyly that when he went visiting there was no telling what time he might be back. And, no, she did not know where Miss Bridewell was.

Lisabeth hesitated on the doorstep. 'Could you please wait up for him, Birdie? Stay with Daisy, would you? And when he arrives home would you ask him to come down to the cottage to see us? It's important, Birdie. *Please* stay with Daisy and *please* give Rhys that message.'

Birdie pursed her lips. She disliked taking orders from Lisabeth and usually found some devious means to avoid doing her bidding without any actual defiance, but here something mysterious was going on and nothing tantalized Birdie like a mystery. She held out her arms to the child, who, after a last hopeless sob, let go her grip around Andrew's neck.

'Why didn't you tell her what had happened?' asked Andrew as they made their way home, she trudging, he limping beside her.

'Because she'll embroider everything and Rhys will get a

410

garbled story, that's why. I've got so much to tell our Mr Morgan that it's best he hears the whole lot all together.'

Andrew stopped in his tracks. Thinking that he was about to say something judgemental about Rhys, Lisabeth turned on him, ready to attack. 'Andrew, don't you think it's time you put away these silly ideas about—?' she began.

He wasn't listening. 'Bollan,' he said suddenly.

'Bollan?'

'Yes, Sis. With all the worry about Daisy I clean forgot. He fell down the cliff, Lisabeth. Tried to get down after us, and he fell. It was instant, Lisabeth, believe me.'

She stared at him in disbelief. Bollan, her friend, who had been there to lean against her and offer a rudimentary comfort when she had no other friends in the world. 'You mean he fell to his *death* and we've just left him there? I mean, what if he was still alive, what if he was just—?'

Andrew shrugged unhappily. 'He landed on a ledge just above the waterline, and was there for ages before the sea washed him away. He was dead, Sis, I promise you that.'

Lisabeth turned blindly to him, a great ragged sob tearing from her exhausted throat. 'Oh, Bollan, what a miserable end.'

His arms clasped her quaking shoulders. How thin and worn she seemed. Her grief made him feel inadequate. Shuddering at the recollection of Bollan's blood-freezing howls as he fell, Andrew said: 'He didn't suffer at all . . . Cheer up, Sis. He was only a smelly moth-eaten old dog . . . He'd had a good life.'

She shook her head against his warm neck, burrowing into the curve like a frightened animal. 'It's not just Bollan, it's you going away and Mr Nye, and—' She broke off, unwilling to confess that part of her misery was the thought of Rhys in Leonie's arms somewhere.

'Mr Nye will be back soon,' said Andrew, misunderstanding. 'And when he does come back you'll have him all to yourself.'

Lisabeth choked back a strangled laugh. She decide to let that pass without comment.

THIRTY-SEVEN

GWYNNE CRIED EXTRAVAGANTLY. 'Five years . . . five years!'
she kept saying as she hugged an embarrassed-looking Andrew.

Lisabeth was all cried out. Cold-faced and bereft, she stood a
pace away on the dock and stared at him with longing and resignation. *I must be glad for him*, she told herself firmly, shoving
away the fear that he might never come back at all. Once he was in
Edinburgh and qualified, the world would be his.

'He'll win the scholarship easily,' pronounced Athol, looming
beside Lisabeth in a musty-smelling grey cloth coat. He wore a
shapeless hat, and his trousers were frayed around the cuffs. 'I
have every confidence in him and, if it's not too presumptuous,
I'll derive a certain pride and gratification from the results.'

'You've been a great help,' Lisabeth acknowledged.

'Thank you. I've regarded it as helping you as much as him.
After all, once he is no longer a financial burden on you, you will
be free to—'

'Excuse me,' said Lisabeth, walking quickly away.

Andrew followed her. 'I say, you two aren't quarrelling, are
you? You know I'd like nothing better—'

'Hush.'

He removed her gloved fingertips from where she'd placed
them over his lips. 'No, Sis, please listen. I've noticed that you
put everybody else first and yourself last. Do this for me, will you?
Consider your own happiness. Mr Nye is a fine man and he wants
you back. I know I hated the idea when you married him but I was
looking at him from a schoolboy's perspective. It's different now.
Honestly, Lisabeth, I'd go away happy if I knew that at long last

412

you were giving some consideration to your own happiness. Life's slipping you by . . .' He paused, rattled by the way she was looking into his eyes without a hint of response. 'I mean, it's not good for you to have people whispering about you . . . Mr Nye could look after you and Aunty Gwynne, too . . .'

'Rhys looks after her very well already,' said Lisabeth through stiff lips. Even the mention of his name hurt.

Andrew snorted. 'I'm disappointed in him. I mean, I saved his daughter's life. You'd think he could have spared five minutes from his hectic life of pleasure to come down and thank me.'

'He's probably not home yet. We mustn't assume—'

Athol intruded. 'It's a scandal the way he neglects his daughter. Off gallivanting while she's beaten by the servants! Hmph! The fellow deserves—'

Lisabeth retorted: 'Gwynne says he's a devoted father, isn't that right, dear? Never mind, I'll certainly have plenty to say to him when we go home. There's so much he ought to know . . .'

Athol cleared his throat. 'Lisabeth, I've been giving this matter considerable thought. You need someone to accompany you when you go to confront Mr Morgan, so I propose to come with you.'

'That's kind of you, Athol, but this can't wait until your return. Andrew thinks that the "sleepy medicine" being forced on Daisy could be laudanum.'

'In which case an accidental overdose could prove fatal,' put in Andrew, immediately the medical student, serious and slightly taller somehow.

'Then, take the doctor with you,' ordered Athol. 'Lisabeth, I expressly forbid you to visit that man by yourself. Especially in my absence.'

Lisabeth was speechless. She looked from Athol's haughty face into Andrew's approving one as Gwynne called: 'Come on, you two, the boarding-flag is up.'

Andrew kissed her. 'Remember what I said. Put your own happiness first. He's a good man, truly he is,' he whispered.

Then they were gone, and Lisabeth stood beside Gwynne holding her hand for comfort in the thicket of parasols and wide summery hats surrounded by sobs and gull-cries and perfume under the hard blue sky (another scorcher!), while the little steamboat pushed itself away from the wharf. The spread of clear marbled water between the crowded dock and the crowded railing grew wider and wider until Lisabeth and Gwynne were no longer

413

waving at Andrew and Athol but were flapping their handker-
chiefs at a distant boat slipping through the encircling arms of the
harbour. The knot in Lisabeth's throat hurt so much that her fresh
tears would not come. *Five years!*

'What an adventure! sighed Gwynne. 'Oh, how I envy him!'
And all the way home in the wagon she talked about the sea
voyages she and Charles had shared. Lisabeth only half-listened,
her heart aching with the pain of separation. Andrew was still a
boy in many ways and when he came back he would be a man,
educated, sophisticated and worldly wise.

'He'll look down on me then, when he comes home,' she said
suddenly as they rattled along the swamp road with its hundreds
of corrugations. A *pukeko* darted across in front of them, flicking
a white tail like a rabbit's. 'Aunty, why is it that only men are able
to have these advantages? Why couldn't we study and become
educated and cultured, too?'

Gwynne was startled by the interruption to what she considered
a gripping story about Charles catching a shark while fishing from
the stern of the *Great Yarmouth,* but she said: 'It's not done,
dear. Ladies acquire skills – needlepoint, jelly-making, quilting
– and if they are privileged they develop a touch for the piano-
forte or an ear for music. Each to their own, you see.'

'It's not at all fair.'

'I don't know, lass,' pondered Gwynne. 'There's a comfort in
it. Nothing much is expected of us. In a way that's lovely.'

New Year's Day had interrupted the shearing season at Mists of
Heaven, and had given the itinerant shearers a rare day off. Some,
like Rhys, had indulged in a flutter at the races but most squandered their wages in the south-west corner of town, in the narrow
streets of shanties beyond the railway depot, where all manner of
delights could be purchased for a few shillings and where back-
yard whisky sold for a penny a tot. All straggled back to Mists of
Heaven in the late hours, and Rhys, slightly hung-over himself,
had to begin the next day by stamping through the bunkhouse,
threatening dismissal if wool wasn't coming off sheep's backs by
the time the sun came up.

As they approached their gate Lisabeth and Gwynne saw the
first wagon loaded with enormous humbug-shaped bales all
stamped with the distinctive peaks-within-a-cloud symbol that
denoted Mists of Heaven. Lisabeth halted Major on a broad
stretch of road to allow the Clydesdales to lumber past with their

load, then clucked him on again, but instead of turning in at the gate she pulled hard on the reins and Major, obviously puzzled, trotted on, past the cockatoo cottages and up the ridge-road.

'We'll both go to see Daisy,' insisted Lisabeth. 'And if you're dying for a cup of tea Birdie can make you one in the kitchen and tell you how much money she won at the races.'

From the long sloping driveway they could see out over the vast shimmering plain towards the blue mountains. It was ferociously hot, even up high, jogging along, and with their large black umbrella to keep the sun off. Waves of heat seemed to bounce at them from the parched land all around.

From the top of the rise they could see, half a mile away and to the north, the huge red-painted shearing-shed which huddled at the centre of a spraddled web of stockyards from where wafted a faint odour of wool, manure and hay and a din of barking and bleating, thousands of voices woven together and pierced by needle-sharp whistles as the shearers sent coded messages to their black and white Border Collie dogs. 'They're busy,' remarked Gwynne.

'The drought looks bad,' said Lisabeth.

At Mists of Heaven itself the lawns were scorched brown, the rose bushes wilting. Even the trees were dusty and yellow. Only the Australian imports looked healthy in this weather – the proteas flourishing with their scarlet cones, the spiky-flowered bottle-brush shrubs and the gums, tall and rustly with their strange ragged trunks.

Miss Bridewell opened the massive oak door to their knock. She stiffened, her narrow lips clamped into a line. There was no greeting.

'We've come to see Daisy,' said Lisabeth pleasantly.

'Well, you can't,' came the terse reply. 'She's fast asleep.'

Not too fast, I hope. 'I'd like to see her anyway.'

'You can't. Doctor's orders.'

'I see.' Lisabeth considered the situation. Miss Bridewell was blocking the entrance, with one hand on the door-frame and the other on the door, ready to bang it shut should Lisabeth advance. 'I suppose Rhys is at the shearing-shed?'

'That's right.' It was a smug reply. Women were not allowed near the shearing-shed.

'Where's Birdie?'

'In the kitchen. But you can't disturb her. She's busy baking afternoon tea for the shearers.'

'Come on,' said Lisabeth to Gwynne. 'Let's go and cadge a cup of tea from her.'

'But you can't—'

'Good afternoon, Miss Bridewell.'

Half an hour later, with the wagon loaded with billies of scalding tea, baskets of buttered scones and trays of apple cake, Lisabeth clucked Major up and pointed him towards the sheds. As she looked back at the house she saw Miss Bridewell watching her from an upstairs window. Lisabeth waved, and smiled grimly when the curtain dropped.

At one side of the shed dusty pillowy sheep were being drafted up the ramps that fed shearing-bays within the sheds, while from the other naked white sheep slid down chutes like pale peas spilling from brown pods into more holding-pens where they stood skinny and shivering on their stilt legs.

Lisabeth drove up to the yards, tethered Major to the split-rail fence and climbed down. Nearby was a long sunken trough of water that steamed and stank powerfully of tobacco and sulphur. Two of the workers were shoving sheep into the trough, one pushing them in at one end and the other ducking them under with a long forked stick as they swam to the shallow end where they staggered out, yellow-tinted, wheezing, but free of ticks and lice.

Because of the noise Lisabeth had to shout to make herself heard. ''E be in there,' the shepherd bellowed back at her. 'But yer cain't—' He pushed back his hat and scratched his head, watching as Lisabeth calmly opened a yard gate and picked her way across the dusty manurey ground towards the clamour of the wool-shed. Nobody challenged her as she tugged back the bolt on one of the outer doors and stepped into the cavernous dim brown room.

It echoed with shouts and was redolent with the sheepy lanolin smell of fresh wool. Around three sides of the 'floor' toiled stooped sweating men, shirts sticking to their backs, arms glistening as they snipped the wool free in long even swaths, holding the sheep by one leg, rolling them over expertly in the crook of an arm while the wide-bladed shears snipped ceaselessly.

At any other time Lisabeth would have been fascinated, but she was tense and angry, her eyes searching for Rhys amongst the many milling people. He wasn't by the wool-presses where the sorted fleeces were heaped and crammed within a wooden frame until their canvas container was bulging under the pressure. He wasn't at the loading-dock, nor at the central tables where fleeces were spread out like rugs, picked over and rolled up. Then she saw him at the far corner of the floor, talking to one of the shearers who had stopped his work for the moment. Lisabeth hurried across, intercepting many startled hostile glances from the men whose paths she crossed.

Rhys was speaking loudly and coldly, and all around him was an eddy of calm into which his words rippled. The other shearers nearby listened as their workmate received the lash of reprimand. 'Every sheep in that pen bears some mark of your clumsiness, Winston. They'll all need tarring – you can do it now before you continue here. Sheep that are cut lose condition, get infected and sicken. I'll not have any more of your butchery. If you can't do your job properly, you can pack your swag and go.'

Winston mumbled something. He had seen Lisabeth's approach and was hot with embarrassment. He was a fellow of no more than twenty with a shock of black hair that blended into his beard like a balaclava.

'No, you're not dismissed, just seriously warned,' snapped Rhys. 'But I'm docking your pay tuppence for every sheep you've cut. So—' Sensing another presence, Rhys turned and saw Lisabeth. His face registered surprise, but there was no melting of his anger. 'What are doing here?' he said.

He hustled her outside, pausing to send one of the men to fetch the food from the wagon. 'Even if you have brought our 'billy-up', you could easily cause a riot in there. Some of those men are as superstitious as old women. Now, what is it?'

She looked at him, guessing that this wasn't a good time to broach the subject. Rhys looked exhausted, his eyes bloodshot, his face dead-looking under the tan, and he hadn't shaved. Nor was he pleased to see her but she had no choice.

Taking a deep breath of resolution, she attacked. 'I've just come from farewelling Andrew to Dunedin—'

'Good riddance,' clipped Rhys.

'– and he was hurt and disappointed that you didn't even take the time to wish him – *What* do you mean, ''Good riddance''?'

'Perhaps you are unaware of what your brother was doing yesterday. Not content with killing one of my children he chose to spend his afternoon taking Daisy on a rock-climb! Of course, the inevitable happened. She fell and was badly bruised. Her legs are black and blue. Yes, I can see you had no idea. So—'

'Did Daisy say that?' gasped Lisabeth.

'The poor child is in no condition to say anything. She was unconscious when I got home last night and still sleeping when I went up to look in on her at midday.'

'Right!' cried Lisabeth, her face white, her eyes snapping indignantly. She was choking with such fury that the words tumbled out of her in staccato bursts. 'First, Andrew took Daisy nowhere. She ran away from her governess. Second, Daisy fell down a cliff when she was alone. Andrew rescued her, and hurt himself in doing so. Third, those bruises on her legs – they're from a *beating*, Rhys. Miss Bridewell beat her with a riding-crop and put her to bed after you left for your afternoon's festivities. Fourth—'

'I don't believe you,' he snorted, eyes snapping with disgust. 'Miss Bridewell beat Daisy? The very idea is ridic—'

'Not only does she beat her,' forged on Lisabeth with raised voice, 'but she tells her that if you find out she's been naughty enough to be smacked you'll beat her far worse.'

The angry denial died on Rhys's lips as he recalled occasions recently when the child had shrunk away from his good-night hugs, how inexplicably fearful she had seemed at times.

Lisabeth was glaring at him, fists at her sides. She hadn't forgiven him for his first remark, and was beginning to agree with Athol that Rhys was neglecting his daughter. Surely he should supervise the nurse better than this? She persisted. 'Not only is the governess beating Daisy, but she's doping her with what Andrew suspects might be laudanum, which will explain why she's so drowsy – and why she's still asleep at noon and possibly why she lost her balance and tumbled over that cliff—'

'This is nonsense,' spluttered Rhys. 'You fly to your brother's defence at the slightest thing, but this is going too far. Miss Bridewell is a reliable and trustworthy person. When she told me what had happened I rode right down with the intention of dealing Andrew a sound thrashing. I notice that you haven't come to me with your story until he was safely out of the way.'

'That wasn't it at all! Andrew was disappointed that you made no effort to come down and thank him for saving Daisy's life. We assumed that since you were out with Mrs Gammerwoth you had other things on your mind, and that's why you made no effort to respond to the message we left with Birdie. She said she left a note on the hall-stand and when it was gone this morning she assumed you must have collected it.'

'There's been too much assuming,' said Rhys, pieces of the puzzle beginning to form together in his mind. 'Come on, let's clear this up. We'll look in on Daisy. Let's walk up, shall we? I want to surprise Miss Bridewell. On the way you can tell me what did happen on the cliffs. Lisabeth, I'm sorry. I've been in a rage – in hell, actually – since I saw you with Athol Nye yesterday. And Daisy had been whining and pleading non-stop to be allowed to visit Andrew—'

'I know,' whispered Lisabeth. She wanted to plead for Andrew, tell Rhys again that the other tragedy, Darius, hadn't been his fault, either, but sensing the tension there she wisely kept silent. All in good time.

Approaching the house from the rear, they walked up the servants' narrow stairs and along the carpeted hall. The nursery door was locked. Rhys rattled the handle in disbelief. 'I've told her never to do this. What if there was a fire?' he said. 'My heavens, Lisabeth, I'm sorry if I doubted a single world of what you told me.'

Lisabeth was glancing surreptitiously along the corridor, thinking how faded her memory must be because she could not recognize this part of the house at all. Ahead was the stairwell illuminated by stained-glass windows, so therefore right here on the left should be the room where Rhys had made love to her in that magnificent canopied bed, but there wasn't even a doorway in this stretch of panelled wall, just a row of framed oil paintings and an enormous oakwood dresser where a collection of antique snuffboxes were displayed. Lisabeth was about to ask Rhys if there was another corridor nearby when she saw a key lying beside an embossed silver snuff-box on one of the upper shelves. Without a word she gave it to Rhys, and he opened the door.

Daisy was lying on her back, staring at the plaster ceiling, so still that Lisabeth at first thought she was dead. So did Rhys. He dashed to her side, scooped her up in his arms and twirled around, hugging her with joy when he realized that his first impression was wrong.

'Papa,' slurred Daisy. 'Papa, my legs are sore!'

'Sorry, angel.' He sat her down on the bed. Her head drooped like that of a loose-limbed doll.

'She's drugged,' murmured Lisabeth, kneeling in front of the child and examining her dilated eyes. 'Daisy, where does Miss Bridewell keep the medicine?'

'Don't . . . know.'

'I think I know where it might be,' Rhys said. 'You stay with her. I'll go and look.'

'I'm sleepy, Lisabeth. Where's Andwew?' said Daisy.

Lisabeth smoothed the soft yellow curls, not trusting herself to speak. From the washstand she brought a cloth wrung out in water which she dabbed on the child's swollen feet. She was bathing Daisy's hands in the same way when the door opened and Miss Bridewell walked in. Behind her in the doorway was Leonie Gammerworth. Both paused in astonishment.

It was Leonie who spoke. 'We heard noises and thought Vashti was awake.' She sauntered into the room, glossy as a leopard in an elegant brown and white striped taffeta gown with a wide hooped skirt and a bonnet shaped like a cluster of white butterflies perching on the back of her head. 'Hello, Vashti dear. Miss Bridewell tells me that you've been a very naughty girl.'

'Miss Bridewell has been telling people a lot of things, haven't you?' said Lisabeth, standing up. 'But I imagine she left out a few details, such as the whippings she gives the poor lass.'

'Children should be chastised. It does them no harm,' remarked Leonie airily. Her smile was frosty and her eyes as brown and hard as the panelling in the hallway. 'Vashti can be an extremely precocious child. If you ask me, she *needs* whipping occasionally.'

'Then, I hope that nobody does ask you!' cried Lisabeth, incensed by the casualness of her cruel remarks. 'How dare you suggest hitting a defenceless child, and how dare you come here and criticize! If you don't like Daisy, you should stay away from her, and from here, too!'

Leonie looked as flabbergasted as the governess, but only for a moment. Recovering quickly, she laughed. 'I see,' she purred in her throaty voice. 'The peasant girl doesn't like being patronized. I do understand, my dear. Perhaps it's you who should run along home to your grubby little vegetable patch, and to your quaint husband who can't decide whether he wants a wife or not. Looking at you, I can't understand his indecision. He made the correct move when he threw you out.'

'He didn't throw her out. She left,' said Rhys from the doorway. 'What are you doing here, Leonie? I thought I made it absolutely plain yesterday that—'

'Now, Rhys, I knew you were speaking hastily,' Leonie cut in. 'I came out here to give you a chance to apologize.'

'Really?' He turned to Miss Bridewell who had been standing just inside the door, a spectator to the skirmishing. 'Now, Miss Bridewell. What's this?' he demanded, holding out a large purplish-brown bottle. 'I found it in your room and it has no label on it.'

Her watery eyes wavered. She bit her thin lower lip. 'It's . . . It's cough linctus, sir. Mild and harmless, I assure you. I take it when I have one of my throats coming on.'

'Do you, indeed?' He glanced at Daisy, but her eyelids were drooping and her shoulders slumped. Lisabeth was sitting with one arm around her, whispering to her and stroking her hair.

Following his gaze, the governess pleaded: 'Don't believe a word of what *she* tells you, sir. I'm the one who looks after Vashti. I know what really happened. I've told you the truth, I vow I have!'

'Then, you won't mind proving it,' Rhys told her as he extended the bottle and a spoon he had found with it. 'Let me see you swallow a dozen spoonfuls.' When she backed away, shaking her head, Rhys coaxed in the same dispassionate voice: 'Come on now. If it's harmless, you wouldn't mind taking twenty spoonfuls.'

'It . . . it'll scour me,' blurted Miss Bridewell.

'A little discomfort,' shrugged Rhys. 'Come on, drink it.'

'No! No, you can't force me!'

'Can't I? A couple of servants from the kitchen to hold your arms and a funnel down your throat? I don't think there would be any problem.' Leonie began to protest, but Rhys silenced her angrily. 'That's what you did to Daisy, didn't you, Miss Bridewell? You forced her to drink this laudanum. You stuck the spoon in her mouth and held her nose until she stopped kicking.' He drew a deep shuddering breath, his face so violent with anger that Miss Bridewell cowered in anticipation of a blow, but instead of hitting her he lowered his voice to tell her she was dismissed. 'Go right now. Don't bother packing – I'll have Birdie take care of that. Just get out of my sight. You, too,' he added as an afterthought to Leonie. 'If your views on child-rearing are so compatible, you might care to offer this wretch a ride into town. You'll find plenty to talk about.' To Lisabeth he said: 'Let's take Daisy down to the kitchen. Birdie might know how to sober her up.'

'Aunty Gwynne is certain to know,' Lisabeth said.

'Of course. I forgot she was there.' He laughed. 'Lisabeth, I think I'm going to plead family responsibility and all that and beg Gwynne to take over Daisy's care.'

'Nothing would please her more,' Lisabeth assured him.

* * *

421

'Well, Lisabeth, what about you?' asked Rhys later that evening. They were alone in the cool mellow library. Upstairs Gwynne was reading Daisy a bedtime story (no 'Buggane' tales, Rhys had decreed), while in the cosy little bedroom beyond Birdie was packing up Miss Bridewell's personal effects. Rhys said, 'I can tell that Gwynne is reluctant to move in. She's always had a phobia about white stone and every time she visits she gazes around fearfully as if she expects the walls to cave in on her, but I think I can talk her around.'

'I'm sure you can.' Lisabeth accepted a stemmed glass of Canary wine, which she held carefully while he settled on the sofa beside her. She sipped it, watching him over the rim of the glass to see how he drank, imitating him.

'Then, what about you, Lisabeth?'

'I'll go back to my cottage. I prefer it there, anyway. Only, if Andrew wins this scholarship, I shall save the rent money and find out if there is anywhere a woman can go to gain a proper education. Please don't laugh at me!' She rushed on so hurriedly that a splash of wine slipped over the rim and down to her fingers. 'I'm serious, Rhys. I've always envied Andrew being able to go to college, learning all those fascinating things he used to tell me about. Half of it I could never understand and the other half only made me hungry for more. I want to learn, to study . . . Why are you smiling like that? Do you think I'm being preposterous?'

'Not in the least.'

'Then, why are you laughing?;

'Because you can study right here, in this room. It's yours. Use it.'

'I couldn't . . . I wouldn't know where to begin.'

'I'll show you. Let me select books for you to read, show you how to make notes as you go along, teach you how to study and absorb what you're reading. I'd love to do that. We could study together.'

Lisabeth stared into her glass. The idea was intoxicating, but it was too much. Impossible.

Rhys was sitting so close that she could feel the warmth of him, very subtle, such as the sensation received when one walked quickly past a fireplace. One hand was behind her, along the sofa back. She was sitting primly, both hands holding the glass, knees pressed together under her faded green poplin skirts.

His hand moved forward, cupped the back of her neck. 'I want you to move in here with me, Lisabeth.'

The demand did not surprise her. She was expecting him to ask her, wanting and fearing those words, but what paralysed her with dread was her own indecision. The wrongness yet rightness of it disorientated her. Her heart was like a nervous bird crouching in fluttering fear. Hardly breathing, she stared into her glass, unable to reply, and she was still sitting like that with Rhys leaning forward, his face only inches away from hers, when Gwynne bustled beaming into the room.

'She is a bonny lass, Rhys, and a credit to you. After all she's been through she can laugh and chatter away, bright as a button, too, now that laudanum has worn off. I thought she'd never go to sleep.' Gwynne was radiant, and looking at her Lisabeth thought: *She feels needed again. It's a tonic to her.*

A small distance apart from Lisabeth now, Rhys said: 'Do you think you'll move in, then?'

Gwynne sucked her lip. 'I thought that over on the way downstairs. It's what Mr Stafford would have wanted, isn't it? He was so fond of you . . . always thought the world of you, he did. Yes, once I realized that Mr Stafford would approve, the idea suddenly seemed perfect.'

Lisabeth recalled Charles's unremitting, envious loathing and marvelled at the elasticity of Gwynne's mind, but her smile was affectionate as she said: 'That's wonderful news, dear.'

'Let's celebrate!' Rhys suggested, standing up. 'This calls for something really special. A splendid occasion *avec ceremonie!* Let's have one of your incomparable egg-nogs, your Christmasy ones with whisky and sprinkled with nutmeg. I'll send Birdie down so that you can give her some pointers – hers are terrible, but don't tell her I said so – and then we'll all sit around in the parlour and drink a toast to the future.' He shepherded her to the door. 'Lisabeth and I will be along in a minute. I want to show her something first.'

He closed the door and turned to face her. 'Answer me one question. Have you any intentions at all of going back to Athol Nye?'

'I did have,' she said. 'I was anxious to do the right thing. Andrew was eager that I should go back to him, and I—'

'Andrew is not relevant to this,' he said, hiding a flare of irritation. 'Answer the question, Lisabeth.'

'Very well. I'm not going back to him. I'm going to ask him for a divorce, but I don't think he'll—'

'That's all I wanted to hear. Come,' he said, holding out his hand to her.

Upstairs in the corridor Rhys instructed her to watch as he braced his shoulder against the enormous dresser and heaved at it with all his concentrated strength. Groaning with reluctance, it scraped along the floor and gradually, inch by inch, a doorway appeared from behind it.

'Your room!' said Lisabeth. 'No wonder I couldn't see it earlier.'

'Our room,' he corrected her, unlocking it with a key he had taken from behind a book on one of the library shelves. The door swung wide.

Lisabeth entered in bemusement. The room was exactly as she remembered it, and it had obviously been untouched since that night. Dead ashes heaped the grate, mould encrusted the inside of the tea-cups on the tray, and the remaining chocolate cake had crumbled to black dust. The bed was rumpled, the towel she had used to dry her hair lay where she had dropped it on the rich floral rug. The room was musty, cool but airless, and Lisabeth had the weirdest feeling of dislocation as she gazed about, at the dust-furred canopy, the pier-glasses, grime-dulled, that reflected the room back at her.

'I used to imagine that you were here with Azura,' said Lisabeth. 'I used to torture myself thinking about this room.'

'So did I. That's why I never could come near it. But I did do something. Remember how you locked me in? Come and see what I contrived to remedy that.' Leading her to the garderobe, he showed her how the door opened only from this side. He moved through, and she followed, glancing around at the empty clothes-racks, the shelves for shoes and hats, and under the skylight the washstand, pink marble like the slab on which a rose-patterned slipper bath stood. 'This is another door I had installed. Fetched a workman from Wellington so that it would be absolutely confidential.' Pressing a knob on the wall he smiled at her surprise as a panel moved back, opening up the way into the next bedchamber, a smaller, less opulently furnished one than the room they had left but still so large that one of the cockatoos' cottages could have comfortably fitted within. Windows opened to a wide view of cliffs and ocean. The room smelt of roses and orange blossom, warm with sunshine. There was a bureau, two huge wardrobes and a four-poster bed with a fur rug flung over it.

She had not said anything to encourage or discourage him. He said: 'I've thought it all through. As long as we're circumspect nobody will think it odd if you and Gwynne come to live here.

424

You may occupy the large room, and this will be mine, officially at least.' He paused, then continued softly: 'Nobody knows about the connecting doors and nobody ever will.'

Lisabeth thought about an endless succession of delicious nights and felt giddy. 'People do talk,' she insisted. 'Mrs Gammerwoth will have a field-day. I don't know if I can endure the vicious gossip that would be generated.' But even as she spoke she was thinking: *Why not? Would Andrew really get to hear any of it, being so far away?*

'There'll be gossip, all right,' Rhys promised her. 'But not of the tone you fear. I'll broadcast all around town the information about Miss Bridewell – in fact, I have to, in case she seeks employment with another family. The province will be aghast, Lisabeth, and nobody will think it amiss if I call in my relatives to help look after Daisy.'

Yes, Andrew will hear of it, thought Lisabeth. *Athol will make sure he hears every detail.* 'I don't know,' she began, then faltered. She had been idly studying a row of paintings which hung above the headboard of the large bed. Five, there were, all coastal scenes executed with dash and flair, conveying more atmosphere than intricate detail. There was a tantalizing familiarity about the style. 'My pictures!' she cried, realizing that here were the paintings Mr Archibaldiston had purchased from Athol's exhibition 'on behalf of the Southern Cross Galleries'. Rhys had arranged it! He had made her famous and launched her career.

'You!' she croaked, and he wondered if she was angry. 'You bought them! Poor Athol was furious, I was astonished, and all of Canterbury Province flocked to buy my paintings all because you played a trick on me!'

'It wasn't a trick. I wanted some of your work.'

Lisabeth began to laugh. 'That's what you would do, of course. Instead of sending one of the shepherds, or five assorted shepherds, servants and acquaintances, you had to give the errand to the country's most influential art-dealer. Oh, Rhys.' Collapsing, Lisabeth rolled over on the luxurious fur, helpless with mirth.

Rhys locked the door and strolled over to where she lay, still shuddering with laughter. 'I'm glad you don't feel cheated.'

She shook her head. Tears smudged her cheeks. 'What poor fools people are – hurrying in droves to buy my work so that they could boast to their friends that Mr Archibaldiston himself greatly admired my work! No, Rhys, I don't mind. I love the joke, and the fact that you went to such extravagant lengths – especially

425

when you had every reason to hate me,' she added in a whisper he didn't quite catch.

'Mr Archibaldiston liked your work. He said you had a deft delicate touch and a certain way with colours, so don't denigrate yourself. Many famous artists accelerate their careers by manipulation. Even Leonie's lap-dog used to pay people to attend his concerts, to applaud loudly and to throw flowers on to the platform. It's a legitimate part of the show.' He leaned over her and nuzzled her face, and she sighed and placed one hand behind his head. 'I want to make love to you here and now,' he murmured in a low voice that sent a spasm of response quickening through her belly.

'What about Gwynne and Birdie?'

'Not them. Just you.'

Still laughing, she stroked his face, touched his dimple with a fingertip which he captured and gently bit. 'Ouch! But won't they be waiting for us?'

'Probably,' said Rhys, lifting her skirt and unrolling her stockings. 'I should have asked Gwynne to bake us one of her plum puddings or a fruitcake to celebrate with instead. That would keep them occupied for hours. I'd rather do this justice, Lisabeth, but I want you so agonizingly . . . I can't wait another moment.'

He was untying the strings at the waist of her knickers when she suddenly stirred and pushed at his shoulders. 'No, Rhys, please! What if there was a result, an *outcome* of our lovemaking? Rhys, we musn't take the risk.'

'There's no risk,' he said earnestly, pausing to reassure her. 'Believe me, Lisabeth, I'll do nothing to endanger you in that way. I love you; I want you for our whole lifetime. We'll have children I hope, but not now, not until the right and proper time, so—'

'I trust you,' said Lisabeth. Then he was pressing his lips against the warm curve of her belly and she forgot about Athol Nye, forgot Gwynne and Birdie and the egg-nogs, forgot everything except why she was here and that Rhys was parting her legs now and kissing her, silvering her with delectable stripes of his tongue, and despite her nervousness she was shuddering with such glorious tremors of ecstasy that her instinctive protests died in her throat and her fingers tightened in his hair.

'You are mine, aren't you?' he demanded against her neck as he fitted his body against hers. 'I'd hate to go to all this trouble if

426

you were going to run away like you did last time.'

That made her laugh of course, and when she said, 'I do love you, Rhys,' it was a happy declaration, as such words should be.

'Then, promise you'll stay,' he urged, thrusting into her and melting in the sweetness that took his breath away. If she responded, he did not hear the words; he knew that they would overcome all obstacles. Afterwards as she lay in his arms, still loosely entangled with him, he kissed her damp forehead and shushed her exhausted sobs.

'You'd be a fool to leave me,' he told her, mock-seriously, but this time he noticed that she made no reply. Propping himself up on one elbow, he searched her face, saying: 'Well, Lisabeth? Will you move in here where you belong?'

Lisabeth bit her lip. 'I want to. Believe me, I want nothing more, but—'

'Then, do it,' he interrupted seriously.

'Please don't rush me, Rhys,' she pleaded. 'I need to think it over carefully.'

He frowned, then his face cleared. She had given him her answer just now, by giving herself to him, and if she wanted time to think he could afford to humour her. 'Take as much time as you like,' he said lightly. 'Just as long as you promise to answer "yes".'

She laughed. 'I'll bear that in mind,' she teased.

427

THIRTY-EIGHT

GWYNNE WAS SO DELIGHTED with her position at Mists of Heaven and the new purpose in her life that she tried to coax Lisabeth into accepting Rhys's invitation to come, too.

'Even for just a few weeks, until Daisy has settled,' she suggested. 'The poor wee lass needs all the love and comfort she can get.'

'I know . . ,' said Lisabeth doubtfully.

'If you're worried about Mr Nye, then don't be, lass.'

Lisabeth was astonished. 'I thought you were eager for me to go back to him. And you know how he disapproves of my association with Rhys.'

'With good reason, too,' retorted Gwynne surprisingly. 'Rhys told me that he had words with our Mr Nye. Accused him of marrying you for your money and then treating you like a drudge. It were years ago, he says, but Mr Nye has never forgiven him for it.'

'I can imagine!' But Lisabeth still would not make a decision about living at the big house. Gwynne was ensconced in a room above the stables (her phobia about the white walls proving an insurmountable block, even to Rhys's persuasions) and, though this gave Lisabeth a perfect reason to move in to be close to Daisy, still she hesitated. Andrew was very much on her mind.

She wrote to him the moment the wonderful news about the scholarship arrived. The letter would reach him before he left for Edinburgh, and in it she told him all about Miss Bridewell's dismissal and the decision Gwynne had made to move in with Rhys. 'She seems to think I should do the same because young Daisy needs caring folk around her,' Lisabeth added casually.

428

'And this may distress you, dear, but several disturbing things have come to light about Mr Nye, which makes me think very seriously about him.'

Fingers crossed, she posted the letter, hoping that if it arrived when Athol was there Andrew would not show it to him.

Athol remained in Dunedin for several weeks visiting with his relatives, and on the day he was due back Lisabeth rowed across the harbour to Sumner from where she would take the coach for Lyttelton. It was another limpid morning, warming up gradually for the searing afternoon it would become. The harbour was sprinkled with half a dozen canoes, each with a lone Maori fisherman, and as Lisabeth rowed past them she rested on the oars to wave greetings. Maori tribespeople were filtering from the interior to stay with their relatives on the coast and share their harvest of food from the sea, for inland the province was brown and dying, hurting in the drought.

At the jetty Alf and Joe were scrambling over the hull of a cutter so newly launched that the masts and rigging had not yet been fitted. 'Lisabeth! It's been too long,' said Joe, while Alf smiled shyly and hurried to tie the rowboat up for her. 'Come and tell us what you think of our latest beauty. We're calling her *Red Jacket* and we hope to race her, don't we, Alf?'

'*Red Jacket* isn't a very feminine name, even if it is your favourite brand of tobacco,' teased Lisabeth. 'But, truly, she's impressive. So sleek. I'm sure she'll fly across the water like lightning.'

'Greased lightning,' amended Joe, sitting down on an upturned barrel. From a sack on top of a coil of rope he withdrew a clay pipe and a tin of tobacco. 'How's Rhys managing? I hear that things are bad down south. Farmers are selling off everything to buy imported grain to keep their best sheep alive. There'll be a real crisis if there's no rain soon. These are grim times.'

'It's bad everywhere. Rhys is worried, too.'

'And you? You seem upset, on edge.' He glanced at her quizzically over the soft flare of flame. 'Great news about the scholarship. Always some good news amongst the bad. Just as well, eh?' He began to walk beside her as she moved towards the road. 'Are you going to visit Ma? She's baking a batch of Kentish Huffkins. Apple and cinnamon buns. Scrumptious. Save some for us, though, won't you?'

Lisabeth flushed, though she knew his teasing was of a gentle brotherly kind. He cared about her, and the knowledge made her brave. 'Joe, I need your opinion.'

'Don't have much of that.' He grinned.

'But you're honest.' She squinted against the glare off the water. 'Aunty Gwynne is moving into Mists of Heaven.'

'Against her superstitions?'

'That's it. She's agreeing to go only if she sleeps apart, in the stable quarters, and Daisy will be alone at night.' She could feel herself flushing again, so hurried on. 'Rhys wants me to live there, too, help with Daisy and so on, but I'm worried that people might gossip.'

His grin broadened, and he pushed his hat back on his mop of dark curls to distract his mirth. 'Lisabeth, people have been gossiping about you as long as I can recall, but people gossip about everybody. Aren't you past worrying about that?' He glanced at her stricken face. 'I see. It's Athol Nye you're worried about.'

'It's Andrew, actually. As for Athol, I'm on my way to meet him now, to tell him that I'm never going back to him.'

Joe whistled between his teeth. 'Good for you. And don't worry about your brother. He's living his own life now. I say, Mr Nye could be unpleasant. Would you like me to come with you?'

'You're a friend, a marvellous friend, but no, thanks, I'll manage.'

'Then, take care.'

She planned to tell Athol right away, in public, but jolting up the Zig-Zag in the tiny coach she wondered whether she would be safe anywhere from his anger. The thought of an ugly exchange terrified her. She prayed that he would be calm, aloof and distant.

'Where's your wagon?' he wanted to know. 'You said you'd be coming to collect me.'

'To meet you,' she corrected him. 'We'll take public transport. I don't mind.'

'I do,' he carped. 'It means annoying delays. Look at the queue of people waiting already. We could be here until noon. Really, Lisabeth, this is most inconsiderate.'

'Then, we'll go by train and I'll pay the extra,' said Lisabeth. 'Did you have a pleasant voyage?'

'I was nauseous all the way,' he complained, explaining away the grey hue of his complexion and his sour demeanour. 'We were served a very questionable roast duckling at the hotel before departure. I'm afraid that nobody has quite Mrs Stafford's excellent gift with poultry. As I was saying to Andrew, I do look forwrd to providing her with an incomparably appreciative audience for her skills.'

The thought of having to sit opposite him every mealtime for the rest of her life turned Lisabeth's stomach. *Tell him quickly*, she thought. 'You may not have a chance to sample her cooking again, Athol,' Lisabeth began tentatively as she watched two gulls squabble over a scrap of pork rind. They were in a crowded space of wharf now; most of the steam-packet's passengers had been met by friends and family, though there were a few stragglers, mostly scruffy discouraged-looking fellows – on their way back from the goldfields, Lisabeth guessed.

'What do you mean? She hasn't—?'

'She's moved into the Morgan homestead, to look after Daisy. The governess had to be dismissed, and Aunty Gwynne jumped at the chance to take her place – Daisy really only needs companionship, so the duties won't be too onerous. Aunty Gwynne says it's paradise up there. Such opulence after the tiny patched-together cabin.'

'All right for some,' said Athol.

'Uncle Charles used to say that, and rather too often, I'm afraid,' Lisabeth commented lightly.

'What's that supposed to mean? I say, Lisabeth, there's something very off-handed about you today.' He pulled his chin back against his Adam's apple and looked down his finely shaped nose at her. 'I must say I'm a trifle disappointed in the warmth of your welcome. I expected you'd be thrilled about Andrew and grateful for the professional assistance I gave him. He won't need any of your money, now, will he?'

A fishing boat was sailing past the wharf, the creaking of its mast audible above the cries of the gulls that yapped and nagged above its wake. Lisabeth watched as she said: 'I'm delighted of course, but even though Andrew no longer needs financial help I won't be keeping any of the money.'

'Why not?' Putting his carpet-bag down, he seized her forearms, and before she could wriggle away pinched her hard so that she winced with pain.

'What nonsense is this, Lisabeth? What *is* the matter with you?'

Pulling free, she stepped back a pace and glanced around to see if anybody was staring, but the clusters of people nearby were busy with their own reunions in their parasols' oases of shade. Nobody had noticed. 'How dare you?' she hissed. 'How *dare* you hurt me?'

431

'I dare because I have a right,' he pronounced pompously. 'Your well-being is of concern to me, and if you seem to be doing something outrageous I react out of that concern. Now, kindly explain what you meant.'

Instead she said with malice: 'Rhys was so impressed by my kindness to Daisy that he's asked me to come to Mists of Heaven to help look after her.'

'That's his excuse,' sneered Athol. 'Lisabeth, I expressly forbade you—'

'What's *your* excuse?' she interrupted heatedly. 'What's the reason behind this concern for me? It *is* the money, isn't it? You coached Andrew because you wanted to make absolutely certain he'd be given the scholarship, and why? Because you—'

'Enough!' His cheeks were livid with indignation. '*You* made use of *me*! You asked me to coach Andrew and now you propose to make a mockery of my good intentions.'

Lisabeth opened her mouth to argue but decided not to bother. They were squabbling with real hatred; it permeated their voices, distorted their faces. 'I came to tell you that I'm not coming back to you, Athol. You can see now, surely, that we'll never be together again. I'd like a divorce, please.'

'You conniving bitch!' he spat at her, darting out his hand to fetch her a stinging blow on the cheek. He drew back, knotting his fists in frustration. 'You forget your duties, madam.' While she staggered, gasping, to regain her balance, he added loftily: 'You're my wife, my chattel, and my patience is at an end.'

If he had said, 'Come, I'm taking you home where you belong.' she would have felt real fear, but oddly it was he who seemed skittery now; he was staring at her with an expression of regret. When he pulled out a handkerchief from his jacket and dabbed at the corner of her salty-tasting mouth, she understood why. She was bleeding, people were surreptitiously glancing at them and he was now sorry that he had hit her. This dabbing away of blood was his apology, she realized, and with that knowledge came relief. Now she could rejoice that he had hit her so hard, for she had won a power over him that she urgently needed, while in her heart unfolded the conviction that she had judged him correctly; he desired her money and wanted her labour but had never really loved her.

'If you agree to give me an annulment – to swear in court that our marriage had never been consummated – I'll give you eight hundred guineas from the sale of my land,' she told him. 'I'm keeping some put by in case Andrew needs it but, as for the rest, you're welcome to it.'

'You want me to lie for money?'

'Isn't that what you're doing already? Pretending to care about me when you patently do not?'

He shook his head. 'Oh, Lisabeth,' he said sadly. 'You'd sell your land to be free of me?'

'To Mr Fox.' The idea had just occurred to her, and she was so delighted with it that she did not notice the baffled hurt in Athol's voice. It was a perfect idea! Thomas Fox would be jubilant to get his land and would be a foe turned grateful, so no more scurrilous pamphlets would appear. Athol would have the money he craved, and she would have Rhys.

'I don't believe you,' said Athol. 'You'd never sell to him.'

'He's an old man. I feel sorry for him.' Licking her lips cautiously, she said: 'I'll go now. Write me a letter when you've considered my offer.' And without a further word she walked away, threading her path between the knots of people and on towards the main street of Lyttelton where she would wait alone for transport back to Sumner. Gusts of wind stirred the dust around her high-buttoned boots as she walked, and the sun beat so hotly on her shawled back that she regretted not bringing Gwynne's ugly old black umbrella. Her face was sore and her gums ached and there was still a warm salty taste of blood in her mouth, but for the first time in her life she was completely free from fear, hatred or resentment and was conscious only of a warm expanding glow of happiness. She couldn't wait to be curled up beside Rhys on the library sofa, telling him all about her adventure.

To her dismay he was aghast. 'Fox? You'd sell to him? Forget it, Lisabeth,' he ordered, pacing the maroon and mustard patterned rug. 'I'll not have that evil old troublemaker peering over the hedge, spying on everything that goes on here. First he'd be up to his old tricks of bribing the servants, and then—'

'I'm sorry,' muttered Lisabeth, scarlet with humiliation. 'I'll thought it would be a good idea.'

'And it's not. What would be a good idea is for you to make up your mind about moving in here. My patience is wearing thin, Lisabeth. You're fobbing me off with one transparent excuse after another.'

'But if Athol were to agree to an annulment,' she offered, leaning forward eagerly, 'then we could—'

433

'Do you know how long that could take?' he exploded. 'Dash it all, Lisabeth, it would be years before you're free. He won't let go of you willingly, and if you're at the cottage alone he's likely to come pestering you to change your mind.' His voice grew harsh with urgency. 'Please, Lisabeth, the time to move in is now, while there's a good and valid excuse. If you prevaricate much longer, I'll have to hire a nursemaid to sleep near Daisy, and once that happens . . . Lisabeth, I *need* you.'

'I know.' Her face was full of a tenderness that matched his own, but her eyes were troubled by doubts. She bowed her head and fiddled with the fringed ends of her lemon-coloured sash. 'I wish it were that simple, Rhys.'

'I don't understand. What else could it be?'

Unhappily she began to pour out her reservations and fears about stirring up a fresh brew of gossip, of how she longed for proper respectability. Rhys listened gravely until she said: 'Really, it's mainly Andrew's opinion that worries me. He wanted me to go back to Athol, and he's so moralistic and conservative, Rhys, that I fear that when he hears about—'

'Great heavens, Lisabeth!' Rhys was gaping at her in furious disbelief. 'Do you mean to tell me that our lives are to be ruled by that young whelp's approval?'

'Not exactly,' she defended hastily, stung by his description of Andrew. 'But I'd be so much easier in my mind if I knew that he was happy about what I was doing. I thought that perhaps I should gradually tell him that —'

'Why bother? Why tell him anything? Damn it, Lisabeth, that damned young whelp has no business at all intruding on your life now. He's *gone* and a damned good riddance, too, so face up to the fact and let go of him. Cut those apron strings you've wound around him for far too long. You dote on him far too much, while *he* doesn't care tuppence about you, whether you're happy or not.'

'He does, too!' she flared, her nostrils pinched white. Indignation gushed hot through her brain. 'Andrew does so care! Before he left he made me promise that from now on I'd put my own hap—'

'To hell with what he said!' Rhys bellowed back, irritated beyond endurance by the way Andrew seemed to manipulate his sister even at this distance. He stood squarely in front of Lisabeth and grabbed her upper arms, lifting her to her feet and shaking her for emphasis as he roared: 'Do you understand me, Lisabeth? I don't even like the sound of his name. I don't want to hear it again, and I don't want to hear one word about what he thinks or says or—'

'Well, you should!' she spat back, her eyes narrowed and her mind goaded with blind anger. 'You should care, Rhys. He's your son, Rhys, your *son*! You fathered him when. . .' She faltered. Even in mindless rage she was unable to drag out the mention of Mary and the affair that had poisoned her life with such bitterness.

Rhys was gaping at her, wordless. The silence was awful. It was moments before the echo of her own voice reached her and she realized what she had done.

I didn't mean it! she thought in whirling panic, but there was no way to retrieve the damaging words now. His fingers slackened their grip on her arms, then fell away. She wanted to speak, to say something – anything – to break the terrible silence, but her mouth was dry and her throat rigid.

Rhys felt ill. He stared a challenge into her huge dark eyes and met the unanswerable truth there. He couldn't breathe.

Gazing back at him, Lisabeth read the horror in his face. With a sob she pulled away, turned and dashed from the room. He scarcely noticed her go.

'Sister Dear,' wrote Andrew from Capetown. *'Thank you for your congratulations and for the news in your most Welcome letter. I am in excellent Health despite the most Earnest efforts of this Vessel which is Determined on the most Uncomfortable path across the Oceans, seeking out Tempests that douse us all with Freezing water. A Scotsman on board informs me that the Climate in Edinburgh is Extremely bracing though others warn it is Abominable. I cannot understand much else of what Emerges from his mouth, it seems for the Most part a Ferocious Garble. I fear I shall need a Translator to Communicate with the Natives. . . .'*

There was not one word about herself, Rhys, or the reaction she was hoping for regarding Gwynne's move to live at Mists of Heaven and her hint that she might do the same.

Crumpling the letter in her hand, she gazed out across the dying orchard to the scorched hills. Whereas in other years the air would be full of the chords of bleating and the soft wholesome scent of fresh-gathered hay, now there was only dust and silence. A single gull wheeled noiselessly in the vivid sky, and the hot autumn sun painted a swath of shimmering haze along the road where a flock of sheep were staggering and stumbling towards the distant swampland.

Not a single word! despaired Lisabeth, scanning the letter again. There was no mention of Gwynne's new position, just a message of love for her, nor any comment about the letter Rhys had sent thanking Andrew for his part in saving Daisy's life. He'd written the night the governess was dismissed, a touching generous letter which he'd read aloud to herself and Gwynne. Why hadn't Andrew mentioned that?

Either he doesn't mind what I do, or he detests the idea so much that he can't bring himself to mention it, she fretted, gazing towards the blue mountains and their whipped-cream topping of billowing clouds. *Perhaps Rhys was right. Perhaps I should let go of Andrew completely.*

This thought was one she had always shied away from. It frightened her. He needed her, she would tell herself. She was all Andrew had in the world, wasn't she? That was the way it had always been; the two of them together giving strength to each other no matter what adversity came their way. Even temporary separations and quarrels born of misunderstanding only served to strengthen that deep bond they shared. Or so she had continually reassured herself.

Smoothing the letter out in her lap, she read it again, still searching for some hint she may have missed. There was none. The letter was all of him, his news, his hopes and his plans, with only a brief message of affection scrawled hastily at the close. She sighed and crumpled the paper in her fist. *You are right, Rhys,* she thought.

Not that the realization would do her much good. Since that ghastly evening communication between her and Rhys had abruptly stopped, for apart from one formally worded note asking her to come up to the house to discuss 'certain matters' there had been nothing. Unwilling to reopen the subject of Mary and the long-ago hurts, she ignored the summons and, though she half-hoped he would call on her, he had not been near.

From Gwynne, who called with Daisy most days, Lisabeth learned that Rhys these days was a man ridden by serious worries. 'Birdie says he paces the floor most nights, and he's out in this fearful sun every daylight hour God sends, yet he's so exhausted that he can barely speak. Birdie told me that he drops asleep at the dinnertable, and once she had to whisk a plate of soup away, just in the nick of time, for fear that his face would fall into it. There's whispers of bankruptcy, you know.'

Lisabeth looked uncomfortable. 'Surely Mists of Heaven is safe,' she protested, though her heart stilled as she recalled how many once-prosperous landowners were being forced to walk off their land. Three in the last month had committed suicide.

Gwynne sighed. 'It's that white house,' she mourned, shaking her head. 'Bad luck and ill tidings, that's what it's brought Rhys from the moment he laid the first stone.'

Rubbish, thought Lisabeth, but she replied lightly: 'I suppose all the other station homesteads are white stone, too, then? It's just an unlucky season, that's all. As soon as the drought breaks all the worry will be over.'

That had been weeks ago, and still the hot dry weather continued, unremitting and torturous. This afternoon was a sizzler with waves of heat beating off the cracked crazed ground while those heaped white clouds in the distance only tantalized with their withheld promise of moisture. Even the strong wind soaring in from the sea offered no relief but scorched her hot face and dried the breath in her parched throat.

Now the flock was straggling past beyond the withered fruit trees. Limping pathetic creatures that lurched and gasped in a piteous manner. Sickened, Lisabeth called to the young Gullick lad who herded them.

'Ay, it's cruel, ma'am, to drive them along,' he agreed. 'But Mr Morgan's an 'umane fellow an' he'll not drive these off a cliff the way farmers are doing to their flocks elsewhere in the province.'

'Would people do a thing like that?' Lisabeth was incredulous.

'Not Mr Morgan. He said we're to slit every throat in the proper way so the poor wretches don't suffer more than—'

'But why? Why kill them?' Bile rose in her throat as she recalled the time, long ago, when Rhys had cold-bloodedly shot the Maoris' horse. 'Yes, that would be his response, wouldn't it?' she said bitterly.

'There's nowt else for it when there's no feed left an' nothing more to do. Mr Morgan wept when he give us the orders. These were some of his prize ewes, an' look at them now. Some blind, some crippled, all half-mad. Been gnawing each other's wool, they 'ave. Terrible, ain't—?'

Lisabeth could bear this no longer. She was already dashing back towards the cottage, blinking away tears of distress. *Poor Rhys*, she thought. *What agony he must be going through.*

She knew exactly where he would be. Yesterday Gwynne had reported that lately Rhys was obsessed by a theory that there might

437

be a deep hidden spring in the peninsular crater below the ring of broken stones. Though the rest of Mists of Heaven was burned to a brown crisp and the rivers had all dried to mud, here was a hollow of ground that retained a faint dappling of green. For the past week Rhys had laboured there alone shifting rock and scraping away powdered soil, hoping against all reason that water might be tapped somewhere below the thick crust of boulders and volcanic soil that lined the crater bowl.

Nervous of his reaction to seeing her, she decided that they would meet as if by chance, and to make it appear that she was enjoying a solitary excursion she packed four honey and sultana muffins in a clean cloth and tucked them into a willow basket beside a jar of ginger-beer. As she puffed up the hill her face grew damp and pink below the wide brim of her yellow hat, while her yellow and brown striped hems were soon bloomed with dust stirred up by her boots.

From the sea the wind still beat strongly, bearing gull-cries and the hollow surge of waves. Huge boiling clouds were scudding over the ocean, those maddening rainclouds that had taunted the province all summer by advancing in a rush over the land then changing their minds and retreating to dump their precious cargoes of water far out at sea. Glancing up at them now, Lisabeth knew that she would never take clouds for granted again. They were cruel, capricious and fickle, not the inanimate objects she had perceived them to be in the past. Look at how dark and grey they were today, practically guaranteeing rain, yet Lisabeth had lost count of the number of times she had seen them look like that, times when her heart had swelled with false hope.

Pausing at the crest of the ridge, Lisabeth bent and flexed her back to relieve a stitch in her side and to catch her breath. From here she could see a peep of her cottage roof, the spread of glistening water across to Sumner and the other headland. A ship was one steady focused spot in the blinding haze. She wondered if at this very moment Joseph Day was rowing out to guide it across the bar.

On the other side of her vantage-point the walls of the mansion glowed like silver in the sunshine. A thousand points of light winked from the mullioned windows. In the yard Daisy was laughing while Gwynne tried to catch her with a hand-held wooden puppet, the one, Lisabeth guessed, that was shaped like a crocodile. Daisy's squeals sounded like the squeaking of a door-hinge. The lawn was an ugly brown, mangy as a moth-eaten fur like the Christchurch cricket oval where in the early days of the drought Rhys took his one relaxation from work. All this fine weather made for perfect cricket, he had joked to Gwynne, back when it was still a joking matter.

Shading her eyes, Lisabeth scanned the contours of the headland. Was that Polka, tethered under a tree on that ridge, sharing the pod of shade with a dozen tightly-packed sheep? Picking up the basket, she marched towards the tree, her stomach quailing with apprehension.

What would he say? Would he even want to talk to her? It could be that he was so heartily weary of her resistance that he had finally lost all desire for her. Love could wear out, she supposed, and with that notion came fear that quickened her footsteps.

She was halfway along the headland path when suddenly she stopped, distracted by a soft thud on the brim of her sun-hat. Another came, and another. Glancing down she saw a scattering of penny-sized splodges appear like bruises on the powdery earth around her. Her heart stopped and the breath caught in her chest as, hardly daring to believe it, she looked up at the great dark hammock of cloud that was slung overhead. A single huge rain-drop batted her on the nose, then another.

Wildly she gazed around her. All up and down the coast it was raining. Rain sprayed over the inland meadows as the clouds lowered to embrace the foothills. A grey curtain dropped between her and Sumner. It was raining there, too.

'It's raining!' she yelled. 'Rhys, it's actually raining!' Hitching her skirts up with her free hand, she dashed towards the tree through the puddles of thin mud as the warm glorious rain plastered her dress to her body. It was coming down in torrents now.

The shelter, when she reached it, was no shelter at all, for the force of the rain was stripping the last brown leaves from the tree and the sheep were milling around snatching at these pathetic scraps of food. Lisabeth set her basket down in a low fork of the tree before tugging off her hat and dashing the water from the brim. Polka nickered and nosed up at the sodden cloth, so she wedged the basket up in a higher fork out of reach of his inquisitive lips and tucked her hat over it like a roof.

She could not see Rhys. Such was the force of the rain that it sent up a thick haze of mud-splashes, and such was the volume that the sides of the crater were already running with brown water like an enormous circular waterfall. But she could hear him. Above the excited bleating of the sheep, the roar of the water and the muffled grumbling of the ocean she could hear his hoarse exhilarated shouts of joy. 'You beauty!' he was screaming. 'You bloody wonderful beauty!'

Careless of the torrents that loosened every step from under her, Lisabeth scrambled over the lip of the crater and went bumping and sliding down the mud-chute towards the sound of his voice. Through the dense rain she did not see him until she was quite close, and when she did she scrabbled for a grip on an outcrop of rock and dragged herself to a halt.

He was completely naked. His arms were uplifted as if beseeching the heavens and his face was raised, eyes closed now and lips parted so that the warm downpour bathed his face and flowed over his body like wine. Lisabeth guessed when she saw his beatific expression that he was silently offering thanks for the life-giving rain.

In awe she watched him. Only in her imaginings had she ever seen him fully naked, and she marvelled at how much more beautiful he was than she could have anticipated. His shoulders were no surprise with their width and packed strength, but she noted curiously that muscles overlaid his ribcage and his waist and hips were unexpectedly narrow, swelling to thick powerful thighs. His calves were corded with sinews and veins like his forearms, while his feet were long and pale, oddly vulnerable. Most fascinating to her wondering eyes was his belly, flat, not rounded like hers, with a centre stripe of dark down leading to where his penis swelled, softly engorged by some of the joy and excitement that was flooding his body. *I love him utterly*, Lisabeth exulted, thinking that nothing in the world could be as splendid as his pale, perfectly proportioned body that stood as still as a piece of temple statuary slicked with wet polish under the ragged grey sky.

Hunched against the rocky outcrop and soaked to the skin, Lisabeth would have been content to stay there shivering as she watched him, but after a few moments he lowered his arms and opened his eyes. When he saw her he laughed aloud, but she shrank back, shy at being discovered.

'Lisabeth!' he cried, loping over and drawing her reluctantly to her feet. 'Isn't this miraculous? You do know what it means, don't you? My sheep are saved, the wheat will grow, the tussock will regenerate, the land will come to life again!' He kissed her, an enthusiastic smacking on the cheek that he might have given Gwynne. 'Isn't it marvellous?'

'I'm so happy for you,' said Lisabeth. Her clothes felt like a ton

440

of wet bandages, and she could feel rain coursing over her scalp.

He glanced back at his nudity, then grinned at her. 'I had to celebrate this properly. When the rain started coming down hard, and I knew it wasn't another false promise, I remembered what Joe Day told me about old Braddock stripping off his clothes and capering around in the rain. I'd always thought he was a crazy old coot to do that, but now I understood how he must have felt. My heart almost burst from joy and suddenly I had to feel that rain flowing over every part of me so that I became part of it and it part of me. I wanted to drink it in through every pore in my body. It was one of the most spiritual, physiccal and emotional experiences I've ever had, but then to open my eyes and find you here. . . .' He paused, and the smile faded as he wondered why she was here. 'Is everything all right, Lisabeth?'

'If you want it to be.'

'What do you mean?'

This wasn't how she'd rehearsed it at all, but the moment was here so she rushed on. 'I've come to say I'll move in with you, Rhys, today if you like, if you still want me to, that is.'

'Want you to? If I like?' His whoop, so like Andrew's, nearly deafened her. Seriously he added: 'You're quite sure? You've thought everything through?'

She nodded.

'You know, what you said really rocked me. Then later I began to understand all the things that had puzzled me for so many years: your antagonism, your bewildering reaction to some of the things I said, even my feelings about Andrew. We all dislike the ingredients of ourselves that we see in others, and if I face honestly up to it there's a great deal I've recognized all along in him. I'm still stunned by the news, but I'm glad you told me.'

'Yes,' she said doubtfully.

Putting away the subject, Rhys said: 'All past and gone, all water under the bridge, hey? You're here and I'm here and this is a magnificient day. The best day of my life!' And whooping again he scooped her up and swung her around, then he set her down again, grinning wickedly. 'Or should I say "almost"?'

'Almost?' she whispered, smiling, overflowing with relief that everything had been glossed over so effortlessly. Gazing lovingly into his face, she beamed with reflected happiness. His cheeks were shiny with moisture, his hair and moustache were slicked down as if with macassar oil and his eyelashes were glued together in wet clumps, but he looked so glowingly beautiful that she was suddenly timid of him. 'Your skin is cold,' she murmured.

'This is almost the happiest day of my life. It *will* be the happiest in a minute,' he told her, still grinning wickedly. Then he swept her tightly against his body so that she could feel the stirring, exciting hardness of him through her sodden skirts while his fingers began to wrest undone the buttons of her bodice. 'Almost,' he promised, bending his mouth to cover hers and smothering her protests with a kiss as, moving more rapidly now, he tugged the last fastening free and shucked the gown from her shoulders. With impatient jerks he plucked the string lacings of her camisole undone, and then the rest of her garments peeled away as easily as casing from a tangerine.

'There, now,' he said, deftly bundling her clothes and placing them with her shoes on a raised shelf of rock where they would not wash away. 'Here we are as God made us, in the finest clothes we could ever wear.'

That wry description made her laugh, and in the gurgle of laughter her nervous apprehension dissolved. It took an effort of will not to cover herself instinctively, not to shield her body from his gaze of open admiration, but once her nerves steadied she decided this was fun, joyful fun. When he opened his arms she flew into them without hesitation, slipping willingly into his embrace.

Gently he laid her down on a smooth platform of rock. It was surprisingly warm; baked by the sun all day, it retained its heat and made a pleasant couching-place for them. Lisabeth lay back with a sigh, a familiar aching sweetness flowing through her bones, dissolving all her strength. 'I love you utterly,' she whispered.

'This is a better way to celebrate,' Rhys was saying as with glee he traced a line of kisses down her neck and across to one breast. 'Lisabeth, you'll make my life perfect.'

'We'll build a perfect life together,' she corrected him. There would be complications and obstacles, she knew, but as the rain beat on her face she felt ritually cleansed of all her problems. Like the dust they were for the moment washed away.

She laughed. He was tickling her nipple with his tongue, teasing her. She opened her thighs, inviting him, and when he saw that she was offering herself so freely he groaned with delight. 'It's a new life,' he declared. 'A new life for the sweet earth and look at us, slippery as babies – it's a new life for us, too. Oh, Lisabeth, I want so much to marry you.'

'Why?' she teased. 'I'll have to be respectable, then. I'll be Mrs Rhys Morgan – no, *Councillor* Morgan's wife. A grand lady. There'll be none of this frolicking in the meadows with the master. Oh, no! I'll wear sober gowns and spectacles and sit all day in the study reading serious books.'

He chuckled, his hands stroking the rain-slick from the insides of her thighs so that she squirmed with delicious sensations. 'You do that! Closet yourself in the library, and I'll come in on the pretext of tutoring you, then I'll throw you on to the sofa, tear off your spectacles and sober gown and do this, and this, and—' He laughed as she playfully slapped at his hands.

'What will the servants think?'

'They'll be puzzled when we go for picnics on rainy days, that's for sure!' He smiled down at her as she wound her legs around him. 'You are a hussy! I'm longing to be properly married to you. Apart from all the silly things – being able to buy you crinolines and pretty gowns that button down the back and as many pairs of shoes as you can cram into the garderobe – I want you for a far more basic reason. It's hell not being able to make love to you properly. Just you wait, Lisabeth Maitland Rennie Stafford Nye. I'm going to love you full of babies. You'll be constantly pregnant and always smiling. It'll be wonderful.'

'But then I won't have time to study!'

'We'll have time to do anything and everything that we want. Lisabeth, darling, the world will be ours!'

'It already is,' she murmured.